TRAITOR
OF THE
DROWNED EMPIRE

Also by Frankie Diane Mallis

Daughter of the Drowned Empire
Guardian of the Drowned Empire
Lady of the Drowned Empire
Warrior of the Drowned Empire
Traitor of the Drowned Empire
Solstice of the Drowned Empire: A Drowned Empire Novella
Son of the Drowned Empire

Coming Soon
Queen of the Drowned Empire (Book Six)

TRAITOR OF THE DROWNED EMPIRE

FRANKIE DIANE MALLIS

HODDERSCAPE

First published in Great Britain in 2025 by Hodderscape
An imprint of Hodder & Stoughton Limited
An Hachette UK company

The authorised representative in the EEA is Hachette Ireland,
8 Castlecourt Centre, Dublin 15, D15 XTP3, Ireland (email: info@hbgi.ie)

1

Copyright © Frankie Diane Mallis 2025

The right of Frankie Diane Mallis to be identified as the Author
of the Work has been asserted by Choose an item in accordance
with the Copyright, Designs and Patents Act 1988.

Cover images © Shutterstock.com

All rights reserved. No part of this publication may be reproduced, stored
in a retrieval system, or transmitted, in any form or by any means without
the prior written permission of the publisher, nor be otherwise circulated
in any form of binding or cover other than that in which it is published and
without a similar condition being imposed on the subsequent purchaser.

All characters in this publication are fictitious and any resemblance
to real persons, living or dead, is purely coincidental.

A CIP catalogue record for this title is available from the British Library

Paperback ISBN 9781399736343
ebook ISBN 9781399736350

Typeset in Plantin Light by Manipal Technologies Limited

Printed and bound in Great Britain by Clays Ltd, Elcograf S.p.A.

Hodder & Stoughton policy is to use papers that are natural, renewable
and recyclable products and made from wood grown in sustainable forests.
The logging and manufacturing processes are expected to conform
to the environmental regulations of the country of origin.

Hodder & Stoughton Limited
Carmelite House
50 Victoria Embankment
London EC4Y 0DZ

www.hodderscape.co.uk

For Julia, who's stronger than she knows.

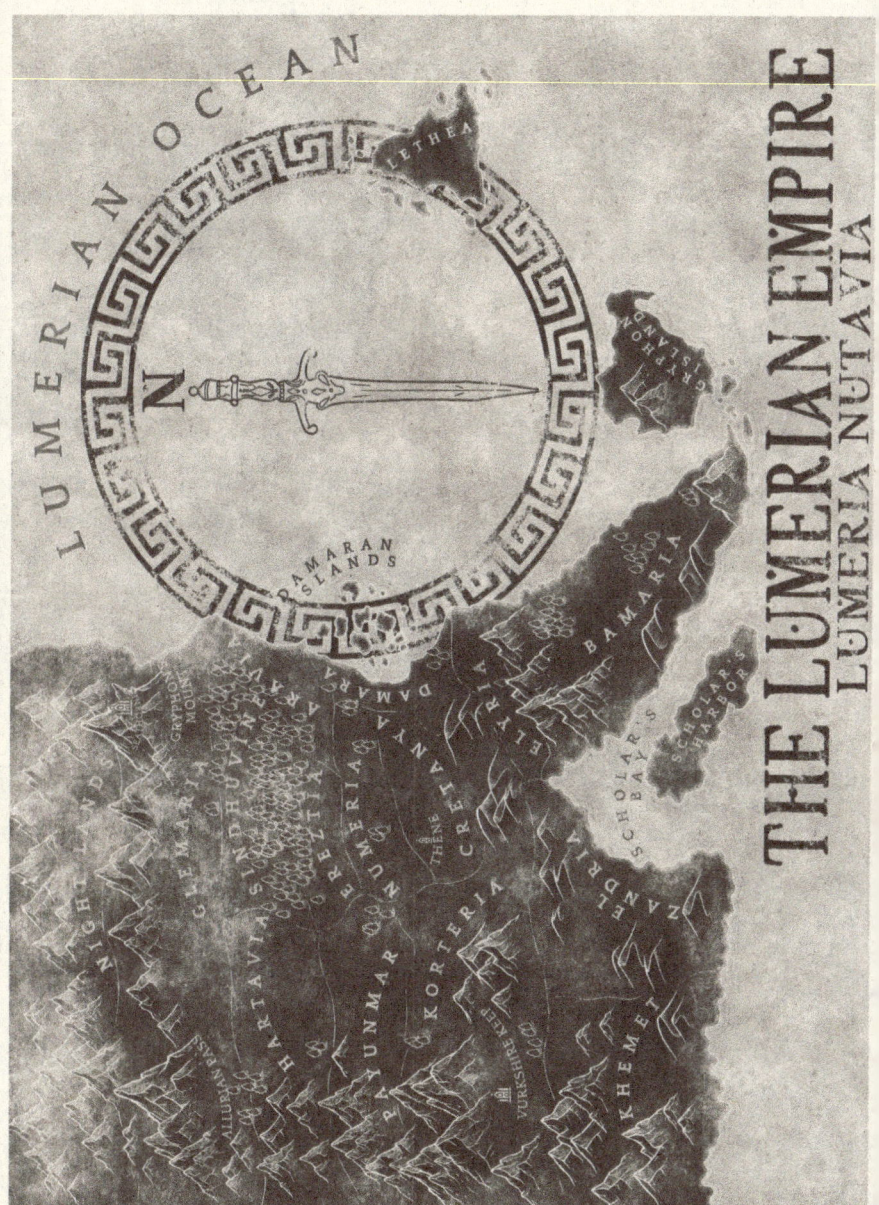

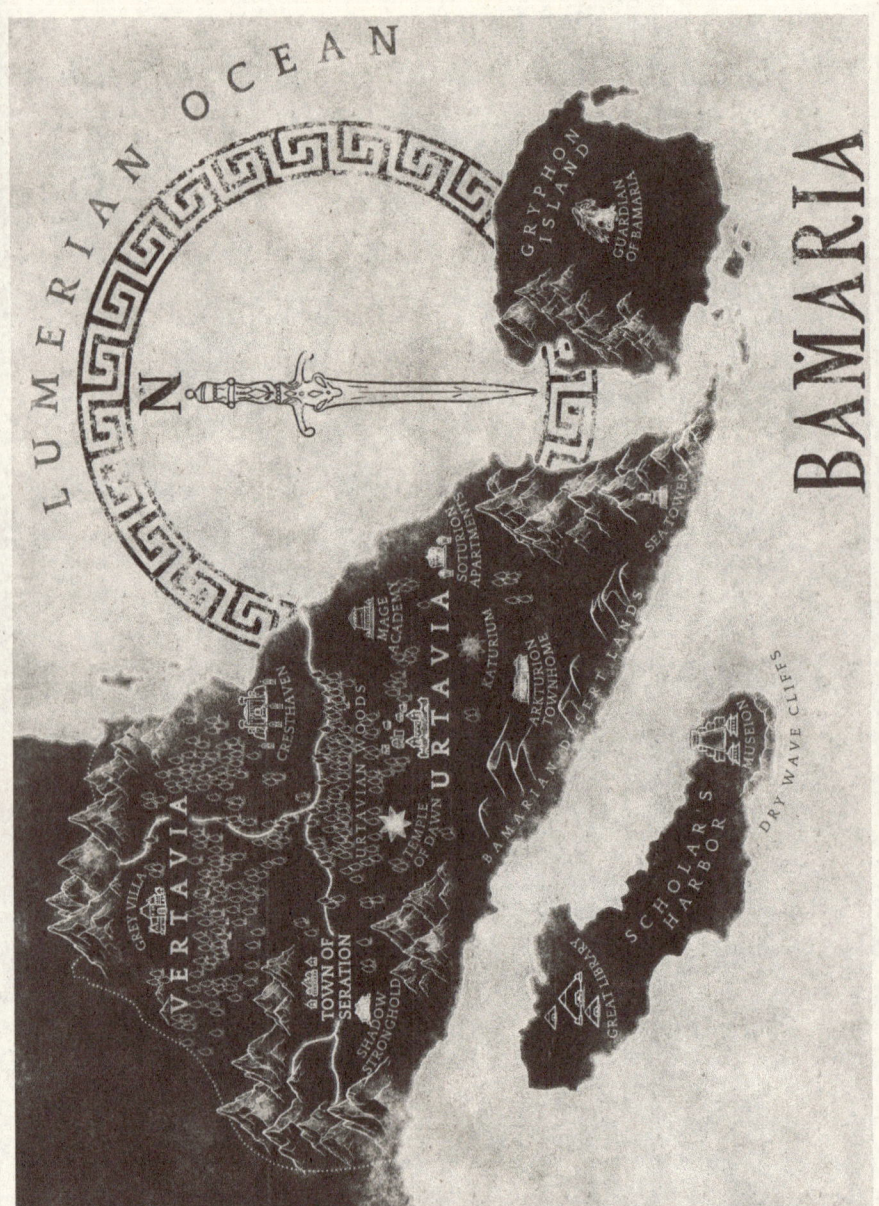

Content Warning

Dear reader, please be advised that this book includes the following topics before you begin reading:

- grief
- misogyny
- violence and gore
- sexual assault
- references to off-page rape
- torture

PREVIOUSLY IN
WARRIOR OF DROWNED EMPIRE

The new Arkasva Batavia, Lady Arianna, has been consecrated as High Lady of Bamaria. And Lord Tristan Grey, the Heir Apparent's new betrothed, is ready for celebrations to die down, and for a chance to stop performing for the crowds. But mostly, he's ready to finally grieve his cousin Haleika who was turned forsaken by the soulless akadim, then killed in the arena by his ex-girlfriend Lyriana Batavia, and her suspected lover, the forsworn soturion, Rhyan Hart. But Tristan can't do any of these things so long as Imperator Kormac remains in his country. Not even the shocking death of his nephew, Brockton Kormac, has pulled him home from Bamaria, or away from the villa owned by Tristan's grandmother. But the Imperator has a task for Tristan. As the most celebrated vorakh hunter in the Empire, he is given orders for something else to hunt: Lyriana and Rhyan. Still in love with Lyr, Tristan agrees, if only to find her and make sure she's safe. But Tristan's whole world is turned upside down when a vorakh hunt later that night reveals his worst fear. Tristan himself is vorakh and just had his first vision—a new detail about the night his parents were murdered by a mage under the thrall of visions, one with a beauty mark who swore Tristan's parents would regret his existence when he grew up and they saw what he truly was.

In the caves of Glemaria, Lyr and Rhyan help Meera recover from her akadim kidnapping, while hiding from Morgana and Aemon, as well as Rhyan's father who has just returned to his Seat. Rhyan's memories of his past life as the fallen God Auriel are haunting his dreams. He can't stop revisiting the death of his past-life love, the Goddess Asherah, Lyriana's previous incarnation. But a newly magic-powered Lyr is facing her own demons as she struggles to accept the fact that not only was Brockton telling her the truth: that Jules was alive—but that Jules has been suffering and alone for two years. Lyr's anger at the Empire, and at herself, is coming to a head as she is consumed with the need to find Jules, and exact vengeance on those who hurt her.

Morgana's own memories of her past life as the Goddess Ereshya, Moriel's consort, are also haunting her dreams to the point they are making it hard for her to remember who she is. The strength of her dreams can be attributed to the indigo shard that she tricked Lyr into giving to her. Despite Aemon's request for the shard to be returned to him, she has refused, and tries to accept her fate as an enemy of her sisters, but not yet a full ally of her lover Aemon, the reincarnation of Moriel. When Aemon leaves her alone in the Allurian Pass with his servant Parthenay, Morgana must decide her next move, and begins to focus on the shard and her ability to wield it. But she's unsettled by the demons around her, including what appears to be a newer breed—akadim that are smaller and more human-like in their ability to think—but just as vicious as the others.

Knowing a battle is coming soon, Lyr has thrown herself into training, both soturion, and mage, now that she has her magic, and possession of Asherah's stave. But her power has come with some strange effects. When Meera falls into a vision and Lyr rushes to help her, she finds herself trapped in the vision instead. There she sees the Emperor's arena and three wolves chasing down a lion. Lyriana grabs an old shield from the ground to protect herself, and then hears Jules's voice, realizing Jules is the lion, just as indigo and orange lights appear. Lyr comes out of the vision and faints, leaving a worried Rhyan and Meera to care for her. Though initially fearful that Lyriana now has vorakh as well, the three suspect that the Valalumir light in her heart, part of the Red Ray placed there by Mercurial when they made their bargain, is able to heal. But this comes at a cost to Lyriana—she must take on whatever pain or sickness she touches. Confident of her new abilities, and the knowledge that Jules is in the capital, Lyriana is ready to make her move. And she'll need to be quick. The Emperor has recently called for a Valabellum, a day of deadly games in the arena reenacting the War of Light. The games will draw everyone from the Empire to the capital, where Jules is. But with Imperator Hart's soturi close to finding them, they must first relocate to a new hiding place.

Rhyan travels with Meera to a new location first—since he's only able to travel with one person at a time. Lyr waits behind with the gryphon they acquired, but is soon surrounded by nahashim sent by Rhyan's father. She escapes on the gryphon, and reunites with Rhyan in their second location. But they quickly discover the nahashim were a trap, and Rhyan, Lyriana, and Meera are captured and bound by Rhyan's old friends: Dario, a soturion serving the Imperator, and Aiden, an apprentice to Glemaria's Master of Spies.

Dario, looking to spread division amongst them, tells Lyr of Rhyan's past crimes, and secrets he's been keeping from her. She learns the soturion he killed in the arena was not only his best friend Garrett, but Aiden's soulmate. Aiden breaks Rhyan's nose in anger, but an akadim attack forces their captors to release their binds and ally together in the fight. The five barely escape on their gryphon, but the momentary truce ends, and Dario and Aiden bring them to Seathorne to see the Imperator.

Back in Bamaria, trials are held for the Valabellum as Tristan is urged once again to find Lyr and Rhyan for the Imperator. He knows he must follow orders, despite his fear of his vorakh overwhelming him. He keeps seeing visions of his parents' death. But after the trials, he has a new concern. Galen, his best friend and Haleika's lover, has won the trials, and reveals he wants to face the Emperor in retaliation—an act likely to get him killed.

North in the Allurian Pass, Morgana begins to take on the power of the indigo shard, ordering the akadim to serve her, though still grappling morally with her role in all of this, and who she really is: Lady Morgana, Lyr and Meera's sister, or the Goddess Ereshya, Moriel's consort, and Asherah's enemy.

Lyriana, Rhyan, and Meera are brought before Imperator Hart for interrogation. Lyriana and Rhyan dodge questions about Meera, and what happened to the indigo shard. They try to hide Lyriana's abilities from him, knowing any knowledge he has can be used against them. But when he brings in Arkturion Kane, the brutal warlord he's marked for marriage to Lyr, another Guardian is revealed. When Kane touches Lyr's skin, her heart heats up—a sign of a reborn Guardian. Kane is revealed as the reincarnation of Shiviel, God of the Yellow Ray, an even more brutal monster than Moriel.

Rhyan is imprisoned, and Meera is sent away. Lyr wakes up in Rhyan's old bedroom, being looked after by the Imperator's new wife, and Rhyan's ex-lover, Lady Kenna. An unlikely alliance forms between Lyr and Kenna, who both agree that they want to protect Rhyan, and free him from the prisons.

Lyriana meets alone with Imperator Hart to negotiate. He reveals that he knows the truth about Vrukshire, that Lyriana and Rhyan are responsible for Brockton's murder, a fact that he learned from Imperator Kormac himself. Kormac has been keeping Lyr's role in this a secret because he still intends to use her to claim Bamaria. Imperator Hart promises he can protect Lyr and Bamaria from this fate, if she does the following— marry Arkturion Kane, and attend the Emperor's Valabellum in order to steal a shield from his Throne Room. He even offers to rescue Jules for her. Lyr is wary of his bargain, especially because it means Rhyan will be forced back under his father's rule. But when the Imperator's nahashim shows her a vision of the shield she's meant to steal, she recognizes it from her vision, and realizes what it is—the orange shard, another piece of the Valalumir—and she knows the reason she saw the indigo and orange lights in the arena. Aemon and Morgana are going after it, too, and if they succeed, they will have two shards of the Valalumir in their possession. Lyr has no choice but to accept, but only after she negotiates Rhyan's freedom from prison, and a private meeting with him to explain her decision. Imperator Hart agrees, and makes Lyr sign a contract with her blood, one that forces her to submit to his every word and command.

The Afeya Mercurial comes to see Rhyan in the cells, and confirms Kane's identity as Shiviel. He also reveals that Auriel and Asherah weakened Shiviel's soul in such a way that he remains weak through every incarnation, even now when he's Kane. Otherwise Lyr wouldn't have survived their encounter. Mercurial also reveals to Rhyan that Meera's reincarnated identity is Cassarya, Goddess of the Blue Ray. This means they only have one Guardian left to identify: the Guardian of the Violet Ray, the Goddess Hava. Mercurial tells Rhyan he's already found her, once. He also warns that Lyr's new healing powers are tied to her ability to call on kashonim with Asherah. When she does this, she is calling on a power known as *Rakashonim*, a magic so strong and volatile for a mortal, that it was the cause of death for Asherah. And if Lyriana continues to call on it, without the aid of the red shard, the shard she was supposed to find per their bargain, she will be in mortal danger. He urges Rhyan to leave Seathorne and to take Lyriana with him. But before he can learn any more, his father arrives to inform him of Lyriana's bargain. Learning that Lyriana has finally submitted to Kane, and that Rhyan himself must also marry someone of his father's choosing, anger takes over him. He can feel Auriel's energy rising to the surface, and swears that if his father harms Lyriana in any way, he will kill him, not just in this life, but in every life, and again in the afterlife—a threat his father seems to take seriously.

Lyr and Rhyan reunite and argue over his father's motives, and their arrangement with him. Rhyan worries about the role Jules is playing in his father's manipulations. He knows how desperately Lyriana wants to rescue her, and worries it's making her easy to manipulate. But tension flares between them as Lyriana confronts Rhyan from hiding that Kenna was his lover, and that he never told her what happened with Garrett, or the night his mother died. Too fearful for her safety, Rhyan tries to convince Lyriana to leave with him. But they finally agree, that as painful as it will be, they have a duty to protect the orange shard from falling into the wrong hands. And with the Valabellum, and both Imperators after them, this might be their only way to do so. Rhyan however, has new suspicions about his father's motives in rescuing Jules, and fails to tell Lyr what he learned about *Rakashonim*.

Lyriana's engagement to Kane is announced, as is Rhyan's to a Glemarian noblewoman, Lady Amalthea, who seems to make him uncomfortable. They are thrown into Glemarian society, appearing at public events to show off their engagements which protects them from Ka Kormac, and also dispels any rumours of their alleged love affair. Lyr resumes soturion training, though she is forced to pretend she's still powerless. In the evenings, Lyriana, Rhyan, Meera, Dario, and Aiden prepare to steal the shield, studying blueprints of the Emperor's Palace, and the schedule of soturi on guard duty.

Unable to reach Lyriana and Rhyan now that they're under Imperator Hart's protection, Tristan turns his attention to saving his best friend. But when Galen uncovers a series of failed bribe attempts by Tristan to disqualify him from the games, he no longer trusts him. Galen refuses to leave, determined to face the Emperor for what happened to Haleika. He doesn't care about the consequences. Imperator Kormac, aware of

Tristan's actions, promises him Galen will be safe, but only if he apprehends Lyriana and Rhyan in the capital.

Back in the North, Aemon returns to the Allurian Pass with a guest, a chayatim, one of the vorakh previously enslaved to the Emperor. The mage has visions, and a noticeable beauty mark. Aemon introduces Morgana to Andromeny, his older sister—the vorakh who murdered Tristan's parents.

As the weeks of preparation for the Valabellum pass, Lyriana and Rhyan feel the strain of being unable to talk, or see each other in private. His father's spies are everywhere. For a month, they parade around Glemaria and attend balls with their betrothed partners, pretending their relationships are genuine. Every touch Kane gives Lyr makes her sick, but her contract with the Imperator leaves her unable to refuse. Luckily, his advances remain on the dance floor.

While Lyr has done everything she can to keep the Imperator happy, and prepare to steal the shield, Rhyan has been conducting his own research into *Rakashonim*, and trying to understand what weakened Shiviel, so he can save Lyriana in this lifetime. Sneaking out to Asherah's tomb, he finally remembers what happened. Shiviel had captured Auriel, and Asherah came to his rescue. Together, they cut his soul in half, separating him from his power. The act created a small child out of Shiviel's soul: a secret eighth Guardian. His father finally tells him that he knows about *Rakashonim*, and that it will kill Lyriana if she continues to call on it for power or healing.

Just before their departure, Mercurial returns, violently reminding Lyr of their deal and the pain she will suffer if she does not claim the Red Shard for herself. Unable to see a way out of her bargain, or to stop Morgana and Aemon from claiming more of the Valalumir's power, she cannot agree. Mercurial tells her that Rhyan's still keeping secrets, including the fact that her power can not only kill her, but everyone around her.

Lyriana and Rhyan attend a ball the night before the Valabellum in the Emperor's honor. For the first time in months, she must face Imperator Kormac and her Aunt Arianna. A dance with Imperator Kormac confirms the truth—he knows she's guilty of murder. And he's been keeping one more secret: Rhyan's vorakh. He orders her to end her engagement to Kane, and resume her wedding to his son, Viktor—or he will have Rhyan arrested for vorakh.

Before Lyr can act, masked warriors from the Valabellum arrive at the ball. Tristan watches in horror as the soturion dressed as Moriel, the warrior who will, according to tradition, die enters. It's Galen. Imperator Kormac again demands Tristan's loyalty in exchange for his friend's life. But before everyone, Galen murders the Emperor.

The Palace enters a lockdown, but Rhyan finds a way into Lyr's bedroom. At last he confesses the secrets he's been keeping: his memories of Auriel, his nightmares about Asherah's death, his research on *Rakashonim*, why he had to kill Garrett, and finally, his suspicion that Jules is the reincarnation of Hava, and that's why his father is willing to rescue her—because he's collecting reincarnations of the Gods and Goddesses. Rhyan also reveals the truth about Lady Amalthea and Lady Kenna. His father was forcing him to sleep around after he spent a year refusing to court because he'd fallen in love with Lyr. Amalthea was the first, and Kenna was the one who allowed the practice to stop. With no more secrets between them, Lyr and Rhyan reunite, their love stronger than ever. Later in bed, Rhyan proposes marriage.

Imperator Kormac is chosen as the new Emperor, and sends for Tristan to reveal the Empire's darkest secret. The vorakh Tristan arrests are not stripped and killed, they are made to serve in the Palace as chayatim. Tristan is taken to a room full of chayatim he personally captured. Galen is being interrogated and tortured by them. When Jules enters, revealing she is alive and a chayatim, Tristan is offered one final chance to save Galen: use the lockdown to bring Rhyan and Lyr to the new Emperor.

Tristan finds Lyr's room, and reveals to her and Rhyan what he saw, as well as his own secrets—he's vorakh. Lyr and Rhyan agree to help him save Galen and Jules. As they leave, Dario, Aiden, and Meera join. Dario and Aiden manage to admit they were forced to obey Rhyan's father through blood contracts, and they were on his side all along. The six of them enter the interrogation room, and manage to get a hold of a badly beaten Jules and Galen. They escape the Palace and fly to Cretanya on gryphon-back, then seek shelter in the inn owned by the in-laws of Rhyan's Uncle Sean.

Lyr accepts Rhyan's marriage proposal, and together they guard their friends and family throughout the night. But then Imperator Hart's nahashim finds them. The group of eight escape to the woods, but Imperator Hart uses his blood contract to order Lyriana, Dario, and Aiden to freeze, and allow his nahashim to strangle them. The only way to break free of his orders is to allow a day to pass, or to create physical distance between them and the Imperator. Rhyan rushes at his father, uses his vorakh, and they vanish. It works. Lyr, Aiden, and Dario are able to move again, and Meera, realizing she is Cassarya, discovers she can control the snakes and sends them away. They all return to the inn and wait for Rhyan to resurface. But time passes and he doesn't return.

Jules has a vision: Rhyan's been captured by the Emperor, tried and found guilty for having vorakh. Since the Valabellum was canceled, Rhyan will be publicly stripped for entertainment instead. Lyr knows that all of her friends and family are in danger, wanted for crimes against the Empire, and half of them are injured or weak. But if she can get to Rhyan fast enough, they can escape. He can travel with her, but he can only take one. Lyr vows to go save him alone, and leaves Dario to protect the others.

Lyr steals an ashvan and rides furiously back to the capital, but there are too many soturi standing between her and Rhyan. She decides to call on *Rakashonim*, but she needs every ounce of strength she can get. So she breaks into the Throne Room, and steals the shield, killing the Blade, the Empire's warlord, in the process. Just before she fights her way out, Morgana enters, followed by akadim who can walk in the sun.

Everyone in the Throne Room is murdered, everyone except Lyr. She can hear Rhyan being brought out to the arena, and begs Morgana to let her take the shield and save him. But Morgana refuses. She'll allow Lyr to touch the indigo shard and absorb some of its power, but nothing more. Out of time, Lyr accepts, and calls on *Rakashonim*. She fights her way into the arena, killing anyone who tries to stop her as Rhyan is mercilessly stripped of his magic. Lyr reaches the dais, and using her magic, carries a deathly weakened Rhyan through the arena. But before they can leave, Morgana and Aemon's akadim attack. As Lyr fights them off, one demon gets to Rhyan. Lyr calls on *Rakashonim* once more to save him. But suddenly finds herself beside the statue of the Guardian of Bamaria, with no way to get to Rhyan. Screaming, she breaks off the onyx head of the gryphon and throws it into the water. Her power intensifies, and she threatens to unleash a deadly tsunami, until a voice stops her, and someone appears, speaking in High Lumerian. The God Auriel, Rhyan's previous incarnation, has regained physical form.

Alone in the woods, a forsaken Rhyan attempts to stop the transformation to akadim by ending his life. When he cannot, Asherah appears to comfort him, but without physical form, she can do little to stop what's happening. His transformation to akadim complete, Rhyan goes in search of his first kill. He finds a mage who seems familiar to him. But instead of attacking, he finds himself agreeing to serve her, as she places a collar around his neck, joining their power together in kashonim. He asks her name, and she answers, "Ereshya".

THE FIRST SCROLL: AURIEL

CHAPTER ONE

RHYAN

The clock tower struck the new hour in Numeria and I groaned.

Fucking Numeria. Fucking stupid Lumerian capital.

How was it possible I was back here? How was I already away from Lyriana? Away from my friends? How the hell had I already been separated from them—and after I'd just gotten them back? After, for a moment, for a brief shining fucking moment, it felt like things were working out for me.

For one night they had.

I'd gotten away from my father's iron grip. Away from the Emperor. I was with Lyr, and she was safe and she was mine and she was loved. And so was I—as long as I was with her.

I was *everything* with her.

And finally, I knew the truth—knew that Aiden and Dario, my best friends, didn't hate me. Gods, they'd even forgiven me for Garrett. For leaving Glemaria and abandoning them. For all I'd done in my escape. For everyone I'd hurt. Everyone who'd died because of me.

And we found Jules. We fucking found her, two and half years after she was taken. We got her safely out of the Palace. Got her to freedom. And more than that. Meera was safe. Hell—even Lord Tristan freaking Grey was on our side now.

It was all working out. All coming together. And by the Gods, the only thing left for me to do was free Kenna, get her away from my father. Away from her father, too—that monster, Arkturion Kane. Shiviel. But I'd already reached too high.

I *always* reached too high.

I leaned my head back against the hard stone wall of my prison cell. The tiny square I'd been locked in was cold and drafty, and the damp and musty hall leading up to it smelled like shit. In a larger cell, a few rows down, prisoners banged on the walls. Coughing, and groaning in pain. Some were crying. Some were just screaming.

Closing my eyes, I tried to forget where I was. To forget everything from the last few hours. And everything coming in the next. The horror I knew I'd face. And the pain. The pain which was inevitable. I only wanted one thing now.

Lyr.

To see Lyr. See her in my mind, and remember the way she looked last night, so raw and beautiful. I could almost feel my body still tangled with hers, could almost feel, even in the damp cold of the cell, just how Godsdamned warm I'd been in her bed. Warm inside her, around her, on top of her, beneath her. We had connected in every way possible. Our bodies, our minds, our hearts. Our souls. And I was smiling, and so was she. And we were happy. For a moment, we were happy.

The backs of my eyes pricked with tears. Fuck. I shook my head, and swallowed, my throat dry and rough.

I was happy? What a fucking joke. Happy. Happiness wasn't for people like me. Happiness wasn't my fate. It never was. I should have known better. I should have known my father would come for us. Should have known that in the end, above all else, he'd come for me. And most of all, I should have known he would succeed. Now he had. Now it was done. And now nothing else mattered. My time was up.

Gods. The bindings were so fucking tight, I could barely breathe. My father wasn't taking chances this time. Not after I'd broken through his double binding at home. Not since I nearly killed him while behind bars. I guess I should have been flattered he found me to be such a threat. But to be honest, it was hard to feel anything else beyond dread.

I knew there'd be no reprieve. The trial they held for me in the Palace had been swift. Barely even worthy of meriting the formality of being called a trial. Accusation, evidence, conviction and sentencing were presented briskly, without emotion.

All in under a minute.

It was a farce. And yet—ironically, I was actually guilty.

Though, what other outcome could have been expected? When I'd grabbed my father, traveled with him away from Lyr, from my friends—from my ... From everyone who'd become my family, I was so afraid, and terrified for them, I wasn't thinking straight. I only knew one thing: I had to stop the threat. I had to save her. I had to save them all. He had fucking nahashim with him, and the giant snakes were going to suffocate Lyr; squeeze Dario and Aiden to death. And there was nothing I could do. Because my father had control over the snakes, and he had total control over their prey. Lyr, Dario and Aiden had all been bound to follow his word, forced to follow his commands. He had blackmailed them all into signing a blood contract, compelling them into complicity with their own demise. Nothing broke me more than the look on Lyr's face at the moment, at the sheer panic in her eyes as she realized she was helpless. The moment she realized that despite her strength, and the power she'd fought so hard to find, she was unable to fight back.

There was only one thing I could do. Only one way to help. Get him away from her. From all of them. Get him far away enough to break the power his words held.

So I ran at him with all I had, and I jumped, holding onto him like my life depended on it. Apparently, my life *had* depended on it. I just didn't understand why at the time. I could still feel my stomach tugging as we traveled. Feel the strain in my arms from holding my father against me. And the sudden weight in my boots when we landed, the strain in my calves. The sinking feeling that followed. Because it turned out the jump I'd made was too short—we hadn't traveled far away enough to break his hold. He laughed when we landed, confirming as much. The threat hadn't stopped.

So immediately, without thought, without recovering my strength, I jumped again. Right into Numeria, right into the Empire's capital. The most dangerous place I could have gone.

My father's face said it all. That what I did had worked. I'd broken his hold. I'd saved my friends, saved my family.

I'd saved Lyr …

Unfortunately, as I was reminded by my current surroundings, I'd been unable to save myself. We were seen by dozens and dozens of witnesses. Their testimony wasn't needed though. The Emperor—the newly crowned Imperator Kormac—already knew my secret. Knew I was vorakh. He'd already told Lyr. And with my sudden display of forbidden magic upon landing in Numeria, so did everyone else. No more hiding.

I was sentenced. And before the end of the day, before the sun set again, I would be stripped. At least, that was technically my punishment. A stripping of power and magic. But everyone at the trial knew the truth—knew what was really going to happen to me.

Because the procedure wouldn't end there. It would end in my execution. My magic would be ripped out of my skin, torn from my muscles, cut out of my organs, and sucked from my bones. They'd take it all, take everything that had made me who I was, until it was gone, until I was dead. The Examiner from Ka Lethea had gone over the procedure already, explaining in such detail what would happen that I'd nearly vomited. He said I might survive, that it was possible. But I could see the lie in his eyes. I knew. We all knew. One did not survive these strippings, no matter how strong they were, no matter how hard they trained. And I had trained. Really fucking hard.

I suppressed a cry and sucked in a breath, but the movement was labored under all of my bindings. I guess this was my final rope. The one I wouldn't be tearing apart.

A tear rolled down my cheek—one I couldn't even wipe away since my hands were bound. Fuck. I was running out of time. The countdown was on. I took a deep breath and shook my head. It was okay. It had to be okay. I mean I could live with it. Or ... *die* because of it. I laughed. Bad time to make a joke. Another tear fell, and I swallowed again, my throat painfully dry, as I tried to steel myself.

I just had to focus on what mattered, on what was important. If it saved Lyr, if it saved her life, I could bear it. It would be worth it. If she was free from my father, free from Kormac, then I could die. I could face down my death with honor, and without regret. As long as she was all right.

I nodded, to no one but myself. She was all right. And she would continue to be—even without me. There was no question about it. Lyr was strong. So strong. A fucking Goddess. She would bring the Empire to its knees when she was ready. And I was so fucking proud of her, of how powerful she'd become, how fierce. She amazed me constantly. I still remembered when I'd first fallen in love with her. Gods. I thought she was so beautiful. So beautiful I'd never tire of seeing her every day. Of seeing her beauty. Her smile. Her eyes. Her body.

I'd been right. But I'd underestimated myself, underestimated her. I hadn't tired of her—not once, not even close.

Instead, I felt insatiable. Like I was starving. I wanted more. More time to see her, to admire her. To talk to her, to listen to her, to hold her ... to ... fuck. To everything with her.

My chest heaved, and I bit my lip, my stomach twisting.

She was so much stronger than she realized. Stronger than me in some ways. I needed her, like I needed air to breathe. But the truth was, she didn't need me. Not to fight for her. Not to protect her. She'd survive this. She would. And she'd move on. She'd done it before. And much as that stung, much as I hated the thought of her with anyone else, the thought of someone else holding her at night, talking to her, kissing her ... it was strangely comforting to know. To know that one day she'd have love again, and safety, passion, partnership ...

More tears fell.

When I was gone, she could survive however she needed to. Just as long as she did. And I'd watch over her, and I'd wait. Wait for however long it took for her to join me in whatever world was next. It would hurt. It would really fucking hurt.

It already did.

But that was okay, too. Because it had to be. Because I'd spend an eternity waiting for her if I had to. If it meant she could have a long, and happy life—even if that was a life without me in it. Still, I would wait.

My vision blurred, and a door opened down the hall. Fresh shouts coming from outside sounded within the walls of the Palace prison. The noise exploded as it rushed towards me.

Great. A full audience was gathered in the arena. And if it was possible to believe from their auras, from the frenetic energy pulsing through the walls, it seemed as though they were even more starved than I was. They'd expected blood today—expected violence, gore and entertainment. It had been promised to them before the Valabellum games were called off. Before Emperor Theotis was murdered. Before

Emperor Avery replaced him. Well, they could cheer up now. Because they were going to get their wish—my blood. Hopefully, I'd make a good show. One they'd remember.

It was a small comfort that Lyr wouldn't know about this in time—there'd be no way for word to reach her of my fate before it happened. Not with how fast they were moving. Not while she remained in Cretanya. It was better that way. Better that she stayed far away from here. Better that she stayed safe and was spared from seeing me like this, along with everyone else I loved. Everyone except for Kenna who was still here. But she would persevere. She was strong, too.

Boots marching across the floor echoed against the walls as they headed toward me. I recognized the approach of my father at once. The sound of his gait was familiar. And hateful. Unwelcome. The force of his aura followed.

His shadow loomed over me before he came into view. I straightened as best I could beneath my chains, and blinked rapidly, until my tears were dried. I wouldn't cry. I wouldn't shed one more Godsdamned fucking tear. Not in front of him.

A moment passed as we stared each other down, and I let my full hatred for this man, this sorry excuse for a father, wash over me. I remembered his crimes. All of them. If I wasn't bound, if I could still access my aura, I would have blasted it at him. But I had to settle for a glare, for the constant growl that curled my lips in his presence.

At last, he stepped up to the bars, his eyes narrowed. "So, Rhyan, this is it. You've finally done it," he snarled.

I noted that despite his bravado, he still kept somewhat of a distance from the bars, and from me—unlike the last time he'd had me in this position. Back in Glemaria, I'd been bound and locked up. Thrown into the deepest levels of the Glemarian dungeons. And I still found a way to choke him. He still remembered, and he was cautious, afraid to get too close. I was behind fucking bars, chained to the wall, three bindings spelled across my body, and still ...

I guess I could take that as a small win. I'd take anything I could get at this point.

"What is this?" I asked, my voice raw. I glanced pointedly behind him, no longer wanting to look at him. His face made me sick. "Making your final goodbye?"

Slowly, he shook his head, and I caught sight of some gray hairs in his beard I'd never seen before. His eyebrows narrowed to a deep V. "Something like that I suppose. And thank the Gods."

"I wouldn't thank the Gods," I growled.

"I certainly won't be thanking you. Because it was you who finally pushed me to this point," he continued, ignoring my words. He was always ignoring my words. Refusing to hear me. Even this time—the last time. I guess there was one benefit to death. I wouldn't have to experience this again.

"I tried to avoid this at all costs," he continued. "To my own detriment at times. To Glemaria's. And I did all of this for you."

"For me?" I laughed. "Fuck. Off." I gritted. "You're always the fucking martyr, aren't you? The savior, the hero and the victim. Are you not tired of your own Godsdamned gryphon shit by now? Of your constant lies? Because I sure as hell am. So just go fuck yourself. Because you did this. You chose this. You always chose this."

"I did no such thing," my father said. "I could have turned you in plenty of times over the years." His mouth tightened. "I didn't. I kept you safe. Protected! You were the one who compromised everything. You were the one who got yourself caught."

"And I'd do it again!" I yelled.

"Would you now? Let me guess. For her?" he taunted.

I snarled, daring him to say her name. Daring him to speak of Lyriana in my presence.

He shook his head, and laughed. "That's it, isn't it? It's always for her."

My hands flexed at my sides, at least, as much as they could. "Yes," I seethed. "It is. And you better fucking remember that! Because everything I said still stands. I meant every word when I swore to you that if you hurt her, if you harmed one hair on her head, there would be nowhere safe for you."

"And nowhere I can hide?" he asked mockingly, repeating my words from a month ago. So he had remembered that, too—good. But right now, he was trying to goad me, I could see it in his eyes, feel it in the storm of his aura. His anger. His hatred.

He shook his head, his eyes narrowed. "All of these threats you make for her are useless. You seem to forget in that small feeble mind of yours that *you're* the one in danger." He scoffed, "And yet, here you are. Helpless. Bound. And soon, you'll be stripped. Your threats mean nothing. Your words mean nothing. And your legacy will mean nothing. Because I will find her, trust me. And when I do, there will be hell waiting for her. She will do my will, and Kane's, and so much more. She will have no choice. She'll be in his bed and anywhere else I fucking want her. She already signed her life away. To me."

"No. She'll find a way," I said. "And you'll lose. She's stronger than you. Stronger than you know." I smiled, my lips wide like a madman's. "She's stronger than me. And she'll be the end of you, if I can't be the one."

His eyes narrowed further, but his chin twitched—one of his agitated tells. I was getting to him.

I straightened. "You're afraid," I said. His aura shifted, the change unmistakable. "Aren't you?" I laughed hysterically. "I'm about to be taken to the wolves, stripped of my clothing, of my power, of everything—all in front of the whole Godsdamned Empire. I'll be executed on your orders," I yelled.

"Dead within the hour," I choked out. "And yet, you—*you*—are more afraid than I am."

His nostrils flared, his neck reddening. "What makes you so sure? Hmmm?"

"You bent the knee," I spat. "You submitted to Avery fucking Kormac." I shook my head, feeling farther than Lethea with what I expected to be my last moments. A countdown to the end, a countdown that was almost over. But this was worth the time I had left. I stepped forward, the small amount my chains would afford me. Barely inches from the wall, and nowhere near the bars. But it was enough.

"You didn't give me up all these years because you cared about me." My voice cracked, and for a second, I hated myself for it. Hated myself for knowing what this man was. Knowing he was far worse than any akadim or demon of the ancient world. He was far more sinister. Because, at the very least, the other monsters presented themselves as such. They were honest in their monstrousness. They wore no masks. They were naked.

But this man? The one who raised me, who claimed the title of father—he was different.

Because in some small corner of my soul, something deep inside me still craved his love, still wanted him to love me back. To be proud of me. To care about me. And he didn't. He never did. I watched him kill my mother right in front of my eyes. I wanted to stab a knife through his throat and cut him limb from limb. And I still wanted him to hug me, and comfort me. Even now. I wanted him to tell me it would be all right. That dying would be easy. That it wouldn't hurt. Or Gods, tell me that he'd made a mistake, that he spoke to the Emperor, and he was going to break me out. He was going to save me. Let me go.

He wasn't going to do that. It was clear now: he never cared. If I was being honest with myself, it was clear a long fucking time ago.

But hearts are fickle things. And hope sometimes takes too long to die.

"You may not care about me," I gritted my teeth. "Or love me. I know that. But I'm still your son. I'm still your fucking son!" I roared.

He paled, but kept his mouth shut.

I shook my head. "That might not mean anything to you. I know it doesn't. But it means something to the rest of the world. To the Empire. And you look pathetic! You look weak handing over your own blood! You're doing this now," I said, "because you're losing. Because you lost your bid for the Throne. You'll never be Emperor! And I swear to you, after this, you won't remain Imperator much longer either. My death will be your downfall."

"Shut your Godsdamned mouth," he said, but he still didn't come any closer. "You know nothing! Foresight and vision were never part of your skillset. You were always so cocky, so sure of yourself when you had no reason to be."

"I had reason," I said.

The shouts outside were growing louder now, more frenzied. Calling for action, for violence. For blood.

My blood.

I closed my eyes, my body starting to shake involuntarily. It will be over soon. It will be over soon.

But when I looked at my father again, he actually looked sick. Regret? Guilt? A change of heart?

No. He'd never change. He was incapable. It was just as well. I had to accept that he was who he was. But I was also going to make sure that in my final moments, he knew exactly who I was. I was going to make sure he didn't forget what I'd promised. I wanted him to remember every day for the rest of his life, that the oath I'd made, that the threat I'd sworn, would still stand. That it would be enforced long after I was gone. My death would not stop justice from finding him.

My heart pounded then, a sudden warmth growing inside me, shooting out through my limbs. And just like that, I had a final burst of energy, of strength. The chains around me rattled, the nails in the walls coming loose. Not enough to break. Not enough to free me. But enough to cause fear in my father.

It was like the moment I'd made my decision, the moment I'd chosen to spend my last moments here on earth doing this, protecting Lyr, protecting my love, my partner, my *mekara*, something had taken over me, was helping me, supporting me. The same thing I'd felt when I first swore my oath against him.

Ancient power. The strength of a God. A kind of kashonim that went beyond this realm.

Auriel. My past life. My soul.

I held my father's gaze, holding it for what I swore would be the last time. "I promised you pain," I said, but I no longer sounded like myself. My voice had changed, and power beyond what I could hold vibrated through my words. "I promised you an eternity of suffering if you hurt her. An eternity of being hunted, life after life. I meant what I said. And just because I'm gone," I swore, "Doesn't mean I won't keep my oath. My death will not make you free of me."

His chest heaved and he stepped back, his eyes widening. "Rhyan!" He held a note of warning in his voice. But I recognized the truth of what lay beneath it.

Fear.

"Not Rhyan," I snarled. "You know who you're speaking to now, don't you? Not your son—not the boy you spent a lifetime trying to scare. I am more. I am eternal. I am Auriel. I am a God. And you know it. You've always known it. And still, you played with destinies beyond your control." I took another step forward, the chains straining against the wall, each one rattling, cracking. One nail popped, and rolled across the floor, stopping at my father's boot. "I want you to remember in the end, when you're all alone, when your people have abandoned you, and you're forced to admit how pathetic and weak you truly are—that you did this. You killed your son. Just as you killed your wife. And soon you will die. If not by my hand, then by one who I will choose to avenge me."

His nostrils flared. "Enough! Enough!" He scoffed, "Auriel! Like I'm to believe you. I've had a lifetime of your ramblings, Rhyan. Of your insolence, and your refusal to take ownership of your choices. Your mistakes. Your weaknesses. You want to speak about who plays the martyr, victim and hero? Well get a Godsdamned fucking mirror. And take a look! But do it soon. Because your time is done." He was losing control, he sounded on the verge of hysteria. "Do not tell me my fate when you didn't have the vision! When this was never your vorakh! I know! Not because of your mother, but because I have common fucking sense. And you don't know anything about how I'm seen! Or how this will look! Or how I will succeed! Now shut your mouth! Shut your Godsdamned fucking mouth! It's time to meet your fate, *Rhyan*."

He'd emphasized my name, saying it again like he was trying to summon me. To make sure it was me. Just me.

"Don't worry, father. I'm ready. At least, I can rest assured that my doom won't take so long. I'll be gone by nightfall. And I'll be at peace. But I promise you, your doom will last an eternity. I swear it to you. *Me sha, me ka.*"

The doors opened again, the sound echoing in the hall. Boots marched across the floor. A death march—mine. A line of soturi made their way to my father, and then passed him, making room for more and more. Each one had their sword out, their guard up.

My entourage was here to take me to the gallows. Out to the pole.

I guess it was a compliment that they perceived me as such a threat. Such a danger.

Look at that. I was receiving all sorts of praise since I'd entered this prison.

My father turned away, addressing the soturi all while their small, fearful eyes sized me up. Some soturi I recognized. Some I'd even bruised as I'd tried to escape my trial, fighting every second until I was locked into this cell.

But in that moment, the feeling of strength left me. Whatever part of me that was Auriel, that was larger than me, returned to wherever he had been summoned from. I collapsed against the wall, sinking to my knees, the rattling chains now still and silent.

I was drained. My time was up. So I cleared my mind of everything. Everything except for Lyr. Lyriana. *Mekara*. I would think of her, and just her for these final moments. Her sweet scent. Her sweeter taste. The hint of lemon and vanilla against her skin. The feel of her arms around me, the soft sound of her breathing in the dark of night. Her cries of passion when we came together. Her infectious laugh when we played. The way her face glowed when she smiled. Or she was discussing a topic she was excited about. The translation debate. High Lumerian. Dancing. The proper time to drink coffee—which was always, according to her.

And I would remember the first time I told her I loved her. The way she looked when she said she loved me, too. The way she radiated with light when our bodies joined. And our souls.

The feel of her against me, skin to skin, warm and sleepy in the morning, or drifting off at night, safe and tucked against me. Collapsing against my body, exhausted from training. Exhausted from other things. The way she dragged her fingers through my hair. Her lips across my throat and neck. Her hips shimmying, dancing, undulating. Her hands in mine, fingers threaded together. The gentle jingling sound her bracelets made. The way she called me "partner" when she was mad at me. The way she called me Rhyan when she wasn't.

Her wild, beautiful hair in the moonlight, as dark as a raven's. Her hair in the fire of the sun. Batavia red. Asherah's red. Lyriana's red.

Lyr.

Lyr.

Lyr …

CHAPTER TWO

LYRIANA

"Shhh. Hey. Hey," Rhyan spoke softly, his arms protectively circling around me. There was only the moon and the stars for light as we stood beneath them. "I've got you. I've got you. Deep breaths. It's all right." He pulled me closer, and I buried my face against his armored chest while my hands remained protectively wrapped around my body. "Breathe with me. Come on, Lyr. You can do it. It's all right. I've got you. You're safe with me. I swear."

My breath hitched, a sense of dread washing over me. I wasn't safe. I wasn't …

Thunder clapped, the crash echoing as lightning struck in the distance.

Rhyan slid his arm behind my knees, and scooped me up until he was cradling me against his chest. He walked forward, his boots sinking into the damp sand of the abandoned beach. The Guardian of Bamaria stared out into the water beside us.

A clap of thunder echoed across the shore. The Guardian's head flickered, going in and out of existence, vanishing and reappearing in such rapid succession, I felt dizzy just looking at it. Until it stopped. Until a headless gryphon loomed over me.

I blinked, and its head was back, its onyx eyes trained on the ocean as usual. I felt strange. Panicked. This wasn't what I remembered of that night. Because that's what this was—a memory.

Breathing still felt difficult as I clung to Rhyan, watching the tides come in, their watery surface reflecting flashes of starlight.

The air cooled even further, and rain fell softly around us, landing in thick, fat droplets that pattered against the sand.

"You see the waves?" Rhyan angled his body, offering me an easy view of the Lumerian Ocean. "The waves," he said again, his voice a whisper. His arms shifted and tightened against me. "Just watch the waves, rolling back and forth. Back and forth. Nice and easy. Just keep watching. I've got you. You're all right." He nuzzled my cheek. "Mekara."

I shook my head. "You didn't call me that last time." The raindrops pebbled against my forehead, falling into my eyes until my vision blurred. "And it wasn't raining." I remembered that night all those months ago so clearly. It had been cooler than it had been in weeks, marking the start of the fall season. We were celebrating Days of Shadows. Waves had been crashing against the shore. And after two years of silence, I'd broken my blood oath. I'd told Rhyan the secret I was prepared to die for. I'd told him about Meera's vorakh. A storm had been brewing in the distance, making the waves crash, agitating our seraphim. But it hadn't been raining. Not like this—not when we'd been here together. Alone.

Rhyan shrugged, continuing to hold me and stare into the dark of the water. "Does it really matter? We can make the memory whatever we want."

"Yes," I protested. "It does. We can't just change them. My memories of you matter."

"The past hasn't gone anywhere."

"No," I cried, a sinking feeling in my heart. "But you have. Don't do this. Don't change the memories. They're all I have now. All I—" There was another more visceral memory, the memory of what had just happened. The thing that could not be changed, could not be undone. I had a strange feeling—a sensation filled with the horror of it all—as reality crashed into me, forcing me to remember. It was breaking the spell on us. "No. No."

"What is it?" Rhyan asked. "Partner? What's wrong?"

I shook my head. "Memories are not enough. We were supposed to have more time together. We were supposed to have decades, years. We were supposed to make more memories. Do more things. We were supposed to—"

Marry me.

I sobbed. "This isn't the way it's supposed to be between us. It's not right. And it's not …" I was choking on my words, my chest heaving. "It's not enough. Rhyan, this will never be enough. I don't want this. I don't want any of this. I only want you. You. Here. Now."

"I am here, Lyr, I'm right here." His eyes dipped to my chest. To my heart. "There. And I'm here. Holding you."

"No … Rhyan! You're … You're not here." I tightened my grip on him, shaking my head wildly, the tears were burning my eyes. "You're not with me. I tried. I tried so hard. But I couldn't find you."

A raindrop fell onto his forehead, slipping down the length of his scar. Slowly, it descended down his cheek. "Lyriana," he said, his voice full of emotion. And then his eyes dampened, tears welling and running down his face.

"Rhyan!" I sobbed. "Where are you? Where did you go? Tell me where to find you! Tell me how to help you. Heal you. Save you." I pushed myself out of his arms, until I was standing before him, grabbing and shaking his shoulders. "Tell me!"

His gaze hardened, his lips tightening, as his already pale skin seemed to whiten. "Oh, Lyr. My Lyriana. I didn't want it to be true. Not yet. But I'm not here." Something shone in his eyes. Like his own memories had returned. "And I'm not … I'm not all right. I'm … I'm somewhere else now. Something else." The muscles in his jaw flexed, and he looked away, his gaze refusing to meet mine. The scar that ran through his left eyebrow darkened, lengthening down his cheek. It was angrier and redder than I'd ever seen it. As if his father had just freshly carved it into his skin.

He had done that though. That was exactly what he'd done tonight to Rhyan—and worse. He'd turned him over to the Emperor. Carved into him. Hurt him. Tortured him.

Stripped him of his magic. His power.

There was a flash of blinding light. A scream of pure, unbridled pain. The sound of a whip flying in the air. The whoosh of a Valalumir star soaring.

I stilled. The memories. The truth. They were returning with more force. We didn't have much time left.

"It's okay," he assured me. "Partner, just ignore them. Forget them all. Don't listen. Don't look. Just stay here with me."

"I can't. I have to save you," I cried.

I reached for Rhyan's face, and traced the scar from his dark eyebrow down to his cheek, feeling him shiver beneath my touch. I reached the edge of the scar, the edge of the line I knew so well because I'd traced it with my fingers a hundred times. Because I'd kissed it just as many when we were together. But the scar didn't end where it was supposed to—tapering off to clear, pale skin. It ran all the way across his cheek, expanding, and lengthening, reaching for his earlobe, and slithering toward the line of his jaw. My eyes widened as even more red lines began to appear, crisscrossing his face, circling around his neck. His eyes were on mine, blazing and green as emeralds, his chest heaving.

His aura swept over me. But it felt foreign. Not like his, not like anything I'd ever felt from him before. Rhyan's aura had always been like a soothing cold, the peace of being tucked safely into your bed on a snowy night. He was fresh air when I needed a breath, water when I was overheated from exertion. And always, always my anchor in the storm.

But the aura I felt now was icy, and violent. And above all else, dripping with a nauseating fear.

In the distance, the waters of the Lumerian Ocean began to recede further and further from the shore, exposing more and more rock and sand beneath it.

Rhyan watched calmly as the water surged towards the horizon, its waves rising higher, reaching for the night sky. Thunder clapped and I could feel the waves preparing to break, preparing to rush at us. There was enough power brewing now, enough magic in the air for me to realize exactly what was coming.

A tsunami. One that wouldn't just cover the island, or Bamaria. It would be enough to drown us all. To sink the whole Empire.

A second Drowning.

"Rhyan," I said, taking his hand, our fingers threaded together. "We have to go! We have to get out of here." But my voice sounded distant and far away, barely audible over the roaring tides. "The storm is coming. Now. Hurry!"

Blinking slowly, his green eyes bored into mine. Emerald. Beautiful. But sad and resigned.

"Lyr. Mekara." Rhyan shook his head. "Even you can't heal me now."

He turned his back on the abandoned shoreline and held his arms out as the waves rushed forward, racing toward us. The waters surged, swallowing the rocks on the beach, as it covered the ground, moving faster, and rising higher.

"RHYAN!" I yelled.

He frowned, suddenly taller as he looked down at me. And I realized, to my horror, his eyes had changed. The green of his irises that I'd dreamed of for years, the green I knew so well, that I loved since I was a girl, had been replaced with red. The glowing red eyes that only meant one thing.

Akadim. A demon. Death.

The waters burst behind Rhyan, the waves reaching like tentacles for his body, until it wrapped itself around him. Trapping him, binding him.

His hand reached out for mine one last time. "Lyr ... I love you."

And I screamed, as the water swallowed him whole, pulling him beneath the tides. "RHYAN!"

There was a burst of light behind my eyes, the sound of thunder crashing, and rain pouring.

I jolted awake, my eyes soaking wet. I was already sobbing, hugging myself, my entire body convulsing.

"Rhyan! Rhyan!" I cried out his name, but the sound was choked, barely more than a strangled whisper. Still shaking, I tried to take in my surroundings. To remember where the hell I was.

I was in a cave, laying on a blanket I didn't recognize, not far from the mouth. I was close enough to see outside, to see the beach in the dark. And I remembered. I was on Gryphon Island. For the first time in months, I was back in Bamaria. My home country.

And sitting at the edge of the beach, its onyx stone glistening as the rain covered its body in heavy sheets of water, was the Guardian of Bamaria. Tall, and regal, the gryphon's body pointed to the ocean, to the waters of Lumeria. For a thousand years it had guarded our shores, and watched over our land. It was the first to spot visitors traveling by boat—those coming from the North, and those visiting from the East, from Lethea.

But no more. Its eagle head was gone. In my rage, I'd stabbed the Guardian, and beaten the stone until I'd decapitated him. I tossed its head into the water ... and then ... Gods. The water had receded. A tsunami *had* been brewing. Enough to destroy the island. To destroy the Empire.

To bring a second Drowning.

But I'd stopped. I'd let go of my *Rakashonim*. Let go of the burning fury and anger that had fueled my Goddess power and strength. My connection to Asherah. We had been seconds from destruction. From the pain finally stopping. But I'd let it go. I'd released the waters, the storm ... I had released everything.

But only because ...

A crackling sound had me turning my head. The torches within the cavern had been lit. But not by me.

My heart thundered, and I walked deeper into the cave, following the lights through its labyrinthine halls. They were familiar to me and left a stinging ache in my chest.

I had come here once before. With Rhyan.

The night the akadim attacked Bamaria. The night of Valyati. The night we'd lost Haleika and Leander. The night Rhyan revealed to me his vorakh.

And it was on that night, in this cave, that he first told me he loved me.

I'm in love with you. And no matter how wrong, or how much it scares me, there is no oath in Heaven or Lumeria that could stop me. Lyr … Lyriana, I love you.

My vision blurred, more memories from that night haunting me. And before I knew it, my hand had fisted, and I was punching the wall, slamming my fingers into the rough rock. I didn't care that it bruised my knuckles. Didn't care that when I hit it again, I scraped my skin. Nor did it bother me when after my next punch, I'd started bleeding. I didn't care that it hurt.

Because nothing could come near the pain exploding in my heart.

My grief was like a rage that had nowhere to go. Nowhere to be released. I needed a way to unleash the pain. The sorrow. If I didn't, I'd combust. I'd dissolve.

I raised my arm again, ready to let loose, ready to break my Godsdamned fingers if it made this pain go away.

But the sound of footsteps echoing around the corner made me still. My hand snaked toward the hilt of my dagger. Heart pounding, I rushed forward, slipping out my blade, and pointing it at the intruder.

"Lyriana!" Auriel appeared from behind the shadows, his arms full of sticks and loose bramble. "By the realms. You're awake." His eyes dipped to the blade. His eyebrows creased together. "And … armed."

Blinking, I stumbled back, and sheathed the dagger at my hip.

Auriel. Auriel was real. He was really here. I hadn't imagined him. I hadn't hallucinated. This was all happening. Even the parts of the night that had been a nightmare. My breath came short with the knowledge of it.

"Don't be alarmed," he said quietly. "It's just you and me here. I brought you inside the cave. After the … the waters settled, the rain began to fall. Pretty abruptly."

I simply stared, dumbfounded. I'd dreamt of this man. I had memories of this God. I'd even loved him. In another life. Before I'd known Rhyan, before I'd loved Rhyan. I'd known and loved Auriel when I was Asherah. Loved him before I was me.

Ani janam ra.

But all I could manage to say in response was, "You carried me in here?"

The muscles in his jaw worked. "I did. And I found that blanket for you. I'm sorry I wasn't at your side when you woke. I've been—well," he lifted his shoulders, something sheepish in his expression, "gathering wood. I wanted to build you a fire. Keep you warm. You were … so cold when you fainted."

"I fainted?"

He nodded slowly. "You did. Right after I—well, after I told you who I was. How are you—I mean, are you …" He made a frustrated face—like he was trying to remember how to act as a mortal. As a human. Alive. "Are you feeling any better now?" he asked at last.

"I don't understand," I said. "You're Auriel? Auriel the God. You're my—" I shook my head. "You're Rhyan's …?"

"Yes. And yes. I am him. I share the same soul as Rhyan, the same memories. Except, I don't have *his* memories exactly—not yet, at least. But he has mine." His lips quirked into a very Rhyan-like smile. Unsure, self-deprecating. It was like a blade through my heart. The opposite of what I'd expect from a God. He pushed the sticks out in front of him. "I haven't had to make one of these in a thousand years." He eyed the torches. "I kind of forgot how. Plus being in a physical body, I'm starting to remember all the limitations that come with it. More than I recalled." He furrowed his eyebrows. "At least, it feels like more than last time. It's harder to move."

I blinked, not sure how to react or what to say.

He continued, "And it feels harder to think, too, and to remember everything I knew before. I know who I am," he nodded, "and I remember where I was—before I came down. Here," he specified. As if there was anywhere else. "But my memories of being here, of being alive last time ... they feel like they're almost locked away. Even the ... the knowledge I know I had—right before I came to you. It's so close, and so far away, the things I know that I knew before, things that were important ... it feels like I lost it." He sighed, his aura flaring, emitting an almost cloudy, foggy sensation. "Luckily, these were easy to light." He jerked his chin at the torches. "And I'll figure out the rest. Come. Follow me. I'll have you warmed up in no time."

He brushed past me as he returned to the mouth of the cave, just beyond the blanket where I'd been sleeping.

Sleeping. Sleeping! Sleeping while Rhyan was—after he'd been—

My chest tightened, and I clutched at my heart, reality sinking in.

"Lyriana?" Auriel asked, his face schooled with concern.

"He's gone, isn't he?" I asked, my voice breaking.

Auriel dropped the sticks into a pile, and wiped his hands together, before nodding slowly. He frowned. "I wouldn't be here otherwise."

For a moment, I felt a dizzying lightness, like I'd left my body. Like I was floating above myself, seeing everything from a great distance.

A laugh burst from me, slamming me back down, and then another laugh came, until I couldn't stop. Tears were running down my face, so hot, so fast I couldn't see in front of me. I couldn't stop crying. And I couldn't stop laughing.

Hysterical. That was the word for this, right? I was hysterical. Mad. Farther than fucking Lethea.

Because a God! An actual fucking God—my soulmate, the God that I had loved in a past life—was standing here before me, wearing golden armor, and wondering with great difficultly how to build a fire for me out of sticks.

And by the Gods if he didn't fully look the part. If that didn't make the whole thing even more absurd. Soft golden curls sat atop his head, and his eyes blazed, beautiful and green, otherworldly with light. His golden armor, too rich and fine to be from this world, was shaped the same way as Rhyan's black leathers, perfectly covering his muscular torso. He wore what appeared to be a new soturion cloak. It was wrapped around his waist, and flowed out from the shoulders of his armor like a cape. Elegant, freshly pressed, and fitted to perfection. Oddly, he had no weapons, but he was wearing a traditionally styled belt with seven leather straps, golden Valalumirs embedded at the bottom of each one. And laced up his thick, muscular legs, were soturion-issue sandals made of soft, worn leather.

An ancient God of the celestial realms. A Guardian of the Valalumir. Auriel, God of the Green Ray. And here he was, standing before me, a pile of old sticks between us.

I laughed even harder.

"Lyriana," he said, his voice softened. "Are you—" He started forward, his hand lifted. Gold cuffs circled his wrists, gleaming in the torchlight. And his skin—tan. Too tan for

Rhyan—for someone from the North. He was certainly not from the cold and snowy region of Glemaria. Then again, he wasn't even originally from this world. "Can I—?" He stepped forward—both arms extended. Like he meant to hug me.

"Don't! Don't touch me!" I stumbled back, clutching my chest. My stomach twisted violently. I couldn't take it. And at that moment, I couldn't bear it to even look at Auriel. Look at his features that were all somehow Rhyan's, but not-Rhyan's. It was like the Guardian in my dreams, his head flickering in and out of existence. Looking at Auriel was like looking at Rhyan and then being immediately reminded that I wasn't. He was Rhyan, and not Rhyan. Rhyan, but not-Rhyan. It was painful enough as it was. A cutting reminder of my new reality. I didn't think I could take being touched on top of it.

"Lyriana," Auriel said.

"Don't!" I yelled again.

He froze. "I-I won't." He held his hands up, revealing his palms were thick with scar tissue. Burns from the fire. From holding the Valalumir as he fell. There were patches of raised skin, some pink and leathery, the edges still red. Other parts of his hand looked like they'd been flattened—the skin taken out in these almost flame-like shaped indents. There, his skin was almost white. I could almost see exactly how the light would have moved as he fell, how the flames would have licked and seared him.

I can cool you with my waters. You don't have to burn.
You're the fire.

I clutched at my chest. Gods! GODS! I couldn't breathe. I couldn't fucking breathe. My knees were buckling, my stomach burning.

"Hey!" he shouted. "Lyriana, I need you to take a deep breath. Come on. You need to breathe for me. For *him*. Lyriana, can you do that?" He started forward again.

I stepped back, my entire chest tightening further. It was almost exactly something Rhyan would say. Something Rhyan had said. But not quite. Everything about Auriel was like looking at a reflection of Rhyan through water. Him, but distorted. Him, but wrong.

"Please," Auriel begged. "Let me—I'm here to help you."

I shook my head. No, no, no. I could stand it—the thought of being touched by someone that wasn't Rhyan. Even if I knew it was part of him, the old version of him, part of the same soul I loved, I didn't care. It didn't matter. I wanted Rhyan. I needed Rhyan.

Rhyan.

Rhyan.

Gods. Fuck! My chest hurt, growing painfully tight. I still couldn't breathe. I couldn't fucking breathe. Everything inside of me felt violent and empty. Like my heart had shattered, like it had turned to glass and every shard was trying to cut me from inside. Like I was going to die. I truly felt like I was going to die. The panic this time wouldn't subside. Not without, not without Rhy—

My knees shook, my hands trembled. This pain, this rage, this feeling of dying was going to burst inside of me. End me. It hurt so much, so badly. I couldn't take it anymore. I couldn't fucking take it.

I was only half aware of Auriel, of the way his eyes filled with concern. I blinked, my vision darkening. And when I focused on him again, his expression was murderous, like he was seconds from rushing to me. Like there was something to fight—some enemy to kill to make me breathe again. To make things better.

There wasn't. Because I was my own enemy now. And yet, even I knew I wasn't going to last like this. The pain intensified. And suddenly, it all came to a head. I gasped, taking in an explosive breath that bled into a scream.

My hand flew up, and I punched the wall again, smashing my already scratched-up knuckles, widening wounds that were already bleeding. Sharp pain rushed up my arm, and blood gushed onto the wall.

I drew back, ready to punch again. Ready to smash my fingers, break my arm ...

"Stop!" Auriel yelled. "Stop! His eyes widened. "You're bleeding." He stepped closer, reaching for me.

"No! No!"

"Lyriana, let me—" He frowned, biting his bottom lip. Then his nostrils flared, and there was a determined look in his eyes like some decision had been made. "Enough of this. Come to me. Now." An order. Not a request. "Show me your hand." He took another step.

"I said," I seethed. "Don't touch me."

"You're hurt. And you're going to hurt yourself more if you don't stop."

"You think I care about that? That I care about any of this? That anything could matter to me after Rhyan—after I—" Another sob tore through me, and I couldn't finish, couldn't get the words out. I sank to my knees. Auriel dropped too, kneeling in front of me, his eyes searching mine.

"Tell me," he said, his voice desperate. "Please. Tell me what I can do. Tell me how to help you."

"Help me? HELP?" I screamed. "You can't help, Auriel! No one can. Especially you! Because you ... You!" I shook my head. "You've already ruined everything." My tears fell harder.

"Ruined?"

"Yes! Ruined!" My entire body deflated, any semblance of energy I had, any force of will to survive was gone. "Why?" I sobbed. "Why did you stop me out there?" I thrust my arm out, pointing beyond the cave. To the ocean. To the place where I'd destroyed an ancient statue, where I'd summoned a tsunami in my rage, the power of *Rakashonim* burning inside of me. The power and strength of a Goddess, of the Valalumir itself. The waves were coming. World-ending waves. Continent sinking. "Why didn't you let me do it? Why didn't you let me end it?"

Because after all I'd seen, after all that had happened—I didn't want to be here anymore. I didn't want to feel this. And I didn't want to live in a world that was this cruel, this unfair. I didn't want to live in a world that could enact such evil.

But above all else, I didn't want to live in a world without Rhyan.

"I could do no such thing," Auriel said. "Not when it comes to you. Lyriana, that's not why you, why Asherah, first came here a millennia ago. And it's not why you came here again, why you came this time as Lyriana," he said, his voice gentle. "This is not who you are. This is not the work of the soul I have known for an eternity. You were not meant to destroy." His eyes blazed. "Asherah, you were meant to heal."

My blood heated. I was so Godsdamned sick of being called Asherah. Of having to put my life aside for the one she had lived. Of having to be here now with her love, her soulmate. And not mine.

"I'm not Asherah!" I yelled. "Not anymore. I haven't been for a very long time. Do you hear me? I've changed. We all have. So who the hell are you to tell me what I was or wasn't meant for? You don't fucking know me!"

"I do."

"You don't—"

"I DO!" he roared, his face reddening. "You seem to think that just because you're not currently Asherah that it doesn't make you her. Did you forget that her soul and her light are connected to and bound to your body? That those are the essences from which you were born? That your fate is connected? She is informing your heart, and your mind. She is your soul, and she is influencing, in every second and every way, the very being who calls herself Lyriana! You think that me being here now, isn't proof of that? Isn't proof to you that Rhyan isn't completely gone either? That he's not completely lost? That the part of him that was made from me still survives because I do?"

"Part of him? Part of him! A part of him isn't enough. A soul isn't enough!" My hands fisted, punching my knees. "Neither is an incarnation. Or you! Just him. Him! And he's not here," I cried. "He didn't survive. I can't touch him. Smell him. Kiss him." My voice cracked. "I'll never hug him again. Hold him. Be held." I shook my head. "And I'll never talk to him! Never see him smile, or hear *his* laugh. I'm not going to see him heal and grow and live his life. I'll never get to see what he might have become." This feeling that had begun to grow in my chest, intensified. More painful than a tightening. Sharper than the shards slicing. My heart was tearing itself into pieces, ripping apart bit by bit. "I don't care if you're connected. I don't! Because you are not a replacement for him. And you never will be! Not for me. Not ever! I don't want you."

"Well, you're no replacement for her either!" Auriel yelled. "But I still came here. I came here for *you*, Lyriana!"

"Why?" I cried. "Why would you do that?"

"Because, you called out to me. Because I heard you, heard your cries. Your distress. I heard them from worlds away. From another time. And when I sensed your despair, I didn't hesitate to act. To risk everything. Because I felt your pain, too. I felt your heart breaking like it was my own." He slammed a fist to his heart, his voice shaking. "I don't know how I did it. Because it shouldn't have been possible. But I did. My heart broke. For you. So I came. Somehow, I traveled through a dozen celestial realms. I broke the laws of time and space to reach you. To stop you from ending it all. Because of you—just you—I did the impossible. I took on my body again. Pushed my way through Heaven and Earth, just to stop you. To help you. To be here with you. Again."

I gritted my teeth. "Gods. You sound just like him." I pulled my knees into my chest, burying my head against them. I squeezed my eyes shut. "Fuck. I can't … I can't do this. I can't be near you. I can't talk to you, or listen to you." I was barely getting the words out, I was choking on them, crying out every syllable. "Every second is a reminder that he's not here. Every second is a reminder that I failed him. I failed him in the worst possible way! I swore to him I wouldn't, but I did. I lost him. I wasn't strong enough. And he suffered because of it. Because of me. And now he's gone. And it's my fault. And nothing I can do will fix it, nothing will bring him back," I sobbed.

Even before tonight. I'd dragged him into this. Into going after Jules. Into making a deal with his father. Into working with him. Playing the game until the very end.

I'd killed him. And there it was again—the panic, my chest collapsing in on itself, feeling like I couldn't breathe. And it wasn't just my heart ripping apart that would kill me this time, or the way my lungs had forgotten how to work. I felt like the walls of the cave were going to close in on me. Crush me. Suffocate me.

I needed Rhyan. I needed Rhyan.

"Lyriana, listen to me, and listen carefully. I see where your mind is going. And I know, because mine has done the same in the past. You need to stop. Right now. It wasn't your fault. You didn't do this to him," Auriel said. "None of what happened last night was your fault. Nor anything that happened before. My memories are hazy, but this I remember. I saw it all. I saw what it was like between you two. I saw what happened in the arena. And I swear to you, I know you did everything you could, I know you pushed yourself beyond your limits. And, I know he knows that, too. I promise."

"But I didn't. I didn't. I could have made better choices. I could have been faster. I could have—"

"He remembered," Auriel said, suddenly looking distant. "He's been so connected to me these last few months—more than any of my other incarnations. After he learned the truth of who he was, it was like a bridge opened between us. He remembered the pain. Our pain. My pain. What it was like to lose you. To lose Asherah. Even after all of this time, it doesn't go away. The memories. The hurt. They … leave a scar on your soul. And you were in danger, so he did what he had to do to save you. To stop the threat. If you could talk to him now, he would tell you the same thing. He would tell you he'd save you again, knowing the outcome, knowing what would happen—he'd still do it. Still save you. Every single time. If he could, he'd tell you he has no regrets."

"But he can't tell me. Not anymore. He's …" Not alive. Not dead either. "He's …" My throat dried, my hands shaking. "He's akadim," I said, finally looking up. The word was like acid in my mouth, every syllable burned as I said it. I could taste it, feel it crawling over my tongue. I wanted to vomit. *Akadim. Akadim.* "He is. Isn't he? I saw it happen. Saw his soul being eaten." A weight settled over me, crushing me. "Surely, by now the transformation's complete."

The muscles in Auriel's jaw flexed. "He is."

More tears fell. "How long?" I asked. "How long has he been akadim? How long have I been asleep?"

Auriel coughed. "It's been a few hours. I think that … the shock of seeing me didn't help. And you had overused your magic, your *Rakashonim*. It made you pass out. It was too much. The magic is delicate, but volatile on its own. And it had been called on too many times. You had no more power in you by then, no energy left. After I reached you, you simply fell over."

"I hardly have any energy now." I barely even felt like I could stand. I shook my head. "It doesn't matter. I don't

... don't care. I wish I'd gone with him," I said, my voice a whisper.

"No," Auriel said. "No, you don't. And don't you ever say that again. However much you love him, he loves you more. I would know. I felt it. I still feel it." He pressed a fist to his heart. "He wouldn't want that for you. Everything he did, every choice Rhyan made in his life was to protect you. You must believe me." His eyes fell to my hands again. "Now enough of this. Fight me if you have to. Insult me. Hit me. I don't care. But I'm not sitting idly by and watching you bleed. Whether you like it or not, I'm cleaning up your hand."

I squeezed my eyes shut, feeling so fucking weak. I wanted to fight, and yet, there was no more fight inside of me. "Do what you will to me," I said. "I don't care."

"Well, luckily for you, I do. Don't move."

I lifted my head higher, numbness seeping through me, as Auriel held his cloak out of the cave, letting it collect rain. Thunder clapped in the distance. Lightning illuminated his body from behind. His hair seemed like it had curled even more from the humidity—just like Rhyan's did.

When he decided that his cloak was sufficiently wet, he returned to me, kneeling at my feet, and gently washed the blood from my knuckles before going into his belt and miraculously pulling out a sunleaf. He popped it into his mouth, chewing until it was paste—his eyes on mine the whole time, as if daring me to rebel, challenging me to refuse him.

Then he spat out the leaf, now cured, into his palm, and gently rubbed it onto my skin.

I'd barely been aware of the sting, of the pain, even as he washed my skin. But the relief I felt was instantly palpable.

I stared at the floor, at the blanket he'd scrounged up, and at the small piece of cloth he'd ripped from this cloak to bandage my hand. When he was done, he sat across from me, his back to the wall. A long silence passed between us. Our breaths mingled with the sound of the rain, the crackling of the fires, and tinkle of water dripping into the cave.

"What are you thinking?" he asked.

"I have to kill him," I said, my voice empty. The truth that had been buried in the back of my mind, the one I'd screwed tight in a box, because I never wanted to open it. "I have to find him. Don't I? And kill him."

"No," Auriel said, his eyes full of alarm. "Lyriana, no. You can't do that."

I shrugged. "Maybe I can't. I might not be strong enough." Akadim had the strength of five soturi. Even the weakest and smallest ones could overpower you. Coming across an akadim who hadn't trained in combat was still a near-impossible kill to make. But taking on Rhyan as an akadim? Rhyan was the strongest warrior in the Empire. And he knew all of my moves, my weaknesses, my tells. He'd trained me himself. Fighting him was going to be like taking on a small army. "He'll be impossibly strong. He might even be the strongest akadim that ever existed."

"That's not what I meant," Auriel said. "I meant—" He frowned. "I ... Realms." He squinted, like he was in pain and shook his head. He'd lost his train of thought—his memories really weren't accessible to him now.

"It doesn't matter if I'm strong enough. Or ready. I never will be. But I still have to try." I sniffled. "For him." A fresh bout of pain washed over me, like a wet blanket sinking into my heart, weighing it down. "Because I can't allow it. Can't allow him to live like this. Do you understand how horrible this fate is for Rhyan? What being an akadim will do to him? The part of him that was *him*? Alive? He could be hurting people. Killing them. Or—"By the Gods. I couldn't fathom where my mind was going next. Because Rhyan was always so careful with me, so concerned with making sure I was okay every step of the way when we were together. Whether it was our bodies joining, or him healing me, or training me. He never did anything I didn't want him to—that I wasn't comfortable with, or ready for. That I didn't say yes to.

The idea of Rhyan not taking those things into account—not caring, the idea of Rhyan fully acting like an akadim, Rhyan doing what akadim did ... I couldn't even form the word for what it was. Couldn't put Rhyan and *that* into the same sentence.

My stomach twisted violently, and I leaned over the blanket, throwing up all over the floor. Bile burned my throat as I heaved again and again.

Auriel rushed to his feet and moved behind me, collecting my hair in one hand, and rubbing my neck with the other. He really was trying to take care of me. Trying to soothe me. Like Rhyan would have.

Fresh tears fell down my face. "I just can't let him be like this. Being an akadim would have been his worst nightmare. He's too gentle for this life. He cares for people too much." I shook my head, "He won't always show it, but he does. He can't stand the thought of hurting someone. Especially someone innocent. He can't even stand to let people down. When he thinks he's failed someone—even when things were clearly out of his control, even when he did everything he could, even if he did everything right, the way he beats himself up—" I froze "*Beat*-past tense. He ... No. No. I can't let him be like this. I can't allow him to be a monster."

"Maybe he doesn't have to be one," Auriel said.

"I don't think either of us are getting a choice in the matter anymore." I wiped my mouth, and spat, leaning away from Auriel's touch. Then I rose to my feet. "I have to go," I said.

"Go? Go where?"

"Numeria. The capital. That's where Rhyan was when he turned. He might still be there. If he's not, he won't be far."

"You can't leave," Auriel said. "Not now. Not yet. You're still drained, your magic depleted. And the rain out there ..." He shook his head. "You need to wait."

"I already waited," I said, my body at the edge of the cave. "Too long."

Auriel took my hand again, and led me back to the blanket. "Please. Just wait a little longer. Until the sun rises. Or at least, wait until the rain stops. Recover your strength, then we'll figure it out."

I wrapped my arms around myself, listening to the rainfall, the truth of it all weighing me down.

When I'd made my choice earlier tonight, I'd bet on the fact that I'd reach Rhyan before he was stripped. Before it was too late. I'd bet that I had enough magic power on reserve to get to him, to fight my way to his side. I thought that if I combined the magic of the red light inside my chest together with the shield containing the orange shard—Ereshya's shard—I could do it. I'd have enough light from the Valalumir supporting me. And I would call on *Rakashonim*, embody the full power and magic of Asherah, take on all of the strength of my past self, and fight my way to him. Save him.

I'd given everything I had. Risked everything else I could. Everything. But it hadn't been enough.

I hadn't been enough. I'd been too slow. Too weak. Too late. I'd failed. Failed him when he needed me most.

I never should have gone after the orange shard, never should have tried to steal the shield. I should have used what I had—relied on my own strength. My own fury and love. I should have gone straight to him. Even if I'd lost limbs it wouldn't have mattered. I could have reached him first. Before he was stripped. Before the akadim came.

That Godsdamned fucking shield. I was so sure I needed it. Needed to let its ancient power surge through me. And in the end—all I'd done is trade it back to Morgana. Given her another damn shard of the Valalumir. Traded for Rhyan's life so I could escape the damn Throne Room. The room Morgana had blockaded with akadim.

And then, my enemy, my sister, Aemon's lover—Moriel's lover—betrayed me again.

Because it was their fucking akadim, their monsters, who'd taken my love.

And I hadn't returned to the inn for my family and friends as I'd promised. They didn't know yet what had happened. Not to me. Not to Rhyan. Nor the orange shard that we'd been trying for a month to steal.

And even worse, now, there was a small army of newly formed akadim hunting in Lumeria. Rhyan amongst them. Akadim unlike any I'd seen before. Akadim who could walk in the day.

It was becoming increasingly clear what had to happen next. My friends, and my family had to be kept safe. Protected. Not just from the Empire. But from Rhyan.

I'd have to return to Numeria. I'd have to hunt akadim. Hunt down the man I loved.

Because even if killing him would destroy me, even if I lost my life doing so, it was better than the alternative. Better than letting his demon-self destroy whatever remained of his soul, and all that remained of his memories—all that remained of us.

I didn't know now if any of his soul remained or existed in any form. I didn't know what happened to a soul after it was eaten. I didn't know how this worked. He was Auriel. But Auriel wasn't him. Thinking about it was too confusing. But if there was any chance that Rhyan wasn't completely gone, that some part of his soul survived, even a mere slither of the light that Rhyan once was—I wouldn't let it be tarnished. Not while I still had strength.

Memories weren't enough. None of this was enough. I disavowed this life. This fate. And I was fully ready to release every deal, promise, oath, and duty that had ever been thrust upon me. Everything I had ever agreed upon, or sworn to, was now void. None of it mattered anymore. Not my hopes, my dreams. Not my future. Not when Rhyan was gone.

But, I could do this. I could do this much for him. For my lover, my best friend, my partner, my soulmate.

My *Rakame*.

I would wait a little. But only a little. Just enough to recover my strength, enough to move forward. And then I'd go. Myself. There would be no "we" as far as Auriel was concerned.

I knew what I had to do. Kill the akadim Rhyan, stop the threat it posed to his soul, stop him from doing further harm—save anyone who might come across him now. Save everyone else we loved.

I stood again, returning to the cave's threshold, my body taut, and ready, the rain pouring down beside me.

If I couldn't save Rhyan's life, if I couldn't heal him, couldn't restore his soul, or have him back, then I could honor his memory.

I would slay him.

CHAPTER THREE

MORGANA

I rose naked from the river, letting the water sluice from my bare skin. It glistened in the moonlight, as I wrung out my hair, feeling more refreshed than I had in hours. More energetic, and more powerful, despite how much magic I'd drawn on through the night. I'd never been this strong. Never this precise with my power. And never with this level of authority. It was heady. Addictive.

And it was all thanks to a fresh scar that appeared on my right wrist. As of tonight, I had three. One for my Revelation Ceremony when I became a mage. One for the kashonim I'd formed with the apprentice I left behind in Bamaria. And the third, Aemon had sliced into my skin tonight when I claimed my shield. Ereshya's shield. Ancient and bronze and full of power. We had finally liberated it from the hands of the Emperor. No longer could they draw upon that magic, that energy. No longer could they use the orange shard embedded within to enact their will. My shard, the one which represented my light of the Valalumir, was back where it belonged. But more than that. I didn't just possess the shard, and the shield. Because also within was Ereshya's blood. Blood that now flowed through my veins.

The tides had turned overnight. Lyr wasn't the only one who could call on *Rakashonim* now. She wasn't the only one who could join her power with that of her past self. From now on, I could embody the full strength and power of the Goddess I once was. The queen who'd ruled over the akadim a thousand years ago.

Maraaka Ereshya was back and with a vengeance. I'd felt this intense connection to the shard and my shield the moment I laid eyes on it. But now, after weeks and weeks of dreaming of Ereshya, and remembering my past life, remembering coming down here, getting used to a mortal life, deepening my relationship with Moriel, and fighting in the War of Light, I felt her presence like she was alive. Like I was her. Like the line between us had vanished.

I'd placed my shield on the grass just beyond the water while I'd bathed. The orange light emanating from its center rose up to meet the clear protective dome I'd cast. The effect had created small bursts of rainbows to illuminate the night. It was startlingly beautiful, but also a powerful reminder for no one to touch the shield, or touch any of my possessions. Not that I expected anyone traveling with me to dare. I'd hardly given my court permission to look at it. Even now they barely dared to look at me. And they were all completely under my thrall.

Between the moonlight and the refraction of the shard, my naked skin glowed with every color of the original Valalumir light. At that moment, I was an eternal flame come to life. I stepped onto the grass and retrieved my stave—more than aware of the red eyes covertly watching my every move. Trying not to, but being unable to drag their gaze away. With a flick of my wrist, I released the dome. The rainbows vanished but the orange light of the shard continued to glow, mixing its illumination with the moon until it filled the clearing with its color. Moontrees looked like the sun, and the grass had turned to bronze.

I summoned Lissa, my maid. She stepped forward from the shadows, holding out a towel in her hands. I nodded for her to approach and slowly took it from her, wrapping it around my body.

The sense of being watched began to grow. Now that I was somewhat clothed, the akadim, my army, felt freer to look upon me. To look without incurring my wrath. But even so, their subdued growls and heavy breathing still carried an undercurrent of vicious violence. It was as thick as the scent of the spices that filled the city every summer. I could practically taste it now—their lust, their violence. But I stood easily, knowing that every single one, every deadly akadim waiting before the river, wouldn't dare disobey or attack me.

Especially one.

The one I'd coveted. The one I'd wanted most. He was who I'd needed for what came next. The most powerful warrior in Lumeria. After Aemon, he was the strongest, the deadliest the Empire had ever seen. And now he was mine. My soldier. My general. An unstoppable beast.

Lord Rhyan Hart.

I looked out at them all in the meadow. My akadim wore silver collars around their necks, binding them to me. I gazed almost transfixed at the mix of colors in the night. The red of their irises, the silver of their collars, and the orange of my light. It was all a reminder of the power I'd accrued. The power that was owed to me—that I deserved. I'd been born the second daughter to the Arkasva, born second in line to the Seat of Power, and only now did I realize how unnecessary that title had been.

How beneath me.

I didn't require a Laurel of the Arkasva. I wasn't like Lyr who had always craved it, or like Meera who had devoted her life to withstanding its weight and burdens.

What I had was better. A crown. A shard.

Because for me they were weightless, freeing. Offering me more. More than I'd ever dreamed of.

I'd been up the whole night gathering my forces, collecting my akadim, bending them to my will. And I'd barely slept the night before that. Not since the death bells rang for Emperor Theotis. Not since I'd gotten a whiff of the death tolls I knew would ring again for Imperator Kormac, the new Emperor Avery. And yet, I wasn't remotely tired.

"My clothing?" I asked Lissa. "Everything's clean as I asked?" She'd been instructed to wash my dress and cloak in the river, something she had to do manually without magic since she was human. I could have washed them myself with a thought. But I'd wanted to give her a task away from the akadim she still feared. We were on our way to meet Aemon, our king. He was with the rest of our assembled court—newly made akadim, vorakh we'd rescued from the Palace, and some Lumerians who'd already joined our cause. I wanted to ensure that when I arrived, I made a powerful entrance as queen.

"*Ma-Maraaka*," Lissa answered timidly. "Y-Yes. Everything is clean, just as you asked." Her eyes furtively shot toward the akadim standing only a few feet away, waiting for my next command. I'd saved her from their violence, given the order that she was not to be touched. But I didn't think anything would take her fear of the creatures away, it was in her nature.

"Thank you," I told her, trying to offer a reassuring smile.

But Lissa could not return the gesture.

"Hold my clothes out for me," I told her.

She retrieved them at once from her basket as I reached once more for my stave. With a wave of the twisted sun and moon wood in my hand, my garments were dry.

I turned the stave on myself, drying and curling my hair, and adding black liner to my eyes, and red to my lips. I'd never been able to perform glamour magic before—the art was incredibly difficult, and only mastered by a few who studied for years. Apparently, it had been more of an art form in Lumeria Matavia. And one retained and guarded by the Afeya. But now that I had the orange shard, now that Ereshya's blood was mine again, glamour and spell work I'd only dreamed of performing came to me with ease.

I dropped my towel on the ground, naked once more. Knowing full well that the akadim—new and hungry and still ready to attack Lumerians in every way—would hunger and lust. And yet—they could do nothing. Would do nothing. Not without my permission.

Parthenay, I commanded in my mind. *Come.*

A moment passed, and then another. And then finally the former chayatim that loyally served Aemon reached my side.

Her eyes narrowed and the golden Valalumir star on her cheek—a sign that she'd previously served the Emperor—lit up. Her gaze roamed down my body, then back to my face, as her lip curled in disgust. *You called*, she thought bitterly.

I laughed. "I did." I pointed to the ground. "I need you to take my towel back to the carriage, so Lissa might dress me."

Your towel? She looked murderous as she spotted it on the ground. Then she shook her head. "I am Aemon's Second. Not your lady-in-waiting."

I glared. *You mean* Maraak Moriel. *Not Aemon.*

Her aura withdrew. "Forgive me," she said.

"Forgive me, *Your Majesty*." I stepped forward, and could feel the walls of her mind going up. She'd been chosen by Aemon for a reason, one that had caused him to free her from the Palace, from her life as a chayatim—even before he rescued his own sister who'd been enslaved. Parthenay was a master at mind-reading and according to Aemon, had been the strongest vorakh of that kind ever to live in the Palace. She could break down even the most advanced mental walls, and read through layers upon layers of protection. But not even all of her years of training could keep me out of her head. Not when I possessed my shard.

Maraak Moriel's Second, I pushed the thought back to her. *That means that you're to be wherever he's not. And you are to do what he would do. And right now, he's not here to pick my towel up for me.*

He is a king, Parthenay argued.

And I am his queen. And I promise you, he'd love to take the opportunity to find me like this. He would have dried me off himself. Just as he bathed me when he first revealed himself as Moriel to me. Were he here now, he wouldn't hesitate. So, be his Second. Do your duty. Pick. It. Up.

Her aura sparked, full of a defiance she couldn't hide. But at the same time, much as she railed against me, she couldn't disobey. She picked up the towel, immediately turning away to hide her face.

I smirked. *Look at me, Parthenay,* I commanded. *I didn't give you leave to turn your back on me just yet.*

Her mouth was tightening as she turned and faced me. *Very well. I'm looking.*

My eyebrows narrowed. *If you ever contradict me again in front of my soturi, or fail to address me properly, I will feed you to them myself. Now go. We're nearly at the meeting spot.* A forest beyond the western border of Numeria. Aemon had gathered his forces to await me right on the edge of Paynumar.

We would have been there sooner if you hadn't stopped for a frivolous bath, came her retort. Instantly I knew I wasn't meant to hear that thought. She was trying to hide it—as she'd hidden so many of her thoughts and intentions before. She was good at it, she had been the best. But not anymore.

Her eyes flashed, and I suspected she was aware of the mental invasion, aware of what I'd done. And what it meant.

"Your Majesty," she said politely, and curtseyed before rushing off to the carriage.

I let Lissa help me into my dress, adding my belt back to my waist. She laced up my sandals, and then pulled my cloak over my shoulders before handing me the crown I'd fashioned for myself. I settled it back on my head. And then for the final piece. My shield. The orange shard of the Valalumir. I strapped it to my arm, barely even aware of its massive weight. And then, fully outfitted, I approached my army.

Nearly three dozen of the demons.

"Akadim," I called out. Their red eyes moved to mine at once, their bodies shifting with a frenetic energy. They'd been forced to be still for too long. "*Teka! Teka el ra Maraaka.*"

Despite the growls, they obeyed, each one kneeling on the ground. I took them in, seeing the hunger in their eyes, the violent desperation in their faces. Nearly all had fed by the time I found them. But not enough—not enough to satisfy an appetite that had just been born. And almost none had yet to feed on what they truly wanted. Lumerian flesh. Lumerian souls. Lumerian blood. I wasn't just keeping them from moving, I was keeping them from acting on their instincts.

When I'd found Rhyan, newly changed after sunset, he'd had blood on his chin, dripping from his lips. There was blood and worse caked under his nails. He was rabid. But I could tell he hadn't killed anyone yet. Just animals.

Eventually, I'd have to let them loose. They'd have to kill. They'd have to feed. It was their nature—and it was the only way to continue growing my army. To get the numbers I needed for what was to come. It was a necessary evil, but the only one I'd allow.

Because there was one thing akadim did that mine wouldn't be doing.

I'd forbidden rape in the Allurian Pass. I'd saved Lissa from such a fate. And I'd save more. For this was a new breed of akadim. Daywalkers. Demons who were able to walk in the sun. They were smaller than the others, but just as strong, just as violent and vicious. With one added trait—they could think logically, they could plan, and they could organize.

They could choose not to immediately give in to their baser instincts. And with all the work I had for them to do, all the tasks that must be completed for the war, rape would be far from their minds. Or at least, they'd have little energy left for it. And if my commands were disobeyed they wouldn't escape my wrath.

"Rise," I commanded. And my soturi followed, growling under their breath. Their teeth gnashed in agitation, their claws fidgeting at their sides. Their newborn appetites were still ignited, and I could feel it in the air. They were ready to unleash themselves, lose control.

I wasn't going to let them.

I eyed Rhyan's red eyes, only shocked for a moment that they were no longer that startling shade of green. He was taller than the others, naturally—he'd been so in life. Bigger, too. Stronger. And I wasn't the only one who saw it. Already he seemed to have become something of a silent leader amongst his companions. I could see the others looking to him for guidance, looking to see if he had followed my orders. And when he did, they did as well.

He was going to be very, very useful to me; to the war.

"We march for the final leg of our journey," I said. "We shall meet your king. *Maraak Moriel.* When we reach the border it will be morning, and you'll be able to rest. You'll be able to feed."

An akadim snapped their teeth, and then another. One howled at the moon, and a shiver ran down my spine. I shouldn't have mentioned food.

When they all began to howl, their claws snapping at their sides, my heart thundered. A lifetime of fear rushed through me. But I was Ereshya now, their queen. A Valalumir at my side and the power of a Goddess running through my veins. They couldn't hurt me. Not if they tried. And with just my thought, the shield emitted a blinding orange light. And they stilled, their mouths snapping shut as they tried to avert their gazes. Some even moaned in pain.

But Rhyan remained stoic—even as an akadim. He stepped forward, and lowered his chin in obedience. Like a good boy.

"Let's go," I said. "You will follow behind Lord Rhyan. He's your Arkturion now."

"*Maraaka Ereshya*," he said in that haunting deadly voice he'd acquired. The voice of an akadim. Of a monster. And yet, underlying it, there was the barest hint of a northern lilt.

I narrowed my gaze, and turned around, marching ahead, feeling him and the others behind, their red eyes boring into my back.

CHAPTER FOUR

JULIANNA

Thene's clock tower struck again. A new hour had begun. I reached for the ring finger on my left hand, feeling for the thin scar that wrapped around the base. It mimicked a piece of jewelry I would never wear. A ring I'd only wanted once, with one person. I circled it, again and again, and I took a deep breath as the bells rang. The sheer sound of the timekeeper shouting the hour was so normal, so mundane. But I'd come to hate them. I hated the reminder that every time I heard them—heard those Godsdamned bells—that another hour of my life had been stolen. Another hour that was no longer mine.

I'd started to track them when I was taken to the Shadow Stronghold after my arrest. I listened carefully those first few hours after my Revelation Ceremony when I was still a prisoner in my own country. I knew my situation was dire, I was imprisoned by the Imperator, the only man who outranked my Uncle Harren, Arkasva and High Lord of Bamaria.

But I'd thought, at least, I'm still on the grounds of my homeland. At least I'm within the borders where I was born. So I'd started bargaining in my mind. Believing that every hour I remained there was an hour of hope. An hour in which I stood a chance of being freed.

But I wasn't.

I was taken to Lethea for testing, and then Numeria for torture, and the hours continued to ring and pass and be announced, over and over until they formed days, until they formed weeks, and then months.

Then years.

I traced the scar slowly, circling the raised skin. A wedding ring without a wedding. A ring that wasn't a ring. A blood oath without the person I'd sworn it to.

But even after all this time, I'd remained true to my promise. Even in those moments when it felt impossible, when I didn't want to anymore.

I looked out of the glass window, the city coated in night. Another chime, another bell. My heart pounded with every ring. Every reminder that time was still moving and slipping away. Night had fallen hours ago. Too many hours. And there was still no hint or sign of Lyriana. Or Rhyan.

Neither had returned. Neither one had sent word. There'd been no news at all coming out of Numeria. No confirmation if Rhyan had been stripped. We had no idea if Lyr had saved him; if she needed to be saved herself.

Or worse.

It was like Numeria had shut down. Gone silent.

The clock tower rang out its final bell, and the note lingered in my ears longer than usual, echoing before the sound faded. Before the room fell back into silence.

I turned from the window, facing my five companions. My constants since I'd escaped the Palace. Meera Batavia, my cousin and the former Heir Apparent in Bamaria. And two more Bamarians with us whom I'd known my entire life. Perhaps the last two I'd have expected to be part of a plot to defy the Empire, particularly Lord Tristan Grey. His Ka had always been close with Ka Kormac, and he himself had spent years cozying up to the Imperator as his star pupil.

"The Great Vorakh Hunter," we'd called him. And not in a good way. And beside him was our childhood friend, Soturion Galen Scholar.

Once I'd come to, able to stay awake, and remain alert without panicking, I'd been sneaking glances at them all, mentally charting the ways in which they'd changed over the years. And the ways they looked like no time had passed. Like everything that I'd been through had just been a dream. Or a nightmare.

Meera's ash-brown hair was longer than before, her body thinner, and her face more gaunt—more haunted. There was an equally haunted look in Tristan's and Galen's eyes. Though Tristan still moved like himself, like I remembered. He had a casual arrogance in his demeanor, one not unusual amongst the nobility. But while he carried himself the same physically, his aura had shifted, had diminished somehow. Smaller. I could almost smell the guilt in his energy field.

As for Galen, he'd grown to twice his size, become even more handsome, his dark arms had thickened dramatically with the muscles of a soturion. Muscles that were currently torn up and bruised from a night of torture at the Palace. Because somehow, unbelievably, he was the man who'd murdered Theotis. At least, he'd been the knife used to deal the killing blow. I didn't need to hear the whispers that had been drifting in the Palace hallways for weeks. Anyone with half a brain knew who had actually orchestrated the assassination. Avery Kormac, nephew to Theotis, Arkasva of Korteria, Imperator of the South. Our new fucking Emperor.

And then there were the two Glemarians, men I'd only known of from letters exchanged between me and Rhyan. Letters that stopped when I was taken.

Lord Dario DeTerria was closest to where I stood. He was a burly soturion with black curls that fell to his shoulders, and dark eyes that remained narrowed in focus.

The other was an equally muscular man, but he was a mage. Lord Aiden DeKassas had the pale skin of the North with auburn hair, and a shockingly large gryphon-like nose—but one that beautifully fit his face. Rhyan's best friends. Two of them, at least.

We were all spread across our small room at the inn, and had been silent for the last two hours. Meera was sitting on the bed next to me. Dario stood before the door, looking like he was about to attack anything that moved. Aiden and Tristan both had their hands poised on their staves, ready for battle. And Galen, like me, stood still in a corner, his eyes alert, observant, but wary.

In the silence, somehow louder now without the bells, my stomach churned violently. Because now a truth we'd been dancing around for too long felt ready to consume me. The hours had been passing, and still we remained in a place where we'd already been found once. Distance wouldn't save us. Nor would Meera's and Aiden's wards. We would be found again. I knew imperators. Too fucking well. And when it came to Kormac, he didn't let anything go. Not any insults, not any power, and certainly not anyone in this room. Especially me, his favorite *pet*.

Every second we remained here, every second we waited, we were more in Godsdamned danger. No one wanted to admit it, but it was so fucking clear.

Rhyan wasn't coming back.

And neither was Lyr.

The scar around my finger heated, suddenly burning against my skin like a warning. I traced the shape of the ring again, my heart pounding harder. I was trying to stay calm—trying to have hope for the first time in forever. I was out of the Palace. Away from my tormentors. I'd seen Lyr, and I was with Meera—family I thought I'd never be with again. But any second now, it would all be ripped away.

We needed answers. I had a feeling that until we could confirm Rhyan's and Lyr's fates, Dario, who'd been left in charge, wasn't going to budge. There was a stubbornness to him I'd never seen before.

In the end, it was Tristan who said it, the thing I couldn't. "It's time for a new plan. We need to make a decision."

"A decision?" Dario snapped. "About what? What kind of room service to order next?" He spoke with the same Glemarian lilt Rhyan had—but with a much deeper accent. Combined with his stubbornness, there was something almost feral about him. He was missing the polished mannerisms ingrained in most nobles.

"You know what I'm talking about," Tristan said, his voice darkening.

"Do I now?" Dario challenged, turning his body toward Tristan's. His hand was already at the hilt of his sword, and his shoulders lifted as he tensed, his biceps flexing.

Galen stiffened, moving beside his best friend in a protective stance. He'd been like that with Tristan ever since we were kids. Always on guard.

Tristan's lips curled as he stepped forward, ready to retort.

But I couldn't take it anymore. This stubbornness from Dario wasn't getting us anywhere, except into more danger. And I didn't care what experiences he'd had before—how much training he'd completed, or time out in the field he'd spent as a soturion. When it came to our new Emperor, I was the expert.

And before Tristan could say anything, I shouted. "Yes! You do, Dario! You know exactly what he's talking about." It was the first thing I'd said in hours.

Everyone's eyes turned back toward me. Since my rescue, they'd all had this look on their faces whenever they saw me, whenever I spoke. Like I was broken, or about to break. Maybe it was both—like they expected me to break further.

Except for Dario. He didn't even flinch as he whirled in my direction, his jaw clenched. "Excuse me?"

"You know we need to make a decision!" I said, my voice shaking with a rage and fear I'd been tempering for hours. "Stop playing dumb. We need to decide what to do next. We should have decided a long time ago."

"You know Godsdamned well we needed to be here," the soturion snarled, his aura suddenly full of fire. It blasted from his body, warming the room. "That they need a place to come to when it's over."

"It is over! And they're not here."

"Your point?" he asked.

"I think you know that we're waiting for something that isn't going to happen," I said. "We all are. But it's so obvious. Lyr should have been back by now."

"You don't know that. You have no idea what kind of timeline they're on. How fast they can move or what obstacles are in their path," Dario said. "She left it to me to keep you safe and that's what I'm going to do until she walks through that door. Until she's back here—and Rhyan with her."

"And if she doesn't come?' I asked, my voice going cold.

His aura flared, like a burst of fire. "You think I haven't thought of that possibility?" he yelled. "That I haven't been running a thousand outcomes for them and us in my head as we waited? They could be delayed for a thousand reasons, they could be on their way now, injured, needing just a little more time."

"Or they might not be coming back at all," I spat.

Dario snarled.

"She's right," Meera said, her voice cold. Her lip trembled and I could feel my own terror for Lyr ramping up. Going into the Palace, even armed, even ready to lose it all—still meant losing.

I felt callous with what I had to say, because Gods, the thing I'd most wanted when I'd been taken was Lyr. To see

Lyr. I missed her so fucking much. But I'd learned by now, you just don't get what you want in life. And this was no different. We had to accept reality. Because if Lyr had been captured, if Rhyan had been stripped—what chance did we stand? It was only because of them we were free to begin with, and we had just barely made it. If they'd fallen …

"Any events in the arena would be long over by now," Meera said. "Whatever did or didn't happen is done. And Imperator Hart knows where we are. We're on borrowed time."

"I'm not leaving Lyriana behind," Dario said. He moved toward the small table where we'd had our meals, and slammed his hand down on it. "Or Rhyan." His voice cracked.

Meera shook her head, moving toward him. "No one is saying that," she said. "Do you think I want to? That I can stomach leaving my sister? Not knowing where she is or if she's safe? That I'm not losing my fucking mind right now? You think I'm not just as worried about Rhyan as you are?"

"No one is suggesting that you're okay with any of this," Aiden said coolly.

"No," Dario said, stepping back into the middle of the room. He turned his head slowly, his dark eyes meeting all of ours, "you're all just saying that it's time to go. That we give up and leave Lyriana and Rhyan behind. Well, we're not. Because that's not how this works."

"What do you think this is?" I yelled. "Protocol training at the academy? There's no turion for you to answer to, no chain of command to follow. Right now, there are no rules. Except for one. Survive!"

"If Rhyan were here," Meera said quietly, "he'd say the same thing."

"If Rhyan were here," Dario gritted through his teeth, "we wouldn't be having this conversation." His eyes reddened. "We're waiting. Just a little longer. You don't know how strong he is, or Lyr. They'll be here. He'll be here," he said again. "He has to." But he no longer sounded convinced.

And then, as if in answer, there was a sharp knock on the door.

Dario rushed forward to check the peep hole. "It's Cal." He unlocked the door, cracking it open just an inch as he examined the hall. Satisfied, he pulled the old man, one half of the elderly couple who owned Auriel's Flame, inside the room.

"Any news?" Dario asked, his voice now filled with desperation. "Rhyan? Lyr?"

"There's a rider downstairs," Cal said somberly, his white bushy eyebrows furrowed. "A soturion with the seal of Lady Kenna Hart. She bid me show this to you as proof. She has urgent news from Numeria—but she was ordered to deliver it directly to you, and only you. If you verify her seal, I'll send her up."

"Show me," Dario said.

Cal nodded, placing a small silver ring in his hand.

Dario's face hardened, his jaw clenching before returning it. "Bring her."

A moment later, a soturion in the dark leathers of Ka Hart appeared in the threshold of the door. Her black hair was braided down her back, but dozens of wisps had escaped, and even had leaves stuck to them, like she'd ridden an ashvan here as fast as she could. Her cheeks were flushed pink, and there was a tear in her green soturion cloak.

"Brianna," Dario said.

Aiden shot across the room as well.

"What happened?" Dario asked. "Where's Rhyan?"

"Here," she said, handing him a leather pouch, the kind used to transport scrolls. "Something happened," she shook her head. "Kenna went to great trouble to get word to you. As did I."

Dario shook his head. "What do you mean something happened? Why is Kenna sending me letters? What is this? What's going on?"

"It's all in there, Dario," she said, turning piercing blue eyes on him. "Everything." Her mouth tightened. "Just read."

"Bri," he begged, shaking his head, "Just tell me. Tell me, please."

"Brianna?" Aiden asked, his voice oddly formal despite the emotion wavering beneath it.

But the soturion, Brianna, shook her head again, and closed Dario's fingers around the missive. "I'm sorry. I can't stay. Not even a minute. I have to get back to her quickly, before I'm seen. The Palace is in lockdown. The whole capital. I barely made it out. My lady needs me. Just … just read. Okay? And do what she says." She nodded at Aiden. Then her blue eyes glanced sadly around the room. "Be careful. Be safe." And then she rushed back down the hall.

"Bri!" Dario yelled, but Aiden closed the door and leaned back against it, his eyes closing slowly, his face drawn.

Dario silently went to sit back on the bed, staring at the case, turning it over in his hands.

My heart raced, my stomach churned. The answers were in there. The answers we needed, that we were fighting over. I wanted to throw up.

"Well?" Tristan asked. "Read it!"

"Dario, please," Meera said. But he was still, turning it over again and again.

Aiden approached slowly, kneeling down before his friend. "Dar? You want me to—"

"She sent it to me," he snapped.

Aiden nodded. "Okay." Something unspoken passed between them. "Okay."

Taking a deep breath, Dario opened the case, and pulled out Kenna's letter. A minute later, his hands opened, the parchment falling to the ground as he stared ahead, his eyes vacant.

Rhyan was an akadim. Rhyan was an akadim. *Rhyan* was an akadim.

The minute Dario dropped Kenna's letter, Aiden had picked it up, trying to read it out loud. But he couldn't finish it. His voice broke mid-sentence as his emotions took over. So Galen had to read as Aiden stumbled back against a wall. He seemed glued to it now, minutes later, unable to move, unable to speak. He wasn't even blinking. Just standing eerily still, his face pale as a corpse.

Dario's eyes were watering and red, and his hands were trembling, the tendons in his arms taut. Without a word, he walked over to the nightstand by the bed. He stood with his back to all of us, his shoulders tensing, and then his fist flew, smashing through the wooden table. He pulled his hand out as blood and shards of wood fell to the floor. He'd hurt himself. Some pieces of wood were sticking out of his palm. But we were silent with him. Like grief had stolen our voices. The only sound in the room had been the remains of the table collapsing.

Meera was the first to spring into action, tending to him—pulling out splinters, and demanding Galen bring her a damp wash cloth to clean the cuts across his fingers and knuckles. Dario just stared blankly, his face turned in my direction, while Meera applied sunleaves.

I slumped back onto the other bed, numb and unsure what to do. The news about Rhyan was too awful to comprehend. And yet, somehow, there was still even more than that to digest. Vorakh—so many more than just me—had escaped, and akadim had attacked. Akadim had breached the capital. Akadim who'd managed to kill beneath the sun, who'd come out before it was night. Akadim who had targeted Rhyan. I couldn't decide which felt less believable. That Rhyan had been attacked, or that it had happened in the daylight.

And then ... there was Lyr.

Lyr was missing. Vanished. *Gone*.

Gods. I couldn't breathe. It felt like my heart was twisting in on itself. I tried to convince myself that it was a good thing that no one knew her whereabouts. Because if the Emperor had captured her, if the worst had happened, Kenna would have known. I was sure of it. Emperor Avery would want everyone to know he had her—especially since he'd long been obsessed with her. The little game between him and Imperator Hart had been going on for years—both wanting to dominate her, to possess her. I had to trust in the fact that no news coming out of Numeria about Lyr meant they still didn't have her.

And yet if the Emperor hadn't captured Lyr, if Imperator Hart didn't have her—why hadn't she come back here? Why hadn't she gotten word to us herself? Why had it taken a message from Kenna for any news to reach us at all? Lyr knew where we were, knew we needed her, and that we'd be waiting, worried. Where the hell had she gone? Or was she hurt? Lying helpless somewhere? Had an akadim dragged her off as well? Gods. Had she gone after Rhyan?

Again, I reached for my ring finger, desperately feeling for the thin scar. I traced the line, again and again. Over and over, searching for comfort, for strength. A reminder of what I'd sworn.

I needed it now. Needed to remember the promise I'd made to him.

But already I could feel the pain in my heart, and of my companions, crashing down on me like the waves of the ocean in a storm.

Lyr was gone. Lyr was gone. And so was Rhyan.

I stood up, facing everyone. They were all like ghosts, lost in their own universes of grief.

"We need to go," I said. "Rhyan isn't coming back, and Lyr—" My voice caught. "Imperator Hart knows where we are. Kormac's soturi are crossing the borders as we speak, if they haven't already. They're going to find us. Trust me, I know. They did it to me before. And at this very fucking inn." A memory flashed of the last time, but I pushed it down. "You think you know what kind of monsters our new Emperor and his brother are. But you don't. You have no idea. I do." I wrung my hands together, finding the scar around my ring finger again. "What you saw last night was him being civil. Easing you in." I narrowed my gaze on Tristan and Galen. They'd been there when I was first dragged into the Yellow Room. "He's so much worse than anything you've imagined. I'm the one they've enslaved for years. I'm the one who spent the most time with them. And believe me when I tell you that if they catch us again, it's over. If they catch you," my throat tightened, "you'll wish you'd never been born."

"You think I don't fucking know that," Dario yelled, his Glemarian accent so thick, his words had blurred together. "I do! I grew up in an Imperator's shadow. I know what the Emperor's like. But we're pretty damn fucked. If we stay, we'll be found. And if we go, we can only run for so long— especially when there's six of us. They'll be looking in the wilds, expecting us out there like last time. And before morning, I promise, more nahashim will arrive—and they won't be the kind so easily enchanted by whatever snake lady magic Meera performs."

"We at least need a head start," Tristan said. "Buy us some time."

"And go where?" Dario roared. He rose to his feet. "No, I mean it, Tristan! Where the fuck do we go? We can't go north, or anywhere loyal to Imperator Hart. And we can't go south—because who the fuck can we trust down there? Your grandmother? Your betrothed? Who else did Kormac buy out? They own Bamaria, they own Elyria, and now with the fucking throne beneath his ass, they own the whole Godsdamned south."

I flinched.

Tristan cocked his head to the side, his neck turning red. "So we just stay here like sitting ducks? Waiting for them to pick us off one by one?" he yelled. "You're so damned stubborn. I know we lost Hart—" He frowned. "Rhyan. And I'm sorry. I really am. He didn't deserve that—any of it. But *we* have a chance, and Lyr's still out there. So let's go. We'll find the next inn."

"Right!" Dario said. "Sure. Another inn." He folded his arms across his chest. "All six of us at midnight just show up at their door. That's not suspicious at all."

"We could pay them," Tristan said. "Everything I have."

Dario laughed bitterly. "Of course. Ka Grey and their silver coin. I doubt that even your purse is enough to buy silence against the Emperor. Especially if his soturi are already there. Keep your money."

"Don't act like you didn't think the same," Tristan snarled. "I know of the wealth of Ka DeTerria."

"Shut your face," Dario said.

"We'll split up," I said.

I crossed the room to Kenna's discarded letter, and its leather carrier. We'd been so focused on what she'd written, no one had acknowledged the gift Kenna had given us. Three vadati stones. I held them up. "We have these. We'll split into three groups of two. Stay in contact with each other. Lyr was right—travelling in smaller groups lets you move faster, hide easier."

"But it still doesn't give us anywhere to go," Dario said. His voice had weakened, like his heart was breaking. "What good will these do if someone's in trouble and we don't know how to get there, and without Rhyan, we won't be fast enough to make a difference. We can run, but we need to be honest about the fact that there's nowhere to go."

My stomach turned.

Because that wasn't true. There *was* somewhere for us to go. To people who would protect us—who would hide us. But it meant I'd have to admit who I really was. Admit my true name.

I'd sworn I never would. Sworn I'd never go to these people for help. Not after we'd been betrayed. Not after their plots had failed. And not after ... not after I lost him. The cost of working alongside them was too high. And yet ... we'd already paid the price.

The scar around my finger burned and I reached for it, circling the mark, knowing it was a warning. But was it for or against my plan? My breath hitched. Admitting this would open the wound I'd so carefully stitched back together. But it was either this or go back to the Palace, back to serving Kormac. To resume my life as his pet. I couldn't. I couldn't do it. The choice was do this, or die.

"I know somewhere we can go," I said finally, my voice catching. "Someone who can help. They'll take us in. Hide us. Protect us. I swear. Just ... give me a minute to talk to Cal and Marisol."

"You know someone in Thene?" Aiden asked, suspicious. "Who?"

"It's complicated," I said. "I don't—I can't—Fuck. Just let me talk to Cal and Marisol. They know how to contact them. Just trust me. I'll explain later."

"I'll go with you," Meera said.

"No," I shouted, my chest tightening. "Just me."

I reached for the doorknob, but Dario was right beside me.

"Dario, no," I said.

"I'm going. And I'm not fighting with you, Julianna," Dario snarled. "I already lost a friend tonight. We don't know where Lyriana is. I'm not risking it. I'm not losing another."

"We're not friends," I said coolly.

His eyebrows narrowed. "I didn't call you my friend, did I? But Lyriana left me in charge, left me here to protect you. To protect everyone. And I did." His hands fisted, a tear slipping down his cheek. "Instead of going to save my best friend, I was protecting you. Instead of having Lyr's back, I was watching yours. So no. We're not friends. But I'm protecting you just the same. Because that's what Lyriana wanted. And because I know Rhyan would as well." He tied his hair back with a leather strap, his hand replacing mine on the doorknob. "Now you go and say what you must to Cal and Marisol. But no more discussion. Soturi from the Palace could be here any minute. So I'm coming." He met Galen's eyes. The only other soturion amongst us. He took two of the vadati stones from my hand, giving one to Galen, and the other to Meera. "I'll call if there's trouble. But you should gather your things so we can be ready to go when we return. And if we don't—don't wait again."

I glared at Dario.

But the scar around my finger heated, burning like it was calling to me.

Survive. Survive. Survive.

The promise. The oath.

My throat was dry as I swallowed.

"Walk behind me then," I snapped.

"As you wish," Dario said, his words clipped.

I clenched my fingers around the vadati still in my hand, needing something to hold onto. I headed down the hall and then down the stairs, my heart thundering, stomach churning with Dario in the shadows behind me.

Cal was at the front desk by himself. But the door to their office was open. Torches were lit. Marisol was nearby.

His white bushy eyebrows lifted when he saw me, and he quickly stood from his seat. His eyes were red, too, and I had a feeling that Brianna had been instructed to share the news with him. He and Marisol were more connected around the Empire's underground secrets than most could guess.

"How quickly can you get word to *El Zan Vylette*?" I asked before he could speak. Before I lost my nerve. "We need their help." I hadn't said those words out loud in over a year. I hadn't even allowed myself to think of them. To remember they existed.

Cal frowned, and I could see the questions in his eyes. He knew how I felt. Knew my reservations about trusting them. But he was smart enough not to do anything but nod, and gesture to Marisol, who'd just come out of the office. She sniffled, and put on a brave smile in acknowledgment.

"We need to make a call," he said.

Marisol's eyes jumped to me, and she let out a shaky sigh before nodding. "Yes. Of course."

"We can reach them," Cal confirmed, looking between me and Dario. "There are several I can vouch for. You have my word. Give us a moment to see who answers first." He walked toward her, and they vanished behind the door, closing it shut.

Dario moved beside me, looking confused. "What is *El Zan Vylette*?"

"It's a long story."

"Well I'm all ears."

I pressed my lips together.

"Julianna, please," he said, his eyes meeting mine, red and tearful. "I can't—I'm going to lose my mind if I have to think about Rhyan. And I … I need to get to safety. Need to get you and everyone else there. So please, just tell me. Give me something I can fucking focus on."

I rubbed at my ring finger, tracing the scar, my stomach turning. Because this did mean safety. Except when it hadn't. "*El Zan Vylette* means the Purple Sun."

His eyes flashed. "I can translate," he gritted.

"Fine!" I turned away.

"I'm sorry," he grunted. "Julianna, do I need to beg? What or who is the Purple Sun? What does that mean?"

I closed my eyes. "It's …" I took a deep breath, preparing to make him swear a blood oath, swearing he wouldn't tell a soul what I was about to reveal. Because it could get him killed. Because it could get me killed. Because it had gotten *him* killed. I met Dario's eyes. "Once you know this," I said, "you can't unknow it. So if you abandon us—"

"I won't," he said, his eyes filling with fire. "I'm not leaving you."

He started to reach for my hand, and on instinct I pulled back. I didn't like to be touched. Not without warning. Not by most people.

"I didn't mean—" Dario took a deep breath, his hand making a fist. "Sorry, I won't touch you. You have my word. I shouldn't have even—It's just instinct." He stepped back, and held his hands up as if to reassure he'd keep his word. He frowned, his eyes searching mine. They softened. "You know you're safe with me, right? I promised Lyriana. But more than that, I remember when Rhyan wrote to you—the friendship you two had—it meant a lot to him. He was so determined to get you out; you have no idea. So if he—Fuck. If he's not here, and Lyr isn't … I am. And I know I'm not what you want. Or who." He exhaled sharply.

I looked him over. He was sincere. I'd been around enough men to know the difference, to know which ones spoke out of their ass, spoke to get something, and then the few rare ones who spoke true. Ryan had been one. And Dario was as well.

He looked miserable as he met my gaze. "Rhyan's better at all of this than me. Look, I don't know what you've been through, or what to say to you to make it better or how to help. I only know how to protect, and how to fight. So for you, I will. I swear it. I give my oath to you, Julianna. *Me sha, me ka.*" He pressed his fist to his chest, tapping it twice, before flattening his palm across his heart. "I will keep you safe."

I looked around the foyer of the inn. We were still alone. Cal and Marisol were the only people nearby. And they already knew my secret.

I swallowed roughly. "Fine. The Purple Sun comes from an old Ka's sigil. It's a shortening of it, a kind of code." My heart pounded. "The sigil was a purple Valalumir star in front of a golden sun. When shortened it becomes the purple sun."

Dario's eyebrows knitted together, his eyes squinting in concentration. "Purple Valalumir. Golden sun." He shook his head. "I don't know that one."

"There's few who do anymore. The Empire tried to erase every image of it, burning any banner or flag depicting it. They even cut its mention from our scrolls. They started in our library at home. Then they destroyed every sigil they could find after they executed everyone in the Ka."

"Executed?" His eyes widened in alarm. "You mean ... Ka Azria of Elyria?"

And there it was. Ka Azria. The Ka that had been a scary story for us as kids. The tale used to keep Lumerians in line, to remind them what happened if you concealed vorakh. Even if you were noble. Even if you were Arkasva. It didn't matter, anyone with forbidden magic would be found and exposed, would suffer the consequences, and so would everyone else who had kept the secret. Even I'd believed the stories as a girl—believed that Ka Azria had broken the law by protecting their vorakh family members. I believed that the whole Ka had conspired to keep the secret in defiance of the Empire. I even thought, at one point, that they had deserved their punishment.

But it turned out that vorakh had had nothing to do with their murder. It was about power. Everything was always about power. Clearing the way for Ka Kormac to rule the South, to open the borders for their occupation of Bamaria.

I took a deep breath. "*El Zan Vylette* is a network of Elyrians across the Empire still loyal to Ka Azria. They reject the High Lord of Ka Elys as their Arkasva."

"Okay," Dario said slowly. "Okay, so they're a rebel group." His eyebrows furrowed. "There are groups like that all over Lumeria. I learned about dozens of active groups in the last year alone. People who don't believe their Arkasva is the rightful Heir to the Seat of Power, that the bloodline is false, or that their leader is corrupt. But that doesn't explain why they would be willing to hide fugitives like us."

"They're not," I said. "Not fugitives like us." I met his eyes. "Like me."

Dario frowned. "Like you?" He shook his head. "I don't understand."

"*El Zan Vylette* isn't like the other groups. They don't just reject the Elyrian Arkasva. They're working to restore the Seat of Power to the rightful heir. The Heir of Ka Azria." My ring finger burned.

His mouth tightened, his eyes narrowing as he took in my words, before he scoffed, "But that's impossible. After the Blade came, none of them—"

"Survived?" I exhaled sharply. "No. Not in Elyria, they didn't. But no one knew that Arkasva Azria had another heir, because he kept his lover a secret. She wasn't Elyrian, but more importantly, her duties kept her away. At the time, she was the Second to Arkasva Marianna Batavia, the High Lady of Bamaria. She was her sister, Lady Gianna. And so, when she bore the Arkasva's child, the child who would become Heir Apparent, she was kept secret, too, to save her life. And after Ka Azria, she was raised in the Bamarian Court with her cousins."

"The Bamarian Court." Dario's eyes widened. "You," he said, his voice barely above a whisper. "It's you."

I nodded slowly. Cal and Marisol opened the door. They nodded once. It was done. We had a safe house to escape to. A way to hide from the Emperor. But it meant going back to the people who'd cost me everything. The ones who could be salvation, if they didn't damn me again. I just prayed that this time was different, this time they'd save us.

Because I was the Heir of Ka Azria.

CHAPTER FIVE

JULIANNA

Cal and Marisol wrote down the address for Dario, spending several minutes showing him a map of Thene, tracing out different routes, and pointing out prominent landmarks along the way that he'd be able to spot, even in the dark. We were lucky we didn't have to go far, but it was going to be dangerous.

Dario looked like he was in shock, and I couldn't tell if it was because of what I'd revealed, or the sudden flip in Cal and Marisol's demeanors. Despite their innocent appearances as the sweet elderly inn owners, they were tough—they had to be. They'd long been part of several underground movements. They were the most involved in *El Zan Vylette*, but I'd heard rumblings of another movement in the North they supported. One that had recently gained traction. It was possibly why Kenna had trusted her rider to find us here.

Cal and Marisol were incredibly well versed in who to trust within the city, as well as knowing which routes were patrolled by Ka Zarine's soturi, and at what times they changed the guard. But we had an extremely limited amount of time before those rules were gone. Once Kormac's soturi crossed into Cretanya, there was no telling where they'd go first, or how they'd organize the search. They'd be everywhere. And they'd be ruthless.

Every second that passed, they were getting closer.

My stomach turned again, and I met Dario's eyes.

"I've got it," he said confidently. "I'm going to show this to the others, then burn it."

Cal nodded, pushing the map toward him before he looked at me again. "Marisol will gather some things to take with you. We've been ready, just waiting for you to ask."

They'd tried to help me last time I was here. They'd tried …

I rubbed at the scar of my blood oath again, and nodded. "Thank you."

A minute later, we returned to our room. Dario wasted no time barking out orders and directions.

"We're splitting into three groups," he said. "That way we'll be less suspicious on the road. They'll be looking for a large group traveling together. We'll all have a vadati to remain in communication. Galen, you and Tristan are together. Aiden, you'll go with Meera. I'm taking Julianna."

I started to object. "No. I should go with Meera. I should be with my cousin."

"No," he said. "That doesn't make any sense. We have two soturi between me and Galen. Aiden's been guarding Meera for the past month. It's the best way to divide based on everyone's strength at the moment." He slammed the map on the table, and the parchment with the address of the safe house. "This is where we're going. It's all arranged thanks to Julianna. They're expecting us." He slid his finger across the map. "Memorize the address and I'll show you the different routes to get there. We're not going far, but we can't take any direct paths or we'll be seen. Now we have five minutes to memorize this and we're leaving. Kormac's on the way."

Tristan frowned. "And we can trust these people to hide us and not sell us out?"

Dario's face hardened, his eyes flashing on me before he turned back to Tristan. "Yes."

"I feel like we're missing some really crucial information," Tristan said, looking back and forth between us.

"You're going to be missing crucial limbs if you don't shut up and start studying," Dario snapped. "Look. Pack. And go. We'll explain when we get there." He nodded at me.

He was keeping my secret. Keeping the others from overwhelming me before we had to run.

"Tristan, let it go," Galen said. "Cal and Marisol have protected us this far. And so has Dario. If Jules says there's a way, then there is." He nodded in my direction, and our eyes met—something unspoken passing between us. Galen and I had always had an understanding. We were the ones on the outside of our little group growing up, looking out for our people. Tristan for him. Lyr for me. And now we had a new one. A shared experience of being Kormac's prisoners.

I looked away, trying to focus. Trying to prepare to run again as everyone else caught up.

The minutes that passed were few, but they felt like hours. Dario went over each route. Thene wasn't a big city, maybe around the same size as Urtavia. But where Urtavia was sprawling, broken up by woodlands, the academies and soturion housing, Thene was laid out like a grid. There were tons of closely laid out waterways and crosswalks, streets full of buildings and alleys. There were lots of places to hide, but just as many that could allow you to be seen. We needed intricate paths, constant changes in direction to avoid being followed. But we needed to make sure that those paths didn't add too much time to our travels. Every second we spent out there we were in danger.

Taking everyone's word that they knew their routes and the landmarks to look out for on their way, Dario burned the map and the parchment holding the address. The remains were discarded in a bowl, as he reviewed the password we'd need to be allowed inside.

A sharp knock on the door came out of nowhere.

I stilled, my heart leaping into my throat.

Dario was at the door a second later, checking the peep hole and slamming it open. He ushered Cal inside quickly, and closed the door behind him.

"What is it?" Dario asked.

"It's Kormac," Cal hissed, his mouth tightening, "they're here."

"Where?" Aiden demanded.

"Down the street. They're heading in this direction. About a dozen. Others have already been spotted on the crossroads and waterways. You have minutes to get out, maybe less," Cal said, out of breath.

"They outnumber us, but it's dark and they don't know the area; we can use that to our advantage," Aiden said. "They're more likely to stick to the main roads, and markers. Do you have a back door?"

Cal nodded, then he shoved two large leather packs into Dario's arms. "Supplies for all of you." Then his eyes swept across the room at us all. "Follow me. Now!"

We scrambled out the door, following Cal down the hall away from the stairs that led to the exit. Instead of going down, we climbed up. Once there we turned a sharp corner that led into a dead end. Cal reached up to tug on a rope hanging from the ceiling.

"Stand back," he ordered. He pulled the rope, which dislodged a rectangular piece of wood. It fell to the ground, and then following it, a rope ladder with wooden steps unraveled. The night sky was above, and a cool breeze filled the hall. "This will take you to the roof," Cal said. "There's another ladder we keep up there. You can lower it to the ground leading into the back alley. Use that to head into the park, get to the woods, and disappear."

Dario strapped both of the supply bags to his back, then reached for the rungs without hesitation, climbing up with ease, even with his cut-up hand. His legs vanished into the ceiling seconds later. He moved surprisingly fast for someone so big.

Cal drew me forward. "You next, sweetheart." He leaned in. "I'm sorry we couldn't protect you better before. Or your friend."

I swallowed, my throat tight.

"I wish a different outcome for you this time. Be safe," he said. His gaze flicked to Dario, then back to me. He smiled, like he approved of Dario, then he stepped back. "Now go."

I nodded, my fingers grasping the first rung. But before I could step onto the ladder, there was a scream from downstairs. Marisol.

"Let me call my husband! Wait! You can't just barge in! NO!" Marisol yelled.

The soturi were here.

"Go!" Cal yelled, racing down the hall. "GO!"

I reached for the next rung, stepping up onto the bottom step. But the entire ladder swayed, and I froze. Marisol screamed again.

"Climb, Julianna!" Aiden urged. "Go. Hurry!"

Cal's angry yells carried up the stairs as he raced toward his wife.

I knew what I had to do. I knew what was at stake. But at that moment I couldn't.

I didn't know what happened. Or what triggered it. But suddenly I could hear Emperor Theotis whispering in my ear. Admonishing me for running. Pulling my hair painfully, ripping clumps out to make his point. And I could feel

Imperator Kormac—Emperor Avery—bending me across a table, lifting my skirts, calling me a bad pet.

I couldn't breathe. I couldn't move. All I could think was that last time I was here—I had tried to escape. We had tried to escape. But we'd been caught. And I'd been dragged back to the Palace. And he had been … he had …

"What's going on?" Dario yelled. "Julianna, why aren't you climbing?"

"I-I can't," I said, my voice shaking. "I can't move."

Galen stepped forward, placing a hand on the ladder. "I'll help you," he said. "I'll climb up with you. Okay? Remember those rocks we had to climb down that one time? At the far end of the beach behind Cresthaven?"

I almost laughed. "The one Tristan led us to when we thought we were lost."

"That's the one," Galen said.

"And I said he made bad life choices." I practically sobbed the words.

Galen laughed. "He still does. Now remember, I didn't let you fall then. You won't fall this time either."

I swallowed. More shouts rose from downstairs. I could hear my heart pounding, thundering in my ears. I was holding everyone up. It would be my fault. My fault we were captured. My fault they were dead.

"I've got you," Galen said. "I'm going to put your hand on the next rung, and I'm right behind you. Okay? Jules?"

Jules. My name. It pulled me back. I nodded at Galen. "Okay."

A second later he was behind me, urging me up, his hands light against my waist until I felt him on the rungs right below me. The ladder swayed and dipped with every step we climbed, but Dario was at the top, holding onto the ropes, trying to keep it as steady as possible.

I climbed and climbed, my stomach churning the entire time. Fresh air from the roof blew on me, as more shouts came from outside. I could hear a soturion down the street, laughing. I froze again. But a pair of large strong hands wrapped around my arms, and hauled me up onto the roof.

Dario stumbled back, clasping me to him, then reached for Galen's hand, pulling him up beside us. He grimaced, but shook it off. His hand had to be hurting.

The ladder shook as the next person began to climb.

"Go," Galen said. "Take her to safety. I'll stay back, make sure the others get out."

Dario bit his lip. I could practically see the inner battle raging in his eyes—the need to protect me, versus the need to stay behind and guard the others. Because Lyriana had asked him to, because it was what Rhyan would have wanted. But also, as I was beginning to see, because it was just the kind of person he was.

So much more like Rhyan than I'd realized. The thought alone made my heart ache.

Dario set down the bags Cal had handed him. Inside were soturion cloaks, the kind that would help us all blend into the night, and camouflage with our surroundings. And a thin stave of sun and moon wood. Dario grabbed it, shoving it into his belt, and then he reached for a spare cloak. "These are for you," he said. "When we get to the bottom." He took my hand, pulling me toward the edge of the roof overlooking the alley. The ladder was bunched into a pile that he quickly released.

"Thank you, Galen," I said quickly. "For getting me up here."

He shook his head, like it was nothing, his broken nose highlighted in the moonlight. "Hey," he said, "I've got you, Jules. We go way back. Plus, us fugitives need to stick together." He winked, and smiled softly, the same smile he'd had since we were kids, running around together in the Bamarian Court. And for a second, I could see us so clearly. Young and innocent, so unaware of the horrors of this world. Or the fates awaiting us as we grew up. We were just running on the beach behind Cresthaven, splashing in the waves. Laughing. Having fun. I'd forgotten. Forgotten so much as I tried to survive. I'd tried not to dwell on the past, or dwell on what I had lost. Otherwise the memories—especially the happy ones—made me feel like I couldn't breathe.

Galen eyed Dario. "Keep her safe."

"On my life," he swore, a hand to his heart. Then to me, Dario asked, "Can you climb? Or do you want me to carry you?"

I eyed the alley below us warily, looking between it and him. We still had a long way to climb down. And the ladder wasn't the sturdiest thing. I'd already frozen once.

My cheeks flushed as I shook my head. "Can you?" I asked.

He didn't answer, just slung my cloak over his shoulder, and stepped off the roof, steadying his feet onto the ladder rung just below, then gestured me forward. "Sit down for me, right on the edge, right there."

I did as he asked. Without warning, Dario wrapped his arm around me, dragging me forward by the waist, tugging me off the roof. I bit back a yell, wrapping my arms around his neck, and my legs behind his back, my pulse racing. His jaw muscle clenched as he took on my weight, adjusting me so I was more secure, and more fully against him.

I exhaled sharply, squeezing him.

"You're doing good," he said quietly. "Now just hang on. I've got you."

He placed both hands on the ladder, and I locked my ankles around his back, my fingers clasped together. Then he started to move, climbing down almost as quickly as he'd climbed up the first ladder.

I was prepared to flinch, or feel that awful gnawing sensation in my stomach that came just before I went numb. The feeling that almost always came when I was touched.

But nothing happened. I almost felt ... safe. My heart thundered with every step he took. The cold damp wind blew my hair into my face, remnants of a storm from the coast. A moment later, Dario was untangling me from his body, and setting me down.

He handed me the stave, and then he pulled the spare cloak off his shoulder. He went to work at once, wrapping the material around my waist and then drawing the excess up over my shoulders, draping the ends over my head like a hood.

"Are you ready?" he asked, breathlessly.

"Ready."

He took my hand, and we were off.

We raced down the alley, heading across the street, away from Cal and Marisol's yells. Away from the screams coming from the inn as the soturi burst into guests' rooms looking for us. Another shout came from the ground. More soturi in the streets, patrolling the waterways as they hunted us. My heart hammered and Dario ran faster, leading us into the park nearby.

I looked back, just once, and spotted Meera and Aiden heading for the ladder.

We moved past the park, into the trees, snaking in and out of them, Dario grasping my fingers as he ran ahead. I had to leap over brambles and avoid small bushes, while barely keeping myself from tripping over the uneven terrain, but Dario kept a firm grasp on my hand.

"We need to get back on the street," he said when we finally paused. "This is as far as we can go in this direction."

I doubled over, my chest heaving, my breaths coming in rapid bursts. I wasn't used to this much movement—the Palace wasn't exactly interested in keeping us strong.

"Let's move," Dario said.

But I clutched my chest. "I need to catch my breath."

His mouth tightened. "Deep breath," he commanded. "Not these little ones. Okay? In through your nose, out through your mouth. We have to keep going."

I tried to do what he said. He gave an encouraging nod, and after a moment I felt my breathing steady. I stood up and he adjusted the hood of my cloak, ensuring it covered my hair completely. Then he tugged me forward out onto a waterway lit faintly by torchlight.

The street was empty as we crossed it. Dario quickly led us through a maze of alleys and empty waterways, behind a block of small shops. We were about to come out of its shadows when Dario pushed me against the wall, his hand over my mouth.

My stomach churned, pain gnawing at my insides. I gritted my teeth, ready to bite his hand off when I heard something. Voices.

"The bitch couldn't have gone far." A soturion.

There was an answering laugh. "Considering how many times the Bastardmaker's had her on her back, I think she's gone far enough. She better be worth that reward we was promised."

I closed my eyes, my hands shaking.

"Shhh." Dario's hand took hold of mine, of both of them, and pressed them to my stomach, squeezing gently. Our eyes met, and he moved his hand from my mouth, breathing slow and even.

The first soturion sneered. "Oh she will be. This one they pay for—and they pay well. If she gets any farther, she'll be worth even more for our trouble."

"Is that so? We should find her then," said the second voice. "And hide her for a bit—we could probably double the price, and take the rest of the year off."

Two sets of footsteps echoed in the abandoned streets, coming closer, and closer.

My pulse raced. Dario slowly leaned in toward me. He released my hands. Then he drew his hood over our heads. His body pressed against mine, so close I could feel his chest rising and falling.

The soturi's laughter grew louder.

Dario cradled my head, pulling me against him, still making shushing sounds. I buried my face in the crook of his neck, inhaling, surprised that despite all we'd been through, he still smelled pleasant.

"What's this?" said the first soturion. His voice was so clear and so close, I knew they'd reached the alley and could see us.

My heart thundered, and my vision was going out of focus. They saw us. They fucking saw us.

Dario slowly pulled my face against his, his lips just barely brushing against my cheek. "Shhh," he said again.

I squeezed my eyes shut, my entire body trembling.

"Ah," said the second soturion. "Leave 'em. Wish I had a girl against a wall. But I want that money more. Come on."

The first soturion laughed. "Give it to her man. Do it for us!"

They both burst into laughter, but soon the sound faded, their footsteps vanishing.

Breathing heavily, Dario pulled back, and instinctively, I pressed my hands to his chest, pushing him away.

"I'm sorry," he said, his face contorted in pain. "I'm sorry."

I shook my head. "I didn't mean to—" I looked at my hands. "It's fine."

"No, I shouldn't have … but I-I just didn't know what else to do to hide you. Are you okay?"

"Please, don't. It's fine." And surprisingly, I meant it.

"We need to run again," he said. "Final burst. Okay, Jules? Can you do that for me?"

It was the first time he'd used my nickname. I nodded.

And we ran out of the alleyway and turned. Dario led us down the length of the street, passing the buildings that hovered over the block until we reached the next one. Checking for soturi, we crossed the waterway and ducked into the next alley, moving through the dark, and then back out to the torchlit street. Five soturi appeared, and Dario pushed me back.

We hid in the shadows of the alley until they passed; luckily they hadn't noticed and were moving away from us, not closer. The minute the coast was clear, Dario took my hand and started sprinting, racing down the block, crossing the waterway and ducking into an alley.

"How much farther?" I asked. I was out of breath, and my legs were cramping. I knew Dario had slowed down for me considerably—more than considerably—and I was barely keeping up. But I was pushing myself to my limit, and I didn't think I'd last much longer.

"Just another minute," he said. "Come on. We're almost there. You can do this."

He led me forward. Thene's temple lay in the distance. The tall building was covered in golden sculptures of seraphim wings. We ran past it, and then up a small hill surrounded by trees. It was the home of our contact with the Purple Sun.

We reached the top of the hill, my stomach painfully tight, my calves burning, and my feet so sore they felt ready to fall off.

A wall encircled the two-story home, almost like a fortress. Someone very wealthy lived here.

A soturion approached the gate. "The hour is too late for visitors. The sun unseen. Go."

"Dawn approaches," I said, answering the code. "And the sun rises."

"And what color is the sun?" he asked.

"*Vylette*," I said.

The gate opened at once, and we were shown down a waterway and up a small set of stairs that led into the home.

Our host, an elderly mage, didn't show his face; I appreciated his secrecy. He was patient as we explained that four more of us were on the way, and that soturi from Ka Kormac would be searching the country for us.

We were shown into a small room to wait for our friends. The elderly mage disappeared briefly, returning with glasses of water for us, as well as a plate of bread, cheese, and sliced apples. He promised to bring more food, telling us they'd started to prepare meals for us once they got the call. I couldn't eat, but I was thirsty and drained my glass. I immediately refilled it as Dario took a plate for himself and piled everything onto it.

He sat, and held the plate in front of me, offering me whatever I wanted.

I shook my head. "What's taking them so long?" I said. "We weren't that far ahead."

"They'll be here," Dario said.

"But what if—"

"They'll be here," he repeated sternly.

But the only person who appeared was the mage to refill our water jug and to put out more fruits, and another serving of warm bread, this one accompanied by several dips.

Before I knew it, the hour was called again.

"Where are they?" I asked Dario, my mind already running through a hundred terrible scenarios.

"We should call," he said.

"That could be dangerous." We'd been waiting, desperate to make contact, but our voices coming through the vadati could be deadly if they were close enough for a soturion to hear. If they were hiding, one call could ruin their cover. The whole idea of the vadati was starting to feel more and more dangerous and foolish.

"Give me the stone," Dario said. "I've had to do this before—make a call without alerting anyone else."

I handed it over, and he took a deep breath before he held it close to his mouth. "Aiden," he said. He spoke as quietly as he could and still have the stone pick up his voice. "Aiden?"

White clouds filled the clear stone, starting to turn blue, but then they faded. It had connected. But Aiden hadn't answered.

I reached for the stone. "Meera," I said. "Meera?"
Nothing.

"Let's try Tristan and Galen," he said. But a knock on the door stopped us. It creaked open revealing a red-faced Meera and Aiden bursting into the room, out of breath.

The door closed and Meera looked frantically between me and Dario. "It's just the two of you? Just you two?"

"Yes," I said.

"Shit," Aiden cursed. "Shit."

"What?" Dario asked. "What's wrong?"

"Did Tristan call you?" Meera asked, her voice frantic. "Did you hear anything on your vadati?"

"No," I said, looking at Dario. "We didn't hear a thing. Not even when we called you two."

"Fuck," Aiden said. "He tried to call us. But when we tried to answer, all we heard was a scream. His. And Galen's." Aiden pushed his fingers through his auburn hair, groaning in frustration.

I clutched my chest. "You haven't heard from them since?" I asked.

I was suddenly dizzy, and had to walk over to the wall, holding onto it to keep from fainting. Because I knew—I knew they'd been captured. Ambushed by the Emperor's men, just like I had been. Dragged back to the Palace by his soturi.

We'd been so close to escape. So close to freedom.

"Julianna?" Dario asked, coming to stand beside me. "Are you ... are you okay?"

I shook my head. "We can't stay here. They'll torture our location out of them."

"Gods," Meera said. "What do we do? How do we help them?"

"We don't," I said, feeling numb. "We can't. As soon as they finish using them to get what they want, as soon as they finish their interrogation—it's over. They're dead."

CHAPTER SIX

TRISTAN

"Lord Tristan Grey," drawled the Emperor. "Thank you for joining us."

My eyes sprang open, blinking rapidly, my heart pounding as I sputtered and struggled for breath. I couldn't breathe—I couldn't ... I coughed violently, water dripping from my mouth. I was soaked in it, the ice-cold water dripping down my face, running into my eyes. It was everywhere, up my nose, down my throat. I was distantly aware that they must have dumped a bucket over my head. I coughed again, desperate to clear the airways, to breathe. I gasped, blinking more water from my eyes. My tunic was soaked, and the water was dripping down my pants and onto the ... onto the ... dungeon floor. One I recognized. The Yellow Room. The room where they'd brought Galen. Where I'd found Jules. Where I'd learned the truth of what happened to the vorakh I'd arrested.

I was back in the Palace.

My stomach clenched, as I finally cleared my airways of water with a desperate gasp. But panic was rising through me, exploding inside. I could barely move. I was immobile, helpless, and sure that if my heart didn't slow down soon, I would die.

"You can stop struggling now," the Emperor said. The former Imperator Kormac had traded his black and gold robes for purple. "Save your strength. You're chained to the wall." He shook his head, his black eyes narrowed. "And you're bound. You won't be escaping this time. Not again. Hart is dead. His friends are gone. And Lady Lyriana seems to have vanished completely." He laughed cruelly, the sound quickly joined by another as a soturion with thick muscles stepped out from the shadows.

The Bastardmaker.

A fresh wave of panic descended and I coughed, terrified I'd choke. Some of the water they'd splashed on me had gone down the wrong pipe. My ribs lit up with pain, and my chest tightened. My cough ended in a pathetic whimper. Fuck. Fuck! My arms had been shoved above my head, and thick metal chains were shackled to my wrists. Another set had been wrapped around my feet. I couldn't move. I couldn't relieve the pain. I couldn't even fucking scratch an itch. And on top of it all, I was bound, cut off from my magic. I could feel it—feel the hot burning ropes crisscrossing around my body. I couldn't see them, but they were there.

So much was happening, I didn't know where to focus. All I knew was that everything hurt. And no matter how I tried to shift or breathe, I couldn't find relief. Despite the ice-cold water still dripping from me, I was sweating against the heat of the ropes. My arms were strained, full of pins and needles from their positions, and yet, my wrists were on fire—cut-up from my restraints.

By the Gods, I was seconds away from passing out. On top of it all, I was so fucking sore. Everywhere. No inch of my body had been spared. Like I'd been beaten within an inch of my life.

I *had* been beaten within an inch of my life. When I'd been caught in Thene. When we'd been found.

Me and ...

"Galen," I groaned, my chest seizing up. "Where's Galen?"

"He's here, too," the Emperor said. "Right where I left him." He jerked his head to the side, my eyes following. My stomach sank.

Like me his arms were chained over his head, and his legs shackled. But his face ... Gods—his face. His left eye was swollen shut, his already broken nose had been broken again. Blood dripped from his nostrils, spilling into a split lip. And his arms ... they were hanging from their chains at a strange angle like they'd both been broken. He was barely recognizable.

And then I heard an awful snap in my head. A memory. The moment Galen's arm was broken by the soturi who found us. The scream he emitted when they did it. The scream when he knew we had lost.

The last few hours rushed back to me. Waiting in our room. Lady Kenna's letter. Our escape. And our capture. We'd been the last ones to escape from the inn—to climb down the ladder into the alleyway. Galen had wanted to wait—to make sure Jules and Meera got out first. We had our route memorized, both of our faces concealed beneath soturion cloaks.

We'd made it nearly halfway to the safe house without incident. Moving fast but carefully. Blending into our surroundings whenever we could.

But there was one walkway we had to cross. We never made it. Five soturi had found us. Galen sprung into action right away, as I reached for my stave. I cast a binding on the soturion nearest me, while Galen fought another—shoving his dagger into his gut. The soturion had stumbled back, but three more had joined them. We never stood a chance. Our cloaks were torn off when they wrestled us to the ground. And they knew. Even if they didn't have our descriptions, my face was too Godsdamned known.

"Galen," I said again, weakly. He hadn't answered. My stomach twisted violently. Why wasn't he answering? Had he heard me?

But then his right eye moved, only his right eye, the other was swollen too tightly shut. His dark iris was bloodshot as it focused on me. A tear ran down his cheek. Puffy and bruised. And I felt my own eyes water.

He was my best friend. He'd been there for me my entire life. As kids, he'd always been able to distract me when I was sad about my parents. He was the first one who invited me to play when the other kids were afraid of me. Afraid of my grief, afraid of the outbursts I had because of it. My anger had been unchecked back then. Until I learned how to feel it, how to let it go. Galen showed me how. He'd been the first one to acknowledge my rage, to validate how I felt. He didn't run when I was angry. He'd stay by my side—not to try to fix it, or change it. He let me be. And that was all it took—being seen, being understood. By a friend. I learned how to socialize, how to appear normal, unbothered. Because of Galen, because he saw me. And throughout all the years, Galen was there—by my side. Always. Until he chose to become a soturion, while I was studying to be a mage.

We'd been through so much together. So many nights, so many parties. First kisses, first drinks. And then we'd been together for all the loss. He was the only one I could turn to when I had no one else, when I was alone in my grief for Haleika. He was the only one who understood. The only one who felt my pain. The only one who saw me.

Another tear fell down his cheek. And then another.

"Galen?" I asked again, my stomach clenching. Something was wrong. Something was very wrong. Why wasn't he answering me? Why wasn't he speaking? "Galen?"

"Oh," the Emperor said, clicking his tongue, "you slept through that part. Unfortunately, he can't answer you."

I shook my head. "What do you mean he can't answer me. Why can't he—" My stomach churned, my throat tight. The backs of my eyes burned as a rage unlike I'd known since I was a kid burst through me. "What did you do to him?"

"What did *I* do?" The Emperor held up his hands. "*I* did nothing. Your friend here, on the other hand, escaped from justice after he murdered my uncle."

"With a dagger you put in his hand!" I spat. Galen had wanted to kill the Emperor, he'd wanted revenge for Haleika. And he'd done it in the end. But we all knew the truth. It was the Imperator all along, manipulating us. Creating a hole in his uncle's protection, putting Galen into position—using him for his own twisted ambitions.

The Emperor clicked his tongue. His black beady eyes narrowed into something dangerous, and predatory. He was a wolf now, more than he'd ever been before, and strung up like this, cut off from my power, I was his prey.

"Tristan," he shook his head, "you really shouldn't say such things. Otherwise, one might think you're not trustworthy. Not capable of keeping your tongue to yourself."

Galen wheezed, his mouth screwed shut, his shoulders shaking, nostrils flaring. Snot ran down his lips, mixing with the blood already caked there. He was crying. My best friend was crying. I'd never seen him cry before. Not even after Haleika. But instead of his cries, or any kind of words, he was moaning, this strange, wet sound I didn't recognize.

"Show him," the Emperor said, jerking his head at his brother. "Show Lord Tristan what happens when traitors don't keep their mouths shut."

Galen's entire body trembled, as his sobs wracked through his chest. The Bastardmaker strode toward him, the giant wolf pelt he always wore on his back bouncing with every step. The grotesque head of the dead wolf, and its lifeless eyes stared at the ceiling as his hand wrapped around Galen's chin forcing his head up.

"Open your mouth, boy," the Bastardmaker snarled. And when Galen didn't comply, he shook him. "Open your Gods-damned lying traitor mouth."

Galen's eye closed as the Bastardmaker wrenched his lips apart. The same awful sound exploded, the painful moan, it was louder now, more ragged. He tried to turn his face away, but the foreign sound he was making intensified, like he was trying to speak but couldn't. Like he was in pain but couldn't express it.

Behind his lips were his white teeth—a few were missing. But behind them, there was ... nothing, just black where there should have been—where there should have been—

Bile collected in my throat. And I started to gag.

They'd cut out his tongue. They'd cut out his fucking tongue.

My stomach spasmed, my ribs cracking. And this time it wasn't bile. Vomit rose up my throat. But I was unable to lean forward. My vomit had nowhere to go. Some of it stopped in my mouth, but the rest went back down, choking me. I heaved. Sweat coating my face. My stomach was on fire.

I threw up again, choking.

"Myself to fucking Moriel," the Emperor drawled.

Tears blurred my vision, and I could feel myself getting ready to heave once more. The vomit was in my nose now and I couldn't breathe. I couldn't fucking breathe.

I was faintly aware of the sound of my chains unclasping. My hands fell at my sides. I collapsed to my knees, just as it came up again. My guts spewed across the ground as the Emperor stepped out of range, keeping his black leather boots clean.

I coughed, and spat, still heaving up everything inside of me. The taste of throw up was coating my tongue, and the horrid scent was plastered inside my nostrils.

The Bastardmaker released Galen's mouth, and patted him on the cheek. Fresh tears fell from Galen's eyes, his mouth quivering before he sealed his lips shut.

"Why?" I gasped. "Why would you do that?"

"Tristan, Tristan," the Emperor said. "I thought you were smarter than that."

"He did what you asked him to. What you wanted."

"What *I* wanted? Tristan, do we need to go over this again? I did nothing. I am grieving for my uncle. Hold your tongue."

"Why! Are you going to cut mine out, too?" I asked.

"You didn't murder my uncle, did you?" he asked. "But I do need to punish you. You've really disappointed me these last few days. These last few weeks. After all these years, all the investments I made into training you." He snapped at the Bastardmaker. "Bring him some water."

I eyed Galen, terrified. My feet were still shackled. And I was still bound.

"I'm sorry," I mouthed.

Galen shook his head, and looked away.

A silver goblet was shoved into my hand. "Drink," the Emperor commanded.

I filled my mouth, washing the taste of vomit from it. I spat the first mouthful to the side and then drank deeply, feeling the coolness of the water as it traveled down my burning throat.

I was given a wet towel and used it to wipe my face. Then I blew my nose. Snot and other awful things came out. I coughed again, still feeling sick.

"I thought you'd be my star pupil," he said. "After all, you were so eager. So open to learning, to being trained. And why wouldn't you be? You hailed from the educational jewel of the Empire. You said you wanted to fight alongside me. You told me so yourself as a young boy, you felt called to protect the vulnerable. You wanted to make sure no one suffered again what you had—make sure no one would be torn apart by a rogue, violent vorakh," he growled. "And what did I do? I taught you. I supported you. I gave you all the tools you needed. And how did you repay me?" he yelled.

I was shaking too hard to answer. I could see myself at nineteen, so eager to learn. Standing in the grass outside of the Grey Villa, watching with intent as the Imperator's mage showed me how to capture vorakh, how to hunt them down. And all the while, the Imperator watched, a dark gleam in his eyes I hadn't understood at the time.

"Huh? How did you repay me?" He stomped down on my hand and ground his heel into its center.

Bones cracked.

I screamed.

The Emperor kneeled before me, taking my chin in his hand, squeezing so hard I thought my jaw would snap. "You squandered the opportunity I offered you. Freed dangerous vorakh, freed murderers," he pointed at Galen, "and then as if that weren't enough, you absconded with the vilest forsworn scum of the Empire." He shook his head. "Where," he threw my head back, "were your loyalties?"

"I'm sorry," I cried, scrambling to sit, cradling my broken hand to my chest. "I'm sorry."

"Shut up," he snapped.

This time the Emperor stalked toward Galen.

"No," I said. "No, don't!"

"I said, shut up!" He smiled then, the most evil, wolfish looking grin I'd ever seen as he looked between me and Galen.

Something inside me went cold—a terror I hadn't known since I was three. Since I was trapped in the cupboard, helpless as my mother fought against the vorakh that would kill her.

"You hear?" he asked. "You hear how your friend knows his place? How he knows now to be silent. Because he knew that the moment he put his blade inside my uncle's belly, inside your Emperor's stomach, that he no longer had a say in his life." He pulled out his dagger.

I opened my mouth to scream, but the Emperor's eyes widened in warning.

I closed my mouth, and he nodded. Then he turned his blade, striking Galen in the stomach with the hilt.

Galen paled, his mouth forming a soundless O, as his body convulsed.

"Now, here's how this is going to work. I'm more than aware of your treachery, your treason. But luckily for you, I still need you. Your face. Your position. You have a job to do." He walked back toward me, keys jangling in his hand. "I need you to prove yourself to me. See—I trusted you before. And I was wrong. I need you to show me I won't be wrong a second time."

He reached behind me, one ankle freed. A moment later the next. And somehow that was worse. An acknowledgment that I wouldn't be free. That I couldn't run, because I was too weak, too injured. That no one was coming. No one would save us this time.

"Well? Ready to prove yourself?" the Emperor asked.

I shook my head. "Why would I prove anything to you?"

The Emperor frowned, his eyebrows furrowed in confusion as he shared a look with his brother. "I can think of several reasons. Keeping your tongue. Keeping your cock."

I shuddered. Then he shrugged. "How about keeping your friend alive?"

Galen shook his head, his eyes wide. I knew that look. He didn't want me to agree. No more bargains. No more deals with a demon. But it was his life. And if there was the smallest chance that I could do it, could buy him time, I would.

I lifted my eyebrows, trying to explain. To tell him I had to. That he was worth it. That I'd take the risk, accept the pain, if I could save him. All this time, all I wanted was to save him.

Galen frowned seeing the decision in my eyes, and shook his head one more time. Just once more.

I met the Emperor's cold eyes. "What do I do?"

"Take off your shirt," the Emperor purred.

"What?" I asked, a knot in my belly.

"I said," his aura flared, nearly blasting me back against the wall, "take off your shirt."

It was like ice had been injected into my veins. Every part of me was going cold—every limb shaking with fear. I tried not to think about it. What it meant, what was going to happen. Only the logistics. Because I could barely do it with a broken hand. Even with my good hand I was too injured, too sore all the way down my arm. I tried to grab my shirt and lift. I didn't even make it to my chest before agony shot through my muscles and my hand fell down. I gritted my teeth, a moan of pain escaping my lips as I did it again. Fuck. I started to cry, unable to stop myself. My right hand was destroyed. And my arms barely had the strength.

A sob wracked my body as I gripped my shirt again with my left hand, and lifted, pushing past the pain, lights exploding in my eyes as I lifted my arm over my head.

Sweat broke out around my neck as I tugged and twisted, trying to push my head out of the material. It took me a full minute. But it was off. I dropped it on the floor and swayed for a moment, fearful I'd faint again. The thing was covered in blood, dirt, sweat, and vomit.

"Good boy," he said. "Now," he stepped back, and pointed at the floor. "Crawl."

"But my hand—"

"I said, crawl."

I sank to my knees, and used my left hand, and right elbow. "Ah," I cried out.

Galen made a pathetic moan in response, like he was trying to tell me no, trying to tell me to stop.

I wanted to. Fuck, it hurt so much to move my hand, to put any weight on my arms. But I lifted my knee, and thought of Galen smiling. Of us getting out of here. Finding a healer, the best in the Empire. Someone who could help him, who could fix this. Then I lifted my elbow, seeing us on the beach, splashing in the water. I moved my knee again, and saw Galen trying beer for the first time and grinning as I'd spat mine out. Another elbow. Galen confessed his feelings for Haleika to me. And I hugged him, wanting them to be together. They kept coming, images of Galen before, happy and healthy. Images of Galen after—healed, alive. I crawled and crawled, my stomach turning. I was a shivering, sweating mess by the time I reached his boots.

"Now kiss them," he said.

So I did. Leaning down and kissing each one. There was still vomit on my tongue. But now there was sweat and specks of dirt caked to my lips.

"They're a little dirty," the Bastardmaker said, striding toward his brother. He kneeled before me, pointing at the Emperor's boots. "Maybe you should clean them up."

I sat back, confused, looking for the towel they'd given me.

The Bastardmaker laughed. "With your mouth."

Oh. I squeezed my eyes shut, swallowing back bile, and then I bent back down, extended my tongue, and licked. I had to work to keep from throwing up again. From gagging on the scent of shit beneath his heels, the stale aroma of urine. I didn't know what I was licking or tasting. I couldn't. I just knew I had to do this. Had to finish, had to breathe through my nose and not throw up. So I licked and I licked, tears burning my eyes, Galen's moans in the background.

And I did the same on the other boot. Licking, and gagging, and holding it in, crying with every inch.

"What do you think, Waryn?" the Emperor asked. "Clean enough?"

The Bastardmaker laughed. "They have a certain shine to them."

Suddenly, I was hauled to my feet, and dragged toward Galen so we were face-to-face.

"You want to live?" the Emperor asked him. "Keep your eye open."

Galen's nostrils flared, his lips screwed together, shaking, but he kept his eye on me as instructed.

The Emperor's eyes narrowed, sliding from my head to my waist. "Take down your pants," he said.

"What! No." I shook my head. "Please—"

"Take. Down. Your. Pants."

Galen cried out, the sound awful. His chest heaved, but he kept his eye on me.

Using my left hand, I reached for my waist, and undid the laces, letting my pants fall open.

"I said down," the Emperor said.

So I pushed on them, and they fell to my knees, leaving me otherwise naked.

"Go on," the Emperor said, his black eyes on my cock. "Grip it. Nice and firm."

My breath was shallow as I did, moving my left hand to wrap around myself. I was going numb. I couldn't feel a thing. Not even the pain radiating through me. The Bastardmaker moved closer, watching intently. His hand snaking down to his hip and then lower. He was turned on.

"Galen," the Emperor said. "Look at what your friend is willing to do to save your life."

But Galen only glared, the look on his face saying if he could speak, he'd be cursing right now.

"You're not looking, Galen," the Bastardmaker said. "You're not looking where you're supposed to." He took his face again, forcing it down, forcing him to stare at my cock.

"Are you satisfied?" I gritted through my teeth, terrified of what was next.

"Satisfied?" the Emperor asked. "Can one ever be satisfied?"

My chest heaved. "What more must I do for Galen to live?" I asked, my voice small and trembling.

He made a sound low in his throat. "Oh, dear Tristan. Nothing. Because you see, Galen's a liability. He knows the truth, and unfortunately he has neither a face, nor a name that is of use to us now. My uncle's murderer must be punished. Justice must be served. So, Galen will be named a traitor and made into an example."

"B-But," I stammered, "I did what you asked. I—" I'd followed his directions. Fuck. FUCK! I did everything he asked.

"This was merely punishment for your betrayal," the Emperor drawled. "Not a bargain for his life. You'll be signing a blood contract with the Bastardmaker, doing whatever he commands you from now on. I see now you needed a far tighter leash than we first gave to you. You will have tonight to heal, get a cast for that hand. Tomorrow night, you'll return to Bamaria. There you are to begin your duties." He ran his knuckles down Galen's cheek. "And poor Galen here," he jerked his chin at his brother.

"NO!" I roared.

But the Bastardmaker's sword was pointed right at Galen's waist. His eyes widened, and his face tightened like he was bracing for what was about to come. The Bastardmaker's muscles tensed as he pulled his arm back, and then with a rageful cry, he drove the sword into Galen's side.

I screamed, but no sound could escape my lips. I was three years old again, terrified of the vorakh tearing my parents apart.

Galen made a final pained, wet, wheezing sound, like he wanted to scream, but he couldn't. His eyes lifted, focusing on me as the sword drove in further, the point tearing through him. Blood dripped down his side, his body convulsing as it was impaled. Left to right.

"Galen," I screamed in silence. "Galen!"

For a second, there was a light in his eyes as they reached mine. But the light vanished, his head rolling forward.

My heart cracked in two.

"You can take your hand off your cock now," the Emperor sneered, his eyes dipping between my legs with disdain. "You'll need it. You have papers to sign."

CHAPTER SEVEN

LYRIANA

Wind howled across the shore, as I wiped at tears with the back of my hand. My heart thundered as loud as the rain. It was still pouring, pounding against the cave. I gripped the rough-hewn stone of the wall, feeling the cold of the wind and raindrops against my face. My stomach was twisting, growing more painful with every second I stayed back.

Rhyan was out there. Rhyan was out there—an akadim. Alone in the world, without his soul. He could be hurt. Or he could be the one hurting someone. Every scenario made me ill. And I knew every second I delayed, that I waited, that I allowed him to exist in this state—it was only prolonging my suffering, My grief. And his—in whatever way that he was connected to the part of him that still existed. The part of him that I had to believe still existed. Auriel said it did, and so did my heart.

"Lyriana," Auriel said. He came up behind me where I stood at the mouth of the cave. He'd given me some space. Let me be for a while. Grieving. Waiting. But I was done.

"I can't do this," I said. "I can't wait. Every second that passes doing nothing, letting Rhyan suffer, feels like torture."

"There's nothing you can do for him. Not yet, at least."

I whirled around on him. "Yes, there is! Gods! Of course there is."

All I could see when I closed my eyes was the look of pain on Rhyan's face when he told me he was dying. All I could feel was the utter horror of seeing him powerless, being killed, changed, taken by an akadim.

"Look," I said, "I know you haven't been mortal in a while, and you forgot how time works down here, but it's passing and quickly, and it's not in my favor. And it's not in his!"

"I can feel the time passing," he said quietly. "It's faster than you know. I feel the mortality wrapped around me. But the storm is still out there, and you're still recovering from using all of your power. Have some patience. The storm will end soon," he said.

"Patience?" I gritted through my teeth. "Patience!"

I stepped beyond the threshold, right outside the cave, and the storm was even louder. Waves crashed against the shore, as raindrops fell in thick, heavy pellets, beating against me. I was soaked within seconds. My hair, my tunic, everything. My soturion cloak would have protected me. But it was gone. I'd given it to Rhyan before ... Before.

My boots slid into the sand and another round of thunder clapped. Lightning struck, bringing the beach to life. The headless gryphon's body was illuminated in the distance, before darkness descended again, and the wind began to scream, blowing wildly.

"Wait!" Auriel yelled, stepping out and reaching for my hand.

I dodged, avoiding his touch.

"Lyriana! You can't go out there like this."

"Morning's practically here," I snapped. "I didn't agree to anything more. I'm done. I don't care about the rain. I don't care about the consequences." I just had to get to Rhyan. Just find Rhyan. Do something!

"Well, I fucking care! And that isn't just some rain. It's a magically induced storm—brought about with ancient magic—magic *you* summoned." More thunder exploded.

"Semantics," I shouted over the noise. "Rain is rain!"

"Oh! You want to play that game?" he asked. "How about we don't? How about, despite what happened last night, you find a way to act semi-reasonably?" he huffed.

I turned away from him and kept walking.

"By the realms!" he shouted. "Where the hell do you think you're going to end up, other than back here, and soaking wet?"

"I'm not coming back. I'm either going to find a seraphim, or I'll take a boat to the mainland, whichever way I find first. But I will find a way. I already told you. It doesn't matter. Nothing matters. Except finding him."

"Lyriana, please. Just listen to me—"

"No!" I shook my head, taking another step away from him. "I'm sorry you came all this way," I yelled over the rain, marching forward. "But you did your job. You came to me when I called. You stopped the second Drowning. So, congratulations. It's just a storm now. But it's over. You can go home."

"Oh can I? Well, thank you so much for the permission." He rushed in front of me, blocking my path. Rain pelted off his armor, and his golden curls flattened against his head.

I pushed my hair out of my face, screaming over the storm. "You're welcome! Tell the Council of Forty-Four that you did your duty. And while you're there, you can tell them to leave me the fuck alone. I'm finished serving them. I don't care how far we go back, it's over. And then when that's done, you can go back to her like you want. Go back to the version of me you actually want to be with."

"The version of you! The version! Realms! Do you even hear yourself now? You think I traveled through multiple dimensions to spend a few hours here? You think I risked my immortality, and the scorn of a council that banished me once already, just to leave you like this?"

"I don't care what you did! You're not stopping me," I yelled, and then I spun on my heels, running for the shoreline, my arms pumping at my sides, my eyes half-closed to keep the downpour from my eyes.

The Guardian of Bamaria lay ahead, just against the shoreline. In the rain it was just a mass of black rock, the only thing visible in the dark like this.

"LYRIANA!" Auriel roared, his voice like thunder clapping in the storm. Until the actual storm drowned him out.

The waves of the ocean rushed toward me, drenching my already soaked boots. It was so dark, and the rain was so heavy, that as I looked back, I could no longer see Auriel.

I raced to the front of the gryphon, my feet just beyond its paws, seeing clearly now the damage I had done to its body, the place where its head once met its neck. I pumped my arms at my sides, willing myself to run faster, but the sand was caking against my boots, slowing me down. And my calves were beginning to burn. The naturalness I'd begun to run with since I'd claimed my magic, the ease with which I could now move, was gone. I was starting to feel out of breath. Hours had passed since I'd called on *Rakashonim* and come here. I could feel it with every step I took now. Auriel was right about one thing. My magic was still depleted.

But I was used to working without it. Used to relying on my own strength. My own muscle, my own grit.

Tear the fucking rope apart. Just like Rhyan taught me.

I reached the other side of the Guardian, and I knew once I passed it, I'd lose him. If he could still see me in the dark and the rain, he wouldn't be able to see through the statue. Up ahead, I spotted a hint of sunlight, growing and expanding against the water. But there was no boat or seraphim in sight. It didn't matter. I'd keep running. I'd find something eventually. Anything—anything to get me off this Godsdamned island. Maybe even call on *Rakashonim* again when my magic replenished. After all, it fucking got me here, maybe it could take me away.

My legs were shaking over the uneven terrain. But the Guardian was behind me now, and Auriel was even further back. I spotted a small dune, and was prepared to leap over it, but something jumped in front of me. One second, I was several feet past the stone gryphon …

And the next, my body was slamming back into its onyx form. I gasped, winded, but before I could scream—

"Caught you," Auriel said, out of breath.

"You were behind me," I said, dumbfounded.

"Well, I caught up," he growled, his hands restraining mine. "It's called running faster." His fingers tightened around my wrists, pressing them harder into the statue.

"What are you doing?" I yelled.

His eyes darkened, but his aura flared like a fog around me. "Getting you to listen to me. I said to wait."

"I can't!" I twisted my hips, and kicked, wrenching my hands from his grip. But before I could gain even an inch of freedom, he pressed himself forward, trapping me between his body and the statue. "I have to find him."

I slammed my arms, my hips twisting to get out of his hold, but it was to no avail. Auriel might only be in mortal form, having trouble being back in this body, struggling to remember what he once knew, or recover the strength he once possessed. But he was hardly at a disadvantage. Even Rhyan's hands had never been like this. Like fucking steel. I could only imagine the sheer power he wielded as an actual God. Auriel at full strength had to be unstoppable.

"Lyriana, you're in no state to do so! What do you think is going to happen if you find him now? He's a newborn aka-dim, he'll be hungry. Ravenous! Out of his mind. And even if he remembers you, it won't be him, it will be something else, something soulless. And I promise you, you're not ready for that!"

"You don't know that! I'll do whatever it takes, and I know I can. Because I did it before! I had to kill a friend who became akadim, minutes after it happened."

"When you were in the arena! When your life was threatened! And so was Rhyan's. It's not the same thing!"

I snarled.

"Just work with me," he said. "Because I feel like there's more to this. Something bigger is happening. Okay. I came because you called me. I did. But still—even that shouldn't have been possible. There's some reason I'm here. And I want to know what it is."

But we already knew the reason. It wasn't just for me, to comfort me, or help me. It was because I was more powerful than I'd known, than anyone had wanted to admit.

I could destroy. I could change the land. And the Council didn't like that. Didn't want another Drowning. There was no other reason. Rhyan was gone. Becoming an akadim was irreversible. It was a state that ended in only one way—death.

A death that would kill me. A death that already had in some ways. Because as much as I was running around in this body, breathing, crying, and running, my heart was broken, my soul splintered. It was no longer mine. It had gone wherever Rhyan's had. I might as well have been an akadim, too. At least, then, we'd be together.

"Auriel!" I yelled, still struggling. "Godsdamnit. Get off of me!"

"I said," his voice dangerously low, "wait, Lyriana."

"And I said," gritting my teeth, "to get off."

"I would if you'd listen to me. But you won't! So you know what, if you want to be stubborn, then go ahead. Run." His lips curled. "Do it. But I'll be right behind. And when I catch you I will take you over my shoulder, and I will carry you into the cave. And then I will hold you down myself until the rain stops."

Fire blazed in me. "You wouldn't."

"Oh, I think I would. Because if you want to know something, I'm getting just a little bit offended at your welcome of me. I think I might enjoy carrying you back there. And if you run, I will do it." He cocked his head to the side. "You understand how seriously Rhyan took his oaths? Well, let me tell you, he learned that from me, and he's far more reasonable! So listen carefully. You're going to stop fighting, and you're going to let me help you. I'm here to keep you safe, to figure things out until we can actually do something about all of this. You might not know this, but Heaven isn't exactly a place you can just come and go from. Normally the only way out is by being born. And that's not what I just did. I'm here for a reason, and we're going to figure out what that is." The muscles in his jaw ticked.

I spat at him, but he moved his head aside too quickly. I knew he was a God, but I was still stunned at how impossibly fast he moved without warning, and how unnaturally powerful his reflexes were. And yet, underlying it all was the way his aura felt, clouded, and confused, like he'd been weakened in some way.

I spat again for good measure. He barely blinked as he dodged.

"Well, you're feisty. I'll give you that." His eyes were sparkling, almost mischievously.

"I didn't ask you to give me anything!" I yelled. "I don't want anything! Just for you to fucking let me go!"

"And we already went over why I think that's a bad idea," he snapped. "Typical. I was trying to be gentle with you back there. Patient. I understand the pain you're in—better than you know." His voice cracked. "And I really am here to help you. But you won't accept anything I say. You're too stubborn."

Auriel made a sound low in his throat. "By all the fucking realms. The latest one in a millennium, and for all the tiny differences, you might as well be an exact copy of the original."

"The latest one?" I shouted.

"Latest incarnation. Most current expression of Asherah." Auriel shrugged.

"I am not a copy!" I slammed my wrists forward without warning, breaking free of his trap. Within seconds I withdrew my dagger, and slid it firmly against his neck, then grabbed his shoulder, pushing the blade against his skin, just enough to tell him I was serious, and I held it there, until I had him pressed and imprisoned against the stone.

"Who's a God now?" I asked.

His green eyes widened in surprise and then with far too much amusement considering he had my knife at his throat.

"Well done," he said, his gaze sweeping down the length of my blade, and then the rest of my body. As if he were Rhyan. As if we were back in the training room together and he was teaching me. The rain had flattened his golden hair, and was running down his face in thick rivulets. But somehow, even with all the similarities between them, it didn't make him look any more mortal to me.

"Your form, your technique," Auriel said, "and your element of surprise is really top notch. As expected. But ... Not. Good. Enough." He flicked his wrist and my blade fell to the ground. A second later Auriel had my arms trapped again at my side. He pulled me against him, and spun us until once more I was pressed into the stone, my breath coming in quick heavy bursts.

"I can still take you!" I snarled.

He laughed again. "Predictable."

"What is?"

"This. You. After all—you are her. I knew you'd get all riled up and angry if I argued with you, taunted you just the littlest bit." He shook his head, a smile spreading across his face. "And you think I don't know you."

I wanted to scream. Because he was right. And because it was exactly like something Rhyan would do. It was exactly like something Rhyan had done on more than one occasion. Arguing with me, teasing, even flirting to keep me present, to keep me from panicking. Spiraling.

He always knew what to say, what to do, how to bring me back from the brink when I'd needed it. But this was different. Because this time Rhyan was on the other side of the brink. And I'd be damned before I let Auriel distract me from what I had to do next. "Let. Me. Go."

"I believe we've already covered this section of the argument, but by all means if we must visit it again in the near future, then go ahead, and let me know. I'll even give you a head start." He winked.

I glared in response.

He sighed, making an exasperated sound. "Lyriana, look, I know this is difficult for you, to lose him like this. I do. But you must believe me when I say that nothing that happened last night was your fault. It wasn't. But it did happen, and it was awful, and traumatizing, and now? You're not thinking straight."

"Yes I am!"

"You tried to summon a tsunami!"

"That was right after it happened."

"Which was hours ago!"

"Oh fuck you. Just stop. Okay? Just stop! I'm not ready for the comfort portion of this. Don't you see? I don't even have time to Godsdamned grieve for him—or try to remember him properly! This isn't over yet. My friends are still in trouble!" I screamed. "They're in danger! And Rhyan ... Rhyan is—" The Godsdamned tears were back. "I have to do something about Rhyan." Find him.

Kill him.

My stomach twisted with fresh pain. I was dangerously close to vomiting again as I realized that the last time I would ever see him, or touch him, it would be as a monster. The last time I would ever put my hands on him would be the first time ever that I wasn't trying to bring him comfort, or pleasure, or healing. It would be to kill.

I'd seen his red eyes in my dream. I could imagine what an akadim Rhyan would look like. And just like that, with that image burning into my mind, the fight left me again. I stopped struggling.

Slowly, Auriel released my hands, and stepped back. He held his hands up as if in surrender, once more revealing the scars that covered them. Eyeing me warily, he took a slow step back, treating me like I was a wild animal.

I slumped against the Guardian, my eyes closed. The feeling in my heart was splintering. I felt like I'd just gone through every emotion in the world in the last few minutes. Panic. Grief. Anger. Now, I felt like I was on the verge of despair.

"Auriel?" My voice was small, and pathetic.

"Lyriana."

"Are you sure?" I asked. "Are you sure he's akadim?"

"*Meka*," Auriel said gently. *My soul*. "I am. I am sure. His soul ... it's ... it's not here. I promise you. I'd know. I defied so much more than was possible, but even I couldn't be here now if his soul was. And yet ... it didn't go to the place one would expect."

"What place? The celestial realms? Heaven?" Or was it just gone? Eaten. Mangled and destroyed by the akadim. Gods. I couldn't even voice those fears out loud.

"In a sense," Auriel said. "It's not quite that. It's hard to explain in language down here. The mortality I'm cloaked in is making everything more difficult, making me work harder to move, to think. I can't stop feeling like I'm forgetting something important. Something else. But what you're asking me, these are ... concepts that just don't exist in this world."

"Can you try to explain," I begged. "Please."

His mouth tightened, but he nodded. "Rhyan's soul would have met with mine if he'd passed. We share the same origin, history, the same life force. But we don't share a personality. Not officially. He would have become a part of me in some way, joined me or ... *returned* to me. He'd remember being me, remember all of the lives he'd lived. But he would still be Rhyan." He frowned. "Think of your family. Your sisters are your sisters—always. Whether you're in the same room or not. Nothing changes that."

There was a sudden pang in my chest. For Morgana. Morgana who'd led the akadim into the capital. Morgana who'd tricked me into stealing the indigo shard. Morgana whose presence stalled me from getting to Rhyan—whose akadim murdered him.

I pushed thoughts of her away and nodded at Auriel, desperate to follow along, to find some glimmer of hope in his words.

"It's like I'm in another room, and if Rhyan had ... had passed traditionally, he would have returned to the room with me."

"So you'd be in the same place?" I asked.

"Yes. And he would continue on in the next world as Rhyan, albeit in a less-physical form, but he would have gone to his own realm, his own Heaven you might say, to exist as himself—somewhere that would make him happy, someplace where you could be with him, too. Forever. But at any point if he wanted, he could be ... absorbed by me. Or by any of our incarnations. He could even—if he wished— watch what's happening here. Watch over you. I'm sure he'd be doing that now if he weren't—well, where he is. But he'd always be able to return to himself. He'd always be Rhyan. With every incarnation—every lifetime lived—my soul only expands. I simply become more."

"So you all continue to exist?" I asked. "I'm Asherah. But after I ... when I die at the end of this life, I won't just become Asherah again—unless I want to be? I'll still be Lyriana?"

Auriel nodded. "If you choose, then yes. Imagine if you will, Lyriana at two years old, and Lyriana at seven, at twelve, sixteen ... The younger versions of you never died. But none of them exist now. They're all here—inside of you." He gestured to my chest. "In the celestial realms, the other versions can step out of your body, and exist separately on their own. Rhyan would be me, and not me. But he'd be home. Back in Heaven. And he's not. If there's one thing I'm more aware of than of Asherah, it's all of my lives, all of my incarnations and all of the souls that are born of them. I know them all well. But Rhyan and I, we were close, and yet, I could not sense him at all. That's how I know he's akadim. Which means his soul went somewhere else."

"Somewhere else?"

Auriel swallowed roughly. "Somewhere else."

"Where?" This was the first time I'd ever heard discussion of souls going somewhere after being eaten. Of them not being simply destroyed as I'd always been taught. The idea that Rhyan was just somewhere else, lost, away from me—it wasn't comforting, but it was maybe better than the idea of him being destroyed, having been eaten, and not existing at all.

Light began to fill the horizon. Sunrise was here, the sky was full of red, golden light. The rain softened, the drops growing sparser. It was letting up, the storm ending. Suddenly, the first warm glow of morning sun was shining across Gryphon Island, illuminating the rain.

"Lyriana, I think that—" Auriel froze. His eyes met mine, moving back and forth, his mouth falling open. "By the realms." His voice filled with awe. "Your hair. Lyriana, your hair."

I glanced down. It was soaking wet, plastered to my armor. Under the sunlight bursting through the drizzle, it was bright, fiery red. Batavia red.

But at that moment, I saw what Auriel did.

Asherah's red.

"You," he gasped. "You look just like her, like my love. You look just like yourself." He reached his hand forward, taking a lock between his fingers, examining it with reverence. "Alive."

I remained still, my heart pounding. Something was happening to me. Something was shifting inside. I was *remembering* Auriel. Remembering more than a flash of him on a beach, remembering more than just feeling a kind of reverence for his name.

I was remembering that I loved him. And just like he'd explained, that every incarnation made from his soul, expanded him, I felt like my heart was expanding, too. With love.

Auriel wasn't Rhyan. He just wasn't. But ... every second I spent with him, he felt more familiar to me. More ... *mine*, in a way I couldn't explain. Our souls were tethered together, and though I didn't remember most of our history, or even our other lifetimes together, I could feel the weight of it all on my heart. I could feel our connection to each other like it was a living, breathing thing. Like our souls had always been in conversation, always seeking the other. That's what happened to me and Rhyan. We'd been kids, and drawn to each other even then, never understanding why.

My heart pounded. My body felt lighter.

And at last, the rain stopped.

Auriel released my hair, both of us breathing heavily. And then his fingers, callused and scarred like the rest of his hand, closed around the edge of my chest plate.

"You especially look like her, like yourself, wearing this." Auriel released a shaky breath.

Asherah's armor was made up of connecting golden Valalumir stars. What appeared to be diamonds mixed with starfire in the center of each star, was blood.

"By the realms." His eyes widened, filling with tears, the muscles in his jaw tensing as he stepped back again, both hands fisted. "That's not a replica. That's the original. Hers." He exhaled sharply. "I can feel her energy still attached to it. Sense her blood inside, mixed with mine."

"And my blood, too. It's how I've been calling on her. Calling on *Rakashonim*."

He reached for my chest plate again, his knuckles suddenly whitening as he gripped the edges, shaking it. "He gave this to you. Didn't he?" His eyes darkened. "Mercurial."

I nodded slowly. "He made sure it was put in front of me on my birthday. And then he made sure I wore it."

Auriel hissed. "That traitorous, two-faced, falcon-headed bastard!"

I blinked, surprised at how quickly his anger had flared.

Auriel's gaze was distant, his eyes watering as he looked away. "I ... I buried her with this. Or I thought I had. I did everything I could to make it impossible to unseal her tomb. Impossible to disturb her, or ... the shard she guarded within. Not without being told the secret by me. Without being told where the lock was. The answer to opening it was written in stone that could only be read in moonlight."

The sun revealed my secrets, so I hid them with the moon.

"And the items needed—those were also supposed to be impossible to come by. A key I'd crafted with my own magic and kept on my person. Then there was my soul—which I knew was likely to return. And at last, my blood, which I thought was safe. But, Mercurial deceived me. He'd kept her chest plate. And now, Asherah's tomb has been opened."

"I'm sorry," I said softly. I'd seen how Rhyan had been affected by it. How upset it had made him. Because he remembered. Because he was Auriel. And then even after that night, he'd dreamed about it. He'd had nightmares for weeks. Reliving Asherah's death—my death. "We had to."

"I know you did." He sighed heavily, looking defeated. "When my own time came to an end, I designed my tomb in such a way, no one would ever disturb it. I knew I had to find the means to keep what I stored inside safe."

"Your tomb?" I blinked, and my throat tightened. "Auriel, where is it?"

He swallowed roughly. His eyes moved past me, sliding back and forth. His hair had started to dry, and in the morning sun, the curls shone with gold. His eyes were even more green in the light. More like the green of Rhyan's eyes. My heart thundered.

"I believe," he said slowly, his voice shaking, "that you're standing right in front of it."

I spun around. The Guardian of Bamaria. The gryphon! All those years, Rhyan and I had wondered, researched, speculated. All the theories of what it could mean. I had thought it might be possible last night, thought there was some significance to it, some reason I'd come here of all places. To the symbol most closely associated with Rhyan, and with the God he once was.

"Auriel," I said, a small surge of hope beginning to simmer in my chest. "Do you think there's a reason I came here last night?" A thousand more questions filled my mind. But before I could ask any of them, a dark shadow swallowed the sun above us. A shadow moving fast. There was a screech in the air. A sound I hadn't heard in months.

A seraphim. It landed not far from us, its golden wings gleaming in the sunlight. A blue jeweled carriage sat atop its back. The bird settled and the carriage door sprung open.

I tensed, instinctively moving in toward Auriel, my hand snaking to the blade at my hip.

Five soturi jumped to the ground, their boots thudding into the sand. The silver armor of Ka Kormac was strapped to their chests. And in each of their hands, a starfire sword flickered with flames.

"What are you doing out here?" came a shout. One soturion stepped before the others, his aura blasting with a predatory viciousness. His beady eyes immediately marked him as a close relative of the Bastardmaker. "We have reports of a disturbance at the Guardian. Hands up, now! Both of you."

"Shit! Look!" shouted a second. "Look at the hair!"

The first one's eyes narrowed. I was sure that he was the leader of the five. The turion amongst them. "Myself to fucking Moriel." His hand tightened around his sword. "That's Lyriana Batavia."

Auriel angled his body protectively in front of mine. His movements were slow and methodical. His eyes never left the five soturi.

"Can I borrow this?" he whispered. His hand was warm on my hip, his fingers closing around the hilt of my dagger.

I was already going for my sword, our hands brushing together.

"Apparently," he hissed, "this version of my mortal body wasn't accessorized with a blade."

"Take it," I said as the metal scraped against my sheath. "You remember how to use it?"

Something in his aura darkened as he tossed the dagger into the air, and caught it with expert precision, his fingers tightening together as he thrust the blade forward. "I remember."

"Lady Lyriana Batavia," barked the soturion, "you are under arrest, by order of His Majesty, Emperor Avery for the murder of Arkturion Pompellus Agrippa. You are accused of orchestrating the murder of Emperor Theotis, for inciting an insurrection, breaking your oath as a soturion, colluding with vorakh, and for a whole fucking list of treasonous acts too long to recite." He jerked his chin and the others began to stalk forward. "Don't even think of running. You'll be dragged before His Majesty, and may the Gods bring justice upon you. Now, hands in the fucking air. Seize them!"

CHAPTER EIGHT

LYRIANA

"I'll take the fuckers on the right, you go left," I hissed.

Auriel jerked his chin in agreement. "I'm at your command, Lyriana." Then he cried out, emitting an ancient warrior's call as he sprinted with a speed that only Rhyan could rival. My dagger gleamed in his hand, ready to strike.

His opponents lifted their swords as Auriel moved between them. There was glee in their eyes as they watched him race into what should have been a trap. But I could see what the soturi had been too slow to realize. He stilled, allowing the soldiers to close around him. He'd done it on purpose, letting them believe he was trapped.

Auriel spun on his heels, his elbow bent, arm lifted to shoulder level. If I'd blinked, I'd have missed it. By the time he'd turned in a full circle, he'd slashed the throats of both soturi. The wolves dropped instantly, their blood splattering red onto the golden sand.

At the sudden realization of what he'd done, the soldiers that were headed for me ran faster, their auras spiking with anger.

One wolf snarled, his boots kicking sand behind him, "Drop the sword, girl." He was Ka Kormac, but with a rare show of dark hair, cropped short.

"Now!" shouted the second, his hair fully shaved off.

"Drop it!" said the first. They were both before me, spreading apart, attempting to trap me between them. "You were warned. We have orders to kill you. And we will gladly carry them out."

"So did the Blade," I sneered. "Now he's dead." I caught sight of Auriel racing toward the leader. The turion drew his arm back, then threw his sword like a javelin, aiming straight for Auriel's heart. He ducked. The sword soared over him, the blade just barely skimming across his back before it smashed into the Guardian. There was a sharp clanging sound, before it fell to the sand.

My sword clashed with my enemy, the metal ringing. I gritted my teeth, my muscles straining as I thrust and thrust, until I pushed him into retreat. With another swing of my sword, he faltered, thrown off-balance.

I shifted my weight away from him, opening a space between us just big enough to spring my blade forward, the point lined perfectly with the weak spot in his armor, just below his belly. I had him, right where I wanted him. Then ... He blocked at the last second, his blade slicing against mine with surprising violence. Hand shaking, I was forced to readjust my grip. But the setback gave him just enough time to gain the upper hand, and thrust. I ducked low, barely missing the hit and raced behind his partner.

In the distance, I caught sight of the turion fighting sword to dagger with Auriel. The turion reached into his pocket, and retrieved something small as he continued to swing. A vadati stone. Shit! Shit! It was already glowing blue. If he connected the stone to another general, everyone in Bamaria would know I was here. And then, so would the Emperor.

"Auriel!" I screamed. "The stone!"

I ran forward, leaping onto the back of the soturion with the shaved head. My sword was already at his throat.

He shook beneath me, and for a second, I almost faltered. Because what did it matter? Rhyan was gone. Killing this man wouldn't bring him back. But then I saw Rhyan's eyes in my mind, burning with intensity, and I heard his voice, as clear as when he first said these words.

If you need to defend yourself—strike first, think later.

I slid the blade across his throat, pushing in until he made a gurgling sound, and I jumped down, my boots hitting the sand the same moment he collapsed.

"Lyriana!" Auriel yelled, still in combat with the turion. "Behind you!"

Three more seraphim had flown in. The Godsdamned turion had already called for backup.

"Auriel! Take him down!" I screamed, just as the dark-haired soturion returned for me.

"You bitch!" he growled, his black eyes moving wildly back and forth between me and his dead ally. "You fucking bitch!"

I raised my arm, bracing myself. There was a clash of steel on steel, and then another. My feet scurried back and forth furiously as I met each thrust.

"Who's the golden boy?" he taunted, blocking my blade. He jerked his head toward Auriel. "New lover already?" His tongue dipped across his lips. "That's cold. Heard that instead of Kane you were fucking Rhyan and he's barely in the grave. What? He didn't satisfy you? When the golden boy's dead, can I have a ride?"

A rage burned inside and I screamed, rushing forward, taking the hilt into both of my hands. Caution was gone. Sanity, too. There were no thoughts in my head of fighting well, or even winning. I didn't care. Only my anger and grief and need for revenge seemed to matter. I needed to gut him. To make him pay. And I didn't care about the price. It wouldn't bring Rhyan back. It wouldn't change things, yet, I needed him gone. I got close enough to land my hit. Too close to make my mark safely.

Strike first, think later.

I skewered him like I needed to, forgetting that my left was exposed.

But he hadn't.

I screamed in pain as his blade sliced through my bicep. The cut wasn't wide, but it went fucking deep—I swore I felt it touch bone. Fuck. Sweat burst at my forehead as I pushed through the pain, gnashing my teeth. And then my sword pierced through his stomach.

His eyes widened in shock. "No!"

I threw my weight forward until I felt his body give into my weapon, my blade slicing past muscle. Then there was a pop as the sword's tip pierced through his back. Blood filled his mouth, and I held his stunned gaze until the light left his eyes.

"Lyriana Batavia!" came a scream. Another squawk. More seraphim carriages filled the sky, their wings casting shadows in the sand.

"Drop your weapons. Put your hands up." The call came from above. "You're surrounded. Surrender now and live to see trial in Numeria. Fight, and you die today."

I tugged at my blade, but it remained stuck inside my opponent. Blood ran down my arm, dripping from my fingertips like raindrops. I leaned back, holding on tight and kicked his stomach. My sword slid free and I stumbled backward.

For a moment, the horizon tipped sideways, my vision blurring. My skin heating. Fuck! The beach had filled with seraphim, their carriages unloading more Kormac soturi.

A sudden scream filled the air. Auriel was still locked in battle with the turion, their bodies so close I couldn't see who was winning. With another shout of pain, the turion collapsed at Auriel's feet, his eyes still open in death. The hilt of my dagger protruded from his chest. Auriel, despite using a smaller weapon, had managed to sever his armor.

In one swipe, he released the weapon. Blood spurted across the fallen general's silver chest plate.

I reached for the sword of the dark-haired soldier before me, and then ran for Auriel, stopping only to collect the weapons of the other soturion I'd defeated. I was sweating profusely, and out of breath. My arm was burning, and there was a sudden wave of dizziness that washed over me. But I was determined to take every sword I could carry. We had to get out of there and we needed every resource we could find. The beach was filled with wolves. Another five rushed toward us on foot. Seconds later, five more leaped from their carriage.

"Come on," Auriel shouted, his hand gesturing wildly to me. "To the seraphim! Run!"

I raced for it, wildly thrusting four swords into my sheaths and through my belt loops. With my uninjured arm, I strapped the last one to my back. I bit my lip to keep from crying as my arm continued to throb, the pain burning like fire. Drops of blood splattered, leaving a trail behind me.

In front of the carriage, Auriel reached for me, his hands firm on my waist as he lifted me up and pushed me inside. But already five soturi were upon us, swords out.

I crawled forward, reached over the ledge for Auriel. "Get in!"

He stumbled back as a soturion grabbed hold of his neck. His meaty hands wrapped around him, squeezing violently, as another trapped Auriel's right arm, forcing it back at a disturbing angle.

He grunted in pain.

"Get off him!" I screamed, and smashed the hilt of my sword into the nearest skull I could find. Auriel's face reddened, his airway cut off, as he struggled to free one hand, attempting to twist the fingers of his first captor. But the bastard was holding on for dear life, choking him even harder. I dug my hands in to help, desperately trying to free him, even as I felt the injury from my arm spreading.

Fuck. I had to do this. I pulled harder, until I finally managed to snap one finger. But it wasn't enough. I reached for my blade again, preparing to strike, but Auriel's eyes met mine. For a second, they were full of desperation, and then his lips curled into a vicious snarl. His eyes moved to my hands then lifted up, signaling for me to let go. I frowned but did as he asked just as he threw his head back, knocking out the soturion behind him.

Coughing, Auriel reached for me, his fingers tight around my wrists as he leapt up into the carriage. I pulled him onto the floor, and together we slammed the door shut. I'd barely bolted the lock, forcing it into place, before the metal started to shake. The bastards were pulling on the knob, trying to rip the door off its hinge. Auriel thrust his body forward, both hands on the door as the bolt rattled. Glass shattered, exploding across the floor as a blade pushed into the window behind us.

Auriel wrapped his arm around my waist, practically lifting me against him to pull me away from the glass. More shadows filled the windows.

"GO!" I screamed at the seraphim. "Fly!"

"*Volara!*" Auriel yelled. He reared his elbow back and then launched his fist through the window.

The carriage floor vibrated, rocking side to side as the seraphim rose to her feet.

"Come on, come on! *Vra! Volara!*" I yelled. But we were still on the damned ground.

"They're on the wings!" Auriel spun wildly on his heels, and grabbed the sword I'd strapped to my back, the metal singing as he withdrew it and returned to the window. His eyes narrowed, moving back and forth across the glassless pane. He wrenched his arm back, adjusting his hold of the sword just so, then hurled it through the window.

Screams exploded outside, the sound ending in a heavy thud. Auriel crouched on the ground, picking up the largest shards of broken glass, and with a speed that was almost hard to comprehend, he approached a second broken window, flinging shard after shard at the soturi.

The floor tilted, the entire carriage was shifting as the seraphim stood, preparing to take flight. She was agitated, but I didn't blame her. Another sharp tilt of the floor flung me against the wall. My head slammed into a cabinet. Heart racing, I looked out of the window just in time to see the seraphim rising. We flew, ascending higher and higher, the shore falling away from us. In the middle of it all was the Guardian's headless body, growing smaller and smaller as we rose.

"We need to tell it where to go," Auriel said, rushing to the window. "Fuck!"

"What?" I yelled.

"They're following. We have three carriages on our tail."

Where could we go that was safe? Safe enough to hide?

Auriel turned to me, our eyes locking. And we both seemed to know the answer at once. Nowhere. I was wanted across the entire Empire. And he wasn't supposed to exist.

"We just need to get ahead of them," Auriel said. "Then it doesn't matter where we go. As long as we get there first. So pick something."

"Elyrian outpost," I blurted out.

"You sure?" Auriel asked.

I nodded. It was the first thing I could think of. The outpost took us west to the Bamarian border. If we could outfly the enemy, we could land and vanish into the woods. We'd be near the brothel where Rhyan and I stayed. They'd kept us hidden before. Maybe they would again.

The carriage shifted, gusts of wind blasting through the broken windows as the seraphim turned west. I lost my balance, falling into a seat. My vision doubled, sweat pouring down my forehead and back.

Auriel rushed toward me, crouching low, as he took me in. "Lyriana! Your arm! What the hell happened back there?!"

I shrugged, wincing. "I stabbed a soturion through the gut."

Auriel's eyebrows knit together with concern. "I see. And did you stop to think when you went in for the kill about protecting your flank?"

"No," I seethed. "I was thinking I needed to kill him."

"Kill him, but not keep yourself from injury?"

I looked away.

Auriel scoffed. "I know for a fact that you're a better warrior than that."

"Really? Are you sure?"

"Yes. I'm sure. Just like I know you, I know this." His jaw muscles flexed as he reached for the shelf above my seat, hauling down one of the first aid kits always kept on board. He pulled out a cloth to tie around my arm and staunch the wound. "We're going to have a little discussion later about your survival skills."

"Maybe not while we're being chased through the sky by a wolf legion."

"Maybe." He tightened the cloth, and pressed his hand to the wound, applying more pressure. I gasped at the pain, biting back a scream, as he pressed. "But we're definitely having a talk. And the next time you think about letting one of those bastards get in a hit on you just so you can exact your revenge, or whatever the fuck that was back there, think of Rhyan. Do you think he'd want you acting recklessly on his behalf? That he'd want to see you hurt?"

My chest tightened. Because I had thought of Rhyan. And somehow, that had almost made it worse.

"Hold this right here for me," Auriel said, replacing his hand with mine. "Tight! And don't move! It's deep. I'll need to take a closer look once we land." He stuck his head out of the window, calling orders to the seraphim, urging it to calm down, while simultaneously telling it to fly faster.

The wind gusted in thick howling waves through the carriage, the walls rattling as we picked up speed.

"By all the damned fucking realms," Auriel yelled.

"What?" I asked, already standing and heading for a window. "What happened?"

"I said don't move!" He crossed the cabin, running to another window, sticking his head out. "Oh! Fuck!" Then he screamed at the seraphim, "*Dorscha! Dorscha!*"

"What? Auriel, no! Why are you telling it to go down?" I yelled. By the looks of the landscape beneath us, we were just barely on the easternmost edge of Urtavia. Nowhere near Elyria, or anywhere remotely free of soturi. But we were already starting our descent.

"Because," Auriel yelled, then his eyes widened. "Shit!" He shot back over to me, wrapping me in his arms, until my entire body pressed against his, my face buried in the crook of his neck.

"What—" I started, and the carriage jolted.

An awful wailing sound screeched across my ears. My stomach lodged itself in my throat and Auriel tightened his arms, pulling me even closer. Realization settled over me with a kind of silent finality. We were no longer descending.

We were falling. The wolves had struck down our seraphim.

"We're going to die," I whispered.

"We're not," Auriel hissed. "We're not!" He took a large gulp of air. "Do you trust me?" he asked.

"I don't know."

"Good enough."

We were hurtling toward the ground now. My entire body seized up, my stomach pinching in painfully.

Auriel lifted me against him, taking on all of my body weight. I squeezed my eyes shut, as fear wrapped around me.

"Hold onto me," he commanded, his hand sliding down my back, urging my legs to wrap around him. "Don't let go."

"AURIEL!" I screamed, as he leapt through the window with me. For a second we were airborne. My arms tightened around him, my heart stopping. And then we were falling, just as fast as before.

"Hold on," Auriel gasped, stretching his body until we turned midair, his back facing the ground. "I've got you— I've got you—"

There was a quick burst of something that felt like magic, like a cloud that stilled our bodies, but then there was a sickening thud and all the air whooshed out of me.

"Lyriana?" Auriel gasped, breathless.

Slowly, still filled with terror, I opened my eyes. I was sprawled across Auriel's body, our limbs entangled. I barely dared to breathe. My body still felt like it was falling, my stomach still dropping. My arm screamed where I'd been stabbed. But we weren't moving anymore. We'd hit the ground. Auriel had taken the brunt of the fall, absorbing the worst of the impact.

"Auriel?" I asked. "Auriel!"

His eyes were open, green and blazing, and staring up at me. "Lyriana," he croaked.

"We're alive?" I asked, gasping for breath. "You're okay?"

He winced, clearly winded and in pain. "One word for it." Something flickered in his aura, dark and foggy. It was even cloudier than before. He gritted his teeth and turned his head. "Realms. I feel mortal."

Our seraphim had fallen not far from us. Her wings twisted, her eyes closed. A sword pierced her heart.

"No," I cried.

"She's dead," Auriel said. "Nothing we can do."

My eyes watered, as I nodded against his chest, and tried to breathe. But the fear was beginning to leave my body, replaced by exhaustion. My body began to tremble, every shake sending a new shock of pain down my arm. "How? How are we okay?" I asked.

"I jumped," he groaned. "It restarted the fall, closer to the ground. So we had less time to build speed. And ... I used a little magic to give us a boost at the end, slowing us down further. But I think ... I used up what I had. For now." He frowned, looking me over. He winced again, looking almost as if he were having trouble breathing. He was clearly in more pain than he was admitting to, but I could see in his eyes he was far more concerned with me. "Can you move at all?"

I nodded, and gingerly rolled off him, giving the world a moment to right itself. As I stood, my vision doubled and my ears filled with the sound of rushing water. I swayed, closing my eyes as a rush of nausea flooded through me. My body felt so hot. Almost feverish. I blinked hard, forcing back the tears in my eyes before Auriel could notice.

"What about you?" I asked quickly, diverting his attention from me. Auriel was motionless on the ground. He still looked like a God. A fallen God. But it was more than evident, seeing him like this, just how mortal he was. "Can you move?" I asked.

His chest heaved, his face and neck still red from exertion, but he reached for my hand, and sat up, taking a few labored but deep breaths. Then slowly, I helped him to his feet. "I guess, I can," he said breathlessly.

Our fingers entwined together, the gesture as startling as it was natural, and something pounded in my chest. "You're sure?"

Auriel nodded, smiling softly, until his eyes dipped with concern to my arm. The cloth was matted with dirt from our fall as well as my blood, still seeping from the wound. Quickly, I placed my hand back over the bandage.

"Looks a bit different since the last time I was here," Auriel said with a smirk.

Urtavia's main streets and shops were not far from where we stood. The Temple of Dawn was in the distance. I could just make out the rounded structure of the Katurium looming beyond. In the opposite direction, there was a small neighborhood designated for soturion housing. Several small apartments had been built at the end of the waterway beside us.

"If we go through the city," I said quietly, "we have a better chance of blending in. Enough people will be out that we could disappear into the crowd. Make our way toward Elyria." It was still early, but I knew we were just reaching that time of morning when Bamarians would be heading out to restaurants for breakfast. Most vendors would have opened their shops for business, and any street sellers would be calling people over to their tents.

Auriel placed both hands around my face, brushing loose strands of my hair back. In the chaos of our flight and fall, my hair had dried. And now, it was a huge, frizzy mess of waves and curls.

And bright fucking red in the morning sun.

"Not with the way you look right now. We need to hide your hair," he said, already unfastening his armor and tossing it to the ground. He unbuckled his belt next, and began unwrapping the long swath of green material folded around his waist. He tossed it to me, and I quickly tucked it into pleats beneath my belt, then drew the excess material up around my shoulders and over my hair as Auriel refastened his belt and armor. Then he touched my arm, his fingers gently dancing over my skin, careful not to touch any part of the bandage. I clenched my jaw, determined not to let him know how much pain I was in. Or how dizzy I was starting to feel.

"Your arm is hot," he said. "I need to clean this properly. Check for infection."

But I pulled out of his grip.

"Not here," I said, gritting my teeth. My skin was growing clammy. I could feel my hair sticking to the sweat on the back of my neck, and my stomach twisted again. "Not out in the open."

Auriel frowned, ready to argue, until shadows loomed overhead. Three seraphim carriages flew right over us.

I stilled, barely daring to breathe as they passed. Canopies of leaves and branches kept us hidden for the moment, but they'd find us soon enough—especially once they located our fallen seraphim.

"Were they the same ones chasing us before?" I asked, reaching for my blade.

Auriel squinted. "I don't know. Doesn't matter. We have to view everyone we see as a threat now. Follow me." Threading his fingers through mine, he ran, leading us both into the trees, as the sounds of seraphim and soturion boots hitting the ground reached us.

"That's the one!" came a shout. "Search the carriage and perimeter. "They're close."

My pulse thrummed so loudly I could hear it in my ears, when suddenly, the clock tower began to sound. But it wasn't an hourly call. The bells were ringing out a new pattern—one I'd never heard before. It reminded me of the bells we played for akadim—but this was different. Darker. A new kind of warning.

Auriel spotted a small clearing ahead and led me to its edge, carefully keeping us obscured between the branches of two suntrees. My chest heaved as I leaned back against one, Auriel sliding beside me.

The ringing had intensified, growing louder and louder, until they stopped abruptly.

A tree branch snapped in half not too far in the distance. Someone was coming.

Auriel didn't hesitate. He took my hand again, urging me forward, his feet practically flying until we reached another grouping of trees. Then he pulled me against him, just as blue sparks lit up the sky, glowing through the cracks of the leaves and branches above us. Flattening ourselves against the trunk, I watched in horror as dozens of ashvan riders rode past. More than I'd ever seen take to the sky at once. Every time one passed, a new one appeared until the view was nothing but the constant shimmering of blue lights.

My eyes widened, trying to make sense of it. Not even during akadim attacks in the past had the riders been summoned in such great numbers. For my entire life, every hour on the hour, the ashvan flew over Bamaria, looking for threats, and checking for akadim. But it was obvious in the way the horses raced across the sky now, obvious from the sheer number that had been activated that this was a hunt. For me.

The bells started again. Once more ending abruptly, but instead of silence, their rings were replaced with a sound that made me jump. A male voice, its volume amplified to an alarming degree.

"Attention, citizens of Bamaria. This is Turion Dairen Melvik, Bamaria's Second, acting Arkturion for Waryn Kormac."

I stilled. Aemon's Second, and cousin. The man who'd relished in punishing me my first day of soturion training—the bastard who'd relished in punishing me any chance he got.

What the fuck was this? I knew we had amplifying spells. They were often used in the arena or at large parades and events in the temple. But I'd never heard of one being cast out through the bell towers. I never knew we had the capabilities to project a message out to the entire country at once.

Because if we had, why had we never used it before? Why hadn't this been a part of our protocol when there was actual danger? When there were akadim on the loose? Or when my sisters had been kidnapped? When Haleika and Leander had been—Fuck.

All this time, and they'd never bothered. Instead they'd waited to use this on me? The last person in the world to be a threat to my own people.

My hands clenched. The lives that could have been saved if this had been implemented. The wastefulness of it all!

"Do not be alarmed at what I tell you," Dairen's voice boomed. "The Council of Bamaria is instituting an immediate curfew for the entire country. No one is to leave their home until further notice. All university and academy classes are canceled. Everyone must return home now. You have fifteen minutes to seek shelter indoors, or face arrest. The forsworn traitor, Lyriana Batavia, former Heir to the Arkasva, murderer of the Emperor and Lumeria's Arkturion, is at large in Bamaria. She was last seen in Urtavia with an unknown soturion male. Be on the look out. Lyriana has dark brown hair that turns red in the sun, tanned skin and hazel eyes. Her soturion companion is reported to have blond curly hair, and green eyes, wearing golden armor. Report any sightings immediately. And, Lyriana, I know you're out there, so listen closely. We will find you, we will find your associates. And you'll wish we hadn't. Choose now to turn yourself in and surrender. Resist, and your consequences will be dire. Anyone found assisting her will face the same."

"Auriel," I hissed. My body felt hollow. I knew they'd consider me a criminal and a traitor. That they'd hunt me and my loved ones down. But the reality of it, the nearness of it, felt completely different. I was injured, and I didn't even have the benefit of an energy boost from any Valalumir shards to fight back.

I wasn't even sure I could call on Asherah again. Not anytime soon. I had hardly any energy left, and my arm was steadily becoming more and more painful with every breath I took.

"Just focus. Keep your hood up," Auriel ordered. "And your head down. Follow me."

"What about you?" I asked. I could try and hide my hair and face beneath my cloak, but Auriel was completely exposed. Every soturion who survived the beach had seen him. One look from them and it was over.

He frowned, then bent down on one knee before me, ripping another piece of cloth from the bottom of his cloak. When he stood, he took my dagger once more and cut two slits into the fabric, before he placed it over his head, sliding it down across his temples. The slits became eye holes for him to see out of. And the remaining material covered his head, masking his curls. He finished it off by tying the ends in the back. There was no hint of blond, or any other way to identify him.

Except for the green eyes. And the familiar shape of his jawline.

My heart panged. It was so much harder to see him like this. Harder to not see Rhyan looking back at me.

"Ready?" he asked.

I blinked, my throat dry, then followed his lead deeper into the woods where the silver moontrees had grown together in tight clusters, the ground thick with twisted tree trunks. We raced over them, and continued on, reaching a slope in the ground that would lead us down to the Urtavian river.

I could hear boots against the ground. Someone approached.

"Hold on." Auriel led us into a controlled run. We were moving quickly, light on our feet, but not so fast that our breathing gave us away.

Above the trees, the ashvan continued to circle over the woods, forcing us to remain in the shade when we weren't sprinting between clearings, and leaping over bouts of uneven ground. We reached the end of the woods, where the trees were growing more sparsely. A waterway was close by.

I tugged on Auriel's hand. "Auriel," I hissed. "The city."

"We need to blend in," he said. "Pretend we're soturi until we find a hideout."

I shook my head. "They'll notice us," I pointed at his mask. "You're not exactly blending in."

"We need to try," he said. Then he stilled, his shoulders tensed.

Boots stomped on dry grass only a few yards away.

"Get behind me," he mouthed. "Now."

We switched places, just as a soturion stepped out of the shadows, brandishing his sword. He wore the armor of Ka Batavia.

"Lyriana, I presume?" he asked. His eyebrows raised as a slow smile swam across his face. "And you must be the male companion?"

Auriel gave me one look, cursing under his breath, and ran, my blade already in his hand. He crossed the distance, picking up his speed before bending his knees and leaping at the last moment. Their bodies collided in midair and fell in tangles to the forest floor. The soturion rolled on top of Auriel, landing a punch to his cheek.

I started forward, reaching for my sword, ready to jump in, when a second soturion's hand slid across my mouth and another hand crossed my waist from behind, trapping me against him.

"Got her," came a grunt from behind.

I started to struggle, but a third soturion stepped in front of me, a knife in his hand. He wasted no time, placing it at my throat, digging it into my skin. "Hold her tight," he told his friend. "Get a blade out."

I tried to squirm, but was quickly stilled by the edge of the blade. A second later, my captor replaced the knife at my throat with a fresh one. The third stepped back as he pointed his knife between my eyes.

"Lady Lyriana," hissed the soturion behind me, his mouth right by my ear. "You must be silent and still. Or your friend dies."

My heart thudded, my stomach twisting as I tried to decide how to get out of this. How much time did I have to surprise the soturion holding me captive? Could I risk slipping out of his hold, and avoiding the blade of the man before me? I didn't have much time—just enough to reach for my own weapons. Then I could strike.

My left arm pulsed with pain. The skin had grown tight and swollen around my bicep. My fingertips had gone completely numb. I'd only be able to fight one-handed.

Maybe this was it. Maybe this was how it ended.

I began to stretch my fingers, silently moving to the hilt of my sword. But Auriel's soldier screamed, then went silent.

The soturion before me took off along with his knife. Before I could shout out a warning, the man holding me retracted his, and spoke into my ear again, "Not a word, Lady Lyriana," he warned. "And I won't hurt you. I swear it. If you want to be free, stay silent."

"And why the hell would I trust you?" I asked.

"Because," he hissed. "You must!"

I froze. I couldn't see his face. But something about him seemed familiar. The way he kept using my title. Still calling me lady even though I was forsworn, and the way he— Gods! The way he said my name. He'd spoken with a lilt, adding an extra syllable to Lyriana just like Rhyan did.

He was Glemarian.

"Wait here. Don't run. Not yet. They're everywhere," he ordered, racing into the brawl.

His friend hauled Auriel to his feet, his blade to his neck, drawing blood.

"Got him?" asked the Glemarian. "This the blond they mentioned?"

"One way to find out." The soldier reached for Auriel's mask.

"Wait," said the Glemarian, his eyes meeting Auriel's intently. Then he turned to his companion. "Give me your vadati, I'll call it in. Let the turion know we have them."

The soturion's eyes narrowed, but he held his hand out, a clear white stone in it.

The Glemarian looked back at me, only a small flash of light in his eyes. A warning.

It was at that moment that the soturion saw me: armed with my sword, and unbound. His face reddened. "You didn't tie her up? The fuck are you—?"

The Glemarian brandished his sword, and thrust, his entire body poised for attack.

My mouth fell open in a silent scream for Auriel. But instead he stabbed his companion, gutting him, and let him fall to the ground. He stabbed once more, ensuring he was dead. Then the Glemarian raced to Auriel, both hands on his shoulders, shaking him.

"Rhyan?" he asked. "Rhyan?"

Auriel's lips were drawn tightly together, and he shook his head. "No. I'm so sorry. I'm not Rhyan."

"Don't play with me," the Glemarian seethed.

"I swear. I'm not him." He pressed a fist to his chest. "I swear."

The Glemarian's shoulders slumped in defeat. "But you …" He craned his neck, trying to get a closer look. "You look like—your eyes and you're—you're not? Are you sure? Please! I heard about the sentencing, the stripping, and the attack, but no news of the outcome. I was hoping—praying that—"

Auriel shook his head. "I wish I was. But I'm not Rhyan."

"Fuck!" The Glemarian pressed the palms of his hands to his eyes, like he was pushing back tears. "Are you a friend?" he asked, a kind of desperation coating the lilt of his words. "Of his? Of Lady Lyriana's?"

"That I am," Auriel said. "Very much so. Of both."

There were shouts from nearby. Too many voices to track. But they were close. If we didn't run now, we'd be seen.

The Glemarian took a deep breath and gestured. "Follow me then. Now. Hurry." At last, he pulled back his hood, revealing pale, northern skin, familiar dark brown curls peppered with flecks of grey, and soft, forest green eyes.

It was Rhyan's uncle. Sean.

CHAPTER NINE

LYRIANA

Sean put his finger to his lips, and removed the vadati from his pocket.

"Turion Matthias," he said, his voice clipped and short. His Glemarian accent was completely gone.

The stone glowed blue and a voice called back, "Soturion Calden." The dead soturion.

"We're in pursuit of Lyriana right now," said Sean, turning off a pathway, and leading us through another cluster of trees. "She's alone. Heading west from the Urtavian Woods—looks like she might seek sanctuary in the Temple of Dawn."

"I'm ordering my unit to the temple now," said the turion. "Good work."

The stone went white and Sean pocketed the stone.

"That should buy us some time," Sean said, his accent thick again. "Both of you, follow me!" Sean started sprinting back through the trees, heading east, out of the city and back towards soturion housing. The opposite direction of where he had told the turion. One look from Auriel, and we ran behind him.

Sean had us stop beneath a cluster of moontrees that led out onto an exposed waterway.

"We're nearly at my house," he said, "You can hide there—as long as you need. We'll keep you safe." Then he stilled. "Shit. Don't move. Someone's coming."

Sean vanished, loudly shouting at another soldier to draw their attention. I kept my back pressed to the tree, holding my breath. Auriel squeezed my hand.

Sean reported the same false story he'd given his turion—that I was spotted on the other side of the woods, heading into the city. He mentioned needing another sword back at home, then he waved the soturion off.

At that moment, the bells began to ring again. The fifteen minutes were up. Curfew had started.

"Hurry, they'll see us," Sean said, coming around the corner. He pointed across the waterway. "First house on the right." He lifted his hood, carefully covering his hair and eyes. "Be ready to run. On my signal."

He stepped forward, looking left and right. I did, too, checking for soturi, but the waterway was clear. And the porches of the homes before us were empty. He turned, making his way toward a small house. He knocked on the door with three rapid taps. There was a pause. Then two taps. Then one. A code.

I didn't understand. All I knew was that this wasn't his house. Otherwise, he would have had a key.

The door swung open as if on its own. No one stood in the threshold, but Sean didn't wait. He dashed inside, gesturing over his shoulder for us to follow. I sensed someone nearby. But I never had the chance to see who it was because Sean didn't stop running. He led us through a modest living room and then into a small kitchen with a back door which he pushed open, again gesturing for us to follow.

"Wait! Why are we leaving?" I asked.

"We're not. We haven't arrived," he said.

"What?"

"You can't be seen on the waterway with the curfew," he said. "Trust me. The only way to keep you hidden is to go through the houses. Now stay close."

We had entered what appeared to be a small yard. Several dolls lay discarded in the grass, like a child had been playing with them but forgot to clean up, perhaps rushed inside by their parents when the bells rang. The yard led into a neighbor's property that Sean had us cross as well. We hopped over a fence, and then another before we entered another home from the back door, entering right into someone's kitchen.

We rushed into a small living room. A green flag, embroidered with the silver sigil of Ka Hart, hung above a fireplace. A second later we popped through the front door.

"Where are we?" I asked.

"Almost there," Sean shouted over his shoulder. "Keep running!"

I lost track of how many houses we'd entered and left. Each time the doors seemed to magically open, or were simply unlocked. We ran in and out, and even a few times, instead of going through the doors, we went through the windows. The houses were so closely built together that all it took was one more step and we were climbing into the kitchen of a new home. Each one seemed to have one small token in it that reminded me of Glemaria. Of Rhyan.

But I was sure it was my mind playing tricks on me. Looking for signs of him. Evidence of his existence. Something for me to focus on while my body screamed in pain. For the first time since I lost him, the pain in my body was overrunning the shattering inside my heart. My arm was still bleeding, my body growing more sore by the second. I was still feeling hot, and sweaty, my head like a deadweight. Exhaustion was quickly catching up to me. And if we didn't arrive where we needed to soon, I was becoming fearful I might faint again.

"Last one!" Sean yelled. "Move! Fast!"

We raced into a kitchen, out through a back door into a tiny yard, and then at last, crossed a property with a small stone gryphon—another sign of Rhyan—beside the back porch. A balcony loomed above on the second floor.

This home's back door was already open, and there was a familiar scent in the air inside. Pine.

The moment we'd crossed the threshold, Sean led us past another door. I could hear the first one shutting, the bolt sliding into place as we were led down a series of stairs into a cool room underground without windows.

"Sean, where are we? What is this?" I asked.

"Basement," he said. "To hide."

The door at the top of the stairs closed, and for a moment we were thrown into total darkness. But then a torch flared to life, the flames hissing. A beautiful mage I'd never seen before began to walk down the steps. She had golden tanned skin like most Bamarians, and long, brown curls that fell softly past her shoulders.

Sean took a second to catch his breath, then rushed for the mage as she reached the bottom step. He took the torch from her hand, and pulled her into a tight hug, before kissing her on the lips. She grinned, and pushed back a lock of brown hair that had fallen over Sean's forehead.

Like Rhyan's hair used to …

"Doors locked," she said. "The coast clear. But rumor is Turion Kevel is making the rounds one street over."

"I'll need to get out there." Sean nodded. "Show my face." He pressed his forehead to hers, his jaw clenched. "You can keep them both hidden until I return?" he asked.

"Of course."

Sean's eyes moved warily between me and Auriel, then back to the mage. At last he said, "Lady Lyriana, this is my wife, Branwyn, of Ka Drona."

Branwyn smiled warmly, and curtsied low. "Lady Lyriana, Your Grace." Her eyes moved to Auriel, and she frowned. "Myself to Moriel. Rhyan? Are you—? No. But I thought— Gods!" Her eyes watered. "By the Gods! Is it you? Rhyan?"

Sean's eyebrows drew together in concern as Auriel sadly shook his head, and removed his mask, revealing his face and hair. And once more, I found myself cataloguing all the small differences between them. And ... the ways they were so completely identical.

I was too aware of the crushing disappointment Branwyn and Sean were about to experience. It was evident from the look in their eyes. Like hope had been lost.

Sean seemed to deflate, even though Auriel had already assured him he wasn't Rhyan. I could see it in his eyes, he'd still held on to hope.

"I'm sorry," Auriel said, but his eyes were on mine as he spoke. "I'm not him."

Sean stepped forward, his eyes moving rapidly back and forth across Auriel's face. "No. You're not, but you ..." He shook his head, almost in wonder. "Who are you?"

"I'm called Auriel." He lowered his chin in respect.

"Like the God?" Sean spat.

"Exactly like that."

Sean's jaw tensed. "Is Rhyan ... Fuck! I heard the reports. Heard there was a vorakh attack on the capital. And that he was—that he was stripped. But I haven't been able to confirm, I mean—Devon's lied more than enough times before. So has Kormac. I know something happened. Something bad. But I also know a Godsdamned fucking lie when I hear it. Lyriana, please tell me. What happened?" His eyes widened, looking between me and Auriel with a sort of silent desperation. "Where's Rhyan?"

I stared at the ground, suddenly afraid to meet Sean's eyes. Like it was my fault. My responsibility.

And it was. It fucking was. I'd sworn I'd get him back. I'd sworn I would heal him. That nothing else would hurt him.

I promise. I'll make the pain go away. And I swear on all the Gods, no one else will hurt you. No one else will lay a fucking finger on you. I'm going to take care of you, Rhyan. I swear!

But he'd been so out of it when I swore, and in so much pain, I wasn't even sure if he'd heard me. If he knew what I'd promised. If he knew I'd broken it. It didn't matter. Because I knew. I remembered.

And I'd failed him. I'd lied. He had been hurt again—and in the end, I hadn't taken care of him. And that ... that was going to be one of my last memories. One of my last moments. Rhyan dying, in excruciating pain, being offered an empty promise. From someone he trusted and loved. Me.

"Lyriana?" Sean asked. "Please. I can't take it anymore. I beg you. What happened to him. Where's my nephew?"

"He was," I said. "He was stri—" My voice cracked. I felt dizzy. I was trying, but I couldn't get the words out but I knew I needed to. Sean was the one person in Rhyan's family he most trusted after his mother. He was the only real parent figure he had left, who actually loved him, cared for him. Sean was the first person who deserved to know. Rhyan would want him to know. And, I knew he'd want me to be the one to tell him. But the words were stuck in my throat. I couldn't. I just couldn't. I felt faint, and like the grief was going to swallow me whole again. Auriel and I had barely discussed what happened. And I wasn't ready. Wasn't ready to talk about it. To say it.

"Sean," Auriel said, stepping forward. "Do you maybe want to sit down?"

Sean shook his head violently. "I do not."

"You might wish to," Auriel said gently.

"Just say it," Branwyn said. "We need to hear. He needs to hear." She'd taken Sean's hand, and he was holding onto her so tightly, his knuckles had whitened.

I met Sean's eyes, every part of me shaking. "Sean, he—um—he—" My vision blurred. Fuck. I couldn't. I couldn't do it. Couldn't say it.

Auriel took my hand, and cleared his throat. "I'm so sorry, Sean, to have to tell you. But, Rhyan was caught using his vorakh in the capital. He was tried and sentenced, then stripped in the arena," Auriel said.

"NO!" Sean yelled. "No. It can't be. Can't be true."

Branwyn cried out.

The tears started falling down my face again, my vision swimming in and out of focus as my stomach pinched in pain.

"Did he—" Sean started, his eyes full of unshed tears. "Did he—oh, Godsdamned fucking damnit. I know it's rare but, did he … Did he survive it?"

"The stripping," I whispered, and nodded my head carefully. "He was so strong, and so brave," I swallowed. "He survived that."

The look of relief in Sean's face was fleeting before his eyes narrowed. "What do you mean—he survived *that*?"

"I tried to save him. I killed the Blade to get to him." My voice broke. "I killed everyone in my path. But there were too many. And I was too slow. He was alive at the end, but just barely. His magic was … they took it. They took it all. I," I sniffled. "So I carried him from the stage. I was going to get him to safety, heal him, heal all his injuries. But we were trapped in the arena, and we couldn't … we couldn't get out—" My voice caught, "the attack."

"The vorakh attack?" Branwyn asked.

"There was no vorakh attack," I said. "It was …" I pressed my head in my hands. I couldn't bear to be the one to tell Sean the truth, to break his heart like mine had been.

Auriel placed a hand on my shoulder, squeezing gently. "The Emperor's lying about the vorakh. The arena was overrun by akadim."

"Akadim?" Sean asked. His eyes widened. "He's killed plenty before. He's strong."

Branwyn wrapped an arm around his waist, her bottom lip shaking.

"He was." Auriel took a deep breath. "So strong. Just not at that moment. I'm sorry. He was turned. He's one of them now."

Sean sank to his knees, his mouth opened, but no sound came out. Branwyn crouched beside her husband, wrapping her arms around him, her face buried in his neck. The look on his face was too much, too raw. Too full of horror and grief. Too painful. I knew the feeling—knew it too fucking well. Knew my face looked the same when I realized what had happened. When I realized I'd been too late.

I wanted to go to Sean. To comfort him. And at the same time, I wanted to throw myself at his feet and beg for forgiveness because I should have stopped it. I should have been faster. Taken Dario with me. Not bothered with the orange fucking shard. Not dealt with Morgana. I should have gone straight into the arena. I could have made a thousand different choices. And surely, surely, one of them was the one that would have saved Rhyan's life. But I didn't know which one. And it was going to haunt me. For now, all I could do was sob, my body swaying. My arm ...

A thunderous pounding on the door pulled me back from my thoughts.

"Turion check. Open up!" The voice boomed all the way down to the basement.

Branwyn's eyes widened. "It's Turion Kevel. What do I do?"

Sean's nostrils flared, as he inhaled a sharp intake of breath, and wiped his eyes. "I'll answer it, come with me, love—so they're not suspicious."

Nodding, Branwyn already started back up the stairs, smoothing back her hair.

"You two," he ordered, "Closet, now."

Auriel helped me to my feet, and we rushed into a tiny closet in the back of the basement. I was pressed against the wall when Auriel slammed the door behind him, enclosing us in total darkness.

The door at the top of the stairs slammed shut, a bolt locking into place, and then I heard the creak of the front door opening.

"Turion Kevel," Sean said, his voice carrying through the house.

The air was warm and still inside the small closet. My head started to swim. I tilted my head back, my breathing labored and erratic. It was becoming more difficult. Everything was becoming more difficult.

"Lyriana?" Auriel whispered. There was a rustling sound, and movement near me that I couldn't see.

"You were called to the city, Soturion Sean. I expected your wife, not you. Didn't you receive your orders?" the turion spat.

"I was on morning patrol when the orders came through. Lost a sword to the river. Came back for a replacement. I'm on my way to rejoin my unit as we speak."

Auriel's arm wrapped around my waist, and I leaned into him, letting him take on most of my body weight. "I feel faint," I whispered.

"It's okay. I've got you. Is it your arm?" he asked.

I shook my head.

Footsteps sounded above us.

"We've had conflicting reports of Lyriana. She's apparently capable of appearing on every end of Urtavia, north, south, east, west at once. Ridiculous. Unless she's vorakh like her dead forsworn lover—"

I stopped breathing. Auriel tightened his hold on me.

"I doubt that," Sean said, his voice tense. "Last I'd heard, her seraphim was spotted in the woods. Quite a way from here. And she's ... well, not exactly one to move quickly. She's the powerless one, right?"

"Not anymore it seems. She took out the Blade with her own hand, massacred a dozen of our men last night in Numeria."

"Did she now?" Sean said, the surprise in his voice real. "Well either way, I would like to return to the field and find her. Before I go, is there something I can help you with?"

"Not unless it involves you returning to your post immediately," he yelled. "Your beautiful wife can walk me through the house."

My throat tightened, a nervous gasp escaped my lips. Auriel kept one hand on my waist, but the other he pressed against my mouth, stifling the sound of my breathing.

"If you don't mind, since I'm here," Sean said coolly, "I'll walk you myself. I'd rather my wife not be alone here with you."

More heavy footsteps pounded on the ceiling, like the turion was walking in circles.

"This is protocol, soturion. I don't like what you're insinuating. Or your insubordination. If you're not out the door in the next ten seconds, you'll be at the pole tonight."

"Turion," Sean said. "We're not hiding anyone or anything here. If you wish to search the house, you may, but I'm going to insist on being present."

"That's three lashes, Soturion Sean," barked the turion. "We could have completed the search by now if you'd shut up."

"I'll accept my punishment," Sean said. "Gladly."

The boots continued to stomp, moving across the room, closer and closer to the kitchen. To the door to the basement. A pair of steps and a door between us. We were in a closet—but that was it. All the turion would have to do is open the door and we were caught. And then Branwyn and Sean would be arrested. And ...

The basement door shook. "Why the fuck is the door locked?" barked the turion.

"I'm so sorry about that," Branwyn said quickly. "There were some small rodents coming inside—I locked the door to keep them out. But I can unlock that for you if you like—though, honestly, the door has been getting a bit stuck with this humidity."

"Unlock it," he ordered.

My heart thundered, and my stomach turned, my body swaying again. I was so fucking dizzy, I could barely stand straight.

"Auriel?" I hissed, prying his hand from my mouth. "Can you travel?"

"No," he whispered, forcing his hand back to shush me. "Not this time."

I squeezed my eyes shut, barely daring to breathe. The front of my hair was plastered to my forehead with sweat. Auriel's body was too hot next to mine. I was burning up. The door started to open.

Shit. Shit.

"Turion Kevel." This was a new voice, more distant. From a vadati? "New sighting inside the Katurium. We've got Lyriana. Arresting her now."

"Turion Abner, bind her and anyone you see with her at once. Lock the whole Katurium down. I'm on my way."

His footsteps moved back over our heads, returning to the front door.

"See you at the pole tonight," snapped Kevel. "Three lashes. Sundown. You miss it—you won't be leaving your house for a week, Glemarian shit."

The front door slammed shut. I pressed my back against the closet wall and sank to my knees, no longer able to hold myself up.

Auriel swung the closet door open, allowing light on me and my crouched position.

"Lyriana?" Auriel yelled in concern, and sank before me. His hand was on my forehead. "You're not just feverish. You're burning up. I thought you felt off in there."

I was clammy, and nauseated. And for a second, I wanted to push his hand away. His skin was too warm.

I needed to cool down. I needed Rhyan's cool touch. His aura. His cold. Him. Just him. I needed Rhyan. Not Auriel. Not …

Auriel craned his neck back, shouting at Sean and Branwyn who were rushing down the stairs. "Help me!" Auriel yelled.

"We need to get her into a bed," Branwyn said, her eyes on Auriel. "Now!"

He lifted me up into his arms, my head cradled against his chest as Branwyn led us to a cot that she pulled out from behind a shelf. Gently Auriel laid me down on it, asking Branwyn to grab fresh water and sunleaves. He pulled back the bandage and I hissed.

"No. Not you. I want Rhyan."

"I'm sorry," he said.

I looked at my arm, bile rising in my throat, my vision blurring. Everything above my elbow was red and swollen. The bandage was soaked through, mottled brown and yellow. Dark blood still oozed from it. Alongside the blood, cloudy yellow pus eked out, making a path down my arm and onto the bed. I swallowed back bile as the smell hit me, like something rotting.

"Shit!" Auriel yelled. "Lyriana, I'm sorry. I'm so sorry. I had no idea it was this bad. We're going to have to clean it out. It's going to hurt. A lot. But I'm going to put you to sleep so you don't feel it."

I shook my head. "What? No. No. I can't sleep. We don't have time for that." My eyes burned—I wasn't sure from the fever or tears.

"Well, we're going to make some." He pushed my hair back from my forehead, and I became aware of Sean. His face had paled, and his aura was exploding with grief. He'd been keeping it clamped down since he'd found me, since the visit from the turion. But now, it was rushing against me. A mirror for how I felt inside. And it was agony.

"Auriel," I whimpered. "Please. Don't. It hurts."

He kissed my forehead. "I know. I know it does, *Meka*. We're going to fix it. You'll be okay. You're going to rest, and we're going to take care of you."

"Not my arm," I said, shaking my head. "My heart."

A tear rolled down his cheek. "We're going to try and fix that, too," he said, his voice hushed. "But first this. Okay? I'm going to put you to sleep now. You won't feel anything."

"No!" I shouted. "No! No! I can't! Please, I need to stay awake. To find Rhyan. To find Meera and Jules! And—"

"Lyriana!" he scolded. "You're burning up with the infection! You're in no condition to fight. You can't even stand up right now. Not until you heal."

"Auriel! Sean! Please, please don't—"

But Auriel's hands were on my face and my eyes were closing. Nothing I did could keep them open.

"No," I gasped. "No."

"I'm sorry," he whispered. "I'm so sorry. I have to."

A door opened and closed at the top of the stairs.

"Branwyn," I said slowly, my words slurred. And suddenly in my haze, I'd remembered something. Something important. "She needs to know. They're in Thene. You must ... warn Cal and Marisol."

"My grandparents? Warn them about what?" she asked, her voice frantic.

I could hear her feet scurrying down the stairs.

"Lyriana?" Branwyn called out.

"Warn them," I said, barely getting the words out. "Warn them that they're coming."

My eyes closed.

CHAPTER TEN

MORGANA

Day broke as we reached our rendezvous in a meadow nestled between the woodlands on the Payunmar border. My akadim, still freshly-made and recovering their sense of selves, knew enough to realize the sun was a danger. Except it wasn't. Not for them. They all growled, their complaints intensifying the brighter the day became. They threatened to run, and look for shade.

But they didn't know how much things had changed. How Aemon, calling upon Moriel's ancient knowledge, had made it so that no time would restrict them. Their collars glowed silver, and the sun shined golden on their monstrous faces as further proof.

Only Rhyan seemed calm, standing at the forefront of my soturi. My new Arkturion. He was still and stoic, mentally putting together the pieces before the others did, understanding that no harm could come to him now. I watched as a few took note, seeing the confidence in his face. He turned slowly, and gave a small nod to his fellow akadim. The gesture wasn't kind, but commanding. Almost like a call for them to relax.

"I give you daylight," I said, confirming their realization, making sure they knew that their gratitude as well as their allegiance was meant for me. Rhyan could command them, but only through my will. "The ability to feed and bathe beneath the light. You may go where you must, and when you need to. You are not like the akadim you knew of before. You are elevated. By me. Now no element of nature shall hold you back."

The looks of awe in their faces almost made me forget they were demons. Almost.

"But," I said, amplifying my voice, ensuring that the handful still looking to Rhyan for guidance, were fully reliant upon me. "I am your queen. You are under my command. Mine."

Parthenay's eyes shot toward me, a flash of anger in them.

"You have a job to do. One to make your lives better and more fruitful. More free. You are a new breed. Evolved. You will eat what you must to survive. That cannot be changed. You will kill, for you must eat souls to live. But," my aura darkened around me, rumbling with the magic of my command, pushing it into their collars, "you are mine. And you will not rape. That practice ends now. I forbid it."

Their growls turned into roars of defiance. Even Rhyan—Rhyan of all people. No, not people. Akadim. But even he looked murderous. He'd been so ravenous and wild when I found him. If he was allowed his freedom, he'd become the most feared akadim to exist. And in all other ways, he still would be.

Parthenay shook her head, blatantly displaying her disagreement. Behind me, Lissa continued to cower as always.

This is insanity. They'll mutiny, Parthenay pushed the thought into my mind. *All the commands in the world will not stop nature from running its course. Look at them even now.*

And indeed, there was a sense of violence and lust filling the air, one I swore I could touch. One I would squash.

I sent a burning flame in response to Parthenay's mind. She jumped back, her face contorted in pain.

They have the command of a Goddess, I thought. *I'm not asking. I'm ordering them.*

But there were several grumbling before me, making their displeasure loudly known.

"Silence!" I yelled, my arms raised, the shield catching sunlight until it filled the woods with waves of orange and gold. "We go now to meet your king, your *Maraak,* and to meet the rest of your fellow soturi."

I stared them down, Rhyan in particular. He straightened like the soldier he was—even in death, looking over the rest of the akadim, his expression full of expectation. All at once, the rest of them obeyed, following me as they were supposed to, and together we walked into the meadow.

Maraak Moriel, Arkturion Aemon, the man known as the Ready, and my lover, stood in the center of it, tall and glorious, his red cloak blowing gently in the early morning breeze. He'd retired his Bamarian armor and now wore a chest plate that fully covered his torso. It was similar in structure to the armor we were familiar with back home. But he lacked the seraphim wings that traditionally appeared on the shoulders.

My heart skipped a beat as I took him in. The first time I'd seen him in his new armor—just last night, I'd recognized it at once. I had seen it in my dreams, in my memories. It was Moriel's original chest plate and vest and like all soturion armor, and my shield, it contained blood inside. Enough for Aemon to form his own *Rakashonim* with his God-self. He could now call on the power of Moriel, embodying him. Fighting with the combined force of the strength of the Ready and ferocity of his past life as a God.

When he decided to call on it again, I pitied whoever faced him. For now, he truly was a God of death made flesh.

He looked exactly like Moriel. Just as he was banished by the Council of Forty-Four, and forced to dwell here.

The armor he'd worn when this all began would be the armor he wore when we finished what had been started.

I carefully eyed the indigo shard—*his* shard. Aemon held it triumphantly in his hand. It was the shard I'd kept in my possession for over a month, withholding it, using it to bargain. I'd used it to dig deeper into my dreams, into my powers, building up my mental walls, learning how to push out thoughts where I wanted them. And now, I was able to push out pain, and pleasure. Whatever I needed. It showed me how to work with the akadim, and reminded me of how Ereshya took control of her legions. Something I knew had to be done. Because I had seen the bigger picture, unraveled the secrets I'd needed to win, thanks to our other ally.

Andromeny, Aemon's older sister. She was the vorakh responsible for murdering Tristan's parents, and until recently, she had been the Emperor's most powerful and coveted chayatim. She saw not just one future, but all potential possibilities, and the Palace had honed her accuracy until she was elite. It was the same reason Aemon had chosen Parthenay to join us. She had been the Palace's most advanced mind-reader, an equal to Andromeny.

Already I could feel myself surpassing Parthenay's skill; nearly matching Aemon's. But, as far as visions went, I understood something most didn't. I'd learned from Meera that even if a vision appeared as a scene that made sense, as a scene that could logically unfold—there was always a deeper meaning disguised within. Some hidden outcome that needed to be interpreted. And now, I realized I could interpret Andromeny's visions. I had the tools I needed to get what I wanted. I had my crown. I had my army. My shard. Ereshya's blood.

Soon, I'd have everything.

My revenge. A broken empire beneath me.

At the moment, Andromeny was in charge of rounding up the vorakh we'd freed and keeping them in line. There were around fifty of them. Fifty former chayatim. Mages and soturi who'd been enslaved in the Palace. Some for decades. They ranged in age and Ka, but they all carried the same look, similar to the one that Andromeny and Parthenay had worn when I first met them.

Exhaustion and worry paired with a brokenness that only came from a life of pain and unspeakable acts. Having come from the dungeons, the chayatim were also filthy, their tattered clothing hanging from too-thin, malnourished bodies. They were bruised, scarred. Some looked exhausted after their march through the night to safety. And I could already tell that many, particularly the women carried wounds that could not be seen. Wounds I would not reopen with the presence of my akadim.

Jules would look like that, I realized, and my stomach twisted. She'd escaped. But I didn't get to see her face. Didn't get to see if she was at all okay. She was with Lyr now, and the thought made my heart pang. I was looking for her, too—using all my resources to find her. For the last year and a half, I did nothing else. And now—I didn't even get to see her free. Nor did I have a chance to see Meera. Gods. For all the foresight I had, and access to secrets and the future, I hadn't expected that—for Lyr to be the one to liberate Jules. For her and Meera to end up on Lyr's side—and not mine. Especially after all I'd done. For all of them.

My chest felt tight, remembering my last meeting with Lyr in the Throne Room. She was half-crazed in that way she got when she needed to protect someone. When she couldn't accept the way things were. Couldn't accept the cruelty of the world.

I'd only seen her like that a handful of times before. At the temple when Jules's vorakh was revealed and she'd been taken away screaming. When Rhyan had been dragged into the arena, his fate already sealed. Whenever anything threatened to reveal the truth of Meera's visions.

But not, I remembered bitterly, when my vorakh was revealed.

Still, there was nothing I could do for Lyr now. She didn't know the truth. She hadn't seen Andromeny's vision like I had. She couldn't accept that it was inevitable that Rhyan would die. That it had been prophesied and fated by a string of events threaded together long before we were born. She couldn't know that nothing she did in that moment, and no amount of power I shared with her, or strength she'd acquired would change the end. I'd seen what would happen. I'd seen that he would awaken as the most powerful and dangerous akadim the Empire had ever known. And I had seen that because of this shift, a spark would ignite. One that would grow into a raging flame. A fire that would engulf all of Lumeria. I could still see the images Andromeny had shown me. The army of akadim. The flames. Rhyan at the head. Arkturion over an army of the dead.

Lyriana would understand eventually—when it all burned down. When the fires flared. And if she didn't—then ... Well, the sides were chosen. It wouldn't change anything for me.

But maybe Jules would come around. My throat dried. Maybe Meera.

I pushed thoughts of them away, willing the pinching in my heart to stop. Because missing them didn't matter. Because missing them only hurt. And right now, my feelings about them, about everything, were of no consequence. The mission was more important. It had to be more important. As was the outcome. And I had work to do. It would be a long road ahead.

I rolled my shoulders back realizing I'd gotten too lost in thought. A mistake I knew better than to make, particularly with the present company.

The eyes of the vorakh, the former chayatim, were on me now, taking me in. They were remembering I was there when they were freed. I could hear my name in their minds being whispered, repeated and moved through dozens upon dozens of thoughts. Some of the vorakh were in awe of me. Some were confused. Mostly though, they were scared. They feared the akadim who stood guard behind me. Little else mattered to them beside that.

Soon, their fear would dissipate. They would relax when they saw the demons work beside them. And their loyalty and strength to our cause and to us would grow when they were fed and clothed and treated fairly. Aemon and I would heal them, we'd give them what they needed, and protect them. It wouldn't be long now before they became the most powerful network of mind-readers and visioners in Lumeria. I smiled to myself. A weapon the Empire hadn't seen coming.

Particularly in Rhyan.

Andromeny had though. But she'd kept that vision secret. Hidden the outcome from the Emperor in a sea of potential outcomes.

Me Maraaka, Aemon purred into my mind, looking over at me. His dark eyes swept down my body, then back up, stopping at the crown on my head, and then his gaze shifted beyond me. To the akadim.

He grinned, pride in his eyes and aura as he extended his arms, inviting me to join him. His fresh *Rakashonim* scar was red against his left wrist. A second, smaller scar ran beneath it.

Ah, my kitten has become a queen. Come. Admire our army with me. And let them worship your beauty. Let them see what I am fortunate enough to worship in the dark.

And in the light, I thought.

He smirked, and I could already imagine his thoughts. The two of us on display. Fucking in front of all of them—a captive audience who couldn't look away. My gasps and moans would fill the sky as our army and court tried to silence their groans, watching us in their own barely masked desire. Aemon taking me from behind—everything on display, everything raw.

My core heated and my stomach tightened, suddenly seeing it clearly, unsure if the thought or images had generated in my own head or his. He could push his own thoughts out. Not just in commands to akadim, but to other Lumerians. Something I realized only recently, he could do for some time. But he wasn't the only one now.

I held my head up high, my heart thundering in my ears in thick, echoing beats. I glided forward, opening my mind just a little more—scanning carefully through the thoughts of our new court.

Lady Morgana Batavia? That's Lady Morgana.

Queen now, I pushed the thought back, and the chayatim who'd thought it suddenly stilled, her aura exploding with shock as her eyes widened.

Wasn't she missing? Kidnapped by akadim? Fuck, are we now kidnapped by akadim?

I was with my soturi, I thought. *You were kidnapped by the Emperor, not us. Now you're free. Now you belong to our court.*

A smile spread across my lips for the first time in public since my Revelation Ceremony. It no longer pained me when I read minds. My shard had seen to that. And I was able to listen to and respond to more than one thought at once.

Morgana and the Ready are together?

They're vorakh, too. They can read your mind. Stay focused. Stay focused.

Gods, I don't want to be here. I don't want to be here.

You are here. My eyes shot to the chayatim thinking the last thought. A young female mage with long dirty-blonde hair. Ka Daquataine from Damara from the looks of her. *You have been freed from your masters. Show some gratitude.*

Her mouth tightened, and she nodded, before staring at her lap, her hands folded neatly.

Apologies, Your Grace.

Your Majesty, I corrected.

Then I was in Aemon's arms, his hands low on my back as he drew me in, and at last I kissed him. Accepting him for who he was, acknowledging what he was. Not the man in the dark, my lover in the shadows. He was my king.

Maraak Moriel.

He bit my lower lip, his tongue pushing past it, as he hardened against me. *I love it when you call me king in your mind.*

I moaned, missing this. I'd gone without his touch for months. Without any touch. It had been far too long.

Aemon pressed a languid kiss to my neck, his hand snaking to my ass in a way that told me my earlier thought had definitely come from him.

Keep that up, I thought, *and you won't hear me call you that again.* Because if he was inside of me, our minds would close, there'd be nothing but silence, nothing but the sound of our joined flesh. The way it had always been.

He laughed. *You'll just have to scream then, out loud. So they can all hear.*

You'd like that, wouldn't you, I thought, and licked the side of his neck, biting his earlobe.

You have no idea how much. "Shall we then, my queen?" he asked, his voice low in my ear. "My strong and beautiful queen."

I smiled. "Yes."

Aemon nodded to Andromeny, and took my hand in his. And at this, our public display of affection and desire, the akadim began to growl and hiss and roar, their voices louder than before. Their claws were snapping, the sharpened edges clicking together, and their lips had been pulled back to reveal their fangs. I lowered my gaze realizing that other parts of their bodies were now standing at attention. The entire scene was grotesque.

Aemon's nostrils flared in annoyance.

And it was at this Godsdamned moment that Parthenay dared to approach us, a look of victory in her eyes.

I told you. They have their natures, she sneered. *They can't even look at their beloved queen embracing their king without wanting to rage and rape. Go back on your command. Before it fails completely.*

Aemon looked at me, his dark brows furrowed before he pulled everything from my mind. Everything I'd allow. My commands to the akadim. The way I intended to rule. It felt like my mind had been scraped, and I nearly stumbled back from the assault. But the thoughts he'd gleaned were nothing I wouldn't have freely given.

His eyebrows knit together in a deep V. *I see.*

I shook my head. *They're my soturi, and they will do as I command.*

I agree they are, and they should. But their nature, he thought, *is another story. Nature cannot be compelled.*

They walk in the daylight! They maintained a more normal body structure. So forgive me, but your argument on nature is null. If they can walk in the sun, if they can evolve to think and plan, why not this? I don't care what anyone says. I've forbidden my akadim from raping. And that's final.

He laughed, looking between me and Parthenay. *Kitten, you have to know, some parts of nature will never be mutable. And this I fear is sealed in stone. To command otherwise endangers your rule. Something I will not have.*

You see, Parthenay thought. *Now tell them.* Her eyes narrowed on me. *Tell them they have free rein, my queen. They'll serve you better when you admit that they can act as their nature demands.*

I caught Lissa's eye, and then thoughts from the chayatim began to shout again into my mind. Their fear was overwhelming now. And for the first time since I'd taken possession of my shield, of the orange shard, I felt pain in my head. One of my old headaches from mind-reading was returning. Fuck.

They will fight better if they're allowed ... certain freedoms, Aemon thought. *A satisfied man always does.* His nostrils flared and he looked away, effectively ending the debate between us.

Parthenay looked elated, her face shifted into the sneer she wore so well.

Aemon stepped forward, positioning himself in front of us, his arms raised. "Look at this most brave and worthy soturi. The fiercest in the land. You have been given an honor. You will fight. You will kill. And you will do so for our glory, for all of our glory. When you have done all that is asked of you, then, and only then you will feed. And you will feed well."

The roars were deafening. I shivered as a chill ran down my spine. Because no one, not even the akadim, had mistaken his meaning.

Aemon, I thought a warning in my tone.

I looked over to find Lissa shaking. The lust and violence coming from my akadim were thick in the air. I'd given my command, but they were ready to burst with Aemon's proclamation.

"Please," Lissa pleaded suddenly. "Your Majesty, please let me leave."

I raised my hand, indicating she should stay. I could only imagine what she had experienced with these monsters before she'd become my maid. But I was not having my lady-in-waiting run off in fear. Not from my own army. I was their Queen. What did that say about me?

"Please," Lissa whimpered again, bending down to draw herself into a ball. The scent of urine filled the air.

Fuck.

"Fine. Go," I waved in dismissal, more than aware her scent had carried to the akadim. They wouldn't mind that she'd wet herself. They were hungry for her in every way possible. And as predators, the fear only made her smell better to them.

I willed her to walk slowly, to walk far, but not run. Partly to maintain decorum. But also, because if she did run, they'd give chase. I had control, I had bound them all to me. But dozens of akadim in a lust-filled feeding frenzy were something else entirely. Queen I might be, Guardian of the orange shard, able to call on a Goddess's strength and power.

But even I'd have to run if caught up in one of their frenzies.

From the look on Parthenay's face, she knew exactly what I was thinking, and she was triumphant.

I would not have it.

The akadim began to shout. "*Maraak! Maraak!*" followed by violent cries of "Feed us! We're hungry! Starving!"

And finally, one that left me cold. "Give us one. Just one to fuck." Roars followed that one.

The vorakh were retreating back, heading deeper into the woodlands that surrounded us. Only Andromeny casting a silver binding around them—the kind used to trap soturi in habibellums—kept them from fleeing.

They cried out against the burn of the ring. But Andromeny didn't care. She was screaming at them now, ordering them to be still, to be silent.

I pushed Parthenay aside, pulled out my stave and conjured a small marble table. I left my shield upon it, a protective dome humming around it, and then I faced my akadim, feeling the brunt of their lust and violence and hunger.

"I know you're hungry. You will be fed. But we have rules in my court. I gave my command," I shouted. "To all of you. And you will obey."

Their growls intensified. And for the first time since I'd collected my army, I could feel their mutiny. Their pushback against their bindings.

You see? Parthenay thought.

In the same moment, Aemon pushed a thought to my mind. *Get them under control now!*

"I will," I hissed.

Kitten. They must rape. We've already changed them so much. Let it be enough.

But I ignored his words. Instead, I whirled on my heels, my eyes meeting Parthenay's. *I do believe that I warned you. Contradict me again and I will feed you to them.*

Her nostrils flared, the challenge clear in her eyes.

Suddenly, Andromeny spoke up—acting like a herald for us—perhaps in an attempt to divert the akadim's attention.

"*Ra Maraak, Ra Maraaka.*" Your king. Your queen. "*Teka!* Bow before their majesties." She turned in a slow circle, eyeing the akadim. They had formed themselves into two small armies. One collared by me. The other by Aemon. "Moriel and Ereshya have been reborn."

The vorakh's eyes widened, their faces stunned. Several looked at each other with questioning eyes, searching for answers that none of them possessed. My akadim fell at once. Because Rhyan bent the knee. He was already the one they looked to for leadership. It was just my luck that the akadim form tended to amplify certain personality traits of the person they used to be. It was a kind of compensation for the parts of them that were lost—the parts tied to their soul. Rhyan had been a soturion with an almost absurd amount of discipline. Now he was an akadim general with the ability to control hundreds of his kind with a single look.

Aemon's soturi knelt, and at last, the vorakh sank down in compliance.

I waited a moment, allowing them to spend some time on their knees, to fully embrace their new roles. And ours. And then I lifted my arm. "Rise."

"Thank you, and welcome," Aemon said, his voice booming and full of all the authority of a God. "Your queen and I have liberated you from your oppressors." He turned to face the chayatim. "From your masters. No longer shall the Empire abuse your abilities, nor will they be allowed to vilify you for how you were born; for magic and abilities you did not ask for. In the world we will build from Lumeria's ashes, no one is born illegal. No one is born taboo. Today we honor you, the sacrifices you've made, the injustice you have suffered."

Someone clapped, and another mage joined in, and then another. There was a cheer rising through the crowd, and a call of victory. My heart leapt.

We were doing the right thing.

Aemon's eyes sparkled. "Each one of you was dealt a fate you did not deserve. But today you have the chance to turn things around. To make a new world. Together, we shall break apart the Empire, brick by brick. You shall have your revenge if you seek it. And together, we'll remake this world into one that honors you and who you are. For being a part of this at the beginning, you will all be rewarded."

More claps followed, more cheers, and several of the chayatim raised their fists.

Behind me, the akadim growled.

I turned, feeling Aemon move beside me.

"You shall also be rewarded," he said. "You will have the power you've been denied. The opportunity to live naturally. To hunt, and feed." His eyes flashed on me then away. "To give into your natures."

Their growls turned to roars, and their teeth gnashed, their eyes glowing red. In the light, their monstrousness became clearer as they revealed their elongated canines. Fangs dripping with saliva pushed past their lips. And if they hadn't already, their natures began to rise—at least it did for those who were male. Everything was on display, and exposed. Between that and fucking Parthenay, I was about to lose all I'd worked for.

I stepped forward, a plan barely formed in my mind.

"You're hungry?" I shouted, facing my army. "I know what you want. But I don't give rewards for disobedience. If you want flesh, if you want pleasure, you'll prove yourselves to me." My eyes found Rhyan's in the crowd. "A demonstration of my benevolence to you. Arkturion Rhyan Hart. Come forward."

His red eyes flashed, and beneath the loin cloth he wore, I could see his own excitement had been ignited. His bloodlust filled the air, and his muscles flexed as he approached.

He bowed. "What do you want with me?" he growled.

"Morgana."

I stiffened. And he seemed to realize his mistake at that moment as well.

So he remembered. Good. If he remembered me, he remembered everything.

I grabbed Parthenay by the shoulders and pushed her in front of him. "You remember Parthenay, don't you?" I asked Rhyan sweetly. "Remember when she attacked you on Gryphon's Mount? Tied you and Lyriana up? Brought you to us against your will?"

A snarl escaped his lips, followed by a vicious growl that made my skin crawl. "I remember." His red eyes settled on her. "You invaded my mind."

"She did, didn't she?" I crooned. "So cruel. You don't like her, Rhyan, do you?"

"No." His irises began to glow, brighter than before. His muscles tensed, as his knees bent, preparing to pounce.

A small stream of saliva slipped from his mouth, and for a second, his eyes shot with venom toward Aemon. He bared his teeth. Rhyan was no fan of Aemon's either.

Aemon shook his head, emitting a sudden burst of power from his aura.

Rhyan's eyes went back to Parthenay, even more lust-filled than before. A lust filled with violence.

"You're hungry, Rhyan? Aren't you?" I eyed his loincloth again, my heart thundering. His cock twitched in response, the muscles in his arms flexing. "Very hungry."

"*Maraaka*," he said in confirmation, licking his lips, taking a step forward toward Parthenay.

I watched Aemon, daring him to stop me, to contradict me. A grin spread across my face.

"Take her," I commanded. "Take her however you want. Feast on her, fuck her, drink her blood." I shoved her forward without warning, watching as she stumbled, and fell to her knees. Immediately I stepped back.

"No—" Parthenay screamed. "No! Aemon! Help me!"

But Aemon didn't move to stop things. Rhyan pounced on Parthenay, moving with alarming speed. He flattened her to the ground, her back hitting it with a thud. He hissed, baring his fangs, before locking her arms above her head, his knees crushing her legs down, and then apart. His eyes flashed for a moment, looking up at me, asking permission, and I nodded, as Parthenay shrieked, attempting to free herself.

With a growl, he opened his mouth, his claws digging into her skin, as he bit down on her neck. His teeth sank into her flesh with shocking violence. Parthenay cried out. Her blood filled his mouth, dripping down her to her shoulder and onto the ground.

The akadim began to roar and howl, cheering and demanding their turn next.

"Aemon, please!" she begged.

"Is this how to address me?" he asked cruelly.

Rhyan's mouth moved, sucking and drawing more blood, before he pulled back, just enough to rip her dress open from her chest to the waist, exposing her breasts.

"*Maraak Moriel*," she cried. "Please, I beg you!"

And suddenly, another akadim broke from the crowd, too excited by what he saw. He rushed at Rhyan before I could stop him, hauling him off Parthenay, his claws tearing through his arms.

Rhyan rolled off to the side, and sprang back to his feet, a deadly look across his face. The second akadim started to drag Parthenay away, but Rhyan was on him in seconds, slashing his chest open and drawing blood. He expertly dodged a hit, then wrapped his hands around the akadim's neck, his foot stomping down on Parthenay's arm, keeping her from running.

The demon's eyes widened in terror as he tried desperately to break free of Rhyan's hold. But he wasn't strong enough. A second later the demon's eyes went blank as Rhyan ripped his head off, and threw it like a cannonball at what remained of my soturi. His silver collar fell to the ground and a stunned akadim picked it up, examining it, while another kicked the head into the woods. Within seconds, Rhyan had kicked the headless corpse aside, and threw Parthenay back on the ground.

"Mine," he growled.

Parthenay screamed louder, her feet trying to kick at Rhyan, but they were completely useless under the force of his muscle. He rucked up what remained of her dress, and began pushing his loincloth aside.

"This is between you and your queen," Aemon said. "Ask her. Beg your *Maraaka* for help."

Sweat was beaded at my neck, my stomach turning. I had meant what I said about forbidding rape. But I needed to make my point. I couldn't back down from Parthenay's insolence.

She cried, "*Maraaka Ereshya!* Please! Morgana! I beg you!"

I held my breath. Waiting just a few seconds too long. To where it had gone too far, but—not far enough.

"Rhyan!" I hardened my voice. "Stop!"

He did. Immediately pulling himself back from Parthenay, his loincloth still covering him. She scurried backwards at once, shaking as she tried to close her dress. No black mark. No invasion of her body. He'd taken some blood, bitten her neck. She'd be bruised all over, but she would be fine.

"Stand," I commanded, and Rhyan listened, wiping the blood dripping down his chin. "Go stand back with the others."

His eyes flashed, and he bared his teeth, clearly agitated he'd been denied a full meal. But like the soldier I knew he was, he obeyed. Then he stalked back toward the akadim and took a seat amongst them. Several shifted away, clearly fearing him now that they'd seen how easily he could kill. Good.

"Gods, Parthenay," I said. "Are you all right?" My voice was dripping with concern. I bent down and swiped my finger across her neck. "You know, I could have let him go all the way. After all, it's in their nature as you like to remind me. You seemed so adamant that they get to rape I thought you'd be okay with helping them out. But," I frowned. "You didn't seem to like it much." Tears filled her eyes. "Calm down. It's just a small bite. It's natural. You're fine."

You Godsdamned fucking bitch! Her thoughts screamed at me.

Your Godsdamned fucking Maraaka.

"Parthenay," Aemon said. "Show your respect to your queen for saving you. Now."

Her refusal was all across her face and aura, but one look from Aemon, and she obeyed, falling to her knees, her hands out in supplication.

A small scar ran across her right wrist.

"You were saying?" I asked, licking my lips. "I think I demonstrated my control—and his—more than well."

"Does anyone else want a chance with her?" Aemon asked, but he addressed his own soturi.

My eyes widened. And two akadim ran forward.

Suddenly, Aemon was chanting under his breath, "*Ani petrova rakashonim, me ka el lyrotz, dhame ra shukroya, aniam anam. Chayate me el ra shukroya. Ani petrova rakashonim!*"

Thunder clapped in the sky, and lightning struck the meadow as indigo light radiated off of Aemon, now the embodiment of Moriel.

Parthenay cowered, as did the rest of the vorakh.

They knew he was powerful. They had no idea just how much.

He took off at a run for the two akadim, his arms outstretched. And I remembered all the times he was called the Ready, all the times he'd been looked upon as a God of Death.

His hands wrapped around the first akadim. And then the second.

There was a crack, and both heads rolled onto the ground.

He'd been even faster than Rhyan.

My heart thundered. I'd known his strength, the sheer force of his power. But seeing it demonstrated like this—fuck. There was no one strong enough to defeat him. Not yet.

"This is the fate which awaits anyone who disobeys my command," he said, turning slowly to face everyone in our court. "As well as my queen's."

Then Aemon pulled me in toward him, his arm wrapped around my back, his hand snaking down my ass. *That was risky*, he admonished.

I shrugged. *Risky?* But inside, my heart was beating too hard. I had almost gone too far. Almost. I shook my head. *A risk can only exist when you have something to lose. I didn't.*

Is that so? he purred, but there was something dark, and violent underneath the seductive tone to his thought. I already knew where this was going.

Yes. I arched my back. *Either Rhyan proved my point, or he didn't. Leaving me to either win the debate, or lose Parthenay. A win no matter what.*

He laughed. *You are a cruel, vicious goddess.* His eyes seemed to sparkle and darken all at once. Then he squeezed his arms around me, tight. Painfully so. He playfully bit down on my nose, and then bit harder, his teeth sinking into my skin, and forcing my mouth open to breathe. *Showing Rhyan's strength worked in your favor. And showing mine has worked in ours.*

Ours? I asked.

He smirked, but his hands tightened even more, bruising me. *Parthenay is my Second. We would not be here today without her. She's not to be harmed.*

I don't like her, I pushed back, willing my nerves to stay grounded. *I don't want her around.*

Parthenay is crucial to the mission. He pulled back, his dark eyes boring into me, his indigo aura pulsing to the point the sky seemed to darken above us.

If she's so crucial to the mission, then when we leave here, I thought, *take her with you. Let her help you.*

Aemon's lips curled. *That's not how a Second works. She goes where I am not. And you should have little problem with her, now that you've shown her how powerful you are. Seen how willing she is to submit.*

So I showed my power. Was I not always stronger than her? I was. And yet, because of you, I cannot cast her aside, I thought, bitterly.

You may not, he thought. *Not yet. Time is crucial, especially these next few weeks as the Empire scrambles to assert its dominance. Now you know what to do. Make your way west to the caves. To the Wall of the Prince. You know where to look. Grow your army as you march. Claim the next shard with your soturi then meet me in the North.*

And Andromeny will seek out the key to our secret weapon, I thought.

Yes. We need her, and the weapon. But the shard must be found first. His eyes flicked to Rhyan, then back to me, before he buried his face in my neck, slipping his tongue across my skin, licking down to my throat. I gasped, feeling him spin me away from him, his hands beneath my cloak, untying the straps of my dress.

"Wh-what are you—?" I asked out loud, I was so startled. He pinned my hands behind my back, and unclasped my belt. It fell to the ground with a sharp metallic thud, and the top of my dress slipped down. Aemon pushed the fabric all the way aside exposing my left breast, and then the right, baring me to everyone in the meadow. Heat rose up my neck, burning against my cheeks.

The akadim on Aemon's side growled, their eyes flashing with fire, and I could sense my soturi drawing closer, while the chayatim didn't seem to know whether to look at us or look away. Though they didn't emit enough shock in their auras to suggest they'd never seen such a display before while in the Palace.

I'd never been shy—not after our first night together. I'd been fucked while Aemon watched, fucked by him in places where we could be caught, or where I knew someone was lurking, watching. Sometimes more than one person.

But ... never like this. Before a full audience, and in broad daylight.

My stomach clenched in fear, even as my core tightened.

If you want to starve your akadim, Aemon's hand wrapped around my neck and he squeezed, *at least give them a meal to look at.* His boot stomped down suddenly by my foot, catching the hem of my dress. It fluttered to the ground leaving me completely naked except for my cloak and crown. I could feel a flush of heat running from my neck to my chest, even as a shock of desire cut through my humiliation.

Aemon? What are you doing?

Come on, kitten. I know you like this. And it has to be done. You can't tease an army of beasts like you did, and leave things unfinished. He unbuckled his belt, and began to lift my cloak from behind. *Plus, don't forget you owe me. You got to keep the strongest akadim as your Arkturion. I allowed you to keep Rhyan Hart.*

Allowed? I seethed. *He's mine! I bargained for him! Because I gave you your*—I buried the thought behind my mental walls, covering it with onyx stone as I drew his hand from behind me between my legs.

Even if I had wanted to fight back, there was no way I could. Not when he was still radiating with the power of *Rakashonim*. Not when he was a living God. And despite it all, I was soaked. Some dark part of me wanted this. Liked the humiliation. Liked being desired.

You're right, I thought, *you did give me what I wanted. So do it then. Fuck me. Fuck your queen. Right here, before our court.* I pulled off my cloak, the only remnant of modesty that remained, and let it meet the rest of my garments on the ground. Now I only wore my crown. From my peripheral vision, I eyed my shield, seeing its orange light rise to meet the sun. *Let them watch. Let them worship us like they used to before the Drowning. But ...*

His cock was thick and heavy against my bare ass, as he leaned me forward, arching my back so he could enter. A pulse built between my legs, and my heart thundered.

The akadim were clapping now, howling into the sky, their control teetering on exploding. Their collars seemed to crackle as if they were struggling to keep them bound. But now that they knew what happened, that disobedience would result in the loss of their heads—either by the hands of Rhyan, or Aemon—they remained compliant.

But what? Aemon thought.

But when I collect the next shard, and I bring it to you, I want one thing in return. My fingers wrapped around his cock, sliding his length between my folds, coating him in my wetness, in the proof I was going along with this. That I was not just allowing, but wanting.

He grunted, slapping my hand away, and kicked my legs even further apart. He positioned himself at my entrance, and gripped my hip, his fingers digging into me.

Name it, kitten. Name your price.

After the next shard is claimed, I never want to see Parthenay again.

Done. He slammed inside of me.

CHAPTER ELEVEN

TRISTAN

"Head up," the Bastardmaker barked.

A sharp pain started in my stomach, its intensity matching the ache in my broken hand as I walked beside him through Cresthaven's Great Hall. Every step more painful than the last.

"I said, head *up*, Lord Tristan," he sneered.

I obeyed, and the pain stopped. Fucking blood contract.

"Now, shoulders back," he commanded.

I did that, too.

"Walk on your toes like a dancer."

I lifted my heels, my teeth clenching, but he only laughed.

"For fuck's sake. I was kidding. Walk like a man."

My heels went down.

He led me up the stairs of Bamaria's fortress. We'd just arrived as the clock tower announced midnight. Twenty-four hours since Galen was—since he—

"But wipe that Godsdamned look off your face. Or forget prancing, I'll make you crawl back to your room."

"Yes, Arkturion," I said blandly, schooling my face to neutral, to the mask I'd been taught to wear since I was a boy. The disaffected mask of a nobleman, of a Lord of Ka Grey.

The backs of my eyes burned and no matter how many direct orders he barked at me, or forced me to obey I couldn't get the image of Galen out of my head. Couldn't stop seeing his swollen face, the pain in his eyes, his gaping, empty mouth. The way his head had fallen forward when the Bastardmaker—when he—

"Left at this hall," he commanded.

I frowned. Left took us to the Heir's wing. Toward Naria's bedroom.

"That's not my room," I said.

He frowned, looking me up and down slowly, his eyes staying a moment too long at my crotch. A wide smile formed across his lips. "No?" he asked. "But it's Lady Naria's." His eyes lit with amusement. "What? You only pull your cock out for your friends? Not for her?"

"Fu—"

"Ah! No!" His hand wrapped around my neck, and the wall hit my back.

I closed my eyes, trying not to cry. Trying not to scream. I couldn't fight back. I only had one working hand. They'd had me seen by the best healers in the Empire, my bones had been reset and already I had some movement back in my fingers. But it was going to take weeks for the soreness to go away.

The rest of my life to forget the memory of how it happened. Of what happened after.

Maybe I should resist. Maybe I should scream. Blurt out the truth, and admit to anyone who'd listen what I'd done. Maybe I could drive him to kill me, too. End my misery.

He sneered and shook his head as if he could read my mind. "Don't even think about it," he said.

My mind went blank. Fuck. Fuck! I knew I had to obey every order given to me now that I'd signed that damned contract binding me to him. But I had no idea it could work on my mind.

"You're not going to get me to kill you. You're not going to join your little friend. No matter how desperately," his eyes lowered, "you want to be with him." He bared his teeth. "Not for," his fingers squeezed around me tighter, "a very," he squeezed again, "very, long time."

"I ... understand," I said, gasping for breath.

"Good." He released me, and I slumped down against the wall, coughing as tears filled my eyes. I clutched at the sling my arm was in, a splint still strapped to my hand to ensure the bones remained in place. "I am taking you to your room. But I thought," he shrugged, "you might want some female ... *comfort*."

"No," I said, my heart hammering. Because I already knew how this game was played. He'd want to stay. He'd want to watch. I'd be unable to do anything about it, unable to make him leave, unable to stop it.

He shrugged. "To your room we go." He pushed me back down the hall and barked out, "Turn right."

Right toward the wing of the Arkasva's Second, the rooms where every member of Ka fucking Grey was now sleeping. The Bastardmaker stopped in front of my bedroom door. But before he could turn the key, the door swung open.

My grandmother stood on the other side, her red lips pursed together.

For a second, I was relieved. So fucking relieved to see her, to see the one person who was supposed to protect me, who had protected me as a kid—taken me in, comforted me after my parents—after they'd—

She stepped forward, her eyes filled with concern when she saw me, taking in the sling, the way I still limped as I walked. My face had been tended to, but it was still swollen and red, still full of cuts and bruises that would take weeks to heal. Before they'd sent me off, a mage had applied glamour magic to my skin, clearing all blemishes. It had to be fading by now. But even if it hadn't, she had to know. She had to see the difference in me, see the pain in my eyes.

Suddenly I was three years old again. A scared little boy, terrified of the things he'd seen, the things he'd lost. I needed a hug. I needed to be protected. I needed my grandmother. Bamaria's Master of the Horse, Arianna's Second. At this moment, she was the most powerful person in the country. The hope that she could do something, that she could somehow save me surged forward.

Gods, could she tell? Could she see it in my eyes? Feel it in my aura? In the way we stood together? Could she see what he'd done to me? Could she undo it? Help me? Fix it?

Her eyes filled with disdain. But too late, I realize they weren't for him, for my captor and torturer. For Galen's killer.

They were for me. For her own Godsdamned grandson.

"Arkturion Waryn," she said. "Thank you for bringing Tristan back to me."

He grunted. "No problem. I think he's learned his lesson," he said.

My grandmother nodded and my heart sank. No—it fucking plunged to my stomach, was drowning. "Please, come in," she said, moving behind the doorway.

He nodded and closed the door behind him

"I hope he wasn't too much trouble for you. The sorts of things young men can get up to. He's normally perfectly behaved. You've been very patient with him."

The sorts of things? As if I were running through the city playing pranks. Stealing purses! I'd just been tortured, and watched my best friend murdered, and she was acting like I'd been an insolent brat in need of a scolding.

"I think we sorted him out," the Bastardmaker said, winking at her, his eyes dipping to my crotch. "We can sort him out more if needed."

My unbroken hand clenched painfully.

"Well, Arkturion, you must be exhausted. Not to worry, I'll deal with him."

The Bastardmaker nodded. "I have one more loose end to tie up here before I find my bed."

My chest tightened.

"Just need to make sure one more time, that your grandson isn't hiding any dangerous criminals from us. We wouldn't want that, would we? Not when he's promised to be a good boy."

"He'll comply," my grandmother said quickly, her eyes narrowing on me.

The Bastardmaker opened his belt pocket, retrieving a single clear stone. White clouds began to fill the center.

One of the vadati stones Lady Kenna had sent us. That one was mine and Galen's. And it connected us to the other fugitives the Emperor sought. The other traitors of the Empire.

"Time to try this again," he sneered, his eyes locking with mine. "Hold out your hand."

I felt like a fucking dog, lifting my palm up, following every order.

He dropped the stone instead of handing it to me.

"Hold it to your mouth," he said. "And call your friends."

"You know they won't answer," I said. "They know I'm compromised."

"They knew you were. Now make them believe you're not," he said. "Cry. Lie. Blubber like a baby. Just do it." *Or else*. I could hear the unspoken threat at the end. The threat he was now openly making in front of my grandmother. "Julianna first," he barked.

My throat dried as I pulled the vadati to my mouth, and said, "Julianna." My voice was hoarse and shaking. I knew they could hear the tears I'd shed underneath. I didn't even have to act. The stone filled with white fog, and a tinge of blue. Fuck. It was connecting, just like it had when they made me do it last time.

"Again," the Bastardmaker hissed, his voice low.

"Julianna," I cried, my heart hammering. "Are you there? It's Tristan. Please. Please answer me. Please."

Blue light filled my palm.

No. No. No.

"Get her to answer," the Bastardmaker gritted.

"Do it," my grandmother hissed, her eyes flashing with anger.

I let out a shaky exhale. "Julianna, I need to know where you are. I-I escaped the Palace. I tried to tell you before, but if you didn't hear me last time, Galen's—G-G—" Real tears fell. "Galen's dead—" My voice cracked. I'd been instructed to tell them, to make sure they knew. And every time I had to say it, it was like the moment was happening all over again. "Please, help me. I don't know where to go. Where to hide. Help me." I shuddered, no longer acting. "I'm so scared. Help me."

The vadati cleared, all the light fading.

I squeezed my eyes shut.

"Keep going," he said. "Call Dario."

So I did. The same thing happened. And again when I tried Meera, and then Aiden, the rest of my co-conspirators now. The stone connected each time, meaning that they were together, that they still had at least one of the stones. But they weren't answering me. No matter how much I begged, how hard I cried, or how desperate my pleas became.

The Bastardmaker wiped his mouth in annoyance, looking between me and my grandmother. "Lady Lyriana," he said, "call her."

My throat bobbed. "But she's missing."

"So we'll find her. The little bitch knows you." He scratched at his arm. "She ran with you. Call her."

"And say what?"

He smirked. "That we have her cousin again. She'll come running."

My grandmother's eyes twitched. Her aura flaring with hatred.

"Lyriana," I said. "Lyriana, can you hear me? It's Tristan. Please answer if you can. Lyr, there's something you need to know. Jules. They have her. The Emperor." My eyes flashed. "The Bastardmaker."

But the stone remained cool in my hand. She couldn't hear me.

"Hand it back," he said.

I returned the stone, feeling deflated.

"Tomorrow you'll go before the people of Bamaria, tell them the new policy. Mandatory testing for vorakh, as well as checkpoints, will be in place by the end of the week. Everyone will be tested again, and subject to further testing at random. Anyone who fails to comply will be assumed to be hiding vorakh, and arrested on the spot."

My heart thundered, and I nodded. I was no longer just the Emperor's dog, scenting out vorakh for him to take control of in the Palace. I was now his puppet, too. Running when he said run. Jumping when he said jump. Forcing nahashim tests on anyone his soturi wanted—whether I found vorakh on them or not. No matter what I did now, I'd be betraying someone. An innocent Lumerian. Or an innocent vorakh.

"See him to his bed, Lady Romula. Make sure he gets some sleep so he can speak nice and clear tomorrow. Emperor's orders."

"Of course." She frowned, her too-red lips were thin and dry as she pursed them together.

His eyes narrowed on me. "And we'll get someone to finish cleaning up your face."

When he was out of the room, the door closed and locked behind me, and one of her silencing spells in place, my grandmother turned to me. Her hand flew before I could react, slapping me across the cheek. Slapping wounds that still smarted and burned. I stumbled, practically slamming into the wall.

"Grandmother," I cried out. "What the—"

"Is it true?" she asked, her voice cold. "You helped the murderer escape?"

"My fucking hand is broken and Galen is dead!"

"As he should be. You idiot. How dare you disgrace the Ka. Our name. Our legacy! You are so Godsdamned lucky that your title and status saved you. After the stunt you pulled, after the scum you associated with, you should be dead now."

I saw Galen's eyes closing in my mind. Felt the cold air on my broken body as I took off my shirt. The rage inside me as I let my pants fall down. I could hear the Emperor's laugh still. See his hands on Jules. The chayatim I'd sentenced. The Yellow Room.

The monster who killed my parents.

You'll regret it when he grows. When you see inside his soul like I have. When you learn what he is!

I shook my head. "I wish I was dead."

She grabbed my neck, squeezing and forcing my gaze to hers. "Hush! You're confused. He got you confused."

I coughed, starting to choke—my ribs moving painfully. "*I'm* confused? Look at you! Or better yet, look at me! Look what they've done to me! Are you even going to ask if I'm all right?"

She released her hold, her nostrils flaring. "You're fine. You're alive."

"And the Bastardmaker's slave!"

She clucked her tongue. "My dear boy. We are all someone's slave until we rise above them. And you, you and your lowborn associations, you are what put us into this mess. I never liked that boy. That Galen. Ka Scholar," she spat. "He wasn't for you. He was dragging you down. Now you listen to me, and you listen well. So you must obey his orders—then you will. But you won't have to do it forever. We are poised for power. I am Master of the Horse, the Arkasva's Second and if you play your cards right, you will be Arkasva. Not that Naria. We are close. So close. But we cannot afford one more misstep."

"One more misstep? One more misstep!" I shouted. As if I'd just been making the wrong choice all along. As if it were my fault, and not our sick fucking evil Emperor pulling the strings all this time. Lying and manipulating me. Torturing me. And now, making me a puppet to go around my own country spewing out his lies. Fulfilling his agenda. I'd be forced to go even more against who I was. Capturing innocent people as the head of his Godsdamned vorakh task force.

My grandmother sneered. "Just be glad now that that boy is gone. And his association is linked with that traitor Lyriana and her dead forsworn lover." She folded her arms across her chest. "It taints Arianna, too, you know. But not us. We're safe. Let's forget this ugliness, shall we? Oh, Tristan. Do not look at me like that. I am protecting you."

"Protecting me? You're protecting yourself," I said. She always was. It was always about her—her and her legacy, her name. I'd just been the last one to see it. To see that I wasn't someone she loved. I was a tool, a means to an end. A way to carry out her ambitions.

And if I did all she asked, I wouldn't be free. At best, I'd just be enslaved to her—like I always was.

"All will be well, my dear," she continued. "You'll see. You're very tired, and injured, you're not thinking straight. Go to bed now. Rest, heal. You can't just keep wearing glamours. We'll start to take our power back tomorrow, when you can present yourself in a manner worthy of Ka Grey. And then I promise you, you won't suffer like this again. I won't allow it."

I blinked back the tears blurring my vision, my stomach twisting. "As you wish, Grandmother." Always as you wish.

She nodded, satisfied, and left me alone. I was sinking against the wall, crying into my fist.

My chest tightened, cold washing over me. My teeth chattered.

The cold. I knew that cold. No. No. No.

Not a vision, not now. Please. Please!

The chills continued, my breathing shallow.

It took me a few minutes, but I realized, it wasn't a vision. It was something else. Panic. Breathing was becoming difficult. I didn't know what to do. I wanted to scream and cry and run after my grandmother and beg her to take care of me—yet some dark part of me hoped I found her at the top of the stairs, so I could push her down.

I clutched at my chest with my unbroken hand, unable to stop my teeth from chattering. My vision blurred, my heart racing so fast it hurt. I felt like I couldn't breathe. Couldn't get enough air. Not inside these four walls, not inside this room. Everything was tight, everything hurt.

I couldn't be in here, couldn't stay here.

I was out in the hall a moment later, stumbling like a drunk, one hand to support me against the wall as I walked aimlessly, moving without thinking, heading toward the corridors which lead into the Heir's wing.

The freezing cold washed over me, my teeth chattering. I was unbound, but I could barely do magic now. Not with my broken hand; not this injured or tired. I couldn't stop shaking or stop the pain in my chest.

A minute later, I was aware of Eric and Bellamy, my loyal escorts trailing my shadow. They didn't speak. I didn't know any more if I could trust them. If their loyalty was to me, or just the coin my grandmother gave them.

I realized I hadn't just been wandering. I'd come to a room. A room I didn't even know I'd been searching for until I arrived and knocked.

A minute later, Naria opened the door, her blonde hair in a loose messy braid. She'd wrapped a robe around herself, her blue eyes fuzzy with sleep.

"Tristan?" she asked, then her eyes widened as she took me in. My injuries. My sling. The red in my eyes. The tears. She frowned. "What? What the hell's going on with you? What are you doing here?" Her voice filled with disdain.

"Naria, I'm sorry," I said, feeling the eyes of my escorts on my back. My stomach turned. "I don't know."

"You don't know what you're doing here?" She placed her hand impatiently on her hip.

"I know we're not—that we don't—fuck." I was trembling. "Please, just, can I come in?" I rested my head against the doorframe. "I don't—didn't have anywhere else to go."

Her eyes narrowed, looking me up and down, then stopping on my broken hand, the splint, and the sling, before staring beyond me, flashing on Bellamy and Eric. She exhaled sharply and let out a sigh. "Fine. Come in."

She closed the door behind me, took my uninjured arm and led me to the bed, sitting me down on the edge.

I burst into tears. "I'm sorry, I'm sorry. I know we're not—that we don't. I just—I couldn't be alone. I couldn't be alone."

She sat down wordlessly beside me. "Your stave?" she asked, sounding almost bored.

"My-my stave?"

"Yes. Pull it out," she snapped.

"What?"

"Myself to fucking Moriel," she hissed. "Cast a silencing spell."

My eyes widened in confusion.

"I'm a soturion, I can't do it," she said. "Neither can my escorts."

I nodded, suddenly understanding and retrieving the stave from my belt, casting the spell around the room with what little energy I had left.

When the small buzzing sound stopped, and faint blue light around the room stilled, I knew the spell was in place. We couldn't be heard.

"What happened to you?" Naria asked. "You're hurt."

"What do you think," I gritted. I had no idea how I looked. But I was sure the glamour was completely gone now and I looked like shit.

"I mean," her eyes flashed again on my hand, then slowly across my face, "do you need medical attention right now?"

I shook my head. "No."

"Okay," she said quietly. "So you came here?"

"I just didn't want to be alone."

"You said." She bit her lip, silent for a moment. "I heard about Galen." She looked away. "It's fucked up."

My chest heaved. There was nothing to say to that. Because it was.

"I didn't think I'd see you again after the Palace," she continued. "Especially after what you did. Betraying the Emperor, escaping with Galen."

"Sorry to disappoint you," I said dully. "I didn't think I'd be seen again either. Apparently my name and face were worth more than my crimes."

Naria's eyes narrowed. "I didn't say I was disappointed to see you again." She frowned. "Is it true? You really ran with Lyr and the others? Or were you taken by them? Held hostage?"

"Depends on who you ask. The Emperor? The Bastard-maker? The Court of Bamaria?"

"I'm asking you," she said. "The truth."

"What does the truth matter? Or what's real?"

"Then nothing matters," she said. "You don't have to tell me. But I am asking."

"Why?" I gritted.

"Because it matters. Because it's real," she said. "Because you came to me. I'm trying to understand."

I looked away, trying to breathe through my nose.

"Did you?" Naria asked again, her voice softer. "Did you choose to run?"

I shook my head. "What if I told you I did? What if I told you that I hate the fucking Emperor, and everyone who bent the knee to him?"

Naria exhaled, her hand tightening around mine. "I'd say it's a good fucking thing we put the silencing spell in place."

I huffed. "Why the fuck does it matter?" I asked. "They know what I did. They know exactly what I'm guilty of. And they don't care. They don't care!" I felt hysterical. "I thought rules meant something, that there were laws in place for a reason—for justice. That I was helping get rid of the criminals. Making my people safe! But all the time, the laws meant nothing. Right and wrong are fucking gryphon shit! Because my best friend is dead! All because he couldn't stand the fact that the Emperor himself made Bamaria unsafe. Exposed us to akadim. Killed the love of his life. My cousin. Haleika! The ones who rule, they get to kill anyone they want, they get to commit murder legally through their laws and their carelessness. Because they have power. But Galen stands up to them; he tries to find a sense of justice, demand fairness. He follows their commands. And he's the criminal?" My nostrils flared. "Oh. But not me. No. Never me! I'm the great vorakh hunter, the little dog bound to the Bastardmaker, licking his fucking feet."

Naria frowned, biting her lower lip in contemplation. "You were a fool to believe that for so long. Justice doesn't come to those who deserve it. The ones in power simply take what they want, and when they want."

"What?" I blinked.

"You heard me." Naria shook her head. "Anyway, some of us are still playing the game, and not throwing a temper tantrum while we do it. Your secrets may have been exposed. But mine haven't." Her nostrils flared. "I intend to keep it that way."

I stilled, meeting her blue eyes. Moonlight poked through the silk curtains, only half-closed around her balcony. There was a soft breeze from the Lumerian Ocean blowing against them, and the scent of salt filled the air along with her flowery perfume.

Her words sank in, and I looked at her almost as if it were for the first time.

My pulse raced. "What secrets?"

"Now you want my secrets? I'm furious with you, you know," she said. "We're betrothed. But you left me behind."

"Your mother is Arkasva."

She laughed bitterly. "My mother is set to become the new Imperator of the South. And her first order will be to annex Bamaria to Korteria. Officially. Ka Elys in Elyria's already agreed to do the same. Temporarily, of course."

"What?" I balked.

"Gods, Tristan. Haven't you figured it the fuck out by now?" Naria laughed bitterly, her eyes blazing. "My mother is evil. She's in bed with the Emperor. She'd put me there, too, if she wasn't so jealous. It's been her plan all along, to do their bidding, to aid them in exchange for power. So she could convince herself that she rose to the top. Your grandmother, too."

My stomach twisted, memories shining in a new light. All the times my grandmother had brought the Emperor into our home. Even after Haleika's murder and public humiliation and execution. Just tonight she was going along with the Bastardmaker even after I'd been clearly tortured. Assaulted.

Forced to watch the murder of my best friend—all while I was, while I was—

Maybe she didn't know *that* part. But she knew enough. Had seen enough. And it hadn't mattered. My feelings hadn't mattered. I hadn't mattered. Not to her.

My eyes narrowed on Naria. "Why are you telling me this?" I asked.

"Because for once, no one can hear me. Because you have nowhere else to go. Because you came here to see me. And because," she shrugged, "because it seems like you're finally starting to get it."

"But you've always been—" I shook my head.

"What?" she asked. "Loyal to my mother?" Her eyes narrowed. "Do you honestly think I had a choice? I thought you saw me. I thought you saw it."

I blinked, because she'd been right. I had—I had seen it—the fear in her eyes, in her aura, the way she changed around her mother. The way she'd shut me down when I brought it up.

She stood suddenly, pacing the room back and forth. "This is so typical. You've had your eyes open to what this Empire actually is for what—a minute? And you can't be alone?" She folded her arms across her chest. "Unlike you, I never swallowed the Empire's lies. Or the lies of the woman who raised me. And unlike you, I've been alone my whole fucking life."

"But you could've spent time with—" I started, my brain struggling to make sense of everything she was saying. To rectify the Naria I'd known, with the one I was starting to see beneath the surface, and the one blazing with fury before me now.

"Spent time with who?" she spat. "My cousins? You really think my mother would have allowed that? Making friends with the people keeping the title of Arkasva from her?"

"If you had told them the truth, they would have helped you. Lyr would have helped you."

Naria looked away, her voice growing softer. "It was easier to make myself hate them. To let them hate me. It was easier to go on without hope things could be different. To know where I stood; where we all stood."

I was silent, so many memories of Naria over the years running through my mind, coming out now in a different light. The way she'd always been apart from Lyr, looking miserable. The way she'd spoken against her father's killer, Aemon, with such ferocity, even though she knew no one agreed with her, only for her mother to loudly denounce her words again and again. Even the way she'd pursued me, knowing of my commitment to Lyr. I could see it now. See how it was all on purpose. Calculated.

"You had to spend nights in my bed just to see an ounce of my discomfort," she said. "And now? Now you finally see the truth? I can't decide if I'm that good, or you're just that stupid."

My stomach dropped. "Why did you become a soturion?" I asked. "I never thought you would."

Her mouth tightened, and she pulled at the ends of her blond hair, twisting them around her finger. "I didn't want to be one. I don't particularly care to be one now. I wanted to be a mage. I wanted to study and do magic. I always did. But she was Master of Education, already in every part of my life, dictating it, controlling it. Being up there on the dais before the Arkmage—being asked what path I'd choose—it was the only time I had a chance to make a choice. The first time in my life I had a choice that she couldn't influence or stop. That she didn't see coming. And it was the only way to get away from her, away from her watchful eye. To gain a moment of freedom, of being able to breathe."

She stopped pacing and sat back beside me, and gestured around her bedroom—the room that was once Meera's. "You can see my plan worked really fucking well."

"I'm sorry," I said.

"You should be. You're stuck here now, too."

She was right. We were both in danger. But as I watched Naria sitting next to me, twisting her hair around her finger, I realized for the first time since I'd left the Palace, I didn't want to scream, or cry, or kill myself. It was the first time being with Naria felt good. It was just us. We didn't have to put on a show. And she wasn't being manipulated by her mother.

"I don't mind as much. Being stuck here with you," I said. It was the most truthful thing I'd ever told her.

She rolled her eyes and I waited for the rebuff. For her to snap at me and tell me how stupid I was being. But she only walked to her closet and reached inside, bringing out an extra pillow. Laying it on the bed, she pulled back the covers and patted her sheets. "Come here. I'll take off your boots, help you into bed."

"I can stay?" I asked.

"That's what you wanted, isn't it?"

Tears rolled down my cheeks. "It is."

"They really hurt you bad, didn't they?" she said softly.

I nodded.

"It's okay," she said.

"Why are you being so nice to me?" I asked.

"I'm not being nice."

I met her eyes.

She shrugged. "You told me once that you cared about me."

Sniffling, I stood up. "I did." My heart pounded. "And I do."

"Well, same. Now come here. I'll look after you tonight."

CHAPTER TWELVE

LYRIANA

I sat beneath the full moon in an open clearing of the woods. The branches of silver moontrees reached for each other, as if they were holding hands. The full effect was a shimmering canopy above an empty stage.

I leaned back on my couch, getting comfortable, feeling the grass tickle my feet. Meera sat beside me, staring ahead.

"The show's about to begin," she said quietly. "Pay attention."

"Oh." I glanced around the forest. There were no other seats. No other indications that we were here for a performance. I shook my head, confused. "What are we watching?"

Meera rolled her eyes. "Come on, Lyr. It was your idea."

"It was?" I asked. "I don't remember." Small lights twinkled within the leaves and branches. The kind we used for decoration at solstice. The kind that had sparkled the night Rhyan first kissed me.

Suddenly, gleaming blue lights flitted across the sky as ashvan ran on their hourly patrol.

I watched their progress, following them as they circled above. The clock tower hadn't rung yet. "It's too early to call the hour," I said.

Meera shrugged. "It's closer to the end than you think."

"What?"

A beautiful mage wearing red robes stepped onto the stage, her long hair falling in thick waves down her back, the color a bright, fiery red. She smiled at the audience, then held her hands above her head in a grand gesture to signal the start of the show.

Meera clapped, then stilled, watching in silence.

A drum began to beat in the distance, and I wondered if the mage might dance. It had been so long since I'd seen a dance performance. Since I'd been in one. But the mage fell to her knees. For a moment she looked up at us, as if startled to see us there, then she threw her face into her hands, and began to sob.

"Lyr," Morgana snapped. She took a seat at the edge of the couch beside Meera. "Gods. Move over."

"Morgs?" I frowned, looking at the armrest my hand was already leaning on. I was pressed against the edge. Taking up as little space as I could. There was nowhere else for me to go.

"You need to make more room," Morgana said, scooching back onto the couch. She fluffed out the skirts of her orange gown, then sat up straight, her body regal.

The mage performing continued to cry, her sobs wracking through her body. The sound began to echo through the forest, until it seemed as if her cries were coming from every direction.

"It's still not enough room," Morgana said. "Move!"

"Morgs," Meera chided, "she's trying."

"Myself to Moriel. Move faster. Father's here."

"But father's—" My eyes widened, and there he was. Walking toward Morgana. He looked younger than when I'd last seen him. The grays in his hair were gone. His face was smooth, missing every line and wrinkle he'd earned over his years.

But even more surprising was that as he walked toward us, I saw something I'd never seen before. He could walk without a limp. He took his steps with ease, holding his head high with the Laurel of the Arkasva on his head. The leaves were a bright gleaming gold, shining as if in the sun, and glowing against the darkness of his hair.

The crying from the stage grew louder, drowning out any other sounds of the forest. The breeze. The chirping of birds. The distant whinnies of ashvan in the sky.

"Father?" I asked, tears filling my eyes. Nearly three months had passed since he'd died. Since I'd seen him. Since he'd been murdered. Since everything else had happened.

But he wasn't looking at me. He was watching the show. Staring intently at the red-headed mage whose entire performance seemed to be nothing more than her crying and wailing. He had no seat on the couch with us, so he perched on the armrest.

"Father?" I asked again. "Father!"

"Shhh," Morgana hissed. "Gods, Lyr. Pay attention."

"I know this show," he said, his eyes on the mage. "Your mother once told me about it." He removed his laurel, and passed it to Meera. "Here. I don't need this anymore."

Meera considered the laurel in her hands, then shrugged and tossed it to the forest floor. "None of us do."

I sat forward, my heart hurting as I tried to catch my father's eyes. I couldn't understand why he didn't have a full seat on the couch. Or why Morgana hadn't made any space for him at all. Why was she forcing him to perch? Why wouldn't she move? Why wasn't there enough room for him? Why were there no other seats?

Morgana stood, and walked away. "I know how it ends."

"I've seen it, too," Meera said. She retrieved the laurel and dropped it into my lap. For a second the leaves shifted, reforming themselves into the shape of a crown, one meant for a queen. Then they resumed their laurel shape once more.

My father looked at me finally, his eyes soft and wet.

"Me bat," he said. "You've been through so much these last few months. You've been so strong."

I started to cry, no longer able to speak. I nodded.

His eyes returned to the stage as he stood up and clapped, shouting what a good performance it had been. But the mage was *still sobbing. The show wasn't over yet. He turned away from the couch, away from me.*

"Wait," I said, my arms extended for a hug. "Don't go."

He turned and shook his head. "I'm sorry. I can't stay long. I'm on the other side now. It's not …" He frowned, and then he flickered. His body vanished and reappeared, like he couldn't hold onto physical form any longer. "It's not allowed anymore," my father said with a sigh. "I had to fight just for this visit. Just for this one show."

His eyes were distant, and my arms fell helplessly to my sides.

"I thought he would be here though," my father continued. "I thought I would give him my blessing for you. But he isn't here tonight. He hasn't come."

"Who hasn't come?" I asked.

"Rhyan."

"W-What?" I stammered.

"You swore, Lyr." Suddenly, Rhyan's voice filled the forest. I spun on my heels, my eyes wild and desperate as they searched for him, but I couldn't find him. Not anywhere. There was no one else. Not even my father, not even the stage and its performer remained. It was just me, alone with the trees.

"You swore you'd make the pain go away," Rhyan said, his voice echoing. "You swore no one else would hurt me. You lied."

My eyes shot open, my hand clutching my chest.

I was in bed. In a basement. Slowly, I remembered that we were at Sean's house. I glanced anxiously around the room. Every corner was dark, like night had fallen. By the Gods—no. My heart pounded at the thought of losing that many hours. Of having been asleep for so long. For having missed too much. For letting too much happen without me. My body felt sore—in the way it did at times when I'd slept too long. When I'd spend too much time in bed.

Gods—please no. There were no windows in the basement, nor any kind of clock or timekeeper—so I couldn't be sure. The only source of light came from a few candles on a small table near the bed.

I swallowed roughly, feeling dehydrated, but not as sick as I'd been before. Before I'd … fainted? No. No.

I had a fever. An infection. I'd been forced to sleep. Forced to lose consciousness, forced to lose out on precious time. Time I didn't have.

By Auriel.

A soft blanket covered my body, and I was already too hot beneath it. My boots and armor had been removed and carefully laid across a small table against the wall. My weapons were there, too. Even Asherah's chest plate.

And next to it all, sitting by itself, was the black leather scabbard Rhyan had gotten me. The one with my stave in it. Asherah's stave. My nostrils flared. That scabbard! That scabbard had been a gift!

I pushed back the blankets, and rushed to the small table, retrieving it. Then, sitting back on the bed, my fingers ran over the smooth leather casing, and traced the golden thread that had been stitched into the image of a sun. Below that were silver threads, stitched into the shape of gryphon wings. The sigil of Ka Hart. Rhyan's sigil.

I swallowed roughly, my throat dry and hugged the scabbard to my chest, careful as I shifted my injured arm. There was a fresh set of bandages, clean and white. There was no sign of bleeding. My skin was no longer hot and swollen. The red streaks were gone. And I no longer had a fever. The infection was gone. Miraculously, it no longer hurt.

A door opened and closed at the top of the stairs, briefly allowing in some golden light. Auriel appeared, his eyes meeting mine instantly. "Lyriana?" Auriel asked. "Thank the realms." He started down the stairs, his feet moving quickly into a slow jog. "You look so much better," he sounded relieved. "How are you feeling?"

I sat up straighter. "How am I feeling? How am I feeling!" I yelled. I gestured at the bed, at the dark basement walls. "You bastard! You Godsdamned bastard!"

"I'm a bastard?" he asked, throwing his hands up. "The hell did I do to you now?" he snapped. "You've been awake for what? A minute?" Auriel shook his head. "Believe me, I haven't had nearly enough time to properly offend you." His eyes narrowed. "Though if you wish, I can certainly try."

"You forced me to sleep. You knew I didn't want to lose consciousness. Lose time!" I yelled. "Gods, Auriel! I fucking told you. I told you I didn't want to! I pleaded with you."

"Yes, well, I can't dispute that," he scoffed. "But let me tell you something, Lyriana. Your fever was dangerously high—even for someone as powerful and strong as you. That stab wound was infected down to the bone. So, at that exact moment, it didn't really matter what you wanted. Branwyn packed it and repacked it three times since you've been asleep, to make sure the infection didn't continue to spread. To make sure you healed. Fucking realms. You're lucky you didn't lose your arm!"

"So what! I can't rest, Auriel! I don't have time! Don't you get it? Rhyan is an akadim! A Godsdamned fucking akadim!" I cried. "I can't even stand to think about what he's doing out there now. Or to think about Meera and Jules, and the rest of our friends. They're all just out there and vulnerable. I have to find them. I have to find all of them."

"And you will! You will. But not yet!" His eyebrows furrowed. "Can't you hear yourself? If I'd let you go out there with the fever you just recovered from, you'd have been captured instantly. Denied medical care by His Majesty, and then what? You would rather waste away in their dungeons? Did you want to stand trial for the murder of not only the Blade, but the Emperor? Stand trial for every other murder they manage to pin on you?" His nostrils flared. "You'd never find your friends. Nor Rhyan. Is that really what you want?"

I closed my mouth, my lips tightening together, refusing to answer him.

"Huh, Lyriana? Is it?" Auriel stalked toward me. "You are Asherah reborn. You are my soulmate."

"No." I violently shook my head.

But Auriel continued, "Her soul is your soul. I know you. And soon enough you will be as strong as she was. Stronger even. But you're not strong enough to fight this, not right now. Not yet. Your body is still mortal. And for some fucking reason, you seem hellbent on forgetting that fact."

"Forgetting?" I shouted. "You think I can forget? That I could watch my lover, my own soul, being torn away from me in the most violent way possible, and I'd just forget the rules of mortality? Trust me, I remember. Of course, I remember. What you don't understand is that right now, I don't care."

"Well you fucking should."

"I can't. There are bigger things happening than me. And if you can't handle that, then you should just leave." I folded my arms across my chest and looked away.

"Lyriana, be reasonable. Please. Whether you'll admit it or not, you needed the rest. The infection has cleared. Your fever, too."

I continued to stare ahead, refusing to meet his gaze.

Auriel made a noise low in his throat. "Fine. Ignore me. I've only been keeping cold compresses on your head, and rebandaging your arm every hour. Just so you know." He shook his head, his lips twitching in anger. "I sat there and held you while we cleaned out your arm. You're welcome."

"What do you want? A fucking medal for playing nurse?"

"I want you to stop fighting me like I'm your enemy. Like it's my fault what happened, or that I'm here. I want you to admit that I have your best interest at heart."

"How many hours?" I gritted through my teeth, my stomach twisting. "Huh, Auriel? How many hours did you force me to sleep for?"

"None. I didn't force you to sleep for any length of time," he yelled. "Your body woke up when it was ready to—when it was healed enough for you to go on."

"How many?" I asked again, my voice dangerously cold. "I didn't just fall asleep by natural means. It was you. Your magic. And if I stayed asleep through all this—" I pointed at my arm, "Then it was because you had a hand in it. So what was it? How many hours?"

His eyes met mine, his jaw tensing. "I stopped counting."

"When?"

"When I counted twenty-four."

"Twenty-four? Twenty-four fucking hours!" No. No. That couldn't be. My chest tightened, panic rising inside me. We didn't have that kind of time. I had to leave. I had to get out of here, find my way north.

"Lyriana!" Auriel yelled.

But I rushed past him to the table that stored my things, grabbing them in a blind rage. I felt farther than fucking Lethea, barely able to see straight I was so mad. I started to fasten my belt around my waist, attaching Rhyan's scabbard. I retrieved my blade next, shoving it through my belt. And bent down to lace up my boots, dizziness washing over me. But I didn't care. I had to be ready.

"By the fucking realms!" Auriel shouted. "What are you doing now?"

"Leaving! Twenty-four hours! Do you know what Rhyan could have done by now? What he could be doing at this very moment—if I'm not there to stop him?"

"I do know! And you won't stop him! Not like this."
"Go to hell!"
He laughed bitterly. "Don't worry. I already feel like I'm there!" he roared.

"If you really want to be sure, try crossing dimensions again. You've broken every other rule so far. I'm sure you'll reach hell soon enough."

"You think I can just cross dimensions?" he scoffed. "That because I'm a God, traveling between worlds and timelines is just something I can do? I haven't been mortal for a thousand years. And by the laws of the Council I shouldn't even be here now, but I am."

"So go then. Go back home."
"I can't!"
"You won't!"

Auriel reached for my shoulders, shaking me, but I twisted out of his hold.

"Stop touching me!" I said. "Just stop! I don't need your help!"

Auriel exhaled, throwing his head back and staring at the ceiling, his shoulders slumping. When he looked at me again, defeat was threaded through his expression as clearly as if he'd raised a white flag. And again the aura that came from him felt like a cloud descending, heavy and foggy, and confused. But above all, mortal. And weak.

"I might not be able to travel like Rhyan," he said, "but I can still help you. Still fight beside you. Protect you."

I scoffed. "I'll protect myself."

"I thought we were past this," he said quietly, and shook his head. Then his gaze shifted to the scabbard at my waist and his face softened. "Silver gryphon wings. Golden sun." There was something almost like defeat in his voice. "That's it isn't it?"

My hand moved protectively around the leather casing, my fingers tightening around it.

"The sigil of Ka Hart. *His* sigil." Auriel let out a shaky breath, taking a stumbling step backward. It was like he was retreating. Surrendering. "You're angry with me," he said softly, "not for anything I've done. But because I'm not him. That's what this is about. I'm not Rhyan. And you can't forgive me for it."

I could hear my heart pounding, like a drum in my ears, the backs of my eyes burning. "No," I seethed. "That's not it."

Auriel's face fell. He pressed his hand over his heart. "Yes it is. And you won't admit it—not even to yourself." His jaw tightened. "So be it. I'm sorry—if that's what you need to hear. I'm sorry I can't be him for you. I'm sorry my name's not Rhyan. I'm sorry I wasn't born in this timeline. Or born into the North. I'm sorry that it's not me who's your lover. Your partner."

"Stop it," I screamed, the panic rising inside of me again, like a nahashim twisting through my insides, squeezing around my heart, my lungs.

"You can't keep punishing me for something that's not my fault. And you can't keep punishing your—"

"I'm not punishing—"

"Yes, you are. That's why you got hurt—"

"I was fighting to survive," I cried. "Fighting for you!"

"And you're a better fighter than that. I would know. I've watched over you in this life. And I've trained and fought beside your soul myself. Fought beside you for centuries. And I saw—saw the moment it happened. The moment you were stabbed. You didn't see, but I knew something was wrong. And this," he pointed at me, "isn't you. You didn't want to rest, or heal, even with a damn hole in your arm ..." He shook his head, his eyes distant. "Fucking hell. There's more. You're blaming yourself for what happened to him. Aren't you? Trying to suffer in return? Even the score?"

"Shut. Up." A sense of dread washed through me.

He stepped back. "Well, let me tell you something, Lyriana, as someone who's been there before—been there more than once—you'll never suffer enough. You'll never hurt enough to defeat the pain, or ease your heartbreak. I know. I know that it will never be enough."

"Auriel, stop! Just stop it." I clutched at my chest. "You don't know what you're talking about." My breath was coming in short, painful gasps.

"I remember what this feels like. I felt the same way when I lost you the first time. When I buried you in your tomb."

I scoffed. "And did you promise Asherah you'd save her before she died? Did you swear to her, promise her with everything you had when she was dying in your arms, that nothing else would hurt her? Did you swear to protect her and then fail? Promise to heal her, seeing the hope in her eyes, only to abandon her to monsters? To let her become one herself? One you have to find and destroy now? Because if you didn't do that, didn't do what I did to him, didn't allow what I let happen to him," I shouted, my entire body shaking, "then you don't understand. You don't!"

"No." His eyes widened, watching me carefully, his body still. His eyes filled with tears, and he swallowed roughly. "I didn't."

I ran for the stairs, my stomach twisting. I needed to get out of there. Out of the fucking basement. Away from him. Away from Auriel. Because if he spoke again, I was going to lose it. I was going to fucking lose it. Already I couldn't stand to hear him speak, to hear the way he sounded like Rhyan—but not. I couldn't stand to hear his tone, and his humor, and warmth. Couldn't stand to hear it all come together into this perfectly packaged, completely familiar voice—one that called out to my heart and my soul. Identical in every way, except for one thing. Rhyan's accent.

He was him. He was him. But not him. Not him. Not even Rhyan was himself now. He was gone. He was …

"I can't breathe. I feel like I can't breathe!" Bile was rising up my throat, and my chest was pounding painfully. I practically fell up the stairs as I ran, my hands grasping for the next step as my feet stumbled behind me.

The door at the top of the landing opened suddenly. Sean appeared, torchlight flickering behind him.

"Lyriana?" he asked, startled. But immediately he reached for me, helping me up the last few steps, and pulling me to my feet.

"Sean, I'm sorry. I'm so sorry," I cried, my words rushing together. "Please. Please, I need to get out of here. I need—I need air. I need to—" I gasped, still finding breathing difficult.

"All right, it's all right," Sean said quickly. "It's okay. I can get you some fresh air." He wrapped his arm around my shoulder, leading me back to the kitchen.

I looked over my shoulder, back downstairs. Auriel had folded his arms across his chest at the base of the stairs. He looked away, but his aura reached for me. It was vibrating, bright and fiery with anger. But also, something that felt like it went beyond sadness.

"Sean, is she safe up there?" he asked, his words clipped.

Sean nodded. "For a little while, Auriel, yes. Ka Kormac is still out there. They're searching homes in the neighborhood, but they came by here already a little while ago. I think we can risk a short visit for her upstairs with protection."

I shook my head, still crying. "I'm sorry."

I'd totally forgotten why I was in the basement to begin with. The soturi were looking for me. And not just soturi from Bamaria—but every soturion in Ka Kormac. Every wolf. And every servant of the newly anointed Emperor. And they were coming here, interrogating Sean. Shit. He'd already been punished for hiding me. Sent to the pole by Turion Kevel. And I'd slept through it. Fuck. It wasn't enough that I'd failed Rhyan. Now I was hurting Sean, the family he loved and trusted most.

I took a step back, suddenly barely able to face him. To take in his curly hair, to hear his accent, to see his green eyes. The subtle ways I could tell that they were related. But beyond that, I could see the way he held his shoulder stiff and in pain. And the haunted look in his eyes. I'd done that. I'd caused that.

"I should go," I said, turning back. "You've done enough for me, Sean—risked so much already. I should just leave—"

"No, Lyriana," Sean said, extending his hand to mine. "Everything's okay here. Branwyn can arrange a ward for you. We have eyes on the streets—friends looking out for us. Remember how we got here—going through all those homes? Every single person whose home we entered is watching out for our best interest. If there's a problem, we'll have far more warning than we did the last time."

"But I'm putting you in danger," I gasped, still struggling to breathe.

"That's my job, Lyriana. I'm a soturion," Sean said. "And I swore my oath to more than just Bamaria. I swore to Ka Batavia. I swore to your father. All of that extends to you. My oath still stands. Protecting you, Your Grace, is an honor I gladly accept."

My eyes watered—for a whole new reason this time. No one had called me "Your Grace" in months. "I'm no longer an Heir to the Arkasva," I said quietly. "Not here, nor anywhere. Not anymore. You don't owe me anything."

"Rhyan loved you." He pressed his lips together, like he was trying not to cry. Then he nodded. "And you need my help. I have more reason than I need to offer my protection. Now, come with me."

I stumbled into his arms, and sobbed against his armor, breaking down so utterly and completely, I thought my heart would shatter. I hadn't let Auriel be there for me. But suddenly, I couldn't help myself. Maybe it was seeing my father in my dream, or just the sheer weight of everything I was carrying. But I gave in, letting Sean take some of the weight.

He tightened his arms around me, hugging me to him. His hand smoothed the back of my hair, like something my father used to do when I was a child. I sniffled, realizing he smelled like pine. Like Glemaria. Like Rhyan. It made me cry harder.

Sean waited a moment, letting me sob, then took my hand. "Let's get you that air. Hmmm?"

I nodded weakly and let Sean lead me through his house, into a sitting room, and then up another flight of stairs to the second floor. He led me down a long hallway, dimly lit by candlelight, and knocked on a door. "Love? It's me, and Lady Lyriana," he said.

Branwyn opened the door at once. I realized that this was their bedroom. Their private space.

I stood back, immediately feeling like I was encroaching on someplace intimate. Someplace I didn't belong.

"Come on in," Branwyn urged, and reached for my arm, gently squeezing it. "Please." Her eyes were soft, but as she looked back to Sean, they seemed to melt.

"She just needs some air," Sean said, his accent thick. "Can you ward the balcony for her?"

"Of course." Branwyn smiled again at me, inviting me inside, trying to make me feel welcome. Then she crossed the room to a set of glass doors, and opened them onto a modestly sized balcony. It was just large enough to hold two chairs and a round table between them. Just enough for two people. For a couple.

I stood awkwardly inside the room as Branwyn moved swiftly around the balcony. Again and again she waved her stave about as she silently created the ward.

"She's a very talented mage," Sean said, watching her with obvious pride in his eyes. "Branwyn makes the most powerful wards of anyone I know. I promise, you won't be seen or heard for miles."

I nodded numbly, glancing around their bedroom while she finished. I didn't mean to do it, but I started obsessing over all of the little details—the pieces that pulled the room together. That made it theirs.

Their bed was large and looked warm, full of thick green blankets—Glemarian green. They were already pulled back, the sheets exposed, like it was ready for them to crawl into at the end of the day. Together. Hanging on the wall above were a set of paintings. One was of a silver gryphon. The other a golden seraphim. They'd been magically infused, and the gryphon and seraphim's wings fluttered softly, their eyes gazing into each other.

Loose scrolls, half-read, lay on night tables on either side of the bed. Both held candles that were half-melted. A few more scrolls remained tucked into leather cases, piled neatly behind them. A cozy chair sat in the corner with a blanket draped across it. One of Sean's soturion cloaks had been tossed onto the arm-rest, and beside it was the dummy used for storing his armor.

Directly across from the bed was a dresser and mirror. Branwyn's jewelry lay scattered over it, along with small bottles of perfume. Hanging from a half-open drawer was a black leather belt—the kind soturi wore while training.

There was an aura to the room—not something I normally felt—an intimacy that existed between them—as thick and tangible as the items within. It was so clear from just seeing the room for even just a moment, how often, and how happily, Sean and Branwyn spent time here together. It was nothing fancy, nothing like I was used to at Cresthaven. But I could feel it. Feel how in love they were. Their energy was attached to the room, existing on its own. I'd had a sense of this once before, the way I'd felt Rhyan's energy when I'd woken up in his old bedroom in Seathorne. The way I'd known it was his room without having to be told.

I never would have imagined this—having lived most of my life in something far larger and fancier, but this was my dream bedroom. Simple. Intimate. Full of love.

I swallowed, turning back to the balcony. Away from the scene. Away from the bed of a Glemarian man happily married to a Bamarian woman.

A gryphon and a seraphim.

Auriel and Asherah.

Me and Rhyan.

Marry me.

I stifled back a cry, reaching for the scabbard at my hip. For Rhyan's gift. And suddenly, I found myself mentally trying to replace all of Sean and Branwyn's things with mine and Rhyan's. Asherah's chest plate would lay on the dresser beside my gold bangles, beside the seraphim wing cuff I always wore. I imagined Rhyan's beat up leathers on the dummy. Tiny love notes he'd leave for me on the nightstand. Extra bottles of suntree paste I could rub on any of his training injuries.

One painting above the bed instead of two—a gryphon and a seraphim together, a sun above and a moon below.

Our own sigil. The one of our kashonim. The one was that was uniquely ours.

I closed my eyes. We'd never have that now.

The sky outside was gloomy and gray, the sun in the process of setting.

Auriel had said more than twenty-four hours. But it was worse than that. We'd arrived in the early morning. It had been more than a full day and a half. Which meant it had been two days since I'd seen Rhyan. Since I'd lost him. I watched the sun go down, realizing that as soon as it vanished over the horizon, that this would have been the exact moment he'd changed. The moment he'd have gone from being forsaken to akadim.

I felt dizzy thinking about it. Nauseated. Was he alone when it happened? Confused? Scared? Was he in pain?

Branwyn stepped back inside the room, replacing her stave at her hip, and gestured for me to come out. But I couldn't move. For a second, I'd forgotten how to walk, my feet heavy and glued to the ground, my mind lost to Rhyan's transformation.

Sean wrapped his arm around my shoulder, and gently led me outside.

"Here." He pointed to a chair. "Sit down. Take a breath. No one can see you or hear you out here. So long as no other uninvited soturi arrive, you should be okay for a while. I'm going to get you some water to drink, and a blanket in case you're cold. Are you hungry at all?"

"I'm not hungry." I sank into the chair, and pulled my knees up to my chest, staring at the trees.

I couldn't even remember the last time I'd tasted food. Rhyan had made me eat that final morning. Back at the inn in Thene. I'd had no idea that it would be our last morning together, that it would be our last breakfast as he'd fed me a forkful of eggs, urging me to eat more. To recover my strength. My stomach twisted, though I wasn't sure if it was in hunger, or simply in pain from the memory. All the times Rhyan had cared for me, all the times he'd made sure I ate, made sure I was okay …

Sean squeezed my shoulder. "I'll be right back, Lyriana. We'll give you some privacy. Okay?"

I tried to nod, and waited for Sean to close the balcony door before I sobbed again. Pulling the scabbard from my belt, I clutched it to my heart, my tears rolling down the leather, making the sun and moon shine.

"Partner." Rhyan snuck up behind me.

"Thank the Gods! You're back," I said.

"Mmmmhhhhmmm," he murmured against my skin, his arms wrapping around me from behind. *"I got some more materials for Meera's soturion uniform. And I brought back more food for you both. I filled two bags with it. She's currently chopping everything up for dinner."*

I leaned back against him, letting him take my weight, reveling in the sturdy feel of his body against mine. Of the strength he projected. The strength I felt just being near him. His skin was still chilled from being out all day on patrol in the Glemarian mountains. But I could feel him warming against me, taking on my heat. He tightened his hold on me, our bodies pressed together.

"I thought you'd come home sooner," I said, my voice hushed.

"I'm sorry, I wanted to."

"No trouble out there?" I asked.

"No. None." His lips skimmed along the side of my neck, leaving small shivers running down my spine. They moved lower, growing warmer, down to my belly, between my legs. *"Other than ..."* He grinned, and I could feel the movement, feel his lips turn up. It made me smile in turn. *"I missed you,"* he said, and brushed his nose against my skin, inhaling deeply. Rhyan pressed a kiss to that very spot at the base of my neck, and then my shoulder, as his fingers moved in lazy circles over my belly.

"I missed you, too," I said, and turned in his arms, our lips meeting.

"Mmmmm," he hummed against my mouth. Then kissed the corner of my lips, squeezing his arms tightly around me. *"I got you something,"* he said, pulling back. He offered a sort of shy smile, like he was embarrassed by the offering. But then he reached behind his back, and placed it in my hands. A black leather

scabbard—the kind used to hold staves. "It's not much, but I saw this and I, well—"

"I love it," I said, stroking the leather. *It was already soft and worn, and the perfect size to fit Asherah's stave.* "It looks just like your old armor, especially with the sigil."

Rhyan was still smiling shyly. "They didn't have any with sigils for Ka Batavia."

"I don't care about that. I love this one. It reminds me of you." *I wrapped my arms around him, kissing him again.* "Rhyan, it's perfect. Thank you."

"Check inside," *he said, opening it for me. The letters L.B. had been painted in gold.* "I had it personalized." *He kissed my forehead.* "I wanted it to feel like yours."

My heart swelled. How did this man always know exactly what to do, what to say? What I needed?

He pushed my hair behind my ears, his palms cupping my cheeks. "I know the last few days have been rough. Since the Allurian Pass." *He shook his head, and smiled ruefully.* "I just ... I wanted to do something to make you smile."

The memory faded, and I cried even harder, remembering Rhyan's lips on my skin. His soft touch. His thoughtfulness. I missed him. I missed everything about him. Being able to whisper secrets to him when we were alone, knowing that no matter what I told him, however awful or embarrassing, he never judged me. He just listened, and he understood. Loving me, and always, always protecting me ...

"You swore, Lyr. You swore you'd make the pain go away. You swore no one else would hurt me. You lied."

My vision blurred, the tears like an avalanche.

The balcony doors reopened, the sound mixing with the wind blowing through my hair. Seraphim birds chirped in the distant sky. And a few yards away, children were laughing. Playing. Being called inside now that it was dark. They had no idea. No idea the world was falling apart.

Sean stepped back onto the balcony with Branwyn, and this time, their arms were full. Between the two of them, they held a green blanket, a silver tray with a clear jug of water, and a decanter of something golden. Whisky perhaps. Several glasses balanced on the tray. There was also a second platter, this one filled with food.

"I'm really not hungry," I said weakly. They'd loaded the tray with far more than I could ever attempt to eat, revealing even more. There was a fresh loaf of bread with several dips, a bowl of nuts, some slices of cake—chocolate. Beside that there were pistachio cookies, hard-boiled eggs, as well as two bowls of fruit, one full of melons, the other berries.

"That's all right," Sean said. "There's no requirement to. But it's here if you want it. If you change your mind."

Branwyn handed the blanket to me and squeezed my shoulder. "I'll be just inside. Call out to me if you need anything, Lady Lyriana. Anything at all. You let me know."

I nodded. "Thank you."

"Oh," she said, "And, um, I wanted to thank you for the warning about my grandparents."

I sat up. "Cal and Marisol? Are they okay?" I blinked rapidly. "Did you hear from them? Any word about my friends, my family?"

Branwyn frowned. "No, I'm sorry—we don't know their current whereabouts. I'll let Sean fill you in on what's happened. Your friends and family evacuated the inn before the Emperor's soturi arrived. Cal and Marisol didn't have any more information than that. They were already gone when I called, and in the process of getting everyone out as a precaution. They thank you for the warning and for trying to help."

"But they're safe," I said, like I was trying the words on—remembering that not everyone had been damned. Not yet. Though a part of me, a part getting louder, was starting to hear the words she wasn't saying. That there was danger. And the fates of my loved ones were unknown. "If you hear anything else, Branwyn, from your grandparents, or if they know anything about my friends, will you tell me?"

She nodded, smiling sadly. "You have my word." Then she went inside, closing the door behind her.

Sean sat down, and without saying anything, poured me a glass of water, and placed it in my hand. I didn't want to drink it, but I was thirsty. So I did.

We sat in silence, the sky growing darker and darker with each passing minute. He lit the torches on either end of the balustrade. Then he heaped together a plate of food, one that seemed to hold one of everything. He slid it across the table to me, before picking up the whisky. Two glasses were filled a moment later, the wind blowing softly with an unusually cold gust.

"This is your home?" I said suddenly, needing to break the silence. Needing to discuss something other than Rhyan. Anything that wasn't currently shattering my world.

Sean nodded. "Of course, why?"

"The way we came here," I said. "Why did we have to go through that maze of houses first?"

"Well, there was the curfew," he said. "Soturi were everywhere and watching. You couldn't be seen."

"No, I understand that part. But the pattern, the homes you entered." I gestured to the house next door. "They were ready for you—like they knew you were coming. And you knew where you were going. You didn't falter once. Like you've done that before."

"I have done that before. Many times." He settled back into his chair. "It's a route that was created around the time I moved here. Every house you entered yesterday—every yard you went through—they belong to a former Glemarian."

I recalled the small hints of Glemaria I'd seen. Gryphons, the scent of pine, like someone had captured the smell of Glemaria in a fragrance. Or maybe they all used the same soap—like Rhyan meticulously did. I could see it all clearly. Their houses were all filled with trinkets of home—their true home. Reminders of the North.

"I didn't know there were so many of you here." Though I should have—especially having met the Northern Imperator. "I'm sorry," I said. "I really only knew of you and Rhyan."

Sean nodded. "We try to stay pretty quiet—out of trouble. We're not exactly welcome. But there's more of us than you think. I mean, it's not like we could escape all Imperators by coming here. In some ways the South was more volatile for us. Kormac knew we could be used against Devon. Luckily, he was occupied with other things. But yes, there are plenty more than just the two—" He coughed, his jaw tensed. "Of us." Sean took a sip of his whisky.

"I never knew, how did you come to live in Bamaria?"

"The same way as everyone else. Forced to leave. Forced out of the North by Devon Hart." He gritted his teeth. "Some of us just pissed him off. Others—like Rhyan—he couldn't control. Some, like me, he considered his political enemies."

In the distance a seraphim squawked, the call growing with intensity as the bird flew overhead. Sean stilled, his mouth tight. I wondered if he missed home. Missed the sounds of gryphons in the sky. Like Rhyan used to.

He turned the glass in his hand, his fingers tapping against the drink before he continued.

"The route was something that began back then."

"The route?" I asked. "You mean stopping at Cal and Marisol's?"

"Not just that. You can't escape Devon's ire just by leaving Glemaria. Too many other countries fear retribution from him as Imperator. And he rewards the return of those he believes have wronged him very handsomely. So the route was formed. Friends, family, Kavim, anyone that opposed Devon were all part of it. It's more than you know. He's not well liked in the North. There's even some other groups with different missions entirely, oppositions and rebellions focused on the South, particularly against Ka Kormac that will also help us out and provide shelter when needed. The policies of both Imperators are deeply unpopular. But there's particular ire with Devon's responses to the akadim attacks over the years."

"He lets them in," I said. "He ignores the threat."

Sean nodded. "The more afraid people are, the more fearful he can make the population, the more he can force them to rely on him. To look to his leadership. Not ask questions. But there are plenty—particularly amongst the educated—who see the truth. Who take the time to see through his lies, his corruption." He took a breath. "Though, the closer you are to him, the harder he can make it to see. He's good at maintaining his image with the Council. Or forcing it, I suspect with blood oaths, blood contracts. But there's cracks. Cracks I took advantage of whenever I could."

He took another sip. "I was always on Devon's bad side, even when we were kids. Even though I was younger, it never stopped me from standing up to him. Keeping him from bullying the other students when we were at the Academy. When we were adults, I wouldn't stay quiet about his policies. His treatment of his wife. And especially his treatment of Rhyan," his voice broke, "I was always after him for the way he treated Rhyan." Sean stopped talking, his fingers clenched into a fist. He looked past me, his gaze distant, his eyes dark green as night darkened around us. "I tried to take him away. More than once. I even made arrangements with his mother, with Bowen, his bodyguard. But I could never quite pull it off. Never get close enough to him to make it happen—not since Devon realized what I was up to. Every time I failed to get Rhyan out of his grasp, to get a better life for him, to bring him here—Devon made it harder." Sean shook his head, staring out at the black horizon beyond the trees. All that remained of the sun now was gone.

"I'm sorry," I said, my voice hushed. Things could have been different for Rhyan. Better. He could have come here sooner—not forsworn. Just as a student. Not been abused, not tortured. We could have come together ages ago, not been forbidden from being together. A whole other life for him flashed before my eyes. And just as quickly, that dream died.

"You wouldn't have known about it," Sean said. "Because Rhyan didn't even know—his father made sure of it. One day, Devon had had enough of me. I'd—well, I'd been drinking, and forgot myself. I just remember screaming at him, telling him every horrible thing about him. What an utter shit of a man he turned out to be. What a monstrous sorry excuse for a father.

"He accused me of all kinds of crap, wanting his Seat, his wife, wishing I was Rhyan's father. I had no designs on his power, or Lady Shakina, but he was right about the latter. If Rhyan could have been my son ..." He swallowed roughly, his throat bobbing, his jaw tightening.

"I was exiled on the spot," Sean continued. "He said I'd be named forsworn if I didn't leave—and he said I'd never see Rhyan again if I didn't. He forced a blood oath on me, then soturi escorted me home, searched my belongings as I packed, and followed me to the border—followed me until I hit Numeria." He bit his lip, shaking his head at the memory. "Honestly, for him, that was merciful. But that's why Rhyan never knew. Never knew that my coming here hadn't been my choice. He never knew that I'd have done anything to stay in the North, anything to be there for him. To save him. I was fighting tooth and nail. But Devon," he let out a shaky breath, "well, you've met him."

"I have," I said bitterly.

Sean made a noise low in his throat. "Eventually, I found my people here. And I fell in love. Branwyn." His lips lifted as he said her name. "But as wonderful as Bamaria was, I always knew that I had to be ready. I knew that a new Emperor could be anointed at any time. A new Imperator for the region. A new Arkasva for the country. One who was not as kind as your father. Or your mother. Laws that once protected us could be rewritten—former enemies of the state pardoned, and former friends named as criminals. Especially while under a cruel and corrupt ruler like Kormac. So we Northerners banded together here. And we practiced—hiding, evading, like we did at home. We knew we needed to be ready. Ready for this day. For yesterday. Ready for whatever else comes next. Because the truth is, when it comes to the idea of justice and freedom," he sighed, "the fight never ends. It just pauses from time to time."

I nodded, and more silence fell between us. Sean refilled his glass of whisky. The glass he'd poured for me was still full on the table.

"Here," he offered, pushing it toward me. "Drink this. But you must promise, you'll eat something, too."

I sniffed the alcohol, and took a sip. Then another. And before I knew it, I'd finished my glass, letting the liquid burn my throat as I swallowed.

"Now eat," Sean commanded, already pouring me another shot. He downed his, then again replenished the drink.

I popped a piece of bread into my mouth, chewing slowly. Despite drinking both the whisky and water, my throat still felt dry. I tossed back my second shot, slamming the glass down on the table in a clear request for another.

Sean obliged.

"This is probably a bad idea," he said, "Especially right after you were sick. Auriel won't approve."

"I don't care what Auriel thinks."

"Well, I'm not sure I approve either. But considering the circumstances—I don't know what else to do. He filled me in, you know—while you were sleeping. Everything I missed—all the details. What actually happened to Rhyan." He looked away, like he was trying to compose himself. Then poured me another shot.

Immediately, I drew the glass toward my lips, Sean watching me carefully. I paused, a sinking feeling in my stomach.

"You're not—" I eyed the glass, my heart pounding, "I mean, this isn't just to make me feel better. Is it?"

"No," Sean said. "It's not."

I set the glass down, my body crawling with uneasiness. "What are you trying to do then?"

"Prepare you," Sean said. "For what I'm about to tell you."

I squeezed my eyes shut and my stomach twisted. It was about Rhyan. He knew something about Rhyan. Something new. Something awful. I could already feel the bile rising up my throat, could feel my body rejecting the news. Rejecting everything. I opened my eyes, and stared blankly ahead.

"Just tell me," I said.

"Your warning to Branwyn was appreciated. She is more grateful than you know for trying to help."

I nodded, my body going numb. "And?"

"And I know you were trying to help your friends, too. We got word about ... what's been happening in Thene. What happened already."

My body started to shiver, and I pulled the blanket up over my shoulders, my fingers tightening around Rhyan's scabbard, running over the embroidery; the sun, the moon. The gryphon. "What?"

"There have been multiple attacks in the city the past two days," he said.

I exhaled, nodding for him to go on, my blood pulsing in my eardrums.

"The first attack came from Numeria. The Emperor's soturi arrived from the capital. Two nights ago, not long after—after it happened—his wolves invaded Thene. They were searching for you. And, from the sounds of it—they were also searching for your friends. Your sister."

My vision blurred. He hadn't mentioned my cousin. No mention of Jules. Was that good? Did that mean they didn't know who she was? Or that Emperor Avery was keeping her escape quiet?

"And?" I asked.

"Your friends left the inn before the soturi arrived. Cal and Marisol sent them away just in time. They gave them the address of some allies—people they trust with their lives to keep them hidden. It's a similar network to what we have here."

"So they're safe?" I asked.

Sean took a deep, slow breath. "We don't know. Cal and Marisol said they got out before the soturi could find them. But they haven't heard from any of them since. They likely didn't stay in one place for too long."

"Why not? If they were somewhere safe? With someone Cal and Marisol trusted?"

"They were. But word is just getting out now that the Emperor arrested the soturion responsible for killing Theotis. They're claiming you hired him."

"What!"

"Apparently, his soturi found him with Lord Tristan."

My eyes widened. "No. No."

Sean frowned. "Cal and Marisol said he was part of the group."

"He was." My heart sank.

"I'm so sorry," Sean said. "He was … he was executed."

"Galen!" I cried out. I covered my mouth to keep from screaming. How much more pain was I supposed to hold. Galen had always been a friend, always kind and gentle and protective. Always at Tristan's side—and even when things between me and Tristan were falling apart, when Haleika's death had come between us—Galen was still there when I needed him. Fuck. Fuck!

"And what about Tristan? What did they do to him?" I asked.

Sean shook his head. "They're saying he helped find and apprehend Galen. He's back in Bamaria with the Emperor's favor."

My eyes widened. No. No he wouldn't betray Galen. He was his best friend. And he'd—he'd fought with us, helped us. He wouldn't just turn around and work with the Imperator—the Emperor—again, would he?

Gods. It couldn't be true. Not after what he'd done, what he'd told me. He was vorakh. The Empire was using him. Making him play along. The way they tried to use me.

I squeezed my eyes shut, feeling like I was going to vomit. I would grieve for Galen. I had to. But when this was over, when I could grieve for Rhyan, too. I'd grieve for everyone when the time came.

I tried to take a deep breath and prayed. Prayed that this was it. I didn't want to grieve for anyone else. Please, please, please let Jules, Meera, Aiden, and Dario be safe.

Sean poured another glass, and offered it to me. "I'm sorry to be the one to tell you this. But the next attack that occurred in the city today—was …" he paused, like he was trying to gather his thoughts.

"Was what?" I asked, my stomach twisting with nerves. I couldn't take much more.

"The next attack the city suffered was carried out by akadim."

I turned in my seat, still clutching Rhyan's scabbard, my grip growing tighter and tighter.

"The akadim that attacked ... fuck." Sean pressed the heel of his palm to his eyes. "Rhyan was there. Cal and Marisol both saw him. In broad fucking daylight. He—" Sean looked sick. "He killed—turned ..." He sighed. "They saw him. And it—Gods, it was a massacre. Right about now ... now that the sun's down, there's at least two dozen new akadim in the world. All created by him."

The sound of despair that came from my mouth startled me. I pressed my hand between my teeth to stop myself from doing it again.

"They all turned?" I asked.

Sean nodded.

They all turned. Because of me. I let this happen. It was my fault. My fucking fault. I'd slept for two days. I hadn't gone right after Rhyan. Because I'd been too weak. Too foolish. Even now I didn't know if I could do it, and I had to. The evidence was right in front of me. Cal and Marisol were in danger. My friends were in danger. Jules and Meera were in danger, and it was coming from every direction. From the Emperor. From Rhyan. Every day I let him live, more would die.

But even now, I could feel myself wanting to crawl back into bed. To pretend I didn't know.

"What about Rhyan?" I said. "He can't—"

"He can't be allowed to exist like this," Sean said simply. "I can't allow it. Not as a soturion who swore an oath to protect people. Not as an uncle who loved his nephew. He can't remain akadim. Not for himself. Not for the boy he was. The man he became, and the man—the man he would have been. He wouldn't want this."

"He wouldn't," I said, my voice barely above a whisper. "That's why I need to leave. I need to … to hunt him." More tears fell, it felt like someone was squeezing my heart, strangling it between their hands.

"You don't have to be the one to do it," Sean said. "I've been fighting a long time. Seen more than my fair share of evil. I can be the one. I can go after him."

"I can fight," I gritted through my teeth.

"No. I know you can. I've seen you in the arena. I heard what you did to the Blade. That's not what I meant. Not why I offered." Sean's jaw tensed. "It's because I've been thinking—wondering what I'd do in your shoes. If it was Branwyn who'd been changed—who'd fallen to this fate. And I can't," his voice shook, "can't imagine having to be the one to stop her—to … to *kill* her. But for Rhyan, it has to be done. He'd want that. Before he hurt too many people. I know it in my heart. I've known him his whole life, loved him since he was a baby. He's my nephew." He shook his head, like he was still convincing himself of what had to happen, what had to be done. "But more than that. He's part of me."

"He's part of me, too," I whispered.

Sean wiped his eyes. "He loved you, Lyriana. He loved you so much. And he trusted you above everyone else. So, if the love you bear for him makes you feel as if you need to be the one to do this—then so be it. I'll go with you. I'll support you in any way I can, watch your back, take care of you when it's over. If you want me to." His eyes darkened. "But if you can't do this, or if you don't want to—please believe me when I say that Rhyan would never fault you for that. And neither would I. But we do need to decide. Because one of us has to do it. And based on what happened today, it needs to happen soon."

I turned away from Sean, staring back at the horizon. At the stars beginning to twinkle in the early night sky. The lights blurred against my tears, and my chest tightened.

"I know," Sean said, "you're worried about your family, your friends. You can go after them. Make sure they're safe. I'll take care of Rhyan. Just tell me what you want to do."

"I don't know. Can you—can you give me some time?" I asked. "To decide."

"You can have the rest of tonight," Sean said, his voice hardening. "I wish I could give you more than that. But for Rhyan's sake, I think it's best this happens quickly, so there's as little damage done in his memory as possible. There's already been too much. And then once it's over, I can … I can properly grieve for him. Honor his memory." He sniffed. "As can you. We'll be able to say goodbye to Rhyan. The way he deserves. After we kill the monster, then we can set him free."

CHAPTER THIRTEEN

LYRIANA

Say goodbye to Rhyan? Say goodbye? The idea felt preposterous. Some part of me still felt like this was a nightmare—a bad dream I'd wake from soon. But it wasn't. It wasn't.

I sat with Sean still, the two of us staring into the dark in silence. I kept contemplating his words, and thinking over what had to be done, making choice after choice in my head. And every choice I made, I felt sicker and sicker. Nothing felt right.

I'd already known what had to happen. What I had to do. But I'd been trying to avoid it. To make it go away. To pass it off to someone else.

I didn't want that either. What I wanted, was it to have never happened.

An hour passed, and then another. I cried. I listened to Sean cry. I drank some more. And I ate. Sean did the same. Finally, when the chill of the night air became too much, when I couldn't listen to Sean's tears any longer without wanting to die, when I couldn't be reminded any longer of Rhyan when Sean's northern lilt came out, we stood up, and both walked inside. Cold, and numb, our eyes red and swollen.

Branwyn was already waiting, and offered hugs to both of us. I could tell from the look in Sean's eyes, and the feel of his aura, he needed his wife. He needed her comfort.

And I went to seek out Auriel.

I took long, slow breaths as I headed down the stairs. Reminding myself that I could get through this. Get through the next five minutes. That was all I had to do. I didn't have to decide anything yet. I didn't have to do anything tonight. Just breathe. Just survive. Five minutes at a time.

Find a way to get through the next five minutes without answers. When you get through them, get through five more. Enough of those minutes become a day, and before you know it, those days become weeks. I've survived for months like this. It's enough.

Rhyan had told me that just after he returned to Bamaria, when we met in the middle of the night at the Temple of Dawn. It was the very first night Mercurial had approached me. The first night of his manipulations.

My hands fisted, remembering the Afeyan's taunts about my use of *Rakashonim* in the arena two nights ago. The Gods-damned immortal bastard.

I'd never forgive him. Never forgive him for the way he stood back when Rhyan needed him, when I needed him. When the akadim attacked, and Mercurial just watched. I could see him so clearly, his blue skin, and his human-like head replaced with that of a falcon. He had refused to help me while I was desperately searching for Rhyan in the attack—desperately trying to save him. And that bastard still wanted me to go after the fucking red shard. To fulfill my end of the bargain. To fully claim my power as Asherah, as a Goddess.

What did it fucking matter now? I'd called on Asherah's power. It hadn't been enough. And the bargain we'd made—his silence about my relationship with Rhyan was worthless now. Because he was gone. And I was forsworn. And from the sound of it, the truth was out anyway.

I found Auriel sitting on the edge of the bed. He was hunched over, his face in his hands. His aura reached out toward me, quietly, almost unsure. But there was something else. It felt different from before. There was no more fire. No more anger. Just a profound, heart-wrenching sadness that seemed to overtake him. The power of his aura was weaker, too, cloudier and murkier than ever. Like it had lost more strength. Lost even more potency.

My heart softened, and our fight—all of the horrible things I'd said to him, the terrible ways I'd acted towards him—came back to me.

Gently, I sat down beside him, reaching for his hand. He didn't move, but he let me take it into my lap, let me entwine our fingers together. I could feel the uneven skin, the scars from the burns that covered his palms. Rough and raised in some parts, and smooth and indented in others. Without thinking I began to rub small circles into his skin with my thumb. It was just like something I would do for Rhyan. Like something I needed to do for him now, but couldn't. What I would give to touch him again. To hold him. To ease his pain.

His words from my dream still haunted me. *You swore no one else would hurt me. You lied.*

"Auriel," I said, my voice hushed. "Rhyan's already made his first kill." I swallowed. "His first …" My throat tightened, "kills."

Auriel frowned, but nodded slowly. "I know. I think I felt it—the moment it happened. It hurt—it injured me. Then Sean confirmed it. We had time to talk while you slept, for me to fill him in on exactly what happened."

I nodded. "He told me about that."

Auriel bit the inside of his cheek, continuing to stare ahead.

"Did you tell Sean who you are?" I asked.

Auriel shook his head. "No. And he hasn't pressed the issue, but I get the impression that he knows exactly who I am. What I am. Even if he has no explanation for it. He's a lot like Rhyan. Perceptive. Maybe too perceptive. But I think, at least, knowing that—it made him feel a little better."

"That's good then. He deserves that. He needs it."

"Though apparently, it's not helping you at all." He made a noise low in his throat, and he looked down. "For you, my existence is having the opposite effect."

"Auriel," I said.

He shook his head. "It's okay. I understand. I mean, I was never meant to replace him, or be some kind of compensation—especially not for you. I just want you to feel better. Because I care. Do you feel better?" Leaning closer to me, he asked, "Did going upstairs help? Getting air?"

Shrugging, I said, "Yes. And no." I frowned. "Auriel, I'm sorry."

He turned his head slowly, watching me with guarded eyes. It only made me soften more. Knowing the effect I had on him. On a God.

On the man I'd once loved when I was Asherah. The man I still loved to this day because my soul remembered his. And the man, or rather, the God, who was all that remained of Rhyan. Because he was him. He was. It became clearer with every moment.

I remembered how I felt after I'd found out the truth. That I was Asherah. Even before I knew Rhyan was Auriel, I'd felt differently towards the God. I'd felt more love for him. I'd felt a supreme sense of love even just from hearing his name. It had become precious to me. Sacred almost. And I'd done nothing to honor that since he'd arrived. Since he'd left Heaven to come here.

"Auriel, I'm sorry for what I said before. For how I treated you. You didn't deserve any of that. Especially not from me."

Tears filled Auriel's eyes and he nodded. "Lyriana." He practically whispered my name, his voice hushed.

"I don't want to fight with you anymore." I squeezed his hand. "You were right about what you said. You were right about everything. I was punishing you. And punishing myself. But mostly I ..." I swallowed roughly. "I didn't want to be the one to kill him. I couldn't bear it. But I also couldn't bear the thought of him going on like this. Of knowing he's out there in the world, existing in this form. Knowing what I have to do—what has to happen to end this. That knowing is almost worse for me, more horrific than the moment when I realized—when I knew that—that he died."

Auriel leaned in toward me, his arms pulling me in for a hug. "Oh, *Meka*. There's nothing to forgive. You were right, too. I don't know exactly what this is like. And I'm sorry. I was too harsh with you before. I'm mortal now—in body, and in mind. I can't—" He shook his head. "I've been struggling to remember so much. To remember everything I knew. Every purpose I had. Since I've come down here again—everything is so harsh, and hard. I feel like I'm trying to run through water. I keep moving my feet, I keep running, and I keep getting nowhere. I think the journey ... it took something from me."

"Auriel," I said, and buried my face in the crook of his neck, content to simply breathe, to just be held for a little. And to hold him, too. Even if he wasn't who I wanted. Or who I needed. He was close enough. The sense of failure I had for Rhyan, the utter devastation that losing him had left me with, made me need to comfort Auriel. I needed it like air to breathe. I needed to do whatever I could for him. At least give to him what I'd failed to do for Rhyan. I held him tighter.

After a few moments passed, Auriel asked more about my talk with Sean.

"He said he would do it," I said quietly, my voice small. "He said he'd hunt Rhyan down. It doesn't have to be me." But even saying the words, my stomach was in knots. There was a wrongness to it. To the idea of hurting Rhyan, or hunting him—even in his present form.

Auriel pulled back, his eyes searching mine. "How do you feel about that?"

I shook my head. "I don't know. I'd already made up my mind to do it the other night. That it had to be done. That it had to be me," I cried, then shook my head, blinking back fresh tears. "But hearing Sean say he'd do it?" I shrugged. "I thought that would fill me with relief. But it didn't. It feels worse for some reason. And I think that means …" The tears started falling. "I think it means that I need to be the one. I just have this feeling, this sense that I have to find him. That I need to go to him."

Auriel's eyes seemed to darken. "But you don't want to."

I sniffled, biting my lip to get the words out. "No. Of course, not. Gods. It's such a fucking nightmare."

Auriel nodded and pulled me back into a hug, his hands moving up and down my spine with soothing strokes.

"Look, it's late. There's nothing to be done tonight. And nothing to be decided. You should get some rest. You need it. And so do I."

I shook my head. "I've slept so much in the last forty-eight hours. I don't think I can."

"You've also been through so much in the last forty-eight hours that you must." He pressed his lips together, watching me carefully. "Sleep, Lyriana. Real sleep. Being down here, I forgot how much a mortal body needs it—how much our magic needs it to replenish. It will help. Any lingering pain, or fever you have. Any weakness or clouding of your mind. In the morning, you'll feel stronger, and you'll be ready to make your next move."

I sighed. "I know. I just don't feel like I can."

"I'll help," he whispered. "Again."

I stiffened.

"Not with magic. I swear. I'll just sit beside you until you're dreaming. Or I can sing to you, rub your back. Whatever you want. Whatever you need to fall asleep."

"Will you—" My throat went dry. And I remembered Rhyan saying something so similar to me after my father died. I needed the same thing as I did then. "Will you hold me?"

Auriel looked relieved. "Of course. Go on. Lay your head down."

I did, and I felt Auriel shift behind me a moment later, pulling me against him. He removed my belt, and the weapons I'd strapped to it. But I took the scabbard, holding it in my hands, and clutching it to my chest. There were fresh cloaks bundled on the table, and some folded clothes. Probably from Sean. I had a sinking feeling that they were spares Rhyan had kept here.

"Do you need anything else?" Auriel asked.

"No."

His arm wrapped around me. "Now sleep," he whispered.

I let out a shuddering breath, and closed my eyes, listening to his slow, even breaths. I was asleep within seconds, realizing only at the last second, as unconsciousness was taking me, that Auriel was still wearing his armor.

And whether it was thanks to the Gods, or Auriel's presence, his body acting like a balm for mine—a deceit of Rhyan's body—I slept. But I didn't dream.

My eyes opened early the next morning. Auriel's arm was still wrapped around me, his hand resting on my hip. Warm. Familiar.

But wrong.

I started to shift away and sit up, but his hand flattened against me.

"Hey," he said, his voice groggy. "You're up?"

"Mmmmhmmm." I turned around, laying on my side to face him. There were some dark circles under his eyes, and his curls were mussed, but otherwise, he looked like he did the night before.

"Hey," he said again, his eyes soft and still heavy with sleep.

"Hi," I breathed. "Did you sleep okay?"

He winced. "Not really."

"Because of me?" I asked, a little embarrassed.

His eyes darkened, grazing down my body, then back up to my face. "Well, I haven't had to share my bed with a mortal in a long time." He winked. "And you kick a lot."

"I do not!" I yelled.

He laughed. "Okay, you don't."

I rolled my eyes, and pushed playfully at his shoulder. He was still wearing his armor, which I imagined couldn't have been comfortable. I sat up suddenly, feeling shy at how close we were and got off the bed, trying to put some distance between us.

But when I looked back, he was struggling to sit up, and wincing. His neck was turning red. Then he flinched when his armor seemed to push against him.

My eyes narrowed. "Auriel, why did you sleep in your armor?"

His lips tugged down. "I forgot to remove it—another mortal body thing I have to remember."

"You're lying," I said. His face was pinched, his words had been clipped. "You're in pain."

"No," he said.

I felt it suddenly in his aura. He *was* in pain. "Then take your armor off," I said.

"Trying to get me naked?" He winked, but it looked like it hurt him to do it.

"Auriel?" I asked.

All the humor he was attempting drained from his face.

Finally, he sat up. But he was moving slowly, and looked like he was having trouble breathing. Like just sitting up in the bed had been too much effort.

"You couldn't take your armor off, could you?" I said, searching his eyes. "You're hurt."

He jerked back from me, his lips pursed together, and his jaw tensed. "I'm fine." Auriel nodded vigorously, as if he was trying to convince himself. "I'll recover. Just some ..." he flinched again, "broken ribs I think. From the fall. And then from that soturion I fought after."

"Auriel," I said. "What the hell! You should have said something."

"I was more worried about you. Your fever really was high, and you—you couldn't stand. And then after—everything you were feeling. It scared the shit out of me. I mean, by the realms, you're so, so mortal."

"And right now," I pushed his golden hair from his forehead. "So are you. I know this is uncharted territory—you becoming human again, but Auriel, what happens to you now? What happens if you—if you die?"

He shivered. "I think we'd better not find out."

"Can I—" I took a deep breath. "Can I see?"

"Lyriana." He looked away, almost embarrassed, his neck reddening.

"Please, Auriel. We're in this together now. You can't just take care of me. At least, if you want to keep it up, then at some point I need to take care of you."

"I'm still a God in a lot of ways. I'll recover."

"And if you don't?" I wrung my hands together. "Look, I can't take care of him. I can't help him. And I need to—I need to do something, and you're hurt. Let me take care of you."

His eyes searched mine, his body still, then finally he lowered his chin, biting the inside of his cheek. "All right." He gestured to his shoulder. "I uh ... I'm going to need some help with my armor."

I nodded, and climbed off the bed so I could stand before him. Then I found the clasps and buckles of his chest plate. Quickly, I unfastened each piece, and removed them one by one, carefully placing them on the table beside my belongings. He'd given me his cloak in the woods, replacing it with a short tunic he'd pulled up beneath his armor.

But when I reached for the ties behind his neck, Auriel's gaze was distant. Like he was embarrassed. He didn't want me to see him in pain. Didn't want to reveal weakness.

I crawled back onto the bed, moving behind him so he could compose himself. It was so like Rhyan. I remembered the first time I'd seen him hurt. That fucking asshole, Brockton, had beat him up in the arena, had bitten his eye, bitten through his scar. Rhyan had been so unwilling to let me care for him. So guarded. Even after that, it took him months to fully open up to me, to trust me with his vulnerabilities. His secrets.

I ran my hands soothingly down Auriel's shoulders, feeling the warmth of his skin, soft and taut over his muscles. My fingers brushing lower, finding smaller scars I hadn't seen, markings of a war from another life. Then I fully unlaced his tunic, letting the sleeves fall down his arms. What remained of the cloth slid down the front of his chest, exposing him down to his waist. Carefully, I shifted myself back off the bed, and came to stand before him.

For a moment, in the dim flickering light of the basement, I had to compose myself. Auriel was beautiful, and I had the opportunity to look more closely and carefully than when we'd been in the forest.

The muscles across his chest and abdomen looked like they'd been carved from marble with an exquisitely practiced precision. Like his body had been dreamt of by a master artist. Rhyan's had been the same way to me. Perfect in my eyes. Perfect in every way. But he'd always been mortal. Real. Warm. Mine.

Auriel though—while almost identical, somehow still looked like a God. Otherworldly. Not from any single feature I could identify. He just was. Even now—even injured. The only thing marring the perfect sculpting of his chest were large, angry-looking red and purple bruises. And on the right side of his rib cage, there was a sharp-looking lump, like the bone was out of place and trying to force its way out. Everywhere else that wasn't bruised or broken was scratched up and red and irritated.

Without thinking, I ran my hand down his chest, my fingers splaying across the worst of his injuries, and smoothing over the skin stretched across the broken bone.

Auriel's body stilled except for a shuddering breath. "Lyriana, wait!" he said. "Wait!"

But it was already happening. My hand had warmed with fire, and my heart glowed as the red ray of the Valalumir, the light inside my chest, came to life. Light spilled out of my tunic, golden and warm, spreading and illuminating the entire basement. Within seconds, the darkened room had been filled with a luminous, golden glow of light.

Auriel's eyes widened. His bruises began to shrink, the red and purple fading back into the tan color of his skin. His rib cage shifted, righting itself, the lump vanishing.

And I shuddered, barely stopping myself from crying out, feeling the pain he'd been in. Taking it on as I healed him, as I once again used *Rakashonim*.

As I took on more, I started to gasp, feeling my own ribs crack and break and bruise. Not really. They were fine—it was the effect of the healing—the need for the energy to exist somewhere, for there to be balance. What was created could never be destroyed. I bit back my scream. I wasn't hurt—but the pain was real enough.

"Lyriana!" Auriel yelled in warning. "Lyriana stop. Don't!"

But I couldn't let go, couldn't pull my hand away. The pain in my ribs was growing more and more tense.

"Wait!" Auriel yelled.

And then ... something else was happening. Something far bigger was beginning to heal.

His aura.

It had felt larger than life to me when he'd first appeared, when I had no idea who he was or what was happening. But in that first moment, before I fainted, he had *felt* like a God.

Since I'd woken in the cave, Auriel had felt more human, more fragile. His aura weakened. He'd looked every bit an immortal, looked exactly as I would have imagined an all-powerful being. But he'd mentioned moving slower, having trouble adjusting to the physical world. And I'd seen it.

Seen him struggle with his mind slowing down—forgetting what he knew in the other realms, forgetting the knowledge he possessed as a God. Even sounding unsure of how he'd gotten here, or how he might leave.

The light began to spark between us—bursting like fireworks, growing brighter and brighter, until it hurt to look at him.

And then, I felt it. The moment his aura healed.

There was a sudden dimming of the light and strength of mine. My power. My knees shook, then gave out.

"Asherah!" Auriel yelled, jumping to his feet and catching me. He scooped me into his arms, and laid me back on the bed, his eyes wide and blazing with green. The color was more vibrant than before. It looked more like Rhyan's green in the sunlight. Now ... even in the dark, it was an exact copy. As if the light from the green shard of the Valalumir itself was behind them.

"Asherah. My love." His mouth opened, then closed and he stumbled back, another burst of light exploding from his body.

"Fuck," he yelled, and fell to his knees, his hands opening and closing helplessly. "You're the fire," he said. "It's inside you. *Rakashonim.* In your heart."

"Auriel," I said, reaching my hand for him. But I couldn't move. The effect of the healing had taken its toll.

His breathing was heavy as he stood up, and then the room darkened again, the only lights which remained were the flickering flames of the candles.

"By the realms—by the fucking realms," Auriel yelled, rushing to my side, and taking my hand in his. "Lyriana? Lyriana, please. Please. Are you okay?" He kissed my knuckles.

I nodded. "Just a little tired. Again."

He kneeled at the edge of the bed, and squeezed my hand. "Do you know what you've just done?" he asked. "You healed more than my body. You—oh shit. Oh shit!" He was breathless, his eyes wild. He let go of me then, and stood, stumbling backwards, until he hit the wall.

"What? What happened?" I asked weakly.

"I remember," he cried out. "I remember now. Fuck! You healed—you healed my memory, too. I ... I'm not cut off anymore. The light. It's the light. The Red Ray! By the realms! The Valalumir itself."

I frowned, not sure what that meant—he was almost babbling. "Are you okay?" I asked. From the look on his face, I couldn't tell if having his aura in full force, and his memory of being a God while mortal, was good or bad. Or if ... somehow, I'd done something wrong. Something that hurt him.

Auriel shivered. "I'd been trying to remember this the whole time. Since the moment I felt my power drain. I could feel it—at the edge of my mind, but I couldn't touch it." He gasped. "It will happen again, soon. But I know now why we've been fighting. What I was trying to say without knowing it. I know now why it feels wrong to you to go after Rhyan. Why it feels wrong to let Sean do it."

"What do you mean?" I asked.

"Lyriana," he gasped. "I was so close to remembering back at the tomb. To telling you everything. But my mind was already clouded, weak, and with the sun in your hair like that, and Asherah's chest plate I forgot."

"Forgot what?"

"Rhyan doesn't have to die." His throat bobbed, his entire body vibrating with the knowledge. "It's been hidden. It's been hidden for a thousand years. It was forgotten. The knowledge lost. Buried. But, I remember. I remember now. We can save him, we can save his soul—the part of my soul that's his. The personality that's Rhyan. Lyriana, we can bring him back—restore him from the state of being an akadim."

"What?" I sat up, my heart thundering. I shook my head. "Auriel, don't say that. Not unless you mean it. Absolutely mean it. You cannot joke about this."

"I'm not." His eyes were wide and blazing with fire and emeralds, and then the light left him again. His chest heaved, gasping for breath as he sank to his knees. "I buried the knowledge with me. In my tomb. That's why you were drawn there. That's why you were brought there. You were desperate to save him, to heal him. And with all the power you'd called on and wielded—you thought you'd failed. You hadn't. You went to the source. I remember now. I think that might be why I'm here. To right the wrong. To fix a mistake we made a thousand years ago." Tears were falling from his eyes, streaking across his cheeks. "There's a way forward for Rhyan. Lyriana, there's a cure."

CHAPTER FOURTEEN

LYRIANA

A cure.

For a moment, I felt like my heart would burst. Like I could leave my skin and fly. Like for the first time since I saw Rhyan in the akadim's arms—anything was possible.

Auriel crossed the room, and knelt before me at the edge of the bed.

"Are you sure?" I asked, my heart thundering. "I can—" My voice shook, too many thoughts, too many emotions racing through me at once. "I can heal him? Auriel, truly?" I grasped at his arms, pulling him up to the bed to sit beside me, my fingers digging into his flesh before I could stop myself.

Auriel was luminous then, like the light I'd used from the Valalumir to heal his body had become a part of him, shining through his limbs. In that moment it was as if the Red Ray had been stored inside of his heart—not mine.

"Truly. There's a way," he said.

I lifted my hands, looking back and forth between them and Auriel—his form now fully healed. "How? Is it with *Rakashonim*?"

He shook his head, his eyes wide. "No. Not with *Rakashonim*. That's powerful. And maybe the thing that could come the closest. But it's only because of what you're drawing upon.

The Red Ray of the Valalumir. With it, you can wield unfathomable levels of power. And you can heal with it—like you've done before. Like you did just now. But to restore a life to someone who's been turned akadim, to call their soul back to their body, to heal and restore it?" He sighed. "Calling on *Rakashonim* alone—it would kill you. And it wouldn't work. The cure requires more."

"More how?" I asked. "Tell me what I have to do. Tell me everything."

Auriel frowned, his blond eyebrows knitting together. "What do you remember about the creation of the Valalumir?" he asked.

"The light itself?" I said, frowning. "Created by the God Canturiel?" I shook my head. "I can tell you what I know about it—if that's what you mean. But, if you're asking if I remember its creation as Asherah, I can't. I don't have any actual memories of that time—or even being a full-fledged Guardian. I don't remember Heaven. Or being a Goddess. None of those memories have come back to me. Not in full." I looked away. "So far my memories as Asherah have been sparse. Glimpses of my life down here—like seeing Auriel—I mean," I bit my lip, "seeing you, on the beach before the Drowning. And then again in battle."

"That's okay," he nodded. "But to do this right, you're going to need to understand everything I'm about to tell you. Especially because I'm afraid with my current mortality, I'll forget again."

"Okay," I agreed.

"What exactly do you know of the light's creation?" he asked.

"Only what I've read in the Valya."

Auriel's eyes widened. "The Valya. Yes—the Valya. Wait—" He grabbed my arm. "There was more than one translation that survived. Right? Which scroll did you read?"

"Well, there's two main ones," I said, unsure where he was going with all of this. "The Mar Valya which was discovered right after the Drowning became the standard for translations and copies. That's the most common. But then there's the Tavia Valya, found a hundred years later, preserved in a chest. I've read both."

"*So,*" Rhyan said, "*tell me your best academic observations of the translation debate.*"

I sat up. "Are you serious?"

"*After you guiled me into an art history lesson, you still think I have no interests outside of push ups and punching people?*"

"*No. I ... I just never knew anyone else who cared about the debate.*"

"*Now you do. So tell me.*"

I blinked, looking back at Auriel.

His throat bobbed. "The Mar Valya was missing an M, wasn't it? Changing the meaning of *Auriel janam Asherah-diam.*"

"Auriel knew Asherah as two," I said, my voice hushed.

"I recognized you the first moment I saw you," he said, his voice flooded with emotion. "The Valalumir was the brightest, most powerful light to ever be created, and it dimmed in your presence. I still remember like yesterday. Remember seeing you. Remember the way that you brightened the room. Remember the way my heart had beat faster. The way I couldn't take my eyes off of you. Before I knew your body, I knew you. I remembered that our soul was in two. But once, it was whole. And I knew what you were to me that first instant. More than a thousand years ago in the Hall of Records. Once I saw you, no oath I swore mattered. No duty. Because you and I were something far greater. We were *mekarim.*"

"Soulmates," I said.

Auriel's face tightened, his eyes watering. "*Mekara.*" *My soul is yours.*

"*Rakame,*" I answered. *Your soul is mine.*

For him, she's brighter than the brightest star in Heaven. That's what Rhyan had told me that night in the Temple, describing the way Auriel had fallen in love with Asherah. My heart thudded.

"Both Valya translations, however," Auriel said, "are incomplete. They're missing part of the story. The Mar Valya and the Tavia weren't the first to arrive on these shores. There was another—one that was whole. One that contained the truth. I would know. Because I wrote it. Auriel's Valya."

"Auriel's Valya?" I practically yelled.

His eyebrows drew together, as he nodded. "In the scroll, I told the truth about the light. About its creation. It wasn't a burst of inspiration like they've told you. The light wasn't just some idea that Canturiel sang into existence one day. It had a purpose, a design. Only that knowledge was lost. Because every copy of my Valya was destroyed before my death. Every copy except for one. The one I buried inside my tomb."

"On Gryphon Island? There's a copy of your Valya?" My eyes widened. "With the cure for akadim inside it?"

"Not the cure itself, but it speaks of it, yes." He took a deep breath. "The truth is that Canturiel was asked to create the Valalumir by the Council." He closed his eyes, like he was trying to remember carefully. "It was designed as a kind of weapon. One that did not harm, but one that restored our enemy, banishing the evil from their hearts. The Valalumir itself was the cure." His green eyes blazed now, full of determination, his hand taking mine. "It was created for this very purpose."

"By the Gods," I said.

Auriel nodded. "But the akadim immediately recognized how powerful it was, and tried to steal it. See, they had been corrupted, but they weren't interested in returning to goodness, only in increasing their power. Their souls twisted until only their base needs remained. Hunger. Lust. Violence. They had no interest in returning to their former states. They made a plan and nearly stole the light from Heaven. Once that happened, we were summoned. The light was taken to the Hall of Records. The Guardians were selected to watch it. And the akadim were banished to Earth."

"And then no one else was allowed to go down there," I said.

"No. No one else. Until us. Until *we* happened. We were chosen to guard the light, to spend eternity protecting it, never to fall in love, never to take our attention from it. But … well you know how that ended. We tried for a long time to ignore it, to ignore our feelings. But love won over duty in the end. I couldn't stay away from you—it didn't matter what oath I'd sworn. And we were caught, and you were banished." Auriel's voice cracked, the pain of Asherah's fall still affecting him. "I watched you from above. I watched mortality make you ill. And I watched you recover your strength. You did the impossible. You renewed your purpose and continued to fight—leading the charge and diving into the battle against the darkness. You were so brave, and so strong. But so was the enemy. And I couldn't stay away. Not from you. And not from the true purpose we'd served. The light. It was never meant to be locked away or hidden. Kept from those it could help. Those it could heal. The Valalumir was always meant to save akadim. So we did what we had to."

"Wait." My eyes widened. "Are you saying—Auriel, are you saying we fell on purpose?"

But the truth of it was already in my heart. Yes, we'd been betrayed. But we'd also allowed it to happen. Had been willing to risk eternity to do so. We'd risked everything to be together, and then risked that to save who we could.

"We did." Auriel shuddered, exhaling. "We did. We were brought before the Council to be punished. But they banished you, only you." He blew air out of his nose. "See, they understood how to actually hurt us. By keeping us apart. I begged them. I beseeched them on your behalf. On everyone's. But they denied me. So I had no choice. I waited as long as I could for the right moment. I watched over you, and when the time had come, I stole the light, and I fell. For you. And for the world. For every soul that had been lost. To show the Council they had been wrong to lock it away. That they were wrong to let humans suffer for their own cowardice."

I could barely breathe. My heart was pounding so hard I could hear it thrumming in my ears. "Then what happened?"

"The light couldn't handle the atmosphere. Couldn't sustain itself in the material realm. It turned into a crystal. And I panicked. I only managed to save one sliver of light. Yours." He reached for my heart, his palm gently resting above my breast. "I placed it inside you."

I rested my hand beside his, feeling my heart beat. Feeling the ghost of another heart. Another life. The same light pulsing inside it.

"I made a mistake," he said. "And I've been paying for that mistake for a thousand years. What I did fractured the Red Ray. The part of the Valalumir that held the power to call their souls back. I separated it from the part that could heal the body."

"You said the other night that I was meant to heal. That's what the Red Ray does."

Auriel nodded. "I did. And you *are* meant to heal. Heal the world. But I made the work harder for you—for everyone. Every day we went into battle together, and we fought, and every chance you had, you would use your strength, and you would use the Valalumir, and the light you carried inside to heal akadim."

"How?" I asked.

"With the Valalumir itself," he said. "After the Drowning though, when it shattered into seven pieces, that was when we learned it was the red shard that was most important. But it had weakened. When the light was whole, it could heal hundreds at a time. It restored thousands of souls. Anyone could wield it. But when it fractured and became crystal, and the light became part of you, it made you part of it. You became the only one. You became the fire."

You're the fire.

"And if I had the red shard now?" I asked. "Could I heal the akadim? Could I heal Rhyan?"

"Yes," Auriel said. "You could."

"Do you know where it is?" I asked.

Auriel nodded. "I do."

I started to stand—ready to go get it this second. Wherever it was. I didn't care.

But Auriel held my hand, and I sat back down.

"It's not that simple. I gave it away. Before I died. For its protection." He sighed. "After I buried Asherah, I knew Mercurial had betrayed me." He stood and walked over to the small table, picking up Asherah's chest plate, staring intently at the linked Valalumir stars made of gold. In the center of each star was a diamond mixed with blood inside, giving it the appearance of starfire. It was my blood—Asherah's and Auriel's.

"No one should have been able to open your tomb," he said, his voice shaking. "Tombs were never meant to be opened." He shook his head, his eyes on me now, green and full of fire. "But more importantly, you were guarding the indigo shard—even in death. I was positive when I'd constructed the tomb that no one could unlock it. I expected that my soul would reincarnate. But no one would have a drop of my blood. Nor would they have the key."

"Except Mercurial," I said.

"Except Mercurial. Because he stole this." Auriel held the chest plate up, then cradled it to his heart, his eyes sad and wistful. "Every precaution I took was to prevent this day from coming. To stop what I'd foreseen. I didn't know when. I didn't know how long it would take. But I knew one day, Moriel would return. I knew his soul would reincarnate, and he would remember. And when he did, I knew he'd allow nothing to come between him and the indigo shard."

"That was my fault," I said. "We opened the tomb. We thought the red shard was inside."

"I know you did. I know," he said quietly. "That was also because of me. When I left the North, I knew I needed to find another way to protect the red shard. Your shard—the most precious to me of all. Tombs could be opened. Items stolen. I wouldn't bury it with me. My only other option to guarantee its safety was to hide it somewhere, and with someone who would never die. Someone strong. Someone who would never ever hand it over to anyone else—whether they asked, begged, pleaded, or bargained. Even if they were an incarnation of my soul in the future."

"Who?" I asked. "Who would agree to such a thing?"

"The Queen of Khemet. Queen Ma'Nia."

"The Afeyan Queen? The Queen of the Moon Court?" I asked.

The sun revealed my secrets, so I hid them with the moon. That was what Auriel had written on my tomb—on Asherah's tomb.

My heart thudded, and suddenly I remembered hearing Asherah's voice months ago.

Do not head for the stars. What you seek is with the moon. Asherah had told me herself. And Mercurial had confirmed it. But in all the chaos of the last month, we'd been unable to seek it out. Unable to escape, to go South. And now ... now I was realizing that what Mercurial had asked me to do, all of this time, was impossible. I was never going to claim the red shard. Not on my own.

Not without Auriel.

I started to breathe heavy, my chest tightening, something burning inside me. A fire. A fire unlike anything I'd felt before—not from Mercurial's torture. Not from his contract. And not from the light burning inside of me. Raging.

"What is it?" Auriel asked.

I placed my hand over my chest, barely breathing. "When Mercurial put the light inside of me, when we made our bargain, this was what he wanted from me. What I've known I'd have to do since that night. Fulfill a favor. Claim my full power. Claim the red shard."

Auriel nodded slowly.

"And all this time ..." Fresh tears burned my eyes. "All this time, the task was impossible. Because Ma'Nia would have never handed me the shard. Nor Rhyan. That was the bargain you made, right? Only you? Only you—your hand could take it back from her."

Auriel's chest rose and fell, his eyes turning red, as he looked away, the wheels turning in his mind. "Fucking realms."

I forced myself to keep breathing, to try and stop myself from panicking, from realizing fully all the pieces coming together.

"Auriel?" I cried. "You said you couldn't have come here if I hadn't called you—if I hadn't been in such despair, so in need of you."

"That was the only way—and it was still a long shot that I even made it. Only because of who you were to me. Your soul. And mine. Because we're *mekarim*."

"You also said that if Rhyan's soul was still here—you wouldn't have been able to come. That you couldn't be here at the same time as him."

He frowned. "Yes."

"By the Gods. *He* did this. Mercurial. He made this happen. He knew he had to draw you out. And there was only one way to do it. All this time, he's been taunting us, teasing us. Acting as if we haven't been listening, haven't been fulfilling our duties." My vision blurred. "But that Godsdamned fucking Afeyan! He's been using us like puppets the entire time. Pushing us together—forcing us apart."

Auriel's eyes widened. "He knew. Fuck. He knew the bargain I'd made."

I nodded. "He planned it all along. Mercurial!"

Light flashed in the basement, a thousand Valalumir stars sparkled around the ceiling, rotating in small circles. Mercurial's aura.

And then he appeared right before us, his body nearly naked, blue skin taut over smooth fine muscles. A silver loincloth between his legs, golden sandals wrapped to his knees. His cat eyes peeked out from behind his falcon head. "So, you finally figured it out."

"Mercurial!" Auriel seethed, his hands flexing.

"Ah, old friend. I've been talking to your newest one these last few months. It's a pleasure after all these years to see you again in your original form, and—" His eyes dipped down Auriel's body. "Back in your original flesh."

Auriel was across the room in seconds, his hands around Mercurial's neck.

But the Afeyan vanished and reappeared on the other side of the basement. "Uh-uh-uh." He waggled his finger back and forth. "You're going to need to listen to me, if you want to help Rhyan."

"Don't you dare!" I yelled. "Don't you dare speak his name!" It was him! He'd killed him. He'd made him akadim, he'd set us up from the start.

Mercurial laughed. The blue feathers around his face elongated into silky, black hair that fell to his waist. He shook his head, and his falcon features were replaced with his usual more human-like features.

"You knew!" I shouted. "You did this! You did this to him!"

His nostrils flared. "I did what I had to." He raised his eyebrows, peering again at Auriel. "As you can see, my little plan worked."

"Little plan!" I screamed, moving forward without realizing it. I was seeing red, my hands twitching, fingers desperate to wrap around the hilt of my sword. I only had one goal. Stick the blade through Mercurial's belly, and watch him bleed out.

He laughed, the sound bell-like, and disturbing. "You will kill me, my remembered Goddess," he said. "You swore you would. But not today." He lifted his hand, and pulled all the stars back through his palm. "You'd better go," he said. "Quick. There's company at the door."

And just like that, a violent knock sounded above us.

I froze.

"More soturi?" I hissed. "I don't understand, why are they back already?"

Mercurial smirked. "Why bother to come here at all?"

I glared at the Afeya—of course he'd answer a question with a question. "I know they're looking for me. But they already questioned Sean and Branwyn."

"Hmmm, so they did. Personally," he twirled his hair between his fingers, "I don't think they liked their answers very much. Besides, old Seany boy isn't exactly a native of this country—nor without a criminal record. A false one created by Devon, but a record nonetheless. One your current Arkturion would be more than happy to dig up."

The Bastardmaker. Fuck. But I had my answer. "It's because he's Glemarian. Because Rhyan was," I gritted my teeth. "And because he was associated with me." They'd be in danger as long as I remained here.

Mercurial nodded slowly, a feline smile spreading across his face. "Exactly. And, they'll be a bit more thorough than the last time—since they're out of leads and ghost sightings of you across the city. They'll come down here this time," he said. "Tear the place to shreds. Having been named a forsworn traitor by the Emperor himself, your Arkturion's big brother, I'd run if I were you, Goddess."

The knock sounded again, and I could hear footsteps coming down the stairs, light, and airy. Branwyn's.

"Where's Sean?" I asked, my heart thundering.

Mercurial laughed again. "Oh, Sean's not here. He left in the middle of the night."

"What! No! He wouldn't. He was supposed to—"

"Wait for you to give him an answer?" Mercurial laughed. "No. Sean's many things, but like Rhyan, when he senses a problem, he can be a little … impulsive. Couldn't wait for you. Anyway, I think we both know what you would've decided."

"No," I breathed. "No."

Mercurial shook his head. "Sean will find him. I promise you that. He's one of the best trackers in the Empire. In fact," he examined his fingernails, changing the color from a cold silver gray, to a vibrant yellow. He flashed them at me, then blew the color off. "Sean was the only one capable of tracking Rhyan down when he was forsworn in the wild." He laughed. "Your little Emperor should have had *him* hunting vorakh, instead of Lord Tristan."

I gritted my teeth.

Branwyn opened the door. I could hear the creak from above.

"Move aside, woman," shouted a soturion.

"Excuse me," Branwyn said.

"I said, move!"

My eyes widened as I realized that if Sean was gone, Branwyn was alone, and unprotected. And if the soturi were from Ka Kormac she was in danger. Not just for harboring us. But for existing.

"How many?" I asked Mercurial. "How many are up there?"

Mercurial closed his eyes slowly, and tapped his chin. "Five. I think you can handle that."

I looked at Auriel, and he nodded. "Just give me a sword."

Mercurial laughed. "I'm surprised. Not trying to ask me for any favors. For any help. For Branwyn's protection. Or to get word to Sean?"

I gritted my teeth. "I'll do it myself. If you think I'm going to willingly work with you ever again, then you gravely miscalculated."

"Choosing to work with me isn't an option. You're bound."

"And Rhyan's gone!" I shouted. "Considering my bargain with you was to protect him, to keep our relationship hidden, I'd say we're done."

He stepped forward, his hand on my heart.

Auriel started forward, rage in his eyes, but with a wave of his hand, Mercurial created a protection barrier blocking Auriel from reaching us.

"You feel that heat? That pulse? It's not just the Valalumir inside of you! My contract remains. You think Rhyan's temporary death ended it? No. It does not. We're not finished here. We're not until I say we are," he seethed.

My eyes narrowed as I stared the Afeya down. "One day I'm going to find out. I'm going to learn the truth about who you're working for; who you serve. And they won't be able to save you." My voice hardened. "For what you did to us—to him—I will kill you." I pressed my fist to my heart, pressed again, and flattened my hand across my chest. "*Me sha, me ka.*"

I expected Mercurial to look surprised or offended. But he only nodded. "Oh, don't worry, I already told you. I know you will. In fact. I've always known you'd be the end of me." He tilted his head, the movement bird-like, before his eyes flashed. "Now go. Save Branwyn. Oh, and Auriel?" The Afeya turned and waved his hand, releasing the barrier between them. "A word of advice."

Auriel stumbled forward. "Advice is the last fucking thing I need from you," he seethed.

"Tsk tsk," Mercurial tutted. "Dare I remind you that one of us has been here the past millennia, our memories intact, and one of us has been napping in a tomb?"

"You know if you're looking for rest, I can arrange that," Auriel said through gritted teeth, his grip tight on my dagger.

"You really are the exception to the idea of things getting better with age," Mercurial said with a sniff. "I simply wanted to tell you that Queen Ma'Nia may need some convincing before she agrees to hand the shard back over to you. Or even open the door when you arrive. After all, it's been a millennium, and she's grown quite used to the power she siphons from it. You'd do well to remind her of the cure. Remind her of the existence of that knowledge. You know her feelings on that. Better than anyone." He winked, his body vanishing. His eyelashes floated in the void, before he vanished completely.

In the hallway above, Branwyn screamed.

CHAPTER FIFTEEN

LYRIANA

Within seconds, Auriel and I had replaced every bit of armor on our bodies, and retrieved every weapon we could find. We were armed now with not just our swords, daggers, and Valalumir stars, but with every spare weapon Sean had left down here. Everything we could carry, we'd strapped on.

My eyes met Auriel's, his green irises blazing.

"You're strong enough?" I asked. "Healed enough to fight?"

He reached for my shoulder, and pulled me in, his forehead pressing against mine. "I am. I swear." Releasing me, he searched my gaze. "And you, *Meka*? You're going to fight?" he asked. "The way I know you know how?"

I exhaled sharply, pulling back and nodding. The fuck I was. Now that I knew there was a way forward. Now that I knew I could save Rhyan. Nothing was going to stop me. Not this time. This time, I would become their worst enemy. Be the fire that engulfed anyone in my way.

"It's all Ka Kormac," he gritted. "All bastard wolves."

I understood his meaning. They were our enemy. The kind of men who wouldn't hesitate to harm Branwyn. Or me. It was us or them.

Them or Rhyan. I gripped the hilt of my sword. "Let's go."

Auriel dipped his chin in respect, then reached for his blade, and tore up the stairs, his boots barely touching the steps.

Branwyn screamed again and there was a sharp thud on the ground.

I raced behind Auriel. The door flew open and we exploded into the kitchen.

Branwyn lay on the ground, groaning in pain. A soturion was bent over her, a fistful of her hair in his hand.

If you need to defend yourself—strike first, think later.

I did.

"Get off of her!" I screamed, and thrust out my sword.

The fucker didn't even have time to realize we were there. Not before my sword pierced his neck. His eyes widened. He would be dead in the next thirty seconds. I pulled back the blade and kicked his torso so hard he flew into the door. Auriel was already fighting two of the others. A sword in either hand, parrying and attacking all at the same time.

I sank down to reach for Branwyn and help her to her feet. She seemed shaken, but she was strong, immediately finding her balance.

"You're okay?" I asked quickly.

It looked like all the color had been stripped from her face. Drops of blood were seeping down the front of her dress. I couldn't tell if it was hers or the soturion's. But she didn't appear injured. Only a little bruised.

Branwyn nodded. "Sean's gone!"

"I know. We'll protect you. Go upstairs! Lock yourself in your room!"

She shook her head in protest. "Lyriana."

But I grabbed her shoulders and turned her toward the steps. "Now! Go! And don't open the door no matter what."

Branwyn nodded, and fled, the same exact moment Auriel killed his first opponent.

I spotted the group's turion. He reached into his pocket, reaching for the vadati I knew he had on him. If he called for backup, the house would be surrounded in minutes.

This time though, I was ready. No more hesitation. I pulled my arm back and arced the blade downward with everything I had. One stroke was all it took.

His hand flopped onto the ground, the vadati dropping with a thud as blood spurted from his arm. He screamed, sinking to his knees, pathetically grabbing at the stump where his hand used to be.

I grabbed the stone, wiping the soturion's blood from it and placed it in my pocket before the other soturion could reach. Another thrust of my blade, and he was dead, too, my sword sinking through an opening of his silver armor. I was getting good at this—finding their weak spot. The spot just above their belts. Like I'd done to Brockton. Like Galen had done to Theotis. I pushed in, and in, and up, using all I had to apply pressure, until the light left his eyes.

I turned back to the one-handed turion, cursing at me and demanding the vadati back. I shook my head, and I ended him as well.

Auriel's second soturion dropped and he cleaned off his sword on the soldier's cloak. Sweat coated his forehead, dampening his curls. He turned slowly, gazing at the dead soldiers at our feet.

His eyes met mine. "All good, *Meka*?" he asked, chest heaving.

I shrugged. "Not a mark on me. Oh. And I got this." I showed him the stone, letting the clear white quartz roll across my palm.

He nodded, his head bobbing up and down as if in shock. "Good."

"We need to check on Branwyn," I said, and immediately, I raced up the stairs, Auriel following on my heels.

"Branwyn!" I knocked on the door. "Branwyn? It's just us. Me and Auriel. You're safe now. They're all dead."

There was a pause, and then the door to her bedroom opened, very slowly, her stave pointed between my eyes.

I held up my hand. "Just us. I swear it." I pressed my fist to my heart.

Her eyes moved behind me, searching, scanning, but then she nodded and opened the door completely. We rushed inside, and that pang I'd felt before pulsed through me again. Seeing their bedroom. The room that was evidence of their love, the room so full of their intimacy, the walls that contained their private moments.

My heart pounded. This future wasn't lost for me. It wasn't lost for me and Rhyan. Not yet.

"I'm sorry," Branwyn said. "I should have known they'd come. I should have warned you. Sean left in the middle of the night," she confessed. "Lyriana, I'm so sorry. I tried to tell him to take his time. To talk to you again. But he's been—Gods, Rhyan meant everything to him. He thought it was for the best."

I smiled sadly. I think in my heart, I'd always known he would. That he'd see this through—that he wouldn't allow such a task to become a burden for anyone else. Only it didn't need to be this way. But first, I had to make sure Branwyn was safe.

"Why did they attack you just now?" I asked. "I'm the one they're looking for, but they didn't come here for me this time. So what other reason do they have to do this to you?"

Branwyn's face fell. "They've been doing that regularly, harassing Sean for some time now. And me, because I'm his wife. Ever since—" She bit her lip. "Since Arianna took the Seat of Power," she admitted. "We've been seeing an increase in Korterian soturi coming around here, asking intrusive questions. Interrogating Sean and other Glemarians. They want to know why they're here, why they left home." Her mouth tightened. "Like they have any right to speak coming from Korteria. The soturi of Ka Kormac here are not under Bamarian control. I don't think they ever were. But they used to fall in line—or at least appear to. Now it's all changed with Waryn Kormac as acting Arkturion. He's given them permission to be their worst selves, to be more hateful, and violent. They see Arianna as an extension of the Imperator. Or the Emperor now, I guess. We've been missing real leadership since your father—" she paused and frowned. "I'm sorry."

I waved her off. "It's okay. Go on. Tell me."

"Since we lost your father, *Bar Ka Mokan*, more Kormac legions have arrived. They've been occupying houses, forcing us to give our spare rooms to their soldiers. Sometimes even the main bedroom if that's all there is. I've heard horror stories. Families being forced to give them all of their food, to hand over any resources they have, clothing, medical aid—sometimes weapons. It's all taken by their soturi." Her nostrils flared. "They take whatever they want. It's been happening more frequently in mage households. I think they started in the homes where they didn't expect anyone to fight back. Where they could easily overpower. But it's coming to the soturi homes lately, too. They won't stop because they don't care about us. They don't care about anyone who isn't them. They've been focused so far on our friends—those who weren't born Bamarian. And the soturi of Kavim that, well … Kavim without any hints of nobility. My status has afforded some protection for Sean. But I can see that that's ending, especially with Avery on the Throne."

"I'm so sorry," I said, anger building inside of me. I'd been watching Ka Kormac enter the country for years, watching as more and more of their soturi began to occupy the city, the country. I knew it was bad. But I never considered the full extent of their harassment, of the damage they could inflict on our people. And all along, Arianna had been going along with it. Signing off on it. Worse. She had murdered our father. Had even convinced Meera to abdicate to her.

I'd known since that night, since I saw the tattoo of the black seraphim on her arm that Bamaria would suffer. But I didn't think things would change this much. I didn't think she'd burn our country to the ground, all while offering the remaining burnt embers to Ka Kormac.

With her help, our enemies had conquered Bamaria, and they'd done so without lifting a single sword. Now, it was poised to fall. All because of her. I had no idea how far her betrayal had gone.

My hands clenched. "I knew they were occupying the city. I didn't realize they were in your homes, or that they were stealing from your families. I should have." Should have known their cruelty would be worse to our people than it had been to us. My family had suffered greatly under their rule, but we were still nobility, still able to find ways to work inside the system. Bamarians like Branwyn couldn't. "I should have known it was like this," I said. "Because I know exactly what they are."

Branwyn shook her head. "What could you do? You were not Arkasva, nor Arkturion. And then you were away, and for good reason. You had to save your sisters."

My sisters. Morgana and Meera.

I'd only saved one.

Branwyn's eyes swept over me. "Lyriana, it's not your fault."

But it felt like it was. This was my country. These were my people. And they deserved safety. Privacy. Dignity. They deserved to keep their own resources for their families, to not have foreign soldiers invading their homes stealing from them, intimidating them. Especially the wolves. It was going to stop. Somehow, I was going to find a way. I was going to banish them from my country.

I had far more than one wrong to right. But Rhyan was first.

"Branwyn," Auriel said, "I'm sorry for all that's happened. But this is important. Can you get in touch with Sean?"

She pressed her lips together, and shook her head. "I don't know. We have one illegal vadati that we keep in secret. It's shared between us and our friends. Everyone on the route you took to get here. There's a handful of allies that it can connect to across the Empire. We use it to communicate, but it always depends on who has the stone." Branwyn's eyebrows drew together. "I told him to take it with him. But he refused. He wanted to keep it here, in case anyone else needed it more than him. In case you did."

"Fuck," I said. We had a spare vadati, but now there was no way to contact him. "Branwyn, I need you to trust me on this. We can't explain right now, and this is going to sound farther than Lethea, but I need you to believe me."

Branwyn nodded. "Okay."

"You need to get in touch with Sean. Tell him to abandon the mission."

"What?"

"Tell him there's another way. Tell him I said not to hurt Rhyan."

But before I could explain further, another knock exploded against the front door.

We all froze, barely daring to breathe.

"Are there any wards in place?" I asked.

Branwyn shook her head. "I was about to before they—"

The knock sounded again. Louder, more violent this time. The walls upstairs shook with the force.

Auriel's jaw clenched, his brows furrowed and I knew we had the same questions. Were these soturi looking for the men we just murdered? For Sean? Or for us? Or worse—just here for Branwyn?

My throat dried, my stomach twisting.

Blue light erupted from my palm. The vadati I'd stolen from the dead turion.

"Shit!" I hissed. Auriel clapped his hand over my mouth. "Turion Tiberius," came the call.

I closed my hand around the stone. "We need to go, now!"

Auriel was already making his way to the balcony, reaching for my hand, and gesturing for Branwyn.

But she shook her head. "If I don't answer the door, they'll surround the neighborhood. They could hurt everyone we're friends with—all of our allies. The number of soturi out there now—we don't stand a chance."

"Come with us. We'll take the route," I said.

"No. I need to be here. I'll try to get word to Sean. But I need to let the soturi find me."

"Tiberius!" shouted the soturion. The pounding started again.

I took Branwyn's hand, urging her to come with us, but she shook her head sadly. "You need to get out. If I stay, I can hold them off. They'll be distracted by the carnage."

So I pressed the stone into her hand. It was all I could do for her.

"It's okay," she said. "They won't suspect me. I'm a mage. They know I can't fight."

"What will you tell them?" I asked.

But Auriel's eyes widened as he nodded slowly at Branwyn. "The truth," he said. "Tell them it was me. The soturion on the run with Lyr. I'm already wanted—this won't change things. But it'll give you protection. Turn me in. Say you hid up here out of fear—that I came by looking for a place to hide, but you recognized my description. And you refused me."

"Auriel." Branwyn's face fell.

"Do it," I said. "And please, tell Sean not to hurt Rhyan. Trust me."

"I will."

"And Branwyn," I wrapped my arms around her, "be careful."

"You, too," she said, and opened the door to her balcony.

"Come on," Auriel said.

The front door burst open.

"Now!" Auriel hissed.

We raced onto the balcony, and Auriel leapt without a thought, his boots landing softly in the backyard.

My breath hitched, looking over the balustrade. I was still afraid of falling—especially after the last time I was in the sky.

But Auriel held out his arms. "*Meka!* Jump! I'll catch you."

I pushed one leg over the banister, and then the other.

There were yells now coming from the house. Tears burned behind my eyes. I jumped.

I landed in Auriel's arms a second later.

But before I could scramble to my feet, he took off, racing to the neighbor's house, knocking on the back door and rushing inside.

"Red Gryphon!" he shouted.

A soturion who looked to be about Sean's age rushed to meet us. "Red Gryphon?" he asked, his Glemarian accent thick.

"Yes. Sean's gone. Branwyn's alone—she sacrificed herself so we could get away, so we could sound the alarm. We killed five wolves. But there's more. She needs help. Now!"

The soturion nodded. "I'm on my way. I'll warn the others."

"Thanks," Auriel said, and in a flash we were back outside. I was still in his arms.

"Let me down," I said. "I can run."

Auriel released me, but his hand wrapped around mine, our fingers entwined.

I didn't know if Auriel had memorized Sean's route in reverse, or Sean and him had spent time going over it while I was recovering. I started to suspect the latter as we raced into backyards, jumping in through windows, and climbing back out. All the while Auriel shouted "Red Gryphon" in each new home. It made me think that Sean had lied to me. A little. He'd made up his decision the moment he'd heard the news. He was always going to go after Rhyan. And he was preparing Auriel, giving him a way for us to escape when he was gone.

My heart was racing when we reached the final house. We were back at the waterway, about to cross into the forest.

I looked back, and my stomach sank. The street was full of soturi. They were spreading out, going one by one to each house, pulling people outside, their swords out and ready to attack.

If we hadn't taken Sean's route we'd have been caught by now.

"There's a port at the edge of the forest, right?" Auriel asked, racing forward. "I've been studying the modern maps."

"There is. Right at the edge of Urtavia proper." Right where the trees ended, and the waterways and shops began.

I leapt over tree trunks, and loose branches and bramble as we raced through the trees, sprinting faster and faster. There was a clearing up ahead, and shouts in the distance. Chanting. Then we stopped, just at the edge of the forest.

The city was full of Lumerians. A mob had formed—not unlike the one I'd seen all those months ago on Auriel's Feast Day. The day Rhyan had returned to me. The first time I'd seen him in three years.

"*Shekar Arkasva!*" came a shout.

I stilled, my chest tightening. False Arkasva. It was what the Emartis used to say about my father. Before they murdered him.

But the chant continued. "*Shekar Arkasva!* Unseat Arianna!"

"Skin the wolves!"

"Arianna's a fucking traitor!"

"Kormac's a tyrant!"

By the Gods. Bamaria hadn't turned on us. They were seeing the truth.

And then fireworks exploded into the air, taking on the shape of a glittering seraphim. Not a black one. Not the symbol of Arianna and the Emartis, the rebels who murdered my father. But a red seraphim.

Batavia red.

Bamaria was rebelling. Uniting.

But then the wolves came.

Soturi in silver armor were everywhere, swords out, my people screaming and fighting back.

"Lyriana!" Auriel said. "Now! We need to run."

Because just at that moment, with countless soturi swarming the city, we'd been spotted. And not just by any Kormac wolf. But worse. We'd been seen by Turion Dairen. And he recognized me at once.

His mouth opened, shouting my name at the same instant he started to run, and reached for his pocket. For a Godsdamn vadati stone.

"Fuck!" Auriel snapped. He was already tugging me away, and then without warning, he lifted me into his arms, pushing into the crowd before us, crashing into people, until they finally parted and we made our way to the port. He pushed me into the carriage, and climbed in behind me.

I looked out of the window and saw Turion Dairen not far behind, his vadati glowing blue.

"Fuck. Fuck!" Auriel shouted, then closed all the windows and practically barked at our seraphim. "Gryphon Island!"

The floor tilted, and then we were off, heading back to Auriel's tomb.

CHAPTER SIXTEEN

LYRIANA

The seraphim barely had time to touch the sand upon landing, before Auriel flung open the carriage door, and leapt onto the beach. Sand sprayed out from the bottom of his boots and our seraphim squawked in annoyance.

I raced behind him, but he was heading to the seraphim's face, stroking its beak, cooing in High Lumerian to calm it down. He'd yelled at the poor bird the whole flight to keep up a brutal pace. But it was necessary. We were going to be surrounded in minutes. And this seraphim was our only way to escape. We needed her to stay.

"Go! To the tomb!" Auriel yelled, one hand resting between the seraphim's eyes. She closed them, starting to look more content.

I turned. The Guardian of Bamaria wasn't far.

The black onyx stone shone in the sunlight. Its head was still missing, probably lost to the ocean by now. I felt guilty about that—especially now that I knew what it was.

I reached the front of the tomb, standing between the gryphon's massive front claws, and stared up at its taut muscles, leading to a neck without a head.

Auriel joined me a moment later, his face drawn as he looked up at the statue he'd created. At the place he'd chosen to make his final resting place a thousand years ago.

I placed my hand on Auriel's shoulder. He startled, as if he'd fallen into a trance. Then he shook his head, like he was attempting to clear his mind. "I didn't recognize it at first. When I had you—" he looked away, embarrassed. "When I had you pressed against it."

"Too dazzled by my beauty?" I teased, trying to keep things light.

He chuckled. "I was. But, also in my defense it was dark and raining for the most part. I can feel it now. I feel this void, the absence of where my soul once dwelt. I didn't feel it before, everything was too muddled."

"You can feel that now?" I asked. "The void?"

Auriel nodded. "I would have known immediately if I felt it that first night." He coughed uncomfortably. "But also, and perhaps most importantly, I wasn't expecting the gryphon to be headless." His eyebrows lifted. "The tomb was made to be indestructible. Of course, leave it to you, the newest one, to rip its head off."

"I'm sorry," I said, and I meant it. My hand slid down his arm, taking his hand in mine again.

"I carved this myself, you know. It took days." He turned to me, one side of his lips lifting into a chagrined smile. "I really should be keeping a list of the ways you've offended me, *Meka*."

"Auriel, you know I didn't mean to—"

He laughed. "Don't worry about it." He leaned in closer, our foreheads almost touching again. "I have an eternity to get back at you." He winked. Then he stepped back, surveying the tomb, and holding up his hand above his eyes, blocking the sun. "And truth be told, you did us both a favor."

"What do you mean?" I asked.

"Well, you've already taken care of step one. Removing the head."

"Removing the head?"

Auriel nodded. "Very few could have done it. I'm not sure if I would have had the strength in the end." His eyes dipped to my chest. "But you did. The head is what sealed it together, kept the tomb from ever being opened." He swallowed. "On Asherah's tomb," his voice cracked, "I left the keyhole exposed. That was a mistake. So I did things differently the second time. Though I must say, you seem to have a real talent for breaking into impenetrable tombs."

"Well everyone needs a hobby."

Auriel chuckled, but I could see beneath the surface what this was—a distraction. He was struggling, trying to build his own courage. It might have been a thousand years since the construction of the Guardian—since his death. He might have been in the Celestial Realms with his immortal body for a thousand years, spending all of his eternity with Asherah. But he was alive once. Mortal. And attached to this life. To this earth. This land. This was hard for him.

And for me. No amount of time would heal the wound. The forced separation of death. Even if we were successful with this, with the Moon Queen, with Rhyan—I wasn't sure if anything would fully heal me. Losing him. Watching him die.

My stomach was starting to twist. A new sensation washing over me. I hadn't been here when Auriel came to his final rest. I'd died first.

But suddenly, that no longer mattered. A memory washed over me. Quick, and bright. Like a flash of light.

"You were crying," I said, though I hadn't planned to say it out loud. "You thought you'd failed me. That you failed the cause. But you didn't. You never did. Not once. Not in my eyes, *Rakame*."

Auriel stilled, his eyes watering. "Asherah?"

I stepped back, suddenly shaky. "I-I'm sorry. I didn't mean to. I don't know—" I'd felt that line blur before. Brief moments, where I wasn't sure if I was her or myself.

A shadow crossed the sky. A seraphim.

Fuck. We were out of time.

"Auriel! We need to open it. Now!"

A sharp, salt-filled breeze blew icily against my back, and the water began to rush at my heels. The waves were growing higher, moving faster. Like a storm was coming. Another seraphim flew overhead.

"Can you give me light?" he asked. "The lines are faint after all this time, and difficult to see. My fault—I made it that way."

I reached for the leather scabbard at my hip, and removed the stave inside, fully aware of how Auriel's eyes tracked it—how they darkened. It was Asherah's stave, and I knew he recognized it. Just as he'd recognized her chest plate. "*Ani petrova vala.*"

I leaned in, our shoulders touching. And right where the head had come off, there were a series of words in High Lumerian carved into the onyx, much as there had been on Asherah's seraphim.

I began to read, parsing out the crafted letters, and translated, "None but I, none but Auriel who fell. Auriel who was a God named a Guardian. Auriel who represented the Green Ray. Auriel who took the secrets of the light and the Valalumir to his grave. None but I, none but Auriel alone."

Beneath the words was an imprint.

A hand.

Auriel laid his palm on top, then pressed down, his fingers fitting perfectly into the indentations.

Auriel, himself, was the key.

Green light—emerald green—the very green I would know with all of my soul at the end of eternity, began to emanate from his skin. The light pulsed and expanded, rising up Auriel's golden arm, and then across what remained of the Guardian's black stone body.

Squinting in the overwhelming brightness, I let the light of my stave flicker out, and stepped back. The ground began to shake, and thunder clapped in the sky as lightning struck the ocean behind us. A gale force wind blew against us and Auriel yelled out as he fought to keep his hand on the statue.

There was another clap, and Auriel fell, his back hitting the ground as I rushed to him, helping him to sit up. His eyes widened, and he pointed back at the tomb.

The Guardian's body split in half, both parts sliding across the sand away from each other. I gasped, and stood up, my entire body aglow in green, and reached out a hand for Auriel. He stepped forward and the stones stilled, the light fading just enough to reveal what had been tucked inside.

Auriel. Himself.

Like with Asherah, there was a golden coffin, sculpted into his likeness. The details were so exact, I had to look away. He looked too real. He lay on his back, his hands folded together across his chest. Without any hint of coloring, the blond of his hair, the tan of his skin, his likeness to Rhyan was even more shocking.

Tears blurred my vision.

The carving of his body, much like Asherah's, had a space open beneath his hands. In Asherah's tomb, we'd found her stave in that spot, along with the indigo shard. Moriel's shard.

My heart pounded as I spotted a cylindrical golden case, encrusted with sparkling gemstones of every color. It looked like the sort of ceremonial cases we used to house important scrolls in the temple.

"Auriel's Valya." He reached for the casing, pulling it out from his coffin's hands.

"The secret for the cure," I whispered.

Auriel nodded.

The ground seemed to groan, along with the thundering sound of the slabs of stone grinding against the sand as they retracted. Just as we'd seen in Asherah's tomb, Auriel's was resealing itself, until the stones were once more bound together.

The sound of waves filled my ears. Suddenly Auriel turned, and shouted in terror. "Get down!"

My back hit the ground, but gently. Auriel's arm had wrapped around me, taking the brunt of my fall, his body like armor over mine as the ocean ejected the Guardian's head. There was a cracking sound, like thunder, but the head was restored. The statue, the tomb, whole once more.

"Lyriana Batavia!" Turion Dairen had arrived.

Auriel raced past the Guardian, and I followed. Three seraphim touched down. Dairen led the charge with at least two dozen soturi behind him. Too many for us to take at once.

"You're surrounded," he yelled. "You have no chance of escape. You are under arrest by order of Emperor Avery for the murder—"

Auriel grabbed my hand, and we took off, running in the opposite direction.

"What's your plan?" I yelled.

"Just keep running."

I looked back. They were gaining on us. "Auriel!"

"No," he said. "No! We've come too far."

But I could hear them yelling, their boots in the sand, their taunts rising above the salty ocean wind, the sound of seraphim flying overhead.

The waves began to crash into our boots, soaking our heels. The water was becoming more violent. More storm-like. Yet the sky remained clear.

"What's going on?" I asked, just as Auriel steered us away from the water. But the water kept coming until I was soaked to my knees.

And then the waves rose, just before the shore. They were high enough to tower over the Guardian. These were the kind of waves I thought I'd see crash the other night. When I'd invoked the tsunami.

I looked over my shoulder. There was barely any space between us, and Dairen and his men.

Fuck. Fuck!

"We need to run faster," I yelled. But my calves were starting to burn, my legs moving slower. I hadn't been ready for a fight—not after I'd used so much energy to heal Auriel.

The waves crashed with a thunderous groan, and water exploded like a dam had burst, just behind us.

Auriel squeezed my hand, moving forward. Another wave crashed. He stilled, and turned. A river separated us from the soturi.

"Lyriana," Auriel warned, his voice full of a kind of fear I'd never heard from him before.

The soturi started to scream.

I looked at the water again, realizing that it wasn't water at all that had entered the shore.

It was fire. Blue fire.

And only one thing to my knowledge could do that. A creature I'd never seen before. A *jalamnavim*. A water dragon.

I turned to the ocean, my jaw dropping, pulse racing. A dragon, the size of Sean's house, hovered just above the ocean. Its wings were spread, long and full of sparkling scales, flapping back and forth in the wind. Its eyes focused, and blazed. They weren't so much a color as they were made of fire. Blue flames. It reared its head back, smoke curling from his nostrils, mouth opening to reveal two rows of sharpened teeth.

I could hear Dairen shouting, retreating, telling his men to stay back. He was already moving away when the dragon opened its mouth, and blue fire exploded, engulfing two soturi's bodies whole.

"Um—did opening your tomb summon the water dragon?" I asked.

Auriel shook his head. "Did my tomb require the protection of a *jalamnavim*?" he asked, his eyes wide. "No! It definitely didn't!" His hand tightened around me. "Now I need you to move slowly."

But it didn't matter what I did. Because the water dragon's eyes were on us, its entire head turning in our direction, its mouth opening wider. There was a growl, and then ... blue flames.

I hugged Auriel, feeling his arms tighten around me. Then he pushed me onto the sand, throwing himself over me, his body covering mine.

I squeezed my eyes shut, bracing for the fire, for the end. But it never came. The air grew hotter, crackling with heat. And then it stopped. Just like that.

I dared to peek one eye open. We were alive. We hadn't burned to death. Because someone had saved us. Someone had come. She stood before us, wearing a tight-fitting black dress. Long red hair fell down her back. Her arms were covered in golden bangles that jingled as she shifted. Leather cases, meant to hold scrolls, were affixed to a belt at her hip. Her stave was held high, blasting forth a dome of protection. The blue flames pushed against it, but the dome held.

"Ramia?" I asked.

"Not now," she hissed, her Afeyan accent thick. "I calm him. Quickly. Or you die."

Now both of her hands were raised and she called out, starting to sing a song I didn't recognize.

Auriel sat up, wide eyed, and pulled me into his lap. "We need to get out of here," he said.

"How?" I asked, eyeing the scroll he still held in his hand. Our options were endless beach, death by water dragon, or death by soturi. And none of those options led us to Queen Ma'Nia or the red shard.

"You come with me," Ramia said, looking back over her shoulder. "We ride him. The *jalamnavim*."

"We what?" I asked.

But Ramia ignored me and continued to sing. I started to translate her song in my mind. "The old Gods have returned. The Goddesses, too. Calm down now, water creature. We honor you." She kept singing it, repeating the rhyme again and again.

It was working. The dragon was no longer breathing smoke, no longer growling, but beginning to snake its neck from side to side—the movement similar to something Mercurial would do. But where Mercurial was sneaky in his movements, the dragon merely looked curious. I wasn't sure if dragons could smile, but for a second, that seemed to be what it was doing.

And then smoke exploded as it screamed. One of Dairen's men had launched a sword at its wing, and struck.

"Idiot!" Ramia yelled. The water dragon's hackles raised, its wings flapping as it rose above the water's surface and released a stream of blue fire once more. I clapped a hand over my mouth to keep from screaming. The soturion who'd hit the dragon was gone. Nothing more now than a pile of ash and smoke. Barely even a burning ember remained.

I started to shake. Three soturi were dead, burned alive. And Ramia started her song again. Her voice louder, yet somehow still soothing and calm. Haunting.

"The old Gods have returned. The Goddesses, too. Calm down now, water creature. We honor you."

Ramia snapped her head to the soturi—what remained of them—only a few yards away from us. And she gestured for the dragon to come forward.

"Come to me, come. I seek of thee. Come to me, come and see."

Auriel stood up, moving protectively in front of me. His feet were already widened, and his knees bent into a protective stance. Then he looked back, his eyes moving slowly up my body before stopping at my face. "Guessing you've never seen a water dragon in this life, *Meka*?"

"No!" I barely remembered they existed. Not once in my life had they come this close to the shore. I didn't even know of anyone seeing one. In fact, they were so uncommon, they were mostly referred to by their common name: water dragon. "They're supposed to be farther out in the ocean," I said, "past Lethea."

"Most are. Not all. Some are closer. But him? Him you disturb," Ramia said. "Your little storm dra w him out."

Its enormous body sparkled as it came closer and closer until two large paws hit the sand. Water sluiced from its body, and its wings were raised like hackles.

Dairen started yelling again, his arms up directing his soturi back into formation, commanding them to brandish their weapons and prepare to attack.

Ramia ran forward, placing herself between the dragon and the soturi. Then she held up her hand, another dome of protection.

"I not hold for long. I do this as favor for Mercurial. Get on!"

"What?" I asked, eyeing the dragon. Its eyes were turning to flames again. It was getting ready to strike.

"Now!" Ramia yelled. "Climb!"

"Come on!" Auriel yelled, already lifting me into his arms. He raced forward. "Good boy," he cooed. "Good boy."

Auriel hoisted me onto his back. The dragon's scales reminded me of the nahashim, surprisingly warm.

"Get closer to its head," Auriel said. I did, realizing there was a dip between the shoulder blades that made for a more comfortable seat.

"Did we ride on these?" I asked.

He settled behind me, one arm wrapped around my waist, pulling me against his torso. "We did," he said, his mouth close to my ear.

A small shiver ran down my spine, my stomach tightening.

"Ramia, get on!" Auriel yelled, shifting over to give the half-Afeyan a hand. She was on his back a second later, tiptoeing with an incredible amount of balance before us, before she settled down and patted the water dragon's head.

Auriel tightened his hold on me. "Ready? The dragon's going to move—it will be quick."

Our dragon rose to his feet at once, wings flapping, blood dripping onto the beach and then we lifted, soaring into the sky.

"Where the hell are we going?" I asked.

"I hear you need ride to Khemet," Ramia said, shaking her head. She replaced her stave in a belt, and used one hand to fix her long red hair.

"How did you know?" I asked. Then I scoffed. "Mercurial?"

Ramia winked. "He said you find trouble at beach. So I come." She laughed, and leaned forward, steering the water dragon. We'd been soaring east over the water, away from land, heading toward Lethea. But now we were moving south. She looked back at us again, and seeing we were flying steady, she twisted completely around. "At last. I waiting for you to figure out." She eyed the scroll, still held tight and safe in Auriel's hand. Auriel's Valya. She knew. She knew exactly what it was. She was a librarian who specialized in ancient artifacts and scrolls along with Afeyan writings. But something in the way she looked at the case made think she knew more than she was revealing.

"Figure what out?" I asked, suspicious.

Ramia made a tutting sound and shook her head. "She not pleased to see scroll again. Not after rest destroyed. But good you bring it. You need scroll to work things out."

"Work what out?" I seethed.

Her eyes sparkled. "Save Rhyan. Heal akadim."

"You knew about the cure?" I asked.

Ramia nodded. "Yes. But cure useless for years, lost. Without you—without someone to bear this—" she pointed at my heart, "no cure. This always had to happen." She gestured around us.

"Because the shard was broken. Because part of it is inside of me," I said.

Ramia nodded. "No cure without light." She eyed my chest. "And no cure without shard." She eyed Auriel. "Now pieces come together. But you face Queen first." She shifted forward again, her hand on the water dragon's head. "*Vra.Volara a Khemet*," she said. And we started to turn again, this time moving west. I mentally pictured a map of Lumeria. Khemet, home of the Moon Court was west.

The dragon roared, and blue fire spurted from its mouth.

I stilled, but Ramia laughed. "Happy fire," she said. "He in good mood now."

"He better be," I muttered, seeing the pyramids of the Great Library. They were like tiny points in the distance. We were flying fast, faster than a seraphim and gryphon combined. We'd be passing Scholar's Harbor in no time.

"I fix you when we arrive. Make presentable," Ramia said, nonchalantly. "My mother won't like if you look a mess."

"Your mother?" I asked, shaking my head.

Auriel's eyebrows scrunched together.

"Why would your mother—" I looked back at the half-Afeyan librarian I'd known most of my life. My stomach tightened. "Ramia? Who is your mother?"

She laughed, tossing her head back, the wind blowing through it now. "In Khemet, I not Ramia." Her eyes sparkled with mischief the way they had a thousand times since I'd known her. Since I'd worked with her. "Not just Ramia." Then she smirked, rolling her eyes as she shook her head in derision. "I Princess Ramia," she said. "My mother, Her Majesty, Queen Ma'Nia, High Lady of the Moon Court."

THE SECOND SCROLL: THE MOUTH OF THE AKADIM

CHAPTER SEVENTEEN

LYRIANA

"Princess?" I yelled. "You're a princess?" I shook my head. "But I thought you were—?"

"What? I can't be both princess and librarian?" Ramia winked. "How boring."

I shook my head. "No, I mean—I'm just trying to wrap my mind around the fact that all of this time I've known you as a librarian—and a jewelry dealer—"

"Rare artifacts procurer," Ramia corrected.

"Okay, fine, if that's what you want to call it," I huffed. "My point is that all this time, your mother was the Moon Queen."

"And?" Ramia asked.

"And I didn't know!"

"Lyriana," Auriel laughed. "We're riding on a *jalamnavim* to Queen Ma'Nia's court to call in a thousand-year bargain, and this is your main concern?"

"Not the main one," I said. "Just the latest. Add it to the list."

"So now I'm keeping two lists. Things that are currently concerning Lyriana. And things that Lyriana has done to offend me."

I twisted my neck to glare at him. "Seriously?"

"And now," he announced, "I'm adding *that* to the list."

I shoved my shoulder back into him.

"And that!" he said.

"Auriel!" I snapped.

"Okay," he said, holding up one hand. The other was still around me, grounding me, keeping me from falling off our dragon. "I surrender to you, Lyriana. Truce! Let's be friends again."

"You're impossible," I said.

The pyramids were growing larger as we moved closer. They housed the library where I'd first met the half-Afeyan. It was in the stacks of scrolls where Ramia had first approached me, and then more recently, proceeded to seek me out, multiple times, trying to convince me to wear Asherah's chest plate. The chest plate that she'd given to me on my birthday—on Mercurial's command.

I frowned. "Ramia?"

She looked back again. "Let me guess. A question?" She lifted her eyebrows.

"If I'm allowed. Just … Mercurial is a member of the Star Court," I said slowly.

"Yes. First Messenger," she said. "Why?"

"Well, you work with him—with the First Messenger of the Star Court. But you were born into the Moon Court."

"This all true." Ramia pursed her lips together. "And?"

I suddenly felt like an idiot. I had no reason to expect Ramia to willingly share her parentage on her own. And it wasn't like I'd ever asked. But I should have at least known what court she'd come from. I'd never wondered—never even bothered to consider the distinctions between the three. As far as I was concerned, they were all Afeya. I thought they were all the same. But now, the idea of her working with Mercurial, especially when she was so high-born of another court, was beginning to sound alarm bells in my mind.

"You work with the Star Court," I said. "Is that normal? For a princess to work so closely with a ... a First Messenger?"

"I only half-Afeyan," Ramia said. "Remember?"

"Your father isn't King RaKanan?" Queen Ma'Nia had been married to the King of the Sun Court for centuries.

Ramia made a face of disgust, as if the question were absurd. "How I half-Afeyan if two Afeya parents? RaKanan? No. He not my father."

"So if you're half-Afeya, does that make you half-princess?" I asked.

Ramia laughed and scrunched up her face. "Like bastard? No. My mother queen." She waved a hand in dismissal. "I princess."

"Then ... I mean, who is your father?" I asked.

Ramia snorted. "Some man." She shrugged her shoulders, unconcerned. "My mother lay with him one time. Then I come."

"And that's it? You don't know who he is? What country? What Ka?"

Ramia shrugged, "Who says he has Ka? Not important. I am my mother's daughter. And princess. Who care about father?"

I shook my head in annoyance.

"It's quite common," Auriel said quietly, his mouth still close to my ear. "Afeya do make life-long commitments like the king and queen, but making a promise for life works a little differently when they live forever. They quite openly take lovers on the side. Have other relationships. What counts is they always return to each other."

"Oh," I said. But that still didn't answer my question. I didn't care what kind of commitments Afeya made, or how open or closed their marriages were. However different they were from us in that arena, we had other similarities that I was much more focused on. Like living within the borders of our countries, and forming alliances between them. Showing loyalties to our rulers. I knew the Afeya banded together against Lumeria. But the courts remained separate, not governed under any one entity. There was no Afeyan Empire. Unlike us, none of them had been forced to bend a knee to our Emperor, or any other.

"Does your mother know you work with the Star Court?" I asked, trying for another angle.

Her nostrils flared. "Who you think introduce Mercurial?"

"So your mother works with him, too? With the Star Court's First Messenger."

"Work?" Ramia scrunched up her nose. "Together?" She frowned. "Shared goal. More accurate way to describe."

"And what goal is that?" I asked.

Ramia shook her head. "Not mine to say. I only princess. Enough question. Why not relax? Enjoy ride." She turned then, and the water dragon dragged its tail before lifting over a current, and splashing us from behind.

I turned slightly in Auriel's arms, our eyes meeting. "Do you know?" I mouthed.

He frowned, his eyebrows furrowed together in confusion.

"The goal they share," I whispered.

Auriel sighed, then quietly said, "I think I did once. But I don't right now."

"Should I try to heal you again?" I asked. His aura felt clear, sunny almost, not like the cloud it was when he first arrived. But maybe he still needed more of the red light's healing to remember.

Auriel shook his head. "It's not the same. I'm not forgetting exactly. It's more like ... the magic of the Afeya is affecting me. I'm not supposed to say. And even from my former position—I could learn things I wish to know, discover secrets—but it's not a matter of asking, or looking up the information. It's more a matter of watching. And I wasn't exactly inclined to spend the little time I was not with Asherah, watching the courts these last few centuries."

"What were you watching when you weren't with her?" I asked.

His eyes drifted down my body then back to my face. "You know what."

My cheeks warmed, and I looked away.

"The common goal between them will be told to us directly by the Queen," Auriel said, "if she wants us to know." His voice lowered. "And if she doesn't? No amount of asking will change her mind."

"Maybe we don't need to ask. It's not like the Afeya are following the rules. Mercurial's able to do magic he shouldn't," I said. "He performs magic on his own all the time in front of me."

Auriel frowned. "No, he can't. There are many loopholes they find and abuse, but not that one. That's not possible. The magic binding them is too strong. I promise you—they're not breaking those rules. No Afeya can perform magic without a request."

"But he can," I hissed. "Unless ... the magic he does serves some other purpose or request I don't understand."

Ramia whipped her head around, her eyes narrowed, before she turned back to the head of the water dragon, continuing to steer us toward Khemet.

"He's working for someone," I continued. "And he won't say who. I've asked him, even offered to make another bargain, Rhyan did, too." I frowned in frustration. "He refused us both."

Auriel bit his lip, considering. "It's not the Moon Queen he's working for—not when he's using magic," he said. "It can't be an Afeya. If they could ask each other for what they wanted—they'd never deal with Lumerians. From down here, I'm not entirely sure what he's up to. But, if he is doing magic without a direct request, it's because he made a bargain with a Lumerian, or … someone who was Lumerian at the time."

"At the time?" I shivered. "Like they're something else now? Like akadim?"

"Maybe. Or maybe it's someone who's passed."

I considered his words. "So you're saying that Afeya can continue to do someone's bidding after death?"

"Some bargains take time. Some may have been outlined to outlast the one making the request, whether that's by Afeyan trickery, or the asker's true wish, I don't know. But the Afeya must fulfill their bargains, answer what is asked of them, or do what they promised when the contract is made, no matter what."

But that still didn't feel like the answer to me. Knowing Mercurial's personality—his sudden ups and downs, the way he seemed to live completely governed by his own whims, I couldn't imagine him just serving someone after they died. "Are you sure there's no other way he can be performing magic on his own?"

Auriel's eyes darkened with shadows. "I'm sure. Lyriana, trust me. Let it go. If I knew, I'd tell you. I swear. But as traitorous as he is, he's not our problem right now. We need to be ready to meet Queen Ma'Nia. You should rest while you can."

I gestured around us. "On a water dragon?" The dragon in question was currently looping its body over the rushing tides of the ocean. Between the waves splashing around us, the way the wind caught in the beat of its wings, mixed with the sound of its breathing, the water dragon was the loudest animal I'd ever been on. And as if to make my point, it shot up into the air without warning, screeching like it was a game.

I leaned back into Auriel, my fingers digging into his arms to keep from falling. My stomach lurched as the dragon dove back down, its waggling tail spraying us with water from behind.

No further words were needed as I glared. Point made.

Auriel shook his head, like he was trying to shake out the water now dripping from his hair.

"Okay," he conceded, "maybe its not the most relaxing of transportation. But I do want you to be prepared. The Afeya ..." He sighed. "Their ways, their culture, it's nothing like you're used to."

I looked out at the water, and beyond, as the landscape passed and shifted. My thoughts moved to my friends and my family. And in the stillness, my heart hurt for Galen, and I was worried sick for Tristan.

But my stomach twisted without having any more information about Jules and Meera, and Dario and Aiden. Not since Branwyn had heard from Cal and Marisol. I still didn't know if they were okay, if they'd been near Rhyan's attack on Thene. And a now familiar ache in my arms—from being unable to hold Rhyan—was starting to pain me, but for Jules. I still hadn't hugged her. My eyes watered.

"You see the waves?" Rhyan said in my mind. *"The waves,"* he said again, his voice a whisper. *"Just watch the waves, rolling back and forth. Back and forth. Nice and easy. Just keep watching. I've got you. You're all right."*

I leaned back against Auriel's chest, and tried to breathe, watching the water move, and imagining that soon, soon, I'd have more than a memory. I'd have Rhyan in my arms again. The ache would be gone, and I'd have Rhyan's chest to lay against, his company to travel beside.

Auriel tightened his arms around me, and I fell into the rhythm of his breathing.

I lost track of the time after a while, my mind almost quiet until the water dragon began soaring faster.

"We pass the borders of Lumeria," Ramia called out. "We in Afeya waters."

We were officially entering the territory controlled by El Zandria, the desert land inhabited by King RaKanan, and the Afeyan Sun Court. For half the year, Queen Ma'Nia also resided there. The couple spent every winter together in Khemet ruling over the Moon Court together, and every summer in El Zandria. Being now at the start of the spring season, she was alone, ruling over the Afeya of her home court on her own. From the way Ramia explained things, it sounded like that was going to work in our favor.

"Too many Afeya," Auriel whispered, "are never a good thing."

I swallowed, starting to feel nervous. Ramia turned our water dragon back north, heading for shore. I could feel a shift immediately. The sun, blazing and bright, began to fade. The air cooled rapidly by several degrees. Every sweep of the water dragon's wings brought us further into darkness. Instead of the sparkling reflection of the sun's light in the ocean, it began to reflect the stars. And though night wouldn't fall for hours upon hours, the sky quickly darkened, and the moon replaced the sun as our source of light.

"Is it always night here?" I asked.

"Always," Ramia said. "And always day in El Zandria."

Our dragon lowered, its tail splashing in the water, until it sank to the surface, its body coasting on a wave. We rose with it, the wave growing taller. Another one came and Auriel tightened his hold around me.

"What's going on?" I asked.

"Meeting friends," Ramia said wryly.

"What do you mean friends?" I asked.

"I think," Auriel said, "she means more dragons."

I peered ahead. Rising from the splashing water, came three more water dragons, their blue scales sparkling in the moonlight. Blue fires crackling in their eyes.

Three Afeya rode on their backs, flying just above the ocean, the dragon tails dragging in the water as they circled around us. All three Afeya were female, with silver colored skin, and silver-white hair that fell down their backs. Silver armor that reminded me of fins covered their torsos, though they only covered one shoulder. Translucent white skirts flowed out from their hips, blowing in the breeze their water dragons had created.

"Who dares enter the waters of our queen?" All three asked in unison, their voices melodic as they spoke in High Lumerian. The dragons lowered, flying right beside us, the circle growing tighter. Each one had a golden tattoo across their forehead, a waxing crescent moon, a full moon, and a waning crescent.

"I bring important visitors to see my mother," Ramia said, now speaking in perfect High Lumerian. I'd never heard her speak with such perfect diction or grammar—and realized at that moment, her broken language in our tongue, and even her accent, wasn't a result of High Lumerian—but some other language—one I didn't recognize.

"Princess," all three said in response, and bowed their heads together before Ramia. When they lifted them, their eyes glowed violet. "We were not expecting you. Welcome home."

"Please. Request an audience for me with Her Majesty," Ramia waved a dismissive hand in our direction, "and my guests."

"Tell us their names," the three said together.

"I bring Lady Lyriana Batavia, reincarnation of Goddess Asherah."

"Asherah," the three repeated, their eyes glowing as they continued to circle our dragon, looking me up and down. "Asherah reborn," they said, translating for my benefit, though it wasn't needed. Their eyes met mine and they smirked as if to say, yes it was.

"And," Ramia continued in Afeyan, "I bring the God Auriel."

"Auriel died," said the three. "Auriel entered the Celestial Realms for eternity. His soul has reincarnated—many times. At present, he is known as Lord Rhyan Hart. Auriel may not return here. If Lord Rhyan is dead, then Auriel's next incarnation must be born."

I bit back a cry. The idea of Rhyan reincarnating—entering a new body, a new life with a new name and a new face without me, going on before I could follow—no. No. It was too much.

But Auriel stepped in front of me, his aura and posture imposing. He looked every bit the God he was. "Tell your queen that Auriel's back," he said. "In the flesh. And that I'm here to see her."

Ramia hissed in annoyance. "Did I say speak?" she asked, glaring back at Auriel.

"We do not take orders from Gods," said the three, their voices now agitated.

"No?" he asked, his eyebrows lifted. "Then I request you tell her that I have this." He held up the scroll vial we'd retrieved from the tomb. Its jewels sparkling in the moonlight. "Auriel's Valya. The last one."

"Auriel's Valya," they all repeated. "All copies of Auriel's Valya were destroyed. Every last version per your agreement."

"Yes. Except for this one—hidden and locked away until all knowledge of it faded. And you all know there was only one way to get a hold of it. Only one way to obtain the last copy." His biceps flexed, his shoulders tensing. "To open the tomb where it was concealed."

"It should have been destroyed," they hissed. "Not buried."

"I made sure it passed out of knowledge. No one could access it, no one remembered. I kept my word. Will your queen keep hers?"

Ramia's eyes flashed in anger, her expression clearly saying, "Shut up."

But the three seemed to go cold with a quiet fury burning through them. "We shall inform her at once," they said in unison.

"Thank you," Ramia said. The three, and their water dragons flew off. Ramia shook her head, her red hair shining in the silver light. "Meeting off to great start!" She huffed, as she rolled her eyes and turned away from us.

My heart began to pound. I didn't like that we were starting on the wrong foot with the Queen, the Afeya who had possession of the red shard, the one thing I needed most in this world.

But a second later small islands began to appear on either side of us. Afeya lounged across them. Some were dancing. Others were drinking, and diving into the waters.

Our water dragon reared back its head, and huffed.

An ashvan ran past us. But this ashvan wasn't like the ones I was used to at home. It was completely silver, just like the Afeyan triple guard. And instead of running only on a step of magic, an entire bridge had formed beneath its hooves, reminding me of a rainbow, but made entirely of shades of blue.

Another blue rainbow appeared right over us. And then another.

Every ashvan was made of silver. As we moved closer to the shore, I realized there were riders on the ashvans' backs. They were leaping off them and sliding down the bridges into the water.

"Is that how they used to be? A whole bridge beneath them?" I asked Auriel.

He nodded. "Before the Drowning, they were all like this. The bridges would appear all over Lumeria, crisscrossing through the sky. You could even run on them without an ashvan. You had to run before they vanished from beneath you, of course—but you could do it. The small steps that appear now are a sign of the breaking of the Valalumir. The Drowning. And the weakening of magic."

"How do they still do it here? They're close to the water, but so is Bamaria. If anything, we're further east, closer to Lumeria Matavia and surrounded on more than one border by the ocean."

"There's no more magic here than anywhere else in the Empire. Not this far west at least," Auriel said. "It weakens in this direction. I remember that. But the Afeya, at least from my understanding, chose to keep things as they were. To pretend the world wasn't broken, that their magic wasn't cut off."

"But don't they need permission, or a request to do this?" I asked.

"They do. And they have it," Auriel said. "It's a thousand years of small bargains made over tiny increments of time. They've made the maintenance of their world part of the deal. It's not hard for them to keep things going, not with so many Lumerians to bargain with. And honestly, my guess is that it's been this way for so long, very little is needed now to maintain the illusion."

"Mercurial didn't ask me for anything like that," I said. Then I frowned. "He actually—he never told me what he wanted in exchange. What the full price would be."

Auriel frowned, glancing at Ramia who was being offered bouquets of water lilies by Afeya who'd come out to greet her. Most were floating nearby in the water, and those too far to approach were tossing single flowers up at her. She smiled, gathering the bouquets, and letting the petals fall into her hair.

"Whatever it is," Auriel said, looking back at me, "Whatever Mercurial wants from you, it's not good."

I looked up at the moonlit sky, feeling disoriented. I was fully aware it was only midday as my eyes followed the glowing blue bridges that crossed back and forth. It was mesmerizing, the way they formed and dissolved as silver ashvan raced across.

And for a second, I felt my stomach tug, like I was traveling and my vision blurred, replaced with a flash of memory.

A blue bridge rolled under me as I rode a golden ashvan beneath the sun. Red hair in a thick braid had fallen across my chest, and I flicked it back over my shoulder. Auriel rode on a twin ashvan, sweat beading his forehead, his curls damp, his eyes hooded, and green, and full of desire. For me.

A desire I matched between my legs. My core was molten lava, hot and consuming, coiling inside me.

His lips curled knowingly into something dangerous and seductive, a promise of later, a promise of pleasure when we were alone.

My breath hitched and I was back in my body, blinking rapidly, determined to ground myself in the present. But my heart was still beating fast. I took a deep breath. We were nearly at the shore. The Moon Queen's Palace lay ahead. I'd seen renderings in scrolls. Paintings hanging in the pyramid that were devoted to the Afeyan texts. But it was even more mesmerizing in person. The palace soared into the sky, and I had to crane my neck back to see even just a hint of the opened roof. I counted about eighteen levels, and each one seemed to be without any walls. From every angle, every floor was completely open to the night sky. It was unlike anything I'd ever seen. Each floor was held up with gleaming columns bordered in silver. Rows upon rows of them. And zooming in and out of every level, were pure white seraphim. Afeya began to emerge between the columns, appearing on every level. They all paused before white marble banisters, leaning over on their elbows and watching our approach. I was in awe.

A dock of white quartz took form, leading to the palace's promenade. Our water dragon came to rest before it.

"Lyriana," Auriel said, his voice suddenly nervous. "Um, I should tell you something. Before we go."

I frowned. "What?"

But Ramia shook her head, water lilies flying from her locks. "No time. Come. Now." She stood up with surprising grace—even for her, carefully walking across our dragon's back, and down onto the quartz of the dock. She dropped her flowers slowly, leaving behind an aisle of petals.

My nerves jumped again.

"Tell me whatever it is later?" I asked Auriel, while also hoping he'd offer me some reassurance as my heart thumped. But his gaze was distant now. His features were taut, and his eyes seemed filled with worry. He shifted me forward, and slid off to the side before coming to stand at the dock. He reached for me, pulling me up to my feet, and lifted me off the dragon, settling me down beside him.

"Sure. Later," he said, and took my hand, our fingers linking, and together we followed Ramia to the promenade. I could feel at least a thousand pairs of eyes watching, even if I couldn't see them all.

Three more water dragons emerged from the palace, miniature in comparison to ours. They were followed by a dozen silver ashvan, each one carrying a rider. They were all adorned in silver dresses, but no two had the same skin tone. The entire rainbow seemed to be represented. My eyes kept jumping, unsure where to look next. While they all had human bodies, only a few of the riders had human heads. The rest reminded me of Mercurial. One rider had the head of a ram, another the head of a bull. One rider even had the features of a lion, their skin orange, a majestic mane falling to their feet. And they were all stunningly beautiful.

Ethereal music seemed to call my soul back to another time. Another life. Not one I could put my finger on. Many of our songs now were originally sung in Lumeria Matavia—the compositions only slightly changed over the centuries. But this felt like something new—a different time, maybe even a different world. More instruments joined the melody, and then voices. I couldn't see where any of the musicians or singers were, or if they were even real. It felt like the music had been summoned from the ether.

The song grew in volume, the music coming to a swell, and on the same note, everyone fell to their knees, including Ramia. She sank down like she was dancing, and gestured for me and Auriel to follow.

Mist swirled at the edge of the palace, changing color with every second that passed. It began as a bright, vibrant violet that darkened to indigo before brightening back to blue. It continued to shift through the rainbow, every color of the Valalumir. Much like the eternal flame we kept in our temples. When the mist turned red, it vanished, leaving in its place the figure of a tall, beautiful Afeyan woman.

"Queen Ma'Nia," Auriel whispered.

I'd never seen her before—nor seen a single rendering or picture. I'd heard she held an otherworldly kind of beauty and like all Afeya, she was capable of changing her appearance, glamouring herself to fit any mood that befell her. But for some reason I couldn't explain, I had the distinct sense that she was in her natural state—because her resemblance to Ramia was startling. There was no doubt they were related. Had they not been Afeyan and immortal, had their ages not been impossible to determine, I'd have guessed they were sisters before mother and daughter.

But slowly, I began to take stock of the differences between them. A small tweak of the nose, a shift in the plumpness of the mouth. The main distinctions came from the fact that

Ma'Nia had startling violet eyes. Her hair was a vibrant red I hadn't expected. But where Ramia's red was something closer to mine in the sun, the Moon Queen had a purple sheen to hers, one I suspected was a perfect match for her irises in the right light.

She stepped forward, wearing a dress made of thousands of pearls strung together. They jingled with every step she took, swishing back and forth across her body as she approached us. She wore nothing beneath them. Every step revealed new expanses of skin, while simultaneously hiding other parts of her. You could see everything and nothing all at once.

She stopped walking, taking her time to look us over. Her head tilted to the side as if she were considering her next move. Something flashed in her eyes, and then she straightened, gesturing for us all to rise.

Ramia stood first, and walked slowly to her mother. The Queen pulled her into an embrace, then drew her daughter beside her.

"Mother, I present Lady Lyriana Batavia of Bamaria. The reincarnation of—"

"Asherah," Queen Ma'Nia said, her voice melodious and soothing. "Asherah again." Violet eyes roamed up and down my body. It felt like she wasn't looking at anything physical, but rather that she was seeing my soul. Seeing Asherah's essence. The thing Auriel said made me her. The thing that he recognized.

I lowered my chin. "Your Majesty," I said.

She held up a hand, and I closed my mouth, suddenly unsure what to do.

The queen turned to Auriel, and storm clouds appeared above the palace. There was a heart-stopping clap of thunder, and lightning struck. Her violet eyes burned.

"Auriel," she drawled, her voice low. "In the flesh. An impossibility. You had your life and you lost it, never to return here again. And yet you stand before me now." She shook her head. "After all you've done," her eyes darkened, "you have the nerve to return to my lands."

"Your Majesty, I beseech you," Auriel started, but Queen Ma'Nia held up her hand again, and Auriel's mouth closed at once. As if she controlled him.

"You are not welcome," she said. "And you never will be."

"Be that as it may, we made a bargain," he said. "A thousand years ago we made an agreement. I'm here to honor it."

"To break it," she snapped, stepping forward, her eyes zeroing in on Auriel's Valya. The true Valya. The one that contained the truth about the cure.

"How do you suppose that? I kept my word," Auriel said. "I broke no vows. Only one copy of my Valya remained, and it was buried with me. Untouched, unread, and forgotten. All knowledge of it faded, dying with my body."

"Until today," the Queen said. "It's so rare for something or someone to return from the dead. But it seems we have not one, but two resurrections before us."

Auriel's jaw clenched, his eyes boring into the Queen's with an unbridled anger I hadn't seen from him before. An anger she seemed to match.

"You are lucky I have not thrown you into the playground with my monsters," Queen Ma'Nia said. Her eyes sparkled. "I may still do that."

Auriel's nostril's flared. "You said that last time, too."

My eyes widened. The playground?

"And then you threw me in anyway," Auriel said. "And I survived."

"Clearly." She tilted her head to the side. "Go. Leave here. I have no interest in seeing you, or in treating with you. Unfaithful."

"You are calling me unfaithful! How dare you. You know you cannot send us away!" Auriel snapped.

"Can I not? Can I not do as I please in my own court? You have no jurisdiction here. Not anymore. Your power is not what it once was, Auriel, Guardian of the Green Ray. You are diminished from what you once were—no matter how much the light from her breast tries to heal you."

I shook my head, feeling desperate. We had to enter. We had to get what we came for. I didn't care what animosity there was between Ma'Nia and Auriel, or how stubborn the Afeya could be. I was not leaving here without the red shard.

Auriel held up his scroll. "Then our bargain is broken. I will make copies of the Valya again. Share what I know."

"Share what you know?" The Queen lifted an eyebrow in challenge. "What you know is worthless. Have you forgotten? It's been a thousand years. They won't believe you. They'll say it's a myth. A story. It will be dismissed."

"You don't know that," Auriel sneered.

She shrugged. "Maybe. Maybe not. It won't change things. You see, some knowledge is priceless. This knowledge, these writings you clutch in your mortal fist, is not. It is worthless without the missing piece." She gazed at my heart, and red light reflected in her violet eyes. The red ray of the Valalumir. "Go, Auriel. I did not invite you here."

"No?" he seethed. "But Mercurial made sure I became flesh. He pulled a lot of damn strings to bring me back."

Queen Ma'Nia stiffened. "Mercurial, First Messenger of Her Royal Highness, Queen Ishtara, also has no jurisdiction here. Whatever he did or did not do will not sway my hand. Go north if you seek Mercurial."

"I have every right to ask you to return what I gave you. That was our deal!" he shouted.

"You had the right to ask. And to receive. But only in your original body."

"This is my original body!"

She tilted her head, tapping her chin. "I can see that it is. And yet—there's something different. This body was not born."

"Neither was I born last time," Auriel shouted.

"I need some to think. Time to consider. To decide if this truly honors our bargain."

"We don't have time," I yelled.

"Shhh," Ramia hissed.

But I didn't care anymore. They had a bargain, and Rhyan's life was on the line. She was going to fucking honor it and I was going to do whatever it took to make sure of it.

"I need your help," I said. "I am begging you. A Goddess is begging a queen. Mercurial acted to bring us here today, and I know you share a goal."

"So?" She threw up her hands. "You're here. He succeeded. That does not mean my hand must be forced. I have something you want, sure, but what do you have that I want? Why would I help you, Asherah?" She peered at me from the corner of her eye. "What could a mortal with only part of the Valalumir in her chest offer to me—when I hold the original shard? What favor can you offer in exchange for it?"

"You know that it's mine," I seethed. "And your magic will force you to acquiesce to Auriel."

The Queen only shrugged. I wanted to rip her hair out. But that wasn't going to get me anywhere. I couldn't lose more time. I had to save Rhyan. Find him before Sean did. Before Rhyan hurt anyone else. I knew what I had to do. The one thing no Afeya could refuse.

I lifted my chin. "Give Auriel back the shard. And I'll make a bargain with you, in exchange."

The Queen's eyes flashed with interest.

"I'll make a deal," I said. "You name the price."

"No," Auriel said. "Lyriana, no."

"Yes," I hissed. "You have my word. Make me a deal, and fulfill your end of the bargain with Auriel. Tonight."

She laughed, a finger curling around her chin. "True love will make you indebted to all of us before the end. But having the word of a Goddess, even if she comes in a young form, is quite interesting to me. Very well." She gazed out at the other Afeya on the shore, their eyes blinking in the night, watching me, giggling into their hands.

Ramia shook her head at me, the movement almost too subtle to see.

"Bring her to me," the Queen commanded. "Now!"

"No!" Auriel yelled. But two Afeya materialized out of nowhere grabbing my arms and dragging me away from him.

Auriel followed behind us, I could feel him at my back and then he suddenly made a sound of pain as he was forced to stop his approach.

The Queen held up her palm, a shimmering silver light taking form as a Valalumir star.

I sucked in a breath. I still remembered the night I accepted my contract with Mercurial. The way the Valalumir had sparkled and shone. The blinding pain when it entered my body.

But that had been the Red Ray, the original light of the Valalumir. What the Queen offered was only a portion of her soul. Not the light itself.

"Lyriana, don't," Auriel yelled.

The Moon Queen held up her hand once more, and Auriel was silenced. She turned the star back to me, letting it spin and twirl as it floated above her palm, every bit as mesmerizing and dazzling as Mercurial's had been.

Some part of me railed against this, my stomach turning in warning. But I couldn't take my eyes away, nor could I back down. Not with what was at stake.

"Well?" the Moon Queen purred. "Are we in agreement?"

"That depends. What are the terms?' I asked.

Her eyes flashed, focusing again on my chest, like she was seeing my contract with Mercurial, like she was reading some fine print I'd never known about.

"First," Queen Ma'Nia continued, "you will fulfill your agreement with Mercurial. What I want from you cannot be done until his wishes are complete."

My stomach turned. Shared goals, indeed.

"Then," she said, "you will grant mine."

"Another vague favor?" I sneered. But my skin was crawling with fear.

The Queen's eyes narrowed, looking beyond me. "Shhhh. Calm yourself, Auriel."

I followed her gaze, Auriel's mouth remained closed, but his face was red like he was trying to yell and scream. He shook his head when his eyes met mine, full of alarm.

"I'm sorry," I mouthed, and turned back to the Queen.

She smiled. "Vague? Have patience. I will tell you what I want, and what you will do if you wish to save your lover." Her eyes flashed, a cat-like smile on her face. "Your most recent lover."

My hands clenched. "Name it."

She waved her hand, showing off silver-painted nails. She blinked, and they turned amethyst, then silver once more. "You, Lyriana Batavia, are going to do something we've all greatly desired for centuries. You are going to lift the curse upon us. You will remove the bindings that force us to bargain, that have forced us into a singular immortality for a thousand years. Unable to die, unable to start anew, to begin fresh, to live different lives, to reunite with our loved ones in the Celestial Realms."

I blinked, for once realizing how immortality itself could be a curse.

"You want to be mortal?"

"Yes," she said.

"You'll be able to do magic still—any kind of magic you want, but freely?" My heart pounded with a warning. They'd have nothing stopping them, nothing to control the power they'd have, no way to rein them in. Until they died. Whenever that happened. It could be dangerous. The knowledge they had, the years of practice and perfection.

"We can do any magic we want at last, wherever we want and whenever we want. And … when we so choose, when our work is complete, we will wither and die, and be reborn."

I bit my lip. "How long will you remain before that time comes?"

"Only one bargain tonight. No more questions."

"I lift the curse and give you free rein, all so you can fulfill the oath you were supposed to in the first place," I said, my hands clenching into fists. I shouldn't have even had to bargain. But here we were. "If I unleash you on Lumeria," I said slowly, "I want something in return."

"The shard to save your love, your *mekarim*, isn't enough for you?" she asked sweetly. Then smirked. "Oh but it is … I can smell it. But, as I am a gracious queen, I will offer you a gift. After you lift the curse, all Afeya in the Moon Court may be summoned to fight on your behalf. We shall," her eyes sparkled, "become your soturi."

I balked. "You'll fight for me? In battle?"

"Once. You may call upon us once. One battle. Choose wisely. Many lay ahead for you."

My pulse pounded, my mind reeling. "I can command you as my army for one fight, and you'll fulfill your end of the bargain with Auriel—tonight?"

"We shall begin proceedings, and I shall invite you inside, along with him. What you do next will determine the outcome. But without our bargain, we won't even begin negotiations. Not tonight."

"H-How do I lift the curse?" I asked. It was a thousand years old. I didn't even know it could be undone. "I know it's a question, but if you want me to do this—I need to know how."

"Why don't you ask Auriel, hmmm?"

"Ask Auriel?" I frowned.

"You see," she continued, "Auriel is more than just the God who fell from Heaven. The God who stole the Valalumir from the sky. He is the God," she spat, "who cursed our kind. Who sentenced us to exile, to immortality, and to an eternity of making petty bargains in exchange for power. He is the God who exiled us for a thousand years, forcing us to hold all knowledge of the universe in our hands, but to only access and touch it when asked." Her eyes glittered with something in between venom, and pride. "Canturiel may have created the Valalumir. But after the War of Light, it was Auriel who cursed and thereby created the Afeya."

My mouth dropped open as I turned, stunned, to Auriel. "You," I whispered. "You were the one who cursed them? You made it so they could only do magic if asked?"

"And therefore binding us," the Queen hissed, "to an eternity of fulfilling favors. Without release. Without death." Some of the Afeya watching us began to yell, cursing at him, and booing.

Auriel blew out a sharp breath and nodded slowly. "Turns out … Yes. That was me."

By the Gods. He hadn't just written the Valya. He'd written the curse of the Afeya. No wonder we weren't being greeted warmly, or allowed inside. And while I knew I'd never forgive Mercurial, his bursts of anger around Rhyan were starting to make more sense.

A sudden rush of magic forced me to face the Queen again.

"Now are we in agreement?" she asked. "I can send you both away and Auriel can try to claw his way back and bargain with me, find another water dragon willing to carry him here, seek another of my daughters who may offer him her favor. Or, you can agree to finish what he started, agree to free us from his curse, and we can begin negotiations."

My heart slammed into my throat. A shadow of a warning settled inside of me. If I freed them of their curse, they'd be like Lumerians. But more. They'd become Lumerians who held all knowledge of the universe. The danger they'd pose to Lumeria unrestricted, free to do whatever magic they wanted, and when they wanted—the idea terrified me.

But not as much as walking out of here without my shard.

I took a deep breath. "You will fulfill your end of the bargain with him. All of your terms with Auriel will be fulfilled. I will find a way to break the curse. And I will call upon your army for a battle of my choosing," I said.

"Yes."

"Then we are in agreement," I said and squeezed my eyes shut.

Blinding silver light filled my eyelids as a sharp pain of ice so cold it was hot—like the silver rings in the habibellum pierced through my chest.

Fire and ice were dancing inside my heart and I gasped, feeling faint, my knees buckling.

Ramia grabbed my arm, shaking her head. "I told you to let me do talking." But she brought me stumbling back to Auriel's side. He wrapped an arm around me at once, pulling me against him.

The Moon Queen laughed. "Asherah would have known better." She shook her head. "You see," she continued, "I was bound to fulfill my agreement with Auriel, however distasteful I find him. However unwelcome he and you remain, and will always remain in my court. Not after what you two have done." Her head tilted to the side, in an agitated twitch.

"You didn't have to trick her," Auriel shouted. "You didn't have to do any of this! We had an agreement. We had a bargain!"

"I know," she said. "We did. But you cannot blame me for trying. After all, when someone can give you what you want, why not take it?" Her gaze settled on me, condescending and full of disdain. "I heard you were easy to bargain with. But I had no idea you'd fold so quickly." She raised her arms high. "I should have asked for more."

I snarled. Fuck. I didn't even have to bargain in the first place. And now, I'd be unleashing Afeya into the Empire—all so the Queen could do what she'd always sworn she would. Having her army on my side for a battle was good—but the fact that I could only use them once? And who was to say they wouldn't join the other side the moment the battle was done?

The Queen grinned widely, knowing she'd won. Knowing that whatever we walked out of here with, she'd taken something more.

"Let's proceed shall we? We have guests," she announced. Then to us, she winked. "Now, you may come inside."

CHAPTER EIGHTEEN

LYRIANA

"Auriel!" I hissed.

"Yes, *Meka*?" he asked me, his voice low.

We were being led into the palace by the Queen's silver-skinned sentries, walking down the long quartz dock as waves lapped along the edge. When we reached the promenade, the crystal beneath our feet shifted to moonstone, as we walked inside. There were long swaths of pure gleaming white, interrupted by sudden flashes of bright, glowing blue. Every step we took seemed to create another spark. It reminded me of the ashvan back home, the glowing blue lights that erupted beneath their hooves. The ethereal music continued to play—still without any sign of musicians or the accompanying singers, until we arrived in what I believed to be Queen Ma'Nia's throne room.

We paused before a small pool of water, the moon perfectly reflected inside. Beyond that was a dais where Queen Ma'Nia stood. Ramia was perched beside her, sitting on a chaise much like the one she had in her office at the library.

"Don't you think it might have been important to tell me that it was you? That you did all of this?" I asked, weakly gesturing around.

"Well," he hissed back, "Considering you were there when it happened, I forgot I had to. Until we were about to dock."

"That's when you decided to tell me? You waited until the last second! Gods! You could have warned me."

"Well technically you knew," he seethed.

"I didn't! I wasn't there! That was Asherah! How many times do I have to tell you? I barely remember anything."

His eyes darkened. "Well I tried!"

"Yes, you waited until the last possible minute. You really tried so hard!"

"Oh, don't act so innocent yourself. You remember more from back then than you think. More than you're willing to admit."

My cheeks flushed. He was right. There were times when I felt like her, when I felt like I was her as I looked at him. Even just moments ago, I had a memory of being Asherah. Of Auriel looking at me with unbridled desire. And I remembered feeling a matching need for him, for his body. The need to claim him and be claimed. I felt it coursing through me. Heating and tightening down my stomach, between my legs.

And I could still feel it now, despite what we faced.

We were surrounded by the Moon Queen's full court of Afeya, but I shook my head, glaring at Auriel. Because once again, there was important information I didn't have—information I needed. He'd been the one! He had cursed the Afeya. Every problem I'd ever had with them, every run-in—was all Auriel's fault. And now because of it, because Queen Ma'Nia had been able to use that knowledge against me, I was in another Godsdamned Afeyan bargain.

The sensation in my chest brought about by the contract had already calmed, but like last time, I felt its presence. I was aware of it there, pulsing, turning, shimmering with every beat of my heart.

Auriel's eyes were on my chest, staring at it with as much worry as Rhyan's had when I'd made my first contract.

I groaned. "Whatever I do or don't remember is irrelevant. Because I didn't remember this!" I gestured around us. Not once in any Valya I'd read had it mentioned it was him. Nor in any of the history books. They always just said that the Afeya were cursed. Passive.

I took a deep breath and looked slowly around the room, at the tall white and silver columns, the open ceiling with the moon above, and the sea of faces in the shadows watching us. Little stars exploded in the air. The Afeya's auras being pushed out.

"I can't help it if I have a thousand years of information to sort through—most of which was barely accessible to me after I arrived."

"But then you remembered," I said. "It all came back to you."

"And right after we had to flee for our lives. Believe me, I'm not trying to keep secrets from you. Okay? I swear. But in case you didn't notice, we haven't exactly been on vacation these last few days. You're the most wanted traitor in the Lumerian Empire. Every other person we meet wants to kill you. All I've been doing is trying to keep you alive."

"I can keep myself alive!" I nearly shouted.

"You can." He leaned in toward me. "But for a little while there you weren't."

"And somehow, despite all of that, I still think you should have told me! You should have told me you were the author of the curse before this! Before we were sailed into the country of the very people you condemned," I snapped. "Before I made another bargain! Now I'm indebted and tied to Queen Ma'Nia. Another Afeya and a whole other court. And we're trapped inside a palace of Afeya who've had a thousand years to be mad at you." And me by association, unless there was even more I still didn't know, or remember.

"Well maybe," he gritted, "that's why I didn't mention it."

"You should have!" I hissed.

"And if I had, you wouldn't have made a bargain?"

I groaned. "I didn't know! She knew what she was doing and I wasn't going to risk not succeeding. Nor wasting any more time. Not when it comes to Rhyan."

"Realms!"

"Have you two quite finished?" Queen Ma'Nia asked, sitting back in her throne. The seat was so wide she was able to sweep her knees up beneath her. Delicate feet peeked out from her pearl skirts, and a large pearl, one the size of my big toe, was fitted around hers, attached to a silver ring. "If not, by all means, continue this lover's quarrel."

"We're not—" I closed my mouth. We weren't lovers. But we weren't … not … exactly either.

"Not lovers?" The Queen shrugged. "Maybe not in these bodies. Not yet. But these iterations of your minds? You're close. I've never seen two souls so intertwined. So deeply connected." Her violet eyes flashed, and I felt naked. "Nor have I ever seen two souls who are so in love."

My throat dried, and I stared ahead, afraid to look at Auriel. Afraid to meet his gaze.

"Perhaps, had you cursed yourselves, you'd still be Asherah, and this fight could be over."

My chest squeezed. I hated that thought. I knew there was pain in our past. Rhyan had felt it so keenly in his dreams. He'd felt Auriel's memories like they were his own. Losing me. Losing Asherah. And I knew that the part of my soul in the Celestial Realms, that part of me that was still Asherah was up there, alone, missing Auriel. Pained. But if we'd never reincarnated—Rhyan never would have existed. Would have never been born. And that was a world I didn't want to be a part of—no matter what it cost.

Auriel's eyes softened as if he read my mind, then he faced the Moon Queen and cleared his throat. "I know it's been a while since we last spoke, Your Majesty."

The Moon Queen nodded. "It has been some time," she agreed. Then she laughed. "For you. Not so much for us. You see, time moves differently here." Her voice had slowed, becoming something hypnotizing and melodic. She ran a finger down the length of her thigh. "Very differently than what you know." She wiggled her big toe and the pearl shone. "When I married my husband, RaKanan, King of the Sun Court, something quite strange happened. We mixed together the elements and energies of the moon and sun, not just with our bodies, or in our beds." She held Auriel's gaze. "But together we joined the spirit of those entities, threaded together their timelines, and cycles."

"Timelines?" I asked. "Your Majesty?"

She laughed again. "Yes. One cycle of the sun within El Zandria and Khemet is the equivalent of the full turn of a moon beyond our lands."

I froze, parsing out her words. "One cycle of the sun?" I shook my head. "But it's night here. Night fell long before it was supposed to." We were at sea for hours. But we still had plenty of time before sunset. "There is no sun."

The Queen clicked her tongue. "Night did not fall. It cannot do such a thing here. It just was, as it always is. In Khemet, the night is eternal. Just as the sun never rises in El Zandria." She gestured to the east. "The day simply remains. But time moves. Hours pass and they mark the cycles which appear stagnant to us."

So a constant moon, and a constant sun, but still there were twenty-four hours. One cycle, one day. Sunrise to sunrise again. Was she saying—Gods, was she saying that a day's cycle was the equivalent of a moon's?

"I'm sorry," I said, sweat beading at my brow. "But ... you're telling me that if we spend a day here in Khemet, a month will have passed in Lumeria?"

The Queen nodded. "Even just traveling through our waters, crossing through the coast of Bamaria to El Zandria, you entered our timeline. Nearly half a day has passed for you here. Yet weeks have passed out there by my count."

Weeks? Weeks! No, no, no. That couldn't be! It couldn't. Fuck. That meant I'd missed weeks of finding my family, of being able to tell them where I was, what had happened to me. Weeks I'd lost that I needed to find Rhyan. Sean could be with him by now and I had no idea if Branwyn had gotten through to him, or if he believed her.

"That's nature," the Queen sing-songed. "Ask your soulmate, your *mekarim*."

Endless levels of floors between the columns, rising up and up, began to fill with faces. Afeya leaned over the banisters, some were hanging from them, their feet dangling in the air. And all of them were laughing and giggling. Their auras were flung out, away from their bodies, leaving shadows and clouds and stars exploding everywhere I looked.

I took a deep breath, my pulse pounding through me. Two Afeyan contracts beating in my heart against the light of the Red Ray.

"Now," she said, flicking her nails. The color changed from silver to a shiny maroon, and then back. Swinging her feet to the ground she stood, the pearls of her dress shifting and jingling. "I am bound to fulfill my end of the bargain and hand Auriel back the red shard I've protected." Her violet eyes flashed. "For you. But before I do, you must understand why this has happened. What role you played, and what role you still might."

I eyed Auriel nervously. I didn't want a fucking history lesson. Not when every second here counted like a Godsdamned hour. But if it was what it took to get the shard, then so be it.

I lowered my chin to the queen. "I'm ready to listen."

"Very well." Queen Ma'Nia nodded. "Akadim were fallen Gods and Goddesses," she said. "They'd found a way to defy the Council. To have more power. More will. Their intention was innocent at first. But the power twisted them, turning them into monsters full of violence, and lust. Their souls could not withstand the evil in their bodies. And so they left, retreating to a kind of resting place."

"A resting place?" I asked. "Is that where Rhyan is? The part of his soul that's still him?"

"It is," the Queen said. "His soul is with the others who've been eaten, taken, lost. Akadim hunger for more than flesh, and blood, and sex. What they desire above all else, is what they once were. They miss their souls. They seek them out. They're starving for them. Desperate for the feel, for the memory. For the life force within. It drives them mad. The only relief they can receive is the devouring of someone else's soul—even if the feeling of life and wholeness is only temporary. And there the souls remain, trapped for years, decades. Sometimes longer—only passing when the akadim that took their body dies, or ... when their life course, had there been no interference, comes to an end."

I shuddered. So Rhyan could be trapped for decades. Alone and cut off, unable to pass over—not until his human body would have naturally aged out of life.

"And some, back then," the Queen added, "lived centuries. So to stop the cycle, and save more from falling, from suffering through an eternity of this fate, Canturiel created the light. And it healed them, restored their souls. Granted what they most wanted. To be whole."

I nodded, desperate for the Queen to continue.

"But some of them did not wish to go back to the way things were. Some disagreed with the rulings of the Council. Some were simply drunk on their power. Others had simply fallen too far. Become too corrupt and monstrous to seek redemption, to even desire it. And so they tried to steal the light. To prevent it from taking any more of their army. The light remained untouched, unused for years, sitting under your watchful eye. And Auriel's. Until the day it wasn't—until you both were banished, the light stolen, the light no longer unbroken. You tried to continue with the original mission as Asherah. You didn't want to kill. You didn't want to further trap souls in the cycle of reincarnation. So you used the cure. Auriel would fight in battle, as would you, but your main mission was to use the Valalumir to heal as many akadim as you could."

I gasped. "I was healing them in the war. Restoring their souls?"

The Queen nodded. "It was honorable work you did. I will not deny that. You saved many. Restored families, lovers, mothers and fathers. But the work is difficult and slow. And without its strongest warrior in battle—you—in the end, you were losing the war. Losing too many of your kind. When you should have killed, you tried to save. Many defected, many saw the lost cause for what it was. So, in the final battle before the Drowning, we refused to fight with you—because we could see the outcome. See the loss you refused to acknowledge. We could not promise you our people, nor send them off into what we believed to be a massacre. We honored life. Not death. Our intention was to protect those who'd sought safety with us. Seeking refuge in our lands, our kingdoms. And still, Auriel cursed us for this. Cursed us for trying to save lives."

She pointed at the pool, at the image in the water of me and Auriel together. With a wave of her hand, the pool rippled, distorting our image, and something resembling a ghost of Auriel rose above the water.

He was furious, his face red. He wore his armor, and there were open cuts and bruises along his muscled arms. Mud coated his boots.

"I curse you," the ghost Auriel yelled in High Lumerian. "I curse you to immortality. To an eternity of remembering what you did, and of facing its consequences. You will live forever. Until you step foot once more on dry Lumerian land. And as you can see, that will never ever happen. You did not honor our agreement, you did not answer our call, or come when asked, though you swore to do so. Therefore, you will never do anything again without first being asked. Without permission. Your magic that you used so freely is now only yours by request. You'll be forced to serve others, to answer their calls, to honor your agreements, your bargains. You have an eternity now to answer the call of others in need—your fate for your refusal to answer mine."

The ghost of Auriel faded, and his likeness returned to the pool, along with mine.

"That's why you asked him to destroy any mention of the cure?" I asked. "Because we'd lost in battle while using it."

The Queen nodded. "And now, I fear you're going to do the same thing as before. Damn us further. Mercurial may wish for you to have the shard returned to you for his own purposes, and you wish to have it to heal your lover." Her eyes flicked to Auriel. "That is—your current lover. You are consumed by your desire to restore the soul of Lord Rhyan Hart, Auriel's current incarnation."

"I am," I said.

She waved her hand in dismissal. "And will you heal others?"

"Of course," I said. "How could I not? The akadim are victims of their circumstances, like Rhyan. There's not one who wished for this, or asked for this fate."

"You speak the truth," she said. "But what I need to know is if you're strong enough to do both. To heal as you always meant to—to remember the innocence of the souls when weighed against the evils done by their monstrous counterparts. And, I need a further guarantee. You may heal with the shard, restore akadim. But you may not do so at the expense of other lives. Moriel already has his shard, as does his lover Ereshya. And if they acquire more, you and your people are doomed. One more shard between them, one more ally gained, and the world will end."

I shook my head, and felt Auriel move before me, his body tensed.

"You may save Rhyan's life. Restore his soul. Heal him. And you may do so for others if given the chance. But akadim breed more akadim. Every akadim you allow to live kills another. Makes another. Eats another soul. The cycle is endless, and completes itself faster than you think. You must stop the threat as you've been taught. And whether that is by taking the akadim's life, or restoring it—you must stop the threat. Do you understand me?"

"I do," I said. "Of course." My heart was thundering.

"Your words are quite as pretty as they always were," the Moon Queen said. "I've known your soul a long time. So I know, like Auriel, you keep your word. But you can also be soft-hearted. If Lord Rhyan Hart's soul cannot be restored, he will prove to be one of the most dangerous, and destructive forces the Empire has ever seen. Worse than the rise of Moriel. A prophecy exists even now. Visions shared by three. He has the power, as do you, to destroy our world. To cover Lumeria in fire. You must not let him. And your feelings for him must not cloud your judgement."

"They won't," I said.

"We shall see." The Queen clapped. "We shall find out through some play."

"What do you mean?" I asked.

"No!" Auriel threw his body in front of mine. "Your Majesty! Don't do this!"

And from the endless balconies above, Afeya leaned forward, their eyes wide and excited. And completely focused on me.

"You shall pass a test, Lady Lyriana," the Moon Queen said, sitting back on her throne. She lifted her feet back up to rest.

Ramia's eyes darted to me, her expression full of fear.

"But you already gave your word to Auriel! And I've already made a bargain. Your contract sits inside me."

"I didn't say those were my requirements. I warned you. I am doing my part. I have invited you inside for negotiations. Auriel may take back what he gave. But I must first know you're strong enough to do what must be done. What must ultimately be done if it comes down to it. And the only way to know for sure is through a test."

"What kind of test?" I asked.

"Before I agreed to bargain with Auriel." She waved around the throne room, "I made him do the same—prove his word and his worth. He had to survive my playground. You survive now, and I shall trust your word. You survive, and my contract with Auriel shall be fulfilled tonight."

Auriel rushed in front of me and brandished his sword. "She's given you enough! And I can vouch for her strength. She was prepared to slay Rhyan as an akadim!"

"So she's said. Now, she'll prove it."

His sword clashed to the ground, and slid away from his feet, just as a gale force wind pushed him to the side, forcing him to stumble back against a wall.

The same wind pulled at me with invisible hands that dragged me forward. I dug in my heels, using all the muscle I'd earned, and that my magic had enhanced. But it was no use. My feet were perched at the edge of the pool.

The water vanished, revealing a large hole in the ground. It was too dark for me to see the bottom. A deep roar sounded from below—a horrific cacophony of noise unlike anything I'd ever heard before.

Something was alive down there. I stepped back, true terror rushing through me. I had no idea what could make such a sound. And I didn't want to know.

Straining, I tried to step back, to keep myself from falling forward.

But then the edges of the pool began to widen, the floor retreating beneath my feet. I gritted my teeth and stumbled back, fighting against the unnaturally powerful wind that was determined to propel me forward.

I stepped back, and then stepped again, using every bit of power I could muster.

But the edge of the pool was under my toes, my balance failing as the floor vanished beneath my heels.

A scream exploded out of me, my stomach rising to my heart, as I fell straight down. Not into the pool. Into the Queen's playground.

CHAPTER NINETEEN

LYRIANA

My feet hit the ground, and my knees buckled, my entire body shaking as I stumbled forward. My palms slammed against the dirt floor, my skin scraping across random debris as dust flew into my eyes. I groaned in pain, disoriented, and reached blindly around, trying to sit up, but I grabbed hold of a loose rock that only cut deeper into my palm. I spat into the back of my hand and wiped at my eyes, desperate to see. There wasn't much. The terrain was filthy, and uneven, riddled with random sticks and rocks. It seemed to go on forever, the edges of the room vanishing into shadows.

Gingerly, I shifted back on my heels, and blinked, tightening my core as I found my balance and stood. I brandished both my dagger and sword, tight in my hands, the blades reflecting moonlight that poured in from above. I took in my surroundings, surveying Ma'Nia's playground. Endless swaths of rocks were strewn across the dirt field, broken up only by a few small hills. But that was it, no sign of the creature I knew stalked me.

There was a soft groaning above, and the ceiling began to close, returning the floor of the throne room to its original shape. Now only a small circular opening remained above my head; right where the pool had been, casting me into an even deeper darkness. The Afeya watching from above, peered down as they leaned over their balcony ledges. Some of the Afeya lay on the floor of the throne room, their hands gripping the edges of the pool, their heads leaning over to watch me.

Their excitement and bloodlust, the energy of their auras pulsed with a kind of morbid curiosity that twisted my stomach. If I died I'd be nothing more than entertainment to them. Entertainment that they were far too eager to observe. Because if I failed—it was nothing to them. I'd reincarnate, I'd return. And I'd end up in this shit-hole again.

The hell I would.

I took a deep breath, and instantly regretted it, the smell was horrific. Whatever lived down here clearly had for a long time—shedding, eating, and relieving itself.

A smoky snarling erupted in the shadows. I went still, barely daring or wanting to breathe, and turned slowly, tuning out the throne room's cheers and applause.

The snarl came again. Foreign, monstrous, and deadly. It wasn't human or Afeyan. And it wasn't an akadim either. I didn't get the feeling I had when near them. Whatever was down here, this was something else. Something I'd never encountered before.

The knot in my stomach tightened.

"Behold," Queen Ma'Nia shouted. "Goddess Asherah, Guardian of the Valalumir has been reborn. Once a great warrior and Arkturion of old—let's see how she faces off today against one of her lost, ancient foes."

I turned again, searching desperately for my opponent. I didn't like this. Not knowing, not seeing. And I didn't like being so damn exposed. There was nowhere to hide, nothing to use to my advantage aside from the weapons on my body. I couldn't use the terrain in my favor, or climb to higher ground, or use anything beyond a small rock as a weapon if needed.

The cheers and applause suddenly shifted to encouragement. But not for me. They were urging the creature to come out, taunting it to attack.

And it seemed to listen. It snarled again, the sound low and vicious. I still couldn't see it. But I knew it had moved closer to me. Its scent of decay had grown stronger. I nearly gagged as I tried to identify the stench, to recall the sound of its snarl. But nothing I'd faced or read about came to mind. Pulse quickening, I turned again, feeling the distinct sensation of being watched in secret, of eyes set upon me. An answering sniff in the air told me that the creature was now scenting me out.

Fuck.

But a minute passed, and still there was no attack. No sight of my foe.

"What is this?" I yelled. I was losing patience, my fear growing with anticipation of its reveal. If this thing was going to play and hide and seek with me, the least Queen Ma'Nia could do was tell me what the hell it was.

Fresh laughter filled the throne room, the sound echoing in my playground. But through the noise, Auriel was shouting, desperately calling my name, trying to tell me something, trying to warn me.

"What is this?" the Queen mocked. "You mean to tell me you still don't know? The smell hasn't brought you back? Your memories are weaker than I thought." She laughed. "You haven't read Auriel's Valya, have you?"

"Haven't exactly had the time," I snapped, my fingers tightening around my weapons.

"Lyriana!" Auriel called out. He said something, a word in High Lumerian that I didn't recognize. Someone screamed over him as he tried again. But the beast's snarl had me snapping my head, searching for it in the dark. I could tell that the snarl had come from the same place as before, the beast hadn't moved—but this time, it sounded completely different. More of a growl, but not from any animal I'd ever heard—not even the one I'd just heard. Maybe animal wasn't the right way to describe it. It was more like scraping bones together.

I shivered as I stepped in the direction of the noise, sweat beading my forehead, and lifted my sword.

A gate creaked, my hand trembled. This was it. The thing had been inside a cage. That was why I hadn't seen it yet. That's why it hadn't charged. So Ma'Nia could fucking taunt me.

Metal cranked against metal as it lifted, and rolled back, causing the chinking chains to echo in the dark.

Steady. Steady. I repeated the words like a mantra.

Whatever was behind the gate, it was going to charge— before I could even see it. I had to be ready to fight. And whatever came into view, I had to face it. For Rhyan.

And just like that, I felt him. Whether it was his soul somehow reaching out from the void, or my imagination, it didn't matter. A cool calm aura washed over me. The sensation of being snuggled up beneath blankets, held tight against a warm body. Rhyan's hand on my belly. His lips against my ear.

Partner.

The sensation vanished, and the shadow came towards me.

The snarls came again. There were two of them, sounding off simultaneously. In the darkness, two sets of eyes appeared. Two yellow eyes. Two white.

Two sets of eyes … two snarls … Had another joined? Had it been waiting in the cage behind the other?

My stomach turned. And then the beast came into view under the light of the moon. Just one beast.

I moved back on instinct, my eyes widening as I bit back a horrified scream. It was seven or eight feet tall, the same height as an akadim. Its body was equally wide, and covered in gray fur. At first glance, it looked like a giant fucking wolf. But instead of a fluffy tail, there was a nahashim, stretching and shrinking with each breath the beast took. Its scaly body curled and then extended into a violent thrust, its head shifting forward, fangs glistening before it hissed right at me.

But that wasn't what had created the second sound. The one that sounded like bones. Whatever this thing was, it had two heads. Two fucking heads! They were squished together, like they were both trying to occupy its neck at the same time. One was a kind of wolf, with cruel yellow eyes, long sharp fangs protruding from its opened mouth. Two white horns, reminiscent of a bull, but sharpened at the tips, poked out of its temples. The second head was the one that sounded like bones. And now I knew why. It was the skull of a wolf. It had matching horns, like it was the other's twin, just lacking muscles, skin, and fur. And though this skeleton head looked and smelled like it had been dead for ages, its glowing white eyes told me that it was very much alive.

"Does this bring back memories for you yet?" the Queen asked. "Memories of another life? Do you recall the last time you faced a chimera?"

A chimera? That's what this abomination was?

That's what Auriel was trying to say.

I'd never heard the term before. Never learned it in any of my studies. But as I tested the word in my mouth, something began to tickle the back of my mind.

A flash of memory. A knowing. I had seen this monster before. Auriel had been right to worry. With two heads, and a nahashim for a tail, it was going to be impossible to kill.

Both heads opened their mouths to howl. Their yellow and white eyes set on me as its front paws, full of elongated, sharpened claws pawed the ground. The chimera was preparing to attack, acting more bull than wolf. It made a huffing sound that ended in a vicious growl. And then, it charged.

I dodged rolling onto the ground out of the way before jumping back to my feet. I didn't know where to strike or how to defeat this thing. Was the skull head always there? Or had its original head been slain, and replaced by that abomination?

I looked behind me, trying desperately to better understand the lay of the land. If I could figure out how far back her playground went, I could use it to my advantage. I could build up momentum when needed, and use the wall in my favor—just like I used the bindings in habibellums.

The hiss of the nahashim had me tracking its movement more clearly, but uneasily. I still remembered how venomous its bite had been. How paralyzing. The power of its squeeze. Forget the two heads. I could be paralyzed and unconscious within minutes from one snake bite.

Dead.

I ran back, hearing its snarls turn into a haunting, echoing howl that left me chilled to the bone.

Then with a quick steadying breath, I raced forward, lifting my dagger and sword, but fear took hold of me as I got too close and I dodged to the side, just barely missing the graze of nahashim teeth against my arm. The shadow of two sets of horns loomed over the small pool of light in the pit's center.

My audience of Afeya booed in annoyance. And someone, one of the Afeya leaning over the pool's edge, had thrown an apple at me.

"Are you going to fight?" the Queen asked. "Or just play?"

I glared, skewered the apple on my sword. It sliced down the center, and hurled one half back at the Afeya. But the other, I threw into the dark, and heard the distinct sound of it hitting a wall. So there was an end to this playground.

But before I could find it, the beast hissed calling out to me. "Asherah."

My body went cold. The chimera charged. My heart thundered as I held my ground, my body trembling with fear. I couldn't jump on it from behind, and not from the front.

Which left one option.

So I waited, and waited, sweat beading at my brows as I prayed my plan would work.

The chimera was nearly in my face, before I dodged again, letting it pass me, my feet scrambling into a sprint. I ran toward the wall, blindly reaching until I found it. Taking a few steps back, I ran, jumping up and kicking my feet against it to gain momentum. I flew backwards, and twisted, my body colliding with the beast's middle. I gripped its roughened fur and climbed onto its back as it roared, its hind legs kicking and bucking. The nahashim tail hissed, striking at me with a sudden and horrifying speed. I barely managed to kick it in the face and avoid its bite. But the chimera bucked again, jumping from its front legs to its back. I bounced, nearly flying up before I landed against its spine, my thighs clamping down.

With an ear-piercing roar, it threw me to the ground and I just barely managed to curl into a ball and roll to safety.

I was so dizzy, the room was spinning as I fought my way back to my feet. Fuck! How the hell did you fight this thing?

Every trick I knew, and every other beast I'd fought felt inadequate. All the fights I'd been in, all the monsters I'd faced and I'd been woefully unprepared for this.

Suddenly, the chimera called to me again, and my blood ran cold as it hissed a name at me.

Not Asherah. It didn't call me by that name this time. Or Lyriana. It was something else—another name, in another language I didn't recognize. A name I could barely hear over the laughter of the Afeya.

I blinked, my vision shifting. I wasn't in Queen Ma'Nia's playground anymore.

I was in a forest, surrounded by tall trees full of green leaves. The trunks and branches were a pure brown. Lighter than pine trees in color—but these weren't the same. I didn't recognize the species at all. Not from any scrolls I'd read, nor any paintings I'd seen, or memories.

A man screamed, pulling my attention toward him. My heart raced with more fear than I'd ever known before. I ran, tearing through the trees, faster and faster. I needed to reach him. To save him.

A chimera had pushed him up against the trunk, trapping his body with theirs while two heads growled in his face, and two sets of teeth snapped.

He paled, shaking with terror. He wasn't a warrior. He was ... a prince. The word popped into my memory. And some protective instinct woke up inside of me. I'd never seen this man before. I didn't know his name, or even where we were. What continent, what year. But he was familiar to me. Soft brown curls sat atop his head. And on first glance, I couldn't help but notice that he was extremely handsome. He had full, soft-looking lips, a strong squared jaw, thick dark eyebrows, and kind, gentle green eyes. No aura, and yet ... my soul called out to his. It longed for him with a yearning that already had me aching. My heart thundered. Instantly his soul responded to mine, his voice in my head.

Ani janam ra.

Rhyan!

But this wasn't Rhyan. And yet—it wasn't Auriel either.

This was a whole other life, I realized—another incarnation they had—we had—experienced. It was after the Drowning, I was sure of that. But I didn't know anything more. Not his name. Nor mine. Nothing. But I knew his soul. Auriel was in that body. Rhyan was in that body.

And I felt my love for him, for all of them rise and grow, for Rhyan in three different forms, deep in my chest. I needed him, needed to be with him, to protect him and save him. Rhyan. Auriel. The prince.

I raced forward, my limbs speeding up with pure determination. While in this incarnation, Rhyan was no warrior, neither was I. Yet it didn't stop me. Even when I realized I didn't have a weapon.

For some reason, it didn't seem to matter to me—or my incarnation. But my fingernails suddenly lengthened and sharpened, leaving me with two large hands, my nails as large and sharp as daggers. I was the weapon. Without hesitation, I sliced through the chimera's tail, cutting off the nahashim. Its black eyes closed and its body fell to the grass, curling limply and rolling before stilling with death.

The beast roared and the chimera turned its ire on me—giving the prince just enough time to slip out of its hold. He started toward me, his eyes wide. He wanted to fight. To protect me, too. But he couldn't—not in this life. Not yet.

I shook my head. "Run!" I screamed, my voice strange and accented. It almost reminded me of the way Ramia spoke. "Now!"

The beast lowered its skull and charged at me. I extended my claws, and with a battle cry, I stabbed out the eyes of the head nearest to me. Because that was how to weaken and defeat a chimera.

I knew that much. Remove the tail. Remove the eyes.

The vision faded. I gasped as if I'd just come up for air.

By the fucking Gods. For a second, my heart felt like it was splitting in two. In those brief seconds, I'd seen another one of Rhyan's lives, and I'd fallen in love with him all over again. With the prince. Seconds I'd been there, and already my heart was tearing itself apart. Some part of me was empty, missing him already, missing his face.

I'd never see Rhyan as the prince again, not in this life. But his soul? Yes. Yes I fucking would.

A plan began to form in my mind. I glanced behind me, sensing a wall a few feet away. If the vision was accurate, and my memories of that life were true, I'd need to cut off its tail first. Then go for the chimera's eyes. That meant I needed to make sure the beast ran ahead of me.

"Come on!" I yelled. "I'm right here!"

The beast howled again, its two mouths coming together in a kind of demonic harmony. The sound made me want to scratch my ears off.

I widened my stance, and braced for its charge. It took off, its two mouths opened wide, the nahashim tail stretching and curling forward.

Steadying my hand, I held my ground, my entire body beginning to tremble as the chimera drew closer and closer.

Two sets of teeth snapped, and I could smell its breath. The stench doubled.

With a cry I jumped to the side, just as its body would've trampled mine. My sword lifted high and came crashing down, splitting the nahashim in two.

The snake's eyes closed, its severed body crashing to the floor, twitching before it stilled—just like it had in my vision. A furious and pained roar erupted from the chimera. Followed by another—an ear-piercing scream made out of bones.

One body part down.

Heart pounding, I took off. The chimera in the vision had two live heads. No skeleton. I didn't know what that meant. Was it a different species? Or were both heads simply alive? Either way, the yellow eyes were closest to me. Within seconds, it was in range. I thrust my dagger through my belt, and unleashed a second sword—holding both together above my head. Then I ran, my arms already burning as I repositioned the hilts, thrusting the blades forward and stabbing the wolf head through both of its yellow eyes.

I released my hands, but the chimera rushed at me, and my foot slipped on a loosened rock. I hit the ground, landing between its front paws and curled up into a ball, the beast rushing over me. Its back foot stomped on my elbow, crushing the bone while its nails cut through my skin.

I screamed, my throat raw with the force of it. Fuck! I bit down on my lip, unable to stop screaming in pain.

Already the chimera had turned around, and was heading back toward me in a rage. Both of my swords were still sticking out of the live wolf's eyes. I didn't have time to get back up. Fuck. I didn't even have time to slide out of the way. I reached for my dagger and rolled out just before it ran over me, and managed to slice its front paw.

Nausea roiled through my stomach, the pain only getting worse, and I swore I could hear Auriel admonishing me. *"Really, Lyriana? We just fixed that arm."*

I cursed at Auriel, still not quite sure whether his words were real or a fevered imagination, and slid my back against a nearby rock, tears in my eyes, as I tore at my cloak to rip off a piece of cloth, just enough to make a sling. I gripped the dirtied and sweaty material between my teeth, pulling the ends and crying out as I tied them together, tightening my arm to my chest. Fuck. FUCK, that hurt.

And meanwhile, the Godsdamned chimera bucked, leaping onto its back legs. Gritting my teeth, and knowing I couldn't stay in place, I jumped back up, my right arm screaming in fresh pain from the movement. Cold sweat was dripping down my neck, and biting pain continued exploding down my arm.

Auriel screamed my name.

The chimera turned to face me again, the white eyes of the wolf skull tracking my movements. And it was then that its other head, the wolf head, slumped forward. One of my swords fell out and clanged to the ground.

The skull head watched it happen, its white eyes glued to the movement. I watched too. Watched my sword spin on the ground, covered in thick goops of blood.

I was already moving, ready to attack again, but so was the chimera. Its paw landed on the fallen blade, and kicked it out of reach, leaving me face-to-face with its white eyes.

I reared back, as its breath hit me, and long fangs dripped with saliva—just inches from my mouth. It unhinged its jaw, bones cracking and rubbing together as it howled. My skin went ice-cold. Its white eyes were beginning to glow until a shadow crossed over them. Slowly the whites of its eyes were replaced with black. The shadows began to lift, and fade, the light returning in reverse, forming the shape of a waning crescent, before its eyes returned to pure white. It was the phases of the moon. Its eyes had just cycled through them.

Before I could understand what that meant, it slammed its skull into mine.

Stars burst across my vision, and I cried out. Auriel was yelling for me. The Afeya were cheering for the chimera. And Queen Ma'Nia was urging them on.

Dizzy, and nauseated, my ass hit the floor. My head was pounding. The beast lowered its head, as its breath was growing hotter and hotter. Oh, fuck. Could these things breathe fire, too?

Smoke curled down its nose, exiting where nostrils might have been if it were alive. I threw my hand back, trying to regain my balance, and I hit the wall. Shit! It had trapped me. I could barely see straight, and the pain in my right arm had moved through my hand. My fingers were either screaming, or going numb.

Red embers formed in the skull-wolf's mouth.

Shit, shit, shit! It was going to burn me alive. I couldn't move. Couldn't escape. My heart sped up like it was trying to experience every last beat.

The skull lowered its eyes to my level, my breathing becoming erratic. My pulse racing.

But just then, I realized how close the other head was. I could reach for my second sword. It was still embedded in the wolf's eye.

I shifted across the ground, reached for the hilt, and rolled under the chimera's massive body just as its flames licked the wall. I landed on my back, and I raised my sword, piercing its belly, and stabbing up and up until I had to sit, pushing harder, and praying that its anatomy was like other animals; that its heart was above me now.

The chimera stilled, then screamed. A sound I knew I would never forget.

Its legs wobbled. Blood spurted from its belly, dripping across my face, then drowning me in it—along with other inner body parts and fluids I didn't want to consider.

I pulled the sword down, and started scooting back and back, moving as quickly as I could, scrambling to get out from beneath its body.

The chimera released one more ear-piercing, bone-shuddering screech before it collapsed across my legs.

I gasped, winded from its weight. I still couldn't move my arm, and could barely see with my face covered in blood and guts. Fuck, it was so heavy. But at least it was just my legs. I would have suffocated if it had landed on my chest.

I watched its body shudder, while I leaned back, desperate to free my legs.

There was one final exhale, a rattling hollow sound. And the chimera stilled.

Moaning, I used my good arm to lean on, and then freed one leg, before kicking the beast and releasing the other.

I scooted back, my legs too wobbly for me to stand.

The chimera was dead, and Queen Ma'Nia was standing over the edge of the pool, her violet eyes murderous as she stared down into her playground.

"Release her!" Auriel yelled. "It's dead. You made your point! Now get her out of there."

The Queen shook her head, her mouth tight, before she stepped back, and I turned on my side, vomiting onto the ground. My power spent, I collapsed beside the beast.

CHAPTER TWENTY

LYRIANA

"Lyriana? *Meka?* Open your eyes." Auriel loomed over me, his eyebrows furrowed, his face anxious.

I sat up and moaned, my stomach twisting into knots. Fuck. Everything hurt. I shuddered, remembering the weight of the dead chimera on my legs, and the vision I'd had in the Queen's playground. Gods. That chimera could have killed me. If I hadn't had that vision, hadn't remembered that past life, it would have.

I looked past Auriel. We were on a bed, in a large rounded room, surrounded by floor to ceiling windows, all without glass. Seraphim were chirping, and ashvan flew by, running across blue rainbows.

White columns painted with the phases of the moon filled the space. It looked exactly like the eyes of the wolf-skull. Like the bone-chilling half of the chimera, just before he attacked.

I looked down at my body. I was dressed in armor, my tunic, cloak, and boots, though my weapons and chest plate were missing as I gingerly tested out the movement of my right arm, wincing in preparation for pain. But it moved with ease.

In fact, it felt fine.

"You're healed," Auriel said quietly. "You're completely healed."

I frowned. "How?" Then I grabbed the front of his armor, terror washing over me. "How long was I out this time?"

"No time at all," he said, taking my hand and squeezing it. "Not really—considering. About an hour in our time."

I shook my head. "Our time is Moon Court time. What is that? Like a day in Lumeria?"

Auriel shook his head. "Don't think about it. What matters is you're okay. And the chimera is dead."

"And the Queen?" I asked.

"She's the one who healed you, cleaned you up."

"The shard?" I asked.

"The exchange will happen in private. She doesn't want the court to see her handing over such a powerful weapon."

"Won't they know anyway? They're Afeya."

Auriel shook his head. "They can know, like they can know anything. But they won't know immediately. Remember—they have to be asked. If they don't see it, they won't know it happened. And unless they come across a Lumerian who asks for this key piece of information, or something related to it, they might as well remain in the dark."

"You're sure?" I asked. "She'll keep her word this time?"

"She has to. The same way a blood oath will find a way to punish you if broken, a bargain broken by an Afeya will also have disastrous consequences."

"She could delay. Find a loophole. It feels like she's tried every other trick or method of extortion she could find."

"I know," he agreed. "But she won't. Thanks to Ramia. And much as I hate to fucking say it—thanks to Mercurial."

"Bastard," I spat.

"Agreed." His eyes searched mine. "But he wants you to have the shard, and in a way, because of her goals, so does she, even though she doesn't want to relinquish the power." He sighed. "*Meka.*" His eyes searched mine. "I was so fucking worried for you with the chimera. I know you'd never seen one before—not as Lyriana. You never learned what to do."

"I remembered," I said.

He squeezed my hand. "Asherah?"

"No," I said. "It–they?" I shook my head. It didn't matter. "The beast said a name down there that I didn't recognize, but it pulled me into memories of another life. I was on the other side of the Lumerian Ocean I think. And Rhyan," I met his eyes, "You. You were there. A prince. You didn't know how to fight in this life. I killed the chimera in the vision. To save you." To save Rhyan.

"The other side of the ocean?" he frowned, then his eyes lit up with a mix of nostalgia and joy, a slow smile spreading across his face. "I remember." His voice lowered. "I remember you in that life."

"What was it?" I asked, a sudden vision of Rhyan, of Auriel, as the prince flashing through my mind. My heart pounded. For all three of them now. "Who was I?"

But Auriel shook his head. "That's for another time. What we need now is to remember what we can of your life as Asherah. She's the one who wielded the cure. That's the life that has the knowledge you need. That Rhyan needs."

I swallowed. "What if I don't remember?"

"You will. With the shard in your possession, you will. And if not, I will tell you." He winked, and pointed to the Valya that he now wore in its case on his belt like a librarian would. "I'll tell you everything. We'll get it right." Then he frowned. "She'll be here in a minute. The Queen. She senses you're awake."

"I need to stand," I said, releasing Auriel's hand. "I'm not meeting her again, laying down. Not after what she just fucking did to me."

Auriel stepped back, and retrieved Asherah's chest plate. "I feel the same way. Here, let me help you with this." He swept my hair to the side and then laid the chest plate over me, before hooking it into place behind my neck.

Together, we sheathed my weapons, sliding my dagger and swords back onto my belt. My hand swept over the stave, still tucked safely in the leather case Rhyan had gotten me.

"I didn't even think to use this," I said. "With the chimera."

He made an amused sound, low in his throat. "You're more warrior than you realize." His hand swept across my back, and then we both straightened. An ashvan of pure silver with a white mane, and a rider with burgundy hair flew toward us. The blue bridge soared ahead and landed in the room. The Queen pulled on ashvan reins made of pearls before dismounting.

"Well done, Lady Lyriana," she said.

"Your Majesty," I gritted through my teeth. "Do you have my shard?"

"Right to the point, I see," she said, her eyes darkening.

"I'm ready to leave. Your dealings with Auriel are over."

She laughed, tossing her head back.

"What's so funny?" I demanded.

She straightened, and grinned slowly. "My dealings with Auriel are not over. Not even close, Goddess. Nor have they ended with you. For you were there. Auriel may have spoken the words, he may have authored the curse. But whose magic supported him? Hmmm? Who was by his side? Who was the reason why the light could never be whole? Why it was stolen in the first place?" She stepped toward me, moving into my personal space. "It's you." She pointed at my chest, at my heart. "You. His soulmate. His *mekarim*. It was always you who caused all of this. You were the fire. The fire who sealed the curse into place. But the same fire that shall undo it. When you're ready.

"My ashvan will take you to the vaults in the Yara Vale, found between the peaks of Anessi, and Vrenya. The mountains which you'll find in the center of the Shevagni Mountain Range. That is where I've kept the shard. I've given instructions for you to be permitted inside. For my guard to disperse upon your arrival, and to allow you to take what is yours. Then you'll be granted leave from my country via the Yara Vale north into Korteria."

Korteria. Ka Kormac's land. The home of Vrukshire. Of Brockton. My throat went dry.

"Ramia will meet you at the vaults, and show you in. We'll need Auriel of course. After all, he is the key. And then, you must find Lord Rhyan. His akadim form must be killed, either in a way that removes him from this world completely, or calls his soul back to his body. But it must happen. You cannot falter. For in his current state, he is working hard for the enemy. And growing closer and closer to bringing about our doom." Her eyes blazed. "Asherah, you must stop the prophecy."

If Lord Rhyan Hart's soul cannot be restored, he will prove to be one of the most dangerous, and destructive forces the Empire has ever seen. Worse than the rise of Moriel.

The vision held by three.

"I will," I gritted through my teeth.

She handed the reins of her ashvan to me. "Go. Claim the shard. Claim your power. And when your obligation to Mercurial ends, you know where to find me."

One battle. For one battle, I'd have a legion of Afeya at my command.

I nodded.

Auriel hoisted me onto the ashvan's back, and then climbed behind. He wrapped his arms around my waist, pulling me against him and I coaxed the ashvan forward, commanding it to fly. A blue bridge glowed against the floor, and our ashvan took off, running faster and faster, until we were flying out the window, wind pushing against us. We rose toward the moon, flying higher and higher, as the bridge circled toward the top of our tower and turned north. To the vault. To the red shard.

And to Rhyan.

CHAPTER TWENTY-ONE

LYRIANA

A series of mountains lay in the distance, each shadowed in the ever-dark of Khemet's night. But green-topped mountains, lit by the gold of the sun, shone behind the peaks. The hills of Korteria. My first sighting of Lumeria in what felt like weeks. There it was already day. We still remained under the shroud of night in the Moon Court as we began its descent.

My heart flew into my throat, as our ashvan ran faster, the ground rising up to meet us. It felt like we were heading for a crash landing—the way gryphons descended.

The horse touched down, walking us across the grassy terrain. The valley lay ahead between the darkened mountains: the Shevagni. Seven distinctive peaks loomed above, each one topped in gold from this angle. A gold that glowed brighter the closer we came. The sun of Lumeria. I marked the valley between the centermost two mountains, the two that I assumed were Anessi and Vrenya. Between them was the Yara Vale. And the vaults. The red shard.

My heart began to beat faster, and I felt the slightest lift in body temperature. Every shard I'd come into contact with had caused a physical reaction. The indigo had unleashed my magic. My first viewing of the orange had caused the light inside my heart to heat up so painfully, I'd passed out.

I tried to brace myself for how I'd react to the red shard at last. To the one that was mine.

Auriel stilled suddenly beside me, his body tense. "We're being watched," he said quietly.

"Her guard?" I asked.

"I would expect. I can't see them, but I can feel them."

A shiver ran down my spine. I could sense them, too. "She'll keep her word?"

At this Auriel stretched his neck, his nostrils flared, and his jaw set with determination. "She has to."

"What do we do? Just walk in?" I asked.

"Follow me," Ramia said, her ashvan touching down beside us. She rode on a mauve-colored horse with an amethyst mane. Beautiful. "You right on Lumerian border. You back home soon. But you need Afeya to guide you inside vaults."

"Ramia," I said curtly.

She scoffed, dismounting. "Ramia? You mean Princess Ramia. I remain princess in Khemet."

"Did you know?" Auriel asked her, his voice shaking with anger. "Did you know she'd throw Lyriana into the playground?"

Ramia's eyes flashed. "You should. She did same to you—no?" She shook her head, wrapping her ashvan's reins in her hand.

"She didn't have a chimera last time," Auriel said. "Where the hell did she get one?"

Ramia rolled her eyes. "We have procurer of rare animal who travel. Farther than Lethea."

"Mercurial," I said, and shook my head.

"Bastard," Auriel cursed.

"Bastard who convince my mother to give what you want. Red shard."

"Because Mercurial wants it for his own Godsdamned purposes!" I snapped. "And your mother had no choice with Auriel's bargain. Not in the end."

"Hmmm," Ramia said, sounding unbothered. "Why else do anything other than get what wanted?" The shadows darkened with every step we took. The foothills of the mountain base rose higher and higher. Leaning against a hill were three golden lamps, the kind we used in the Great Library. The rods towered above all three of us, the tops curving into hooks from which an amethyst hung.

Ramia handed one to me and winked. "You do magic now, yes? Light lamp."

Despite it all, I laughed. I'd been looking forward to doing this for years. I still remembered the absolute humiliation I'd felt when I'd returned to the library after my failed Revelation Ceremony. The lead librarian, Nabula Kajan, had been so excited for me to finally light my own.

Of course, Ramia had known that.

I swept my hand over the stone three times, just like the librarians, and chanted the spell for light. "*Ani petrova vala.*" Purple light shimmered across the crystal, and then I spread it to the others. Auriel grinned proudly. Ramia winked again.

"Come." She continued forward, the Yara Vale coming to an end as the bases of Anessi and Vrenya both met. "Through here," she said. "Vault inside." She held up her hand and pressed it against the mountain. A door formed against the rock. Silver with golden etchings, again showing the phases of the moon.

Ramia pressed her hand to the door. The etchings began to gleam, radiating with light, and with a slight groan, the sound of rock shifting, the door opened, and we were led inside.

I held up my lamp, casting the room in a faint purple glow. The ceiling was made up of a series of arches that appeared to have been carved straight into the rock of the mountain. Each one glittered as we walked past, heading toward another pool in the center of the room. Beneath our feet was a waterway made of glass. Luminescent blue water ran beneath us.

As we got closer to the pool, I realized there were dozens of waterways, each one jutting out from the room's center, leading into darkened caverns.

"Each a locked vault," Ramia said. "Many secret."

"Where's mine?" Auriel asked.

"Straight ahead," she said. "Put hand in pool."

"The pool?" I said warily, already having too much experience with pools in the Moon Court.

But Auriel shook his head. "It's okay, *Meka*. I remember this. The water takes my hand print." He kneeled over the edge, and dipped his hand inside. The water sparkled and stilled, and when Auriel pulled back, an imprint of his hand remained.

One of the waterways lit up. "Follow path."

Auriel swallowed roughly, and rolled his shoulders back. "The last time I was here," he said, "I was grieving for you." He smiled sadly, and walked forward. The vault led us down a dark corridor. Our only source of light was the amethyst lamps which turned the waterway purple as well. Finally, we came to another silver door, rounded, and designed in the same style as Ereshya's shield had been. But instead of a crystal at its center, there was a hand print. Auriel's. Just like there'd been at the tomb.

He pressed his palm to it, a perfect fit. A silver light glowed, and the door dissolved, revealing a small stone room, a rounded quartz in the center, and sitting atop was the red shard. My shard. It had been shaped into a sword.

"You designed it yourself," Auriel said, clearing his throat. But his voice was coated in emotion. "You wanted it to be effective. To cure as many as possible."

"What do I do?" I asked.

"You stab the akadim," he said. "In the heart."

I stilled, my throat dry, chest pounding.

Auriel urged me forward. "Go on. Take it. Claim it. It's yours. It was always yours."

I approached the quartz, my eyes fixed to the sword. Carefully, I reached for the sword, and lifted it off the table. My fingers wrapped around the hilt, settling on the handle like it had been made for me. Made for this body, this incarnation. All at once, golden light poured out from my chest, bursting from my armor, illuminating the vault. Flames erupted down the length of the red blade.

My heart thundered, and warmed. My entire body heated. But it was comfortable. Like I could finally take the heat. Like I was always meant to be this way. I held the sword up higher over my head. It was heavy, but I had the muscle to withstand its weight. Then with the fires still burning up and down, I thrust the sword forward, swiping it left and right, testing it out.

"How does it feel?" Auriel asked, pride in his eyes.

"Fine," I said, surprised, and frowned. It was strange. When the red light entered me, it was blindingly painful. Being in the mere presence of the orange shard had made me faint. And now, I just felt ... normal. Like me. Because this shard, this light, it was part of me. It always was. The fire could no longer burn me. I was the fire now. I was complete.

The flames vanished from sight and High Lumerian writing script appeared down the length of the shard as fresh energy moved through my limbs.

My name was written into the crystal and steel. Lyriana Batavia. A match for my dagger. And my stave.

"You look just like Goddess Asherah," Ramia said. "Fierce and powerful. Mighty soturion."

It was what she'd said to me months ago on my birthday, when I'd first tried on Asherah's chest plate.

"Thank you," I said, with a laugh—knowing she'd done so on purpose. She'd known all along we'd get here. My eyes narrowed then, something niggling in the back of my mind. "You also told me I looked like an Heir Apparent."

Ramia scoffed, her eyes sparkling. "No. You look like queen."

Suddenly, Mercurial's cryptic words, uttered months ago, right after he'd placed the light inside my heart, ran through my mind.

When the time is right, you will strike and have your revenge. And then you will retake the throne of Bamaria.

We don't have thrones here, I'd told him.

The ghost of a feline grin appeared within the vault. Glittering Valalumir stars lit the ceiling—always a sign of his presence. I shivered.

"You will," he hissed into my mind. The very same words he'd said that night.

My chest heaved, the weight of it all pressing down on me.

But as I looked at Ramia, I realized that Mercurial had only made himself known to me. The words we'd exchanged remained between us.

The stars vanished, and I turned to Auriel. He'd pressed his lips together, like he was trying to keep his emotions at bay. His eyes had reddened, watching me, Asherah reborn, her golden armor across my chest, her stave in my belt, and now the red shard, in the sword she'd forged. The sword she'd used in battle. The sword I'd use to heal. He sniffled, his jaw tensing, and then he laughed.

"Come on," he said, wiping his eyes. Then he reached for the hilt of his sword. "Let's get Rhyan back."

CHAPTER TWENTY-TWO

JULIANNA

The black eyes of the nahashim blinked slowly at me, its tongue poking out pathetically as I held its tiny body in my hands.

"You're not hungry," I said firmly.

The snake hissed, baring blunt fangs that couldn't hurt me—no matter how hard she tried. And she had.

I sighed. "You literally just ate dinner." The snake hissed again.

"Fine," I groaned, and placed her back into the box that had become her bed.

"You want me to do it?" Dario asked. "Julianna," he added at the last second.

I hadn't even noticed him come into the room. I stood up and wiped my hands on my dress, already looking away. "If you don't mind."

"Mind? Me?" he said, his voice dripping with sarcasm. "No. I love serving crushed bugs to baby nahashim."

"How nice for you." I strode out toward the balcony. I still gagged just a little every time I had to hear the snake eat. And swallow.

A cool breeze blew against my face, but the sun was shining warmly enough, I could almost taste summer. Almost.

We were weeks into the spring season, and staying in yet another safe house. In Korteria of all places. Cretanya in the end, Thene in particular, had been a nightmare. I should have known. That's where I'd been the last time my life fell apart. Where I'd escaped to, where I'd been free for a moment with … Seth. But that had all been taken from me in the most brutal way. It was all I could do to go on—to survive by not thinking about it.

I reached for my ring finger, for the blood oath I'd made him before he died.

I'd sworn I would survive, promised I'd live, even without him. And I had. I fucking had.

Even after the soturi came to our inn—again.

Even after two safe houses in the city were compromised. After a brutal akadim attack left dozens dead. Worse, turned. Dario had had to get us out, and we'd fled the country in the middle of the night—not even saying goodbye to Cal and Marisol.

But I was still here. Still alive, still somehow surviving every day. So I guess that was something. And now I was hiding in the country of my worst enemy. Kormac's country.

Our new host was a loyalist of Ka Azria, a wealthy member of *El Zan Vylette*. But they weren't Elyrian. As expected by our location, they were Korterian. Born and bred, going generations back. They just also happened to be one of the few that didn't support Ka Kormac, who thought they were overstepping their power and that what had happened to Ka Azria—to my Ka, to my family, the family I'd never known—was wrong.

And while he'd been nothing but kind, protecting us, housing and feeding us, I didn't fully trust him. Not that I trusted anyone completely.

Because as of a week ago—there was no Elyria. And no more Bamaria. Not according to our new Emperor. Because of the recent instability, rising akadim attacks, and growing concerns about vorakh living amongst us—the new southern Imperator, my aunt Arianna, had decided to unite the southern border. My homes, the home I'd been raised in and loved, and the one I was supposedly destined to rule, had both been turned into something called New Korteria.

It was temporary, they said. It would dissolve the moment we were safe. What a joke. That day would never come. And if it did, I already knew there'd be some horrendous attack or distraction to delay it. I guess it didn't really matter that I was here. We were all Korteria now. Everyone of us along the southern border.

Go figure. They made my aunt announce it—so Bamaria didn't revolt. Elyria under the rule of Ka Elys had been basically Ka Kormac all along. And why would Lord Viktor, the Emperor's son and newly consecrated Arkasva of Korteria ever take issue?

Arianna may have been given the title of Imperator, but it was worthless now. All the power lay here with Kormac. Like always.

I clutched my stomach. We were fucking surrounded. Even *El Zan Vylette* was laying low, it was going to be pretty hard to remove Ka Elys from power and place me on the Seat when they currently didn't have a country to rule. But what did it matter? What did any of it matter? Rhyan was long gone, an akadim. Galen was dead. Murdered. Tristan back under the thrall of the enemy, their puppet once more. And Lyr—Lyr had been missing for almost a month now. It was time to stop pretending we lived in Lumeria anymore. Or that we were remotely free. The whole Empire was going to be New Korteria soon.

Dario stepped onto the balcony. "May I join you?" he asked formally, his Glemarian accent thick.

I continued staring out at the green hills, the white flowers beginning to sprout in the meadows.

In the distance there was a growth of purple flowers I didn't recognize. The color was mesmerizing. And for a second, I lost myself in them, wanting to go out there and pick a bouquet, place them in a vase and stare at them for hours.

Because they were violet. Because I was Hava, Goddess of the Violet Ray.

I groaned and shook my head. Another title, another identity that sounded impressive, and might have been interesting to me at another time. All I saw now was more ways for me to be used, hunted.

I'd remain Julianna and nothing else. I wasn't the Heir. I wasn't Hava. I wanted to be no one. I looked away from the flowers.

"It's a beautiful day," Dario said. "Maybe ... maybe you'd like to take a walk in the fields?"

"No."

"You should get outside. Stretch your legs."

I glared back at him, gesturing around us. "I do believe that we are outside."

His mouth tightened. "You know what I mean. Out there, out in the open, where you can breathe, be surrounded by nature, its smells, the way the air moves. You're so cooped up in the house. You're always in the house."

"I said no." My voice hardened.

"Okay. Sure." He looked away, his jaw clenching. "Sorry."

"Did you need something?" I asked.

"No, I-I just—I wanted to see how you were doing."

"I'm babysitting nahashim," I said dully. "It's not that exciting."

Meera had become obsessed with the snakes since she realized she could control and communicate with them. It was part of her identity as the Guardian of the Blue Ray, Cassarya. Admittedly, it was a productive pursuit. Her ability had saved our lives. Several times.

As soon as we arrived at our second safe house, a nahashim had appeared. Another the next day. All sent from Devon Hart. He was trying to find us, before Emperor Avery did. I couldn't decide which man was worse. Luckily, neither had their hands on us—yet.

At first, she sent the snakes away, purposefully confusing them so they'd go back into the wilds and leave Devon's service. But then she'd realized she might be able to do more than just confuse them. We attempted to send one back to Glemaria. Not for Devon. But for Kenna. And it worked. Since then, messages had been passing back and forth between us regularly.

When Meera had intercepted his latest attempt she'd realized the snake was pregnant. So now we had two newborns. And I was on babysitting duty, while Meera sat with the mother. She'd sent the snake on a mission to find Lyr, again, and it had just returned this morning—with nothing. Fucking nothing.

Was she dead? But if she was—wouldn't we know? They'd want us to know, whoever killed her.

"Um," Dario started, then stopped. He'd been like this for weeks. Trying to talk to me, then stopping, when I didn't answer, or waved him off. I hadn't meant to be mean to him. I just—I didn't have the energy most of the time to talk to anyone. It was clearly getting to him, upsetting his confidence. Which was leading to more and more moments like this.

I wish he'd just go away. Leave me alone. I didn't want anything, or anyone. Just peace.

"Aiden wanted me to tell you," he started again, "um, he said he could have some more magic lessons with you tonight after dinner, if you want."

Aiden had become my mage professor, making up for all the time I wasn't in the Academy. In the Palace, I'd learned only one kind of magic. Visions. How to control my vorakh, how to relax into it, interpret it, even cause visions to come by request. It was a far cry from what Meera had been experiencing. But now that I had my own stave, I was making up for lost time. When I wasn't being tutored by Aiden, I was helping Meera with the nahashim, learning to communicate with them, too. And teaching Meera how to have her visions without pain.

I turned to Dario, meeting his dark eyes. "Aiden could have told me himself."

"He could have, but I was here, so I did. Do you want me to te—"

"No." I shook my head. "I'll tell him when I see him." I trained my eyes back on the trees in the distance. "How much longer is Meera going to be?"

"I don't know. I think she's trying to get the nahashim to go back out and search for signs of Lyriana."

I sighed. When all the searches for Lyr, and ... for Lyr's body, had turned up empty, she'd trained the snake to listen for conversations about her, to record them and report back. The only problem—the conversations were everywhere. Some of the talk had died now. Rhyan's stripping and the attack in the arena were slowly fading as people began to discuss New Korteria, and the mandatory vorakh testing happening. Lyr was assumed dead.

I shuddered.

"We'll find her," Dario said, reading my mind.

"Like she found Rhyan?" I spat.

Dario paled. "Good day, Julianna. Enjoy the balcony." He bowed formally, and walked back inside.

Fuck. "Wait," I said. "I'm sorry."

"No." His mouth tightened. "No need to apologize. You're not wrong."

"But I shouldn't have said that. Rhyan was my friend, too. And I didn't mean—"

"It's fine. I, uh—don't know what I was thinking coming out here."

He walked back in the door.

I threw my hands into my hair, unsettled by the interaction, but I couldn't move from the spot I was in, couldn't say anything to change it. So I didn't.

Meera joined me an hour later, both nahashim infants curled around her wrist.

"He likes you," she said quietly. "You don't have to be so cruel to him."

"I'm not," I snapped. "I said nothing cruel. I just … don't say much at all." My stomach turned, but then I shook my head, angry. "Why should I? What do I owe him anyway?"

"You don't owe him anything. But, Jules. You can be nice. We're all in this together. And he is proving time and time again how willing he is to protect us."

"I protect us. I got us this house, and it's because of me we got the last two. We'd be in the Palace now, locked in the dungeons or the Godsdamned Yellow Room, if it weren't for me."

"Jules." Meera's eyes widened. "No one disputes that. And we're all grateful. But, we also might be locked away in Seathorne if it wasn't for me."

I exhaled sharply, leaning over the balustrade.

"We're all doing our part," Meera continued. "Our best. The situation is shit no matter how you look at it. We're just … trying. Especially Dario."

"What do you care?" I asked. "Why does it matter if I'm nice to him?"

Meera's brows drew together, her hazel eyes thoughtful. "It doesn't. I have no designs on this. It's just, right now, we need each other. It would be nice if we were all getting along. If we all trusted each other a little more."

"Fine." I watched people moving through the small stone streets of the town beyond the hills surrounding the house. People were just going about their daily life. Hardly aware that so much evil lurked around them, above them. Was that unique to Korteria? Were the Bamarian's just as unaware they'd been conquered? Soothed by Arianna's lies? Comforted in the false belief they were safe because of Tristan's vorakh testing?

"You know he won't …" Meera started, and looked away. "Dario would never hurt you."

"He's a man," I said, my voice barely above a whisper. "He can hurt me."

"He could. But he's one of the few that I know won't." She lifted her arm, and stroked the backs of the babies. Their bodies arched and curled, both of them opening their mouths and making tiny hissing sounds that were, admittedly, kind of cute. But only a little.

"No news about Lyr?" I asked.

Meera's eyes grew distant and she shook her head. "She's out there. She's just … hidden somehow."

The clock tower began to chime. My heart thundered. Another hour of my life gone. Stolen.

I shook my head. "I thought the whole point was that nahashim could find anything, anywhere."

"They can. I even—" Her mouth tightened "I sent one on a mission to—to find Her Grace." Lyr's title, if she were married to Kormac. Meera wiped at her eyes, and blinked. "Nothing."

"It doesn't make any sense," I said. "Maybe the snakes are being intercepted, like you're doing to Devon Hart's."

"But we would know, they wouldn't be returning to us. They can find anything," she said, like she was reciting something she read in a scroll. "There's nowhere they can't go. Nothing they can't find. I mean, for Lyr to be unfindable— she'd have to—she'd have to not exist in our world. But she does."

"She does," I said. "She's somewhere, somewhere out there in time or space."

Meera frowned. "Time?"

"What?"

"You said time." She squinted, her mouth open.

"Just a saying," I said.

"No. It's not. She's somewhere in time. She's—By the Gods. I think—I think I know where she is."

I leaned in toward her. "Where?"

"The snakes keep coming back, and each time they turn around at the southern border here. Where Korteria and Khemet meet. The Moon Court."

"So? Maybe they're just being turned around by the Afeya," I said, confused.

"But they should still be able to enter. Nahashim are from the old world, from Lumeria Matavia. Like the Afeya. They wouldn't turn them away. They'd ignore them, or welcome them in. Not confuse them and send them back. I remember reading once that time moves differently there. That ..." Meera frowned. "Oh, come on. No! I didn't read it. The knowledge isn't public. It was in one of my trainings to become Arkasva. That's it!" She shook her head, looking wild, slamming her hands down on the banister. The snakes slithered up her arm, settling in tiny coils on her shoulders. "The Moon Queen married the Sun King, and it changed time in their realms. A day is a month there. And a month is a day."

"And the last sighting of her was on the beach of Bamaria. With a water dragon," I continued. Something that hadn't been seen by anyone on the shores of the Empire in as long as I could remember. They supposedly spent most of their time near the Afeyan lands. And Lethea. I encountered them on my travels there. But ... if they also spent time near El Zandria and Khemet ... almost a month had passed since Lyr's last sighting. And the snakes were getting turned around the Korterian border. Turned around when they reached Khemet.

"She's in the Moon Court," I said.

Meera nodded breathlessly. "She is. Gods, yes." She clutched her heart. "Yes. I knew it." She shuddered. "I knew she wasn't dead."

My heart thundered, my own relief at the news washing through me in waves. I'd hoped she was okay. Prayed. But I'd barely allowed myself to think of her. Hope, I'd found, was a dangerous thing. Because it made you want, made you desire. And when you wanted things, you could lose them.

I'd been numb for a long time now. So long. After losing my home. My family. My freedom. And then … Seth.

It was miserable not wanting. I hated it. Deep down inside of me, I wanted to want. I wanted it more than anything. wanted to feel alive. But I just … I just didn't.

"Oh," Meera cried out. And all at once, the warmth of the sun shining down on us was gone. Freezing cold air blasted against my skin. A cold I knew too well. Meera's aura. A vision.

I grabbed her hands, pulling her body back against mine and slowly helped her to the floor, her head in my lap.

"Meera, breathe," I commanded. "Relax. Remember what we went over. Let it come to you. Don't fight it."

Her hands twitched in mine, starting to resist me.

"Relax," I said. "Deep breaths. Inhale. Exhale."

She gasped a choked-out sob, her chest rising and falling, but her breathing slowed, her facial muscles released, and her eyes began to move rapidly back and forth behind her eyelids.

A moment later, her eyes opened, and she sat back up, gingerly holding her head.

"Thank you," she said shakily. "That was … the least painful one yet."

"Good," I said. "I'm glad. You're getting better at this." I frowned. "What did you see?"

Meera pushed her hair back off her face, and slowly rose to her feet, slipping the nahashim back into their boxes.

Her aura darkened, like a storm, and my stomach twisted. "It was Rhyan," she said. "I saw him as an akadim, marching with an army on Glemaria. Under the sun."

"Daywalker?" I asked.

She shrugged. "Maybe. There was water flowing beneath his boots, he was on … on the cliff where Asherah's tomb lies. On Gryphon's Mount. The water turned to fire, and then it—it spread across the Empire."

I had a sinking feeling in my stomach. I knew that image.

"So Rhyan …" I said slowly.

"Could destroy all of us." Meera's voice shook. "There's something—he's getting more powerful. More dangerous. Closer to … to a weapon of some sort."

I swallowed roughly. Fuck. Poor Rhyan. And Lyr. How was this world so fucked up?

"Do you think … do you think she's in the Moon Court for him?" I asked.

"I think so. And whatever she finds there, she's going to have to use against him."

"Gods."

"Um," Meera crossed her arms over her chest, still clearly cold from the vision. "I think I'm going to go lie down."

I nodded. "Take your time."

"And since I already had one today, I don't think I'm going to be up for anymore visions tonight. You should study magic with Aiden."

"Okay." I watched Meera leave the common room behind. We were occupying one wing of the safe house. A common room, a small library, a bathroom, and two bedrooms. One I shared with Meera, and one for Dario and Aiden.

I sat down on the couch, my mind still on Lyr and Rhyan, and their fate. Their undeserved fate. What had drawn her to the Moon Court? And did it relate to Meera's vision?

I lost track of time, and realized I still needed to tell Aiden that I would study with him tonight. But before I could go, the door opened, and Soturion Alistair, the owner of our safe house, walked in.

"My lady," he said, lowering his chin in respect at once. Like I was an Heir. Or Heir Apparent.

He'd tried to call me "Your Grace," when we first arrived. I'd broken him of that habit, but this one seemed to stick.

"Soturion Alistair," I said, rising to my feet.

"I don't mean to disturb you," he said. "But a guest has come. One of us."

Us? There was no us. We had nothing in common. There were just the people who wanted to use me for my bloodline. Who thought that I could fulfill some need in their life because of who my parents were. And then there was me—literally using that just to survive.

"I'm a little tired," I said.

Alistair's brows drew together. He was older, the blond in his hair now gray. His muscles were more lean than stocky. But I couldn't forget that at the end of the day he was Korterian and a soldier. A wolf.

"If it is a quick meeting," I amended.

"Would you like one of your companions to accompany you?"

I looked back. Not a lot of options. Meera wouldn't be up to it just yet. And I didn't want to ask Dario. Not after our last interaction. Aiden? But I'd have to go through Dario to get to him.

"No," I said, "I can come on my own." I paused. "You're sure it's safe?"

"It is. This is a long-time member of *El Zan Vylette*."

"Very well," I sighed and followed him out of the room and down the stairs. He led me into a drawing room with two long couches. A middle-aged woman stood at once, nervous hands twitching together, her blue eyes widening as she saw me.

"Oh," she gasped. "Your Grace."

I started to shake my head. But what was the point?

"May I present," Alistair said, "Lady Aliyah of Elyria." He gestured to me. "And of course, Her Grace, Lady Julianna Azria."

I stiffened. That name.

"My dear," Lady Aliyah said. "You look …. By the Gods. You look so much like your father."

I blinked. That was a new one. I looked like my mother. Like a Batavia. Like Lyr and Meera. And Morgana. No one who knew me now had ever known my father. Or the truth.

I had a feeling she was just saying it to say something. Make conversation, pretend we were actually connected. I doubted I looked anything like him. But I nodded graciously. "Thank you." I drifted to the couch and sat down before any more formalities were announced.

Alistair and Aliyah sat across from me, silent for a moment. She had a determined look in her eyes, one that I immediately recognized and distrusted. I'd seen it before in the men at the Palace. It was the look of someone who wanted something from me.

"I can't tell you what a wonder it is to sit across from you, Lady Julianna. To know that Ka Azria's time to rise grows ever closer. I know you are busy, so I will get right to the point of my visit. A long time ago, I was tasked with an important job. I've been putting together money for you," she said. "For a very long time."

"Money?" I asked. "To do what?" Help me get to safety?

"To put you on the Seat of Power, of course," Aliyah said.

My stomach sank. Of course. What else did these people ever want from me? My power so they could secure their own? I sat up.

"You say it's nearly time for Ka Azria to rise, but how will money do that? There's no Ka Azria right now. Gods. There isn't even an Elyria to take over or back. It's New Korteria now. So I ask you, how will your money change all of that?"

"There's much it can do. We can buy favor, bring more nobles to our side, and of course, there's the need for soturi—"

I shook my head. I'd heard enough. And I was done. Done wasting my time on fantasies, and done being used. "I'm sorry," I said. "Can we do this another day? I'm just—not feeling well."

Aliyah frowned, looking hurt.

"My lady," Alistair said, and I could hear the anger simmering under his words, "Lady Aliyah has gone through much trouble to arrange this meeting."

Fuck. And by extension, I supposed, so had he. This safe house was only open to us because of who I was—or rather, who everyone else wanted me to be. They only cared about the Heir of Ka Azria. Julianna Azria. Not Julianna Batavia.

"Tomorrow," I amended, trying to sound as gracious as I could. I even smiled. "I would love to speak more tomorrow. And hear of your plans. But I truly am not feeling well."

"Oh," Aliyah looked relieved. "Of course. I understand, Your Grace. I'll return tomorrow."

"You're too kind. Thank you. Please, excuse me."

I drifted back upstairs on my own, unsettled by the conversation. With nothing more to do, I returned to the balcony, looking out at the hills, the town. The whole conversation just now had unsettled me. Reminded me that our time here was limited. A choice would have to be made soon, with, or without Lyriana. Because as soon as Alistair realized I had no intention of taking back the Seat in Elyria, our little home here, would be gone.

I closed my eyes, trying to relax, trying to temper my heartbeat. But my eyes opened, alarmed by a strange noise below the landing. Aliyah leaving? I looked beyond the hills and down below. There was nothing. But then that sound came again. A metallic clanging, like something had snapped into place. And then something else, like rope shifting. Like someone was climbing.

I looked over the edge, at the base of the building below. I'd been standing out here so many hours every day and I'd never seen anything unusual. Alistair's grounds and home were well protected. There were hills detracting visitors, and walls, and even a sentry at the door.

Yet there it was again. That strange sound. And then … a grunt.

My stomach dropped and I stepped back, moving slowly back inside the room, reaching for the balcony's glass doors.

A hand appeared on the balustrade. And then another. A head full of blond hair rose up wearing silver armor. Armor that looked like a wolf's pelt. I shut the doors, just as black eyes, identical to the Bastardmaker's, spotted me.

I locked the doors, my heart racing as I ran, tripping over the boxes where the snakes slept.

The glass shattered. I reached for the door, leading to the hall where Dario and Aiden were. I just had to scream. Just one scream.

A hand wrapped around my mouth.

I bit down, and they released me. "Dar—"

A cloth covered my mouth, some potion layered into it. One I'd experienced before. At the Palace.

He'd found me. The Emperor had found me.

My eyes widened, one last time, my heart racing, as I watched my fingers pull away from the doorknob. And then I lost consciousness.

CHAPTER TWENTY-THREE

JULIANNA

I awoke with a start. My hands were bound behind my back, my body bouncing on a wooden plank. It was dark out, the moon above. It took me a moment, but I realized I was in the back of a wagon, being wheeled along the stone streets of Korteria. A rough woolen blanket had been shoved over me. And from the sound of it, an ashvan was walking down the street, dragging me along.

My head ached, and I could feel my body had been scratched and bruised all over. My elbow and knees and the backs of my legs were aching, with fresh cuts burning. I tried to sit up, realizing then that my feet were also bound. Shit.

I sucked in a breath, trying not to cry as I let my awareness move between my legs, my body trembling. It wouldn't have been the first time I was unconscious when they—when Kormac—

But there was no soreness, no strange sensations there.

Although there would be soon if I didn't get out.

The wooden walls of the wagon around me were about as tall as I was from the looks of it. I tried to stand up, managed to hold my balance for about two seconds—enough to learn that the walls only reached my chest—which wasn't much better—before I fell over again. Unable to brace my fall, my head slammed into the ground.

"You hear that?" came a voice.

I stopped breathing. Did they hear me? If they thought I was awake, or trying to escape, they'd only come back here and make it worse.

"Just went over a rock," came another voice. "Hit the wheels or some shit. *Vra.* Faster, you stupid horse."

"How much fucking farther?" asked the first.

"We're near the border for Cretanya. The others are meeting us there. We'll stop for the night, have some fun. Bring her to the Palace in the morning," said the second voice.

I started to shake. No. No. No. Not again. I couldn't do this again.

"Emperor's going to pay us quite well for his favorite pet," said the first.

I seethed, my hands trembling. That fucking nickname.

"Much better than the vorakh task force," the second agreed.

Wind rustled through the trees and the wheels began to slow as we shifted off the stone ground onto grass, moving into a woodland.

I started straining against my bindings. Seeing if I could rip through the rope around my wrists, or kick off the ones around my ankles. But there was no give. None at all.

My only opportunity to escape might come from the moment they stopped. At some point, they'd release the back wall to pull me out. It would be a small moment. A blink of an eye. But if I could get my legs free, maybe I could run. But that was a huge maybe.

I closed my eyes. Fuck. How the hell had they found me?

Was it Lady Aliyah? No. Alistair would have vetted her. Someone with her that couldn't be trusted? But these were Kormac soturi, loyal to the Emperor, enemies of *El Zan*

Vylette. I didn't think I'd been betrayed by any of my "supporters" though it had happened before.

I tried to think. As if knowing how would stop this from happening. But I needed to know. Needed to know if I truly couldn't trust anyone. My stomach turned.

Was it possible that it was one of the chayatim from the Palace? That was most likely. They could have a mind reader wandering Korteria, just listening. If it was someone who knew me, knew my voice, it would have been easy. Gods. Weeks of turning nahashim away and staying inside to avoid this very situation. Being all cooped up as Dario would say. And here I was. I'd done everything right. Again! And it still wasn't fucking enough to save me.

"Shhh, whoa. Stop!" the first soturion yelled out.

"The fuck?" asked his companion.

I heard a whooshing sound, and then a scream, and a thud.

A sword was withdrawn, the metal singing in the air. "Show your face, you fucking bastard!" It was the first soturion.

I sat up, peering into the dark, my eyes straining. Something moved in the trees, shifting. A body. A soturion's. My captor held up his torch, shining it up at the branches and I caught the profile of the man there. A strong broad nose, and curls tied on top of his head.

Dario!

My heart leapt.

He pounced from the tree, falling on the captor that remained. They both moved out of my sight, until all I could hear were grunts of pain, and the awful sound of flesh hitting flesh, followed by the singing of metal as swords were drawn.

Dario cursed, and then cried out.

There was something that sounded like a punch, and then some rustling noises and grunts. The second soturion was awake.

"You bastard," he roared. "I'll have your guts for this!"

"Not if I have yours first," Dario taunted.

My breathing grew shallow and pained. Dario was strong. I knew that. But it was two against one. And these men were motivated by something more powerful than anyone realized. Money. I had to get out.

I inched my way across the floor, my shoes just barely sliding over the wooden planks beneath me. I reached the back of the wagon, and sucked in a breath, bracing my body. Then with all I had left, I slammed into the wall, again, and again and again.

"Shit, she's up! Get back there. Grab her!"

"No," Dario roared. There was a slapping sound. Someone hit the ground, and the back wall of the wagon was pulled back.

I stared into the black eyes of the man who'd kidnapped me. Who'd climbed the tower, chased me back inside the balcony. He reached for my neck, fingers gripping my throat as he pulled me off the wagon.

I couldn't even scream, or kick my feet as they dangled in the air.

A shadow appeared behind him. The hilt of a sword slammed into the man's head.

His eyes rolled back and he collapsed, releasing his hold on me.

Dario caught me in his arms before I could fall, and a second later, he cut my bonds, freeing my hands and dropping to his knees to release my feet.

He took my hand in his and we raced to the front of the wagon. My other captor was laying on the ground, barely moving, his eyes still open, watching Dario with absolute hatred.

"They're on their way, you fucking bastard," the wolf said weakly. "More soturi from the Palace. You took the Emperor's pet, and he wants her back." He coughed.

"You look like you're in pain," Dario said calmly.

"Fuck you," said the soturion.

"Dario," I hissed. "Kill him. He's seen you and me."

His nostrils flared, but then he stood over the soturion, reached down for his dagger and handed it to me. "Hold this."

He brandished his sword, holding it over the man's stomach. His boot slammed down on the man's torso, making him wheeze. The movement pushed his armor up, exposing more of his midriff.

"No! No! Please," begged the soturion.

Dario's eyes narrowed. "Since you said please." He lifted his sword, and instead of impaling him, slit his throat.

I gasped and turned away. Dario reached behind my knees, lifting me into his arms and placing me on the back of the ashvan.

A second later, he'd sliced through the straps tying the wagon to the horse, and then he climbed up behind me. "*Vra. Volara!*" he yelled. He tugged on the reins, one hand snaking around my waist, forcing my back against his front.

I tensed up, even though it wasn't our first time touching, nor the first time our bodies had been so close.

"Hold on to me," Dario said.

I hesitated. I hadn't touched a man by choice since Seth.

And when Dario and I had escaped the inn. I grabbed hold of his arm, and squeezed my eyes shut as the horse reared back, lifting and kicking its front legs, and then we ran.

Only this ashvan didn't fly.

"Fuck. *Volara!* Fly!" he yelled.

"He's too old," I said. "That why they had the wagon on him."

"Shit. Okay. Hold on," Dario said, turning the ashvan around. We raced through the trees back out through the woodlands that led to the Cretanyan border.

Within a few minutes we had reached the stone road again.

"Stop!" I yelled.

Dario slowed the horse. "What?"

"Out on the road," I said. "They're there. Ka Kormac."

Dario eased our ashvan forward, just enough to peek out from the woods. Sure enough I was right. There were at least two dozen of the wolves out there drinking, dancing, parading up and down the street.

"It's Viktor's Arkasva celebrations," I said once the horse had stepped back into the shadows. "They're never going to end."

Dario sighed. "We can wait for them to pass."

I shook my head. "They're going to be out there all night. And if they see us—if they see me," I swallowed, "you need to kill me first."

"Jules, that's not going to happen."

I craned my neck, finding his eyes in the dark. "I mean it. I'd rather die."

And as if to prove that the entire universe was against me—our horse decided that that moment was a perfect time to whinny.

Dario stiffened behind me, his aura flaring. I stopped breathing. But we'd been caught.

"Yo, there's an ashvan nearby," came a shout. "Who wants a ride?"

"Into the woods!"

"Go," I hissed under my breath. My fingers dug into his arm. "Now!"

Dario turned, shout-whispering orders to the ashvan, backing us further from the street, deep into the wild bramble of the forest floor, and then we were running, tearing through the trees, low hanging branches cutting up my cheeks and arms, leaves sticking in my hair.

My heart pounded with every step the ashvan took. With every sound I heard that couldn't be explained by our horse. Dario only slowed when he came toward a small mountain pass, its ridges barely outlined in the night sky above the trees.

"Let me see if we can take shelter there," he said, leading us forward.

We walked on for several moments, and the woods grew still. Too still. And suddenly I remembered the other threat still out there. Just as grave as Ka Kormac.

Akadim.

I gripped Dario's arm even harder. But the trees grew sparse, leading into a clearing that sloped down into the valley just before the mountain pass.

"I think there's an opening," he said quietly. "Is your stave on you?" he asked.

I touched my belt, first feeling the dagger he'd given me and then—yes. They hadn't taken my stave. They probably hadn't even looked for weapons, assuming the Emperor's pet didn't have any. I didn't know whether to be insulted, or relieved that they had barely touched me.

"But I can't do much," I said, suddenly embarrassed. I should've been in my third year of mage studies—about to become an apprentice, taking on my own novice and deciding what I wanted to specialize in. Instead, I was struggling through basic spell work with Aiden. But, Dario also knew that.

"Can you call light?" he asked. "If not, I'll light a fire."

I bit my lip. It was such a basic spell. "I'll try."

"It's okay," Dario said. And only then did I realize Dario had been directing us through the woods in almost total darkness, leaving the torches behind so we couldn't be followed. He hadn't faltered once, just kept going, using all his senses to keep me safe. I pulled out my stave, my hand shaking.

For a second, I saw my first stave—my original stave—falling out of my hand, hitting the dais and rolling onto the floor of the temple. The Bastardmaker coming and carrying me away.

I stilled, my hand shaking. I saw it every time I picked up a stave.

"*Ani* ..." My throat caught. Fuck. Come on. "*Ani petrova vala.*"

Heat warmed in my hand. Sweat beaded my brow. And a small light flared. I exhaled in relief.

"That's perfect," Dario said. "Thank you. Can you hold it up as we go in? I need to check for a nest."

We moved into the mouth and I immediately spotted some kindling. Dario released his hold on me and leapt off the horse, rushing over to it, sparking a small flame and then igniting a fire.

"What if that attracts them?" I asked.

"If it does, it can also kill them."

"What if—" I bit my lip.

His eyes darkened. "What if the akadim is Rhyan?"

I nodded slowly.

Dario looked away, breathing hard through his nose. "Then I'll kill him. What else can I do?" But he looked ready to vomit as he spoke. I felt a similar sensation. He returned to the horse's side and reached for my hand, helping me down. Our fingers threaded together. I stilled, expecting to feel something wrong, or off. Unwanted. But, like his other touches so far, my body didn't seem to mind.

We walked through the cavern, ducking under low stone formations. The entire cave was rather small, and from the smell of it, sulfuric—but not full of the stench of decay or dead bodies. After a quick inspection, Dario deemed it safe, and started gathering any remaining loose sticks or kindling he could find to build out a bigger fire.

The days had been getting warmer, but the nights were still cold and I shivered, watching Dario bring the flames to life. When it was set, he looked up at me, and frowned.

"You're cold."

I shook my head. "I'm fine."

"Here," he said, removing his armor and belt. He began unraveling his cloak, pulling all the folds from around his waist out and then bringing it over to me, draping me in it.

I stilled. "You didn't have to—"

"No. It's okay. You need it more than I do." He frowned, watching me, his face red against the fire.

"I'm not that cold."

But he shook his head. "Are you okay? Did they hurt you back there?"

My eyes burned with unshed tears, and I was suddenly so, so fucking angry. Why should I be upset? That was probably the best I'd ever fared in Kormac's hands. They'd drugged me, bruised the shit out of me and cut me up as they dragged me unconscious from the house. But they hadn't beaten me, or humiliated me. Or raped me. So why was I on the verge of tears? I'd been through far fucking worse.

Dario reached out a hand. "I'm sorry, Julianna. I got to you as fast as I could."

"How—" I narrowed my eyes. "How did you find me? Did you hear them take me?"

His jaw worked and he looked away. "I should have. I could have sworn I heard something. And I went to the room to check—but then—well, I didn't think you wanted to see me, so—"

Shit. I almost lost my fucking life because Dario was actually respecting my boundaries and trying to give me space.

"But then I went in a few minutes later." He hissed through his teeth. "And you were gone. We tore the house apart. Meera prepped a nahashim to come find you. But then I remembered the babies in their boxes. They saw what happened to you—saw that man grab you and drag you off the balcony. I took off after you at once, running and tracking every clue I could find until I found the wagon."

"You tracked me? Using nothing more than a vision of me being kidnapped?"

"Well, I could make some deductions based on their methods and the fact that no one else had seen anything. I had to make some quick guesses. Thank the Gods I was right. If anything had happened to you—" His hands fisted.

My throat went dry. "You would have broken your promise to Lyr?"

Dario grimaced. "Yes." His eyes met mine. "But more than that, I would have lost it. Because I—" He paused and I could see the uncertainty in his eyes. "Because I care about you," he said softly.

I looked away. I was tired. My body ached. My brain felt heavy and stuffed, like my head was full of wool. But it wasn't either of those things that was making me feel exhausted. It was far more simple than that. It was feeling. Just feeling. Feeling anything. I had worked so hard during my time in the Palace to become numb. To everything. My body. My mind. My heart. To feel nothing, just so I could survive. Keep my oath to Seth. And now, I realized that for the past month, I'd been feeling so much. Like I was using muscles I hadn't tried to use before, or had forgotten. And I wasn't sure I was ready.

"Are you hungry?" Dario asked after several moments of silence between us. "I have some food in my pack."

I turned back to him and nodded. I was hungry.

"Have a seat," Dario said. "I'll give you everything I have."

"What about you?" I asked.

He shook his head. "Don't worry about me."

I started to sit down, but suddenly cried out. Now that we were still, that the threat was gone, my injuries were catching up to me. At least a dozen cuts and bruises, it felt like.

"Can I look?" Dario asked.

My heart started thundering. My stomach twisted. It suddenly occurred to me how alone I was with him. How at his mercy. But he held up his hand. "I'll only look, I swear. I won't touch you. Not unless you say it's okay."

"Okay," I said, eyeing his hands, and slowly inched his cloak off my shoulders.

He reached for a pouch on his belt and came to kneel before me.

"Show me where," he said quietly. "Oh, hold on."

He pulled out a small cantina of water and splashed it over his hands, rubbing them together. Then he pulled out a jar of golden sunleaf paste, and popped the lid, sticking his finger in. His eyes narrowed. "You have a cut on your cheek." His jaw tensed. "May I?"

My heart thundered but I nodded. "Yes."

He brushed the salve across my skin. Already the burning there felt soothed.

"Is that okay?" he asked.

"It feels better." I swallowed roughly, and showed him my neck, pulling my hair back.

His eyes followed my movements, scanning the injuries there. "May I?" he asked again.

"Yes."

He nodded, putting some salve there as well. I nearly sighed in relief. "Where else?" he asked.

I showed him the other side of my neck. And again, he asked, "May I?" before applying the salve.

I swallowed, knowing what came next. They hadn't all been monsters in the Palace. Some had been nice. Gentle even. At first. Asking permission, showing respect. But the end was the same. Always. What they wanted from me. What they expected in exchange for the smallest of kindnesses.

The backs of my eyes burned, and I was suddenly breathing heavily through my nostrils. But it was time. Time to get it over with. I began to untie the tops of my dress.

Dario watched with rapt attention as I let the material fall down, exposing my breasts in the firelight.

He sucked in a breath, his eyes widening, darting to my nipples. His chest heaved, his jaw working, before he met my eyes again.

"Wh-where?" he asked. "I don't," his eyes narrowed, "I don't see any cuts."

I almost laughed. "They're elsewhere. I figured I'd just give you what you wanted up front."

Dario's face fell. He looked like I had punched him in the stomach. He practically reared back from me.

"What I–what I wanted? What—"

"You want something from me, don't you? I've seen the way you look at me." I ran a hand down my breast, my fingers slowly caressing my nipple. "Not just today, but for the last few weeks."

Dario turned away, his face red. "That's what you think of me? That I came after you to get something in return?"

"Isn't that what you want?" Rhyan had trusted him. So had Lyr, and so did Meera. And to some startling extent, so did I. Even that first real night together, when we'd had to escape, when I'd told him my secret, told him who I was, I felt I could trust him. But … I just … if he was going to be like the others, going to use me, I just needed to know. Needed to stop guessing, stop wondering, and know without a doubt if I'd been wrong.

"Gods, Jules." He turned back to me, his eyes on mine, his hand reaching for me.

And there it was. His hand would be on my breast, in a moment, he'd be laying me on the floor, rucking up my skirts. I was ready. Ready to gloat. Ready to bask in being right. But most importantly ready to retreat, to go to that place I had to in order to survive, to not feel.

Only Dario didn't touch me. His fingers closed around the straps of my dress as he pulled them back up to my shoulders, reaching around me for the back pieces and tying them again until I was covered.

His nostrils flared, his breath still heavy. "If you have any more injuries," he said coldly, "I'll treat them. But that's it. I won't touch you in any other way."

I believed him. And yet, I scoffed. "Sure."

"I won't. I gave you my word, Julianna. I swore I would protect you, that I would keep you safe. I gave you my oath."

I shook my head. "I saw the ways your eyes darkened, the way you looked at me just now."

"Because you're beautiful," Dario said, lifting his hands up in surrender. "Is that what you want to hear, Jules? What you need from me? An admission? You need me to tell you that the first time I saw you, I thought you were so Godsdamned beautiful it hurt? Because it did." His nostrils flared, his jaw muscles working. "Yes. I want you. Okay? I do. But I will not act on it. Because what my body desires doesn't mean shit if you don't want it, too. Not ever. Especially not tonight. You owe me nothing. I would have come for you no matter what. I would have come for you if you hated me. Nothing would have stopped me."

My stomach turned. I could hear the hurt in his voice that I didn't believe him. That I hadn't trusted him. Had thought him little more than a Kormac. Only I had believed I could trust him—I knew he wasn't like that. Dario wasn't just some man. He'd been my companion for a month. My protector. What the fuck was I doing?

"I-I feel this pull towards you," he said quietly. "Being with you," his voice cracked, "it would mean something to me. More than you know. You, of all people, never have to fear me."

I squeezed my eyes shut, almost nauseated by what I'd done. Old fucking habits. Fears.

"They really ... hurt you," he said, "didn't they?" Not the men tonight. But the Palace. The last two and half years.

"They did." He wasn't Ka Kormac. He wasn't even close. And he needed to know that. Know that I was sorry. And that I did trust him. Slowly, I pulled up the skirts of my dress. Not so anything could happen between us, nor to test him any further. But because I trusted him. I trusted him enough to show him the proof–the physical proof.

He watched warily as I pulled the fabric to just below my hips.

There were several raised pink lines across both of my thighs. Lines that had come from a very thin whip, used to humiliate and torture me.

Dario gasped, looking more closely, his hand fisting again, his nostrils flaring, the muscles in his jaw clenching. "Those aren't from tonight."

I shook my head. "From before."

"I'm sorry."

"I'm not showing you for pity."

Dario's eyes darkened, something still and murderous behind his irises. "I don't pity you. I understand you." He met my gaze. "The man who did this to you," he said slowly. He was seething, almost too angry to get the words out, "Does he still live?"

"The man?" I said, and shook my head. "You mean the men. There's more where this came from. Other scars I carry."

A tear rolled down my cheek. That hadn't happened in a long time. Not for this. But it had also been a long time since anyone had seen my scars with my permission—seen them and looked sorry. Not excited. Not eager to add more.

"The one who did this," I gestured to the top row of scars, "who started it, he was killed. By Lyr actually."

"Good," Dario growled.

I shook my head. "No. She didn't kill him enough."

He nodded slowly. "The others who hurt you?"

"They live."

His neck reddened, his gaze sweeping back over the scars. "Not for long. Not after they meet me."

I met his eyes, and for the first time since I'd seen him, I truly began to see the kindness behind them. The generosity. The care. The protectiveness. I thought I'd seen that back at the inn. Seen that I could trust him, and yet, this, this was something else. Like I was seeing a glimpse of his soul. His eyes, were so dark, so endless looking, I thought for the first time in what felt like forever, that I could lose myself in them.

I blinked. A different set of eyes flashed in my mind. Just as kind, protective, passionate.

Seth's.

My heart clenched, and I was suddenly pushing my skirts down, smoothing the material over my legs and crossing my arms over my chest.

Dario shifted onto one knee, his hand fisted. "You tell me the next man I come across who hurt you, who touched you. And I will kill him. Thoroughly. *Me sha, me ka.*" He pressed his fist to his heart, tapping it twice, then flattened his palm across his chest, eyes blazing.

I nodded, and held out my arm, where I'd been scratched by a tree. "This is from tonight."

"May I?" Dario said.

I nodded, and he continued addressing my wounds, covering my arms, and my calves, and one scratch between my shoulders.

When he was done, he helped me fold up his cloak into a bed, and covered me, making sure I was comfortable.

"What about you?" I asked, sleepily.

He shook his head. "I'm going to watch over you, Jules. All night. Go ahead, close your eyes. You're safe."

And I did. Because for the first time in forever, I believed it. I believed him.

CHAPTER TWENTY-FOUR

TRISTAN

My grandmother lifted her wine glass high in the air, my grandfather behind her, already drinking. We were in Cresthaven's ballroom, the entire Council present, along with our new Imperator, Her Highness Arianna Batavia. My future mother-in-law.

But of course, the Bastardmaker was here, too. Standing close. His black eyes were on me, commanding me, reminding me. Like I needed a fucking reminder at this point. He could leave. He could leave me alone forever. And I'd still know what to do. Shoulders back. Head high. Smile. Pretend everything was fucking fine. Convince everyone that I was happy. That I agreed with what was happening to my country, to my people.

To vorakh like me.

I was his puppet, unleashing chaos with a smile. And, of course, most importantly of all, I had to show that I was happy. Not grieving for Galen. Or acting as if the murder of my best friend wasn't still tearing me apart a month later. That I still wasn't waking from nightmares of the Yellow Room, Galen screaming with no sound coming from his lips, my hand shattering. My soul breaking.

"To my grandson, Lord Tristan." My grandmother lifted the goblet to her lips. All the Council Members and nobles of

Bamaria followed. She grinned, her lips now the same color as the wine. "He has made the Empire proud. And he has made us safe again. Ever since he's become the head of the vorakh task force, Bamaria—or rather," she winked at the Bastardmaker and then Arianna, "New Korteria, has never been greater. Thanks to Tristan's efforts, we've arrested two dozen criminals from our streets in just the last three days alone. All shipped off to Lethea where they belong."

I downed my glass in one go.

Naria took my hand in hers and squeezed. We'd grown closer over the last month. For the first time in all the years we'd known each other, we were actually becoming something that felt like friends. While every other aspect of my life was going to complete shit, Naria was starting to become the best part. The only thing getting me through the day.

"Just a little while longer," she whispered. "Then we'll have done our duty and we can retreat to our room."

I nodded, trying to calm my breathing. My grandmother was still grinning, then her eyes flashed on mine and she deposited her glass on a tray floating past her. Her fingers full of silver rings and precious stones sparkled. The Bastardmaker crossed the room, and took her hand. She grinned even wider. I could only make out part of their conversation, something about overflowing prisons. And a new contract to build more—using Ka Grey silver.

I was going to be sick. But suddenly, the door to the ballroom slammed open. The room filled with silence, every noble turning in the direction of the disturbance. At who had entered.

"I was just wondering ..." It was Lord Eathan Ezara, the former Second to the Arkasva. Harren Batavia's cousin. He'd been about to take the Seat of Power in the interim between Harren's death and Arianna's consecration. Until the Emperor threw him from the Seat.

Without a role on the Council, I hadn't seen him at Court in months. Though as Lyriana's cousin, he remained a noble with considerable power.

It was startling just then to see him in blue robes. For as long as I could remember he was always in gray—the color worn by the Master of the Horse. The color my grandmother was now expected to wear. Only of course, she'd had her robes made of silver.

His eyes crinkled as he smiled at Arianna and bowed before her. "Your Highness, pardon my interruption," he said. "But I was just wondering. Since the task force has been so successful under Lord Tristan's leadership, and since we have yet to experience another akadim attack in these lands in months, if things are as safe and great as you say, at what point does Bamaria become Bamaria again?" His voice hardened.

Arianna smiled sweetly—too sweetly—and plucked a glass of wine from another floating tray. Her red hair had been curled on top of her head, her golden Laurel of the Arkasva delicately laid across her brow. And now, as Imperator, she wore a golden border through her black robes.

"Lord Eathan," she said. "First, let me welcome you back to Court."

"Your Highness," he said again, slowly eyeing the room. "And my question?"

"Unfortunately, that is a question best left to the Council, a Council you no longer sit on. I would offer more, as I hold you in such high esteem. You have served our country well and for many years. But we don't want to act too hastily. After all, that's how mistakes are made. And when you have akadim, and now vorakh running wild, committing acts of terrorism, we must proceed with caution. Lord Tristan is doing admirably. But there are more vorakh out there, more threats to stop, and unifying with Korteria is keeping us safe. But I thank you for the question."

"Were we not already unified? Under the Lumerian Empire?" he practically barked.

"These are trying times. And I would advise you to accept my answer." Her aura flared, leaving a startlingly icy chill down my spine.

"Of course." He stepped back, and from the corner of my eye, I watched as the Bastardmaker gave a signal to another soturion, one of the sentries on duty. A silver wolf.

Eathan stepped into the crowd of nobles.

I wanted to scream at him, warn him. But I couldn't. My blood wouldn't allow it.

I turned to Naria, my eyes desperate. We had to help him. Do something. But she shook her head. "We can't."

The wolf stepped forward and grabbed Eathan's arms from behind.

"What are you—"

The soturion covered his mouth, and dragged Eathan from the ballroom.

Hardly anyone looked up. But the mood had changed. Everyone's aura suddenly dampened, being pulled back, held close.

"That'll be us next," Naria hissed. "If we don't play the game."

"We're not playing the game! We just do what they tell us to do."

"And we're alive because of it," she said. "Eathan asked one question. One. He framed it innocently enough, and you saw what happened. Now just stay calm."

I tapped my foot. We'd been having these parties almost every night for a month. Celebrating Arianna's consecration as Imperator. Celebrating the decision to bring Bamaria and Elyria together under New Korteria. Pretending Arianna actually wanted that, or our people liked the decision. And worst of all: pretending it was temporary. And it didn't stop there. We had another celebration when Viktor was made Arkasva of

Korteria. And another yet again to mark the Emperor's first month on the throne. Next thing I knew we'd be having a party because the Bastardmaker took a really clean shit. Anything to keep the Council distracted and happy. Anything to keep them from asking questions like Eathan.

"Mind your thoughts," Naria said quietly. "You don't know who's listening."

I sighed. It must have been all over my face. And she was right. Someone wasn't listening though. Someone was watching.

The Bastardmaker crossed the room. "Smile. It's a party."

I smiled, like an idiot.

Some time passed, musicians played, and water dancers traipsed through the ballroom to perform several songs. Drum beats echoed against the walls, and I drank two more glasses of wine.

I was about to call over Bellamy, have him send word to Galen that we should get some real alcohol later. Like we usually did. Then I remembered. The sorrow crashed back into me, nearly knocking me over.

I eyed my grandmother, desperately hoping she'd at least let me retire for the evening.

But she shook her head, her eyes cold.

"We have one more surprise for you all tonight," Arianna announced. "I know that in our positions we are often not able to see what our people do. And sometimes it can be hard to understand where they're coming from, or their needs. We represent them, and we care for them with our leadership, and our policies. I think to do so effectively, it's important that we connect with them as deeply as possible."

I eyed Naria suspiciously. Where was this going?

But she only shrugged. Since we'd actually started having real conversations, I'd learned that her mother kept her in the dark about nearly everything. That one of the reasons she always seemed angry, was because she was actually nervous, never knowing what Arianna would ask of her next.

"I'll let Arkturion Waryn share with you what's going to happen next," Arianna said.

The Bastardmaker walked into the center of the ballroom, a dangerous gleam in his eyes.

"We have with us three accused vorakh," he announced.

I paled.

"Now they are only accused," he said. "Which means, they have a chance to prove their innocence. And as you don't usually get to see the way this happens, I thought it best to use this opportunity for a demonstration. Further proof of how strong Bamaria is. How strong New Korteria can become. And how the betrothed of your Heir Apparent, Lady Naria Batavia, is able to do this for you."

Fuck. Fuck. Fuck!

"Lord Tristan, come and show everyone just how skilled you are at protecting your people."

I joined his side, using all my willpower to keep from trembling.

The Bastardmaker leaned in, whispering in my ear. "And this time you only have to hold your stave, not your cock. Smile."

I grinned, my stomach roiling.

Soturi, all in silver, marched through the doors, each one holding the ropes of a bound mage. Two women, one man. They all seemed to be around my age, probably still at the Academy, studying.

And completely undeserving of what was about to happen.

"Well," he said, "go ahead."

I cleared my throat. "I usually apprehend at the time of a vision or when they're in the act of using their vorakh. It can be hard to say when the ability is docile."

"But you're our star hunter," he said, and snapped his fingers. A black box floated into his hands. "Now," he said, pulling back the lid. A black nahashim poked its head out and hissed. "Go and hunt."

My stomach clenched in pain, fear choking me from the inside. I'd never touched one. I was just the face of this task force. Yes, I'd had to arrest a handful of vorakh—the ones having visions in front of me. Like I always had. I'd had no choice—not when there were witnesses. But this—I'd never done this, and I did not want to touch this snake. This snake that was primed to sniff out the very thing I had inside, that I had to hide.

"Do it," the Bastardmaker hissed. And pain shot through my arms and legs. I had to obey.

I picked up the snake, shocked at how hot the scales were in my palm.

"Who shall we test first?" he asked, his voice booming. "Accused criminal one," he pointed to the first woman, tanned skin, with blond hair that reminded me of Naria's, "accused number two," he pointed to the woman in the middle. She had a long narrow face, sleek black hair, and her entire body was shaking. "Or accused three?" The man. Not a mage I realized as I looked more closely. He was built like a soturion, with brown hair and eyes, the same color as mine.

Everyone in the room began to call out different numbers. Most seemed in favor of the blond woman. And I had a sickening feeling why.

"Well?" he asked. "Who will it be? Where do your instincts lead you?"

"Three," I said. The male soturion. Immediately the men in the room began to boo and show their disapproval. Several of the wolves even howled.

The Bastardmaker huffed in obvious disappointment. "Interesting choice," he drawled, his voice low. Then he shrugged. "Remove the ropes, keep the binding. And take his robes."

The man began to shake, his eyes wide. "No. Please."

But a mage, one in Ka Kormac colors, was already taking the ropes away with their stave, and then one of the soturi ripped his robe right off his back, leaving him completely nude. There were a few gasps. My grandmother had the decency to turn away. But Arianna looked delighted, her eyes sparkling as she took in the man in his current form.

Breathe. Breathe.

I walked forward, unable to look him in the eye. If I did, I'd give it all away.

"Please, please don't." His voice shook. "I don't have vorakh. Or any magic. I'm just a soturion. Please."

Vomit rose up my throat, and I swallowed, placing the nahashim against his face.

It slithered up to his eyes, and then its body vanished within.

The man screamed in pain, his body convulsing as a black mark in the outline of the snake appeared in his cheek and began to slither. He screamed, convulsing, and the two women beside him started to cry in fear.

And I could do nothing, couldn't stop it, couldn't help. I just had to watch as it moved through him, violating him, hurting him, searching deeper and deeper. Until at last, the snake began to slither its way back up to his face. His neck reddened, his body breaking out into sweat that dripped from his forehead.

Suddenly the snake flew out of his mouth, landing, slippery in my hands. I stared down at it in horror. It turned its head, and I swore it stared back at me. That it was reaching up, trying to touch my face, to slip inside me and expose my secrets. Its tongue shot out, black eyes shining, its head rearing. I rushed it back to the Bastardmaker, throwing the snake into the box as the man retched, vomiting on the floor. Several nobles backed away, making horrified sounds of disgust.

I was going to vomit next. I was actually going to vomit. But the Bastardmaker stared at me firmly. "Swallow," he commanded.

I did. My throat burning. My stomach twisting.

He examined the snake, looking into its eyes, a sudden frown on his lips. The man was innocent. The nahashim found nothing.

"Guilty," he announced.

"No," groaned the man.

The vomit came up again. "I-I'm going to—"

The Bastardmaker rolled his eyes. "Go then."

I ran from the room, Bellamy and Eric on my heels, running to the nearest bathroom I could find. I was barely inside, before I collapsed on the ground and heaved.

CHAPTER TWENTY-FIVE

JULIANNA

The next morning, Dario and I took our ashvan from the cave and headed into the nearest town, keeping our heads down, to look for food.

Because I'd been taken, that meant our safe home was once again compromised. Dario said that Meera and Aiden were already preparing to flee when he'd run out after me.

We had no idea where to go, or where they were. We'd run out of options for *El Zan Vylette* in both Cretanya and Korteria. Which meant Meera and Aiden had to find another solution. A safe place to go before we could reunite. Dario said the plan was to send nahashim to find us once they had things in order.

But there'd been no word from them yet, which I tried not to read into.

Dario and I quietly gathered supplies. More blankets with the little bit of money he had on him, and food. We returned to the cave quickly after and waited.

The next day was the same. No news. I was growing more worried. What if something had happened to Meera? To the only family I had left. I was so anxious that Dario and I barely spoke. We'd come to a kind of understanding, and maybe even a level of comfort around each other. But we weren't touching. Nor were we bringing up the awkwardness of that first night, of me accusing Dario of ulterior motives. Or the oath he swore—to kill any of the men who'd raped me.

On the third day, we ventured out, sticking to crowds, and laying low. We tried to listen for news. For any possible mentions of Meera and Aiden being captured, or Lyriana finally being seen. But suddenly, there was a scream in the square. A man shouting. He was barely past the age of twenty. Like he'd only gone through his revelation ceremony this past year. Suddenly his shouts of protest turned to a scream of pure, unbridled pain.

Dario took my hand, his fingers tightening over mine, moving me away. But it was too late. I'd seen what was happening. What we'd known was happening all over the country to countless innocent people. What Tristan was currently the face for.

The vorakh task force. A mob was forming around him, their auras vicious and wild. They were bloodthirsty, flinging accusations with abandon.

The man, boy really, had been stripped naked by them as the mob grew in size and intensity. They were all yelling, calling him a vorakh.

I moved closer to Dario, starting to shake. A soturion in silver, one of the Kormac wolves, stepped behind him, and grabbed hold of his arms.

He screamed, struggling to get away until a bone snapped. His arm broken.

Another soturion stepped into the circle, holding a small box.

A nahashim.

The crowd cheered, and screamed as the box lid was removed and the snake inside was thrown at the man. It landed on his bare chest, slithering up to his face, and then— it slipped inside his eyelid.

His screams pierced through my heart.

"I'm getting you out of here," Dario said, pulling me away. His fingers threaded through my hand, his arm around my shoulder, as he guided us into the shadows, my heart pounding.

We were back at the cave shortly after that. I had to dry heave, until my stomach calmed. Dario sat with me, silently rubbing my back. But only after asking if he could.

I brushed the tears from my eyes, and slowly sipped on the water he'd gotten for me.

"You're okay, Jules," he said gently. "You're all right. You're safe."

I shook my head. "No I'm not. Nor are you. Not as long as we stay here." I met Dario's dark eyes. "Don't you see it? They've won. The takeover's complete. I'm not in the Palace anymore, but I'm not free. None of us are. And, the truth is, I never will be. None of us will. Not against the whole force of Ka Kormac. Dario, I, don't know if I want to find Meera and Aiden," I said, quietly.

"What?" he asked, "No, don't say that. Of course, we're going to find them."

I shook my head. "No, I mean I don't want to. Not unless it's outside of the Empire. If they wish to, they can join me there, but I'm done trying to just survive here. I'm done being afraid every minute, waiting for them to find me, to exact their next law of cruelty. I want you to take me west, to the human lands. To Dobrava."

"Jules," he frowned, "your home is here."

"Home? What home!" I yelled, my stomach twisting. "I'm from a country that won't recognize I'm alive. Heir to a Seat of Power that are both been usurped, my family killed. And more than that! I'm from two countries that don't even exist anymore—that are both now New Korteria. I'll be killed if anyone finds out the truth, or worse. Returned. I've been enslaved and raped repeatedly for years. All by the same man who's now in charge of everything. And now—they're taking people off the streets. You said you care about me. That you'd protect me. Take me away from here."

"If you want me to," he said. "I'll take you. But, Jules. Are you sure you want to run? You don't want to fight back?"

"Do I look like I can fight?" I snapped. "I can barely do magic outside of my vorakh. And I'm not strong. I'm not a warrior. I can't fight these soldiers."

"You could be trained," he said. "I'd train you. If you wanted."

I exhaled sharply. "Sure."

"You could," he said fervently. "Lyr did. She had no magic at her Revelation Ceremony, and she learned to kill akadim anyway. You have magic. You could learn too."

"And save one person. Maybe? Maybe save myself. Once? But what would be the point? The fight would never end."

Dario stared at the flames burning before us. "You're right. It wouldn't end. The fighting never stops when it's you against the world. An army, a soturi makes it better. You can cover more ground." He stilled, his eyes blazing as he looked me over. "But you know what has an even bigger impact, and could save more lives, help more people than me and a hundred soturi ever could?"

I blinked. "What?"

"Being a leader," he said. "Being a good leader. Like an Arkasva. Making changes for the country, standing up against the Emperor."

I scoffed. "Oh right! Of course. An Arkasva! That sounds nice in theory. But in case you haven't noticed, we're lacking good Arkasvim at the moment. We don't have them."

"We could," Dario said slowly. "We could. What if you claimed your birthright? What if you became High Lady of Elyria? Took it back from Kormac and Ka Elys? Jules, you could make things better."

I stiffened. "No," I said, my voice hard. "I won't do that. And I don't want to talk about it. Not being Heir. Not being Hava. None of it."

"Why?" Dario asked, his aura pulsing with energy. "You have the chance to have power in this world. Too many have that who don't deserve it. But you do. You could take it."

"Because I tried once before and I failed. Okay? These titles mean nothing. The same as all of these little fucking rebel groups. Did being Hava stop me from being a slave? Did being Heir to the Arkasva save me from being, from being raped?" Or stop them from killing Seth. …

My hand trembled, and I picked up a stick beside the fire, tossing it in, watching the flames crackle, my heart hurting. Fuck all of this. Fuck the Empire. Dario was speaking nonsense. Dreams of delusion. I didn't want it, I didn't want any of it. For the first time in years, I had the tiniest chance to be Julianna again. To just be myself. But I couldn't do that under the Emperor's rule. No matter what country I was in, what it was called, or who was Arkasva. Even if it was me in the end, sitting on the Seat of Power.

Because I knew Avery Kormac. And I knew I wasn't a leader. I could barely do magic. Barely run more than five minutes without needing to sit down. And I was supposed to lead a Godsdamned country? One that would have me arrested when they knew what I was, one that would shrink in horror when they learned what was done to me?

Dario inched closer, careful not to touch me.

"Can you drop this? Please?" I asked. "I'm not going to rule. Whatever my birth father says, it was never my destiny. If you want a new Arkasva, talk to Meera. She at least was trained."

"You could learn," he insisted. "You could train, too. You're smart, and you're kind."

I glared.

"Not always to me," he lifted an eyebrow. "But you are. I see you. I see your heart. You don't want to see others suffer, and you wouldn't, to the best of your ability, allow anyone else to. And if there's something you don't know, you can get advisors or your council to help you. Meera would help you." He looked away. "I would help you."

"Dario, I just want to leave. Are we really having this conversation now?"

"Well, we could be sailing the Lumerian Ocean, but since we're stuck in this cave, with nothing else to do." He shrugged.

I sighed. It would never happen. Not for me. But when he explained it, the steps I could take, the way he sounded so sincere, like he believed in me, it almost seemed possible. Almost.

"I wouldn't be enough," I said. "You know that. You know how things work here. All my inner strength, and all my claims in blood would be worthless, nothing without soturi backing me."

Dario leaned in. His aura filled with fire. "If the day comes when you make your claim on Elyria, I will fight for you. I will be your Arkturion, protect your land, protect you, until it's secure. And if you want me to go home after, I will. But if you want me to stay, then I'm yours."

My mouth fell open. I'd accuse him of joking, but I'd spent enough time with Dario by now to know—he was serious. "You'd do that?" I asked slowly. "You have no connection to Elyria, or anyone from there. None at all."

"Not true." He grinned. "I know you."

"That's not enough."

"Well, for me it is. Because like you, I also hate to see suffering. It doesn't matter that Elyria isn't my home, or that it's not connected to me. It still needs to be protected. And why not? I've spent years of my life fighting for my own country, but doing so under a corrupt ruler, one who's done nothing but hurt me, and my friends for years. I'd easily fight in a new country for a good ruler." His eyes flashed. "Especially if she were you. There's ..." he coughed. "There's little I wouldn't do for you."

I feel this pull towards you.

"Can we not talk about it anymore?" I asked.

Dario nodded. "Of course. I just—thought I'd tell you how I feel."

I laid down on my makeshift bed, watching Dario closely. "Will you—would you lie down beside me?"

His face softened so completely I almost wanted to cry. Like he'd been waiting for me to ask. He crawled beside me, his body still careful not to touch mine. He shifted onto his side, his hands resting under his head as our eyes met.

We couldn't go back to Alistair's. But Lady Aliyah had gathered money. And Kenna was working with her own rebel groups back in Glemaria. If I had Dario by my side ... No. I needed to stop. These were dreams. Worse. Fairy tales. I shook the thought away, and matched Dario's breathing. We stayed like that, our eyes watching the others for hours. There was nothing else to do. And neither of us seemed willing to move, or break the silence. Until we eventually fell asleep. Not talking, not touching. Just watching.

When morning came, sunlight streamed in golden rays through the mouth of the cave, a cold wind blew inside, and a sharp hiss broke our silence.

Dario grabbed his blade, rushing at it, half awake, but then the snake dropped a scroll it had been carrying in its mouth.

He grabbed the case, and unraveled the parchment, his eyes leaping across the page as he read. And then he laughed, his eyes filling with joy. It was the complete opposite of the reaction he'd had to the last scroll delivered to us.

"What?" I asked. "What is it?"

"It's Meera and Aiden! They found somewhere to stay. Nothing special, just an inn that's cheap, no questions asked. But still! They're safe. They left the address for us. And there's more." He grinned. "There aren't many details—we'll need to speak to them in person. But according to this, Kenna sent good news about what's happening in Glemaria. And—" He walked back to me and crouched down on the blanket. "And a second nahashim returned to them, one of the ones sent to find Lyr."

My eyes widened, my heart thrumming. "What did it find?"

Dario grinned. "She's alive."

I burst into tears and threw my arms around him. He pulled me close, holding me until my sobs slowed.

"What do you want to do?" he asked. "I'm at your service. Do you want to head for the border? Or do you want me to take you back to Meera and Aiden?"

"Take me back to Meera and Aiden," I said. And Lyr. "I'm not leaving. Not yet."

CHAPTER TWENTY-SIX

TRISTAN

The protests were growing worse. The people were starting to riot. There were mobs forming in the city, screaming about New Korteria. About Ka Kormac's occupation. About the way their soturi was starting to overshadow our own. There were complaints pouring in from soturi whose homes had been invaded by Ka Kormac. And complaints of worse crimes happening during those invasions. Reports that left me ill, and sick to my stomach.

The biggest protests though were centered around the vorakh task force. The Emperor had sent word that he wanted more arrested. More than perhaps we even had. The other night when those three accused of vorakh had been dragged into Cresthaven, all three had been innocent. Publicly humiliated by being stripped naked, and tortured. And all because of an accusation. And despite their innocence, despite the proof by nahashim, the Bastardmaker had sent them to the newly constructed Bamarian prisons. They were only half built by the mages, not yet fit for anyone to live in for a single night, much less the weeks I knew they'd be there, but it didn't matter. Kormac's wolves had to meet their quota. Avery needed more slaves.

I didn't know what to do. I felt like I was losing my mind. But luckily, there was no ball tonight. Nor a parade—those were being restricted now thanks to protests. Arianna was finally getting a taste of her own medicine. But barely. So when the Council meetings finally ended for the day, and the soturi out hunting vorakh made their final report to me, I was beyond grateful to retreat to Naria's room and lie down.

I crawled onto her bed, and fell asleep hours before nightfall.

Sometime later, I woke up with a start. My eyes opened, but closed nearly at once as cold seeped through my body and I was sucked into a vision. No. No. No.

The door opened. Fuck. I tried to still my body, but I couldn't. I couldn't stop shaking. Couldn't stop the vision from taking over.

"Tristan?" Naria asked. "Tristan!"

No! No! I couldn't answer. I was being swept away, my surroundings gone, and within seconds, Naria's voice faded from consciousness.

There was a flash of yellow light.

Yellow. Too much yellow.

I looked around. I was in the ruins of an ancient temple and there were people shouting. No. Not people. Gods. Two of them. And a Goddess with flaming red hair.

I was little, my body barely a boy's, and I was naked. And cold. So cold. I reached for a blanket on the ground and covered my body, holding it tight around my shoulders. But still I shivered, afraid. Everything felt new and strange and harsh.

A God lay on the ground, unconscious, a yellow crystal hung from his neck. He wore the armor of a warrior. He was familiar to me, though I also knew I'd never seen him before.

He'd been powerful. Deadly. Someone strong enough to destroy the world.

And I was scared. Because I felt the death he'd wrought inside me. It felt like my soul had been torn in half. Like my body was splitting. Tearing apart. Everything hurt.

I wanted to crawl to the God. I wanted him to protect me. I wanted to crawl back inside of him. But he wasn't waking up. His eyes wouldn't open.

I looked behind me. Another God, this one awake, his eyes an almost blinding shade of green. Curls spun of gold on his head. The Goddess was beside him.

I shook my head in confusion and pain and cried out, my voice small like a child's. "I ... I can feel it. My death. My birth. All at once." I had died. But I'd also just been born. What was happening to me? "It's so much," I said, tears falling down my cheeks.

"We had no choice," the God whispered.

The Goddess watched me with concerned eyes. "It must feel so confusing," she said gently. "But you're going to be all right. I swear. You don't have to be alone in this. I know the role I played. And I'm sorry for it."

I stared at my feet, poking out from the blanket. My hands opened and closed in my lap. Then I lifted my arms. My skin was so new, I was almost pink.

"Are you hurt?" the Goddess asked. "We can't stay here. But we'll take you with us. Protect you. Can you walk?"

We can't stay here? Why can't we stay here? Anger rushed through me, fiery and overwhelming, ready to consume my small body. I pulled the edges of my blanket closer. I still didn't understand. Where were we? Who were they? And why did I want to crawl into the arms of the God who seemed to shine the color yellow?

I glared at the God and Goddess. "You said you had no choice. But what is it that you have done? What am I?"

The Goddess began to cry, but I felt no sympathy for her. "You were part of the God known as Shiviel," she said, "Guardian of the Yellow Ray. Now you're not. Now you're new."

"New?" I asked, horror filling me. "I'm not new. I can feel it. I'm ancient. I always was. I can feel where you cut ... where you cut me apart." Shiviel. Shiviel. I had to get back to Shiviel.

I could see it now. Heaven. Earth. The Hall of Records. The Light. The War. I wasn't new. "I remember," *my voice shook.* "Remember too much. I can't be new. I've been here for so long. If I were new, I wouldn't have died. I wouldn't have felt it. My death."

"You're right," *the God said.* "You are ancient. We were brothers once. We protected each other. And I swear I will protect you now. I will amend this. You don't have to be afraid."

"Why should I believe you?" *I spat. They were the ones who had cut me.* "I sense memories. Of another world. Another plane of existence. Of light. A light that did not burn." *It was becoming clearer. All of it. Who I'd been. Who I was. A Guardian.* "But I am not Shiviel. Not anymore. I am ... other."

A light flashed. Yellow. Yellow light. Blinding. Too much.

A woman tore through with wild, unkempt black hair, and a beauty mark above her mouth. The vorakh who murdered my parents.

"NO!" *I screamed.* "NO!"

"I'll still get you," *she said.* "I'm close now. Closer than you know." *A smile spread across her face, one embedded with a promise. Of death.* "You won't get away from me this time, Turiel."

My eyes sprang open again, and I was kicking and flailing and shouting. "I'm not Turiel. I'm not Turiel!"

"Tristan," Naria said. "Tristan, stop! It's me! It's Naria."

I gasped, coldness clinging to every inch of my body.

"What the hell," she said. "What's wrong with you?"

"C-Can you get me a blanket," I asked weakly.

Rolling her eyes, she walked to the closet and pulled out a spare. She climbed into the bed with me, wrapping her legs around mine, her arms across my waist as she pulled the blanket over the two of us.

"Body heat will help," she said quietly, her eyes searching mine.

I burst into tears. "You know what you just saw?"

She nodded. "I know. I've known. I figured it out."

"And you didn't tell anyone?"

She leaned over and kissed my forehead. "Obviously not. I'm not an idiot. I'm not going to tell anyone." She pushed back my hair, her face softening. "It's okay. I'm here with you."

I buried my face against her neck and breathed in her floral scent, trying to push the vision out of my mind. But when I closed my eyes, I saw the vorakh again, and all I could hear was her telling me she was coming to get me.

Coming to get Turiel.

CHAPTER TWENTY-SEVEN

LYRIANA

"Careful," Auriel said, reaching for my hand. I'd lost my balance, stepping onto a series of rocks at the top of a Korterian hill. The grass had grown so tall the rocks were hidden, and I'd been taken by surprise more than once as we crossed the border back into Lumeria. And back into a regular sense of time. A task made more difficult since my boots were still wet from crossing a ravine at the Afeyan border.

I grasped Auriel's hand, and took a deep breath, my free hand sliding reassuringly behind my back over the hilt of the red shard.

"You're all right?" he asked.

I shook my head. "Fine."

But my heart was pounding. An entire month was catching up to me all at once. I felt the time passing with every step, and I wondered if this was what it was like for Rhyan after a jump. Feeling so much distance speed through his body.

The Queen's warning was fresh in my mind. I had to end Rhyan's akadim existence. No matter what. Either by restoring his soul, or ... no. I wasn't even going to think about the alternative. I was going to heal him.

But first we had to find him. Only I had no idea where to start. And Korteria was the last place I wanted to do it in. Not after last time I was here. Not in the country most loyal to the Emperor. I took a shuddering breath, pressing on up the endless hill, but exhaustion was trailing after me.

I could see it in Auriel's eyes, too. Every step we'd taken beyond Khemet's border, had been one where I could literally feel the passage of time catching up to me. I couldn't explain it. I'd been in the Afeyan lands for a day. But I could sense all the changes around me now that I'd missed. The warm air that coasted along the breeze. The slight shift of the color in the clouds and sky. The growth of fresh green leaves and the scent of flowers blossoming were everywhere. Spring had just barely sprung a day ago for me. But Lumeria was in the midst of the season. An entire month lost.

Auriel stilled suddenly, his ears perked. And a second later a Korterian time keeper rang the bells announcing the hour. Ashvan riders would be on patrol any second now, over the border. They'd be searching the ravine, and the hills. Flying right over us.

"We need to hide!" I said.

Auriel grabbed my hand and ran, pulling up the hood of his cloak. I did the same, running faster until we reached a series of suntrees. The clock tower continued to chime. It was midday already. We moved deeper into the brush, finding the tree with the longest branches, the most leaves, and then pressed our backs to it. I tried to focus on my breathing, as the blue lights of Lumerian ashvan formed in the sky, and the horse's jewel-toned bodies raced across.

At last, the clock tower stopped. I waited for the final round of ashvan to pass.

Only they didn't. Two riders landed beyond the trees. I pressed my head back against the trunk, stilling my breath and my body. From my peripheral vision, I could see Auriel's face pale. His eyes remained on the riders, their silver armor flashing in the sunlight as they dismounted their horses. Swords drawn, they started toward us.

We could fight them. Easily. But when they didn't return to their posts, their turion would know immediately that something was amiss. And we needed secrecy to begin our search. Any increase in soturion presence was only going to complicate things.

Without warning, Auriel turned to face me, pressing his body against mine, his hand sliding down my hip, drawing my leg around his waist.

"What are you doing?" I hissed.

He reached through Rhyan's leather scabbard and pulled out my stave.

"Buying us time," he whispered. The way we were positioned, they'd assume we were lovers sneaking off for a moment alone. "Have you ever done glamour magic?" he asked.

"No," I said, starting to panic.

"Who's out here?" a soturion yelled. "Name yourself."

Shit. Shit!

"Try," Auriel whispered. "Make our armor silver, turn your hair blonde."

Blonde? Blonde like Ka Kormac. Everyone knew I had dark hair that turned red in the sun. It was my most identifying feature. I didn't know what I'd missed in the last month. But I was pretty sure that I was still wanted by the Emperor. And if these men were looking for me, it would be the first thing they'd check. Having blonde hair and silver armor—they'd never suspect who I was—especially if they didn't know my face. If these soturi had been assigned to patrol here, then it was unlikely they'd ever been stationed in Bamaria or seen me before.

I closed my eyes, recalling the spell I'd read about while I was studying mage magic in Glemaria. Aiden, the spymaster's apprentice, was the most gifted in this arena. And I'd seen him do it multiple times. I took a deep breath and tried to mimic his movements, imagining my hair blonde, and my armor and Auriel's both silver.

I chanted the words under my breath, my heart pounding, but nothing happened. Glamour magic wasn't the sort of thing you could just call on without practice, without intense skill.

"Shit," I said. "It didn't work."

Auriel squeezed the back of my neck. "It's okay. Try again."

I did, repeating the spell and the movements, but I was starting to panic. Either this worked, or we fought and risked exposure.

"The shard," Auriel said. "Use it."

My eyes widened and I reached behind my back again, repeating the spell. Warmth immediately filled my chest, and rose up my spine. Silver, the same exact shade of Ka Kormac's armor, spread across Auriel's torso.

"We see you!" shouted the soturion. Two sets of footsteps sped up.

My breathing grew heavy, but the same silver now spread across my torso, even changing Asherah's chest plate.

"You did it," Auriel said breathlessly, pulling out a lock of my hair from beneath my hood. From the corner of my eye, I could see that it was pure golden blonde.

"Come on out," said the soturion. "We know you're in there."

With a heavy sigh, Auriel pressed his forehead to mine, his lips just a breath away from my mouth. I gripped his hip, and his eyes opened, suddenly locked with my own. My memory flashed to that day on our ashvan, a thousand years ago, Auriel's eyes hooded. Asherah's desire—my desire, pooling between my legs. My throat went dry.

"Look what we found," said the first soturion, speaking with an unusually high-pitched voice. "Having some fun?"

The second one laughed. "Do you think he'll share?"

Auriel snarled under his breath, but then whispered, "Let them see your hair."

Their footsteps approached, and within seconds, two sets of hands grabbed his arms, hauling him off of me as he cursed and shouted.

The second soturion who had the beady eyes of the Bastardmaker, and an unkempt blond beard with scraggly hair, pulled a blade against Auriel's neck.

The first one, with the higher pitched voice, stalked toward me, a knife in his hand, pointed at me. He wrapped his fingers around my neck, the edge of his blade, dirty and rusted skimmed across my jaw and then to the hood of my cloak. I stiffened. He pushed it back, revealing my new golden blonde hair.

The soturion smiled in approval, twirling a lock around his unwashed finger. "Pretty." He grinned, his disgusting breath making me want to gag. But on the plus side, he'd let his dagger move. With my neck no longer in danger, I swatted his arm away with barely any effort. I had my sword withdrawn a second later.

The moment I made my move, Auriel did as well, easily head-butting his captor. The soturion's knife fell to the ground, and Auriel swiped it, pressing him back against a tree. He used his free hand to withdraw the soturion's sword. A second later, he'd whacked him over the head with the hilt. The soldier collapsed instantly.

And almost at the exact same moment, mine fell, too.

I gasped, out of breath, and Auriel rushed to me, wrapping me in his arms.

"*Meka!*" he said, his eyes scanning me up and down. "Are you all right?"

"I'm fine," I said. "Truly. Auriel that was brilliant—having them see my hair first."

"They should be out for a while now," he said, spitting on the soldier who'd fallen at my feet. "Disgusting shits." He craned his head back, his lip curling in disgust. "We should take their horses."

"I don't think flying's a good idea," I said. "We'd be noticed too easily—especially in the daylight."

"But we can ride them on the ground. Get us into town—it'll be faster than walking, and it will slow those bastards down after they wake."

I nodded. "That's actually a good idea."

He winked. "I have them from time to time. We just need to keep our glamour up. But once there we can start listening for any stories of recent akadim sightings. See if we can find any clues leading us to Rhyan. And by the time these two wake up and return to their post, we'll be long gone. They'll never find the two blondes who snuck away from patrol." He tugged gently on my hair. "You actually look good in this color."

I scoffed, highly doubting that was true.

But his eyes softened. "You've had it before. Other lives." He pressed his lips together but then his gaze rolled over one of the fallen soturi, and he grimaced. "Let's get some supplies."

He removed the man's dagger, and then started picking all the Valalumir stars off his belt. I followed suit. We relieved both soturi of all their weapons—and their money too, for good measure—then we hopped onto their ashvan, and rode down into Korteria.

It was late afternoon when we arrived on the edge of Vrukston, a small town at the foot of the hills. Auriel and I slowed our horses, moving carefully through a tiny woodland.

Soturi filled the streets—not surprising since nearly every man in Korteria became a soturion. There were hardly any mages in the country—which was partially because they didn't respect them. But also because of their geographical position. They were landlocked with both of the southern Afeyan countries. Their western border was shared with the human lands, and their northern and eastern borders were up against three other Lumerian countries. It was the water of the Lumerian Ocean that strengthened our magic, that let it work. And while they weren't the only ones on the western front, they certainly seemed to have embraced their fate the most—not even attempting to bring more magic into their daily life. The construction of waterways bringing in ocean water would have easily solved the problem. But they hadn't even done that, they'd chosen to fight instead.

Looking more closely, I could see the mentality extended to nearly every aspect of their life. Two women walked briskly carrying two large buckets of water.

And in a nearby open stall, another woman sat weaving cloth. No use of magic at all. Even the buildings were constructed far more roughly than any I'd seen at home or in the other cities and countries I'd visited. The homes were shorter, the walls sometimes uneven, and lacking any sort of finessed design.

Magic hadn't been used to build them, but actual physical labor. And if I were to bet, I was sure that we wouldn't find any mages inside the town.

It made the Emperor's recitation of the law to me after my Revelation Ceremony all the more infuriating. Because he'd claimed I needed magic to be part of our society according to his twisted interpretation of the law. Of course, the purpose was to punish me and my Ka. But still, seeing the lack of magic now was infuriating.

Auriel dismounted and came to the side of my ashvan, taking my hand and helping me down. My hand tingled where we'd touched, and I quickly brushed my palm against my cloak, peering ahead.

We crept toward the edge of the trees, and Auriel frowned, looking me over.

"You should keep your hood down," he said. "With your hair like this, you blend in. It will invite less of them to look at you."

"I hope," I said. "Ka Kormac isn't exactly known for sending women into their soturi."

But I retrieved my stave, and pointed it at Auriel's armor, then mine before training it on my hair. The spell I'd used before had faded quickly since I wasn't trying to hold it. But now, it would need to remain undisturbed for as long as we were in public. I tried to focus on the Valalumir at my back, touching it again to let it fuel and strengthen my spell.

"Too bad Aiden isn't here," I said wistfully. I was pretty damned proud that I'd managed to change our armor believably, and my hair. But I didn't think I could do much more. If I could have made myself a man, that would have been better.

"You're doing a good job," Auriel said. He peered back out through the trees. "Let's go to a pub. We both need food, and it will be dark in there. People will be drinking. It's a perfect place to disappear unnoticed. And listen."

We did just that, sitting inside for about an hour, tucked into a wood table pushed into a shadowy corner. We'd both ordered several beers, just to blend in, but neither of us were drinking. We were more focused on the food—which wasn't great. The stew was bland, and the bread stale. Most of the cuisine I was familiar with back home wasn't available. But we were both starving, and anything was better than nothing. Especially when anything was what kept me strong, kept me ready to fight.

The evening set in, the sky changing color through the window beside us. Outside soturi were coming and going—most seemed to be off-duty, meeting friends for drinks.

A few were out with their families, walking into restaurants for an early dinner. In the nearby square, bets were being placed on fights inside a tiny make-shift arena. We watched several battles end, money being passed back and forth, all while trying to listen for any talk of akadim.

Another soturion entered the fight, but was knocked out almost instantly.

"What if it's too late?" I asked quietly, my nerves jumping. I'd heard endless inane conversations, but nothing even related to akadim. Was that possible? Would the Queen have sent me on the mission to end Rhyan's akadim state if it was already over?

Auriel shook his head. "No. It's not."

"How do you know?"

His jaw tensed. "Remember how I told you I could feel the void of where my soul once was. Feel the absence of it."

I nodded nervously. "At your tomb."

"I ... I think I have that feeling again. But for him. For Rhyan."

"His body," I said. As an akadim it would be void of his soul. "You sense it?"

"I do. It's not strong, but it's the most I've felt since I—since I arrived. He's not gone. In fact, I think we might be close. Or ... closer than we were. Enough I can sense this much."

"Do you think he's in Korteria?"

Auriel frowned. "I don't know. Let's listen. We'll track what we can—but this," he placed a hand on his heart, "might help lead us to him." His eyes swept down the table at my mostly finished plate of food, and empty drink glass, before sweeping over my hair. "The color's fading," he said quietly. "I'm going to get you dessert. See if you can add more glamour."

Auriel headed to the bar, keeping his eyes trained on me as he waited for the server. I pulled my cloak over my lap, concealing my stave. Sweat beaded my brow. Keeping the glamour up was taking more energy than I realized, but a second later, the silver across my armor and Auriel's was refreshed.

A sudden burst of applause exploded from the arena. But before I could see what had happened, the pub doors burst open, and a dozen soturi poured inside.

Auriel quickly grabbed the plate from the bar and rushed back to me. It was a slice of chocolate cake. My appetite was gone though as we watched the soturi swarm the room, lining up at the bar, slamming down glasses of beer, and occupying the remaining tables.

"Lady Lyriana," said a soturion. I stilled, my stomach flipping. "She's dead," he continued. "She died on the beach a month ago. I don't know why they're wasting their time with these searches."

Auriel's eyes widened. I leaned across the table, meeting his gaze.

"She's vanished before," another soturion said. "Turned up later. She's sneaky."

"Maybe. But it's been a fucking month now. And not one sighting. No girl's smart enough to hide that long and not get caught. I don't see the point. Who cares where she is now?"

"She ordered that soturion to murder the Emperor. Killed the Blade. You should care about that."

The bartender placed two pitchers on the counter.

"They were old. Dying anyway."

"She let the vorakh out. Killed a bunch of men at the stripping," came a darker voice. "My cousin was one of them. If she's alive and I find her—I'll rip her fucking throat out."

"I mean, sure—if she's alive," said the first soturion. "But personally, I'd rather join the raids. There's more money there."

I raised my eyebrows at Auriel. "Raids?" I mouthed.

He shrugged, and tilted his head, so he was still facing me, but watching the men in his peripheral vision.

"You know Bannan?" the first soturion went on. "He went on one. Picked up three vorakh. Made enough gold to take a year off."

"A year?" asked a companion.

"How'd he know that's what they were?" asked another.

The first soturion shrugged. "He just grabbed some mages and accused them. No one asked questions, just took his word. They didn't let him join up with the task force—the ones really looking and testing."

Testing? For vorakh? They couldn't be doing that.

"Ugh," said another. "I wouldn't want to do it. Those snakes give me the damn creeps."

My stomach dropped. Nahashim. They were testing innocent people with nahashim. Like they'd done to me. Gods.

"No," said the first soturion, "you don't need to mess with the snakes. They're mainly for the higher-ups anyway. The rich ones, and the unfortunates who come across the check points. We don't handle the beasts. Don't need to."

"No?" asked another.

"No. You just need an accusation. And if the accused bastard can't afford the snake test, it's your lucky day. You get paid."

"I heard you get paid either way," someone chuckled.

"Well now that's tempting. I saw them snakes everywhere last week," another soturion chimed in. "You ever see an exam done? The snake goes right inside you. Under your skin. Disgusting."

The men burst into laughter.

My stomach turned. What the hell had happened in the last month? Since when was this a standard practice?

"The best is accusing a woman. You get to see her all naked and thrashing."

My hands clenched into fists.

"Well they might be opening ranks on the task force soon," said a new voice. "The testing's disgusting, but Lord Tristan has it under control."

They had Tristan leading this?

The first soturion barked. "Emperor's dog always coming through loyal."

"Actually," a new soturion piped up, as he slammed a mug on the counter, several drops of beer spilling out. "I hear what they really need are guards for the prisons, people to build some more, too. They're running out of space to hold the criminals."

"Where are they building?" Yet another soturion had been drawn into the conversation, his hand on the hilt of his dagger, his black eyes eager.

"Bamaria. I mean, what used to be Bamaria anyway."

Used to be? My stomach roiled. What the fuck did that mean?

"New prisons are popping up by the water in Ba—I mean, in southern New Korteria—nowhere to escape. They can build them fast there, they use magic with the labor. Hot as fuck—but I hear there's a nice bonus for new recruits—the ones that get accepted."

"I could use some extra money. A bonus sounds nice," a new voice had joined. "I could definitely round some people up."

All their auras were flaring, their pettiness, hatred, and greed felt tangible enough to make my stomach turn.

"Let me check where Lord Tristan is now—he's scheduled to start traveling with the Bastardmaker soon, setting up new prisons and check-points in each country. But that's the fastest way to join."

Auriel's eyebrows knit together with concern, watching me. "Stay calm," he mouthed. But my heart was racing. They'd just called Bamaria southern New Korteria.

"I don't know," drawled a soturion. It was one who'd spoken before. "Something about this don't seem right."

"What do you care?" asked his friend.

"I don't. I just think we ought to focus on real problems. I know they say they're killers, that the vorakh sends them out of their minds, all farther than Lethea and shit, but we've got real enemies in front of us. That bitch Lyriana is a fucking murderer and she's going to pay for my cousin."

I stilled. Had he been at the stripping? Would he know my face? I was blonde now, and it had been a month. But still ... If he looked too closely, it was over. His aura was rank and moving through the pub in quick, powerful bursts. I could feel his violence shifting toward me.

We needed to get out of there—without starting a scene. For all the hours we'd been here, I'd been the only woman. I'd noticed it, and so had Auriel, but only now that a dozen soturi were at the bar, drinking heavily, did I clearly feel it.

"Well, I hope you find her, brother." A soturion stood and clapped the angry soldier on the back.

"I hope so, too," he said darkly. "I got a gut feeling. She's not dead. Probably still hiding in southern New Korteria. That's my guess. She couldn't go far. She's just a girl, an evil one, but a weak one. She has no power."

I almost rolled my eyes. Right. I had no power, but I'd killed the Emperor, killed the Blade, and his cousin. These fucking men. And it was fucking Bamaria! New Korteria didn't exist!

"You should get assigned down south," another said. "They're taking recruits for next month," he continued. "Need another half legion down there."

"Just to find that bitch?"

"No. The whole fucking Empire's looking for her. It's because the Bamarians are protesting. Not happy with the Emperor's new policies. Fucking vorakh lovers."

"Wait—" one held up a hand, "they like vorakh?"

"No, no one likes them. They're just mad because all the prisons they're building need to be manned. By us. They think we're outnumbering them."

"We are!" someone shouted.

"Prisoners need prisons. And we need homes. So we've been taking theirs. Taking their women, too." The soturion laughed.

"And the best part? Our Emperor made Arianna Batavia the Imperator to shut them all up. She lets us do whatever the fuck we want." He turned in his chair, licking his lips, his eyes on me. "Speaking of fucking …" He stood, taking a step toward me, before pausing, and sizing up Auriel. "Hey. You share?" He raised his eyebrows. "I can buy you a drink in exchange."

Auriel's hand was already on the hilt of the sword, his other hand moving to the one strapped to his back.

I started calculating. Twelve soturi at the bar. One bartender. Six more patrons at tables. Twelve were our enemy, best case scenario. Six for me, six for Auriel. Worst case, we'd have to take on all nineteen. We had the corner, a wall at our backs so no one could come from behind, and a window if we truly needed to escape.

But then a scream came from outside. A blood-curdling yell full of fear.

They'd said one word. And one word only.

"Akadim!"

CHAPTER TWENTY-EIGHT

LYRIANA

My eyes met Auriel's. Only one thought in my mind.

Rhyan.

My stomach twisted as I looked out the window. Night hadn't fallen yet. But I could see the outline of the three beasts coming. They were moving through the town center, their red eyes glowing from afar. They reminded me of the ones that had attacked the Throne Room with Morgana. Shorter than most akadim, but still taller than any man. They were pale, their eyes red. I could see their fangs and their long claws that extended from their fingers.

I reached over my shoulder, touching the blade of the red shard. The cure.

Auriel tracked my movement and my meaning. His mouth tightened and he shook his head. "Not yet. Wait."

The three drew closer. One stopped to draw out a soturion who'd tried to hide behind a bench. He had blond hair that fell to his shoulders, and the kind of muscles that suggested he had been a soturion when he was alive. Maybe even a member of Ka Kormac. One of the demons behind him was full of muscle, and dark curly hair.

I clutched at my chest. I wasn't ready. I wasn't ready to see Rhyan like this. Or to fight him. Or cure him.

How was I going to be ready to stab him through the heart? I knew it was the only way, that it would bring him back—but the idea of doing that to him, of hurting him—even in this form—made me sick to my stomach.

The soldiers who'd crowded the bar just seconds ago were rushing out into the square, while the patrons at the other tables were attempting to barricade themselves in the bathroom, or trample over the bartender in their attempt to hide in the kitchens.

Every instinct inside of me was screaming for me to get up. Yelling at me to run. To hide. And to fight. All at once. My body knew I was in danger.

But I had to know. I had to know before I got out there if I was going to be killing an akadim—or doing something I never imagined I would. Protecting it. Because it was Rhyan.

My breath came short from just the thought. It was starting to feel too real.

By the Gods. By the fucking Gods.

The long-haired demon was deep in battle with the soldier he'd picked up. But now there were more soturi surrounding them, trying to free the man. Another group of soturi were actively trying to attack from behind.

The other beasts continued on through the square, unbothered by the resistance forming around them. They weren't interested in fighting, or killing. I had a bad feeling—like they could sense more meals up ahead. Us. Everyone in the pub.

And suddenly I had a clear memory of Rhyan explaining how akadim chose their victims.

"I take your pomegranate seeds. What do you do? Fight me for it? Or go for easier pickings, reach for more, just as ripe and sweet, from the bowl in front of you?"

I sighed. This had to be a trick question. "I'd reach for the bowl."

Rhyan's good eyebrow lifted. "Exactly. That's what an akadim would do, too. Reach for more, reach for whatever's easiest."

And right now, anyone trapped in the pub, anyone hiding in here—they were the easy pickings. Including me and Auriel.

My throat was dry as all three were finally close enough for me to scan their faces, taking in their features. They were distorted from what they must have looked like when living, but enough that I was sure I'd know Rhyan if I saw him. I'd only ever seen one akadim that I'd known alive. Haleika. And she'd transformed in front of me. But I was sure I'd have recognized her if I'd seen her in the wild. And with this new breed of akadim that could walk in the day, that looked just a little more human than the others, I'd know. I'd know him. He didn't have his soul, but I had his features memorized—every little detail. I'd know Rhyan, I'd recognize him in any form.

And I emitted something between a sigh and a sob as I realized that none of the three akadim approaching were him.

Auriel seemed to realize the same thing and turned back to me—his hand on my shoulder. "We need to get out of here," he said. "Get away from this town before anyone looks too closely at us."

"What about the akadim?" I hissed.

Auriel shook his head. "We can't, *Meka*. I disagreed with Queen Ma'Nia on many things. But she was right about this—we were losing the war, prioritizing the cure over stopping the threat. In the end, neither decision will feel right for you. Or for me. No matter what we choose—it means death for someone. That's the thing about war. There are almost no good answers once you're in it. You want to save everyone." He reached across the table, his fingers grazing my chin. "Especially someone like you." He sighed. "But you can't. In the end, you have to choose. You always have to choose."

I looked out the window again. All three akadim were in battle, surrounded now by soturi. Already two had fallen. One was lying on the ground, his head turned at an angle that told me he was dead. The other was trying to staunch a bleeding wound.

A wound I could heal. A wound that might have never happened if I'd been out there. If Auriel and I had already joined the fight.

My heart hurt. I certainly had no warm feelings towards anyone born to Ka Kormac. As far as I was concerned, they could all go to hell. But becoming an akadim—that was a fate worse than death. No one deserved that. And I couldn't stand by and just let them be killed so violently, and in such a brutal manner. Couldn't allow the akadim to just make more of them.

My fingers tightened around the hilt of my sword.

"Lyriana, look at me," Auriel said. "Look. I don't like it either. I don't like it one bit. But if we charge out there now—we risk everything. You are in just as much danger from the soturi as you are from the akadim. And you haven't even practiced using the sword, aiming for the heart." He shook his head, his eyebrows furrowed. "It's not Rhyan out there. It's not him. I can feel it. We're closer than ever—but not close enough—not to him. And any moment now one of those groups will win this fight. And it won't matter which side is the victor. Because you know damned well that we can't afford to have either group finding us here."

The twisting in my stomach continued, tightening painfully. "I know," I said, my voice small.

"Then follow me. I'm getting us out of here."

"Okay, fine," I said.

"Good girl." Auriel's jaw clenched, his gaze searing into mine. "So here's what we're going to do. We're going to get up, and we're going to calmly head to the door. We're going to remain safe tonight, and stay alive—both of us. We're going to go find him, but we need to be alive to do so. All right? Are you with me?"

I squeezed my eyes shut, and nodded. I was with him. But that didn't make my decision any easier. If the akadim won—we'd have minutes before sunset, before all the fallen soturi rose again as monsters. And if the soturi somehow won—I'd heard horror stories of soldiers after battle. Finding women, and going into a frenzy. It wasn't hard to imagine Ka Kormac in those shoes. I'd heard enough about them, and experienced enough myself to already know that a battle wasn't needed to make them act like that. And there was only one woman here.

Me.

I wasn't afraid of them anymore—they'd never hold that power over me again. But that didn't mean the threat they posed wasn't real.

I stood from the table, and tightened my belt, checking that all of my weapons were in place. My stave neatly tucked into the scabbard Rhyan gave me. And the straps of the sword belt carrying the shard were secure across my back and shoulders.

"Put your hood up," Auriel commanded, taking my hand. "We're going to run when we get out there. Away from the fight. As far as we can get." His eyes locked onto mine. "Ready?"

"Ready," I said.

We headed for the door, taking quick, measured steps, and immediately turned away from the fight, walking briskly from the town, back toward the woodland. The sun was setting rapidly, the sky darkening with every step we took. The trees loomed overhead, not far from us now.

Auriel picked up speed and I matched, my calves burning. The hill had begun to slope up, the incline growing steeper. We passed by two lone suntrees, their trunks thick. They'd grown apart from the rest of the woodland. And in the fading light, their golden leaves had turned bronze. Auriel shifted, his stride pushing just ahead of me.

Just as I was about to pick up my pace, I was hauled back as someone grabbed me. Foreign hands wrapped around my waist. I screamed. Without hesitating, I pushed out of the hold, scrambling to break free, but I was caught again and fell onto my ass, knowing only that the hands that grabbed me weren't akadim.

"Get the fuck off her!" Auriel snapped, already rushing back, brandishing his sword.

"Came back for what's mine," said the soldier.

It took me a second to recognize the soturion who'd caught me. But once I heard his high-pitched voice I knew. The rider from this morning—the one we'd left unconscious at the top of the hill.

And sure enough, his friend emerged from the edge of the woodland, right where we were heading.

"Finally came to," he said.

The two ashvan we'd stolen were still waiting in the woods. Grazing right beside the soturion. With a snarl, he rushed at Auriel.

My soturion dragged me to my feet, his knife at my throat.

"Been looking for you," my captor crooned, shaking his head. He pressed the blade harder, and I sucked in a breath, feeling the pressure intensify. But I remembered his knife was dull—and I'd left it behind. Had it been sharpened, he would have sliced me open with the way he was pressing it into me. But even so, he could still do unthinkable damage. And the position I was in meant I couldn't reach for any of my weapons—not if I didn't want to get hurt.

Auriel's sword met the other soturion's. It wouldn't take him long to win the fight. But then my captor yelled out again.

"Submit. Or I cut her throat."

Auriel froze, eyeing us carefully, his neck turning red. Nostrils flaring, he dropped his blade, his hands up in surrender.

"Don't hurt her," he said, just as the other soturion picked it up and grabbed hold of him, forcing his head back. The soturion's lips curled as he drew Auriel's blade along his collarbone.

I tried to calm my breathing. The soturi weren't a true threat to us. We could get out of this—even if we got injured—we'd survive. But our ability to keep our identities secret could be compromised. How much fucking danger were we in? It was bad enough being in Korteria—but with all these rumors about New Korteria, and my aunt's further betrayal, I had a bad feeling.

Auriel's chest heaved, and he scowled, trying to keep his eyes on me. I could see it in his expression. He wasn't going to play their game much longer.

"You idiots. You should have flown," my soturion said proudly. "All we had to do was track the hoof prints. And what did we find? Our stupid ashvan, all wandering and lost in the woodland. And then, coming right back to us, our new little toy." He jerked his hips from behind me.

Auriel growled. But all I could see was red. If Auriel's patience was lost, mine had combusted.

"Let her go," Auriel shouted. "There's no fucking time for this. Akadim are attacking your men in the square."

"Our men? Not yours?" his soturion asked.

Auriel gritted his teeth. "They're being attacked right now!"

"Is that so? And you two were what?" his soturion asked. "Running away from your duties? Fleeing? Never faced one before now, have you?"

"We've killed plenty," I gritted. "Now let us go!"

Both soturi burst into laughter.

"You? You killed one?" My captor laughed harder, tightening his grip on me. His hand snaked toward my waist, and pulled out the sword I'd stolen. He thrust it back into his scabbard, then did the same with his dagger. Then he opened my belt pouch, his fingers curling around the money inside. He was sloppy when he pulled it out, dropping some of the coins, and letting his hand graze against my hip too long. "Bad girl," he crooned. "Taking what's mine."

The soturion holding Auriel was emptying his pouch, too. And I prayed that that was all this was. They just wanted their things back, wanted to save face after we beat and robbed them. Then they could let us go. Not ask questions. Not cause a scene. Join their comrades in the square and fight.

But any hope of that was dashed when Auriel's captor stilled, his eyes widening. He lifted a hand, and pointed, looking right at me. Like he was just seeing me for the first time. "What the fuck!" he yelled.

Alarmed, I looked behind me. Nothing. My stomach sank, and I looked down. The silver of my armor was fading back to gold. The hair over my shoulder was dark brown, with just a hint of red in the setting sun. Auriel's glamour vanished, and so did any hope of concealing my identity.

"Doesn't Lyriana's hair change color?" my soturion asked.

Auriel's jaw clenched, his hands fisting. He was ready to explode, to kill these soturi.

"Ain't it supposed to turn red?" his friend asked.

My captor spun me around so we were face-to-face. His beady eyes looked over me, slowly raking over my features, like he was hoping my name would appear across my face. Then his eyes dipped below my neck, settling on the shoulders of my armor. Two seraphim wings.

"She's fucking Bamarian." His eyebrows narrowed. "I don't know what color your hair is supposed to be, but I know it ain't blonde. You're her, aren't you?"

I pressed my lips together, my pulse racing.

"Are you her? Are you fucking Lyriana?" he asked again, shaking me. "Are you?"

I wasn't sure what I was going to do next. Lie, or break out of his measly fucking hold and finally kill him for his silence. Because if he knew who I was, our entire mission was compromised. My pulse raced, beating like a drum in my ears. But a second later, any choice I might have made was gone.

Because a growl sounded from behind us, and a pair of red glowing eyes stalked forward. My stomach hollowed in fear, my heart leaping into my throat. It didn't matter how many times I saw them. The horror was always the same. And now it was worse. Because every time I faced one, I was looking for him. For his face. For Rhyan's.

The akadim bared his teeth, quickening his pace.

"LYRIANA!" Auriel screamed, breaking free of his captor. He knocked the soldier out, not wasting any time before tearing down the hill to me.

I broke free of the world, and jumped back, my stomach twisting with a vice-like pain.

Shadows moved in the distance, moving quickly, stalking toward us. Three more akadim.

They were different from the ones in the square. Which meant we were near a Godsdamned nest. Rhyan could be near. Or …

Panicking, I quickly looked them up and down—I hadn't seen his face, but I had to double-check.

Not Rhyan. Not Rhyan.

I didn't recognize any features. But one thing stood. All three wore silver collars around their necks. The akadim in the square had been wearing them as well, but I'd been so preoccupied with the dual threat of them and the soturi, I'd barely noticed.

These three were also on the small side. Like the ones serving Morgana.

Maraaka Ereshya.

That's what they called her. Queen Ereshya.

By the Gods. If these were hers ...

She'd been there that night. The night Rhyan turned. Was it possible?

I brandished my sword, reaching on instinct for the blade at my hip. The akadim who approached me growled, his red eyes glowing as his claws extended. He swiped at my arm, trying to knock out my sword. I dodged, just barely missing his attack, and turned on my heels, reaching for my dagger and rushing to his side. Pulling my elbow back, I launched the blade at his face.

Teeth gnashing, he deflected with a snap of his arm, sending it hurtling back. I ducked. But there was a scream of pain behind me.

The returned dagger had sliced through the soturion's arm. Though from what I could see, it was just a clipping—no major artery.

He'd live.

"Don't lose that," I hissed at him.

I widened my stance, my knees bent, distantly aware of Auriel and the other soturion. He must have regained consciousness because now they were both fighting against two akadim.

Mine started toward me. I dodged, barely missing his claws. Fuck. I wasn't used to fighting them like this. The bigger ones I was used to, the more giant—oddly enough—felt easier to battle. When I didn't come face-to-face with them, they were easier to strike since their bodies were larger. And it took them longer sometimes to reach me since their arms had to go a greater distance. If this was any other akadim, I would have jumped on his back by now. I would have raced past him and sliced his thigh open.

But this one was more like battling a soturion, we were face-to-face. He was quick. And it was clear from his movements that he'd had training. He seemed to sense all of my moves before I made them, and was able to block thrust after thrust and hit after hit of my blade.

I leapt back, just barely avoiding another swipe of his claws. He'd nearly gotten me.

"You serve Morgana?" I asked, hoping to distract him—but also needing answers.

The akadim's eyes glowed and he tilted his head in curiosity, before running forward, both hands outstretched. I attacked his side, blocking his hit, and forced him into retreat. Grunting, I pushed my blade forward, further pushing him back.

"Do you serve Morgana?" I asked again, my voice hard.

"Morgana?" he asked, his voice low. He bent his knees, shifting his weight side to side. He squinted in confusion, then bared his fangs, seeing an opening to attack.

I dodged, spun on my heels, and whirled my blade forward. "Queen Ereshya," I said.

"*Maraaka*," he confirmed.

"She put the collar on you?" I asked, the blunt side of my sword meeting his arm. He used the impact to push me back and steered me around, herding me toward the woodland. Auriel was fighting behind me. And so was the other soturion, who was surprisingly holding his own.

But the one who'd tried to capture me just now was slowly getting up, and inching away. Coward. And he was holding my dagger in his hand. My dagger from the oath ceremony. With my Godsdamned name burned into the metal. Fuck! The dagger meant something to me—we'd been through so much. But more importantly, with my name burned into the steel, it was Godsdamned proof I was here.

It was one thing for this idiot to know my name, to claim that he'd seen me—to say he saw a girl with Bamarian armor. But it was a whole other thing to have actual evidence to show.

"Drop my dagger!" I roared, barely blocking another blow from the akadim.

But the soturion only laughed, his eyes flashing on the steel before sliding across, and reading.

"Soturion Lyriana. I fucking knew it."

"You know shit!" I yelled.

But he continued to stalk away, abandoning both the fight and his friend. My blade clutched to his chest.

Bastard! I hoisted my sword above my head, and catapulted it—not at him, but close enough. The target I'd been aiming for was struck. His cloak. I'd torn right through the cape folded over his shoulder.

"You bitch!" he screamed, murder in his eyes as he faced me again. "I'll fucking kill you! I don't care what the reward is for turning you in!"

"Get in line," I gritted, stabbing my sword. I pierced the akadim's thigh. But I barely made a scratch. Shit. These daywalking demons were small, but their skin and muscles were just as tough as any other akadim's to break through.

"I will," the soturion growled, and he started charging back. Gods. He was bleeding from his arm, and I was currently battling a fucking akadim. Apparently, for him, petty revenge was more important than his actual Godsdamned safety. Or mine. Or his friend's.

The demon turned, grabbing the soturion by the neck and squeezing hard. The Kormac soldier wheezed, his feet kicking helplessly as he was lifted into the air. Then the akadim reached for his armor.

No! No! He was going to eat his soul. He was going to—

I didn't think, I just acted. And I threw my second sword, screaming as I put all of my strength behind it. This time I struck. Not enough to cut the beast's arm off as I'd intended. But enough to impale his bicep.

The akadim roared, his eyes burning with fire. But he didn't turn on me.

He finished ripping the soldier's armor off, tearing through his tunic, and spreading the material open. The akadim pursed his lips together, as white light began to stream from the soturion's chest, a small black hole taking over his heart.

I screamed in horror. Seeing Rhyan again, helpless in the akadim's arms. Injured and dying, the brilliant light of his soul pouring out of his heart. A black shadow across his chest.

I couldn't breathe. I couldn't fucking breathe. My vision blurred with tears and a fire that was raging inside of me. I couldn't see this. I couldn't see this happen again. Even if this soturion was a fucking asshole, I didn't want to see him lose his soul. I had to do something. I had to act.

But I was out of fucking swords. That stupid fucking idiot had taken all of my spares.

I stilled.

Except for one ...

The red shard. I reached over my shoulder, my fingers wrapping around the hilt as I brandished it in the fading sunset. Small flames erupted along the sharpened edge, the crystal glowing as heat spread to my hand. A heat mirrored in my heart. And then I charged, with no more thoughts, except for one.

Stop the threat. Stop the threat.

I stabbed the blade through the akadim's belly, grunting and pushing with all of my muscle. The akadim screeched, his hand opening in surprise.

The soldier fell to the ground, screaming and crawling away, before getting back to his feet. He ran forward, stumbled onto all fours, and then got up again, his arms flailing as he ran.

I used the moment the akadim was distracted to pull my other sword out from his arm.

He hollered in pain, and I retrieved the red shard next.

I pounced, a blade in both hands, crossing the swords in the air, and pressing them both against his neck like scissors. With the right amount of pressure, I could decapitate him. And from the look in his eyes, and the blood spouting from his stomach, he knew it.

But I wasn't going to kill him. Not yet.

"Have you seen Rhyan?" I asked, my chest heaving. "Rhyan Hart? Lord Rhyan Hart. He's an akadim, too. Have you seen him? An akadim named Rhyan. In a collar like yours."

His eyes glowed, blood spouting from his stomach. "You ask too many questions," he hissed.

"Rhyan! Ryan Hart!" I demanded again. "Do you know an akadim named Rhyan? Have you seen him? Tell me and I'll let you live."

"Let me live." He laughed.

"Tell me!" I roared, pushing the blades together. His eyes bulged out, and blood seeped to his shoulders. "An akadim called Rhyan! Rhyan Hart! Rhyan Hart!"

A sadistic grin spread across his face, his fangs protruding past his lips.

"LYRIANA!" Auriel screamed.

I looked back. Both akadim were on the ground. Their heads cut off. Dead. Permanently dead. Their souls lost to the in-between, never to return. Nor pass on—not until the years passed, their natural lives over.

Tears pricked my eyes. Sorrow for the first time at a dead akadim. An akadim I wouldn't be able to save. The other soturion though had survived. He was on his knees, bleeding from a slash to his forehead.

"Too many questions," my akadim growled. "And I'm hungry. So feed me, fuck me, or kill me."

I whirled around, but suddenly, his claws lifted, slashing through my arms. I was standing too close. Again.

I screamed in pain, my hands opening. Both swords fell to the ground. I stumbled back, but the akadim grabbed my waist with both hands.

"Stop!" I yelled. My feet were kicking now, dangling in the air as he lifted me higher, so much higher than should have been possible.

I could hear Auriel behind me, screaming my name, commanding the akadim to put me down. But he sounded distant. Because all I could hear was my thundering pulse. I kicked again, trying to pry his hands from my waist. But it was impossible. He was too strong, and now, my arms were badly injured. I couldn't reach my weapons. I had nothing to fight with. They were all strewn across the ground. My swords. My dagger. The red shard.

But not the stars on my belt.

With a grunt of pain, I bent forward, and ripped one off of its leather strap. My arm screamed in agony as I slashed the star across his neck.

Blood spurted, but not enough. Not fucking enough. He smiled viciously, baring his fangs.

What the fuck!

No matter how many times I cut or injured him, he just kept fighting. And then his mouth opened as he started pulling me in—his eyes on my neck. He wanted my blood.

I kicked wildly, and then froze as something bright red pierced through his chest.

The shard.

Auriel had caught up to us.

The akadim dropped me at once, and I scrambled back to my feet, trying to grab the swords. But I couldn't do more than wrap my fingers around the hilt. I couldn't lift them. My arms were too cut up. And then with my adrenaline slowing, the full force of my injuries came on me. I couldn't control my fingers. I was going numb.

The blade vanished from his chest, as Auriel pulled it out. The demon collapsed.

"Wait!" I yelled. Auriel was already rushing around, gathering my weapons.

"*Meka*, we need to go! Now!"

"But the blade! It went through his chest. What if he turns back? What if he's cured?"

Auriel shook his head. "We don't have time! We don't have time to find out!" Auriel had strapped every weapon to himself, his eyes widening. "Fuck! You're hurt! Again." He hoisted me into his arms.

"Auriel, wait!"

"Lyriana," he growled, "we have to go. More are coming!"

But our akadim was still alive. Still breathing.

I twisted out of his hold, running back to the akadim.

"Do you know Rhyan?" I shouted again, on the verge of hysteria.

"LYRIANA!" Auriel grabbed me, and was running now, back to the woodland. One ashvan remained, kicking at the suntree he was tied to, angry and scared.

The akadim laughed cruelly.

And I tried one more time. "RHYAN HART!"

"Not Rhyan Hart," the akadim said, a sadistic grin spreading across his face. "Arkturion Rhyan."

"Arkturion?" I asked. "Auriel put me down!"

"No!" he said, his voice low.

Because over my shoulder, a new horde of akadim had appeared. Collared. Unfamiliar. Blood was dripping from their mouths, and had been splashed across their tunics. Whoever they'd fought had lost. And now they were running toward us.

We reached the woodland, and Auriel hoisted me onto the ashvan, quickly cutting the rope. A second later he climbed up behind me, wrapping one arm tightly around my waist, and the other he used to reach forward for the reins.

"*Vra!*" he commanded, and the horse, more than ready to run away from the chaos, took off. His hooves stamped through the woodland, swerving around the trees.

"Shit! Shit," Auriel hissed. "They're coming after us. We need to get into the sky, or we're dead. *Volara*," he roared. "Fly! Fly!"

The ashvan raced faster and faster until I caught the hint of blue lights sparking under its hooves. I felt it rear back, its front legs lifting and kicking out, and then we were flying, lifting off the ground. I stared down, numb. The demons had reached the woodland.

But there was only one I cared about. The one Auriel had stabbed. His glowing red eyes were still visible in the dark. He was still alive. Still an akadim.

He hadn't been cured. He hadn't changed. He'd been stabbed with the red shard. With the shard that was meant to cure him. But it hadn't worked.

My heart sank.

There was a logical explanation. There had to be. Like maybe because Auriel had wielded the blade, and not me.

Therefore, the shard was incomplete—missing the light I carried inside. Or maybe it was because he'd missed the heart.

When we found Rhyan, I'd be the one to stab him. I'd have the sword, and my light. I wouldn't miss. It would work. He'd be cured.

But my stomach still twisted. Worry and fear nauseating my stomach. My arms were on fire, and I could do little more than lean back against Auriel and close my eyes.

Because there was another crushing sensation weighing down on me. The akadim had known Rhyan.

He'd called him Arkturion.

CHAPTER TWENTY-NINE

LYRIANA

Cold spring winds whipped my hair in my face, my chest heaving as I took labored breaths.

Arkturion Rhyan. Arkturion Rhyan. He wasn't just an akadim. He was a general. A leader. Gods. That had to mean something awful. Something more than just being a strong fighter. It had to say something about his viciousness as an akadim, about how violent he was. And still, even more than that—it meant he was overseeing the violence of others. Their cruelty. Encouraging it. Directing it.

Had Morgana appointed him? Aemon? Why? To get back at me? At Rhyan? Because we were Auriel and Asherah? Or was it because Rhyan truly fit their agenda? The prophecy the Queen had warned me about. That Rhyan could be even more destructive than the rise of Moriel if not stopped.

I sucked in a breath, and squeezed my eyes shut. Every time I thought about it, every time the words entered my mind, it felt like I was going into shock. I should have known, put the pieces together sooner. He'd been turned by Morgana and Aemon's akadim. Of course he was one of them now. Killing and—Gods. My chest tightened and I blinked back fresh tears.

Auriel's arm was wrapped around my waist as we rode. We hadn't spoken in about an hour. But every time I started to feel panicked, he sensed it, and squeezed me against him, a small reminder he was there. A reminder we were still in this together. That it wasn't over.

There really wasn't anything else to say. Not until we were safe. And from the focused energy of his aura, and the taut way he sat, holding the reins, I knew he was determined to make that happen. To not stop until he could guarantee my protection.

Auriel swore that he recalled a cave formation he'd utilized the last time he was here. Further west, closer to the territory that put us near Vrukshire. But considering the time that had elapsed since then, a millennium, most of Korteria's landscape looked unfamiliar to him. There were towns that hadn't been there before, buildings and forests that had popped up. Forests that had been chopped down. He was unusually silent, watching the terrain like a hawk. I started to worry that he was losing some of his memory again, losing access to the information and strength he had as a God. But it was also entirely possible he'd just never paid much attention to Korteria while in the Celestial Realms. He had no reason to—not when I wasn't there. Or Rhyan. Not until now.

We flew over what felt like an endless number of hills and mountains. They all looked so similar, I could understand why Auriel was confused. But as we moved toward Vrukshire, I recognized the horizon. The shape of the mountains and hills I'd seen from Brockton's room had seared itself into my memory. Each one was filled with suntrees, their golden leaves faint under the moon and starlight. But the last time I was here, they'd been capped in snow.

When finally, another cluster of hills passed beneath us, Auriel called out in relief. "There! That's it! By the realms, that's it! I recognize the formation." The mass of hills was leading toward a small valley. It was nestled between a mountain range full of more peaks than I could count. And to its left lay the tallest of the mountains, a peak said to be the tallest in Lumeria. It curved just slightly, like a fang. *Bovruk* was the official name of the range. But it was more commonly known as Mouth of the Wolf.

"*Dorscha*," Auriel commanded. The ashvan's steps tilted down, and we began our descent. Within another minute, we touched the ground, and our ashvan's blue lights faded into the night. Auriel dismounted, but urged me to stay on and rest as he walked the horse deeper into the valley.

"Much easier to remember the landscapes over here, away from civilization," he said, his voice was light, but there was a levity to his aura. "That town back there …" He shook his head. "Certainly wasn't there last time. And I had definitely never seen that pub before." He waggled his eyebrows up at me.

He was trying to lighten the mood, but it wasn't working. I just stared at the valley, feeling numb. Rhyan was an Arkturion. He'd been an Arkturion for a month. And Bamaria was gone. What the fuck was happening?

Auriel helped me down at the mouth of the cave, leading the way inside. He found some wood already tied together in a neat pile for kindling. But rather than watching him suffer trying to recall how to make fire again after a thousand years, I used my stave to conjure flames. My fingers had begun to feel better, though my arms still felt weak.

Laying out his cloak as a blanket, Auriel sat me down, and immediately began removing mine. He methodically unhooked my armor before he vanished—finding a small spring to wash up a cloth and clean my arms up. He gently applied sunleaves, and bandaged me up, and after making sure I was comfortable and warm enough, he sat down across from me. His eyes swept over my body, watching me. His aura was on edge, and I could tell that now we were safe, and

I'd received first aid, some of the fight and tension was leaving him. And I wasn't sure I liked or wanted to deal with whatever had replaced it. He was clearly biting back his words.

He had something to say. I could feel it in every bone of my body.

"Don't accuse me," I said dully, watching smoke rise from the flames.

"Accuse you?" he said, his eyebrows raised. "I would never just accuse you out of nowhere. Unless I had something to accuse you of." He frowned. "But since you brought it up, why don't you tell me—what heinous sin have you committed this time?"

I shook my head. "I fought poorly. Or I assume that's what you're thinking. That I'm not trying to win." I glanced at both of my arms, scratched and cut-up, covered in shallow wounds. Nothing like I'd experienced when I was injured at Gryphon Island. And even now, the cut that had nearly killed me was completely healed—thanks to the sudden passage of time in Khemet. These in comparison were nothing. They stung like hell, and made lifting my weapons difficult. I could fight—fight hard if it came down to it—but this wasn't the condition I needed to be in when I found Rhyan. When I finally faced him. I had to be ready. And I had to aim true.

"Lyriana," Auriel said gently, "I'm not going to say that. I'm on your side. I know you were trying to win. You fought bravely, you were strong. But—"

"But," I gritted.

"But I think you wanted information about Rhyan more than you wanted to get away. Which I understand. I wanted it, too. I just ... need you to be careful." His jaw muscles clenched. "So does Rhyan." He turned away. "Did you get what you were looking for?"

"I don't know." I pulled my cloak more tightly around my shoulders, like a blanket. "That akadim was one of Morgana's and he knew Rhyan. He called him Arkturion. I didn't even know akadim had rankings."

"They don't," Auriel said. "These akadim are evolved, smarter than any we've ever faced. But they don't have that kind of structure. That's Aemon's doing. It was something Moriel enforced as well." He sighed. "Arkturion Rhyan. That's good."

"Good?" I yelled. "You think that's good? It's bad enough he's an akadim. But now he's a fucking leader for them! A warlord of the undead!" I was already sick to my stomach imagining the horrors he might have committed as a regular akadim. But for the past hour I'd been plagued by thoughts of him as their commander—the atrocities he'd committed, led, and approved of over the past month had to be endless. How was I going to face that?

How was Rhyan going to be able to face that when I healed him?

If I healed him ...

"Yes," Auriel said. "It's very good. It means he's known. It means he's respected. That any akadim we encounter moving forward can lead us to him."

I scoffed. "Right, because they're so agreeable. Do you know how many times I had to ask this one for that information? He knew but he didn't give me shit on how to find him."

"Maybe we need a new tactic. Maybe we need to cure them first," Auriel said.

"If we even can." I looked away, tears blurring my vision. "That akadim was stabbed with the blade. With the shard. It didn't work—did it?" And that had me far more worried than the news of Rhyan's new ranking.

"No," Auriel said. "But I think it's because it was me. The shard was incomplete." He lifted his arm, pointing to my heart. "It has to be you."

My heart pounded as if in response. The light inside me warmed. I was the fire. But I didn't feel like it at that moment. "I hope you're right."

"I am," he said. "We'll find him. I can sense him still. It's stronger now. That's good. I think it does mean he's in Korteria. And if not, we'll go wherever he is. But not until you're fully healed."

I knew he'd say that, but I couldn't even argue with him. He was right. I had to be in perfect fighting condition. And right now I was far from it.

"What do we do?" I asked.

"Nothing. Nothing more tonight. You need to rest. You deserve to rest. You'll heal faster that way. We'll train in the morning. We'll practice with the shard. Make sure your aim is perfect. And we'll continue on. We'll go to each town we can find on the map, we'll listen for any news or rumors of akadim movements, anyone pursuing a moving horde. And I'll keep my senses open. We'll do it every day until we find him. Until we track him down."

I nodded. "Okay," I sniffled, my chest contracting painfully. Being in a cave, sitting by the fire, having my injuries tended to ... Auriel had done this once before already, on the night he'd appeared. But Rhyan and I, for a while, this had been our life. Our own private world. For weeks we'd been on the run, alone like this. Together. And the pain of it, of him not being here with me, of him not being the one to sleep beside me tonight felt like a fresh knife to my heart.

"Auriel?" I said, my voice shaking.

"Lyriana?"

"I miss him," I cried. "So much."

"Oh, I know you do, *Meka*. I know. Come here to me. Come here." But he was already standing, moving to my side, and pulling me against him in a hug. He let me cry against his chest, and rest my head in his lap when I grew too tired.

Then he stroked my hair, and my back, until I finally drifted to sleep. The red shard glowed ever so slightly as it lay beside me, my eyes closing.

The next morning, I woke up early and ready for training. Though the skin on my arms was still healing, the use of my arms, and the control in my hands had returned. For the first time in days, I felt restored.

I used my glamour magic on Auriel to change his armor again. I'd perfected the spell a little more, not having to perform it under as much pressure as before. It was still nowhere near as convincing or detailed as what Aiden could do. He truly was an artist, and I hoped I'd get the chance to tell him that when I saw him again. When I saw everyone again. Wherever they were.

Standing back to check my work on Auriel's appearance, I decided it was perfectly passable as long as no one looked too closely. Auriel appeared to be wearing the standard silver armor issued by Ka Kormac. I decided to also change his eyes from green to black. They didn't suit him at all—but he would definitely blend in with the other Korterians.

After doing a quick perimeter check for any threats—animal, akadim, and Kormac he took the ashvan by himself out to the nearest town. The plan was for him to listen for news, open his senses, and gather food for me. Because he insisted I eat before I trained. Like Rhyan would ...

So I did, knowing there was no way around it—even if I felt energetic, even if I was eager to start. Auriel was just as strict as Rhyan, if not more. So, while I waited for him to return, I practiced the Dance of Asherah, holding the sword. It was something I used to do with Rhyan when I was growing accustomed to even holding a weapon, to building the muscle necessary. He thought it would help if I held it while moving in a way that felt natural to me. A way I had already mastered.

Again, the shard glowed ever so slightly with my movements, like it was attuned to me. And my heart warmed.

Auriel returned to the cave not long after, standing stunned as he watched me dance. My skin heated, and I put the sword down, almost embarrassed. Though I had no reason to be. I was doing an ancient dance—one named after myself. My old self. And by the look on his face, he'd recognized it at once. This wasn't just an Asherah-inspired dance. This was her dance.

Our eyes met, and for a moment, I remembered the way he'd looked at me in my vision. His eyes had held a similar intensity on the hill.

But he quickly shook his head, and the blaze of warmth that had accompanied his aura seemed to calm. He set down the breakfast he'd found, proudly reading off the menu he'd created. I was impressed. It was his first time having to go out on his own since he'd returned. And he'd brought back a proper feast, and most importantly, coffee.

We settled down to eat, but not before I made a point of un-glamouring his eyes, and his armor.

A little while later, when I was fed—and by the Gods, caffeinated for the first time in days—we began training. Hours were spent parrying and thrusting our blades, moving through basic exercises. I was already accustomed to holding the red shard, thanks to my earlier dance session. But I needed to wield the sword, not just hold it. I was paying attention to everything, wholly focused on every movement, every step, every turn. I had to understand the shard's weight and its precise movements. I had to know the speed in which I could use it. The force a stab required. And most importantly, I had to perfect the art of hitting my target.

The heart.

I was determined for the shard to become an extension of my arm, to become as much a part of me as the light inside had been. And with every move I made, I was growing closer and closer to making this happen.

Auriel and I moved through our drills over and over; I was ravenous to learn, to practice. To become a master. And when he suggested we break, I refused. I had to keep going. Every time I felt tired, I saw Rhyan's face, saw the pain in his eyes when I'd picked him up. And the way they'd turned red in my dreams—my nightmares.

It wasn't until we were both dripping with sweat, until my arm was practically numb, and my fingers could no longer hold the hilt, that I relented. We took turns bathing in a nearby spring, careful to give each other privacy. Then we packed up our things, and rode on the back of our ashvan into town. This time, my hair was glamoured to more of a white blond in the hopes of differentiating myself from any stories that had spread about me. I also made a point to change the color of my eyes, black like Ka Kormac. Two soturi now knew I was here, but they had no proof it was me. Hopefully that was enough to keep me safe.

I decided to change Auriel's hair as well, and matched his eyes to mine again. When we caught a glimpse of our reflections in a river, the effect was startling. Combined with the way I'd transformed our armor from gold to silver, if no one knew who we were, they'd think us regular Kormac bastards.

Back in town, we kept our heads down moving from pub to pub, listening to people talk. Listening not just for stories of akadim, but of people going missing. If Rhyan was leading a horde, or an army of akadim in Korteria, then surely, they were feeding. Which meant Korterians had to be vanishing, or seeing more of the demons than ever before. There'd been at least six back in Vrukston. And if we were close, there'd be even more. Especially since I had a feeling the akadim were being encouraged not just to maim and kill, but to make more of themselves. To grow Morgana and Aemon's numbers. But we heard little to back up our theories.

I had another coffee, and so did Auriel. And over the course of the day, we ordered more beers than we could drink, letting them mostly go to waste. Then we stepped in and out of every small shop that had people inside.

It wasn't until dinnertime that night when someone finally mentioned Bamaria again. Or rather, fucking southern New Korteria. There were protests mentioned—though, considering we were moving further west through the country, they might have been referencing the same protests we'd already heard about. It was entirely possible it was just taking longer for the news to travel. But I couldn't be sure. Unless we went back east, I didn't think I'd find out the truth of what was really happening back home.

Eventually though my name did come up. A lot. What we heard were mostly things not worth repeating. Or more speculations that I was dead after having gone missing for a month. The other popular story, besides my death, was that I was pregnant with Kane's baby. That rumor was followed closely in repetition by another rumor about me being pregnant with our new Emperor's baby. And then the Bastardmaker's.

I even heard Rhyan's name thrown in a few times. Apparently, I'd been impregnated by everyone. But the majority of the time Rhyan's name came up, it was less about our affair, and more about condemning him as a vorakh. Gloating over his stripping, and excitement for more to meet his fate. Auriel had to hold me back a few times from punching Korterians laughing over it.

But, I noted, there was no mention of him as an akadim—or even any mention of the akadim attack on the capital at all. The Emperor had truly kept that under wraps, making it all about me, and the vorakh. The story that seemed to be going around Korteria was that Rhyan succumbed to his wounds after the stripping. The deaths I knew had taken place were being downplayed. And the ones acknowledged were being blamed on me and the vorakh they accused me of freeing.

I wanted to scream at them all. They were so fucking worried over a group of people who weren't a threat to them or their lives. In fact, they seemed most afraid of the very people who were the most threatened by the Emperor himself. The people who if found, would lose everything.

And despite the overwhelming presence of akadim we'd seen here just the night before, no one seemed overly concerned or worried about the danger they were in. And the most disturbing—they'd just lost the one thing that protected them from akadim. And thanks to Emperor Avery's lies, they had no idea they'd lost it.

Daylight.

The Lumerians in Korteria were still unaware that under the shining sun, akadim could emerge from the shadows and attack at any moment. But I couldn't say anything—couldn't warn them. Not without drawing attention to myself.

Did information just travel that slowly here? Were they in denial? Or had it somehow been suppressed?

When our day ended, we returned to the cave, using our cloaks to sleep on the ground near the fire, our ashvan tied up just outside. We repeated our routine in the next town, and the day after that in another. Every day we listened, and every day we trained and prepared. The same variations of the same rumors were circulating everywhere we went, everywhere we listened. And still, no mention of akadim. Nor any clues that could lead us to Rhyan. I was starting to wonder if the akadim attack the other night had been in my imagination. Not that I wished for it, but why weren't there more? Why hadn't Morgana's and Aemon's forces made themselves known? It didn't make any sense. They were out there. But even

Auriel had no further sensations of Rhyan. Or the void of his soul from his body.

With nothing else to go on other than Auriel's hunch that Rhyan wasn't far, we continued, moving through more towns, our eyes black, our hair blond, and our armor silver. Our hands never strayed far from the hilts of our swords, we were always on guard both from Ka Kormac and akadim. Though after I'd gotten too many comments about the color, size and shape of "that strange colored sword on my back," the red shard, I glamoured it, too, turning it into something that looked old and rusty. Something worthy of that Gods-damned soturion we'd fought that first night.

Days and days of searching and listening passed and still there was no real news. Only more disgusting rumors about me, or updates on the search for my whereabouts. There were none—a relief.

But soon the gossip turned to the latest stories about the vorakh task force and the mandatory testing that had been rolled out. According to some mages I'd overheard, the protests happening now were focused on the testing, and the sudden uptick in arrests.

Allegedly, unverified accusations were flying now. Anyone could accuse anyone of being vorakh. And though there were nahashim testing for the forbidden magic, apparently now, an accusation was all it took. The accused would be taken to Lethea without a test, and without a trial.

Though I suspected that even that was a lie. Lumerians were being taken, and kidnapped. But I didn't believe they were being brought to Lethea. I'd already overheard the discussion of the new prisons being built. Marring my land, my country with their construction. The bastards didn't care who they took—they just needed bodies, slaves they could control and extort. Vorakh or not, Lumerians were being taken to the Palace and made into chayatim. I was sure of it.

I had to stop underestimating the Emperor. As well as everyone else serving him.

Once it grew dark, we climbed back onto our ashvan and returned to the cave. Days were passing and the pattern remained the same. I was getting antsy, more worked up every time we returned without learning anything new. More word about protests, about Lumerians vanishing. About me missing. Nothing about akadim. It didn't make any sense.

Everyday Auriel was reassuring me it was for the best that we'd found nothing. Because I wasn't ready to fight Rhyan. I still needed more time with the sword. With the shard. I knew it was giving me more energy, and allowing my spells to become more effective, to last longer. The proof was in my new skills with glamour.

At night when Auriel closed his eyes, I read from his Valya, looking for differences between it and the ones I'd studied. Reading over and over anything he'd written about the cure.

And then a week passed. I was getting stronger. Better at fighting with the shard. But more anxious and unsettled by the day. Why hadn't we found him yet? Why, when Auriel was so sure he was in Korteria, had there been no sign of akadim? Not since that first night.

When we returned back to our cave after a second week of fruitless searching, visiting endless towns, and walking through the hills for signs of nests, I broke down. "Where the fuck is he?" I asked, slamming my fist into the cavern wall.

Auriel came to stand beside me. "He's out there, Lyriana, he is."

I shook my head. "It's not like it's that hard to find akadim. Especially a horde—or whatever you might call the number serving him as an Arkturion. Isn't it the whole fucking point that they go out hunting for you? I mean, if we hadn't found him by now, shouldn't he be finding us?" I held my arms up wide, turning in a circle and screaming. "We're fucking prime targets out here! We're alone! We're in the middle of nowhere. The akadim should come running!"

"Maybe let's not advertise that right now," Auriel said. "I mean once word gets out that we're here and we're tasty, the line to sample us will reach the town and then—"

"Stop it! Just stop! You're not going to talk me down by making jokes!"

Auriel bit his lip, the muscles in his jaw flexing. He leaned his head against the wall, his arms folded across his chest. "Okay. I won't."

I exhaled shakily, meeting his gaze. "What if you're wrong? What if he's not here? What if you're feeling something else?"

His eyes softened. "I'm not. I'm sure he's here. I don't know why we haven't found him yet. I wish I did. I wish I had a better sense of him, I wish that he felt—I don't know, clearer to me. But that doesn't change anything. I know what I feel."

"What if Sean found him?" I asked. "What if Branwyn never got through? And he's gone?"

"I would know. I would sense it."

I shook my head. "Or you're just wrong and won't admit it!"

"I would admit," Auriel said, "I think we're close. There's—there's something. Some reason I feel him, his void. Some reason I'm sure."

"What?" I asked dully.

"In my mind. It feels cloudy, not quite like before but like … there's something I'm just not putting together."

I turned away, my arms folded across my chest. "Well, let me know when you do."

"Wait. Aemon is Moriel," Auriel said slowly. "And Morgana is Ereshya."

I nodded in exasperation. "Yes." Because he already knew this.

"They already claimed the indigo and the orange shards. And now they have a horde of akadim under their control led by Rhyan." He started to pace. "Akadim that can move in the day. And akadim that need to feed. And I'd bet on a somewhat regular basis. There's no way that that many akadim are going unnoticed. Especially since over a month ago they committed a massacre in Thene, and before that in Numeria. They have the numbers. They attacked the Palace, the place that is supposedly impenetrable."

"Not anymore," I said. "I also attacked the Palace."

"And you're the only story being spread and repeated. That you attacked, that you freed the vorakh—and yet they're the ones the Empire wants everyone to fear."

"And?" I said. "So what? We know this! We've been hearing confirmation for days. Weeks! It's not like this is anything new, or even the first time they've put out lies, told us what to fear while ignoring the true danger."

"No. But there is real danger. Somewhere out here is a small army of akadim. We met some of them already. And no matter how many lies the Empire spreads, something this big can't just be covered up." He clapped his hands together. "Think about it, Lyriana. We haven't heard shit about Aemon and Morgana. And Aemon—Moriel—he was known as the Ready." Auriel's eyes blazed, like he was on the verge of a discovery. "Lady Morgana was known across the Empire. And akadim are the gravest threat that any Lumerian can face. I mean by the fucking realms. Was there ever a bigger, more violent, or more brutal attack on Lumerians in a single day, than the attack in the arena?"

The attack that killed Rhyan, that turned him. "No," I said.

Auriel nodded vigorously. "No one discussing the akadim seems to have the slightest clue they can come out in the sun," he snarled, his aura flashing with anger. "We literally fought that kind of akadim here—in this country! Why? Why doesn't everyone know that?"

"Because it's just like you said. The Empire tells us what they want us to know. And when the Empire is run by fucking Ka Kormac, of course everyone in Korteria believes it." And probably New fucking Korteria, too.

"Exactly," he said. "It's just like last time we fought. Just like when we battled against the Council, a millennia ago. They control the narrative, the stories they want you to believe, they tell you where they want your attention to go. And you know what stories they wouldn't want getting out?" His nostrils flared.

I shook my head. "No."

"Protests," he said. "Anyone in disagreement with them. Yet, we're hearing about them every day, because they're happening. They're becoming a big deal."

I frowned. He was right. Everyday, in every town, they were discussed. And there was a rumor—albeit a small one—that someone from Ka Kormac had been arrested for vorakh. No one believed he was guilty. Apparently, he'd been in a feud with another soturion. That soturion had made the accusation out of revenge. And that was all it took. He was taken in the night. The soturion who'd made the accusation had been beaten within an inch of his life. And then there'd been a small, yet failed uprising at the home of a local turion. An attempt to free the accused. But it had failed, and everyone there had either been arrested or beaten. Their soturion pay was docked as punishment.

At least, according to the rumors.

"Okay," I said slowly. "They're not completely controlling this narrative. So, what are you getting at?"

"So, Morgana and Aemon aren't working with the Empire. They have a legion of akadim under their control. Two shards of the Valalumir in their possession. Wouldn't it stand to reason that with all that power, and all those moving pieces, that they would be in more stories? More rumors?" His hands fisted. "But they're not. We know what the Empire wants everyone to know. But things have a way of getting out. The truth can't hide in the shadows forever. Aemon and Morgana are lying low. They're preparing for their next move. I don't think the akadim are roaming around Korteria and hunting. I think the ones we found two weeks ago were a fluke, or they were on their way to meet the others. Because I think they're going after the next shard. For *Maraak Moriel*, and *Maraaka Ereshya*. And now I'm convinced I know which one. Because I know Rhyan's here. And I know what else is. The green. My shard."

"By the Gods," I said, my eyes widening. "You're right. Fuck. That's the answer, isn't it?" Shit! Shit! I ran my fingers through my hair in frustration.

If Lord Rhyan Hart's soul cannot be restored, he will prove to be one of the most dangerous, and destructive forces the Empire has ever seen. Worse than the rise of Moriel. A prophecy exists even now. Visions shared by three. He has the power, as do you, to destroy our world.

By handing the green shard to Aemon and Morgana, giving them three, I wouldn't stand a chance against them, not with only one.

"Auriel, do you know where the green shard is?"

He nodded. "It's buried deep. I went for tombs, keys, and riddles when I hid the indigo and the red. But for the green," he smiled self-deprecatingly, "well, let no one accuse me of only having one trick. For mine, I chose nature as my accomplice. Nature and sheer brute force. I used my magic to create a hole, deep inside the mountains of Korteria, as far as the human lands. I buried the shard inside it, and then I closed it up."

"And it's in Korteria?"

He nodded. Then Rhyan was here. But …

"Did you do anything else when you hid the shard?" I asked suspiciously.

"Well, one thing," he said, averting his eyes. "I made it so no one could use magic to reopen the hole. I guess back then I was kind of inspired by the way magic couldn't touch akadim. I wanted something else magic couldn't touch. And I put it in a place where magic was weakest."

"West," I said.

Auriel nodded. "The place can be accessed by anyone, human, or Lumerian, if the spot is known. But you'd have to fight nature, and dig." He frowned. "The hole I made, and the force I used to close it was extensive. Even for me, even at full strength. It would take months, and an immense amount of digging from an entire team of Lumerians with God-like energy and muscle. And that timeline is generous, and only believable if you had a team working day and night."

"What about a month?" I asked. "But instead of strong Lumerians digging, it was a horde of akadim? Including one who had living memories of you. And remembered where it was buried."

Auriel's mouth dropped open. "Fuck. Fuck! That's what they're doing. They're using Rhyan to locate it, and the akadim to dig out the shard. We need to go. Now."

CHAPTER THIRTY

LYRIANA

My heart was hammering, the pieces of the puzzle all coming together. The silence of the akadim, Aemon and Morgana's plans, and the green shard being hidden in Korteria. That was why Rhyan had been made Arkturion.

I eyed Auriel carefully, my body tensed. "We should leave now," I said, ready to run, ready to race toward the shard. Toward Rhyan.

But Auriel shook his head, and pulled out a map we'd acquired on one of our outings. "The mountain is at the westernmost Lumerian border, as far as you can go before leaving the Empire." He pointed.

Even more conveniently closer to Vrukshire than we were now. My heart pounded.

"Shit. That's why we haven't heard of any attacks," I said. "Because they're in the mountain."

"Exactly. And more than that. Akadim can survive a month without feeding. They can outlast starvation by years if they have to."

"You think Morgana and Aemon are starving them?" I asked uneasily.

Auriel nodded. "They would have to, to keep them on schedule, to dig as deep as I buried the shard." His mouth tightened.

I frowned. Akadim were insatiable. Morgana and Aemon might have them under their thrall—but they were still a horde of starving akadim. They'd riot. They'd mutiny.

And if there was food nearby, then they were feeding. They were just doing it quietly.

I pointed beyond the border, feeling sick to my stomach. "They're going to the human lands—where there's no magic. That's who they're feeding from, who they're … attacking. And killing. And … Fuck—they're probably also building their army with them too. Using them to dig." All these innocent people, losing their lives, being turned into monsters, all so they could be enslaved and used by Aemon in his war.

Auriel nodded grimly. "Damn." His eyes reddened and he shook his head. "Lifetimes pass. Some things never change."

"They did this last time?" I asked.

Auriel's gaze met mine, and there was something heavy in his aura. Like a rain cloud that needed to burst. "You still don't remember?" His voice shook.

I shook my head, my eyes watering. "I'm sorry."

He exhaled sharply. "This was exactly how they gained the advantage over us back then. Numbers. They sent ships beyond the continent, ships that were completely empty. They'd return with humans. Food for their army. Food that became the army."

My stomach twisted.

Nostrils flaring, his aura turned from something sad, to something more fiery and more determined. Auriel dragged his finger across the map from the border mountains to where we were now in the Mouth of the Wolf. The border mountains were known as the Wall of the Prince. We were only a few miles away from it.

Auriel cleared his throat, considering. "We can take the horse there, or we can go by foot." He glanced toward the mouth of the cave; there was nothing but darkness beyond it. "But I really don't like the idea of us going at night. If they are feeding—even if they have day abilities—they're most likely still attacking in the dark. When people are asleep, vulnerable. They may be going over the border. They may not. They may have a watch to the east of Korteria. We don't know what we'll encounter. But we need to find out everything. And I'm not risking you at night."

"You're not risking me at all," I snapped. "Nor do you get a say in what I do."

"*Meka*, please. Am I not allowed to look out for you? To care about you? To," his voice cracked, "love you."

I held his gaze, and that feeling came over me again. The one I felt in the Moon Court. The ghost of a memory of him looking at me. His face was full of love. And an almost animalistic passion. One I saw nearly replicated from time to time when our eyes met.

"You mean Asherah," I said.

"No." He shook his head. "You. I love you. When will you understand? It's the same thing." He swallowed roughly, his jaw muscles tensing. "There's nowhere you can go where I won't find you. No face you can wear that I won't recognize. No form you can take that I won't love. Because I know you. I knew what Asherah was to me the first moment I saw her. It was the same with you. Since I've been with you, my love has grown, expanded. I love you, Lyriana. As you are now."

My throat dried. "I ... I didn't realize."

His mouth tightened, his gaze cloudy and distant. "I'm on the other side of things. I see all of Asherah, all her faces, all her lives. And I see you." His eyes met mine. "But you only see Rhyan."

My heart sank at his words. "Auriel."

He shook his head. "No, no. You don't have to say anything. It's as it should be. I think I miss ... I miss her, too. You're a temptation that's hard to resist. Because I see her in you, see that you are her. And yet, you remind me constantly that you're different." He coughed, and stared down at the map again. "I think we should go in the morning," he said, finality in his voice. "Find a place to stay nearby. We need a base, and we need to investigate first. Seek out the mountain. The Prince's Wall. Find out what numbers we're facing. And when we know, when we're ready—we'll strike."

We'll find Rhyan. My heart pounded. I could feel it this time. We'd figured it out. We were really going to find him.

I went to bed not long after that. Auriel took the ashvan out for a ride—he was getting antsy, missing his hourly patrols. And then I felt Auriel standing guard over me, so I could fall asleep first, in peace.

We didn't discuss his outburst or his confession. That he'd fallen in love with me. Not just because I was Asherah. But because I was myself.

I remembered loving him as Asherah. Stronger than any feelings I'd had in this lifetime. But nothing like what I felt for Rhyan. And if I was honest, I simply wouldn't allow myself to feel anything more. To forget my mission. Or slow down. Because anything he felt for me, or that I could possibly feel for him, wouldn't matter once Rhyan was cured.

I woke up in the middle of the night. I couldn't remember my dream. Only that Rhyan had been in it. An ocean between us. Yet I could still see his face clearly. His green eyes had turned red, and his teeth had grown into fangs. He'd opened his mouth, and the waves took him. Again.

I wiped the tears from my eyes, and shivered. My body was so cold. The fire we'd built had gone out.

Auriel stirred beside me, still asleep, blissfully unaware of the drop in temperature. I rolled over to him. He reached for me instantly, his arm wrapping around my waist, pulling me close. His hand found my belly. The place that Rhyan's normally occupied. Something softened in my chest, and on instinct, I snuggled closer to him, burrowing into his warmth.

My heart pounded with the sensation, the sense of safety that I'd been missing, the familiarity I'd craved. I peered back at his face. He was smiling as he dreamed. I'd never seen him do that before. He looked peaceful. Content. He'd been missing Asherah as much as I'd been missing Rhyan. We both needed this. For a few minutes, I listened to the sound of his heart beating. The sound I had listened to as Asherah a millennium ago. A sound that had been imprinted on my soul. Proof he was alive. So alive. And finally, warm again, my eyes closed.

In the morning, Auriel gathered food, and I practiced with the shard until he returned. We packed up what little belongings we had—mostly weapons—and coins we'd stolen during our outings. Then I went through the routine of glamouring our appearances before climbing onto the back of our ashvan.

We kept to the woods and the hills, until we'd reached the small town beyond the mountains. Once there, we found an inn with a spare room. Auriel paid enough to allow us to stay a week. The inn provided a lunch which we took advantage of, and then with the rest of the day open, we began our hike to the mountain range.

We let the horse go then, releasing him from the post we'd hidden him at before entering the town. There was nowhere to keep him in the town. Not without drawing more suspicions toward us. It was known throughout the country that one of the patrol ashvan had gone missing. So we went the rest of the way on foot, fully armed. There was a field leading into a valley, one that led right to the mountain range.

We hiked around the outskirts, and saw nothing. No akadim. But no ashvan either. No seraphim. Nor any kind of birds at all. It was eerily, disturbingly silent.

"The animals sense their presence," Auriel said. "So can I. There's a heaviness in the atmosphere. They're definitely here."

A shiver ran down my spine. I recognized an unwelcome sensation I was all too used to. I was being watched.

"How do you get in?" I asked, craning my neck up at the structure. It looked like pure stone all around. No openings.

"There's a way," he said. "But," he shrugged, "it's been a thousand years. Things shift."

I bit my lip, but my heart was pounding as we moved closer, Auriel touching the mountainside. Yet everywhere we looked, it was the same. Just rock. No sign of life. No sign of entry. Hours passed, and the sensation of being watched never left me. But with the sun setting soon, Auriel dragged me reluctantly back to the inn.

I dreamt of nothing that night. My thoughts on endless rocks, and Rhyan.

We returned the next day, no longer glamoured, retracing our steps, searching for an opening, for any signs of activity.

We decided to climb higher—to get closer. The sensation I had the day before returned.

"We're being watched," I hissed.

Auriel nodded. "Stay close to me." He reached for the hilt of his sword, his green eyes blazing with determination.

We climbed higher, coming to a small rock landing, and again Auriel touched the mountainside. He gasped, almost as if in pain, and his tan skin paled, the green light of his eyes going out.

"Auriel?"

His chest heaved, and then suddenly he looked like himself again. "Sorry, I'm all right."

"Are you sure?" I asked.

But then he stepped back, and stumbled. He'd never stumbled, not on his own. Not like this.

A pit formed in my stomach and the hair on the back of my neck lifted, and a shiver ran down my spine. Something was wrong.

"I just felt—I can't explain it."

I took his hand in mine. My heart was beating faster and faster.

"Was it the void? Did you sense Rhyan? The shard?" My heart hadn't warmed, hadn't heated the way it did for the others once my magic was revealed. But ... I couldn't shake the feeling, or the fear running through me. We weren't alone. "Auriel, I—"

A growl sounded behind. And then another one came from above. And an akadim walked out onto a short cliff near where we stood.

We didn't have time to react, to grab our swords. The akadim leapt, flying up into the air and then soaring as he fell. He tackled Auriel, rolling him down the hill.

I screamed and turned around, only to come face-to-face with another. The sun shone behind him, the light glaring and leaving me momentarily blind to everything but his silhouette. I blinked, stumbling back. He moved, blocking the sun, and my vision cleared.

"Hello, lover," Rhyan growled, his voice low.

I reached for my sword. For the red shard. But Rhyan was faster. He wrapped his hand around my neck, and squeezed, and squeezed, my feet lifting off the ground.

Auriel yelled my name, the sound faint and fuzzy. And then my vision blurred, my breath coming short. I was aware of something clattering to the ground, something falling. Metal. Crystal. Light.

Rhyan's lips, now large and fanged, turned up into a cruel, monstrous smile. My eyes closed, and then I knew nothing.

CHAPTER THIRTY-ONE

LYRIANA

I awoke to the sound of Rhyan growling low in my ear. My back was pressed against him, his arm wrapped around me, keeping me warm. His hand was splayed across my stomach as it was most nights, one finger moving absent-mindedly back and forth, back and forth, soothing my skin. It was a familiar sleeping position for us. Except for the fact that I wasn't sleeping. And apparently, neither was he.

Rhyan was up. And from the way he was poking me from behind, it was clear that all *of him was.*

His breath deepened before I felt the blankets shift beneath us as Rhyan pushed his erection against my ass.

I grinded back. "You're awake," *I said, my voice hushed and heavy with sleep.*

"Your fault," *he teased, his fingers now moving in slow lazy circles across my skin, just barely brushing the underside of my breasts.*

Instinctively I arched against him, trying to bring his hand higher. To feel him cup me there. I wanted to feel his hand squeezing me, his thumb brushing against my nipple. But he kept his hand in place, his fingers purposely taunting me more.

"My fault?" *I asked.*

"All your fault, partner." His voice was low, and scratchy. I arched again, and this time, his hand moved exactly where I wanted him.

I gasped. Moments ago, I'd been sound asleep. "Really? How did I wake you up?"

"By doing exactly what you're doing to me now." His lips skimmed across my neck, leaving shivers running down my spine, and heat pooling between my legs. *"Grinding against me, just enough to torture me."*

I bit my lip and circled my hips back, feeling his cock pulse through our clothes. "I'm sorry, I woke you."

"Mmmmmm." He chuckled, his chest vibrating against my spine. *"I'm not sorry. I liked it. A lot."* His hand slid down my belly, between my legs, until he cupped me. I pushed my hips forward, chasing the feel of his fingers. He was gentle for a second, teasing, and then he pulled me back into him, his hand between my legs dragging my body to his, so there was no more space between us. His knee pushed through my legs.

A surprised moan escaped my lips.

"Just like that," he said, his fingers finding my core.

A whimper escaped my lips and I moved against him, seeking more friction. But between his knee and his hands, he was everywhere.

He worked me slowly, sucking on my neck. "I like waking up like this. With you."

"Me, too," I panted, feeling him twitch against me. I reached over my shoulder with my free hand, grasping his arm and pulling him on top of me as I rolled onto my back. He slid down the length of my body, stopping when his head reached my stomach. He smiled and kissed my belly button, his tongue dipping inside.

Then he pulled up my shirt—his shirt—the one I'd stolen from him to sleep in, until my breasts were exposed to the cold air of the Glemarian cave. My nipples hardened, aching for him to touch me again, to suck on them.

He knew, but he was having too much fun teasing me, slowly kissing his way back up my stomach. I squirmed as his mouth dragged higher and higher. Until finally, after what felt like an endless amount of torture, he wrapped both hands around my breasts, and stilled, his eyes hooded with desire as he stared intently at them.

I bit my lip. "What are you doing?"

"You know what I'm doing, partner." His eyes darkened. The edge of his lips quirked up. "I'm admiring the most perfect breasts in the world."

I raised my eyebrows. "Bold of you to assume they're the most perfect breasts when you haven't seen every pair in the world."

He scoffed. "Bold of you to assume I haven't."

"Rhyan!" I yelled, and burst into laughter.

"Oh shit," he hissed, immediately slapping his hand over my mouth. "Shhhh," he tried to say, but he was laughing too hard to get the sound out. It only made me laugh harder.

"Meera," I tried to whisper against his palm. She was sleeping, but her bed wasn't too far from ours. We'd finally had sex again the other night, our first time since—well, the very first night. We'd made every effort to be as quiet as possible. But there was no way Meera hadn't heard our laughter just now.

And I was right. She'd just gotten up. Shit.

Rhyan squeezed his eyes shut, his shoulders shaking before he collapsed on top of me, and buried his face in my neck. I wrapped my arms around him, pulling him closer, grinning stupidly, trying to keep my laughter quiet.

"Gods, I love you," he said against my skin, still laughing.

I stroked the curls at the back of his head. "I love you."

My eyes sprang open, my breath coming in quick, painful bursts. I was on my stomach, face down, my nose smushed under me. I was in something like a bed—a mix of straw and old blankets that carried a stale, musty scent, like they hadn't been washed in a long time—if ever. I coughed and swallowed painfully, my throat was dry, and my head was heavy and aching. From the damp, sulfuric smell in the air, I knew I was in a cave. Specifically, the Wall of the Prince.

The cave that—

"And what were you dreaming about?" Rhyan asked, in that low, growly voice that marked an akadim. Heart thundering, I slowly turned my head and found him casually sitting on the bed beside me, watching. Chills ran down my spine, fear rushing through my veins. That voice had no soul, and was devoid of all warmth. It was unmistakably the voice of a demon. But more than the fear it evoked in me, was the pain in my chest. Because hearing Rhyan like this, hearing him speak, hearing his lilt, felt like someone had slashed my heart. I could still hear his accent, still hear him beneath the monstrousness.

And somehow, despite it all, despite the growl underlying each syllable, and the way his vocal cords had deepened, he still sounded like himself. Like Rhyan.

I rolled over onto my side, shifting away from him. Everything hurt. I was sore, and there was a sharp crick in my neck. But I couldn't do much more than roll. My arms were bound behind me, restrained with rope that he'd tied tightly from my wrists to my elbows. The position had forced my shoulders back to the point that they were strained. I tried to wiggle, to see if the ropes would come loose or if they had any give, but there was none. Rhyan had been thorough in his binding.

Rough stone walls surrounded us from all sides with only a small opening—like a doorway that led into more darkness and stone. Something awful smelling was in the air, something metallic and sharp, like decay. We were in a private alcove. A single torch had been nailed into the stone, its faint flames flickering, and casting eerie shadows across the room.

And Rhyan had me alone in it, tied up, trapped.

Where was Auriel? Had he been captured, too?

A shiver ran down my spine as more details of my reality set in. I was still dressed in my tunic, and boots. But my cloak was gone, so was my armor, Asherah's chest plate, and my belt. He'd taken all of my weapons. Everything I'd carried on me.

And he'd taken—he'd taken—No. No. No.

Rhyan was leaning back on our bed, one leg stretched out long, the other bent, his arm resting on his knee. In his hand was the red shard. His long, clawed akadim fingers wrapped around its hilt and he was swinging it carelessly up and down, letting the blade arc over me.

I shifted back, as much as I could, my heart pounding. The blade moved over me again with another absent-minded swing.

His red akadim eyes glowed as they ran up and down my body—and I swore I could feel everywhere he looked. Feel my skin tingling, and growing cold. Colder than I already was. He hadn't put a blanket over me, and without my cloak, I could feel just how low the temperature was in here.

Rhyan wore a silver collar around his neck, and a black leather vest across his torso—similar in style to the armor he'd always worn—always favored. Instead of his soturion cloak wrapped around his waist, he wore black fitted pants, and black leather boots. All at once I took him in. His monstrous appearance, the way he'd grown in size in every way—he was at least a foot taller than he'd been the last time I saw him. His muscles had sharpened and widened. And red lines crossed over his skin, which was so much paler than it had been. It even crossed into the wings of his tattoo, the ink stretched now over too much skin.

He grinned, the sight monstrous as two long sharpened fangs glistened across his lips. His nostrils flared, his red eyes glowing.

I struggled to come into a seat, spotting my weapons in a small corner just beyond the bed. They'd been neatly laid out in a row—too neatly. Just like Rhyan would have done. He'd always been neat, always carefully arranging things. It was how I'd known I'd woken up in his room at Seathorne. It had smelled like him, felt like him. But even if it hadn't—I would have known. And looking at the items here, forgetting where I was, what he was—all I saw was him. Rhyan. My Rhyan.

My heart panged. All these little details. Gods. They were still there. These small parts of him that I loved, that were part of what made him who he was. His lilt, the way he organized things so precisely. It was like he was still him. Still Rhyan.

But this wasn't him. And it was my fault. My lip trembled. Because that was all there was. Not his soul, his warmth, his love ... They were gone. And I had to remember that.

But I also needed to remember that I was going to be the reason he was saved. I was going to be the reason that the parts of him that he'd lost, that I'd lost, were brought back. I just had to survive.

I'd never reach the shard with my arms bound, not with his body blocking the blade. But, if I could leap off the bed, I could rush to my weapons corner and reach for a sword—no, I'd be too slow. He'd be on me before I could cut myself free. And that was if I could even figure out how to grab a blade with my restraints. If I was going to free myself like this I needed time. Time I didn't have—not as long as he was in the room with me.

I could try to call on *Rakashonim*. But that felt foolish. The power was great—but volatile, and I still didn't have control over it. I couldn't be sure if it would come, how hard it would hit me, or how quickly it would go through me. Not without the shard in my hand to temper it.

He clicked his tongue, looking pointedly at my weapons, then back to me, meeting my eyes. He shook his head.

"I know what you're thinking, what you're plotting. Give it up," he growled. "You'd never make it in time."

My stomach twisted. "Oh?"

"You're fast," he said. "I remember." He licked his lips. "But not fast enough. You wouldn't get past me. And come on, do you really think I'd let you?" He shook his head again. "I wouldn't. And even if by the damned Gods you managed it, this mountain is full of akadim. They'd have you captured and laid at my feet in seconds. One order from me is all it would take. Trust me. You don't want to test that theory. All the akadim in this mountain are not just loyal to me, they're bound to me, to their Arkturion." He sounded proud.

My chest heaved, my pulse racing too fast. "I-I heard about that. *Tovayah maischa* on your promotion."

He chuckled cruelly, sitting all the way up, his eyes running up and down the blade. It glowed red, catching the faint light of the fire. He tilted his head, and swung it again, the blade arcing just over my body.

"I don't remember this," he frowned. "Your other effects I know. But not this one. Where did you get it?"

"It's um ... a long story," I said, my voice shaking.

"Was it that soturion I saw you with? The blond one fighting for you?"

"Yes," I said, before I could think better of it. I dared to look at Rhyan, meeting his eyes, and asked, "What happened to him?"

He shrugged, nonchalantly, like he wasn't at all concerned. "Ran off. If he comes back, we'll find him." His eyes were fixed on the blade, he was turning every which way, examining it from every angle, letting the steel catch the firelight, and then the reflection of his face. His monstrous face.

I tucked that piece of information away. Auriel hadn't been caught. Auriel was still out there. That was good. He'd come for me. Why did Rhyan seem so unbothered? Was that because he didn't see him as a threat? Was he that confident?

Yes. After all, he'd captured me.

He turned the shard in his hand again, he seemed mesmerized by the crystal, his cure, and rested the blunt side of the blade against his knee. "So red," he said. "And bright."

I sucked in a breath. "It is."

"Too bright." He pulled his gaze away and looked toward me again. There was a light in his eyes, glistening in a way that made my heart stop. That reminded me that he was a predator. And I was the prey.

He started to inch across the bed toward me. There wasn't far to go. He was already taking up nearly all of the space there was. My throat dried as he settled the sword down, carefully placing it on his other side. I stilled as he reached for me. His hand grasped my shoulder, gripping it painfully.

My heart sank. "Rhyan? What are you—"

He pushed me down, and I landed on my back, my arms and hands crushed beneath me.

I hissed in pain, my stomach clenching violently as he leered. His body crushed against my side, then he wrapped a leg around mine, so he was half beside me, half on top of me.

By the Gods, I couldn't breathe. I couldn't fucking breathe. Fuck! This wasn't happening. This wasn't happening. Not to me. Not like this.

Not with Rhyan.

He lifted himself up onto his elbow, and hovered over me, making it plain just how much larger he was—how much more powerful. He'd always been bigger than me. Taller. Stronger. At least, until my power arrived. But I hadn't always noticed the height difference really, or the weight—because I'd always felt so safe with him, so comfortable. He'd always been so gentle with me, so careful. Never once using his body against me. Now the power it exuded, the strength rippling through every distorted, elongated part of his akadim form was terrifying.

I shuddered, and tried to slide away from him. I nearly rolled off the bed.

"No," he said, his hand wrapping around my neck. He pulled me closer, sliding me back to him. Staring down at me, his claws digging into my hair, he started to squeeze. And I coughed, choking, his grip roughened, tightening and I kicked helplessly against the stone strength of his leg over mine.

"Rhy—" I choked.

He released his hold, looking unbothered by the tears in my eyes, and slid his hand up the length of my neck to the underside of my chin. His fingers used to be callused at the tips and blunt, his fingernails always trimmed. But now, all I could feel were the sharpened edges of the claw that spiked from his fingers. Trembling, I tried to look away, but he grabbed my jaw and forced my gaze to meet his. Forced me to stare into their red glow, into the light which was devoid of humanity. Of life. The rest of his body pressed into mine.

"Rhyan, please. Please, don't do this."

"You never answered my question before," he drawled.

"Y-Your question?" I asked. My entire body was shaking. I couldn't think. Couldn't even remember what he'd asked me. Or anything he'd said. Just that I was here, his prisoner. Bound, and weaponless beneath him. And he had my shard. He had the light of the Valalumir—his cure, and I couldn't touch it, couldn't wield it.

The torch flickered and hissed, darkening as smoke undulated. And beyond our alcove more akadim moved about, growling low. They were arguing, and whatever they were fighting about, it was getting louder. More intense. There was a slapping sound, and then another, followed by a roar.

Rhyan squeezed my face, forcing my attention back to him. "What were you dreaming about?" he asked.

"D-Dreaming?" My heart thudded.

"Mmmmhmmmm." His nostrils flared. "I could sense it. The quickening of your pulse, the stirring in your breath." He squeezed my chin harder, forcing my lips to squish together. "Your heart pounding, your hips wiggling." He smirked. "But most of all," his tongue darted out, sliding against the tip of a fang. "I could scent it." He paused, and took a pointedly, long, drawn out sniff.

I stiffened, my entire body tensing.

"You smelled sweet, and musky, and … wet. Makes me think that it was about me." He leaned in, his lips just over mine, his breath metallic. Like blood. "Makes me think it was about fucking me."

I gasped, and shook my head. "I … Rhyan." Think. Think! He wanted to know, he wanted proof it was about him. Fine. But he needed to give me something in return.

"I-I can tell you," I stammered. "But I need you to untie me first."

He chuckled. "Untie you? Just to talk? It's not like I sealed your mouth shut." He released my chin and suddenly he'd pushed me back onto my side and gripped the ropes behind my back.

"What are you—?" I screamed.

He lifted me up by the ropes. My arms burned, and started to go numb as the rope tore into them. Something warm dripped down my hands. My wrists were being cut.

He watched me, literally dangling like a toy for him to play with. My entire body hung, suspended in the air, and slowly, I began to turn as I kicked helplessly. He looked transfixed, and then without warning, he dropped me back onto the bed.

I landed with a wheezing feeling in my lungs before he pushed me onto my back again, and this time he crawled completely on top of me.

I shook my head. "Rhyan, please, please."

"Untie you?" he asked again, his eyebrows lifted. Both of them. Something he hadn't been able to do since his father had scarred his face. He tilted his head, his red eyes running down my body. "You mean these ropes?" He reached beneath me, his hand sliding up my ass, to my bound hands. The rope tugged violently beneath me as he brushed his nose against my neck, sniffing me. He smelled so metallic and sulfuric, like he was part of the cave. So unlike himself. But there was something else that made want to retch. A scent I could only describe as death. He dragged his rough, dry mouth against my skin until he reached my earlobe, wrapping it between his lips.

I closed my eyes, my body shaking. There was a sharp, painful piercing. Fuck. He bit me. I cried out. Warm blood rolled back into my hair, and slid down my neck.

"If you don't like it," he growled low under his breath, "Why don't you just—tear those ropes apart?" He burst into laughter.

A tear rolled down my cheek.

"Oh, come on," he said. "That was funny."

I sniffled before I could help myself. Rhyan would have never said that to me. Never made fun of me. But Rhyan would have also never tied me up. He'd have been the one tearing the ropes apart, killing anyone who got in his way to reach me.

And yet—I wondered if there was some way I could play on our history. To make him remember how we were, how he was. To reach the part of him that Auriel swore still existed.

"Rhyan, please," I begged, my heart pounding. "Please untie me. I need to go. Okay? I just need my weapons back."

His eyes softened. "I know. There's so many akadim here. Akadim who will hurt you. You really do need your weapons to defend yourself."

I nodded. "I do. I do. Against the others, but not you. I won't fight you. If you give them back to me, I'll leave you alone. You know I will. So, can you—can you do that for me?"

"Do that for you? Hmmm." He looked like he was considering it. Then he smirked. "You know I can do a lot for you, Lyr. Almost anything I want," he said, his voice suggestive. "But untying you?" He laughed.

My heart sank.

"No," he said, "I don't think either of us want that. Neither of us want you to leave. Because I can smell it on you." He skimmed my neck with his lips. His fangs sharp against my skin. "I can still smell your arousal."

His hand slid back down my neck, to my shoulder, moving lower. I burst into tears, a sob wracking through me as I felt his hand slide down my chest, toward my heart. He flattened his palm against it. My stomach twisted painfully, and yet at the same time, heat bloomed between my legs.

Gods.

The terror running through my veins was real, and yet, my body was still reacting on some level like this was just Rhyan. The Rhyan I knew, and loved, and trusted. Not the monster, not the akadim lying on top of me.

I squeezed my eyes shut, my entire body trembling, as his hand pressed harder against me. His elongated fingers touching the upper curves of my breasts, his clawed nails piercing the fabric of my tunic.

No. No.

"Please," I whispered. "Rhyan, please, don't." I looked up at him imploringly. His hand hadn't moved, he was still holding it against me, but he was wearing a curious expression now. He looked—Gods—he looked almost human.

"It beats so fast," he said. "Why does it beat so fast?"

"Because—" I started.

His hand slid over my breast, his claws just missing my nipple as he trailed down to my waist. And any humanness in his expression was gone. He was all demon now.

Tears blurred my vision. "Because I'm afraid," I cried with a painful gasp, "I'm afraid you're going to hurt me."

I knew that was a stupid thing to say to an akadim. But I didn't know what to do. How to react. Normal akadim I knew how to fight. Knew how to kill. But I'd never been tied up by one—never been with one that could talk and reason with me.

And I'd never been with one that was Rhyan. The man who I trusted more than anyone in the world. In the universe. The man, who until this moment, I'd believed with my whole heart would never—could never—hurt me.

Some part of me deep inside, was desperately clinging to the belief that I could appeal to him. Rationally. Like some part of him was still in there, and not lost in the in-between. He still had his accent, and his neatness, and fuck—it was dark and off-putting, but his humor had remained.

But this wasn't Rhyan. Rhyan would have never laughed at me, or tied me up.

Or touched me without permission.

"Hurt you?" he asked. "I don't want to hurt you."

I sniffled. "You don't?"

He tilted his head to the side, his eyes moving up and down my body. "I don't."

"You—you won't hurt me?" I asked, my voice small.

Rhyan laughed. "I said I didn't want to. Doesn't mean I won't. That all depends on you. If you're a good girl. Or, if you need to be punished."

"Rhyan, please," I said desperately. "Listen to me. This isn't you. This is not who you are or what you're like. But there's a way to fix this. I can help you."

"Help me?" he scoffed. "How do you think you can help me?"

"I can change you back. Bring you back to life. It can be like before."

"Before?" He shook his head. "Before when I was weak? Before when they took my power from me? No. I don't want to go back to before." He grinned, showing off the full length of his fangs. He'd been resting his weight mainly on his hands, keeping them on either of my head. But now his legs pushed mine apart, and he let his weight fall completely on top of mine.

I gasped. He was so heavy, it was hard to breathe.

"I have everything I want here. Power. Control. Strength unlike any I had before. I have an army beneath me, no laws. No Empire to bow down to. And now," he licked his lips, and pushed his hips into mine, "I have you. I could barely believe it when my scouts told me there was a girl skulking around the mountain. A girl whose hair turned red in the sun. I knew I had to come see for myself. Knew that if it was you, it had to be me who found you. Who claimed you. Because you're mine."

I shook my head. "I am yours. But not like this. Okay. Everything can be different for us," I said. "We can change things together. So much has happened since you went away. And I'll be by your side to get through it all. It will be better for you. I'll make it so. I promise, I swear."

He laughed again. "A promise from you? Why would I trust you? You've broken promises before."

I promise. I'll make the pain go away. And I swear on all the Gods, no one else will hurt you. No one else will lay a fucking finger on you. I'm going to take care of you, Rhyan. I swear.

"I'm sorry, I'm so sorry, Rhyan. I wanted to save you."

"Shhhh." He pressed a long-clawed nail to my lips. "Forget what happened. It doesn't matter now. Because you're here. And you're with me. I'm glad. I should have known you'd find me," he said. He'd spoken low, so low and so soft that it almost sounded like him. Those were his words, Rhyan's words, and his voice … if my eyes were closed, I'd think everything was okay—that I'd imagined he'd become akadim. That his weight was welcome on mine. That I wanted him. That I wanted this. But then he snarled, "Now you're here, now we're together. You can give me everything I want."

My body went cold. "And what's that?"

His growled, low in his throat. "You. Always. I want you." The red of his eyes lit up. "I've been deprived. Starving. You have no idea what it's like. The hunger. The need to fuck. And I've held back. Every time. But you're here with me. Now we can be together. Forever." He leaned in, baring his fangs, his eyes on my neck.

"No!" I screamed, and then I bucked and kicked my legs with all I had.

By some miracle, or perhaps Asherah helping me, I pushed him off and he rolled beside me. I immediately turned, trying to get out of the bed with my hands behind my back. My feet touched the floor and I made it three steps before his fingers looped through my ropes and I was slammed back into him.

"Don't run from an akadim," he hissed in my ear. "It makes us give chase. And excites," he pressed against me from behind, "other parts of ourselves."

I bit back a cry, my body shuddering.

"Then again, that is what you wanted, isn't it? Why you came here? To get fucked by one."

I felt myself recoil with disgust. "I don't. I—no. No."

"Not even if it's me? *Partner.*" He pushed into my back and while I'd become aware of his new height and weight, it was suddenly very clear that every part of him had grown substantially.

"No," I hissed. Godsdamn him. Every time he called me partner, it was like a punch to the gut. I took a breath. "Not even if it's you."

"Come on. You must have been missing me all this time the way I missed you." His hands started to slide up, sharp claws at the end of his nails grazed the undersides of my breasts.

I wriggled just out of his touch. "Rhyan. This isn't who you are. I know you and you wouldn't—You wouldn't do this."

He whirled me around, hands beneath my underarms, then he lifted me up, my feet dangling helplessly in the air as he licked my face, from my jaw to my forehead.

"Wouldn't I?" he asked, and slammed me to the floor. My knees collapsed. I was on my ass a second later, scrambling back away from him. "After all we had together, and all the ways I learned how to make your body scream, you think I wouldn't do the same just because I'm akadim?"

He reared forward, and hauled me back to my feet, one clawed nail ripping down the front of my tunic. The thread popped and my clavicle was exposed.

Fuck. Fuck! I eyed the collar on his neck. The one that bound him, controlled him.

"What about your queen?" I blurted out. "Morgana. I mean ..." I gasped, struggling to think, to breathe, as another thread tore. "*Maraaka Ereshya*. You serve her, don't you. She made you Arkturion?"

"Yes," he hissed. "*Maraaka*."

"Take me to her then," I demanded. "She'd want to see me. She'd want to know I'm here! Take me to her. Now! I'm her sister!"

He laughed, and his claws plucked at the threads on my sleeve, until they popped and the sleeve fell, revealing my bare shoulder. "I know who you are, Lyriana. My memories are not affected. I know who you are to my queen."

"Okay," I said, angling my shoulder away from him. My tunic was fast losing its ability to cover me. He went to work on the threads of my other shoulder. "Then can I see her?" I looked around, like she might pop up at any second. Maybe she would if she was nearby. She'd hear me, even if she wasn't. She'd read my mind.

MORGANA! I screamed internally.

"No," Rhyan said. "You can't see her."

MORGANA! IT'S ME! IT'S LYR! HELP!

Rhyan laughed again. "I know what you're doing. You're shouting for her in your mind, aren't you?"

I just stared. I didn't know how to answer, how to read him. In some weird way, this was almost exactly like talking to Rhyan—but then not. Like when I'd met Auriel. He was so like Rhyan it hurt, but in so many more ways, he wasn't. Yet Auriel hadn't felt cruel—he hadn't mocked or threatened me. He was trying to help me. And actual Rhyan—or akadim Rhyan—he was trying to hurt me.

"Your *sister*," he mocked, "is not here. We're close to finishing our mission. She had to leave for another. To prepare. But she'll return when it's done. When it's ready, then I shall present it to her."

"The green shard," I said, before I could stop myself.

He cocked his head to the side. "Of course, you figured it out."

"I know it's in these caves—buried beneath them."

Rhyan nodded. "We've been digging for weeks. Nearly a month. But I can sense it. My shard. Any day now, it will be free."

My eyes flicked to the bed—to the red shard. He could sense the green—but could he sense the red? Did he know what that was? Had he taken it because he knew, because he remembered—or was it just something shiny, something that caught his eye?

I narrowed my eyes. "And what about Aemon?" I asked. "*Ma-Maraak Moriel?*"

"He's with Morgana," he said. "Tracking down the next shard."

I blinked, taking that in. So neither of them were in Korteria. "Are any Lumerians here?" I asked. Rhyan shook his head. My stomach dropped. "Who's in charge?"

Rhyan laughed again. "Me."

"Just you?" I asked, my voice shaking.

"Are you still afraid?" he asked.

"Yes," I whispered.

"I can smell it, just as I can smell your arousal. Both are sweet. Both are—" His eyes glowed and he growled with a sudden violence I hadn't seen yet. He exposed his fangs and suddenly he lifted me up into his arms, and dropped me back on the bed.

The air left my lungs as I hit the blankets, and a shiver ran down my spine. Growls filled the alcove. Not just Rhyan's.

More akadim. And from the sound of it, they were all trying to push their way toward Rhyan. Toward me.

I eyed the red sword, and quickly tried to shift my body closer. If I could just rub the ropes against it, I could free my arms, I could fight.

But suddenly, someone was on top of me, and I felt fangs on my neck.

I screamed and kicked, feeling the red shard shift and fall from the bed—out of reach. Shit! Shit!

Rhyan hauled the demon off me, and threw him into the wall. There was a horrible crunching sound and a thud as he collapsed.

Two more burst through the alcove's entrance and I yelled out as two more akadim rushed for me.

But Rhyan got there first, cutting them off. He grabbed them, launching them forward. Their heads smashed into the stone walls, making a cracking sound before they fell.

Three unconscious akadim lay at his feet.

"We want her," said one, hovering in the entrance. Unlike Rhyan, he was nearly naked with short black hair. The ones on the floor were also without clothing. Almost none that I could see had any—only the collars. I wondered if that was on purpose—if they didn't care for clothing and Rhyan did—or if he just dressed up because of his title, because he was Arkturion.

Rhyan leaned forward, hissing and snarling at the akadim, his arms outstretched, claws taut.

"Give her to us," shouted the black haired one.

"This one is mine! NO ONE TOUCHES HER!" Rhyan roared.

"Why? We can smell her," said a blond akadim. He bounced from foot to foot, and gnashed his teeth, before sticking his tongue out. It was grotesquely long, hanging down past his chin.

"I don't give a fuck what you cretins smell! Because that smell is for me! She belongs to me! No one touches her. No one so much as *looks* at her. Or I will tear your heads from your necks. Now get back to work! That's an order—from your Arkturion."

A third akadim stepped forward. This one, alarmingly, was missing all of his teeth—yet his mouth still seemed sharp and deadly. His eyes were bigger than the others and had zeroed in on me. "We can't work now. We're hungry, starved. We need to fuck as much as you do."

By the Gods. No. No.

"Why do you get one and not us?" asked the third. "We can share. We can take turns. I'll even leave her arms on."

"NO," Rhyan said. "You know the rules."

The third grinned. "*Maraaka* said no. She forbids it." He touched his collar. "But, she's not here."

"You forget that I am! I enforce her orders!" Rhyan said with an icy violence. "There is no rape."

I blinked. No rape. Morgana had forbidden rape. Did that mean—Gods—did that mean Rhyan hadn't? Wouldn't? And the others?

I wanted to believe it. But I wasn't so sure—at least not since she'd been gone.

Because it was all over their faces. I could feel their lust and violence eking off them.

Maybe my earlier theory about them was right—that they'd been trapped inside here, starving, in every way. Forced to work, not eat, not rape, not kill. Not draw any attention to anyone that they were here. They had one job: dig.

They might have been controllable while alone in these caves. Away from temptation. But now I was here. Tied up. The easiest target in the world. Ripe for the taking.

And however much these akadim were evolved, able to walk in the day, able to think and use logic—however much control Morgana had, that didn't mean their baser instincts were gone. They were just lying in wait.

How far did the influence of those collars carry? I thought before that they were like a kashonim—binding them to her and Aemon. But were they acting more like a blood contract? How far away was she?

"The work is almost done," snarled an akadim—this one was beyond the alcove—and I couldn't see a face. "We deserve a reward! You know we do. *Maraaka Ereshya* doesn't have to know."

"She will know," Rhyan shouted. "You know the consequences of disobeying her. Of disobeying me! Now get out. You have work to finish if you want to even think about eating."

"We haven't eaten in days," came a shout.

"Tonight, you'll be fed. And that's only if no one comes near her again."

"*Maraaka* said no," said a new akadim. He had scraggly yellow hair that fell to his shoulders—but none on the crown of his head. He was still in the alcove, but towering above the others in front of him. "I can smell her cunt from here, and she wants it." Suddenly, his claws were out and he slashed the arms of the akadim in front of him. He tore into our alcove, his red eyes fixed on me, while others began to pour in, invading the space.

Rhyan leapt like an animal, tackling the balding akadim to the ground.

"Get back," he said, one hand around the akadim's throat, the other held up to the others. "Do you need a fucking reminder? What happens when you disobey?"

"No!" cried the akadim. "Arkturion. I'm sorry!"

But he pleaded in vain. A second later, Rhyan ripped his head off, and chucked it at full force into the gathered akadim. Slowly he stood, and walked to the other three who still lay unconscious, and ripped off head after head.

Bile rose in my throat, as I heard the sound again and again. Like the crunching of bones, and tearing into meat. I had to look away before I was sick.

"You want food?" Rhyan asked, throwing the heads at the demon. He wiped his hands together. Then he kicked the remains of the dead at the others. The bodies flew, grotesque and headless. "Feast! Then back to work! GO!"

Most scrambled away, hissing and growling beneath their breath. But there were three who stayed behind. They picked up the remains of the dead beasts, hunger in their eyes. They lowered their heads to Rhyan in a show of respect, and then they rushed off, their claws digging into their dead companions' flesh.

Alone again. Rhyan turned to me. He shook his head. "I need to get down there. We have a schedule to keep."

I nodded, too stunned to respond after what I'd just seen.

But then his words settled in my mind. If he had to get back to work—did that mean he'd leave me here? Alone? If he did, I could cut my ropes. I could find a way to escape before he returned.

He walked slowly toward the bed and picked up the red shard. "I like this one. I'm going to keep it."

My heart sank as he strapped it to his back. But if he at least left the others—

"You can't be here alone," he said. "I can control them. You saw. But they're beasts at the end of the day. So you're coming with me. It's the only way I can keep you safe."

"Where?" I asked.

"To the mines." He hauled me up to my feet, and dragged me against him.

"Can you untie me?" I asked. "Please."

"No."

"I won't ... I won't run away from you. You protected me. Like always. I want to be with you, Rhyan." A tear fell. "You know that. That's why I came to you. To find you. But the others—you saw what they were like. You have to untie me, just so I can defend myself."

His eyebrows lifted.

"Against the others," I said. "Because I'm yours. I won't let them touch me."

"They won't touch you. Because I won't let them," he said and reached below the bed. There was another piece of rope. He looped it around the one already around my arms, and then took the opposite end in his hand.

A leash. He'd made me a Godsdamned leash.

"And I'm not stupid enough to fall for that, Lyr. You'll stay by my side until the work is done. And then, I'm going to make you one of us."

"Rhyan!"

He tugged on the rope. "Come on, partner," he said, his voice cold and cruel.

Then he walked out of the alcove, pulling on my leash until I was forced to walk forward, lest I be dragged. Because this Rhyan wasn't going to stop if I fell.

A heavy rock lay outside the opening of our alcove. He pushed it between the walls, effectively turning it into a door, cutting me off from the room and all of my things. My swords, my stave, my armor. All of my weapons.

The cavernous walls loomed over me, and I could hear grunts in the distance. Rhyan moved forward, the red shard on his back glowing a faint red, before it blacked out leaving me in darkness with no choice but to follow him.

CHAPTER THIRTY-TWO

LYRIANA

Rhyan led me down the length of a long dark tunnel. I nearly gagged with each step. The smells wafting from the ground were awful. There were things I couldn't, and didn't, want to identify. But the main smell I recognized easily—the rancid scent of piss. It was like the akadim just relieved themselves wherever they were. Whenever they wanted.

I was willing to bet that Rhyan's little alcove was maybe the only enclosed space here that didn't smell completely disgusting. Another piece of him that had stuck. His hygiene.

A light flared ahead signaling we were reaching the end of the tunnel, and indeed, we walked out onto a stony pathway. The space opened up beneath high ceilings of dark, uneven stone. The footpath sloped upward, the incline almost breathtaking in its sharpness. And after a minute of walking, it had become so steep I felt like I was climbing up a mountain. I guess in a way I was, I was just on the inside of it. I had to lean all my weight forward to keep from falling. Between my arms being tied behind my back, and the way it attached to the leash in Rhyan's hand, my balance was completely thrown off. It was taking all of my effort to remain upright. Rhyan barely seemed to notice. He marched to the top with ease, his arms swinging carelessly. He didn't slow down, not even once. Not even to pause and look back, to check if I was okay.

My calves were already burning—even with all of my training as I climbed, desperately trying to match Rhyan's new pace. It was more than the fact that he wasn't slowing. Being a foot taller than before, his stride had widened. The ground was so rough, if I fell, he'd keep going and I'd be completely banged up as he dragged me along. Or worse, if he lost his balance, and fell with me, I'd plummet to the bottom. And thanks to my fucking leash, he'd crush me completely.

I tried not to think about it. The thought of falling. But mostly of Rhyan not caring—of Rhyan—*Rhyan*—putting me in harm's way. He was always so careful with me, always calculating our risks, looking out for every kind of danger we might face. I never knew anyone more prepared for threats than him. My chest panged. The Rhyan I knew would have already found a way to escape. He would have scooped me into his arms, gathered my weapons, handed the red shard back to me, and traveled us away from here. Somewhere safe, somewhere where we could be alone, and hold each other and …

Akadim Rhyan grunted, pulling me back to the present. And then literally, by pulling me forward with a rough tug that had me tripping over a small rock.

It wasn't him. It wasn't him. I had to remember that. Whatever features he kept, whatever memories he had, or personality quirks, it wasn't him, he wasn't inside that body. It was only a void for where his soul had once resided.

My feet ached from the sharp incline as I took another step, tightening my core to keep from falling over. Sweat beaded my forehead and the back of my neck. It started to itch. Gods. If only I could use my damn hands.

Finally, the ground evened out beneath me, and the walls opened up. We emerged from what was essentially a collapsing tunnel, into an expansive stone cavern. With each step we took, the ceiling rose higher and I caught the slightest breeze of air from ahead. It was stale, but it was moving.

I took a deep breath, trying not to consider the danger around me, or the danger I was bound to. I just had to survive. Not think. Not worry. Survive.

I had to focus on the things that were in my favor. And from where I stood, I had two. They were small, but they might be enough. First, I wasn't completely alone in this. Auriel was still out there. He hadn't been caught, and that meant he was trying to get to me, fighting to save me. Like Rhyan would have. Like *my* Rhyan would have ...

And second, despite how uncaring the akadim-Rhyan was for my person, however brutal or cruel, he was still just like the Rhyan I knew and loved in one very important way: he would kill anyone who tried to touch me. He already had. So as long as he was with me, no akadim could assault me, no akadim could hurt me.

Granted, that was only because he planned to do so himself—before he turned me akadim as well. My chest tightened. But I breathed through the pain. It was still in my favor, and I had to work with what I could. As long as the akadim under Rhyan's rule remained defiant, remained hard to control, and as long as they required Rhyan's supervision to finish their work—I could avoid being alone with him. I could delay whatever he had planned.

And when the time was right, when I had an exit in sight—if Auriel hadn't come for me first, I'd call on *Rakashonim*.

I just had to survive until then. Gather my strength, my courage and survive. And in the meantime, I'd learn the terrain, learn their systems, their weaknesses, anything. Find a way out of the ropes, and get out.

Rhyan stopped walking suddenly, and I caught up to him, the rope finally not taut between us. I'd been so focused on keeping up, not falling, and watching his back, I hadn't noticed that the path we were on had led to a sharp cliff. I didn't even want to comprehend the fall beneath us, or how high up we were. One wrong step and we'd plummet with no chance of surviving.

I swallowed roughly, taking baby steps back from the edge, as far back from Rhyan as I dared. "Is that the mine?" I asked.

"Right outside," Rhyan said.

And as I looked, I could indeed see the assembly line, a hundred akadim were at work below, grunting and cursing, relentlessly pushing out rocks. Some had stuffed carts full of them, some were carrying the boulders in their arms, and some were rolling them across the ground.

"You're close to finding the shard?" I asked.

Rhyan smirked. "Very close."

The walls shuddered around us and I froze. All along the walls, small cracks were forming, spidering into intricate webs. Small rocks spilling onto the ground. Nothing in this cave was stable, not with all the digging and mindless moving of rocks.

"Is this cave going to collapse?" I asked. Even though I already knew the answer.

Rhyan laughed. "Don't look so worried. The cave will hold until we have the shard. And when it does fall, we'll be long gone. At least, you and I will." Rhyan kicked at a loose rock, sending it over the edge of the cliff. It took an absurdly long time before the echo of it hitting the ground could be heard.

Fuck—we were high.

"What about the others?" I asked.

"They're my soturi," he said. "I'll get as many out as I can. But, they're not a priority. You are, and the shard. Whatever else happens, happens."

The walls shook again as a large groaning sound rose from below. I frowned, not sure I trusted Rhyan's confidence in the cave's infrastructure.

He shrugged. "Let's get down there."

"Down?" I asked, panicked. "How?" We'd had to go through a tunnel just to get up here, and I saw no stairs. Our path wound around a curve and vanished. I looked back to where we'd come from. That was lower ground—maybe we had to go back through there.

Rhyan watched me trying to puzzle it out and shook his head. "Alas, no. That way collapsed a week ago. Plus, the giant boulder they just excavated blocks every other way through."

"So?" My heart pounded.

"You have to cross to the other side to go down." Rhyan pointed ahead to what I guess technically one could call a bridge. It started across the cave at the edge of another cliff, and then it crossed the drop—but the end of the bridge couldn't be seen from where I stood. It must have ended around the curve behind us. I shuddered. It had been made of rope with wooden steps laid out to create the floor. It was thin, only wide enough for one person—or one akadim—to walk across at a time. And it was the flimsiest, most half-assed put-together-looking thing I'd ever seen.

"We have to cross that?" I asked.

An akadim was currently on it, barreling across. Unlike the others I'd seen, he wasn't a daywalker. This one was at least ten-feet tall, a giant even next to Rhyan. His face was monstrous—pale and sharp with all of the classical features of the demons. There was no trace of humanity remaining, not in the shape of his lips, or his eyes. Nor in the way he bared his teeth. I shivered on sight. Fuck. I'd never get used to them. And I was about to come face-to-face with him while completely bound.

The bridge drooped with every step he took, and a wooden floorboard loosened behind him, shifting out of place. Several floorboards were already missing, leaving tiny gaps. The next person—or akadim—who tried to step on it would fall if they weren't careful. I held my breath, waiting for him to finish crossing; waiting to see if the bridge would hold.

He vanished from sight, reaching the end around the curve. Heavy footsteps shook the ground and then he appeared, coming toward us.

"Arkturion," he growled, then stopped as his eyes fell on me. His fangs were out at once, drool dripping down his chin and an erection pushing aside his scrap of loin cloth. "Girl," he said, already reaching for me.

Rhyan caught his arm in his hand, staring the monster down. "Move along," Rhyan seethed, shifting his body protectively in front of mine.

"Want," growled the akadim, his eyes glowing. He lunged forward. But Rhyan pushed him forward, his own fangs bared.

The akadim's eyes widened. He was about to fall off the cliff. He hissed, trying to pry Rhyan's hand away.

"MINE," Rhyan growled. "She's mine. Now move." He tossed him to the side, and the akadim scrambled for the wall—just barely escaping with his life.

He bared his teeth, his eyes drawing my body as his nostrils flared, sniffing out my scent. But finally, he lowered his head, and turned, walking toward the dark of the tunnel.

"Our turn," Rhyan said, and tugged on the rope, pulling me closer.

"There's no other way?" I asked, my heart thumping.

"What do you think?" he asked, leading us around the bend.

"It doesn't look safe."

"Safe enough." Rhyan walked up to the cliff's edge and stepped forward, his boot landing on the first wooden board. The entire structure swayed.

I stood in place. If that bridge broke and we fell—we were both dead.

"Rhyan, wait—wait!"

"Lyr, I said come." He tugged violently on the rope, forcing me forward.

"I'm just—I'm scared."

He rolled his eyes. "I don't have all day."

I shook my head. "Is that how you got me here before? You carried me across this?" Gods, I didn't want to think about that. The idea that I could have plunged to my death unconscious.

But Rhyan shook his head. "No. We were on this side already."

My eyes widened. He had no idea what he'd just revealed. There was a way out, located past his alcove. And if I wanted to escape, that was where I had to go. I had to go back down the tunnel we'd climbed, get back to his alcove.

"You could take me back to your room," I said. "Leave me there."

"I said, let's go!" And suddenly he was in front of me, his eyes flashing with violence as he grabbed my waist, and hauled me over his shoulder.

"Rhyan!" I was bent over him, my ass in the air, and my face up close with the red shard, sheathed to his back.

He stepped onto the bridge and it swayed again, just as there was another wall-shuddering groan from the mines.

My stomach lurched. I had nothing to hold onto, nothing I could do like this, with my arms behind my back, my body bent. I was completely at the mercy of the bridge's structural integrity, and Rhyan.

I squeezed my eyes shut, praying I didn't hyperventilate. Praying more we didn't fall. Every sway, every groan, had my stomach tightening more painfully.

There was another shudder from the walls and the bridge shook. Rhyan paused. I dared open my eyes, praying we were at the other side. I nearly vomited. We were only in the middle, and Rhyan had just loosened another floorboard.

I watched it fall, spinning in midair until it thunked onto the head of an akadim with short red hair.

Rhyan continued forward as the bridge swayed again. I started holding my breath out of fear, gasping when we finally reached the other side.

I practically moaned in relief when he set me down. He just shook his head, like I was being completely ridiculous. Then he tugged me past half a dozen daywalkers, waiting to cross the bridge. Each one leered, sniffing and baring their teeth.

Suddenly I felt the claws of one of the akadim scratch down my back before grabbing my ass, hard. I yelled out in pain.

Rhyan turned. "Who touched her?"

None of the akadim confessed. Rhyan stepped forward, keeping a firm grasp on my leash. And I realized that whoever had touched me, had done me a favor. His claw had clipped the part of the rope near my hands. I could feel a loose thread. I quickly tucked it into my palm, drawing on it before anyone noticed. Another tug, and it started to give, unraveling even further.

When Rhyan finished berating them—allowing them to live this time—my fingernails dug into my palm, holding onto the loose threads.

Rhyan led me down the path, taking me to another bridge. Though this one was made of stone, it wasn't much better. The path was thin, and unlike the rope bridge, this one lacked railings. There was nothing to hold onto or grab if you lost your step.

I was careful to keep one foot in front of the other, keeping a steady pace behind Rhyan, before we descended into another tunnel, and then another, that sloped down and down and down and smelled even worse than the first one had.

After what felt like forever, we were back out in the open on leveled ground. We'd reached the floor with the carts. Looking up, I could see just how high the rope bridge was.

Way too fucking high. And to get out of here, I was going to have to cross it again.

Rhyan pulled me close, before addressing the akadim before him. There were dozens upon dozens, all at attention, all noticing me. "We're nearing the end of our work," he said. "Our sacred work for *Maraak Moriel*, and our queen," he tapped his collar, "*Maraaka Ereshya*. I have ordered a feast for you all tonight. You shall be fed in reward. Your dinner is being hunted for you now."

"Why can't we hunt for ourselves?" one asked.

"You know why," Rhyan shouted. "Our secrecy is important. Now back to work. All of you."

"Why's he get one?" someone whispered nearby.

"He almost got that other one," came a hiss.

I frowned. What other one?

"He's the queen's favorite."

An akadim, with an arm covered in tattoos, stopped pushing his cart and bared his fangs at the speaker. "He is Arkturion. You will obey him, get back to work."

Rhyan glared and nodded at the akadim defending him.

When the wheels started to creak again, he moved on, and led me further into the cave—toward the mines, through an underpass of stone. More akadim slogged through, pushing carts full of rock, while others ran back carts which had been emptied. It was darker here, and the ground seemed to rumble and vibrate as we reached the edge of a pit. Akadim ran back and forth with rock, while others were busy digging with their hands. Others had shovels.

My heart began to warm, a sudden heat inside my chest.

"Ah," I gasped out loud and bit my lip.

Rhyan snapped his head in my direction, his eyes narrowed, then they moved down to my chest, where a small golden light was bursting through my tunic. He grinned, tugging the rope and forcing me closer.

"I forgot," he said. "Your heart can sense these things." He drew a claw down my collarbone, slipping it beneath the top of my tunic, the material already torn.

I sucked in a breath as the sharp edge of his claw scraped against my bare skin. It caught on the fabric, and he tugged, making a ripping sound.

"Rhyan," I pleaded.

But he'd cut my tunic down, letting the remaining flaps fall open just above my breasts.

The golden light grew brighter. More than one akadim stopped working, taking notice.

"We truly are close," he said, almost in wonder. Then his eyes fixed, not to my heart, but to my chest. The tops of my breasts were on full display, and his tongue darted out, sliding against a fang, his eyes hooded. His chest heaved and I could see him straining against his pants.

"What happens after the shard is found?" I asked, hoping to put his attention elsewhere. "Does *Maraaka Ereshya* return?"

He stepped closer. "She's already on her way. She'll be here within a few days. And I'll present the shard to her upon her arrival."

Suddenly, the red shard on Rhyan's back began to glow as an akadim called out a request for an empty cart.

I stilled, praying Rhyan didn't notice the light, or that no one else did. It was bad enough he had the shard across his back. I didn't think he knew what it was. Maybe in his akadim form he couldn't feel the power of it. And I knew he wouldn't recognize the form—neither of us had remembered it was a sword. But still, knowingly or not, he had the one thing I couldn't leave without and I had no idea how to get it back from him.

"Hmmm." He let his hand fall on my shoulder again, then lightly let his claws slide across my bare skin.

I tugged at the rope in my hand, furiously working to unravel it further.

"Don't you need to focus on them?" I asked. "On keeping them in order?"

"My presence is enough to keep them working as hard as I want them to be."

And from the way that they did continue working—with only momentary pauses toward me—I believed him.

I swallowed roughly. The front of my tunic was hanging in two separate pieces and he pushed them both aside, revealing the full expanse of my upper torso, everything above my breasts. I could see it in his eyes. He was growing impatient. His energy had changed. The lust was consuming him, and he was starting to remind me more of the others—of the akadim that couldn't think, couldn't use reason.

"Rhyan," I said, my voice pleading. "What about the rules? What about what Morgana said. No rape."

He made a noise low in his throat and slowly shook his head. "It wouldn't be like that between us. It never has been."

"It would if I said no," I gritted, working the thread more quickly.

"Then don't say no. Say yes. You think I don't remember our last night together? How many times I plunged inside you, how many times I made you come."

Shit. Shit. More threads snapped.

"But the others," I said, looking behind him. "They can see us."

"Let them watch," he said, his fangs skittering across my collarbone. "Let them see me take you. Let them all know you belong to me. I could never claim you before publicly, and I hated it. I hated that I had to stay in the shadows, and keep our love a secret. And then I had to watch as Tristan and Viktor and Kane put their paws all over you, put their claims on you while I had to hide. Well, I'm not hiding anymore."

I tugged on the rope behind me, loosening another thread, and then another. He bent his head down toward me. Fuck. His tongue was on my collarbone.

I was breathing heavily in a way I hadn't expected. My body had been starving for his, desperate, and dying for his touch. But this wasn't it. This wasn't him. Wasn't Rhyan. It wasn't even really his body—but a distortion of it. A mangled twisted joke of what he was.

But yet, my body didn't seem to know that. I was afraid, my body sensed the akadim behind Rhyan, and yet, as dangerous as he was, his touches were igniting a fire inside of me. By the Gods, I didn't want this to happen. But I couldn't stop reacting.

I squeezed my eyes shut, and tugged again. And finally, finally, I felt my shoulders shift. They were sore and numb, but they moved away from the taut position they'd been forced into. My arms tingled as blood flowed freely through them, reaching out toward my fingertips.

"You want me, Lyr," he said. "Admit it. I can smell it."

"Not like this. Not when you're akadim. It's just my body reacting. It's confused."

"Are you sure it's your body that's confused?" he asked, his claws tangling in my hair. "I think it's your mind. Not ready to accept this. To accept us. We can still be together, Lyr. We can be together for real this time. Forever."

My mind flashed to Auriel, to his explanation of the Celestial Realms. An eternity together in these forms, even as we expanded, even as our souls continued to reincarnate, to live more lives, to fall in love again and again. We'd wake up in new bodies, find ourselves with new faces, new names, but we'd always recognize each other, always feel our soul connection. We'd always remain Rhyan and Lyr. Because we were Auriel and Asherah. Because we were *mekarim*.

Unless I couldn't save him. Unless I couldn't bring his soul back from the in-between and let him heal. But I wanted more. I wanted our life, this one. Mine and his.

"Rhyan—no! There's another way."

He laughed. "You're lying. You want this. And you know how I know?" He traced his hand down my stomach to my waist. I snapped my feet together, and pushed my hips back, dodging his touch. "You're wet for me. You always were."

"Maybe I am," I snapped. "But it's not for you. It will never be for you. My mind is not confused! Because Rhyan—the Rhyan I know—would never do this to me. Would never touch me when I said no. I know what you are. And you are not him," I growled, hiding the sound of another thread tearing, the rope loosening further.

He grabbed me, pulling me close, his hand reaching between my legs as he pushed me back against the wall.

Not knowing what else to do, I spat in his face.

He only grinned, and licked my spit with his tongue. "Mmmmm. I miss the taste of you."

My heart began to pound so loudly in my ears it was all I could hear, a steady beating rhythm. I hissed, my fingers moving rapidly. Another thread in the rope had come loose and I had to make an effort to keep my shoulders back, to keep my arms still so he didn't notice.

"You'll put the others in a frenzy," I pleaded, trying to find any sort of delay. "You saw how they reacted already. How many more will you have to kill? It'll delay your work. Lessen the numbers of your soturi. Your power. You won't finish in time for Morgana to return." I pressed myself back, using the rough-hewn stone of the wall to my advantage, to further tear and weaken my ropes. My fingers were getting scraped up, my arms. It didn't matter. Nothing mattered. I just had to get free.

"I'll control them," he said. "And the work will finish." His eyes flashed, and he tongued his fangs, sharp and glistening.

"I'll take you when I want, how I want. And I'll make you scream like you've never screamed before." His hand reached for my tunic, ready to tear it apart. Tear it off. It was the final straw. Rhyan knew—knew how much I hated this. How much it upset me, having my clothing torn, removed.

This was it. No more chances. I had to act now—or never. I chanted under my breath.

"*Ani petrova* Rakashonim, *me ka el lyrotz, dhame ra shukroya, aniam anam. Chayate me el ra shukroya. Ani petrova* Rakashonim*!*"

Heat exploded in my chest, my torso alight with fire as golden light streamed from my heart. My arms broke free, and I pushed him off me with such force, he stumbled back in shock.

"Arkturion," yelled an akadim in concern. But several had already stopped working, watching me with violence in their eyes, and blood rushing to their dicks.

Rhyan's eyes flashed, and I charged forward, punching him in the face.

He stumbled back, and another akadim yelled for his attention.

"Arkturion, there's a problem outside."

A problem? Auriel!

"Deal with it," Rhyan roared, rushing back to me. I shifted again trying to get to the shard. But he was too tall, the sword too out of reach. I ran back, urging him to chase me, and then I reversed course, leaping into his arms, and reaching over his shoulder, withdrawing the blade. It was glowing bright and red.

I held it up, I just needed to position it. Get it into his heart. Nowhere else. I couldn't miss. I couldn't miss. Or I could kill him.

But he was holding me too tight, and suddenly he was running, out of the mines and into the next room where he slammed me against a rock.

The air wheezed out of my lungs and I let go of the sword, hearing it clatter to the ground.

He kicked it behind him and it slid several feet out of reach. No!

"Fine," he said. "I was going to be gentle. But not anymore." He opened his mouth, his fangs out, and he bit down on my neck.

"NO!"

Rhyan was a force to be reckoned with when alive. As an akadim he was unstoppable, even with Asherah's strength.

All I could do was push my hand out, begging him to stop. My palm settled against his leather armor—right over his heart.

And suddenly, Rhyan stumbled back, releasing me. He looked stunned. Confused.

My heart shattered. His eyes. His eyes were no longer red. They were green.

He blinked, looking startled and lost. "Lyr?" he asked. And his voice. Gods. His voice. It was his! *His* voice. Soft and alive, and warm, and lilted.

"R-Rhyan?" I asked.

Then he blinked, and the green was gone, and so was the warmth and any semblance of humanity. The akadim had returned. The void. He looked bewildered, like he knew he'd lost a moment he couldn't account for.

"What the hell? How did you—?" But he paused and shook his head, suddenly aware of the sword on the ground. I ran for it, but he was faster, scooping it up, and flexing his arm before pointing the blade at me and charging. His arm shot out and he grabbed me as I was running away. With a grunt, I kicked out my foot, and tripped him, but we toppled together to the ground. Rhyan landed on top of me, flipping me onto my back.

He gnashed his teeth in my face. "That wasn't very nice."

"Well, I lost my manners," I gritted.

His claws dug into my arm, cutting me open—right where I'd been injured on the beach.

I screamed, and managed to knee him in the groin.

He winced, pausing just long enough for me to escape. This time I didn't hesitate. I ran. I had no weapons, just my strength. But I was unbound, and I had two arms, and two legs, and the stamina to run, and the energy to punch and kick at any akadim that got in my way.

Almost immediately, one got in front of me, and a second later, my fist was in his face, and the path was clear.

I could hear Rhyan screaming my name from behind. He was gaining on me. But he was also helping me escape by demanding everyone back off, and not touch me.

I pumped my arms at my side, urging my feet to run faster and faster, until I was past the carts and the rocks. I was back on the path that led to the tunnel that would take me up to the cliff, and back to the bridge.

"Lyr!" Rhyan roared.

But I wasn't stopping. I only ran faster on the incline, practically flying to the top of the mountain. And akadim stood there, waiting for me.

I didn't slow—I shoved him aside, and he slipped over the edge, catching the rock with his claws.

Then I kept going. Racing past another, before being grabbed from behind as an akadim leapt out of the shadows. He lifted me up, his claws around my waist as I kicked, suddenly finding my feet dangling over the edge.

"Put me down!" I screamed.

"I'll put you down—all the w—"

His words were cut off by the sound of a sword singing, and the wet slap of blood against stone, and the thud of a head hitting the ground. His arms loosened and I started to fall, but a large hand gripped me, claws wrapped around my neck, as I was dragged off the ledge, the headless akadim's body falling and falling.

"I said, don't run from akadim. It excites them," Rhyan sneered.

I waited until he had us turned, both of our bodies firmly away from the ledge and then I reached for his claws, and tore his finger back as my legs lifted and kicked him square in the chest.

He released me, and I slammed to the ground on my ass, but quickly scrambled to my feet, using the half second I'd surprised him to sprint. I ran across the stone bridge, and then finally, I made it to the top.

"Damnit," he yelled. I was coming to the edge of the cliff, to the rope bridge.

Fuck, fuck, fuck. I had no choice. I started running, holding onto the railings, my stomach dropping with every sway. I slowed down in the middle, conscious of where the floorboards had gone missing. And then I felt the bridge dip low behind me, all of the ropes shaking. Rhyan. My heart was in my throat, but I kept my eyes ahead, focused on the other side. Another step loosened and fell just as I reached the cliff.

And suddenly, Rhyan screamed.

I turned back, my heart stopping. His foot had fallen through the bottom. The step that had just dislodged.

One entire leg was dangling precariously off the bridge, while he balanced the other on one remaining step, his knee bent awkwardly, his claws hanging onto the roped railing. He wasn't able to pull himself up—the rope didn't provide enough leverage or support.

I backed up against the wall, my heart shredding into pieces.

There was a groan deep in the mines below, and another shudder of the cave, and Rhyan's step gave out.

He fell, his entire body dangling from the bridge. He was holding on to the ropes, and nothing else. His body was so heavy, and he was so twisted up in them, he'd never pull himself free in time to catch me. I'd be free. I'd find Auriel.

If I ran.

But if he fell to the mines, that would be it. He'd die. Die in his akadim form. Rhyan would never come back to me.

He might kill me if I went back for him. The bridge was already so unstable on its own, I was likely to fall.

And yet, none of that seemed to matter as I found myself running toward him, leaping over the missing floorboards until I reached him.

He looked up, and his eyes were red and soulless, but they were scared, and something inside of them still felt like Rhyan. I widened my stance, one hand braced on the railing, the whole structure shaking and swaying.

"Take my hand!" I yelled, reaching for him.

"What?" he asked. Like he didn't realize we were in the middle of a truce.

"I'm not letting you fall," I cried. "Now take my hand!"

He reached for me, and I pulled, my muscles straining against my injuries. But with a burst of energy, I tugged him toward me as my breath came in quick, painful spurts. He was so Godsdamned heavy, and with the unsteadiness of the bridge, I couldn't find my balance.

"Come on," I yelled, my hands sweating. The bridge swayed again and I tightened my grip, pulling with one last show of strength, using everything I had.

And then he was back on the bridge, landing on his belly before rising to his feet, one hand, large and clawed, tucked in mine.

Our eyes locked. The walls shuddered. And with our hands still linked, we ran to the ledge.

I slammed against the stone wall as far from the cliff's edge as I could manage, about to catch my breath, only to realize Rhyan was reaching for my neck, his eyes glowing.

"I knew you were mine," he growled.

But I pushed him back again, careful it was away from the cliff's edge. He stumbled and I spun on my heels. I raced for the tunnel, running as fast as I could, my feet flying. I didn't stop to look back, or try to make a plan, or fight. I just had to get out—get away. So I kept running, and running. Rhyan caught up fast—as expected. He was on my heels, close enough to breathe down my neck. I bore down into the reserves of the power I had left from Asherah, and I sprinted, my speed doubling—the way I'd been trained to at the end of our morning runs.

I could hear the sounds of a fight up ahead, a scream of pain and then, the most glorious and welcome sight in the world.

Auriel. His golden armor shining as bright as the curls on his head. And behind him, illuminating his body in the gold of a God was the sun.

He held a sword in each hand, half a dozen akadim surrounding him, another half dozen laid out on the floor. His face had twisted with the fury of battle. But his eyes found mine immediately.

"Lyr!" he yelled.

I gasped, so relieved that I stumbled, tripping over a rock. I slammed down onto my hands and knees. Rhyan threw himself on top of me, crushing me.

"Get off her," Auriel yelled. And without warning, he'd barreled into Rhyan, grabbing his shoulders and throwing him back.

"Come on," Auriel said, reaching for my hands. I gripped him, terrified of letting go as he brought me back to my feet.

Then his eyes flashed with green as they eyed akadim Rhyan, and I could see the moment he realized that my sword was on his back.

"The shard," he said, his voice panicked.

But I shook my head. There was no time. More akadim were already coming down the tunnel, rushing to defend their Arkturion—and hungry to attack me. And I was out of weapons. Auriel had gotten this far—but he couldn't take on all of these akadim alone.

The fight was leaving me ... I was starting to weaken. I stumbled, and Auriel caught my arm, holding me up.

"*Rakashonim*," I spluttered. "Running out. Need to go. Now!" Before I fainted. Before I fell over and lost myself to my injuries.

Auriel's nostrils flared, torn between me and the shard, but he lifted me into his arms, and then we ran out into the light, and didn't stop running until we were back at the inn, back in the room, the doors locked and barricaded.

Rhyan and the other akadim had stopped giving chase at the edge of the Wall of the Prince—perhaps under some order by Morgana not to reveal themselves in the town.

But we weren't taking any chances.

"Fuck," Auriel said, sitting me on the bed. "By the realms." He pulled back my hair, taking in my slashed-up tunic, the cuts on my arms, and the bruises everywhere else. "What did he do to you?"

I shook my head and burst into tears, feeling Asherah's power—my *Rakashonim*—running out at last. The effects of my injuries were now exploding across my body.

But worse, worse was the realization of what had just happened. What Rhyan had been like.

I couldn't answer Auriel. Couldn't bear to say it out loud. To make it a reality, to admit what the akadim version of Rhyan had been like, had done to me.

"It's okay," Auriel murmured. "It's okay. I'm here now. We're going to take care of this. You're going to be all right."

I met his eyes, my vision blurred by my tears.

"Lyr, I've got you," he said, his voice so soft, so quiet. So like something Rhyan would say. I looked away, trying not to think about the pain. Trying not to think about anything.

Auriel worked quickly, cleaning my wounds, slapping sunleaves over my cuts and scrapes. He eased me out of my ruined tunic, leaving me in my short-pants and breast bindings. But he found a fresh shirt for me to wear and slid it over my head and arms. Before long, I was covered in bandages.

Except for my neck. He placed the final bandage there, leaning in close, my body shaking. I'd been trying so hard to hold it in. To be strong. To fight what I'd seen; what had happened. And how again, I'd failed. I'd lost my weapons, and every chance I'd had with the red shard, I'd been unable to take it.

The moment Auriel sat back, the dam burst and I let out a sob.

"Lyriana," he said, pushing my hair out of my face. "You're going to be okay. These injuries are nothing next to what I've seen on you."

I shook my head. "It's not that. It's everything else." I looked down, staring at my hand. "It's the way he was." My voice came out as a whisper.

"He wasn't himself," Auriel said firmly. "That wasn't him. That wasn't Rhyan. Rhyan loves you. He would never ever hurt you. You have to remember that."

"I know, I know, but …" But he did. And it wasn't him. Not his body, not his soul, and yet … it still felt like he had. Hurt like he had.

"Shhh," Auriel said. "It's okay, Lyriana. It's going to be okay."

"He was so cruel, and mean," the confession started pouring out of me, "and … I know it wasn't him, but the things he said, the way he acted … he has Rhyan's memories and he was using them against me. Taunting me, reminding me. And …" And my Godsdamned fucking body betrayed me.

He'd even done the worst thing he could—ripping off my clothing. Rhyan knew better than anyone how that affected me after Vrukshire. Rhyan had been the only one I trusted to touch my clothes after that. And even when he was cutting my tunic open, my body still acted like it was him, like it was okay.

Auriel brushed a tear from my cheek, and pressed his forehead against mine.

"It wasn't him," he said. "It wasn't. Just a void, a shell of what he once was."

"It doesn't make it any easier."

"I know. It's okay. Any reaction you have to him is okay. Lyriana, he knows how to hurt you, the evil of the akadim means that he knows things he shouldn't. He has access to Rhyan's memories. But that's not him. It's a demon, an akadim animating his body without a soul. You hear me?" he asked, drawing his fingers across my hand. "The closest thing to Rhyan isn't that monster. What you just saw, what you just experienced is the farthest thing. Rhyan is good—Rhyan is his soul. His *ka*. And that's not what you faced back there. The closest thing you have to Rhyan right now is right here in front of you, *Meka*. Not that body, not that monster. Me. *I* am his soul."

I exhaled sharply, my eyes meeting his in a way that they never had before. Not in this life. I became acutely aware that our foreheads were still touching.

My breath caught, and Auriel froze, his body still as a statue, barely moving except for his hand around mine. His fingers made soothing strokes across my skin. Warm, comforting. Alive. The gesture was so familiar, so like Rhyan. Memories of Auriel ran through my mind. Memories of loving him as Asherah, and of feeling that love now as Lyriana. Of knowing I'd fallen in love with him again through Rhyan. Because he was Rhyan. And that love I'd felt for him, my *mekarim*, was thrumming through my veins, pulsing through my heart.

I leaned forward, just an inch, my lips humming from how near they were to his. I could smell him, the musk that clung to him from battle. And yet, perhaps because he was a God, there was a sweetness underlying it. A scent I wanted to bathe in.

I tilted my head, our lips nearly brushing together.

"Lyr," he breathed, his chin lifting, and that was all it took.

The distance closed between us, and my lips pressed against his. Something ancient and powerful seemed to zap through me, pushing out the pain, pushing out the hurt, the scars left by the Rhyan I'd just faced.

Auriel stilled, my lips tingling just from the barest touch. "Lyriana," he said again, his chest heaving. "What—What are you—?"

Our eyes met, our lips once more a breath away from each other, and I was suddenly lost in the sea of Auriel's green. The green I'd always loved. His eyes were hooded as he watched me, darkening with raw hunger—hunger I'd seen in my memories as Asherah. The same hunger that had been rising to the surface for weeks now.

His aura pulsed around me, pulling me in toward him, bright and warm and full of an unbridled need. A need for me.

And yet, there was still a question in his gaze, a small doubt. He had to know I was sure, as much as he had to make sure I was okay. I could see it—his concern, his worry.

But under it all, I could see something else. His love.

"Lyriana," he said again, his eyebrows drawing together. One final question.

I shook my head. "Don't, Auriel." I pressed my finger to his lips. "Just kiss me."

CHAPTER THIRTY-THREE

LYRIANA

Auriel's lips slid across mine as his hands cupped my face, his fingers brushing against my cheeks. He angled my head, pulling me closer and sucking my top lip between his, his tongue sliding against it. Shivers of pleasure ran down my body, as heat pooled in my core. Then he repeated the kiss on my bottom lip and moaned into my mouth. Like he'd been thirsting for me, starving. Because he had been. And so had I. He pressed another kiss, our lips fitting together like they were supposed to be, like they'd been designed for each other. Two halves of a whole.

"*Meka*," he whispered.

And that was it. That was all it took—a damn burst between us—weeks of pent-up desire and frustration, torment and denial were exploding as we lost ourselves in a frenzy of kisses. I couldn't get enough, I wanted to ravage his mouth, eat him alive.

Auriel groaned as our tongues collided. Every nerve inside me was alive and alight. I felt like I was sinking into my body for the first time in weeks, breathing for the first time since Rhyan had been taken.

I reached for his hair, tangling my fingers in his curls, caressing the nape of his neck as I slid myself onto his lap, my legs wrapping around his hips. I undulated against him, my chest rubbing against his armor.

His hand snaked toward my shoulder, and then down my spine, before lowering me onto my back as he positioned himself on top of me. His knees braced against the bed, between my legs, one hand pushing into the mattress by my head. Our eyes met, as he held himself over me and then he thrust down, his hips pushing against me, his hardened length sliding against my core.

I gasped, gripping his neck, kissing him deeper, and moaning into his mouth. I crossed my ankles around his hips, pulling him closer, urging him to go harder. My own hips lifted, seeking him out, desperate for more friction, desperate to feel his cock pulsing against me. I needed him, I needed this. Gods. I just needed more. So much more.

He pulled back, his eyes meeting mine dark and laced with desire, and with a feral growl, he reared his hips back, and slammed against me.

I cried out, sliding my hands down his back, my fingers digging into his waist, urging him on and on. Whispering in his ear, "Faster. Harder."

"Fuck," he growled into my mouth, circling his hips between mine. He was somehow growing thicker, pushing against me, right where I needed him. "You feel so good. It's been so long." He thrust again, crying out. "So long since it was like this." Then he was kissing me, sucking my tongue into his mouth, leaving me breathless as our bodies strained, pushing, grinding, trying to get closer, trying to feel more.

Auriel slid his hand down my side, finding the hem of the tunic he'd just put on me. He bunched it between his fingers, rucking it back up as his hand slid against my bare skin, sliding higher until his hand cupped my full breast. A second later, he was fumbling with the binding, sliding his hand beneath, his scarred and callused skin left me whimpering, and then mewling when his fingers squeezed my nipple. Pleasure rippled to my core, heat gathering in my chest, warming me from inside.

I bucked and my ankles unlocked, heels digging into the mattress as I lifted my hips up, meeting him thrust for thrust as our tongues tangled.

I was soaked, maybe more so than I'd ever been. My underwear was drenched, my arousal sliding down my legs, and I didn't know how much had been from my confusion with akadim Rhyan, and how much had been purely because of Auriel.

Tightness coiled tighter inside me, and I slid down the waist of his pants.

Auriel cried out, "Asherah. Asherah."

I stilled, my body going cold. Because I had my answer. It wasn't confusion over my encounter with Rhyan that had pushed me to this brink, this need. To this desperation to touch and be touched. To taste and kiss and fuck. And it wasn't because of Auriel either—not exactly.

His eyes widened, and he pulled his hand out of my shirt, immediately shifting his weight off of me, eyebrows furrowed with concern.

"You're kissing her, aren't you?" I asked.

He squeezed his eyes shut, gasping for breath, his chest heaving, and he rolled over to the side, sitting completely up, his jaw tightening.

I scooted back, and sat up across from him.

"I wasn't," he said quietly. "I was kissing you. But also …" He rubbed his face. "Also her. Because you are her. You're you, you're Lyr. You're both to me. And from my perspective, when I'm able to sit back and see things from my immortality, there's no difference." He smiled sadly. "But there is for you, isn't there?"

My eyes welled with tears, my chest tightening. "I was kissing Rhyan."

He sighed. "I know. It's okay. Come here," he said, patting the blankets next to him.

I shifted over, my body craving his warmth still, and he wrapped his arms around me. We sat like that, not speaking, not moving, for several minutes. Until the tears came again and Auriel remained by my side, holding me, rubbing my back, and making quiet shushing sounds in my ear until I was done crying.

Night fell around us soon after, and I confessed everything to Auriel. Everything I'd been unable to vocalize while he'd taken care of my wounds. I told him about the structure of the cave, the way Rhyan ruled over the others, and how close they were to uncovering the green shard. His shard. The way I could feel it, and the way it made the entire cave shake and shudder.

His eyebrows furrowed, listening intently. I could practically see his mind memorizing the layout I'd described, formulating a plan. And then upon his urging, I confessed everything that had happened intimately to me with Rhyan. The things he'd said. The things he'd done. The way he'd hurt me.

Auriel was silent as he listened, a quiet fury pulsing in his aura, his hands fisting in his lap. He looked ready to fight the akadim, to murder him, but he remained still, letting me continue.

When I was done, he sighed, him shaky, but as he took my chin in his hand, his touch gentle. He coaxed my eyes back up to his. "Lyriana, what I'm about to say to you is important. And I mean every word." He took another deep breath, his mouth tight, like he was fighting back his own emotions. "You were brave. And you were strong. You were strong for every second you were there—stronger than most would have been in that situation. Stronger than most could have dreamed of being."

I sighed and cast my gaze down again, my cheeks flaming. "I didn't feel brave. I was afraid."

"Lyriana, look at me."

I looked.

"That *is* bravery. Fighting back even though you're afraid, even if you might lose. You fought back, and you kept your mind. You did the right thing," he said, his voice firm and commanding. "You couldn't have done anything differently under the circumstances. You were smart, you survived, you saved his life, but most importantly—you saved yours. From the moment you were taken, I was out of my mind with worry. I was fighting my way to you—using everything I had. Nothing could have stopped me from reaching you. But you know what? If I hadn't been there?" He shook his head, his eyes sparkling with pride. "You would have gotten out on your own. You found a way to escape. You didn't even need me until the end. You're so much stronger than you know."

"But the shard," I said.

"Isn't lost. We know exactly where it is. Even if he doesn't know what he has on his hands, I guarantee you he's keeping it—he was wearing it for a reason. And I'd bet my eternity that he's keeping it close, very close. The same way he's hoarding your other possessions."

I started to realize how naked I felt without my armor, my chest plate, and my weapons. My tools. My protection. Over the last few months, they'd truly become parts of me.

I bit my lip, gesturing at my body. Even my belt was gone. "He took everything."

Auriel shook his head, and slowly, he reached for me, his hand settling carefully over my heart. "Not everything."

I sucked in a breath, my heart pounding and then warming against his touch. The light inside me had woken. The red light of the Valalumir, the other half of the red shard in Rhyan's possession. A golden glow began to emanate, making the tan of Auriel's skin shine. It had started to warm when his hand was in my shirt before, when he was teasing me, pleasuring me. But here now, his hand still and directly over my heart—it had fully awakened. Pulsing, and flickering with flames.

"You see," he said, taking my hand in his. "So here's what we're going to do. Nothing tonight. You're injured. You need the time to heal. I've done all I can, now your body will do the rest. As for me, I need a few hours to gather more weapons, find you some armor. Then tomorrow night, at sunset, we go back to the cave."

"And do what?" I asked. "Knock on the door? Announce ourselves?"

"Yes," Auriel said. "That's exactly what we're going to do."

I shook my head. "Auriel, come on."

"No, I mean it. You are going to march up to the mouth of the cave. You are going to demand entry to the Wall of the Prince, like the warrior you are, and you're going to tell them that Lyriana Batavia is here. Because your name is power. All you have to do is say it, use the leverage it gives you. You'll be brought inside, and taken to Rhyan directly, if he doesn't come out to greet you himself."

"And what if he doesn't do that?" I asked. "What if they don't listen? What if there's orders to kill me?"

"There aren't," he said.

"How can you be so sure?"

"Because I know Rhyan better than I know anyone else in this world. I know today was hard, and he was—" he sighed, "He was awful to you. But, before he lost his soul, his personality formed—and it was influenced by mine. In the end, he and I are one. And I swear to you, I know some things that will never change. You saw it yourself. Things stuck even with his soul gone—things that formed him, that made him who he was before he was akadim. Things that are so core to who he is, they can't be taken away, even by the void in his body. His hygiene, his organization, his lilt, his strength and discipline, even his humor—albeit twisted by the magic animating him, but it was still there. And most importantly of all, the one thing that will never ever change—that can never be broken or tampered with because of how central it is to his being—is how protective he is of you."

I frowned.

"He didn't let anyone hurt you," Auriel said. "And he wouldn't let anyone touch you. He killed every akadim who tried to. His goals might be twisted now, but he's not just hoarding your weapons for tactical reasons, or because he needs them. Not one akadim is looking at them. Because they don't care. And you know why. You remember the second rule of being a soturion?"

I squeezed my eyes shut, still recalling that day of training. Being alone with Rhyan for the first time in our training room as he patiently explained the rules. Stop the threat. That was the first rule of being a soturion. And then the second rule. I met Auriel's gaze. "Akadim are the weapons."

His jaw clenched as he nodded. "Exactly. And the third rule, follow the chain of command. Rhyan has no need for your weapons. *He* is the weapon, and as Arkturion, especially considering the soldier he was, he's making sure his orders are followed. I guarantee it. He has one reason to hold onto your things and one reason only—they're yours. They remind him of you. Because as twisted as he is now, that never goes away. You say your name and you will have safe passage to him. From there, it's up to you. You say your name, go before him, and then, the fight is on. Everything you need will be in one place—Rhyan, and the red shard."

"And what about you?"

"I'll be right behind you. Watching your back. Fighting any akadim who break through Rhyan's command. He has a lot of control, more than I've ever seen—I don't know how. Losing control over a handful of akadim is nothing. He shouldn't have control over even one."

"It's not just him. It's the collars," I said.

But Auriel shook his head. "No. It's something else. Those only give Morgana control. Still, this will work in your favor. It already did. I'll follow behind you. Watch your back. And while you're with Rhyan, I'm going to get my shard back. Because I'll be damned if after all that, it ends up in the wrong hands again." He eyed me carefully. "Nothing's going to happen to you, Lyriana. I swear. I won't let it."

"And if I fail? If I can't cure him?"

His eyes darkened. "You won't fail."

"Auriel, I need to be realistic. We haven't seen the cure work once. Not that we've had many opportunities." Only Auriel using the shard on one akadim our first night here. All the other Godsdamned akadim have been hiding. Digging in the mines with Rhyan. I drew my knees to my chest. "I know you've seen it happen. But that was a thousand years ago. What if things have changed?"

"This hasn't. The power of the Valalumir—even in its crystal form, even shattered into pieces—it's still as strong as the day it was created. Even now, I can sense the green shard in ways I couldn't even a day ago."

"There was one moment," I said, "between me and Rhyan, when my hands were finally free. I touched him—I touched his heart, and it was like a flash, like he was back."

Auriel frowned, his gaze distant. "You didn't mention that before." His eyebrows furrowed. "What do you mean he was back?"

"Like it was him," I said. "His eyes were green. He looked confused, like he didn't know what was happening.

Couldn't remember where he was. And he—he said my name. Just my name. And when he spoke—his voice was his. Not just the lilt, but the timbre, the tone—everything. It was his voice. There was no akadim inside him when he spoke. For a moment it was like … like Rhyan's soul had returned, like he was looking at me through the monster's eyes."

"That would explain it," Auriel said.

"Explain what?" I asked.

"There was a strange moment for me. I think I felt it," he said. "This was just before you escaped?"

I nodded.

"I was fighting an akadim," Auriel said. "I had the upper hand, I was about to knock him out—it was almost too easy. And then I stumbled and I missed. For a whole moment, I couldn't recover. Like I lost all my strength."

By the Gods. Auriel had said he couldn't be here if Rhyan's soul was. That they both couldn't be here at once. Had my touch called it back?

"What does that mean?" I asked, my heart pounding. "What—What happens to you if he's cured?" It was a question we'd been dancing around. Mercurial had figured out how to activate the impossibly rare scenario that would bring Auriel back—but this had never happened before. What would happen to him next?

Auriel shook his head. "I've been wondering that every day since I arrived. And honestly, I don't know." His jaw clenched. "I just don't know."

I wrapped my arms around him, pulling him into a hug, burying my face in his neck.

"I don't want anything to happen to you," I said, my voice hushed.

"Hey, now. I'm still a God."

I sniffled.

But Auriel cleared his throat, choking back his own emotions and hugged me to him. "I think we're safe tonight. I don't sense that they're any closer than before. Even if they do uncover the green shard—they're under orders to hand it over to Morgana, right? And Rhyan said she'd be here in a few days?"

I nodded.

"Perfect. Plenty of time for me to recover it myself. So how about this, why don't you take a hot shower, and get into bed, try to relax. I'm going to go out and find something for you to eat. And then," he pulled his hood over his head, casting his face in shadow, "I'm going to bring you weapons."

I laughed. "Exactly what I want for dessert."

He smiled, and brushed my hair back, his hand lingering on the bandage across my neck—the place where Rhyan had bitten me, had sucked my blood. Anger sparked in his aura, but he let it go. Then he leaned in and kissed my cheek. "Go on. I'll see you soon."

I grabbed his hand as he stood. "Auriel—wait. About earlier—the kiss … I'm sorry."

He let out a sharp breath, and shook his head, a rueful smile on his lips. "I'm not. I'd do it again. I'd do it all again for you, *Meka*. Fall. Steal the light. Burn my hands. Cross the realms of time and space and defy every member of the Council. All just to be with you—even if only for a moment. Even for just one kiss. In every lifetime, every body, every name, every face." His eyes crinkled. "It's an honor to fall in love with you in every life. I'm yours. Always. But you knew that. My soul has always been yours."

"*Rakame*," I said. Your soul is mine.

He grinned widely, a tear running down his cheek. Then he nodded, squeezing my hand. And he was gone.

Hot food was waiting for me when I got out of the shower, and hours later, when I opened my eyes, I was tucked under the blankets and drowsy with sleep. A sword had been laid on my nightstand. Auriel kissed my forehead, pulled the covers over my shoulders and whispered my name. I fell back asleep.

When I dreamed, I dreamt of Rhyan. Of emerald green eyes, and a soft Glemarian lilt. Of my lover on a boat in the ocean, and waves that were finally calm.

CHAPTER THIRTY-FOUR

LYRIANA

The next night, Auriel knelt before me, strapping the final knife to my thigh. I was covered from head to toe in new armor and weapons. Well—new to me, at least. I didn't even need to use glamour magic to blend in now—I was dressed as a wolf. Silver armor covered my torso, and matching cuffs were at my wrists. Auriel had located a soturion belt with fresh Valalumir stars embedded in the leather straps. Two swords crossed my back, and another hung from my hip along with two daggers, one on either side, and a knife, hidden in two garter belts. If only we'd had these when we were investigating each town. But I much preferred my own effects, my own armor and weapons.

I had tried to ask Auriel how he procured each item, but he wasn't willing to discuss it which made me think it wasn't exactly legal. Then again, it wasn't like these were items one could simply purchase—especially not late at night in a small hillside town on the western border.

He tightened the leather belt of my garter, tugging on the strap to make sure it was firmly in place. His eyes flashed as he looked me up and down, and for a second, I caught a hint of the passion that had burst between us yesterday. His hand lingered on my thigh, giving my leg a squeeze before he let go, and rose to his feet, looking me over studiously, checking that each weapon was in place, and secure.

Exactly like Rhyan would have done—even down to the squeeze, like he needed just one more touch. One more reassurance that I was there and so was he.

My throat was dry as I pulled my gaze away and looked out of the window of our room at the inn. The sun had set and the sky had darkened. It was time to make our move.

Auriel slid his hand over the hilt of his swords, something I'd started to notice he did before battle, a small moment to familiarize himself with the weapons. The rest of his body was preternaturally still. There was something else in the air between us, passing back and forth from our auras—this kind of feeling of finality. Like this was it.

And on some level, deep down in my soul, I knew it was. I wasn't going to get another chance to attack Rhyan, or to cure him. If I failed tonight, it was likely because we didn't make it. Either because I failed to cure him, or I failed myself in going up against him. And much as akadim Rhyan still wanted me, even he was going to prioritize his own survival at some point. I'd spent some time in the morning reading again from Auriel's Valya, focusing particularly on the sections that spoke about the akadim. Sections not included in the Mar or Tavia versions I'd always known. We'd never been taught about this in the Academy since the cure had gone out of existence. According to Auriel's writings, akadim when faced with the idea of becoming mortal again, being cured—reacted similarly to the way we did when confronted with being turned. They saw it as a death sentence.

The moment he began to truly fight back, to use all his strength against me—I was going to need to call on *Rakashonim* to survive. And then I wouldn't have long before it wore out.

Whatever we did tonight—it had to fucking count.

Auriel met my eyes, his jaw tight, and his shoulders tensed. He opened his mouth, like he wanted to say something more, but then he snapped his jaw shut. Instead, he nodded, and flipped up his hood, covering his head, his face darkened in shadows. I did the same, and then quietly, we crept out of the inn, into the silence of the night.

The air was cool against what little skin I had exposed, and felt far colder than it had the last few weeks despite the fact that we were now even further into spring. In another month, the weather, especially this far south, would begin to heat drastically.

I closed my eyes, trying to imagine it. The warmth of the sun on my skin, the familiarity of the heat. Home. Bamaria. Hot and safe. And Rhyan by my side. My Rhyan. It felt like a dream. One I could barely grasp. Especially now I was forsworn, not even allowed back in my own country. Now my country didn't even exist. If Rhyan and I got through this, our best-case scenario—after I found Jules and Meera, and made sure they were okay—was likely exile.

"You all right over there?" Auriel asked. He reached for my hand and helped me climb the hill we were on. They surrounded the town and the inn we were staying at. There had been a more direct path leading from there to the mouth of the caves—but the only time we'd used it, was yesterday in our escape.

Now, we had to be sure that we couldn't be spotted. Our cloaks would have made us invisible to any other Lumerian nearby. But magic didn't work on akadim. And I knew they could see in the dark far better than we could. Still, the cloaks were made of a material that naturally camouflaged with the terrain. I prayed that that would give us enough cover to approach, and catch them off-guard.

Whatever happened, I wanted Rhyan to scramble when I arrived—I wanted to catch him unaware. I was sure he expected me to return. He knew me after all. And the fact that none of the akadim had come looking for us, seemed enough proof of his mindset. But we still needed the element of surprise to ensure Auriel remained hidden. That was key.

We both ducked low as we moved down the hill, moving slow and taking breaks behind trees, looking out for scouts or any sign of akadim.

The Wall of the Prince was close, its mountain peaks only a faint outline in the starlit sky. A small woodland lay ahead, the silver leaves of the moontrees glimmering. Auriel took my hand, and together we dashed from our hiding spot, our boots racing over the ground until we were covered once more by trees. I could see the hidden opening of the cave—the one we hadn't been able to find—until my escape. Two akadim stood before it on guard.

My stomach knotted seeing their red eyes glow against the dark.

Auriel peered around the tree trunk. "Damn," he said. "Not daywalkers."

"No. Those are definitely originals." They were huge. At least ten feet tall, their faces grotesque with large fangs protruding from their mouths. "Fuck." I frowned. "Do you think Rhyan put them out there for a reason? Because of all his akadim—those are the least likely to follow orders."

Auriel's eyebrows furrowed as he continued watching. "They might be a deterrent," he said. "He'd know that's the case. He might expect you to come to the same conclusion."

"You think he'd really try to keep me away?" I asked.

Auriel sighed. "No. But he saw I was with you. Maybe they're for me."

"Or it's a trap. I don't know if I trust them to follow orders."

Auriel leaned his head back against the tree, deep in thought. "I'd say it was a trap, too—but there isn't one inch of that cave that isn't."

"So, what do we do? Stick with the plan?" My stomach turned at the idea of handing myself over to those monsters.

Auriel blew air out of his lips and shook his head. "Yes. But I think we need to kill them first."

"Are you sure? I mean, what if there's a chance I can—"

He shook his head. "No. Trust me when I tell you that I hate this. But you can't save everyone. And you won't save anyone at all unless we get the red shard, and the green before it falls into Moriel's hands."

I frowned but nodded, my stomach twisting. "Then what?"

"Same plan as before. But I don't think you need to knock. Last time, the doors were closed—all the akadim were inside, except for the handful I fought when Rhyan took you. After that, I spent an hour searching the mountainside, climbing up and down—looking for any way in. It wasn't until one came out that I had any luck. If they're there now—then the door is open. We'll take them out, then slip inside. If the way is clear, you'll move through the cave unseen until you find him. Until you can cure him. But if someone finds you, then the first plan is a go. You tell them your name, and you demand to be brought before Arkturion Rhyan."

I took a deep breath. "Okay."

I'd barely taken a step when Auriel grabbed my waist and pulled me against him, crushing me in a hug. I could feel his heart beating even through all of our armor. Feel his pulse in his aura.

"Do not give up," he said, his voice fierce and commanding, but under it all was a wave of emotion. "No matter what. Whatever happens in there, you are stronger than you know. You are strong enough to do this, strong enough to finish this. To save him." He released me, his hands on my face, his gaze intense. He pressed his forehead against mine, and then stepped back, his jaw clenched. "Do not give up," he said again.

"I won't."

"I know." His nostrils flared.

"Auriel," I said, my heart pounding. "Thank you. For everything." I tried to put as much feeling as I could into my words. Because there was so much he'd done for me. It was so much more than helping me get here, helping me find the cure and learn how to wield it. He'd kept me going, kept me from giving up. If he hadn't come to me when I was lost in the initial despair of losing Rhyan—I didn't even want to think what I would have done.

He shook his head. "No need for any of that." And like always, he seemed able to put words to my thoughts. "You would have found a way on your own. You always do. Now go. I'll be right behind you," he said.

Our eyes met, one final blazing meeting. Then I made my move, pushing away from the tree, and ducking low. I moved slowly and silently across the valley, keeping my senses on high alert—making sure I never got the sensation of being watched, or the awful feeling I got when akadim were near. I was aware of the two at the door—but if any others came, I had to know immediately. And, I had to make sure that the two on guard remained none the wiser.

Luckily there was a soft breeze in the air—one coming in my direction from down the mountain. It would keep my scent hidden—just a little longer.

The grass was high and wild and I was able to easily keep my head low, but I was nearly within a dozen feet of the beasts. I glanced back, and saw what appeared to be a very tiny mound of dirt that hadn't been there a moment before. Auriel.

I took a deep breath, remembering my training. My fingers tightened around the hilt of my sword. And I heard Rhyan in my mind again.

If you need to defend yourself—strike first, think later.

Another step and then both akadim stilled, their nostrils flaring. They sensed me.

No more hiding.

I jumped and I ran, brandishing my sword, and leaping before either could react. I landed on the back of the one nearest, grabbing hold of its neck. My thighs clamped down as I hoisted myself up, climbing as high as I could. He roared, flailing his arms to try and reach me while his companion approached. A claw swiped, and I leaned back, just barely avoiding getting cut. The akadim I'd climbed onto growled, and cursed, stumbling back from his friend. He raised his arms, trying to attack me. But I'd already positioned the blade of my sword, both hands on the hilt. My legs squeezed, and I stabbed down, plunging the blade into his back.

His arms flailed, still trying to reach me. Suddenly, he slammed his back into the wall of the cave. I wheezed on impact, the air flying out of my lungs. His head crashed into my belly.

Gasping, I held on, pushing deeper and twisting the blade.

He stumbled forward, and reared back, but I jumped to the ground, just before he collided with the stone again. I ended up on the ground between his legs, rolling forward to safety. But his friend was waiting. He grabbed my shoulders and hauled me into the air, his claws biting into my flesh. I hissed, feeling blood trickle down my arms.

Fuck—I missed my Bamarian armor.

He bared his teeth, roaring into my face. I tensed, unsure if this would alert the others, or Rhyan. But no one came, and a second later, he slammed me to the ground. I landed on my ass, without enough time to move before he flung himself on top of me.

His weight was crushing. My legs were completely immobilized. Kicking was useless, and I realized with horror that this one had no interest—not yet at least—in killing me, or drinking my blood. He was excited in another way. One clawed hand pressed against my chest, pinning me to the ground, while his other hand fumbled to find between my legs. I reached for my dagger at my hip—the closest weapon I could find and plunged it into his side. It did nothing. He didn't even flinch. I pulled it out and I plunged again and again and again.

Finally, he reared back, making a garbled sound of pain. I stabbed once more. He slapped me across the face, just before his eyes widened. A heavy thud sounded behind me.

The first akadim was dead—his body falling over. Auriel stepped out from behind him, looking rather pleased with himself. He reached down, and pulled my blade out of his back, then chucked it at the akadim hovering over me.

It pierced him through the shoulder, and I used the moment to withdraw my dagger and plunge it in again, twisting this time, digging deep into his muscle.

Then I reached for the blade still stuck in him, pulling it out. He seemed to realize he should have called for help at that moment. He was too late. I swung, cutting his neck.

He screeched and reared back, clawing at the wound and blade embedded there. I rolled out from beneath him, and jumped to my feet. The akadim sat back on his knees. Auriel approached, a fresh sword between his hands.

And it was at that moment the demon made a fatal mistake—assuming Auriel was the bigger threat and forgetting me.

He attacked him, swiping his claws at Auriel's arm. Auriel dodged, and just before the akadim could try again, I pulled the sword from his flesh, and lifted it over my head, swinging at his neck one more time.

I lopped through skin and muscle until I hit bone, managing to cut halfway.

Auriel swung next—administering the final blow. His head rolled off.

I grabbed my blades, quickly wiping them on the grass. Auriel dashed toward the cave's entrance, and pushed the rock aside. My heart thrummed as he vanished into the shadows, and then stuck one hand out, beckoning me inside.

No akadim were nearby. He'd been right.

Darkness filled my vision. I could barely make out Auriel's silhouette in the shadows.

He took my hand, and led me further in, until we came to the corridor from where I'd escaped. There were several paths that opened up. But I knew the one we needed lay right before us. It sloped up, leading to another darkened corridor—the one that would take us to Rhyan's alcove, to my weapons. In the distance, a torch flickered faintly. A loud shuddering groan shook the floor beneath us. The walls began to vibrate.

I stumbled, falling into Auriel's arms. The shaking continued. A rock dislodged from the ceiling, groaning before it fell, nearly crushing us. Then another dropped, this one shattering into tiny pieces by our feet. The smaller rocks skittered across the floor.

I threw my hand over my mouth to keep from yelling.

Another earthquake-like rumbling hit. More rocks loosened and fell. Tiny ones at first. And then there was a crash before the cave's mouth.

"Fuck," I hissed. The only exit I knew about was gone—completely covered in rock and debris. The ground seemed to hum, shaking with small aftershocks. And then at last, it stilled. "Gods. Are they all digging at once?" I asked.

I looked around, trying to see as best I could in the dark. We were solidly inside now, well past the entranceway, and not one akadim had appeared. Nor had any seemed to notice that the guards out front were dead.

Auriel's eyes glowed with a sudden bright green in the dark, and he gasped. "It's my shard." He clutched at his chest. "I can feel it. They've broken through the final barrier."

My heart thundered. "How long do we have?"

He shook his head. "Maybe minutes."

"Let's keep going," I said, rushing ahead, and there it was, the rock that stood in front of Rhyan's alcove.

"This is it," I said. "This is where my weapons are." I started pushing at the giant rock, grunting with the effort to move it aside. But as expected, it didn't budge—not even an inch.

Auriel caught up with me, and placed his hands on the boulder. Together, we managed to push it past the alcove's entryway. I cringed as it groaned. If any akadim were in our corridor, they'd hear. But then another shudder ran through the cave, and the grinding sounds of rock and stone were drowned out by the noise of the shifting mountain.

The path to Rhyan's alcove was clear, and I dashed inside, finding the torch stuck into the wall. Auriel went to work on the pile of bramble Rhyan had already assembled to light it. So neatly arranged.

My heart panged. Flames flickered to life, the torch brightening every wall of Rhyan's room. In the same corner was my armor, my weapons. And my stave.

I started stripping at once, unbuckling my belt, and unhooking all the clasps on my silver Korterian armor. Auriel was behind me a second later, the torch lit, finishing the job, discarding my wolfish armor onto Rhyan's bed. Then he went to work hooking all the clasps and buckles of my Bamarian armor, while I focused on my belt, reattaching the leather scabbard, my stave, and my dagger. I switched out my borrowed sword for the one I knew, and trusted, and at last, Auriel picked up Asherah's chest plate, his mouth tight as his fingers squeezed around the gold metal. He let out a shaky breath, his eyes watering.

"Auriel," I said softly.

He shook his head. "It's okay. Hold your hair back for me."

It was already pulled into a soturion-issue braid, but I held it off my shoulder as he asked. Auriel shifted behind me, and laid the chest plate across my armor. His fingers brushed against the back of my neck, as the clasp hooked. When he was done, he kept his hands on me, just a moment longer, his fingers grazing the metal, sliding toward my collarbone. Then he pulled back, and I turned to face him.

He stared at the Valalumir stars, their centers glittering red under the torchlight, before lifting up my hood.

"I'll never get over how it looks," he said, his eyes on the chest plate, "after all these years, it's exactly the same." His eyes met mine. And he shook his head. "Or you." He swallowed. "Only one more thing to make your outfit complete."

The red shard.

But before either of us could say anything, a vicious growl sounded from the hall. I spun on my heels and found an akadim waiting. A daywalker.

He lunged, but I picked up one of the spare swords and threw it like a javelin at his heart. His eyes sparked and then paled as he collapsed to the ground. I stared, wondering if he could have been saved. Gods, the guilt I now felt for each one.

"Hurry," Auriel said, lifting my hood back up. "Before more find us."

We dashed out of the alcove, and started running for the corridor and the tunnel that led to the top of the cliff. It spilled out at the edge, my stomach twisting as I was confronted again with the sudden drop below and the bridge in the distance which had even less integrity than before. More floorboards were missing, and some of the rope was fraying where it had been tied. The knots in my stomach tightened painfully.

"We have to go across *that*?" Auriel asked when he caught up to me.

I nodded, my back sliding against the wall. I pushed Auriel back next to me. All it would take for us to plunge to our deaths would be another shudder of the cave as the akadim continued to dig below.

But they weren't all down there. Across the cavern, three akadim appeared, marching in line, heading for the bridge. Toward us.

"Shit."

"Keep your head down," Auriel whispered, shoving his body protectively in front of mine.

I slowed my breathing.

Auriel squeezed my hand.

The first akadim had blond hair, cropped short. The kind of blond that was unmistakably Ka Kormac. He stepped onto the first floorboard, his red eyes narrowed as he looked across, just missing where we stood. He took a step, and the next akadim moved behind him.

"All soturi to excavation," came a command. It was from below. Not Rhyan, but another akadim, perhaps his Second. "All soturi to the excavation level now."

"Final push," Auriel said. His mouth tightened, and there was another flash of green light from his eyes. "I need to get down there."

The akadim turned back from the bridge, marching back down the cliff, to the mine. We'd get across easily now. But once we descended to the lowest level—we'd be surrounded. At least a hundred akadim stood between us and the green shard. Between me and Rhyan.

"No turning back now," Auriel said.

I leaned my head back against the wall, and took a deep breath. Finally, I straightened and nodded. "Let's go then. This way." I led Auriel around the bend. The end of the bridge was in sight. The rope's edges had been tied around two hefty stakes embedded in the stone.

I stepped forward and grabbed hold of the handrails, but made the mistake of looking down. The hundred akadim were moving below, pushing carts back and forth. Dumping rocks and dirt and debris, and then running their emptied carts back toward to the excavation site, to the pit they'd created.

"Don't look down," Auriel said. "Just go."

I had done this already, twice. I'd even run onto the damn bridge willingly to save Rhyan's life. But now, I felt paralyzed.

"You won't fall," Auriel said. "I won't let you."

"You still have some of that magic to slow us down if I do?" I asked.

"For you," he winked, "always."

I sucked in a breath, and I took a step, then another. The bridge swayed, rocking back and forth. I gripped the banister, the rope rough against my skin, and found the next floorboard.

"Good," Auriel said. "Keep going."

I did, barely daring to breathe. It felt like an eternity, but we made it across. Now all we had to do was reach the lower level, and walk into the mine of a hundred akadim. My stomach turned.

We took careful, measured steps in our descent, moving cautiously in case we encountered any akadim shirking orders. But the way was entirely clear, and it wasn't long before we stepped down to the next level. We crossed over the stone bridge, and began our final descent.

When I reached the bottom level, I pushed back against the wall, my chest heaving.

Auriel came before me and pressed his forehead to mine in the dark.

"Remember, your name is power with him. He's down here and even now—especially now—he'll protect you. Get the shard, stab him in the heart—do whatever you must.

Whatever happens, it ends now. He can't go on like this. And we can't allow two shards to go to the enemy."

I nodded shakily.

"I'm going after the green shard," Auriel said. "I remember where I buried it. I know what to do. I'm going to get it back for you. Draw their attention away, and I'll make my move."

Then he kissed me, his lips soft against mine. There was no lust behind it. Not like before. It wasn't meant to lead to anything or say anything more than it was. A kiss. A show of love. And in that moment, I could feel the love he had for me, feel it rippling through my veins, filling my aura. It wasn't just me he was expressing his love for, but it was also his love for Asherah. For my soul.

I squeezed my eyes shut, and touched the hilt of my sword. If he was strong enough to travel across the realms of time and space to find me, to risk his immortality, and defy the Council of Forty-Four then I could be strong enough to face these akadim. To walk out and call Rhyan's soul back to mine.

And so I did. I stepped out from behind the wall, planted my feet down, and pushed back my hood with a shaking hand. A pair of red eyes fell on me, and then another, and another, until dozens had stopped rolling their carts, until dozens more had stopped moving completely. All to watch me—baring their teeth, their nostrils flared, attuned to my scent.

My heart pounded so loud I was sure they could hear it even above the sounds of digging and excavation that continued.

I held up my arms. "I am Lady Lyriana Batavia."

The akadim growled in response, subtly shifting forward, gnashing their teeth and baring their fangs.

"I demand you bring me to Arkturion Rhyan," I shouted.

Several started toward me, their claws extended either ready to attack or grab me—I couldn't tell which.

But then a voice rose above the noise, growling with a low and powerful vibration. Its command exploded above the commotion. "Make a path."

Rhyan.

The akadim began to clear, scrambling to get out of their Arkturion's way, dropping their heads, and looking away from me. My heart thundered as I realized how right Auriel had been. Even just the day before, they would have looked at me, tried to get closer. Now it was clear that they'd all received their new orders. I was untouchable.

Except when it came to him.

He stalked forward, wearing the same boots and riding pants, the same leather vest as the day before. His red eyes glowed against the silver of his collar, matching the subtle glow of the sword at his back—the red shard.

I stepped out to meet him, my eyes unflinchingly on his.

"Hello, lover," I said.

He widened his arms as he continued toward me and grinned, baring his teeth, his fangs shining. His tongue poked out and slid against their sharpened edges. "Lyriana," he sing-songed. "I knew you'd come back." His eyes dipped down the length of my body before rising to my face. "I see you've been busy. Couldn't resist returning to my bedroom, could you?" He shook his head. "Put on all of your old clothes. All of your old things." He gestured at my armor and weapons. "I liked you better with them off."

"Why? Easier to fight me?" I asked. "When I'm weaponless? Or how about when I'm tied up?"

He sneered. "I like it when there are less things between me and what I want."

"We don't always get what we want, do we?" I said.

Rhyan laughed. "Maybe *you* don't." His eyes narrowed. "But *I* plan to."

"Well, that's nice for you. But I didn't come here to talk," I said.

"No? Good. How about you and I go right back to where we left off? Finish what we started."

I brandished my sword. "We are."

"Lover," his eyes narrowed, "that's not what I was thinking."

I took a step forward. "How about you stop thinking, and fight. And fight me for real this time."

He bared his teeth. "As you wish."

The entire cave shook, a deep rumble that ran through the ground. A seam split right under Rhyan's legs.

All the akadim stilled, their eyes wide.

"Get to the pit," Rhyan shouted. "Something's happening."

Auriel. I hadn't seen him move, but I knew with absolute certainty that he was there. That he'd found his way into the mines.

"NOW!" Rhyan yelled. "Go. All of you."

At that moment, a giant boulder fell between us. A few akadim scrambled out of the way, barely missing being crushed to death.

"I think something's wrong with your fortress," I said, my voice shaking. Above us, the rope bridge fell, the floorboards coming loose, crashing to the ground. A crack broke through the stone bridge, severing it down the center.

"That means we're close to getting what we came here for." Rhyan jerked his chin at the akadim still frozen in place, now visibly shaking with fear. He growled low in his throat, and they quickly shuffled off.

"Now it's just you and me," Rhyan said, withdrawing the red shard from his back. He held the hilt between his clawed hands. Its blade pointed at me.

My chest heated, and golden flames burst around my heart. It felt like the light inside me was calling out to its other half, wanting to possess it—to claim it, but most of all, to reunite and be whole.

I eyed the blade carefully. "I thought akadim were the weapon," I said, pointing my own sword at him, our bodies perfect mirrors.

Tilting his head to the side, Rhyan stretched, his nostrils flaring. "And I thought you didn't come here to talk. Are you sure you want this fight?"

"I'm sure."

He let out a low roar, deep in his throat and then he took off, running for me.

I raced out to meet him, dodging rocks and pebbles that had skittered across the ground, our swords meeting with a clang.

The force of his hit against my blade, made it reverberate to the hilt, tiny tremors rushing through my arm.

I spun and again our swords met. I angled my hips, my knees bent as I thrust, just missing him. His sword stabbed, and I blocked a hit, shifting my body back.

The akadim began to run. The ground was vibrating beneath us, and to my shock the wall behind us was starting to crumble, creating a small opening that led back outside toward the valley. An akadim began to dig, and then crawled through to escape. Another quickly followed.

Rhyan launched himself at me, his blade swinging, the red shard little more than a flash of red and crystal. I dodged, just barely missing the hit. Another spin and I prepared to swing, but Rhyan knocked me back with his elbow, and I stumbled, crashing into a metal cart.

I groaned, peeling myself off and stabbing my sword, just in time to block his next attack.

Breathing heavily, I raced behind the cart and pushed it at him. It rolled forward with a surprising burst of speed, but he stopped it easily with one hand.

"Really, Lyr?" He shook his head and made a clicking sound with his tongue. "That's the move?"

He dashed around the cart for me, but I raced in the opposite direction, letting him chase me until I turned, and stabbed, just barely catching his arm.

He jabbed at me, nearly landing a hit to my stomach, but my own steel came down at just the right moment. Metal slid against the sharp unyielding crystal and I forced him back, breaking free of the hold between our blades for a quick slash of his other arm. And then more rocks began to fall, crashing into the broken wall behind us, where even more akadim were digging tunnels to escape. My heart thumped. I could feel myself growing tired. If Rhyan didn't catch me with the blade of the shard, a falling boulder was likely going to be my demise. I had to end this soon. I had to disarm him, get the shard back. And I needed to know what had happened to Auriel.

I thrust again, aiming for his shoulder and Rhyan blocked, barely having to move that time. Angling myself I feinted to the left, and stabbed right, but Rhyan saw it coming and merely stepped back.

"I thought this was a serious fight." He shook his head, both eyebrows furrowed. "But you're not even aiming for my heart. I don't know, Lyr," he said with a disapproving frown, "it doesn't feel like you're really trying. I thought I taught you better than that."

"You taught me nothing," I snapped.

"You wound me." He pressed a hand to his chest, and made a sound of mock pain. "I taught you everything you know. *Everything* you know," he said, his voice suggestive.

And then he lifted the red blade, sliding it back into the sheath he wore on his back. Snarling, he ran for me, no longer holding back. I held out my sword, but I was so afraid of actually hurting him, of getting his heart with the wrong weapon that I missed and he knocked the sword from my hand.

I yelled out as his hands wrapped around my arms and he lifted me into the air before slamming me onto the ground.

"No!" I yelled. But he'd forced my hands over my head, crawling over me again.

"Well, you weren't fighting. So I thought it was time for something else." His nostrils flared as his eyes zeroed in on the bandage on my neck. He ripped it off and I cried out just as his tongue licked across the bite marks he'd left behind.

I kicked, but it was fucking useless against his muscles.

"Remember how it was between us? How good?" he asked. "Remember how many times I took you our last night together? Again and again in the Palace. And then on the rooftop in Thene."

I shook my head. "Don't. Don't."

"Don't what? Remind you of every time you came because of me? Or don't do it again?"

My chest heaved and my eyes zeroed in on the blade at his back. If I could free a hand, I could reach it. I'd have to hurt him to get him off of me, get into position.

Even now, even in this form, and knowing damn well everything he'd done to me, the idea hurt. But I had no choice. If I was going to save him, I had to be ruthless.

I met his cold soulless gaze. "Can akadim even kiss?" I asked.

He laughed. "We can do all kinds of things." He leaned in. "If you want, we can start with kissing." He skimmed his nose against my neck, then lifted up to meet my eyes again. "Can I?" he asked.

I want to kiss you. Can I?

I bit back a cry, the backs of my eyes burning. How dare he! How dare he tarnish that memory for us.

But I nodded. I knew what I had to do. "Yes."

"See?" he purred. "It was only a matter of time before you gave in."

His mouth pressed against mine, and I almost recoiled in disgust. His lips were cold and hard. Nothing remotely like Rhyan's. In a way, it was freeing—it wasn't him. Not at all. Any lingering confusion I'd had the day before was completely gone. I could still feel Auriel's kiss, soft and gentle and full of love and passion. It hummed under my skin, reminding me of the truth, of what Rhyan actually felt like—what he was like when he had his soul. When his heart beat against mine.

But this Rhyan forced his tongue into my mouth, his fangs scraping against my lips. I softened, willing myself to remain calm, to go along with him.

One of his hands still held mine together above my head.

A tear rolled down my cheek, as my fingers reached for his wrist, stroking his cold skin. I lifted my chest, undulating under him, pressing my hips against his.

I met his tongue with mine, and pulled back, just enough to whisper, "Touch me."

It had the effect I wanted. He released my hands and slid his down my torso, as he kissed me deeper.

I wrapped my arms around his neck, my hands digging into his flesh, urging him on as I let the kiss deepen, my fingers tangling in his hair. Not soft like it once was.

The ground shuddered, another boulder fell. I moaned into his mouth, and I reached for my sword. Rhyan ground into me, his hips pressing down as my fingers tightened around the hilt.

I pulled it out, in one stroke, the tip of the blade suddenly pressed into his neck.

He froze and I pushed back, hard enough to draw blood.

"Lyr," he said, a warning in his voice.

"I told you I came here to fight," I seethed. "And take back what's mine. Now get off me. Stand up, and I won't cut off your head," I bluffed.

His eyes narrowed but he sat back on his heels, and I scurried back, removing my body out from under his. My breath was coming in heavy, my fear rising to the surface. What if I missed? Gods. What if I killed him?

Because while I had no warm feelings toward the twisted monster in front of me, the one stealing Rhyan's memories and using them against me, he was the vehicle I needed to bring him back. To restore his body. His beautiful, strong, kind loving body, the home for the soul I loved, the body of my soulmate.

Slowly, holding the sword out, I rose to my feet. Rhyan did as well, his hands raised in surrender.

I stepped forward, not sure what to do. Did I just stab him? Would he let me?

He gave me my answer with a sudden growl as he lunged. My sword swung, cutting through his arm. But he wasn't deterred. He only looked angrier. There was a violence in his eyes I hadn't seen before. He was past protecting me. He was fighting for his life.

I stepped back but Rhyan was already on me, trying to rip the sword from my hand. I tightened my grip, but he was using his claws to wrench it free, using all of his muscle, ruthlessly twisting my arm, forcing me to let go.

"NO!" I yelled. I heard it before I felt it. An awful bone-cracking sound.

Pain exploded like a thousand knives in my right arm. It hung uselessly at my side as the sword clanged to the ground.

Rhyan had broken my arm.

More than that, he'd broken my sword arm.

No. No. No.

I fell to the ground, trying not to vomit from the pain, reaching for the hilt with my left hand as Rhyan came down upon me. I had no time to prepare, no time to ready myself.

My arm shot up, and the blade pierced through his leathered armor. Something cried out in my heart.

He roared, his head turned up to the ceiling as he reared back.

I'd stabbed him. But not deep enough.

I crawled back to my feet, my stomach twisting with another bout of nausea, the pain in my arm exploding.

Rhyan kicked, the sole of his boot slamming into my left hand. The sword flew back on impact, my hold on the hilt hadn't been tight enough. The red shard slid out of my grip, and the blade sliced through my hand. Blood spurted wildly, the red droplets mixing with the red shard, sinking into the red crystal.

In seconds I'd be weaponless, both hands useless.

This was it. He was going to kill me. My heart thrummed, pulsing a million beats at once, like it could make up for all the time it was about to lose.

And then, just as I was about to give in, light illuminated the blade. It glowed with a bright fiery red, nearly blinding in color—brighter and more vibrant than anything I'd ever seen. Without warning, my mind flashed to another time. Another life. A great hall of golden columns, set against a blue sky and rainbow-colored clouds. Music hummed in my ears, an otherworldly harmony, haunting in its beauty. A brilliant luminescent light glimmered and shone above me. For a moment, I felt at peace. Whole and without pain.

I was in the Hall of Records.

Watching the Valalumir.

A head of golden curls peeked out from behind a column. His green eyes found mine, shimmering with light and love.

There was a jolt in my chest as I was pushed out of the memory and slammed back into my body. Pain lit up my broken arm and my sliced-up hand. My stomach roiled, my throat tightening, like I was about to vomit. My mouth began to move, words spilling out before I could think.

"*Ani petrova* Rakashonim, *me ka el lyrotz, dhame ra shukroya, aniam anam. Chayate me el ra shukroya. Ani petrova* Rakashonim!"

The spell echoed through the cave, my voice sounding foreign to my ears. It was Asherah, siphoning through me in her purest form. To save me. To save us.

I caught the hilt of the blade before it touched the ground. My blood coated the steel and handle. But strength pulsed through me—not enough to erase the pain in my body, but enough to fortify me to the point where it didn't matter, where I was strong enough to stand it.

My eyes met Rhyan's.

With a scream, I ran forward, the blade poised. And I thrust, watching the point vanish beneath the tear in his leathers, breaking into his skin, and then sliding in and in, piercing his heart.

His body stilled, his face frozen in horror.

He gasped, reaching one hand out for me, as if I might hold it. Might hold him.

"Lyr," he said, his voice desperate and helpless. His eyes glowed red with pain. Still akadim. "Lyr," he groaned again. The sword glowed, flames erupting around the blade. Flames that echoed in my heart even as my chest tightened. My aura flared out, golden light doming around us.

I gripped the sword even harder, pushing it further into his heart, before I pulled it out. Rhyan sank to his knees, his eyes still red, but they were losing light, losing signs of life.

"Rhyan?" I asked. "Rhyan?"

The dome of gold vanished, leaving us in the darkness of the mines.

"*Me—Mekara*," he croaked out, and fell, landing on his face.

"RHYAN!" I screamed, falling to the ground and turning him over. Blood poured from his chest—from his heart. I'd struck true. I'd done it—I'd done exactly what Auriel and his Valya had told me to do. I'd done it perfectly. But he was still akadim. He was still akadim. It hadn't worked. It hadn't fucking worked.

I shook his shoulders, crying out and yelling his name. "Rhyan! Rhyan!"

A blood-curdling, animalistic scream, one that didn't even sound human, thundered from my mouth.

The ceiling cracked in two, glimmering stars peeking through the breach. Rocks rained down around us.

His eyes closed, and his chest stilled.

He remained akadim.

Dead.

I'd failed.

CHAPTER THIRTY-FIVE

LYRIANA

The world was breaking apart. Rocks thundered from the cave's ceiling—the fissure widening, letting in more night sky, raining down more chaos. Every crack in the wall was webbing out into more. And all I could do was scream. My vision blurred, blinded by tears.

"RHYAN! RHYAN!"

I could hear what sounded like an earthquake erupting. A boulder rolled down the side of the cliff, spinning right past us, until it exploded against the wall. I couldn't move. I couldn't leave Rhyan's side. Not until he changed. Not until he woke up.

But he just lay there, in his akadim body, his fangs still protruding, his claws limp against his unmoving hands. His skin was still stretched over his akadim height, and he was still pale. Too pale.

Gods. I felt like I was dying. Like I had died right there with him. Every breath hurt, my arm felt like it was on fire, and so did my hand. And my heart—my heart was breaking all over again.

He wasn't breathing. He wasn't moving. He was ... dead. But no, no, no. He couldn't be. He couldn't be! I had the shard, and the light. I'd seen the fire, the golden aura around us. I was Asherah reborn. The Moon Queen had promised me. The Valya had promised me. Auriel had promised me!

Auriel ...

"LYRIANA!" he screamed my name in the distance, his voice carrying through the cascade of crashing rubble. "Lyriana, where are you?"

Another crack formed above, pebbles raining down. A rock dislodged, ready to fall right over us. We'd be crushed when it landed.

I flung myself over Rhyan, screaming out in pain as I rolled us over, crushing my broken arm further as we turned. His akadim body flopped over mine, lifeless with dead weight. I panted with exertion and pain as I continued to push him, shifting him just out of the way, barely avoiding the rock that flattened the ground beside us.

"Lyriana!" Auriel screamed again. "Where are you? Lyriana! Answer me, damnit! We have to go! NOW!"

"I can't," I yelled back. "I'm sorry."

"Where are you?"

"Here. I'm here with him," I sobbed.

"We have to go!" he roared.

But I couldn't. I couldn't leave him like this. I knew the cave was going to collapse soon. I could feel it. And yet, not one part of me could get up, could leave him, could abandon him. I didn't care if the cave collapsed, didn't care if it buried me alive. I wasn't going to abandon Rhyan.

"Lyriana!" Auriel screamed.

Thunder struck, but it was just the ceiling breaking apart even more. I flung my body back on top of Rhyan's, burying my head in his neck, and sobbed.

"Please don't be gone. Please. Please. Don't. Don't do this to me. Rhyan, don't leave me. You have to come back. You have to come back to me. You promised, you swore. You swore you'd always come for me. I need you to do that now, okay? Rhyan, please. Please."

Auriel was screaming my name, and the rocks continued to fall.

They were hitting my back, my head, my arms and legs, raining down around us. But my body had gone numb. Nothing could hurt me. Nothing mattered.

"Lyr!" Auriel cried out. "LYR! *MEKA!* Do not give up on me now! We have to get out of here. We have to take the shards. Come on! I've got the green. Now take the red and let's go! Before you're crushed. Before I can't reach you."

I stared down at Rhyan, my chest heaving in painful, broken spurts.

I couldn't bear it, couldn't bear to leave him like this. But my hand was bleeding, and my arm was broken. I couldn't carry him this time, not like before. My tears were so heavy, they were now rolling down his face. And still, still he didn't breathe. Nothing inside me was willing to move, or leave him. It was bad enough he'd been turned akadim. Bad enough he'd been subjected to this fate. I wouldn't let what remained of him be crushed. I wouldn't allow his remains to be destroyed—I didn't care what form he was in. Gritting my teeth, I looked up, and found an emptied cart used to carry the more massive rocks out of the mines. It had turned over in the chaos and was just big enough to fit Rhyan's body.

And mine.

I jumped up and reached for him with my left hand, blood still gushing. I didn't care. Because I was doing this. I was going to protect his remains. With what little will I had left, I dragged him toward it, grunting as I pulled his body inside, sliding it over the metal, pushing him all the way in, until we both had a makeshift roof.

I started clearing the debris that had fallen on him, trying to clean him up as best I could.

"LYRIANA!" Auriel roared. "Get out of there!" His voice grew louder. He was coming closer. Risking everything to get to me. Again.

"Rakame," I whispered to Rhyan, my voice broken. I brushed his hair back, fingers running through his bronzed curls. He'd kept them as an akadim. Like his neatness, like his strength. And his lilt. They never left him. Never went away.

I kissed his forehead, and placed my hand over his heart, willing it to beat. Willing him to turn back. "Rhyan, please," I cried.

"Lyriana!" Auriel crouched down before the cart, his hands wrapping around my waist, pulling me toward him.

I gripped my unbroken arm around Rhyan. "No. No!"

His green eyes paled, for once devoid of their emerald light. They were sea green, like the ocean after a storm.

"He's gone," he said quietly. "I'm sorry. I'm sorry. But Lyr, you can still get out. Come. Come with me. Survive."

"I can't. I can't. I can't do this. I can't go on like this. I don't want to."

"Yes, you do," he said. "You have to." His voice broke. "Get up. Lyr, get up. You have to get up, and run!"

I sobbed, clinging to Rhyan. As if I could cling to his soul by holding onto him, as if I could bring him back.

"I can't leave him."

"We're going to be crushed if we stay. And I'm not letting you die. Not again! I watched it happen once before and it nearly destroyed me."

"Then you know what it feels like!"

"I do. I do. But it doesn't have to be this way. Lyriana, please. If we die here, the shards will be found, the Empire will go to Aemon and Morgana. So many will suffer like they did before."

"Then take the red shard from me, and go."

"What about Meera?" he asked. "What about Jules? Tristan? What about Bamaria? Do you think Rhyan would want this for you?"

My chest heaved.

"Do you think this is what he fought for? Died for? So you could end it here? Crushed to death? So it could all fall? So his fight meant nothing?"

"No." I shook my head, crying even harder.

"Then get up! Get up and keep fighting. You have to keep fighting."

I didn't want to try. I was done. I was so fucking done. Every time I got back up, and tried again, I failed. Every time it just got worse. But as I looked back and forth between Rhyan and Auriel, Auriel whose heart still beat, who was still alive, and still desperate for me to live, to get up, and go on, I knew he was right. That this was what Rhyan would have wanted for me. It was what I would have wanted for him. I'd done what I could. I'd given him a roof. The last bit of protection I could manage. I kissed Rhyan's cheek and placed my bleeding hand on his chest, right over his heart. Over the wound my sword had made.

I love you, I thought. Praying that he wasn't in the in-between anymore. That he could somehow hear me. That he was at peace. *Wait for me, Rhyan. I'll find you. In the next life.* Me sha, me ka.

"Come on then, come to me," Auriel said.

"He broke my arm," I cried. "And my hand's cut up."

Auriel crawled inside the cart, reached for the red blade, and strapped it to his back. Then he scooped me into his arms, crushing me to his chest as he crawled out and stood.

"Can you run?" he asked urgently.

I nodded.

"We'll fix your hand, and your arm, but you have to swear to me. You'll live," he said. "And you won't give up. For Rhyan."

"For Rhyan," I whispered. Then I took his hand. And we ran.

The rocks were falling harder now. We couldn't avoid getting hit, no matter how much we dodged, or how quickly we raced. The back of the cavern was sinking, the ground shifting and rising beneath our feet. The wall was in sight, the fissures breaking apart, widening, making a way for us.

We burst outside into the night, and I nearly choked on the cold, fresh air.

I stumbled into the grass, my body clenching in pain.

A chorus of bone-chilling growls sounded in the dark.

"Auriel?" I hissed.

"We're surrounded," he said, his body going still. "The akadim escaped when I took the green shard."

"And now they're all out here?" I asked, turning my head and seeing at least two dozen sets of red eyes popping up in the dark.

"Most ran—especially when they saw the light. But not all of them. Lyriana," he said slowly, "You're going to need to heal your arm. Right now."

My pulse pounded in my ears as I stepped back, feeling the cool of the stone wall behind me. "I can't heal a broken bone that fast!" I hissed.

"Well, you're going to need to try."

But a part of me didn't want to. Didn't want to try. Because it was starting to feel like nothing in the whole fucking universe was on my side. I'd made it out. But it was only my body. I'd left my soul inside, clinging to Rhyan.

"Lyriana, come on!" Auriel urged. "Do it. Please."

I took a deep breath and focused on my arm, not sure exactly what to do. I'd never healed myself before. But I did what I always did, what I'd done for Rhyan and Auriel. I saw the outcome I wanted. I imagined the bone was whole, the arm back in place and healed. Then I reached for it with my left hand, still covered in blood, imagining sending all of my power to it. All of the red light inside of me.

Heat began to flicker in my chest, more so than the heat already present as I ran through Asherah's power.

I bit down on my lip to keep from screaming, because fresh agonizing pain raced down my arm, firing through my nerves. And then suddenly, it stopped. I gasped, sweat coating my forehead as the arm straightened and once again hung at the correct angle. I tried to move my fingers. I could. The arm wasn't broken, but it wasn't exactly healed either, and probably wouldn't be for days. It was still tender, painfully so, and sore. But it was enough to withstand the weight of a sword. Enough to know that if I went down in this battle, at least I'd go down fighting.

Gritting my teeth, I took my right hand, and pressed it to the left, to the stab wound cutting through it. Light moved through my veins to my palm, and the wound closed. The bleeding stopped.

But now the akadim were closing in on us.

"I did it," I panted, "but I don't think it's enough. My arm's still weak."

"Better weak than broken. Here," Auriel said, placing the sword in my hands.

I nearly dropped it, and bit back another cry of pain, as I lifted up the red shard.

"Move aside," Auriel commanded. "This is Lyriana Batavia, and your Arkturion gave orders not to touch her."

"That's not going to work," said a voice in the dark. "Not this time."

Because Rhyan was gone. Because his command couldn't be enforced.

I squeezed my eyes shut, my heart clenching. Until there was a bang right behind us.

"Run!" Auriel yelled, taking my hand. His sword was out, ready to attack, but the akadim began running in terror. The ground was shuddering and shaking, more rocks were rolling toward us.

I looked back and gasped in horror.

The Wall of the Prince had collapsed. The cave was gone. The mines. And Rhyan. He was gone now. All of him was gone.

Auriel slammed us against a tree. Most of the akadim were still running—trying to get away from the chaos. But dozens were lined up in front of us, their eyes glowing with violence.

I held my sword higher, my arm crying out in pain, and gritted my teeth.

"What now?" I asked, my body shaking.

"We fight and we—" He cried out in pain, bending over. An emerald green light emanated from his body—it seemed to have started under his armor, coming from his heart.

"What's happening?" I asked, helping him back up.

"I don't—I ... Fuck!" He cried out, the light grew brighter, shimmering with starlight.

"Auriel?" I frowned, only then realizing that he had told me he'd uncovered the green shard, but I hadn't seen it anywhere. Not in his hands, not strapped to his body or armor.

Because I realized at that moment it *was* his armor. It was shaped identically to what he'd worn since he found me—a golden vest that covered his torso. But this one had a green interior.

"It's the shard. Your armor's the shard."

He nodded. "It is. But I'm not doing this. I'm not controlling it—aaah!"

The light began to blaze, growing so bright, even I had to look away. The akadim that had cornered us started to retreat, their silhouettes shrinking into the shadows as they growled in pain and cursed.

It was working. It was fucking working.

And then, all at once, the light vanished and Auriel's voice broke as he moaned in pain, sinking to his knees.

"Auriel?" I asked, sinking beside him. "Auriel?" Our eyes met.

I reached for his arms, sliding my hands down his skin, checking his chest and stomach for injuries—but his armor was intact.

"What happened?" I asked frantically, my hands and eyes desperately searching him all over. "Are you hurt? I can't find a wound."

"I'm not injured," he said, but he sounded weak, like his energy was gone.

I stood up, and grabbed his arms, again hauling him back to his feet.

He stumbled back, slamming into the tree behind us. He leaned his head against the trunk and closed his eyes, his brows furrowed, sweat pouring down from his forehead. "Something's wrong," he said.

"What?" I asked. "Tell me. Tell me what to do! I'll heal you. I'll heal you."

I placed my hands on his face. But he flickered. Vanishing completely and returning. It was like that first night when I was dreaming. Seeing the Guardian of Bamaria's head vanish and reappear.

"AURIEL!"

His chest heaved and he reached for my hands, pushing them down, his face tight in pain.

"Lyriana," he said. "I'm sorry. I don't … I don't think I can stay any longer."

"No!" I cried. "You can't go. Auriel, you can't leave me. I'll fix it. Okay. It's going to be okay." I pulled out my stave, pointing it to his chest, and squeezed his hand. His fingers threaded through mine, squeezing back, only barely.

The akadim were starting to close in on us again, now that the light was gone. Now that Auriel had nothing to threaten them with.

Once more he vanished from sight and reappeared. His eyes had been pale since he found me at Rhyan's side. And now, the blond in his hair was losing its golden shine.

He was fading, fading before my very eyes. He lost his balance, and fell against me. And for the first time ever since I'd seen him, he didn't look like a God. He looked ... mortal. I wrapped my arms around him.

"Auriel," I cried. "Auriel, please." My voice. "Please don't go. I'll heal you. I swear I will." And I was trying, pouring everything I had into him with my touch, imagining him healthy, strong and glowing. A God restored.

He pulled back, meeting my eyes and shook his head slowly, the movement labored, like it was taking all of his energy. "Don't make promises you can't keep."

My chest heaved. No. No. No. It was exactly what Rhyan had said to me after he'd been stripped, when he was—when he was—

"You're not dying," I cried.

"No. I'm not. I'm a God, remember?" He winked. "I wasn't born. I can't die. But my time here is up. I-I'm done. It's not ... not allowed anymore. The Council says it's done. I can't stay here with you." A tear rolled down his cheek.

"It's not done!" I cried. "It's not." I was going to kill the Council when I found them.

He brushed my hair back, his hand sliding down my ear, and then to my neck, dipping lower. His fingers shifted over Asherah's chest plate, stopping when his palm was over my heart.

"It was ... wonderful to be alive again, and to be alive with you. But I can't," he swallowed roughly. "I can't stay." He smiled sadly. "Lyriana. *Mekara*."

"No! Auriel!" My heart stopped beating.

"Even you can't heal me now," he said. Then his smile widened, and his eyes were no longer seeing me. They seemed to be looking through me—to something beyond me. "Asherah," he whispered.

"Auriel!"

But he was gone. My hands clutched at nothing but the air.

His weapons and armor, the green shard, all fell to the ground where he'd stood. All that was left of him now. All he'd come down with had vanished with him.

I was alone. Completely alone. Rhyan was gone. Auriel, too.

And a dozen hungry akadim stood before me.

For a split second, I was still, my chest heaving.

My nostrils flared, every part of me shaking as I held up the red shard and shouted. "Get back!"

But several of them stepped forward, and within seconds, I was surrounded. I grabbed one of Auriel's swords, and though I wasn't healed, I raced forward, slashing with both arms, slicing through stomachs and shoulders and hands and pushing back every akadim that came near me. I felt out of control, blinded by my grief and rage.

I could barely keep track of who I'd fought and who I hadn't because they just kept coming and coming. And I kept fighting.

Until I was attacked from behind. An akadim wrapped its arms around my waist and hauled me into the air, as the others gathered, grabbing my legs and arms. My weapons were taken and thrown to the ground, including the red shard.

"No!" Then I yelled out for help, pleading, begging for anyone to hear me, for anyone to send aid in any way they could, in any realm. But no one did. Not here in Korteria, and not beyond.

The akadim just laughed at me, tugging at my hands, and tearing at my cloak and boots. I screamed again even though I knew I was alone. It was over. No one was coming Maybe my cries would reach someone in town. Maybe someone would hear me, someone would hear me scream, and at least, in some small way, bear witness to my end. At least,

I'd know I tried. Tried to survive. Like Auriel wanted. Like I knew Ryan would have.

So I sucked in a breath, my lungs filling with air as the akadim clawed and grabbed at me. The next scream that tore through me encompassed all of the fire inside, all of the power that remained. All that was in my soul, in this life, in all my lives. The scream that relayed the horror I felt at being brought to this point, to this ending. I poured it all in, screaming it out. Crying. My fury, my anger, my pain, my rage. My fear.

And my love.

It was primal and ancient, and when I finished I was met with the silence of the night. The blowing of the wind through my hair, the twinkling of the stars above, the shifting of clouds in the sky. For a moment, even the akadim had gone quiet.

And then somewhere in the utter silence and stillness of the dark, someone called back to me. One word. My name.

"LYR!"

I gasped, my stomach dropping. No. No. It couldn't be. He was dead. I'd stabbed him, I'd killed him. I'd watched his body go still. He was ... He was—

"LYR!"

The akadim holding me started to panic and suddenly, half of the beasts who'd been grabbing me turned, shifting into formation, their backs to me, creating a line of defense against the oncoming threat.

"Put me down!" I yelled. "Put me down!"

"LYR!" Rhyan screamed, tearing through the meadow.

An akadim ran out to meet him, his claws slashing in the air, but Rhyan slashed back and the akadim fell. He took down the next, and the next, butting his head into the demon. It collapsed to the ground. He spun on his heels and kicked, his boot crushing the beast in the belly. The next one he lifted by the shoulders and flung him to the ground. Rhyan bared his teeth, his fangs glistening in the moonlight. The akadim released me, rushing to attack Rhyan next. He leaped onto Rhyan, claws extending to his face. But Rhyan slammed his head into the monster's, rolled him onto his back, and punched him in the nose, again and again, before he stood, and kicked him aside, like he was nothing.

Heart pounding, I reached down, blindly reaching for the red shard until my fingers felt the cool metal of the hilt, and tightened around it. I stood, brandishing the blade in my shaking hands.

All but two of the remaining akadim had fallen. Their bodies were scattered through the meadow. And together the last demons ran for Rhyan, each one grabbing an arm. He was hauled back, growling and roaring and screaming my name.

His eyes met mine, red and glowing. But he broke free of their hold, and suddenly he had become the one holding down their arms. With a snap of his wrists, he pulled them in front of him, and bashed their heads together.

They crumpled to the ground on either side of him.

And then he ran for me, his movements feral.

I held the sword higher, my hands trembling.

"Lyriana," he said, stopping just in front of me. And this time when he said my name, it was *his* voice. Rhyan's voice. Soft, and lilted, and human and alive. Not akadim. Not akadim.

"Lyr!" he cried. He stepped in toward me, and sank to his knees, his arms wrapping around my legs, his hold tightening.

A shuddering gasp escaped my lips, my heart racing, my body trembling.

His shoulders shook. He was crying, burying his face against my thighs. Like he was trying to crawl inside of me.

Slowly, I removed one hand from the sword, and lowered it down as I reached for his hair, stroking my hand through his curls. They were soft again. Like they used to be. Like they were when he was alive. My heart pounded, ready for him to jump up suddenly and knock me over, to finish our fight in the cave. But his shoulders only shook harder, his tears soaking through my riding pants.

"R-Rhyan?" I asked.

He looked up at me then, his chest heaving with such force, I thought he was hyperventilating. Then he stilled. His eyes met mine. Emerald light shone in them. Green. Not red. Green! The green I'd dreamt of, the green I'd loved since I was a girl. His eyes. Rhyan's eyes.

"Lyr," he sobbed, his mouth opening in a cry of agony. No fangs. They were gone. Just his straight white teeth. His features were so familiar, so like I remembered, like I knew with my heart, it felt like I'd been stabbed in the chest.

I sank to my knees before him, and took his hands in mine. The claws were gone. His fingernails were back, the pads of his fingers round and callused. And the red lines that marked his akadim body, the lines which appeared when his skin had been forced to stretch to fit his new height and size, were gone. His face ... it was *his* face. Human, kind, beautiful. Alive. Gods. Even his scar was back, slicing through his left eyebrow, tapering off at the edge of his cheek. One eyebrow furrowed. The right one. The only one that could move.

I cupped his cheeks, his skin soft, and warm. His eyes moved back and forth watching me, taking me in, only red now in the corners, because he was crying. Because he couldn't stop crying. Because the tears wouldn't stop rolling down his cheeks.

"Rhyan? Is it you? Is it really you? You're here with me?"

"I am." He nodded. "I'm here."

I blinked, my chest so tight it hurt.

The cure. It worked. His soul was back.

He was alive.

"Lyr," he sobbed, hugging me again, his arms crushing me to him. "By the Gods, Lyr. You found me."

And then his lips were on mine.

THE THIRD SCROLL:
THE ARKTURION

CHAPTER THIRTY-SIX

LYRIANA

Rhyan's hands were in my hair, his mouth crashing against mine. We kissed feverishly, desperately, like we needed the other to breathe, like we'd suddenly picked up from the last kiss we'd ever had, racing through the woods all those weeks ago, trying to escape his father. The kiss had been brief, cut short by the fight, and then Rhyan's disappearance. And now we were continuing on, as if no time had passed. As if our parting hadn't been real, as if we'd always been kissing. All of our life.

All of our lives.

With every kiss, every gasp, and sudden intake of breath, our bodies pressed closer together, our arms tightening around each other. I felt like I was drinking water after thirsting for weeks, and when he cupped my chin, his tongue sweeping across my lips and dipping inside, tangling with mine, I moaned in relief.

There was nothing left of the monster who'd kissed me in the cave, nothing even close to the demon who'd used my own memories and heart against me. The idea that I'd even considered what had happened there between us to be a kiss now felt preposterous, because there was no comparison. This—*this* was kissing. This was what it was like when I was kissing Rhyan. The soft ferocity of his lips, the way it felt like he was going to devour me, the way I wanted—needed—to become a part of him.

Even Auriel's kiss had felt wholly different from this—it had been amazing and special on its own, but it wasn't this. Nothing in the universe could be compared to this. To Rhyan. Just Rhyan. My Rhyan. My *mekarim*. The way he angled my face, the way he gasped into my mouth or his fingers tightened against my flesh, the way he said my name, breathing it into me.

My chest heaved as I tried to somehow kiss him deeper, and get even closer. I felt like I'd go mad if we parted. I needed him inside of me. I needed to feel him, but it was more than that. More than the intimacy of sex. I wanted to pull his entire body and soul within me, so I could carry him, so I could protect him and keep him safe. So I could make sure no one—*no one*—ever touched or hurt him again.

"Gods," he groaned. "I missed you," he kissed me again, "so," kiss, "much," kiss.

"I missed you, too," I cried.

"Lyr, Lyr," he said. "I should have known you'd find me. That you'd save me. You told me you would."

My promise. I'd kept my promise. But before I could say anything more, a growl, low and pained, escaped from the lips of one of the nearby akadim. Shit. Not dead. Only unconscious. And from the sound of it, not for much longer.

Rhyan had knocked out every one of my attackers to reach me. I didn't know when the change started, but he seemed to have been acting out his full strength and without weapons. He hadn't been able to kill. Not one.

Another of the unconscious demons huffed through their nostrils, and yet another lying beside him began to stir, his claws making a ticking sound as they tapped together.

My heart thumped, my body tensing. Rhyan pulled back at once, his ears strained, his entire body taut and on alert.

He didn't speak, just started to stand, immediately aware of the danger we faced. He grabbed hold of my hands and helped me to my feet. Automatically his hand went to his waist, as if he'd grab the hilt of his sword—but it wasn't there. He had no weapons on his belt, because as an akadim he *was* the weapon.

"We have to get out of here," I said urgently. I was close to being drained of my magic, my *Rakashonim* had started failing a while ago, and I wasn't sure what Rhyan's strength was like at the moment, or if he was harboring any injuries I needed to look into.

"Is there somewhere safe we can go? Somewhere close?" Rhyan's eyes narrowed as he looked around the Korterian hills in the dark, trying to take in the landscape. We were surrounded by the shadows of the hills and dirt mounds. Small woodland clusters lay ahead, and then east of that, the tiny town where Auriel and I had been staying. The collapsed front cave of the Wall of the Prince lay in heaping piles of rubble behind us.

"Yes," I said urgently. "I have a room at an inn not far from here. Just beyond the hills there's a town."

"I know," he said, "It's the last town in Korteria before—" He frowned, looking back over his shoulder at the collapsed cave. "I remember. It's a small inn." He bit his bottom lip, then looked down at his body. He was still wearing that hateful leather akadim vest—now with a hole where I'd stabbed him. His pants were hanging low on his hips, far too big for him now, and I was pretty sure his feet were swimming in the boots he had on. Akadim tore out of their clothing when they turned as their bodies grew. I hadn't considered how the reverse would leave a person swimming in their former attire.

I kneeled down again before him, pulling his foot free from each shoe. I hated the idea of him being barefoot, but there didn't seem to be much choice. Not if we were going to get out of here quickly.

Rhyan was already undoing the laces of his pants, tightening them at the hip, and rebuckling his belt onto the smallest notch he could manage.

I looked him over, realizing he still wore the silver collar. Another akadim huffed, and one blinked its eyes, the irises still dark in the shadows. Too dark to show any red. We had to hurry. "Come here," I said, and lifted the hateful thing off his head, tossing it into the trees. "This, too." I reached for the vest. I didn't want to see it again. I didn't want the reminder of the moment I'd had to stab him in the heart—even if it was the exact thing that brought him back to me.

Rhyan lowered his head so I could pull it off. With him now naked from the chest up, his skin pale in the moonlight, I started grabbing the remaining weapons Auriel had been using—the ones he'd left behind. I swallowed roughly, my heart clenching as I touched the hilts—they were still warm, like his touch had lingered behind. I handed them to Rhyan, relieved to see that his fingers tightened instantly and instinctively around them as he tucked them into his belt.

Finally, I picked up the golden armor, unhooked the top clasps and handed it to Rhyan.

"Here. You need to wear this. It's yours now."

"By the Gods." His eyes widened as he pulled it over his head. "This is it, Lyr? This is the green shard?" A faint green light began to glow from inside it, lighting up his face and arms. He took a deep breath. "This is …" he said in wonder. "It's what we were digging up."

"Yes. Auriel got it out. Now you can claim your shard," I said solemnly, sheathing the red shard securely against my back. "And I have mine."

He smiled tearfully. "You do."

I took his hand, far too aware that another akadim had turned over and groaned. None had opened their eyes yet—a small miracle. But we needed to leave. Now.

"Follow me," I hissed, and led him quickly away from the Wall of the Prince, toward the nearest woodlands.

"Lyr," Rhyan said.

We'd covered a fair amount of distance. I'd been keeping a brisk, but steady pace, not trying to rush him barefoot.

"I know I don't …" he frowned. "Don't have my magic anymore, but—we can run. We—we should run."

I nodded, my hand tightening around his, my heart pounding. Then we took off, our feet moving together over the hills, farther and farther away from the ruins of the cave behind us.

The hair on the back of my neck stood up. We were being watched. I looked over my shoulder, expecting to see the akadim awake, or worse, giving chase. And if not the ones Rhyan just fought, then surely the others that had escaped the wreckage of the mines. There had to be close to a hundred hiding out here now. I could feel it. Feel the sensations over every inch of my skin that we weren't alone. But, yet, nothing was approaching us.

With every glance back made by me or Rhyan, every time our heads swiveled, scouting the area, trying to see through the dark and shadows of Korteria's hills and trees—there was nothing.

My pulse raced, my stomach turning at every small sound—every gust of wind, every snap of a tree branch. But still there was nothing.

"Where are they?" I asked.

Rhyan's mouth tightened. "I don't know. I'd say they're still under my command," he flinched at his own words. "I mean, that they knew not to come near you. And they would have never—never attacked me. Not before. But that's clearly," he sighed, one hand on his heart. On the spot where

I'd stabbed him. "That's not true anymore." He squeezed my hand a little tighter. "I see the town. Come on."

He sped up—nothing as fast he'd been as when he had his power. But the speed was still incredible, a pace built from years of patience, practice, and determination.

A few torches lit the tiny street at the base of the hill we raced down. My blood pumped, my calves burning. The stressors of the night, the fight, the battles—the way I'd had to call on *Rakashonim*—it was all catching up to me. But at last, our feet touched down on the road, and we sprinted down, moving through the tiny buildings all tucked neatly together.

"This way," I told Rhyan. I pointed ahead to the inn nestled in-between two other buildings at the end of the road. A small mountain cast its silhouette in the dark behind it.

But he pulled us into a small alleyway, tucking me against the wall.

"Did you sense something?" I hissed.

Rhyan nodded slowly. "Do you still feel it?" he asked. "Like we're being watched?"

I did. I tried to open my senses wider. The feeling I had when I was near akadim had completely dissipated. I was sure that feeling had vanished the moment Rhyan's eyes turned green. But—that could be wrong. Maybe I was just confused by his change, and it was making it hard to sense the others.

"I do." I leaned forward, and peered back at the street behind us now, my eyes narrowed. "But it doesn't feel like akadim."

Rhyan pulled me back into the shadows with him. "They were ordered not to come into the town," he said. "By—" He took a deep breath. "By me, but first by Morgana. I don't think they'd disobey her—especially if they still have their collars."

"So we should be safe here?" I asked.

"As safe as we ever are," Rhyan said, pressing his forehead against mine.

I almost laughed. "So not safe at all."

He kissed me. "Let's get inside."

Holding hands, we carefully stepped back onto the street and then made the final sprint in the darkness to the inn. Luckily, no one was at the front desk as I pulled Rhyan into the foyer. Though in the dark, they weren't likely to see much difference between Rhyan and Auriel, aside from hair color. I was, however, hoping to avoid questions about his lack of shoes.

Quickly, my fingers tightening around his, I led him to the stairwell that Auriel and I had used multiple times to get up to our room. And then at last, I unlocked the door, and pulled Rhyan across the threshold, closing every lock and latch behind him.

I reached for my stave, quickly uttering a spell for light, bringing to life all three of the torches embedded in the walls. I set the wards, reinforcing them and watched as Rhyan peered through and then locked each window. I slid a table against the door as an extra measure of safety. The room finally secured, I stopped, and found myself face-to-face in the light with Rhyan. *With Rhyan.*

His eyes watered as he looked around, slowly taking everything in. The two unmade beds, the leather satchel full of men's clothing. A spare soturion cloak. And then the items that were clearly mine.

"So Auriel," he said, his voice heavy. "He was here with you."

"He um, yes," I said, suddenly feeling awkward. "He appeared the night I—the night I lost you." My voice broke.

"I know," he said. "On the beach."

"How did you—?" I asked. "Wait—back in the hills—when I mentioned the inn here, you said you knew about it—I thought you were just talking about the town, and you'd seen the inn. But did you—did you already know I was staying here?"

"Before tonight?" he asked. "No. When I was still … still trapped in that body. But …" He sighed. "There was a moment when Auriel and I—we connected as I was changing. As I was coming back to you, and he was leaving. It was quick. No more than a few seconds, if that. But," he swallowed. "His memories—are mine. He's my past, even if the timeline has gotten somewhat," he shrugged, "loopy. So a lot of what happened with you two, things he did, things he thought, or saw, it's almost like they're becoming my memories. They're trickling into my mind, even now."

I remembered Auriel telling me that Rhyan had all of his memories, he remembered his life as Auriel. But Auriel didn't have Rhyan's. Not yet. Because Rhyan was his future.

But then that meant—Gods.

I met Rhyan's eyes, my heart pounding. "Everything that happened between us?" I asked.

Rhyan nodded slowly, his mouth tight.

"So that includes things like—?"

Don't, Auriel. Just kiss me.

My cheeks heated and my stomach roiled. "Rhyan?"

His eyes flicked to the bed. To my bed. To the very spot where Auriel had laid me down, my legs spread beneath him, our mouths wild and frenzied as they came together.

"Everything," he said, his voice hoarse, "everything that was between you."

I squeezed my eyes shut and shook my head. "I was going to tell you about that. I didn't think—I mean, of course I wanted to tell you what happened, and what it meant to me—but we just only—me and you—" Fuck. I didn't think I'd be having this conversation less than an hour after I got him back.

"Lyr," he said, crossing the distance between us. "Hey, look at me." He cupped my jaw, forcing my gaze to meet his. Green eyes. Emerald green. Rhyan's eyes. I could see now how his gaze connected to Auriel's, how the light inside them linked their souls together, how Auriel almost seemed to be peeking back out, and yet, the look he was giving me now was all him. All Rhyan.

"I'm sorry," I said. "I'm sorry. I felt like I was breaking and I was missing you—and I'd just escaped the cave and—"

He shook his head. "Hey, partner. You didn't do anything wrong. I was dead. Okay? And you went through hell. You have nothing to apologize for. Nothing. For one moment that happened between you and my soul? A moment between you and the God I used to be?" He exhaled sharply. "It's not like it's the first time you've kissed him."

"It was when I was in this body!"

"Asherah," he said. "It's okay."

I frowned, unsure if Rhyan meant I'd kissed Auriel as Asherah, or if he was referring to the part of me that was her.

"Lyr," he said, "Listen. I can see through his eyes what you went through. All of it, it's not all organized in my mind. But it's there. I can see it." His eyes welled with tears. "The way you suffered. Got hurt. And the way you fought for me. Fuck. I thought I couldn't love you more than I did when you found me in the arena. I was dying and even then, I was falling more in love with you, and I thought this—this is the pinnacle, and I can die now knowing that. Knowing how greatly I could love." A tear fell. "And be loved. But, every second since you've saved me tonight—again—has proven how wrong I was because somehow, Gods, Lyr, I love you *more*. I love you so fucking much. And I don't know how in the world I can show you."

"You don't have to—"

"I do. I do. You deserve it. I want you to have it. And I don't know how to express it. How do I explain how grateful I am, how amazed? How I—Gods—how I should be on my knees, thanking you, worshipping you for bringing me back from hell." He brushed my hair from my face. "Lyr, *Mekara*,

I know the circumstances. I see it. And I promise you, every step of the way, you did nothing wrong. And nothing wrong before. You are blameless for what happened to me, blameless for anything that happened after. All that matters now is that you saved me. You brought me back."

"You would have done the same," I said, looking away. "You." My voice cracked. "You wouldn't have had to ... had to save me like this. Because, Rhyan, you wouldn't have failed, not like I did. You would have gotten to the arena faster, you would have gotten to me on time."

"Lyr, no. No. Shhh." He pulled me against him. He smelled like the mines still, a little sulfuric, but also musky—like himself. "Don't think like that."

"I know that we were," I hiccupped. "That we were up against things so fucking beyond our scope of control. And manipulations for things that started before we were born. I know that. I do. But I still ... I still see you on the dais when I close my eyes. I still hear your screams. And I see ... I see the akadim who took you. And it—Gods. It kills me."

"And it kills me," he yelled, "seeing you in the cave tied up, hurt, and scared." He shook his head. "The only difference is I'm the one who actually did that to you. I'm so fucking aware of what I did to you I want to vomit. The things that I thought when I was akadim, the things I did—fuck." His nostrils flared, his mouth tightening. "Lyr, listen to me. Please. If anyone did anything wrong—it was me. Okay, it was me."

"But it wasn't you," I cried. "It was the demon. It was the—the thing that took over your body. It cast out your soul, and then it took your memories."

"I know, I know. It did. But I still—I still have its memories, too. Like they're mine. Weeks' worth of them. All the things I did. All the awful—I mean, I can still—Gods. I can still taste your blood in my mouth." His voice shook and he stepped back, his chest heaving. "Let's ... I mean. Can we ...?" He closed his eyes and swallowed, his jaw muscles working. "I love you," he said at last. "Gods, Lyr, I love you. And I don't," he shook his head, "I don't blame you for what happened to me. Okay. Not even a little." His face fell. "How could you—how could you think that?"

"I don't know," I cried, my vision blurry with tears. "I just—I didn't want it to happen—any of it."

"Me neither," he said, exhaling sharply. "And after all you went through, do you blame me? For hurting you?"

"No," I said. "No. Not for anything."

"No?" He lifted his good eyebrow, his eyes darkening. "Not for tying you up? Dragging you through the caves?" His hand ran down my neck and collarbone, sliding between my breasts. "Or ripping your clothes off? Smelling you. Biting you. Threatening to—to—" He made a noise of disgust low in his throat and turned away.

"No. And you know that already. Because you did all that to me," I said quietly. "Or the thing that was you did. And I still went back for you."

"You pulled me off the bridge," he said, his voice hushed. "I would have died if it weren't for you. And then after you—you pulled my soul back. You brought me back to life."

I moved in front of him. He was struggling to keep from crying.

"I wasn't going to let you die. Not again." My chest heaved. "Rhyan, the fact that you're here now, with me, alive, and healed, and you—you—Gods! You're all I wanted. All I thought about for every fucking second of every day and night since I lost you. I missed you so much I thought I'd die from it."

"I know," he said quietly. "I saw ... saw it through his eyes." He shook his head, his neck red, and his nostrils flaring. "So you don't blame me? Don't fear me now?" he asked. "Truly?"

"Truly," I said. "I'm not confused. I'm not afraid of you. The demon in the cave, that wasn't you, not even close."

He pulled me to him and his hand smoothed down my spine, slowly rubbing up and down, before he pressed his lips to my forehead.

"Well, good," he cried, letting out a shaky laugh and shook his head. "You know, considering how traumatized we are, I'd say this reunion is going rather well."

I sniffled. "There isn't exactly a guidebook for this sort of thing."

"No?" he asked. "You mean, no one wrote a scroll about how to move on when your lover turned akadim, tried to kill you, and then came back to life?"

I laughed. "Someone really needs to get on that." I shrugged.

"They do." Rhyan sighed, his face now solemn. "The truth is, I don't know what I'm doing. Or what I'm supposed to do, or feel, or even what I want to do next. I'm scared. I … I remember the last night we were together. And I was—Fuck, Lyr, I was so happy. Because I was with you." He pressed his forehead back to mine.

I had a flash of that night. We'd just had sex again after a month of being unable to touch. Rhyan and I had finished, but he was still inside of me, looking down and smiling. Happy.

"I was with you," he said. "And then I wasn't. That life I wanted for us—it was stolen from me." His eyes searched mine. "There's only one thing I do know. And it's that I love you." He gripped the nape of my neck. "I love you. And I want to touch you. I want to kiss you. Gods, I want to plunge deep inside you, claim you, mark you. I need to—" He shook. "I need to undo the cave. I need to touch you everywhere the akadim did—kiss every hurt. Replace every memory, reclaim every moment. And then, then we'll figure the rest out." He blinked. "That is—if you—if you still want me."

"Rhyan. Of course I want you."

We both stared at each other then, his eyes hooded with desire, our chests heaving with grief, and love, and fear and … something else. Something that tied our souls together, something primal that needed to be acted upon—proof we were alive. That we'd done the impossible. Found our way back to each other. And now, though there were no more obstacles in our way, and we were together and alone, it felt like a chasm had opened between us. Because as much as we loved and understood each other, and understood the horrors we'd both been through, it didn't change the fact that they were very much real. Very much affecting us. And would be for quite some time.

That first kiss between us, the one that made it feel as if no time had passed now seemed like a distant memory—and instead, the space between us felt oceanic. Like all the distance and horror we'd been through had suddenly manifested itself as a wall.

"Partner," Rhyan said. "Why don't we get cleaned up, and relax. I could—I could really use a shower."

I nodded, relieved. "Me, too."

"Then," he said. "Then we'll figure the rest out."

We headed for a closet where we removed our weapons and armor. The green shard, Rhyan's golden armor, my sword, and the red shard were set down carefully. I used my stave to create an additional ward, and then Rhyan took my hand, leading us into the bathing room and turning on the shower faucet.

I stared at him, half naked in the firelight. His skin looked soft and inviting, the muscles on his chest and abs somehow sharper and more defined. My mouth went dry as my gaze lowered down to his exposed waist and hips. His pants were hanging dangerously low, exposing the V that vanished beneath his waistband.

"You're not hurt," I said, unable to stop myself from reaching for his chest, flattening my palm against his heart. I needed to feel his warmth, feel his heart beating. "I stabbed you."

He flinched. "I remember."

I placed my other hand on him, sliding them down slowly to his hips. "You have no marks at all." Not even from the stripping whip. I remembered those—every single hateful stripe that had been branded onto his body, every place where he'd been invaded by Kunda, where the whip had scoured inside him, tearing out his magic. "Nothing," I said, still in awe. Was this an effect of turning back from being akadim? Or had the light of the Valalumir healed more than that?

"No," he said, his voice growing hoarse, and looking down. His throat bobbed as he followed the path of my hands, my fingers sinking into his flesh, my palms moving lower. "But if you keep touching me like that," he said, "this is going to be a very short shower."

My breath hitched. "You're so beautiful."

"So are you," he said, and reached for my tunic. "Can I take this off?"

I nodded. "If I can take these," I said, my fingers already unlacing his pants.

He reached for the hem of my tunic, hauling it over my head and throwing it on the floor, and immediately, he started tearing at the bindings over my breasts as I shoved his pants down.

His cock sprang free, already thick, and hard. I gasped, and felt his gaze on mine as I took all of him in with hungry eyes.

"Did you miss this?" he hissed, pushing his pelvis forward.

"Yes," I said, and wrapped my fingers around him, stroking him from base to tip.

He closed his eyes, a small noise of pleasure escaping his lips, before his eyes snapped open, watching me stroke him again and again, reveling in how silky he felt. He quickly stepped out of the rest of his pants, his eyes on my bare breasts.

Suddenly, his lips were on mine again, his tongue pushing into my mouth as steam from the shower billowed around us, the reflection in the mirror over the sink basin distorting as it filled with fog.

I started to pulse between my legs, my inner walls already clamping down in anticipation of him as molten heat pooled between my thighs.

He cupped my breasts with both hands, his thumbs sliding over my already sensitive nipples.

"Gods, I missed these," he said. "And you. All of you." His chest heaved, his hips suddenly bucking beneath my ministrations. I had both hands on him now, twisting the head of his cock as I cupped his balls. I couldn't get enough of him. The way he felt, the way he looked. The sounds he was making, the way his hips were moving with urgency, as he fucked himself into my hands.

Cursing under his breath, he stilled, and gently pulled my hands away. "I need to see you. I need to see all of you," he said, his accent now thick and guttural.

My bottom half was still completely covered, and now he was the one kneeling before me, unlacing my boots, and pulling them off my feet, before rolling down the socks beneath and tossing them into the corner.

He looked up at me, his emerald eyes blazing with fire as his hands reached for my waist, his fingers tangling in the laces. One swift tug and they'd come untied. He hungrily reached for my pants as well as my underclothes, shoving them down in one move.

I shuddered, startled at being completely naked again before him. My skin was heated and my arousal started to slide down my leg.

The look Rhyan was giving me though—it was everything, full of awe and wonder, and lust, and devotion.

And love.

He blinked rapidly, his eyes darting over every inch of my skin, like he didn't know where to look first—like he couldn't take enough of me in.

I was doing the same to him, drowning in the sight of his body. His body was so beautiful to me, even more magnificent than I remembered. Because it was his. Because his soul was inside it. Even without an aura, he seemed to glow, lit up with his own kindness and goodness and passion and love.

He was kneeling now before me, and pulled my foot onto his lap. He kissed my knee, his hands sliding up my thigh, pulling my leg closer as his lips followed the path, moving higher and higher.

His kisses were searing against my sensitive skin until he reached the apex. One gaze up at me and my blood heated. His fingers slid over my folds, parting me, before closing over the bundle of nerves at my center. He moved his thumb over me, circling again and again. My hips bucked just as he replaced his thumb with his lips and sucked, his tongue flicking against me.

"Gods," I gasped, nearly falling forward. My knees buckled and I grabbed blindly for his head. My fingers tightened in the curls at the nape of his neck while he reached one hand behind my ass, pulling me closer, locking me in. I was immobile against him, and all I could do was try to hold onto him as ripples of pleasure raced through my body, coiling tighter and tighter between my legs.

One finger slipped inside me and I clenched around him, feeling like I was going to tip over the edge. And in truth, it wasn't going to take much. Despite the pain, despite the uncertainty and the long road of healing I knew lay ahead of us, there was an unbridled joy racing through me—pulsing through my heart, bringing it back to life.

Because Rhyan was here, he was back, and that alone was going to make me come. He added another finger, pumping them in and out, as his tongue laved at my center. He groaned, his fingers curling inside me.

My orgasm tore through me, my back arching and toes curling as I cried out. Still shuddering and shaking, I collapsed against Rhyan, and he gathered me into his lap, my head resting against his neck, our hearts pressed together, and beating as one.

"Fuck," he said, brushing my hair back. He nipped at my ear. "You taste better than I remember."

I blushed. "I thought we were supposed to get in the shower."

"Oh," he said, raising one eyebrow. "We are." He locked my ankles around his back, his cock pressed against my center. The tip glistened with his own arousal. Then his hands were around my ass as I clasped my fingers around his neck.

Rhyan rose to his feet, and a second later stumbled into the shower, still holding me.

He pushed me against the wall, the tiles cool against my fevered skin. At once, I started to arch, grinding against him. His cock pulsed between us, and I couldn't help but reach for him again, sliding the moisture down, and coating him with more of my own. My lips found his neck, kissing and sucking and biting.

I needed to claim him, to brand him, to tell the whole fucking universe he was mine and I would unleash hell on anyone who tried to come between us. I needed every lick and kiss and touch to say that there was nowhere he could be taken, nowhere he could be hidden where I wouldn't find him, wouldn't come for him. No dimension, no timeline, no realm. It didn't matter. He was mine and he always, always would be.

We writhed together, every part of his cock rubbing against me, reigniting the heat inside as we built more friction and pleasure.

"You ready for me, partner?" he asked, one eyebrow raised.

"Yes," I said. "Yes. Rhyan, please. Please."

His eyes narrowed, his eyes flicking down my body and back to mine. "Please what?"

I gripped his face in my hands, pushing my hips so far forward, the head of his cock slid just barely inside.

"Please fuck me," I gasped, pushing forward trying to pull him all the way in, to take him deeper. "Now."

But he pulled himself back, leaving me empty. I was near tears. One orgasm hadn't been enough. I needed more. I needed all of him. I needed to feel him fill me. To make me whole. And much as I needed to claim him, I wanted him to do the same to me. To know it was his body, his soul, his heart and mind, all that made him Rhyan doing it.

But as he watched me writhe and buck, begging him to take me, a vicious glint emerged from the emerald of his irises.

"Where did Auriel touch you?" he rasped, his voice dangerously low.

"Wh-what?" I asked.

"Where," he demanded, "did he touch you? Was it here?" He kissed my mouth. "Here?" He licked my neck. "Here?" He pulled on my breast, squeezing it before he lowered his lips onto my nipple.

"I-I—" I was too lost in the sensations to answer. Too muddled with my own desire for him and confusion to think straight. "I thought—" I gasped as he sucked on my other nipple. I bucked, but he used his body to flatten me against the wall, keeping his hips and cock cruelly away from my sex. One hand slid down, cupping me between my legs.

"What about here?" he asked. "Did you let him touch you here?"

I cried out, as he slid two fingers inside of me, curling and pumping in and out, in and out. "I thought ... ah ... you weren't ... mad ... about ... that."

His eyebrow arched, his nostrils flaring. "I said you didn't have to be sorry for what you did with him. That you didn't do anything wrong."

I frowned.

"And you didn't," he said, softly kissing the tip of my nose. Then he slid a third finger inside, fucking me with a bruising pace. "But I never said," he thrust, "that I wasn't mad."

I panted. "You—you're mad?" I asked. "What the hell is this?" I circled my hips against his hand, greedily seeking more friction, biting my lip as fresh waves of pleasure rounded and tightened in my core.

"Your punishment," he said, his thumb pressing against my center. His forehead pressed against mine, angled and our lips slanted together. "I know you feel guilty."

"I do," I panted in frustration.

"So then, do you want me to punish you?" he asked. "Give us both some satisfaction?"

"Yes," I practically choked out the word "Do it. Punish me. Claim me. Fuck me."

"I do claim you, Lyr. Lyriana. You were always mine. Mine since before the dawn of time." His hand flew into my hair, his fingers grasping my hair at the base of my neck. "And I'm going to remind you of that, remind you that I belong to you, and you belong to me and only me with every thrust. Every touch, every kiss, every time you come for the rest of your life. I'm going to make sure you know it's me. I'm going to make you say it."

"I'm yours," I gasped. "I'm yours."

He pulled my hair at the back of my neck, the sensation more pleasurable than I'd realized, and then suddenly, his fingers flattened and he turned my head down.

"Then watch," he said. "Watch as this cock, *my cock*, takes you and fills your cunt."

He gripped himself, and then slammed into me, burying himself to the hilt in one thrust.

"Fuck," I yelled, as he cursed. I was more than wet and ready for him, but after weeks of deprivation, my body needed a second to remember how to adjust and accommodate his length. It stung for a second, and then I stretched around him, and the pleasure began to grow and pulse, rippling through me.

His mouth was on mine, our tongues dancing as he pumped into me, slamming his hips in and out, again and again.

"Rhyan," I yelled. I couldn't stop. I wanted to say his name for the rest of my life. "Rhyan, Rhyan, Rhyan."

"Yes, Lyr. Yes," he hissed. "Tell me! Say it. Say who's fucking you," he growled. "Who?"

"You. You are."

"And who do you belong to?" he asked.

"You, Rhyan. I belong to you."

"And whose cock are you going to come all over?" he barked.

"Yours," I cried. "Yours."

"Then do it," he growled. "Come on, Lyr. I feel you tightening. You're squeezing me so fucking hard. Come on. Come for me. Come." His eyes flashed, boring into mine. He had the same vulnerable look in them he had the night he died, when I picked him up in my arms, and told him he wasn't going to die. "Lyr," he panted. "Lyr."

And that was all it took. I was coming, falling apart, my body trembling, my throat raw as I screamed, and tears filled my eyes.

"There you go," he said. "There you fucking go." He continued fucking me through every last spasm, his cock twitching inside me. And when my toes uncurled, my body loosening like jelly, Rhyan buried his head against my neck, his hips thrusting faster and faster, moving wildly. It was all I could do to hold on. He tightened against me, stilling suddenly, and then I felt his release spilling inside, spurting with such force, it was already sliding down my leg, mixing with my own arousal.

Rhyan roared my name, and gasped, pulling his head up, fresh tears in his eyes.

I pulled his face toward mine. My ankles locked together, keeping him deep inside me as I found his lips, kissing him. "*Rakame*," I said between kisses. "Your soul is mine."

"*Mekara*," he sobbed. "My soul is yours."

I nodded. "Because we always find each other."

"Always," he said. "Are you okay? Was I—was I too rough?"

I smiled, my eyes watering. "You were perfect." I leaned forward, kissed his tears, and buried my head against his neck, stroking his shoulders and back.

We stood like that together, our breathing slowing to a more manageable rhythm, and finally, he pulled out, hissing through his teeth. I was feeling overly sensitive, too, as I finally touched the floor of the shower, standing before him.

Rhyan hugged me, our bodies still trying to get as close as possible. We only broke apart when the water began to lose heat.

Without speaking, we both reached for the shampoo bottles, and soap, taking turns washing each other's hair, and bodies until there was no hint of the cave left on us, no hint of the fights from earlier, no hint of anything but him and me.

Rhyan turned off the water, and stepped out first, reaching for the towel to wrap around my body. We were careful as we dried each other off, taking our time to give every inch of skin attention, and then we stumbled, exhausted, bleary-eyed and content into bed.

I laid back on the pillows, drawing Rhyan into my arms, his head resting against my breast. My fingers tangled in his hair, and for a moment he tensed.

"What happened?" I asked.

"Memory. Bad one."

"I'm here," I said. "And you're here with me. We're alive, we're together." I soothed the wrinkle he'd made with his brow, until his eyes closed, his breathing slowing. "It's okay. I've got you."

"Lyr," he breathed softly. His eyes were closing, but there was still some tension in his body.

"Rhyan," I said, shifting my hand to massage his back.

"Even after I fall asleep," he whispered, his voice shaking. "Will you still hold me a little longer?"

"I'll hold you, even while you're dreaming."

Golden light emanated from my chest, the Valalumir inside of me had awakened. I drew the blankets up over his shoulders, holding him as close as I could. And when the light faded, his breathing even, I closed my eyes, too.

CHAPTER THIRTY-SEVEN

RHYAN

By the Gods. By the fucking Gods. My chest tightened with such visceral pain, I couldn't breathe. I couldn't breathe. Fuck. Fuck. Everything hurt. Every limb, every organ, like I was being torn apart, sewn back together and ripped through again.

"What's going on? What the hell is happening to me?" I cried out.

Auriel appeared, my mirror image, except with hair the color of gold, and skin nearly as tan.

"What is this?" I clutched at my chest. "What's wrong with me?" I asked.

"Nothing," he said. "Just your memories coming back to you."

"But I haven't forgotten anything."

"No, but you didn't cross over, you still have to experience them."

I shook my head. "Why does this hurt so bad? What memory is this?"

"It's the night you died," he said solemnly. "I'm sorry."

"No. NO!" *But there it was again. The Nutavian Katurium laid out before me. Tears filled my vision so completely, I could barely see. I could hear the screams in the stadiums as I approached, the yells coming from the Palace prison fading behind me. The chains around my legs and arms clinked and clanged with each step I took. Dust flew at my heels, further fogging my vision as I was led into the center of the arena.*

The curses were coming now—the calls for my death, the condemnation, the insults. They rained down on me, growing louder and more insistent with each step. Rising to a crescendo, my father pushed me up onto the dais, my heart thundering so loud, for a moment it drowned out the noise.

Lyr. I was thinking of Lyr. Her name had become a mantra, a prayer, one I was making to her, to a Goddess. I wasn't praying for her to save me. I was beyond hope for that. But for a distraction—some comfort—a moment to forget the pain coming for me, the humiliation, the debilitating fear.

Lyr, Lyr. Lyr, please.

But the roar of the crowd was too much, too loud, too powerful, and too violent. It pulled me back into my body. The chains were removed. My arms felt heavy, almost useless as they were lifted over my head and strung up, tied to the stripping pole. A soturion came up behind me, and I heard the rip of my tunic, felt the material bite into my flesh as it was torn away. My back was exposed. My tattoo on display.

I could almost see it in my mind, as clear as the day I'd gotten it. The gryphon—the one that had saved my life, helped me escape Glemaria, and the rope around its leg. The torn rope. The symbol of my own strength and will, the power I'd clawed and fought for.

A very different kind of rope held me down now. And with my power bound—and the chains still wrapped around my feet, I knew it was the last one. The last rope.

The one I'd never tear through.

I was shivering now, my entire body shaking with cold. There was a breeze in the air carrying a chill from the shore that lay beyond the Palace. But that wasn't what was leaving my body trembling. Being from the North, this kind of cold was somewhat warm to me.

No. The shivers covering my skin came from my growing fear. And within a minute, I was sweating.

The rest of my guests on the dais arrived—each one garnering their own round of applause. Imperator Kormac—now the

Emperor—*and the Bastardmaker proudly stood beside my father, and fucking Kane. And then, of course, what stripping would be complete without the Examiner. Without the one who would execute me in the end*—*Kunda Lith.*

The Emperor sneered, his black eyes full of sickening triumph. He'd won. He'd fucking won. And I didn't think my father knew it yet. Not that I cared.

Because what did any of it matter now?

I looked away, trying to breathe, trying to think of Lyr, to remember her face and her smell and her voice. I needed her in my mind, the only place I could keep her. But she was gone. I couldn't focus, I couldn't lose myself in her because the crowd was only ratcheting up their noise and excitement, their auras pulsing through the arena with a vicious cruelty.

The Emperor cleared his throat, a wolfish glint in his eyes as he swept his gaze over me, then began calling out my crimes. Listing them out one by one.

I scoffed. My crimes.

There were no crimes as far as I was concerned. Being vorakh wasn't evil, it was just who I was. It was power. It was a gift. And loving Lyr? Fuck anyone who called it illegal or forbidden. As if some Godsdamned made-up law could dictate who I loved. As if loving her wasn't my destiny or my entire soul's purpose in being here.

Helping Jules escape? And Galen? Getting them away from the black-eyed monster who stood before me, the one who orchestrated his own uncle's murder, who kidnapped, raped and tortured thousands for his own gain? There was nothing more honorable than freeing them from his clutches.

If I regretted anything, it was that I hadn't freed more from his prisons. Saved more from his grasp. That I hadn't strangled him or cut out his heart when I'd had the chance.

Beyond that my only other regret was that I lived in a world that made doing the right thing—that made being on the side of justice and goodness—a crime.

I held my head up, realizing that that thought alone had given me courage. Had made me feel strong again. That and knowing just how deeply and well I'd loved Lyr, and how much she loved me back, accepted me, all of me.

But a look from my father, from my own blood, the one who captured me, who turned me in, who'd been the one to damn me, and it all went to shit. Even I could only be so strong. My mother was gone. It was just him. And he hadn't just abandoned me. He'd damned me.

Something inside of me broke.

Auriel flashed before me.

"Am I done?" I asked him. "Is it over?"

He slowly shook his head. "No. I'm sorry. I'd trade places with you if I could. But I can't."

Kunda announced the first strike of the whip. Immediately I tensed, and tried to breathe, tried to prepare. I could withstand this, I could bear the pain. After all, it wasn't as if I hadn't been whipped before. Sometimes even just like this, with my father and Kane looking on. I just had to brace myself. I had to breathe.

But then the pain came. And, fuck.

I couldn't do it, couldn't withstand it. I was wrong. So fucking wrong.

I panicked and bit my tongue. I could feel the whip not just striking and wounding, but pulling my magic out of me, like someone had taken a burning poker and sliced me open with it, poking and prodding, searching inside of me, my skin, my muscles, my bones.

I screamed, feeling the whip retreat. Feeling my magic go with it. Part of me. Part of my essence, part of who I was. Part of what made me Rhyan. It had been taken. It was gone.

The crowd roared, and blood dripped down my back as I spat. The whirring in my ears as the whip came again was worse the second time. Even worse was the third.

The fourth strike.

I wet myself.

They cut off my pants next—leaving me nearly naked, save my underclothes.

I heaved my guts up. My stomach roiled painfully.

I was weakening. Dying. Closer to death with every strike. Losing my soul. I knew it was coming. I knew how this ended. No one survived the stripping. No one survived the pain, the rearranging of their insides as their magic was torn out.

I knew there couldn't be much left when my father laughed. By now, I welcomed it. I wanted it to be over. I wanted it to end.

Someone screamed. Someone in the crowd. It was strange—strange that someone else seemed to be in pain—someone who wasn't me. More yells followed, more cries of terror, and then there were cries for help.

I stared at the ground, feeling a ball of sweat collect on my chin. I waited for it to drop, to splatter to the ground, to mix with all the rest of my bodily fluids. It seemed like almost every kind I could make was at my feet. Blood, sweat, tears, urine, vomit. Fuck. All I had to do now was shit myself.

And then the Emperor shouted, "Lyriana Batavia."

My head lifted at once, my heart pounding. "Wh-what?" I asked. But my voice was so hoarse from screaming, my throat so raw, I could barely hear myself. "Lyr," I said. "Lyr." I didn't know if I was talking to her, or asking for her, or simply saying her name because it was all I could manage at the moment.

But then the whip came again, biting into my skin, digging into my flesh, searching through me. My head fell, and a scream tore from me as the whip pulled away, taking more of me with it, along with any conscious thoughts.

The ground swayed beneath me, my vision blurring. There was movement on the dais. Bodies shifting, auras panicking. The Emperor was gone. The Bastardmaker, too. I noticed then, in my peripheral vision, a flurry of soturion boots running away. The crowd was screaming now, but not at me.

"Protect His Majesty!" someone cried out.

"Guard His Highness!" came another shout.

I thought my father had said Lyr's name again, I thought he was speaking to her, but I was so far gone ... I was no longer processing thoughts. No longer able to discern reality from pain.

"End it. Kunda, now," he commanded.

No! No!

But he did it anyway. He took what little remained of my magic, my power.

Blue light flowed from the end of the whip into a box. All of my magic, all of my power, all of me, stolen, trapped and contained. By my father. And a scream tore my throat. A sound I'd never made before.

"I thought I was dead then," I said.

Auriel frowned. "You almost were."

"Why didn't I die?" I asked.

"Because she came," Auriel said, showing me a brief vision of Lyr fighting through the arena, her hair a fiery red, her hazel eyes like golden flames as she stabbed every soturion in her way.

"She kept you tethered to her," he said. "She doesn't even know. She saved your life. No one survives the stripping. But her soul called out to yours, and it was a far stronger pull than the cries your soul made to mine, to yourself, to your original form. In the end, it was sealed in blood, in kashonim. But without that connection—that alone wouldn't have been enough."

I blinked, back on the dais, and suddenly, miraculously, my pain began to lessen. I looked up and found Lyr crouching before me. Beautiful. Strong. Amazing. A true Goddess in human flesh.

"Are you ..." I couldn't finish. I'd started coughing up blood. "You're really here?" I finally managed.

"I'm really here, Rhyan," she said. "I've got you. It's all right. It's over now. It's going to be okay. I'm going to protect you."

But all I could think was no. No. Leave me. I'm done. I'm dying. Get away from my father, away from the men who want to hurt you. But she stayed. And lifted me up into her arms.

And then the akadim came.

I wrapped my arms around my chest, shaking my head. "This part is worse," I said.

Auriel didn't speak. He only nodded.

I was laying on the ground, hidden in the stadium seats, barely able to move while Lyr fought the beasts. The beasts who could attack in the daytime. They'd evolved. Aemon's work. Moriel's evil.

Lyr had left to defend me, to fight them off. To stop the threat. But there were too many.

I lost track of time and space. The next thing I knew, I was being dragged over the rough stone of the benches, and ...

I'd wondered if this was what Garrett had felt. Or Haleika. Countless victims over thousands of years. Was this what it was like? This desperate crazed need to try and hold onto your life, your heart and mind, the inner fight that commenced when you felt your soul being stolen from you? The painful desperate clinging to all you were, all you knew, because it was you, it was yours. And now it was being taken. Everything was being taken.

I thought of Lyr. Over and over. Until the end. Until I didn't think of anything at all.

I awoke in the woods after dark. Akadim. A monster. Starving. Every bodily desire on edge. I was thirsty, and hungry, and horny, and itching for a fight.

Until I wasn't. Until ... Morgana found me. Collared me. Made me her soldier. Her Arkturion.

Morning came, and the sun.

"You remembered who you were," Auriel said.

I shook my head. "Much good it did me."

"It did. You weren't here. You were gone. But what you left behind was powerful. Your discipline, your strength."

I somehow was in my akadim body, but I was also me, outside of myself, and watching.

"You're hungry, Rhyan? Aren't you?" Morgana asked, her dark eyes dipping down my body, to the loincloth I'd found in the night and used to cover myself.

I knew what she was asking of me, what she wanted. And I was hungry. So very hungry.

My cock twitched and my arms flexed, my mouth salivating. I wanted it all. Food, sex, violence. A soul to eat.

"Very hungry," she said with approval. A grin spread across her cold, beautiful face.

"Maraaka," I said and licked my lips, taking a step forward, taking in the sight of Parthenay's slight body. I noted how thin she was, how weak she appeared. It would be so easy to slam her down, to take off her dress, to drink her blood.

No. No. No.

I tried to look away, to hide from the scene. I didn't want to be here again. I didn't want to remember this. But all I did was end up inside my akadim body, looking out through those eyes.

"Take her," she commanded. "Take her however you want. Feast on her, fuck her, drink her blood."

Yes. Yes!

Morgana shoved the girl forward as she screamed, calling out desperately to Aemon for help.

I remembered her—remembered my disdain. Remembered my hatred for Aemon. I loved that I could hurt this girl, for what she'd done to me, done to Lyr, and I loved that I was doing this in front of Aemon. She was his servant and I could touch her. Hurt her the way he'd hurt Lyr. Hurt her while he watched.

I pounced, my nostrils flaring, as I crushed her body beneath mine.

But it wasn't her beneath me. It was Lyr. We were in the cave, in the Wall of the Prince.

"I'm afraid," she cried. "I'm afraid you're going to hurt me."

I jumped back, shaking my head. No. No. What have I done? What have I done?

"Rhyan, please," Lyr begged, her eyes filling with tears.

"Lyr?" I asked. "Lyr? LYR!"

A black box rattled before me, blue light exploding from within.

Lyr screamed.

I woke with a jolt, my heart slamming into my chest, my stomach roiling, sweat coating my brow. I was alive. I was alive again. And mortal. My soul returned. But my power was still gone.

I gasped for breath, my chest heaving painfully.

"Rhyan," Lyr said softly, stirring from sleep. "Rhyan, you're okay. You were just dreaming. I'm right here."

I was still laying on top of her, partially on my side, my head against her breast, her hand on my back. I shifted and turned onto my belly, burying my face in her heart, just as I burst into tears.

I felt her fingers in my hair, then her arms wrapped around me, pulling me closer, holding me.

"Shhh," she said. "It's okay. I've got you."

But I couldn't stop crying. I calmed down a little while later, shifting back beside her. She took my hand in hers, squeezing tight.

"Do you want to talk about it?" she asked.

I shook my head noncommittally. My face damp from all the tears. "I was back there. The night I died."

She pulled me closer then, like she needed the contact and reminder I was alive as much as I did.

"You were remembering?" she asked, her voice breaking.

"Reliving it," I said, managing barely more than a hushed whisper. "Auriel was there, too."

She stiffened.

"I think it was more of the connection forming between us. I don't know. But after I ... I died, I saw my first morning as an akadim again. Lyr, I—Fuck. I did something awful."

She took a deep breath, paling, and even without my magic or my heightened senses, I could hear her heart thundering, feel her nerves on edge. "Did you—?" She closed her eyes, like she was too afraid to ask the question. The question I knew she had. "Did you rape anyone?" she finally asked, her voice hushed.

I shook my head.

Her relief was all over her face.

"But I wanted to," I said.

She stilled, slowly shaking her head, her brows furrowed. "No, you didn't."

I swallowed roughly. "Not me, but you know what I mean. What happened when my soul was gone—when my body became akadim, I remember it all like it *was* me. The akadim had my memories. And I have its. And in my mind and in my dreams now, I remember what I wanted to do. What I came close to doing when I had a chance. It was—do you remember that night on Gryphon's Mount? When we opened your—Asherah's—tomb? And that mage captured us, the one who brought us to Aemon?"

Lyr's mouth tightened as she sucked in a sharp breath and nodded.

"Her name is Parthenay. She was a chayatim mind reader, now traveling with Morgana—she's Aemon's Second."

Lyr pushed up onto her elbow, her gaze intense. "Really?"

I nodded. "Morgana doesn't get along with her. And she makes it known."

"Why?" she asked.

I shrugged. "I don't know if there's history between them. But there is one major difference in opinion. Morgana forbids rape. It was the first thing she told us—commanded. Except that first morning, I don't know, she was making some kind of power play. Proving a point. She called me forward—told me to—commanded that I—well, you know."

"What?" Lyr cried, her aura filling with fire and fury. "In front of everyone?"

I looked away, my cheeks heating, my stomach twisting. "I didn't, in the end. But I came close. Morgana made me stop."

"Morgana made you start," she seethed. "I'm going to— Gods! When I fucking see her again—"

"Lyr," I said, "It doesn't matter why now. All that matters is that it didn't happen."

She nodded slowly, trying to control her breathing. "I know."

"But when I dreamt it, I remembered having her—" I turned on my back, closing my eyes, too ashamed to look at Lyr now. To admit how twisted my mind had become. "I was on top of her. And I hurt her. Because I wanted to. But in my dream, she was—she was you."

"It was just a dream."

'No," I said. "I mean, sure, that was. But it's still real. Especially to me. I still know what happened to you when I was akadim. And it's confusing. Because I half feel like it was me, like I can't trust myself around you. And I want to throw up, and get away from you, to keep you safe from me. And a second later, I want to pull you close and kiss you and protect you. But I feel like it's me I need to protect you from."

"Rhyan," Lyr said softly. "Look at me. Look."

I opened my eyes and turned back to her. She'd sat up, the blanket we'd slept under falling to her hips. Her bare breasts peeked out from the long waves of her hair, red in the morning sun. Her hazel eyes blazed. "What happened to me wasn't your fault. And what happened to you, wasn't yours either. I know who you are." She reached for my heart. "*Ani janam ra. Rakame.*"

"I know you," I said back. "*Mekara.*"

Lyr nodded, her eyes softening. "There's more than one person who needs to pay for what they did to you. And I think it's time to extract payment. Because it's what's right, because it's the justice they fucking deserve for their crimes. Because it will protect others—save them from their evil, their cruelty. And, most importantly for you—for you to take back your power."

My mind flashed on the box in my dream. In my memory.

"Lyr," I said, "When you came to the arena and found me, my father was there. Was he holding a black box?"

She gasped, her eyes widening. "Yes. Kunda was putting your magic in there after he stripped it. I remember—your father took it and ran."

"So he has my magic." My hands clenched into fists, even as a small burst of hope rose to the surface. "Have you ever heard of it being restored after it was stripped?" I asked.

She shook her head. "No. I haven't."

I exhaled shakily. "Auriel in my dream said I should have died when it was over. That you had tethered my soul to yours, you kept me here. You saved my life."

"He did?" Her voice quaked.

"He did. Maybe there's a way," I said. "If I can survive being stripped, if you can bring me back to life, restore my soul after I became akadim, then maybe there's a way I can take back my power—not symbolically. But actually fucking take it back."

"Anything is possible," she said. "If it can be removed, it can be put back in. Just like your soul."

"Nothing new was ever created. Nothing destroyed." The words of the Valya. My lips lifted, just for a second. "Maybe with the red shard, and your ability to heal, it truly is possible."

She gripped the back of my neck, forcing my gaze up to her. "Rhyan, I will find a way. I swear it."

"We'll need to remove my father first. Permanently. He sacrificed me to curry favor with Kormac. But also I think, I think it was because he could never really control me—or

Auriel peeking out. He wanted my power. Wanted it for himself." Despite the fact that I was his son, his flesh and blood. The one person he was supposed to love. My chest tightened as my gaze locked onto Lyr. "He's not going to give it up."

"Not alive, maybe. But dead," she said simply, "he'll have no choice."

My heart thrummed. "He's let too many innocents suffer my fate." My hand clenched. "Allowed the enemy to grow too large, allowed the Allurian Pass to go unchecked, allowed akadim to roam free, all so he could keep the North unstable, so he could keep his power. Continue his tyranny. It ends now."

Lyr's eyes blazed.

"And not just my father," I said. "All of them. Kane, Kormac, Aemon—they all need to be removed from this world."

Lyr squeezed my hand, her aura now filled with a different kind of fire. Not fury, but a kind of controlled understanding of the need for vengeance, the need to right the wrongs done not just to us—but to all of the Empire. A fight that was always coming. And it was about fucking time we met it head on.

"Where should we start?" she asked, a dangerous gleam in her eyes.

I swallowed. "My father. We're going North. It's time. His reign is finally going to come to an end. I need to remove him from his Seat of Power."

Lyr nodded. "You will. And I'll be right beside you."

CHAPTER THIRTY-EIGHT

LYRIANA

My pulse thrummed with excitement and fear. We were going to end the tyranny of Rhyan's father. Ever since the night Rhyan had confessed to me how he'd gotten his scar—since he'd woken from a nightmare so powerful, he'd caused a blizzard to erupt in his apartment—I'd wanted his father to pay. I'd wanted to offer him violence.

And ever since I watched him run from the dais like a coward, his son dying, Rhyan's stolen magic in his arms—I wanted to rip his throat out.

Of course, we needed a plan. Glemaria was well protected with far too many soturi who remained loyal to their Arkasva and Imperator, either out of a sense of nationalism, or fear and coercion. Either way, we needed to think, and that meant I needed Rhyan strong again.

I brushed his hair back from his face, my fingers soft against the furrow of his brow. He was doing so well considering, but when he thought I wasn't looking, there was a haunted look in his eyes. Like he was still seeing the world through the vision of an akadim, still being plagued by the memories.

I sat up in our bed and stretched my arms. "First things first," I said. "Before we do anything. I need to feed you. You need food. A lot of food. I should have already gotten you some." If he hadn't passed out in my arms after the shower, I would have. But I couldn't let go of him. Not once all night. I couldn't leave the room, or be away. Not even for a second. Not after what we'd been through. I shook my head, feeling a pang of guilt anyway. "You didn't even eat last night."

"No?" One eyebrow lowered, his eyes hooded.

"No," I said.

His lips curled. "Oh, you fed me all right," he said. "I ate."

"What? No you didn't."

He grabbed my waist, and threw me onto my back, crawling over me. He kissed my belly, his tongue darting out and dragging across my skin with a kind of tortuous sensuality leading down to my core. I gasped as he nuzzled his nose between my folds, inhaling deeply.

"I. Ate," he repeated, and gripped my hips, leaning his head over to bite one. "You fed me very well."

I covered my eyes with my hand and laughed. "I meant real food."

"Hmmmm," he said, forcing the sound through his lips so they vibrated against my sensitive skin.

"Rhyan," I shuddered, already wanting him again. But despite his sudden playfulness, he did need real food, actual calories and nutrients. Especially now that he was powerless. I remembered all too well what that was like. I reached down between my legs, his head already back there.

He licked me from bottom to top. Then pressed a kiss on the bundle of nerves at my center.

"Fuck," I grunted. But I gripped his head, and pulled him up over me, kissing his lips, and tasting myself. "Rhyan, focus. I need to feed you nutrients. You can have *that* for dessert if you eat everything else first. But we have a problem."

"Besides getting to Glemaria without getting caught and while I have no power?" he teased.

I shook my head, biting back a laugh. "I'm glad you're in a good mood."

"I'm trying," he said, and kissed me again.

"There is the problem of getting to Glemaria without getting caught, while you have no power," I said. "And then figuring out how to remove your father, while also not getting caught—because as much as I want to see him pay for his crimes, and make sure he can never hurt or touch you again—" Something dark flashed in his eyes, the muscles of his jaw working. "I'm not losing you. I'm not risking you. If we do this, we do it right. We do it together. We survive, and we remain free."

"We will. I swear," he said.

"Good. Because perhaps what's worrying me more than you without power at the moment, is you without any boots to wear."

"Right," he said, frowning. "I don't have any shoes. And I can't jump."

"We'll get you boots. Auriel and I had some money we … procured."

"Stole?" Rhyan's good eyebrow lifted.

"Well, it's not like Auriel had access to a bank account." Or me, as the Empire's traitor.

Rhyan laughed. "No. So we'll go and get some boots in town."

"We?" I asked.

"I'm coming with you." He sounded like he meant to be flirtatious, but his voice wobbled, like he was scared—scared of being separated again. It had happened before. In Korteria. I'd let go of his hand when we were jumping together, escaping from his father's nahashim. He'd traveled without me, and I'd been taken by Brockton Kormac.

After a separation like the one we'd just had, I imagined it was hitting Rhyan even harder. It was hitting me, too.

I squinted at his feet. "If you're sure. But so we don't get any unwanted attention, I'll glamour boots for you to wear in the meantime," I said, "before you get real ones. I also ... since we've been here, I've been changing my hair and armor to hide my identity, and blend in. Blonde and silver."

"Like Ka Kormac," Rhyan seethed.

"So no one knows it's me."

"Hmmm." He closed his eyes and nodded. Probably seeing my hair change color through Auriel's memories.

"Also," I frowned, "you are hungry, aren't you? I know akadim don't eat regular food."

He coughed uncomfortably. "I am. I'm hungry."

"Oh." I sighed in relief. "Good. I mean, not good. I don't want you to be hungry. I just—wasn't sure—if there were any, I guess, side-effects of your transformation."

"I'm sure there's plenty we don't know about. But from what I can feel, hunger's not one of them. And I'm positive I can eat real food."

"Okay then," I said, "Let's go. I want to see you eat, and get armored up. Then we can make a plan on what to do next."

"Like meeting up with everyone else. Dario, and Aiden, and Jules, Meera. Tristan. Galen." Rhyan frowned. "Are they here, too? Or nearby?"

I froze.

"What?" he asked. "What's wrong?"

"Well, I lost ... um," I looked down, "I lost them that night." My voice shook. "Dario was supposed to protect them all while I went after you."

"Lost? What do you mean? What happened?" He paled, his eyes moving quickly before they focused on me again. He was starting to remember more details, take in more of Auriel's memories. Then his face fell. "Gods. We were in Thene. They were in Thene!"

"I got word that they all left the inn sometime after I did, to hide from the Emperor's soturi. But ... I haven't heard anything about Dario, Aiden, Meera, and Jules since they left.

I have no idea where they are, or if they're okay. I've been just praying that no news is good news."

Rhyan frowned. "Dario's strong. If he's with them, I have faith that they're okay. He wouldn't betray your trust."

"Not on purpose," I said. "I burned through the blood contract with your father when I came to the arena, I think my *Rakashonim* did. But as far as I know, their contracts are still in effect."

"What about—You didn't mention Galen." He frowned. "Or Tristan."

I sighed, and took his hand. "Galen's dead. He was captured."

Rhyan sucked in a breath, his eyes distant and then he nodded, like he knew, like he remembered. "Galen." His voice shook.

I nodded, biting my lip. I hadn't been able to think much about him. To grieve the way I needed to. I hadn't allowed myself any more room for sadness, any more room for anything that could slow me down. But Galen deserved more. And he'd have it. Soon.

"And Tristan," I said. "Tristan was made the head of some kind of vorakh task force by the Emperor. They're doing mandatory testing now, enforcing them with nahashim at random checkpoints. They're arresting anyone they even suspect of vorakh."

Rhyan's gaze was distant. "They freed chayatim," he said slowly. "That night."

"They did."

He shook his head. "Have to replenish their resources. Shit. Can we trust Tristan?"

"No," I said sadly. "I don't think he betrayed us. I don't think he would now—not after what we did. But I don't think he's acting freely either."

"Damn." Rhyan's jaw tensed. "He isn't. He's vorakh, too." He entwined our fingers together, his eyes on mine. "I saw how haunted he looked that night. He's not free."

"No."

"We'll have to find him. All of them. After we deal with my father."

"And then there's the whole New Korteria thing," my stomach turned, "it's supposed to be temporary, but you know that was Kormac's plan all along. To conquer Bamaria. And now my aunt let him."

"We're going to figure that out, too," he said.

Rhyan shifted, his hand warm as he settled it against my thigh.

I was suddenly very aware that we were both still naked, and in bed. And the small fire Rhyan had stoked inside me from just one lick, was still burning. Our eyes met.

But then I was even more aware of Rhyan's stomach grumbling, and shook my head.

"Food, and boots," I said, kissing him quickly. "Let's get dressed."

A few minutes later, we were ready, clothed as best as we could be, armored up—Rhyan in his new golden armor, the green shard of the Valalumir. And we were armed, including the red shard on my back. Rhyan looked like himself again, like the soturion I knew he was—minus the fact that he had no shoes.

But a moment later, black leather boots appeared around his feet, laced up to his knees. He was barefoot in reality—but, it would keep anyone who saw us from looking twice.

Then I went to work on the rest of our glamours. My hair became an icy-white blonde shade, as did Rhyan's. For a second, my heart thundered. I thought I was looking at Auriel again. I was overjoyed to be with Rhyan. But I hadn't expected to lose Auriel so suddenly. To not have a chance to truly say goodbye. To hug him one last time. To thank him. Rhyan said they'd connected as their souls moved—Rhyan's into his body, and Auriel's back through the dimension that led him home. But I wished I could see or talk to him, just know that he was home and safe, and back in Asherah's arms.

My arms. Because I was Asherah. And Rhyan was Auriel. And every life he'd lived, every life in which I'd loved him in, was precious.

But I let the thought go. One problem at a time. And we had more than enough to deal with.

Another sweep of my stave, and we were both in Kormac silver.

Rhyan's eyes widened when he saw my transformation. "By the Gods," he said.

"You hate it?" I asked, touching my hair self-consciously. "It's not really my color."

He pulled me into his arms. "Partner, every color is your color." He kissed my forehead.

An hour later, we sat in the darkest corner of a pub, Rhyan wearing his new black boots.

He looked longingly at his food as it arrived at the table. I'd ordered everything off the menu. It was his first meal in almost two months. I wanted him to have everything.

There were eggs and bread and dips, berries and melons, pancakes, and fried potatoes. Plates and plates of them.

His jaw tightened, his chest heaving.

"Go ahead," I said. "Eat."

"What about you?" he asked.

"I'll have whatever you don't want. But this is yours."

He reached under the table, his hand seeking mine and squeezing it, his foot shaking. His jaw muscle worked. Then he took a fork, and stabbed it through the plate of scrambled eggs, his eyes reddening as he brought it to his mouth. For a second, he bared his teeth as if he'd extract fangs, then his throat bobbed.

"Sorry. Habit." He frowned.

"It's okay. Take your time."

He wrapped his lips around the fork, then he chewed, making a strangled sound in his throat, his eyes closing. Swallowing the first bite, he sniffled.

"Is it good?" I asked.

He just nodded, too emotional to speak. I picked up my fork, spearing it through the eggs, but holding it up to his mouth, feeding him as he fed me that last morning.

"Here," I said.

He accepted my eggs, then smiled, and in turn, fed me another forkful.

We ate slowly, purposefully. Rhyan wanted to savor every bite. I wanted that, too.

Our waiter had just delivered a second carafe of coffee to our table, when the pub doors opened and a group of soturi stumbled inside, speaking in hushed tones.

"The Wall of the Prince," one muttered. "Just collapsed. How the fuck does that happen?"

Rhyan stilled, and my ears perked up.

"They can't be far, the akadim," said one of the soturi.

"No. There's at least a hundred on the run," said another.

"They're onto the next fucking destination. Godsdamnit."

Rhyan paled.

Their accents. They weren't from Korteria. Each soturion spoke with the Northern lilt of Glemaria.

And the last man who'd spoken, I knew his voice at once.

So did Rhyan.

A set of forest green eyes were now staring at him, and Rhyan was staring back.

"Excuse me," Sean said. "I'll be just a moment." He stood up and rushed to our table, his chest heaving as he approached Rhyan. His eyes narrowed in scrutiny, and then turned to me, his brows furrowing at my hair color, before they lifted in recognition as they swept over my face.

"Lyriana," Sean hissed. "Is that you?"

I nodded carefully, more than aware that Korterians were dining at the pub, and sitting not far from us.

"Thank the Gods." Sean wrapped his arms around me, kissing me on the cheek.

Then he turned to Rhyan. "Auriel?" he asked.

Rhyan blinked. "No. Sean, it's me."

"What?" Sean said, his voice too loud.

Rhyan reached out a hand to his uncle, squeezing it, and said quietly. "Sean, it's me. It's Rhyan."

Sean shook his head. "But you were—you were—" His chest heaved, and he looked back and forth between us, seeing me nod, my eyes watering, before he drank in Rhyan's face again. "Fuck. You were—you were a—"

"I know," Rhyan said again. "I was. But Lyr—" His throat bobbed. "She saved me."

"Branwyn gave me your message, but I didn't believe I … It really is you. It is," he said, his eyes welling with tears. "How? There's no … there's never been …" He wavered on his feet for a moment.

"It's a long story," I said and jumped up.

I stole a chair from a nearby table and placed it behind Sean before he fainted. But he only reached for Rhyan, pulling him into a hug, his hand clapping around the nape of his neck.

"By the Gods. I can hear it. Hear your accent, your voice." He pulled back, looking into Rhyan's eyes. "Your scar. Truly, it's you? My nephew."

"Just with a little glamour in my hair." Rhyan laughed, self-consciously touching his pale blond curls. "It's me, Sean. I swear. *Me sha, me ka*," Rhyan said. "I'm back."

And then Sean burst into tears.

CHAPTER THIRTY-NINE

RHYAN

"Rhyan, Rhyan!" Sean was crying, murmuring my name again and again.

"Sean!" I gasped. "I'm so glad to see you!"

He was rocking me side to side, hugging me so tight I could barely breathe, until Lyr coughed and placed her arms around us. Her hand pressed firmly into my back.

"I don't want to interrupt," she hissed. "But we're starting to draw attention."

I looked up, and sure enough, the bartender, black-eyed like the Bastardmaker, with thin blond hair, was eyeing us suspiciously. And another table had stopped eating, looking over.

Sean stiffened. "We need to get out of here and talk in private. Now," he said, his voice thick with emotion. He glanced at the table, at the stacks of emptied plates. "Are you done eating? Still hungry?" His eyes searched mine, clearly torn between getting us out of there, and making sure I had enough to eat. "I can get more for you if you need it.'

I shook my head, remembering how Sean had done something just like this when he found me in exile. When I was living in the caves, forsworn and depressed. He'd taken me to Auriel's Flame and had Cal and Marisol make everything they'd ever served. It was my first real meal in months. It had been so fucking good. Lyr must have known. Because she'd done the same thing. Gods, I loved her. It made my chest ache all over again, being here with him and with Lyr. Two of the people I loved most in this world.

My eyes met Sean's, steady and forest-green. Home. "I've had plenty."

"I ordered everything off the menu for him," Lyr said.

Sean smiled, his eyes crinkling. "Good girl." He opened his pouch, and pulled out several gold coins and laid them on our table. "That should more than cover it."

"Oh we can—" Lyr started.

But Sean held up his hand. "I got it. And then some, so hopefully they take the money and shut up. Let's go. I have a room nearby."

He pulled up his hood, and led us up to the counter where half a dozen soturi stood watching us. They wore Bamarian armor, but I knew their faces, recognizing them at once, their names slowly coming back to me. They were Glemarian, and each one of them had accompanied me on many of the akadim hunts I'd been sent on when I first arrived and had to earn my keep. In those first few months, when I was Lyr's bodyguard, and apprentice, I was also an akadim hunter on the weekends. The majority of those trips I'd been sent on had been with other Glemarians.

I'd speculated at the time that it was more to do with our experiences hunting the beasts. After all, until Garrett—lured by Aemon—had gone to Bamaria, there hadn't been any akadim attacks in the South. Not for years.

At least, I felt sure that that was the reasoning Lyr's father, Harren, had used when selecting us. But after a while, the missions—particularly when Imperator Kormac—Emperor Avery now—became involved, felt like they had more to do with putting us in danger. Us. And not his men.

I nodded, meeting their gazes. But they frowned as I approached, a quizzical look in their eyes.

They didn't know. Like Sean, they probably believed me dead. I knew from Auriel's memories that I'd—he'd—spent time with Sean in Bamaria. Filling him in on my fate. Sitting with him after he was lashed by Turion Kevel for hiding him and Lyr, and sitting with him as he grieved for me. Unable to comfort him. Unable to explain that he was sitting with a part of me.

My chest panged.

I took a deep breath as I stepped outside, my hand locking with Lyr's.

Sean emerged from the pub a minute later, and joined us.

Out in the open, Lyr's shoulders tensed, her aura flaring with a kind of fiery alertness that was mirrored in her eyes. Scanning the small town. Looking for soturi, for signs of being watched.

And for signs of the akadim that seemed to have vanished overnight.

My stomach turned. Where the fuck had they gone? We'd have to find them, and deal with them soon enough. But I was eager to get off the waterway and main road. I wanted to be in private, and I wanted to be with Sean. In the distance, I could hear boots marching. Only about two sets. Despite our very active presence here—there hadn't been much in the way of soturi. We were too far west, and I assumed that Kormac's view of the border was similar to my father's view of the Allurian Pass.

Besides, we'd done everything Morgana had asked to avoid earning any unwanted attention.

We'd hunted in the west. Hunted humans only.

I had a flash of one laying before me, ripping into her flesh, sucking her blood, and then her soul—turning her.

I closed my eyes, my feet felt like lead.

Almost as if sensing something was wrong, Lyr squeezed my hand, and stepped closer to me.

"We're staying down the road," Lyr told Sean, "at the inn at the end—just under the mountain."

Sean frowned. "Follow me to mine. It's a friend's home. We managed to use it as a base. It's more private there. Safer."

"Okay," Lyr said, her free hand rubbing my back.

I felt her walk forward, my arm lifting, our hands still connected, but my feet weren't moving.

"Rhyan?" she looked back, her hazel eyes filled with concern.

"I—" I could taste the blood in my mouth. I thought the food this morning would undo it. Remove the memory. The taste, the sensation. I didn't crave it. It disgusted me. But I remembered the taste, and the way I'd desired it. It was all still there in my mind. Fresh and visceral.

"Rhyan, what's wrong?" Lyr asked, her voice low.

My chest tightened. I could still feel the way my jaw moved, lapping up the blood, the way my tongue had brushed against the girl's neck. The way I'd done the same thing to Lyr.

"I can't—I—" The words wouldn't come. My mouth moved, the words wanted to be said, but my brain and mouth weren't connecting. I couldn't, couldn't …

"He's having a panic attack," Sean said.

Suddenly, both him and Lyr had wrapped their arms around me, and were moving me forward, supporting my weight as my feet moved helplessly across the waterway. I couldn't even see where we were going.

I could barely hear anything over the ringing in my ears. No. Not ringing. The slurping sounds I'd made as an akadim, the sounds I made as I swallowed blood—Lyr's blood.

"It hasn't even been a full day," Lyr said. "He's still getting used to everything again."

"Was that his first meal?" Sean asked.

"It was." Lyr's voice trembled with worry. "He only changed late last night, but I should've—"

"No. No. It's okay. He'll be all right," Sean said, soothing her. Then in my ear, "Rhyan, we're going to step up a few stairs. Okay? And I'll get you some water." He paused, and his hand lowered on my back, then down to my thigh directing me to the step. "Up you go now."

I stepped up, my new boot hitting the stair, and then the next, and the next, and then there was darkness as we walked inside.

I lost track of everything. My surroundings. Where I was.

"I can't breathe," I gasped.

I felt myself being sat in a chair, and warm arms wrapping around me. Lyr. She crawled into my lap, her hands on my face, palms to my cheeks. Forehead pressed to mine.

"Rhyan," she said. "Breathe. Breathe. It's okay. You're okay. You're alive. You're safe."

I opened my eyes, staring into hers. Hazel. Brown, and green, and with flecks of gold. I shook my head, my chest heaving. "I hurt you," I said, my voice weak.

"No," she said firmly. "You didn't. It's the memory. It wasn't you."

"I tasted your blood."

A door opened and closed. "Here," she said. "Sean brought you water. Can you drink some for me?"

I opened my mouth and felt glass against my lip then cold water sliding over my tongue. I swallowed. Water. Water. Not blood. Not blood.

My armor loosened, and was removed, sliding over my head, and then I felt Lyr's hand snaking inside my tunic, pressing against my bare skin, right over my heart.

"Deep breath," she said. "You're okay. I've got you." She kissed my cheek. "It's okay."

My eyes filled with tears, sharp painful breaths contracting in my chest.

Lyr shook her head. "I'm okay." She pulled her hair off her shoulder, and showed me her neck, the very place where my akadim fangs had sunk in. "See? There's barely even a mark. It's healing."

But I still felt like I was out of my body, my chest too tight. She looked past me suddenly, and frowned, her eyebrows knitting together in confusion.

Then I heard footsteps and the door opened and closed again.

"Rhyan," Lyr said, shifting closer on my lap, "it's just you and me. We're going to replace the memory, okay?"

"What? What do you mean?"

She leaned forward, her chest against mine, and pulled on my neck, dragging my lips to her skin. To the bite marks. I shook my head.

"Put your mouth on me," she whispered.

"What?"

"Put your mouth on my neck."

I tried to shift away. "No. No!"

But she was so strong, I had no choice but to comply. Her flesh was soft against my lips, my face, and she smelled—she smelled sweet. Her usual scent, something like vanilla and lemons, was there against the musk that was just, her. I breathed in deeply.

"Bite me," she said.

"Lyr."

"Bite me," she commanded.

I was shaking. But I did, biting into her flesh. She wiggled a little against me, but didn't make any sort of sound of discomfort or pain.

"Use your tongue," she said.

"No."

"Rhyan," she hissed. "Do it."

I lapped at her skin, at her whole skin, not broken, not pierced by fangs. No blood. Not even a drop of sweat. And the taste, the familiar taste of her, started to bring me back. There was no blood. No violence. Just Lyr. Me and Lyr.

"You're alive," she said. "You're Rhyan. *Rakame.*"

My chest expanded, breath coming easily again, like the spell had been broken. I kissed her, sucking on her neck, pressing tiny kisses up toward her ear.

She moaned, and I felt myself harden beneath her, my hands suddenly settling on her hips, shifting her against me.

"Sean's just outside the door," she said in a gasp. Her chest heaved. "Are you okay?"

I let out a shaky exhale, then took in another breath, meeting her eyes. "I am now. I'm sorry."

"No. Don't apologize." She smiled softly. "No guidebook, remember?"

I laughed. "No guidebook."

"Was it the food?" she asked. "Did that …?"

"I don't know. I think the memories—they just hit me. I know everything that had happened, but some things feel more present than others at times. I can't hold it all at once."

She frowned. "Well, when the next one hits, I'll be there with you. We're going to get through this."

"I know. Thank you." I looked down between us, her legs straddling me and my very obvious erection. I shook my head. "Not normally how I deal with this."

She chuckled. "Hey, whatever helps. I didn't exactly mind. But seeing as how we're not alone—" She kissed me, chastely, hugging me tight, then crawled off my lap to sit beside me.

I took a deep breath, trying to cool down, reminding myself that Sean was just outside the door. Anything else my body was craving from Lyr could wait. But I supposed it was a good thing that it wanted this, and not something else. Not something evil or depraved. It just wanted to be near her, to touch her, love her.

A moment later, I nodded. "Okay. I think I'm good."

She kissed my cheek. "You sure?"

"I'm okay."

"I'll bring Sean in."

A minute later, fully back to myself, I realized I was sitting in a complete stranger's living room, with walls made of darkened wood panels, a stone fireplace, and a flag with the sigil of Ka Hart above the mantel.

Lyr held my hand on the sofa where we sat, and Sean came to sit on a small chair beside us.

"Where are we?" I asked.

"This is the home of an old friend from Glemaria. Soturion Sheldon Daigen. Ka Daigen were loosely connected to Ka Gaddayan."

Kane and Kenna's Ka.

"He joined the soturi of Ka Kormac when he was exiled by your father," Sean continued. "Sheldon's retired now, but still lives here, offering shelter to any of us who pass through. Any of us who stand against Devon."

I nodded.

"How are you doing?" he asked, his eyes crinkling with concern.

I shook my head. "Well, the last five minutes don't paint a great picture. But, I'm alive. So there's that."

Lyr squeezed my hand, her face tightening like she was trying not to cry.

"You were—you were coming to kill me," I said, pulling out Auriel's memories as I looked at Sean.

His face fell. "Only if I had to. I didn't want you to live like that."

"I didn't either." I'd had to do the same thing for Garrett. Kill him. End it. Keep him from this life. But that had been before—before Lyr had found a cure. Before the knowledge had been unlocked, and the red shard taken from the Moon Court. The thought that he could have had a different outcome, that I was saved and he wasn't, made my heart hurt.

"I'm so glad I wasn't on time," Sean said. "I came searching for you. Tracked you down. It took me about three weeks to find you out here. I came alone. When I saw how many akadim there were, how much protection the cave offered, I left, and put out a call for every soturion who wanted to help. Who wanted to stop the threat. And who—who cared about you. Who wanted to help you in any way they could." His throat bobbed as he looked away. "Gods. Thanks to the Gods you got here first," he said to Lyr.

I silently thanked her, too.

Not because I was afraid Sean would have killed me.

I was afraid that as an akadim, I might have killed Sean.

"How?" he asked, looking at Lyr. "How did you do it?"

Lyr straightened and looked at me, her eyebrows raised in question. I knew what she was asking. Permission to tell Sean the truth about who we were. It was the only way to offer a real explanation. And I was done lying, hiding who I was.

"Tell him," I said.

So Lyr did. I watched his eyes widen with shock, and then a kind of calm knowing, like he'd always suspected that I was Auriel, like deep down, a part of him had always known. I listened breathlessly as Lyr spoke. I knew what had happened to her while I was gone, seeing the last six weeks play out in Auriel's memories. But hearing Lyr explain it, I couldn't take my eyes off her. Her courage and bravery, and determination left my heart pounding.

She did all this. For me.

When she finished explaining the connection between me and Auriel, and then the one between her and Asherah, Sean looked pale, his eyes full of tears. He stood up wordlessly and went to hug her, holding her so tight, I didn't think he'd ever let go. Until he did—and pulled me into his arms.

"I want to talk to you," he said quietly. "Later. Just the two of us. Make sure you're really okay."

"I am," I said. "Or, I think I will be."

"Good."

The last time he'd found me in the wild, I'd been too depressed to function or heal myself. But I was stronger now. I had Lyr. Still, I knew talking to Sean would feel good. He always knew what to say, and I'd missed him terribly these last few months. Ever since we left Bamaria to track Meera and Morgana.

Finally, he sat back down and took a sip of water, as I rejoined Lyr on the couch.

Sheldon walked in to check on us. He was an elderly man with a thick Glemarian accent that reminded me of Artem. All bushy white eyebrows. He welcomed us and asked if we needed anything, then left, giving us our privacy again.

"Right now," Sean said, "there's something you should know." He gritted his teeth. "There's much I haven't been able to tell you these last few years, because your father—he forced a blood oath on me. But things have changed, and I think I can tell you this now." He sat forward, setting down his glass of water on the table.

"I put out a call for help when I saw how many akadim I faced all those weeks ago. How much help I needed to get to you." He clasped his hands together. "Soturi from all over the South answered. Dozens who knew you as a boy, dozens more who fought and trained beside you. And every soturion who fought akadim at your side in Bamaria. They all answered the call, ready to defect from their posts and legions. In the end, there was over a hundred ready to fight. I had to ask some to stay behind. There were too many to be able to travel at the speed I wanted. But right now I have fifty soturi with me. And each one is loyal to you. Not your father. You, Rhyan."

"What? What are you trying to say?"

Lyr gasped, and I met her eyes.

I nodded at Sean to continue, my heart pounding.

"Most of the soturi I've gathered are camped out in the woods. We've been moving in small packs to avoid detection by Kormac. Our rendezvous point was in the meadow before the Wall of the Prince, tonight. We were going to strike. And well—you know."

"I know." I swallowed, realizing how close we'd both come to destruction if Lyr had just been one day late.

"We'll still rendezvous tonight so I can share the good news," he said.

"What will you do then?" I asked, a plan forming in my mind. Lyr looked at me and gave a small, firm nod.

Sean shook his head. "We have to figure that out. These men left their posts—they can't simply go home now. Things were getting bad in the South already with the new leadership. Bamaria isn't—it's not what it was."

"What about heading North?" I asked.

"North," Sean frowned.

"It's time. Things have gotten bad enough. Beyond bad. My father's tyranny has gone too far for too long."

Lyr squeezed my hand.

Sean's eyebrows drew together, his eyes searching quickly back and forth between us. "A movement has been brewing in Glemaria for some time. An uprising to stop your father. To remove him from power. Previous attempts failed. Many times. But things are different now. And I think, I think the time is right."

"So do I," Lyr said.

"What he did to you," Sean's voice shook, his aura flaring with anger, "was so fucking awful, that even the most ardent haters of vorakh—have turned away their support." He huffed. "It's one thing to quietly send your son away to Lethea because of vorakh."

"Like that's any better," Lyr snapped.

"No, it's not, I agree," Sean said. "People are hypocrites. But, in this case, it's working in our favor. They were disgusted by the idea of a father standing there as his son was—was—"

"Stripped," I said dully.

Lyr sucked in a breath.

Sean nodded, his neck reddening. "Yes. It kind of opened a door, let's say, for other criticisms that hadn't gained traction before. He hasn't been seen in a great light these last few months. And he knows it. Protests are rising, calls for new leadership. So, he's doing his usual."

I sneered. "Holding a tournament."

Sean nodded. "It's going to be in that arena he restored. You know, the one they called the Pits."

"An Alissedari," I said. The event where I'd killed Garrett. The place where my old life had ended. My throat dried.

"He's going to be there," Sean said. "Out in the open."

"But even with people coming to their senses," I said, "he's still well protected. He has fucking Kane, and his legion. Do you have anyone we can rely on in Glemaria? Not just here?"

Something flared in Sean's aura, something bright and hopeful. He smiled, a genuine smile, and his eyes were sparkling in a way I hadn't seen in years.

"We have someone who's been getting the word out to us for years now, letting us know your father's moves, and any weaknesses we can exploit. Particularly amongst those who serve him in the Glemarian Council."

"Who?" Lyr asked. "Who's in place?"

But I already knew. Of course! I'd asked her to run away with me years ago, when I needed to escape the abuse, when I wanted to save her, too. She refused. She'd always wanted to remain in Glemaria, to be in her home. Because she was going to make things better.

"It's Kenna," I said.

Sean nodded.

"Kenna?" Lyr asked. "By the Gods."

"Kenna's been working to gain support for his removal from power for years. And now it looks like it's time. Your father's going to be in the Pits for his tournament in one week. And he's going to be vulnerable. We can easily infiltrate the arena, surround him. And arrest him. And Kenna has assured us that no one will interfere or object."

"But his personal guard," I said, remembering the way they'd stood there and watched as my mother died. "They can't be trusted. Plus, I know he's compromised the first legion and the Master of Peace."

Sean grinned. "Are you so sure? Because right now he's never been weaker. He's missing one very key element of defense, one that he's going to keep quiet for as long as he can, but it's already too late. Because *we* know."

"What is it?" I asked.

There was something gleeful in Sean's aura as he spoke. "The Ready," he said. "Arkturion Aemon has been spotted in the North with a small army. I don't know what he's up to. But he's not returning to Bamaria, or whatever they're calling it now. He's gathering forces for some other reason."

I met Lyr's eyes, her mouth formed an O as her jaw dropped.

I had a good fucking idea of what he was up to. And I bet Morgana was with him. She'd left us weeks ago, claiming I had things under control. We were so close to unearthing the green shard. They were preparing for battle. Against us. Against the whole Empire.

But we'd just taken two weapons from our most ancient enemies.

Me. And the shard.

"What does the Ready have to do with this?" Lyr asked.

"It's Arkturion Kane," Sean said. "Kenna got word to us this morning. An ambassador from Aemon's camp met with

Kane a week ago. Whatever they said to him, it worked. He defected. He and his first legion have abandoned your father and they've joined Aemon's army."

I sat back against the cushions, my mind whirling. One enemy had weakened. But another had just grown dangerously powerful. Because Kane wasn't just Kane. He was Shiviel, God of the Yellow Ray. Lyriana and I had just begun to match the combined power of Aemon and Morgana. We were together. We had two shards of the Valalumir, just like them. Only they both had their magic. And before long, they would have three shards.

I had to get my power back. And we had to find the others. Dario. Aiden. Meera. And Jules.

Which meant there was truly only one course of action. We had to strike. We had to head for Glemaria and meet my father in the arena.

Because without Kane there, and without his legion, my father was a sitting duck.

And I wanted it to be my hands who took him down.

CHAPTER FORTY

LYRIANA

My heart was pounding so fast I could barely breathe. Sean had somehow just delivered the best and worst news all at once. I could see Rhyan already reeling from it, his eyes wide, his skin pale. Kane had fucking defected. From one enemy to another. He'd always been a source of evil, a scourge across Lumeria. But, unlike the other Guardians, he was the only one of us who didn't have a vorakh, or, access to it.

Although I didn't have a vorakh, I had taken on one of Meera's visions to heal her. And, I had jumped on my own, traveling from Numeria to Bamaria. I felt the weight of the red shard on my back, realizing I hadn't even begun to tap into the full force of power I could draw on.

I met Rhyan's stormy gaze, my hand in his, my thumb stroking his skin.

"What if they find the eighth?" I asked quietly. "And restore their power?" According to Mercurial, we had only survived Kane because of what we'd done as Auriel and Asherah. We'd performed ancient volatile magic to weaken him. We'd severed his soul, creating an eighth Guardian, one whose identity was still unknown to us.

"I was just thinking about that," he said. "I'd bet anything that's exactly what they're up to. That, and going after the yellow shard."

Gods. Every single time it felt like we were gaining on them, covering lost ground, or finding more power, they were still ten fucking steps ahead.

Sean frowned, his eyebrows drawn together in confusion. "I'm sorry. What?"

I swallowed roughly. I had just told Sean the truth—well, part of it. He knew now that Rhyan was Auriel reincarnated. That he'd met the real Auriel when he was with me. And that I was the reincarnation of Asherah. That seemed like enough for him to know in one sitting, just enough for him to understand how it was possible that Rhyan's soul had been restored. But we hadn't gotten into the bigger story, or the fact that we weren't the only Guardians reincarnated. That all seven of us were back. Plus the unknown eighth. And if they were found by Morgana and Aemon, Kane would become our biggest nightmare. Queen Ma'Nia's warning returned to me.

Moriel already has his shard, as does his lover Ereshya. And if they acquire more, you and your people are doomed.

"Sean, there's more," Rhyan said. "I'll explain later. I'll tell you everything."

"You're not the only two reincarnations?" he said.

"No, we're not." Rhyan shook his head. "Everyone came back this time."

"All seven?"

Rhyan's face tightened, but he nodded.

Sean took a deep breath. "Your father's not—"

"No," Rhyan said quickly. "But … Kane is."

"Well," Sean said. "Fuck."

I nodded. "We need to go to Glemaria. It's time. Devon needs to go. I want to see him bound in chains, bound and powerless and thrown into the same dungeons he put Rhyan in. And then, Rhyan needs to reclaim his power. Take it back from him. He's going to need it." Sean stood. "I'm going to escort you both back to your room at the inn to get the rest of your things. Close out of the room as discreetly as possible.

Then we'll come back here. It's more protected. We'll wait until nightfall. Then we're going to cross the western border out of Lumeria. My soturi will be waiting. We'll start sending word out to the others who couldn't come. And other groups who are waiting to help. And then, come morning, we make our way north."

Sean pulled Rhyan back into a hug, his hand tight against his neck, his other hand rubbing his back. Then he looked over his shoulder, his arm extended to him. "Get in here."

I joined them, warmth spreading through my limbs. Safe. I felt safe. And so happy that Rhyan was back with Sean.

"You're amazing," Sean said, his eyes crinkling as they looked at me. "You are so amazing, Lyriana. I cannot thank you enough."

"Rhyan would have done the same for me. For anyone he loved."

"I know he would have." Sean pulled back. Then suddenly, he dropped to one knee. "This goes without saying. But, when I left Bamaria, I ended my oath to Arkasva Batavia. As did all of my soturi. We're now forsworn. But I give my oath, my sword, and my soturi to you. To both of you. To whatever comes next. If you accept me."

Rhyan let out a shaky exhale, and grabbed his uncle's hands, pulling him back to his feet and clapping his back in another hug. "Of course, we fucking do."

"Thank you, Sean," I said.

He shook his head. "No. Thank you. I mean it." His mouth tightened. "Now let's go. Get your things."

I took a moment to reinforce the glamour magic I'd placed on Rhyan, lightening his hair which had started to darken and shining the silver of his armor. I touched up my own hair, and returned the red shard on my back into the rusted old sword I pretended to carry. After removing the sparks of gold seeping back into my armor and Asherah's chest plate, we were ready to go.

We stepped outside, Sean and two more soturi that seemed to appear out of nowhere walking behind us.

Rhyan took my hand in his, and we attempted to walk nonchalantly through the town, back toward the waterway and the main road of buildings that ended with the inn. I glanced over my shoulder, getting an eerie feeling, like we were being watched. And not by Sean. Nor was it akadim.

But we headed inside the inn without incident, our hoods down.

"Afternoon," said the inkeeper. She was one half of a married couple who owned the place.

"Afternoon," I said. "We'll be checking out now." I smiled. "We're on our way, to get the rest of our luggage."

"Oh," she said. "You're paid up for another three days. Do you want me to get you a refund?"

I shook my head. That would take too long, and require her to spend more time with us—looking at our faces.

"Oh no, that's quite all right," I waved her off.

"It was a lovely stay," Rhyan said.

The inkeeper stilled, looking him up and down. "Huh. You know, I don't think I've ever heard your accent before."

I stiffened. Shit. Rhyan looked just like Auriel, especially with the change in hair color. But I'd totally forgotten that he didn't sound like him. Not unless he was using his utmost formal court voice.

Rhyan forced a laugh. "Oh. It comes and goes," he said neutrally.

"He served in the North. Apprenticed in one of their academies. Sometimes it just comes out." I laughed. "Well, we'll be on our way then."

I tugged on Rhyan's hand, hurrying him to the stairs and back to the room where I shoved the door behind us. I leaned back against it and closed my eyes. Fuck.

"I'm sorry," Rhyan said. "I totally forgot—"

"I did, too." I took a deep breath.

"Do you think she's going to be a problem?" Rhyan asked. "I've hardly seen any soturi this far west."

"I don't know. I've come to expect everyone to be a problem." I took a deep breath. "Let's just get our things, and get back to Sheldon's. I'll feel much better once we're there." Once I knew we had an actual guard watching our backs. And even more so once we crossed the damn border out of Korteria. Or New Korteria. Whatever.

We combed through the room, gathering all of my things. And Auriel's—Rhyan's now. It only took a few minutes since we didn't have much—most of what we owned we were wearing. Our armor, our shards, our weapons. And my stave. But there were first aid supplies, extra sleep clothes, an extra cloak that could be used for bedding. I knew now from my travels just how important these resources could be.

One final sweep of the room, checking the closet and under the covers, and we left. I returned to the front desk, and handed over the keys.

"Thanks again for everything," I said, wishing it was her husband here. He was not nearly as interested in the guests.

"Of course," she said. "I hope you'll come and visit us again."

"We'd love that," I said.

"Oh, and I've been meaning to tell you …" Her eyes narrowed. "I love that hair color on you."

My throat went dry. "Thank you."

Rhyan wrapped his fingers around my arm, already dragging me toward the door.

"Bye now," he said formally. "Enjoy the day."

"You, too," the innkeeper called, a sickening smile on her lips.

The moment we touched the ground outside, we were fucked. Five soturi of Ka Kormac waited on the waterway.

"Excuse me," called the leader, the turion I assumed from the looks of him. Blond like they all were, with black beady eyes, and that fucking wolfish gleam in his smile. He was at least a foot taller than the others standing behind him. "We've had some strange reports of akadim in the area. Mind if we speak with you two?"

I watched Rhyan from the corner of my eye. We were armed, and we had soturi waiting in the shadows. If we had to fight, we could. But it would fuck up the plan. And absolutely destroy any semblance of secrecy we had. Before, I'd needed to remain anonymous so no one interfered with my search for Rhyan.

But now? We had to get fifty soturi into Glemaria without word reaching Devon Hart. A misstep here and the plan could fall to shit before we even started.

"I haven't seen any," Rhyan said, his voice still devoid of his accent. "Though there was some odd stuff happening in the meadows. Looks like part of the Wall of the Prince fell."

"Yes," said the turion. "Possibly akadim activity."

"We were just passing through," I said. "Small holiday. We're heading back east though. Back home."

The turion stepped forward. "Home? And where is home for you two?"

"Vrukston," I said quickly. It was the name of the first town I'd visited with Auriel.

"Vrukston?" the turion asked, one hand on the hilt of his sword. "And how long have you been staying here?"

I nervously eyed Rhyan before blurting out, "Two weeks."

The turion frowned. "I see. And you're just now completing your stay at this inn? Enjoy your visit?"

My heart thundered. "We did, very much. Didn't we?" I asked Rhyan.

He nodded vigorously. "It was very pleasant."

"So if I were to ask the innkeeper when you checked in—they'd tell me it was two weeks ago? You didn't check in after that?"

That Godsdamned bitch—she'd already reported us.

I laughed nervously. "Oh, here? Well, sure. I'm sorry. I meant, we've been on our trip for two weeks." I wrapped my arm through Rhyan's trying to look like I was too besotted to remember details.

"Hmmm." The turion eyed me up and down before narrowing his gaze on Rhyan. "Women. Can't remember anything."

Rhyan laughed again. "No. Now, if you'll excuse me, I better get her home. Before she forgets where we live."

"Just one more thing. Your names?" the turion asked.

"Right," Rhyan said. "I'm Soturion Sean, Ka Kolina."

I barely managed to keep the shock off my face. My mind had gone blank when the turion asked for a name, but Rhyan had managed to come up with one that was actually a lesser-known Ka in Korteria.

"Ka Kolina?" the turion bared his teeth. Fuck. He knew we were lying. It didn't matter that Rhyan had given a legitimate name.

"Yes," Rhyan said.

The turion scratched at his head. "I didn't know we had any Kolinas in Vrukston." He held up his hand. "Learn something new every day."

Rhyan lowered his chin. "We'll be on our way then."

"One more thing," the turion said, his dark gaze locked on us. "Just need to see your dagger."

"Of course," Rhyan said. His eyes met mine, his hand on the hilt as he withdrew and turned the blade in his palm to safely hand it over. "Here," he said, placing it in the turion's hand. Barely a second passed before Rhyan spun on his heels, withdrawing his sword, knocking his dagger from the turion, and pointed the tip at his neck.

His opponent had barely blinked before he found himself at Rhyan's mercy.

I had my swords out a second later. A cough signaled that Sean, and the two soturi who'd been trailing us had emerged from their hiding spots.

Five against five. One for each of us.

The soturi glanced around slowly, each one sneering confidently. They thought they could take us.

But then, I watched in horror as the turion touched his ear, and blue light from a vadati began to glow. "We know who you are, Lyriana," he said.

"Now!" I yelled.

Rhyan launched at the turion, slamming his body to the ground, the vadati rolling out down the waterway.

Realizing the innkeeper could be watching, as well as anyone else inside the buildings down the street, I pulled out my stave.

The spell came to me at once. "*Ani petrova chayate lyla.*" Shadows cloaked us in darkness, as if the sun had just been eclipsed, but only where we stood.

Everyone froze, shocked at the sudden nightfall, and then, all ten of us were in battle. I kept my focus on the soturion in front of me, his blond hair shorn so short it was spiky on top.

"Need two swords?" he asked as he thrust.

I blocked the hit with ease, metal clashing against metal.

He shook his head, and angled his hips, preparing to strike again, but I went in for the kill, my vision clear even in the darkness that encased us.

With one hit I knocked his sword from his hand, and with the other, I stabbed just below his armor, hitting flesh. He grunted, his eyes widening in shock as I pushed the blade in, shoving it past muscle.

He coughed, and spat, blood spewing across his armor before I grunted, and pulled the blade out. He collapsed, coughing miserably.

I slid my blade across his throat a second later, and his eyes closed.

Sean met my eyes, his soturion now dead, as well as the other two. Only Rhyan remained, battling the turion.

The Kormac warrior had flipped Rhyan onto his back, and punched him in the face. Rhyan's eye was already swelling.

Sean started forward, and I was already regripping the hilt of my blades, ready to rush in. But Rhyan yelled out, and with a fury I'd never seen from him before, he grabbed the man's head, and shoved his fingers into his eyes. The turion cried out in pain as Rhyan flipped him over onto his back. He punched him in the face, again and again. Rhyan reached for his sword and the turion was dead seconds later. Rhyan got back up, his chest heaving with exertion.

"Come on," Sean yelled. He raced across the ground and grabbed the vadati which was now clear. The connection was gone. The turion didn't have time to announce our whereabouts, but he'd said my name. Which meant others were looking for me now.

"We can't wait for tonight," Rhyan said. "Lyr and I need to cross the border now."

"I agree, and I'm coming with you." He turned to the other two soturi with us. They all seemed to be around Sean's age, in their early forties, with the same brown hair that Sean had—albeit with some specks of gray.

"We'll round up the others," one said. He had a stocky build, and a long scar down his right arm. "Most are still gathering supplies."

Sean nodded. "Everyone needs to meet us as soon as possible beyond the border. We'll be in the first town, Dobrava, at the eastern outpost. They have until sunset—then we head north."

"It will be done," said the soturion. He nodded at me and Rhyan, lowering his chin in respect. "Go."

I quickly gathered my bag, and handed Rhyan's back to him. We pulled our hoods up over our heads, and without another word, we ran.

My feet were flying as we crossed through the shadows that I'd called down, shadows that were still cloaking the dead soturi. My power was becoming easier to use, less taxing. And it was all from the red shard. But even that wouldn't hold for much longer—not with magic being so weak by the border. It was truly a testament to how powerful the shards were that I'd done as much as I had. Even Rhyan had struggled with traveling here the first time, and we hadn't been this far west.

The meadow lay ahead, and the hills leading to the Wall of the Prince.

Rhyan took my hand as we approached the valley. The collapsed cave at the foot of the mountain looked like a tomb. My stomach dropped. If Rhyan hadn't freed himself from the rocks, it would have been his.

He squeezed my hand like his mind had gone to the same place, and at the same moment, I had that strange feeling again, like there were eyes on me. Like I was being watched.

The akadim. It had to be. They could come out in the daylight, and we hadn't seen any since last night, but they were near. I was sure of it.

When we reached the valley, Sean turned, heading north. He was taking us around the mountain. There was no way through. Not anymore. Not that I'd have ever entered the Wall of the Prince again.

When we came to a small woodland, we stopped for a short break, catching our breath, leaning back against the trees.

"You okay, partner?" Rhyan asked.

I walked into his arms, leaning my weight against him. "I'm fine. What about you?"

"Fine," he said, averting his eyes from the cave.

I shook my head. It was so like him. He was the one without power this time. And he was still more worried about me than himself.

"I don't like it here," he said quietly.

"Me neither."

"Are you two all right to keep going?" Sean asked.

Rhyan kissed my forehead, his eyes darkening as he glanced at the cave ruins. He stretched out his legs, then nodded. "Let's do it."

We ran. Our path leading us around the mountain bordering Korteria. After an hour, when my body was ready to collapse we crossed into Dobrava, the human lands. The place where magic stopped working.

I slumped against a tree trunk, leaning my head back and wiping sweat from my brow. A strange feeling crawled up my spine.

A tree branch snapped. There was an intake of breath. Not from me, or Rhyan, or Sean.

Eyes were on us, watching. The same feeling as before. But it was stronger. Much stronger.

Rhyan went preternaturally still, as did Sean, all of us wordlessly sensing the threat and reaching for our swords.

Someone appeared in the shadows, a silhouette of a man, who seemed to be wearing rags. A cloth had been strapped to one shoulder and hung down to his waist. Another appeared wearing only pants from the outline I could see. And yet another appeared, wearing only a scrap around his waist.

The kind of clothing worn by akadim.

Five more appeared, and then a dozen. Rhyan and I slowly inched toward each other—Sean joining us, until we were all back-to-back. "The akadim," I hissed. "The ones that escaped."

"I recognize them," Rhyan said, his voice hushed and shaking.

My heart pounded. I had the red shard, Rhyan had the green. But more and more were approaching, their faces concealed in the shadows, their silhouettes dark.

I started to count, two dozen, then three. And more were still approaching in the shadows. Too many for us to fight at once.

I shuddered, fear gripping me, my stomach twisting like a vice.

Then one stepped forward and called out. "Arkturion. Arkturion Rhyan."

"Yes," Rhyan said cautiously. "Harman, right?"

"Yes," Harman said, his voice surprisingly soft for an akadim. He took another step forward, into a small ray of sunlight shining through the trees. He lifted his arms out to the side. They ended in fingers, smooth and round at the end—not clawed. And his eyes—they were dark, perhaps brown. It was too dark to see. But it didn't matter. Because there was one important color that they weren't: red.

"Your eyes are green," Harman said. He was thickly muscled and tall. A soturion build. His skin was dark brown, and his hair was silky and black like many born of Ka Elys. Carefully, he looked Rhyan up and down. "You're alive?"

"Y-yes," Rhyan said. "I'm cured." Tears welled in his eyes. Tears that I could see were reflected in Harman's.

"How?" Harman asked.

Rhyan's lips trembled, and he shook his head. "I was stabbed in the heart. By my love." He looked over at me. "With a lost shard from the Valalumir. It had healing powers, and so does she. She brought me back."

"It wasn't just you," Harman said. He looked over his shoulder, and gestured. More men, and a handful of women began to emerge from the shadows and behind the trees and some bushes. "My lady," Harman said, meeting my eyes. "You saved us then. Healed us." He knelt down on one knee. And the rest followed. Over fifty former akadim were kneeling before us. "We are yours in gratitude. We owe you our lives."

And then, Rhyan fell to his knees, looking up at me, tears shimmering against the emerald green.

CHAPTER FORTY-ONE

RHYAN

"How?" Lyr asked. She looked stunned as her eyes moved across the former akadim.

I reached up and took her hand. "Lyr, it was you."

Her chest heaved, as she took a few shallow breaths. "But I only stabbed you." She stared out at the crowd, shaking her head, her brows furrowed as she tried to understand. "I didn't think I saved you at first." She took my hand and pulled me up. "Auriel never said this was possible. We were losing in the last war because it took so long to save akadim. We had to do it one by one. How? How could I have turned so many of you at once?"

"Arkturion Rhyan," Harman said, rising to his feet. It was only then that I realized he'd been holding the silver collar he'd worn as an akadim. The ones Morgana had fashioned. It was the collar she'd used to bind us all to her, forming a kashonim that she could manipulate and control. We'd all drawn blood, had it mixed inside the collar along with hers.

It forced us to follow her directives, to comply with her rulings and commands—at least when she was nearby.

But she left weeks ago, taking Parthenay and her maid with her. Lissa. That was her name. I'd already been Arkturion, a leader for the akadim, keeping them on task, giving them their orders. Reinforcing anything Morgana wanted. Or *Maraaka Ereshya* as she was referred to.

"Harman," I said. "May I—" I frowned, a theory starting to come together in my mind. "May I see that?"

"Of course, Arkturion." He stepped forward, slowly approaching Lyr, Sean, and me.

"You," I shook my head, "You don't have to call me that anymore. I'm not—I was never an actual Arkturion."

"That's not what I remember," Harman said.

I remembered him clearly. He'd been paler as an akadim, but now his skin had been returned to a deep brown. I hadn't spoken much to Harman—truthfully, I hadn't spoken to many of the akadim. They weren't exactly social creatures. But I remembered Harman. He did what was asked. And he kept the others in line for me. He'd been … I supposed loyal was the right word.

He placed the collar in my hand and I nearly recoiled. I still remembered the night I got mine. The way Morgana had found me naked and feral in the woods. I was so angry and confused. But she'd collared and calmed me, and by morning, I'd had purpose.

I turned the silver in my hands, watching the hateful metal, and all it represented, glint in the sun. It was more than just a symbol of the monster I'd been, or my obedience to Morgana. It was my kashonim. The one I'd formed with her as an akadim. Like Lyr and I had done as soturi, with our armor and blood mixed together.

Auriel's words from my dream came back to me.

She kept you tethered to her. She doesn't even know. She saved your life. No one survives the stripping. But her soul called out to yours, and it was a far stronger pull than the cries your soul made to mine, to yourself, to your original form. In the end, it was sealed in blood, in kashonim. But without that connection—that alone wouldn't have been enough.

Lyr had saved me from the stripping because she was my soulmate, and because of our kashonim. It had linked us. It had brought me back. And the collar I wore had linked me to Morgana.

"The night Morgana left," I said, my voice hushed, "she wanted to make sure that her commands were followed, that the force of them remained strong, even while she was far away. So a new kashonim was made."

Lyr's eyes narrowed. "To you?"

I nodded slowly, my heart racing.

"Every akadim drew blood and it was mixed into my collar, and in exchange, a drop of mine was given to them. Lyr, I think when you called me back, when you called back my soul, I think—I think it brought everyone back. Everyone tethered to my blood."

"By the Gods," Lyr breathed.

"You were a good Arkturion," Harman said, pulling my attention back.

Several others began to yell out their agreements, affirming his words, some even clapped.

"You were fair," he continued. "You kept us in line. You didn't hurt anyone unnecessarily. You only killed when we were assigned to ... assigned to feed."

I closed my eyes, my stomach roiling. I could still taste it. Taste blood and flesh on my tongue. I wanted to vomit. Especially when I remembered the taste of Lyr's.

"You never killed others," Harman continued, "except when *Maraaka*—"

"Morgana," Lyr hissed. "Her name is Morgana. And she's no queen."

Harman lowered his chin. "Yes, Your Grace."

Lyr shook her head, but I stayed her hand. He was right to refer to her as Her Grace. That was her appropriate address, no matter the status of Bamaria.

"You only killed," Harman continued, "when she ordered you to. And then never again. Not once during all those weeks we were digging and mining. You didn't hunt any innocents, and you didn't go after any of us. You didn't beat us, or kill for fun. You only killed … when you arrived, my lady," he said quietly. "But even then, I know you were protecting Lady Lyriana. Even until the end, you were fair, as fair as an akadim could be. Not kind maybe, but not cruel either."

I exhaled sharply. Not kind, but not cruel. What a way to be described. Though I supposed for an akadim, that was high praise.

"Well, I thank you for that," I said, awkwardly.

"For an akadim," someone shouted. "You might as well have been a saint."

"Arkturion," came a new voice. A blond man stepped forward, he was tall, towering over even me, with lean muscles, and a look that reminded me of Leander. I blinked, suddenly seeing his face as an akadim's.

"Brandes?" I asked. "Ka Daquataine?"

Brandes's face broke into a wide grin. "Yes, Arkturion."

"Just Rhyan," I said. "That's all I am."

"No," Brandes said. "What Harman and all of us are trying to tell you—is—" He clutched at his own collar, staring down and turning it in his hands over and over. "We were gone. Our lives were forfeit. We had been damned to a fate worse than death. To walk the world as a demon. Hunting. Killing. Doing what—what akadim do—what I know we all wanted and felt driven toward—what happened with you and Parthenay that first morning—"

I paled, feeling ready to retch. I'd do anything to forget that morning, to undo it. I looked at Lyr, afraid she'd run, or want to vomit as well. But she looked so steady and sure, and confident. Confident in me. Trusting in me. I didn't fucking deserve her.

"I'm sorry," Brandes said. "To mention it. What we're trying to say is—we all of us—Fuck."

"He kept you from committing the worst crimes," Lyr finally said. "None of you committed rape."

My chest tightened. And for a second, I felt like I couldn't breathe again. Because I'd been close. Morgana had put me in position, riled me up. It wouldn't have started without her. But it didn't change the fact that I'd still participated, that I'd almost done it. That I'd been willing to. Only her command had stopped me.

Not me. The akadim. But still—the memories were mine.

"Yes, Harman said. "And so much more. Not only did you keep us from doing the worst things akadim could do, but you brought us back. You gave us another chance at life."

And several more former akadim began to shout in support.

"I don't know how it happened," someone called out, "but we owe you our lives."

"I'll see my wife and children again."

"I thought my life was over. You changed that," came a shaky voice.

"Because of you, I have the chance to atone, to make things right."

The words kept coming, the thanks, the relief, the sheer praise for me and gratitude that no one had turned into the worst kind of monster in this world. And even more were thanking me because they were human again. Because their life hadn't ended.

"We still have to atone," Brandes said, looking out at the crowd. "Much evil was done by our hands. But that burden has lessened. Thanks to you, Arkturion Rhyan. And the reason we get to do so, that we have a second chance at life, is thanks to you, Lady Lyriana."

Applause exploded at Brandes's words.

But it was Harman who dropped back to his knee. "I can barely live with what I've done, what I've become." His voice shook. "But at least I get to live. I have a chance now to do things differently. You gave me another chance to be human, and to be better, to make up for the sins I've committed whether willingly by my hand or not. And for that reason, I give my oath to you, Arkturion Rhyan. I will fight for you. If you'll take me."

And suddenly, they were all shouting, "I give you my oath."

"I pledge myself to Arkturion Rhyan."

"My loyalty is with Arkturion Rhyan and Lady Lyriana."

"I would have no life without you. I pledge my life to Arkturion Rhyan!"

The promises and oaths kept coming, again and again.

I looked at Sean, who was nodding proudly, then Lyr, taking her hand.

"What do I do?" I asked. Yesterday I'd been a monster, and then I'd woken up alive and guilty and a fugitive and criminal on the run. And now? Now I had a band of soturi asking me to lead them.

She smiled. "You can accept their oaths."

I shook my head. "I can't. I can't ask them to fight for me."

"You're not asking," she said. "That's the thing." She looked out, turning her head to see everyone before us. "They are."

I caught Sean's eyes crinkling as he smiled. "Rhyan," he said. "Listen to me. I understand why you hesitate. You're humble. You always were. And way too fucking hard on yourself. But this isn't about you." His aura flared suddenly, full of pride and hope, bright and warm like the forest in the sun in autumn. "It's about them, what *they* need," he said fiercely. "What if you were out there? Just come back from being akadim, not knowing why. Feeling the guilt of what you became, of being a monster. Plagued with the memories."

My throat tightened. "Sean, I don't—I don't have to imagine. That is what I'm feeling."

"And what are you going to do about it?" he asked. "You're going to fight back. You're going to remove a tyrant from power, someone who hurt you and countless others for decades. Someone who will only hurt more people if he's not removed. So you can become ruler, become Arkasva. You were born to take the Seat of Power from him. So you will. And when he's gone, you're going to go after the next tyrant and the next. You're going to make things better. Make this world better. You have a path forward." He shook his head, pointing at the former akadim. "That's what they want, too. What they need. A path. They're asking you to show them the way. That's all."

My heart pounded. "Can we bring them to Glemaria?" I asked.

Sean held out his hand, taking the collar from me. He turned it over a few times, considering it, then tapped on it with his finger. "I thought this was decorative. Silver," he said. "But this is steel. We can melt these down. Forge weapons." Exhaling sharply, he said, "We'll need to." His eyes roved over the faces of the former akadim. "We've got our work cut out for us. We just doubled the size of your soturi. One hundred strong."

"My soturi?" I asked.

Sean laughed, "Did you think they were mine?" He grinned. "The soturi who came with me—who came to fight—they came for you. Out of loyalty and respect for you. I'm not the one being called Arkturion now, am I?"

Lyr's face lit up. "Sean's right. Rhyan, they want to fight back. And they want to do it with you. We need them. With them, we have an even better chance of winning."

I looked around, taking them all in, recognizing many of their faces, recalling names. I thought about when I had fled

Glemaria after being named forsworn. How I had wandered in exile. How I hadn't been able to see a path, how I'd lost everything.

And how in the end, choosing to be a soturion had saved me. I needed purpose. Meaning. And I'd made my choice. I'd decided to fight evil. To defend and protect. I saw the same desperate hope in their eyes now.

"It's up to you," Sean said softly. "It's your choice to take them with you, just as it's their choice to ask to come along. But if you do, my soturi are already loyal to you—they will cheer at your consecration. Celebrate when you become Arkasva Hart, High Lord of Glemaria."

I bit my lip, his words sinking in. But my stomach was still turning. "If we do this, we only have a week."

Lyr squeezed my hand. "Anything is possible."

My throat tightened. But she was right. So was Sean.

The cheers and shouts were starting to die down. I stepped forward, my eyes sweeping over them. And I took a deep breath, my mind made up.

"Come with me," I said. "If you want. But before you agree to fight at my side, and with Lady Lyriana, there's something I need to say."

Already they were chanting my name, shouting out again. But now, it wasn't Arkturion they were calling me. It was Arkasva. Arkasva Hart. High Lord of Glemaria.

My stomach turned.

"I want you all to know," my voice cracked, and I started again. "I want you all to know that you're free. Your freedom was returned to you for no reason other than it was always yours to begin with. None of you deserved to have it taken away. Not one of you, me included," I paused, my eyes watering, "deserved what happened to them, to us."

Harman's eyes watered. Brandes shed a tear.

"You were cured by the grace and power of Lyriana Batavia. And to understand how, you should know. It's because she is Asherah, the Goddess reborn."

Lyr gasped, her eyes widening. "Rhyan."

I shook my head. It was time. Time for everyone to know. She'd healed them all, done the impossible. And it wasn't going to be the last time. If we were going to do this, I was done with hiding. Finished with secrets. What the Empire deemed illegal no longer concerned me.

"She saved you," I said. "Her magic, her strength. It was she who brought me back and all of you by extension. I am so grateful to her, for more than just myself. For all of you. She is my *mekarim*. My soulmate. I will love her, and honor her and serve her for the rest of my life. So if you want to join me, if you want to fight with me, you fight for her."

Her hazel eyes watered, the specks of gold glinting in the faint light escaping through the canopy of branches above us.

The former akadim cheered, now shouting Lyr's name.

"There is a war coming," I said. "And I need your help to fight it. But you are under no obligation to me, or to this cause. None of you signed up to have your lives disrupted, your souls taken. None of you asked to be changed, hurt, or violated in the ways you were. The way I was." I took a deep breath. "And I hold none of you guilty for the crimes committed when you were not yourself. If you need to hear you are absolved, I say this to you now—you are." My voice shook. "Though I admit, I am struggling to remember the same for myself. But I'm working on it. And I'm willing to work on it beside all of you.

"If you want to go now, if you wish to go home, to go back to your countries, your Kavim, your families, if you want to leave the Lumerian Empire altogether and continue west, know that I understand. And that you go with my blessing, and—" I reached for Lyr's hand, bringing her forward. "You go with Lady Lyriana's. But if you do want to stay, I would be beyond honored to fight beside you. We are heading north, to Glemaria. To take down its Arkasva and Imperator. My father. I am the rightful Heir Apparent. And I'm ready to finally remove my father from power. Something that should have been done a long time ago. For years, he's abused his position, allowing akadim to roam free, terrorizing my people, and everyone in the North. And he's committed other crimes. Too heinous to name. But it's time for him to receive justice. So you all get to choose now. You can come with me and fight. Or, you are free to go."

I felt dizzy as I stopped speaking, like I might fall over. Only because Lyr's grip on me was so strong did I manage to stand. But suddenly, the former akadim were shouting, shouting my name. Calling me Arkasva. Pumping their fists in the air, bowing, kneeling.

"Arkasva Rhyan! Arkasva Rhyan! High Lord of Glemaria!"

Sean sank before me, pressing his fist to his heart, two times, then flattening his hand against his chest. "*Me sha, me ka*, Your Grace, Arkasva Rhyan Hart, High Lord of Glemaria," he shouted.

Everyone erupted into cheers.

I turned away, burying my face against Lyr's as the tears overwhelmed me.

CHAPTER FORTY-TWO

LYRIANA

I held Rhyan tight, letting him compose himself, before he bravely turned to the former akadim, and accepted their oaths. The applause that sounded was the most beautiful thing I ever heard. Because Rhyan deserved it, he deserved their support, and they all deserved a chance to make things better, for themselves, for Lumeria. And this was step one. So many wanted to come forward to thank us, offer hugs of gratitude, introduce themselves, and personally pledge their sword, or skills, or simply their loyalty.

Others had wanted to touch my hands, the hands of the person that had healed them, that wielded the red shard. I still could barely believe it. The cure had worked. Rhyan was saved. And so were all the akadim that had been bound to him. It was a miracle, and my heart wouldn't stop pounding. I tried to stay close to Rhyan through it, to make sure he was okay. He'd never exactly been one to make himself the center of attention. And I knew despite his brave words, and the strength he was exuding in each interaction, he was still unsure of himself. Still carrying the guilt of what was done to him. What had happened.

And questioning his new title. Arkasva.

Soon the numbers of people who wanted to speak to us quickly became overwhelming, and I found myself moving into various crowds as Rhyan was pulled in the opposite direction away from me.

Sean's soturi—now Rhyan's and mine—had been making their way to Dobrava all day long. Which meant that after several hours, there were over one hundred of us gathered together, attempting to make camp for the night. Dozens had gone into the nearest town to try and barter for food with gold. Dozens more had gone into the woods to hunt any local game they could find. Another group had risked going back across the border into Lumeria to purchase more supplies. Spare cloaks, daggers, boots, and armor. And of course, for those who'd been akadim, they needed clothes and shoes.

About a dozen of them who had been taken from human lands and had no magic in them, had begun to melt down Morgana's collars in order to weld the steel into swords.

I was in shock at how much was happening and how quickly. Only a day ago Rhyan had been akadim, and I'd been on the verge of hopelessness and despair. Fighting for my life and his.

And now? Everything had shifted. Our world turned upside down, and for once, it was all in our favor. After months of hiding and being hunted, of being forced to sell ourselves in every way to survive, we had support. We had allies. We had a chance. It was more than I could have dreamed. And I couldn't stop being amazed every time I thought of it.

The soturi who had answered Sean's call were surprisingly well prepared with tents, extra clothes, and weapons which they happily shared with the former akadim. But even after a whole day of bartering, stealing, and sharing, we still were woefully behind in supplies. Suddenly, feeding Rhyan was the least of my worries. I had to find a way to feed over a hundred of us. It was decided quickly that almost everyone would be sharing a tent tonight, squeezing in as many bodies as they could get inside. At least half of the soturi would be sleeping under the stars. Sean was already working out a schedule of who would take overnight guard shifts and where to place everyone, and Rhyan was working closely with him. After the initial shock wore off from seeing the healed akadim, and his new role amongst them, he had taken on this look of utter determination. Like he needed to prove that he was worthy of the promises and oaths given to him today. And given me.

He couldn't see it yet. He was so worthy. And as the hours went on, I could see that there was a part of him that wasn't fully here. It was the part of him that was still holding himself to a higher standard, an impossible one.

The part of him that had had a panic attack just this morning because he could remember hurting me. Remember the taste of my blood.

I tried to talk to him a few times throughout the day, but there was so much to do and arrange, so many new logistical puzzles appearing every other minute. Eventually, I had no choice but to give up and keep working. With so much happening, the day passed in a blur, and the sky darkened. More soturi returned with food, and several bonfires were set for warmth and cooking. And before I knew it, someone was handing me a plate of hot food. I searched for Rhyan in the crowd. I couldn't remember the last time I'd seen him. Hours ago? I asked around, eventually found myself sitting with several soturi, listening as they shared stories from home, from their countries and Kavim. Everyone's spirits were high, and some groups were even breaking out into song. Celebrating the second chance. Singing away the horrors of what they'd been through.

Finishing my plate, I excused myself and began walking through the camp. Every step I took, someone called my name, thanking me, and praising Rhyan.

But Rhyan was nowhere to be found. My stomach turned, and I began asking if anyone had seen him, but everyone's last sighting had been different and ultimately unhelpful. Until finally, I found Sean.

"Lyriana," he said. "Did you eat?"

I nodded. "Where is he?"

"He's already back in your tent," he said. "It's all set. We don't have enough to go around for everyone, but I've made it so you two will have privacy."

I shook my head. "No, Sean, that feels selfish." So many didn't have a roof over their heads for the night. "We can share."

He grinned. "No. You couldn't if you wanted to. Trust me. There's not one soturion here who would dare try and stay with the two of you. Not with their new Arkturion Arkasva, and—well, we haven't decided your title yet. Savior's been thrown out a lot."

"Savior?" I asked.

Sean nodded.

"So Rhyan's in our tent now?" I asked. Why hadn't he come to find me himself? Was he sleeping? "Is he okay?"

Sean shrugged and sighed. "I sent him there a little while ago. He needed a moment. Alone."

Alone. "What's wrong?" I asked.

A sad smile played upon his lips. "Nothing. Everything. It's Rhyan, you know. He's ... he's still taking it all pretty hard." Sean's face hardened, his eyes racing and back and forth across my face. "He's going to do that. Probably for awhile. But he also needs to look strong for the others."

"He is strong," I said, my voice shaking.

"He is, Lyriana. Very. But he's also hurting. He needs to be strong for them, for everyone here. My job though, is going to be making sure he feels it." He touched my arm. "I imagine yours, too."

"More than you know. Now tell me. Which tent?"

Sean shook his head. "He wanted to be alone."

"Which tent?" I asked again, my voice hardening. "Sean, he's been alone. His time is up. I'm going to go see him. Now. So just tell me." I knew Rhyan needed his space at times, but I also knew he had a habit of running away, and isolating himself when the guilt and shame overwhelmed him.

Sean's eyebrows drew together, but he pointed to the center of the camp. A modest sized tent, one of the smaller ones, which was fitting, as it was only for two of us. But someone had placed a flag on top. The sigil of Ka Hart.

"Just be patient with him. As long as I've known him, he's always had to figure things out on his own."

"He can figure out all he wants to. But he's not going to be alone."

Sean's eyes crinkled. "I thought you'd say that. And I'm glad. Go on."

"We have sentries stationed overnight?" I asked.

"The schedule's all set, our borders protected, and scouts are monitoring the perimeter. You can rest. You should rest. You both deserve it." He turned and pointed to the other end of camp. "I'll be over there for the night shift. If you need me, you know where to find me."

"Thank you."

I started making my way through the tents, walking over exposed cloaks that were being turned into makeshift sleeping bags. But I could barely move two steps without being stopped. I debated retreating into the woods and putting on a glamour. But even out here, outside of Lumeria I could barely feel the power of the red shard on my back.

At last, I made it to our tent, the Ka Hart sigil flapping in the spring breeze. The night had grown cold, the wind strong enough to blast my hood off my head.

"Rhyan," I called from outside. "It's me. Can I come in?"

"Of course," he said, but he sounded hollow and stiff.

I pushed the tent flaps apart and walked inside.

Rhyan had folded his cloak into sections on the ground, creating a small bed, just like he'd done on our countless nights sleeping in caves.

"Hey," I said, removing my cloak. I sank down beside him, noting he'd removed his armor and weapons, and once more, had piled them neatly into a corner. My chest tightened.

"Hi." He sounded breathless.

"What's wrong?" I asked, taking his hand.

He shook his head. "I'm just tired. Really tired."

I nodded. "I figured. You didn't come find me."

"I know. I just ... I don't know." He released my hand and turned on his side, facing away from me.

I reached for my chest plate, quickly unhooking the clasps and placing it down beside the make-shift bed. I removed my belt and weapons next, then finally tackled the armor across my torso, until I was down to my tunic and riding pants.

I laid down beside him, shifting until my front pressed against his back. Then I wrapped my arm around him, my hand sliding into his tunic, over his heart.

He shook, then stilled, still turned away from me.

"Will you talk to me?" I asked.

"What do you want me to say?" he asked.

"Whatever you want. Whatever's bothering you."

"It's fine. Everything's fine."

My throat tightened, and there was a painful clench in my chest. "No it's not."

"What do you mean?" He laughed bitterly. "I'm alive. I have an army. They named me Arkasva. And Arkturion. It's a little confusing, all the titles. And, I have you. What could possibly be wrong?"

"You—" I said "What is this? Rhyan, what are you doing?"

He turned on his back, staring at the tent above, refusing to meet my gaze.

"I'm trying," he said, his voice rough. "I am. But I can't tell you how bad the guilt is I'm feeling, how much it's gnawing at me from the inside. Tearing me apart. Lyr, I was a monster."

"You weren't."

He closed his eyes, breathing hard. "But I was."

"But you're not anymore. If you were, would I be here now? Would I feel safe with you? You've seen me afraid. You know what that looks like. And I'm not. Not with you. With you I feel safe. Always."

"But you *were* afraid." His eyes opened and moved toward mine, watching me in his peripheral vision, but his face remained turned to the ceiling. "I can't stop seeing it in my mind. Hurting you. Hurting so many. Killing. Do you realize that some of them out there thanking me, became akadim in the first place because of *me*. Because I'm the one that killed them, that ate their soul, and turned them forsaken. Me!"

"Rhyan, remember what just happened out there? They want to follow you, support you. And it's because you were the one who turned them, who bound them to you that they're human again. What about everything you said about absolving them of guilt? None of them wanted to be akadim. None of them chose this. And neither did you."

"It's a lot easier to say it to them, than it is to say it to myself." He turned to me finally, his eyes searching mine. "I'm just afraid of what's next. Afraid of … confronting my father."

My heart swelled, wishing I could just wrap him up in a hug that never ended. "You won't be doing it alone," I said. "You've fought him before and won. Remember, you're stronger than him."

"This feels different," he said.

I pushed his hair back off his forehead, revealing the faint line of his scar. "How?"

"Because …" His voice broke. "Because he killed me."

"Rhyan." I pulled him into my arms.

"I mean," he said, "I know it was the akadim, brought there by Morgana and Aemon. And it was Kunda Lith who stripped me. Emperor Avery fucking Kormac who sentenced me. But my father—my father put me in that position. He turned me in. He's the one that did this to me. That caused this."

"He did," I said quietly.

He shook his head, his eyes red.

"I always thought," he choked out, "I always thought there was a limit. You know? A limit to his—his cruelty. A limit to where he stopped being him, being evil ... and became ... human. And I ..." He took a shaky breath.

I ran my fingers through his hair, wishing I could do more to soothe him. That I could undo the hurt and the pain. And above all else, I wished with everything I had that I could have changed his fate. That I could go back in time and save him. Keep him from this pain and suffering.

"I was under no delusions about who he was," he said. "*What* he was, even as a boy. I knew. I felt it. In every part of my soul. But ... even from my oldest memories, my earliest ones ... he—he had moments. He wasn't always ..." He sucked in a breath and his eyes grew distant. "He had small moments of clarity, or ... kindness. I don't know. He ... it wasn't as if he never could make me feel like he loved me. Or cared."

I nodded, and took his hand again, rubbing small circles into his skin with my thumb. "I could see that. He could be charismatic when he wanted to be."

His chest heaved. "I clung to those moments, you know, hoarded them into a dragon's pile, obsessing over them, trying to understand. And the moments, Gods, the moments were so small and insignificant now that I look back. Sometimes he just talked to me." Rhyan's jaw tightened, his nostrils flaring. "Like we were close. Like we had a relationship, or a bond or some shit like that. Like he, like he *could*—love. Could ... love ... me." His voice broke again. "His son. Sometimes I thought maybe—maybe underneath it all, he did. He really did. That he just didn't know how to show it." He sobbed. "I believed for so long that he wasn't all evil. Even after he ... with my mother. And all he'd done to me. The country. My friends. I still believed ..." Tears streamed down his face. "I still believed there was a line. That *I* was the line. That my life was the line, the one he wouldn't cross. That at the very end he wouldn't forget I was his son. That at the very, very least, my father, my own flesh and blood, couldn't—wouldn't do that to me," he cried. "But he did."

"Rhyan," I gasped, barely able to say anything more. My heart was breaking for him. It was already broken. Seeing him like this, so tortured, it was shattering all over. I pulled him closer, until his head rested against my breast. "I'm sorry. *Rakame*. You didn't deserve to have him as a father."

"No? Because now I think about what he's like, how he was with me, and then I think about how I was with you—"

"No," I said firmly. "Don't. Listen to me. You are not your father. Not even close. You couldn't be more different if you tried. He became a monster by choice. He chose to hurt you, and your mother, your people, your country, even me. Because that's what he wanted to do. Anything you did as an akadim, was not your choice. Not your will. You didn't ask to be like that. When you're in control, when you're you, and you have the choice to hurt someone, or help them, I know what choice you'll make. Every single time."

He burst into sobs. I pulled him into my arms, his body laying over mine as it did the night before.

He calmed after a while. "I should get back out there," he sniffed. "There's so many who need comforting, have questions. There's so much to do."

"No." I traced the shape of his eyebrows with my fingers. "You get to rest now. Safely. You have a hundred soturi out there protecting you and me. Night sentries on duty. Scouts reporting back. Tonight, you rest. Everyone will understand."

"I want to help. I want to be prepared, and prepare them. I need to know that we're going to succeed. That his reign is coming to an end. That some good will come out of this shit."

"Some good already did. You, Rhyan. Now come here," I said, and pulled him into a kiss.

He licked the seam of my lips, his tongue sliding past them, kissing me deeper. We kissed for a long time. Nothing more happening between us. No progression. Just kissing. Just being together, and eventually, he fell asleep in my arms. I held him, pushing his hair off his forehead, stroking his back, and had just begun to nod off when I felt him move.

"I'm going out there, just for a little. I won't be long."

I sat up, so I could join him, but he laid me back down and kissed my forehead. "You rest."

"I should be out there, too," I said.

"You will be," he said. "We're partners right. So, we're going to take turns. I won't be long. Wait for me."

I kissed him again. "I will."

Two hours later, I felt him crawl into the bed beside me. He pulled me against him, wrapping his arm around my waist, his hand seeking out my stomach—the way we usually slept every night. The way I'd missing sleeping with him for months.

I placed my hand over his. "You feeling better," I whispered sleepily.

"Better," he said, kissing my neck.

The next morning was a whirlwind. Rhyan seemed to be in better spirits, carried by the anger he had for his father, and the promise of his removal from power. We spent until lunchtime mapping out our route to Glemaria. We planned to head north in Dobrava, until we reached the Lumerian border of Payunmar. There we'd cross back into the Empire's territory. We'd been safe all night mainly because most of the surrounding area had been claimed by the akadim who now no longer existed. But moving north we were bound to encounter more hordes since they favored the longer nights here, plus they always saw the human lands as easier prey.

We also wanted to avoid the Allurian Pass in Glemaria, which we knew was infested and quite possibly where Aemon and Morgana were housing more of their undead soturi. Much as I wanted to cure more akadim, it was more important to reach Glemaria. To remove Devon. And get Rhyan's power back. There would be no way to fight against Morgana and Aemon's evil without restoring Rhyan's magic first. So once we reached Hartavia, we'd travel east, then cross into Glemaria. And then, enter the arena.

Sean, now officially acting as Arkturion to Rhyan's Arkasva, and far more experienced in soturi logistics than I was, started nominating soldiers to act as turion and assigning soturi into troops. Those who'd been human and chose to remain were tasked with clothing and weapons and food, any jobs that could be done without great strength or magic. Everyone else continued taking turns running out for supplies, hunting, standing guard in our outposts, or participating in training exercises that Rhyan was running.

We remained in our camp a second night, but with a routine established, and everyone's roles understood, we packed up the following morning, making our way north. We reached Payunmar by nightfall, and easily fell asleep after another exhausting day. My eyes closed with Rhyan beside me, his arms around me, holding me tight. A dozen of our human soturi, having done what they could, decided to travel home on the third day. But not before they all came to me and Rhyan hugging us both and thanking us.

My heart panged as I watched them travel away, but for the first time in a long time, it wasn't from sadness, or anger, or fear. It was from hope. Hope that maybe, just maybe, change was possible. And that they'd be okay. That after all the horror they'd faced, there was still a life ahead of them. And a life ahead for us.

We continued to camp in Payunmar through our fourth night, and then we packed up, and began the slow trek to Hartavia, the country bordering southern Glemaria.

Scouts were sent out to the border, and a few Glemarians were assigned to go inside.

All the reports that came back confirmed what Sean had told us. The arena known as the Pits was being set up for the Alissedari, and there was no sign of Kane or his legion in Glemaria. They had truly abandoned Devon. Sean also began sending out messengers to alert some of the other rebel groups who stood against the northern Imperator that we were preparing to move. And more and more soturi were sending word back that they planned to join us, to fight for me and Rhyan.

Making camp the fifth night, I crawled into our tent. We were two days from attacking. Rhyan pulled me in close, his breathing slow. I turned around to face him, tracing the shape of his eyebrows, running my finger down the bridge of his nose and to his lips. He sucked my fingertip into his mouth, then drew me in, rolling me onto my back. I opened my legs, making room for him. He was hard, and rocking against me. We hadn't come together again since that first night. We'd either been too tired, or we were needed for one meeting or another. Our rest was interrupted frequently by some decision that had to be made about routes, or meals, or shifting soturi to different troops based on strengths. But mostly, with everything happening, there just hadn't been privacy. We were alone, but our tent was rather close to the others. Much as I loved that aspect of our relationship, what we really needed was just time to hold each other, to talk, but tonight, something felt different. Like an undercurrent of magic was stirring between us.

"I want you," Rhyan rasped in my ear. "I want you so fucking bad."

I lifted my hips, gasping as he rubbed against me.

"I want you, too."

His tongue opened my mouth, sliding inside until he was kissing me so deeply, I could barely breathe. I ran my hands up his back, and moaned as he bucked against me.

His hands cupped my cheeks, tangling in my hair, and then ran down my neck as he lowered his mouth, kissing me in the spot where he'd drawn blood as an akadim.

I whimpered as he sucked harder on my skin, my flesh already so sensitive. His hand ran down my chest, pulling on the hem of my sleep shirt.

I reached for the waistband of his pants, loosening his drawstring and slipping my hand inside. He shuddered as I wrapped my fingers around him, already so thick and hard for me.

He growled against my neck, his teeth grazing my skin as I stroked him from base to tip.

"I need to be inside you," he said, his lips furiously kissing their way back on mine.

I was already shoving his pants down, as he pulled at mine, tugging them to my knees. I was about to reach down and get them off completely, when Rhyan lifted himself and reached for my waist, flipping me onto my hands and knees. He gripped my hips, his hand sliding down the curve of my ass, and cupping me.

"Fuck you're soaked," he hissed in my ear.

"I've been wanting you. For days." We'd been too busy, too tired. But my body hadn't seemed to care.

"Me too," he admitted.

"But you—didn't—" I whimpered. "I didn't think you—" He slid his finger inside me.

"Partner," he breathed. "I always want you."

"Why didn't you—ah—" He curled his finger inside, his palm pressing down. I hissed. "Why didn't you take me before?"

His breathing deepened. "I was afraid." He started to pump in and out, his thumb circling the apex of my thighs. Another finger slid in.

I sucked in a breath. "Of what?"

"Me," he said. "Memories. I'm still—still dreaming about it. Being akadim. What I did to you."

I turned, angling my neck so I could find his mouth again, one hand reaching up to stroke his face. "I'm not afraid of you. I love you."

His tongue licked his lips, his eyes hooded with desire as he pressed his forehead to mine, his fingers curling until I moaned.

"In my dreams," he panted, "I wake up confused, like I'm still trapped in that body. And I have you as my prisoner. Tied up." He shuddered. "Scared. Of me." He exhaled, his chest shaking. "It's still like it was that first morning. I want to tell you to run away from me. To save yourself. Leave me. But then," his voice broke, his strokes increasing in speed. "Then you open your eyes, and you look at me. You see me. And you're not afraid," he cried. "And then I remember. I remember you saved me. And then I just want ... fuck. All I want is to hold you. To be with you. Near you. Next to you. On you. In you. But underneath it all, I'm still afraid—afraid I'm not worthy."

"Then look at me now," I commanded, "and hear me. Hear me nice and good." I met his gaze in the dark. "You are worthy, Rhyan, of everything good in this world. *A ni janam ra.*"

He shuddered again, and nodded, his chest heaving against my back, "I know you."

I kissed him, our tongues battling.

"Gods, Lyr," he breathed against. "Can I fuck you now?"

"Yes. Yes."

He slid his fingers out, and gripped my hips, and then I felt him at my entrance, the head of his cock sliding against me, coating himself in my arousal.

"Please," I panted, needing to feel him completely.

"I'm at your command. Always." And then, he slid in, and in, and in.

I cried out, only for his hand to slide across my mouth, sealing my lips shut, and muffling my groans.

"Shhh, partner," he crooned in my ear, his pelvis lifting, his cock hitting a spot that made my eyes close. "My army will hear you."

"Your army?" I bit down on his palm as he started to thrust, remaining buried deep inside me. "I thought you … were at my command."

He moaned. "*Our* army."

"That's more like it," I gasped.

"Fuck. I don't think I'm going to last long," he said.

"Your fault for waiting all this time." I pushed back against him. "But me neither."

"You feel … so … fucking … good." He tightened his hold against my mouth, just as I started to cry out. He pumped into me, faster and faster, pushing with so much force, I collapsed onto my elbows. His hand swept under my knees forcing me down, flat on my belly. The new position pushed my legs together. Rhyan's weight rested fully on top of me, pressing me deep into the blankets. Then his ankles locked over mine. I could barely move. Only lay there and take him as he pumped, his movements growing wild and rabid.

He gripped my hair, pulling my head back, his lips on my neck, as he slid in and out, his hips setting a bruising pace. The heat coiled between my legs was rippling and tensing. I couldn't take much more. It was too good, too intense.

"I'm going to come," I whined.

"Oh, I know you are."

I mewled.

He bit down on my earlobe. "Can you come quietly? Hmmm, partner. Can you do that for me?"

"No." I cried out, shaking my head, burying my face in the blankets. Every part of my body was in contact with his, and after days without this, with Rhyan only sleeping against me at night doing little more than holding me, I was heady. He didn't understand. Just like that first night, he hardly had to do anything to drive me wild. He was alive. He was alive. That was all I needed. And again, I knew I could come just from that. But of course, this was Rhyan. And he knew exactly what to do to make me lose control. To make me scream. And then I started to, unable to stop.

"Give me that loud mouth of yours, partner Come on. Give it to me." His hand wrapped around my face, turning my head and crushing his lips over mine, silencing my cries of pleasure. He breathed into me, his hips jerking. With a groan, I felt him twitch, spilling into me.

That pushed me over the edge. My body tremored, every limb shaking as ripples of pleasure crashed like a tidal wave through my limbs.

Panting, I buried my face in the blanket as Rhyan kissed my cheek, his body still on top of mine. We breathed together like that, his hands reaching up to find mine, our fingers threaded together.

A moment later, I shifted under him, and he slowly pulled out, turning me over and kissing me thoroughly. His hand slid under my head, holding me close. Then he got up, rummaging through our bags for a clean towel. He had a small cantina of water that he poured on top. Then he knelt before me, a wicked glint in his eyes as he cleaned me. Then took care of himself, sliding his pants back up. His lips curled.

"What's that look?" I asked.

One eyebrow lifted. "I was just thinking ... I kind of like the idea of everyone hearing you. Of them knowing that you're screaming for me. That I'm claiming you. You're claiming me. After all the hiding we had to do," he shrugged, "I don't know. I kind of like the idea of them hearing how pretty you sound when I'm deep inside you, when you come for me."

Heat spread across my cheeks, even as the idea started to stoke the fire inside me again.

"And what about you? Will you let them hear you scream for me?" I asked, sitting up. He slid my pants on, licking his lips.

"Partner," he pushed my hair back, "I'm at your command. All you have to do is ask, and I'll do whatever you want." He kissed the corner of my mouth. "Whenever you want."

"Hmmm." I cupped his chin. "Good to know."

"Lord Rhyan." The call came urgently from outside our tent. "Lady Lyriana." It was Harman. He'd been named a turion by Sean and was leading one of the troops currently on sentry duty for the night.

"Harman?" Rhyan called back, then looked me over, making sure I was decent. Satisfied, he smoothed his hair back and opened the tent flap. I followed him out, folding my arms over my chest as the wind blew.

"What's wrong?" I asked.

"I'm sorry to disturb you both. But the camp has visitors."

"Visitors?" I frowned. We'd been unbelievably lucky. No one had found us yet. Our scouts had been too effective, and once we were back inside Lumeria, I'd warded the campsite each night, adding small glamours like fog and additional shadows to keep any soturi on duty away. The only new people who'd managed to find us were Sean's allies, returning with his messengers.

"Who?" Rhyan asked.

"They say they know you two, and insisted on seeing you themselves," Harman said.

I looked at Rhyan, his eyes were narrowed in suspicion. "Did they offer you a name?"

Harman shook his head. "No, Your Grace. There's four of them. Two female mages, one male, and a male soturion. He speaks like you, Your Grace. Glemarian."

My eyes widened, my heart pounding.

"He said to show you this." Harman opened his hand and produced two vadati stones. Stones I'd seen before. Part of a set of three that Rhyan once had from his mother. He'd kept one, given one to Meera, and gifted the other to me. Two of our stones were now in Harman's hands.

I was already back in the tent, pulling out our boots and shoving them at Rhyan as I slipped into mine. I pulled out the red shard, strapping it to my back—I never went anywhere without it, and Rhyan had begun clasping his golden armor on—securing the green shard around his torso.

"Take us to them," I demanded. "Now."

"Please," Rhyan added.

"Yes, please," I said.

Harman held a small torch in one hand, the fire crackling and releasing curls of smoke into the night as we moved through the maze of tents lined up through the campsite. I was stumbling over my feet in my rush to get there—to wherever Harman was leading us.

Beyond the meadow where our encampment lay for the night was a small woodland, with a canopy of moontrees. Two more sentries stood guard, their swords drawn before four figures whose silhouettes were defined in the shadows.

Rhyan started breathing faster, taking in the familiar outlines. One man had curly hair that was pulled half up on top of his head. The next showed off a gryphon-like nose as he turned, revealing his profile, and then two women could be seen, one with long, fine wavy hair, the other with a lion's mane of curls sprouting from her head.

"Let them pass," Rhyan cried out. "Let them pass!"

"Your Grace," the first sentry said. He lowered his sword, and the second followed.

Dario, Aiden, Meera, and Jules all spilled into the woodland, stopping before us, their features catching on Harman's torchlight.

It was Dario and Aiden who caught sight of Rhyan first, going completely still, as they looked him up and down.

"You were dead," Dario said, breathlessly.

"I was," Rhyan said. "Lyr saved me."

Dario twisted his head to me, his eyes watering, his chest heaving. He bared his teeth like so much emotion was pouring out of him he had to brace himself for battle.

"Your Grace," he said to me, his Glemarian accent thick. "Again."

"Again," I said. "I guess." Titles still felt a bit fast and loose. But I supposed Rhyan and I were both Arkasva at the moment—though of which country or how—I wasn't sure.

But Dario didn't seem to care. He rushed over to me, his arms slapping around my back as he pulled me into a bear hug. "Thank you. Thank you!" he yelled. And then he turned to Rhyan, his entire body shaking. "You. Godsdamned. Gryphon shit. Bastard," he sobbed, then pulled him into a hug, grabbing his face, and planting a violently affectionate kiss on his cheek. Then another. Dario wouldn't let go. He just kept kissing Rhyan's face, calling him a bastard again and again as he cried.

Aiden hugged me next, then joined his other two friends. He stood back, his eyes shining. For a moment he was silent, and then a shaky breath escaped from him. "You scared the fuck out of us," he shouted, breaking all of his normal "Aiden" decorum.

I laughed, already crying again, and then Meera flew into my arms.

"Lyr, Lyr! Gods, we were so worried. What the hell happened to you? You vanished on us."

"I know, I'm sorry. I have so much to tell you."

"So do we."

I squeezed my arms around her, holding her as tight as I could. "Gods, I missed you. I'm so glad you're okay!"

"Us, too," Meera said.

"We need to tell them the news," Jules said suddenly.

I pulled back from Meera, looking at my cousin. My best friend. The part of my soul who'd been missing. My heart felt heavy as I took her in. She'd gained weight in the last two months. She looked healthier than when we'd taken her from the Palace. I was grateful. Dario had kept his word. He had kept her safe. Which was all I could ask for. But my heart panged. She was still standing back from me.

Rhyan looked past the circle of hugs he was trapped in with Dario and Aiden, locking eyes with Jules. "Hey, friend."

"Hi," she said, her voice a little shaky.

"What news?" Rhyan asked, turning to smile at Meera. "Hey."

"It's your father," Meera said. "We've been searching for you for the last few days, but we just found out. The tournament has been moved up. It's happening tomorrow."

"Tomorrow?" I asked. "No. We were supposed to have a whole other day to travel and prepare." I paused. "Wait. How did you know we were heading to the tournament?"

"I've seen it," Jules said. A vision. "He's getting scared of the pushback. His people are unhappy. The distraction had to move up. Before any more soturi abandoned him. And there's more that I've seen. I'll explain everything." She stepped forward, slowly taking me in, her eyes wide. Her mouth tightened, the corners of her eyes shining and red.

"Jules." My arms were literally aching from missing her. But after all she'd been through, she hadn't been ready to hug me, or be touched. And until right before I left to go after Rhyan, two months ago, I hadn't been able to risk touching her. She was the reincarnation of Hava and could have activated the Valalumir inside me.

But we didn't have to worry about that now.

Her hazel eyes searched mine, and then she sucked in a shaky breath. "Lyr," she said finally. Her voice broke, "You're okay?"

"I'm okay. You?"

She nodded, then rushed into my arms, wrapping me in a hug.

"Jules!" I sobbed, crushing her against me.

CHAPTER FORTY-THREE

RHYAN

I had about five minutes for my heart to fill with joy as I stood with Dario and Aiden, my best friends. And even more joy as I watched Lyr's aura light up with Meera, and Jules. Jules at last. Gods, it felt good seeing everyone like this, safe, together. Reunited. I wanted more time for all of us. A proper reunion, especially now that I knew my friends didn't hate me. That they never did for what happened to Garrett, or for the way I left Glemaria. We were all okay. But we also had unfinished business, so much more we needed to talk about to fully clear the air.

I imagined Lyr felt the same about her group. My heart panged for her, knowing she'd had to leave Jules behind as soon as she'd found her. To rescue me. Because of me, they'd been parted.

Because of my father, they had.

I took a deep breath, wanting nothing more than to find some mead and bring Aiden and Dario into my tent so we could talk all night. Laugh and joke like we used to. But I already knew how easily this moment could be stolen from us—how fleeting it all was. We had to act first. The Empire was still against us. Morgana and Aemon. And my father had already moved up the timeline for our attack.

We needed to plan. Because I sure as hell wasn't going to let him catch me unaware again.

I turned to Harman. "Wake Sean. Tell him to meet us, and any other soturi you can spare—send them here. We need to meet now."

Harman nodded. "Of course, Your Grace." Then he lowered his chin to Lyr. "Your Grace."

She smiled. "Thank you, Harman."

A few minutes later, Sean came barreling through the camp, fully dressed in his uniform, his sword on his back.

"What's going on? What happened?" he said, his face drawn with concern. He stilled as his eyes swept over Dario and Aiden, then his mouth spread into a wide grin. He laughed and sprinted forward, pulling them both into a hug. "You two!"

Dario, Aiden, and Garrett had all adored Sean. I'd forgotten. They were nearly as crushed as I'd been when he left Glemaria. I stood back, letting them have a moment. And met Lyr's eyes. For a second, they heated with fire, with the same look she'd given me when I was deep inside her. I felt my own answering heat. The scent of her still clung to me. But then she turned back to Jules, her eyes sparkling.

I gave Dario and Aiden the basic rundown of all that they'd missed. That Lyr had found me, cured me, and then how we'd found Sean, and the Glemarian soturi who'd defected to Bamaria. And then the rest of our army, the former akadim.

Aiden couldn't have looked more shocked if he'd wanted to. And Dario, well, he was still fighting all of his emotions.

I was about to ask what I'd missed since I last saw them. Dario had glanced more than once at Jules when he thought no one was looking. But Harman returned with five more soturi behind him. I took Lyr's hand, and we sat down, quickly rattling off everyone's name, title, and relationship to us.

"Now that we're all introduced, the real reason I've brought us together is because Lady Julianna and Lady Meera," I said, gesturing to the two of them, "Have important information about my father's plans." I turned to them, waiting for them to explain.

For a moment, there was nothing but tense silence. Jules and Meera looked at each other before staring back at the gathered soturi.

I realized the problem. They were still keeping secrets. Secrets deadly under the Empire.

But not here. Not anymore. I would no longer abide by their rules. And neither would anyone fighting beside me.

"I want you all to know that Lady Julianna and Lady Meera," I said, "Have my utmost confidence. And Lady Lyriana's. You can speak freely in front of them, trust them. But you should know, that like me, or rather—like I was … before—they're vorakh."

Sean jerked his head toward them in shock, unable to school away the surprise in his face. But I could see that he wasn't afraid, just surprised. He accepted them, and tried to show it, by vigorously nodding his head. "Of course. You are welcome here. All of you."

Three of the other soturi with us, former Glemarians, looked somewhat uncomfortable. I didn't like it, but I understood—they'd spent their lives being taught to fear vorakh. Yet, it was clear from the look in their eyes, and the way they hadn't bolted, that they were open-minded enough to see the evidence before them was stronger than the lies and propaganda of the Empire, and I could also see their faces change as they began to see that we were no threat. I could almost see their minds slowly digesting the news, replacing the stories they'd been told, and accepting them. It made me hopeful, hopeful that more minds could be changed.

However, Harman and the rest of the soturi he'd collected, those who had been akadim with me, had a completely different reaction. They looked almost relieved at the admission.

"I was akadim," Harman said. "A far worse crime is in my eyes than any I could imagine are associated with you. According to the Empire at least. I'm working to make up for what I did, what I was. As are many of us. Lord Rhyan and Lady Lyriana have trusted me. And I trust them, so that extends to you. I don't see why I should fear vorakh. Or hate you. If you don't fear or hate me."

"No," Meera said. "We don't."

"Not at all," Jules said, but her eyes were on me. "I'm so sorry that happened to you."

"Thank you, my lady," Harman said formally. But his lower lip shook.

Dario's gaze moved back and forth between them, his body turning protectively in Jules's direction. I eyed Lyr quickly, who'd also taken note. She shrugged when she met my eyes, then jerked her chin at the group again, pulling me back.

"Well, now that that's out of the way," I said, "Julianna and Meera come with news about my father's plans. The event has been moved up to tomorrow night." A Hartavian clocktower began to chime in the distance. Midnight. "Tonight, actually," I said, when the bells stopped. "Which means we have to push all of our plans up by a day. We need to be ready to make our move when the Alissedari happens."

"And this is based only on visions?" Sean asked. "Not that I don't trust what you've seen."

Meera shook her head. "No, of course not."

"We've also had contact with Lady Kenna," Dario said. "She managed to get a few messages out to us, and they confirmed everything their visions showed. And as you know, I served along with Aiden in His Highness's inner circle, privy to many of his plans. We're ready to speak out against him, and know others who will do the same upon his arrest. Once his influence is over, there are many who will be freed from his control."

The blood contracts. For Dario and Aiden to help us, they couldn't get near my father, not close enough for him to give orders. But I tucked that detail away. We had a hundred more to go through. Visions shared by Jules and Meera, intel from Kenna. And a new plan to make and execute come morning. It was a lot.

"Just one question," Sean asked. "How can we get word to Lady Kenna now and any other allies inside his Court? It's the one thing I haven't been able to manage, and I'm fairly well connected."

Meera grinned suddenly, opening up a small pouch at her belt.

There was a sharp hissing sound and two baby nahashim slid out onto her arm, snaking their way in tight coils to her elbow. "Shhhhh," she cooed, and stroked their backs with a finger. "They can get inside Seathorne, and deliver any message we need. They can also seek out anyone, or anything," she eyed me, "we might need or be looking for. And in turn, I can intercept any nahashim he sends our way. For the last two months, I've been destroying his most effective secret weapon. One by one."

"Meera, that's genius," I said, before glancing around at my council to make sure no one was about to bolt. We'd just thrown them all into a midnight meeting with vorakh and nahashim. But everyone was still. And calm. It was a good sign.

"Once the plan is in place, I'll get word to Kenna," Meera said. "And then we go."

"Okay." I took a deep breath. "Tell us everything you know."

We broke camp before dawn, marching in the dark to the Glemarian border. Lyr's sword, the red shard, shone against her back, her hair glowing red now, even without the sun to change it. She emitted so much power, working with Aiden to glamour our entire soturi in shadows as we crossed into the wilds of Glemaria. It had been left unguarded on purpose by my father. It was one of his cruelties, and thus had become a hot spot for akadim activity, one that left my people unprotected. With all the demons known to the area, and the loyalty he had of Hartavia's Arkasva and people, no one ever came through here.

Until today, when I stepped over the border. I took in the fresh scent of pine, the scent that I'd always loved, that always reminded me of home. I could see the familiar outlines of the mountains rising against the trees. To the left was the Allurian Pass, Aemon's hideout. The mountains where Morgana had taken the indigo shard.

I looked around, stepping on the familiar landscape, even recognizing the field we'd entered. The last time I'd been here was for the last Alissedari. I'd been dropped off in the early morning with every other soturion participating. Wild gryphons had been all over the woods and fields. I'd been with Garrett, fighting to claim a gryphon, and earn his trust, enough that I could get him to fly me to the tournament and compete in it.

This was where we'd been ambushed. Where the akadim had attacked Garrett, leaving him forsaken for hours, turning in silence until he finally confessed what had happened in the arena. And asked me to kill him.

Asked me to let him die as himself.

All because of my father. Because he'd allowed the akadim inside. But that ended tonight.

The clock tower rang out and in the distance a flock of roaring, squawking gryphons came into view as they flew just above the trees. My heart sang. I hadn't seen or ridden one since—since the night before I died.

And right now, Artem, my old friend and Glemaria's stable master, was heading for us, leading the flock. There were about a dozen flying behind him. Dario had been able to send a message to Kenna via Meera's nahashim, explaining our transport needs once we reached the border.

Lyr and Aiden stepped forward, releasing the shadow glamour that covered us, just enough so Artem could see. His gryphon moved into the sunlight and I gasped audibly, seeing its feathers and fur.

"By the Gods," Sean exclaimed. "Is that—"

My eyes widened, my heart leaping. No. It couldn't. It couldn't be. But it was. A wide grin filled my face. Artem landed in front of me, riding on the back of a beautiful newly adult gryphon I never thought I'd see again. Not after he helped me escape from my father. He was unlike any other gryphon in Glemaria, not bronze, or silver. He was red. He flew with bright red feathers. Batavia red.

"How?" I asked. "I thought he went home." The gryphon was born in the Afeyan lands, part of the Star Court. But he'd ended up outside of Seathorne as a baby, and in need of care.

Artem shrugged, patting the gryphon's head. "I think he likes me." His eyes crinkled, looking down at me. "The lad just keeps coming back."

Lyr stepped forward looking mesmerized. "I've never seen one this color."

Jules looked equally enthralled, and smiled. "He's beautiful."

I stood back, my heart filling with joy, as I opened my arms. The gryphon met my eyes, eyeing me up and down, then he started forward, butting his head into my belly, like he was trying to burrow his way in, just like he had when he was a baby. "Hey. Hey now," I said, rubbing behind his ears.

"I missed you, too, buddy." Artem descended, and slapped his knee. His pants were covered, as always, in dirt and straw from the stables.

"Welcome back, Rhyan," he said, his eyes sweeping over me.

"Artem," I said, and opened my arms for a hug.

He shook his head. "I smell like gryphon shit."

I laughed. "You always did." I pulled him into a hug. And he patted me on the back. The rest of the gryphons in the flock began to land, each one touching down and squawking or kicking at the dirt and grass beneath them with their claws.

"He's beautiful," Lyr said, coming over to stroke his feathers. My gryphon looked up at her, and immediately pushed his head into her hand.

I would have called him a traitor, going to her so fast, but I couldn't blame him when I had the same urge. If he was going to love anyone else besides me, Lyr was a good choice. I was glad to see that she seemed to feel the same way about him. Much to my disappointment, she had taken a little longer to warm up to the creatures—though considering her first ever time riding one had been trapped in the arms of Aemon's akadim, right after Parthenay had bound and captured us—I didn't blame her.

Parthenay.

My vision darkened suddenly, the visceral scent of grass and blood and sweat in my nose.

You're hungry, Rhyan? Aren't you? Very hungry.

My mind flashed. Morgana ordering me to take Parthenay. To do what I wanted to her. Anything I wanted. She was underneath me, screaming, and crying. Her blood on my lips. Pain shot through my head, and my chest tightened. My vision blurred. I couldn't breathe.

"Rhyan." Lyr grabbed my hand and squeezed. "Look at me," she said urgently. Her palm rested against my chin, her fingers stroking my cheek.

I met her eyes, my chest still hurting.

"Breathe," she said quietly, just to me. "Breathe. I'm right here. We're in Glemaria. We're alive. We're okay."

I watched her chest rise and fall, and breathed with her, squeezing her hand back.

The images faded, and I nodded. Relief spread across her face, her thumb rubbing back and forth on my hand. We stood there another moment, just watching the gryphon when Lyr squinted her eyes. "He ..." she frowned. "He looks familiar."

"Um," I swallowed, "he's actually the gryphon I had tattooed on my back."

"This is the gryphon?" Lyr asked. She looked quickly back and forth between us and grinned. "I see it."

"Spend a lot of time looking at his back?" Dario asked.

Lyr glared.

"Yes," I said. "And he's Afeyan, that's why he looks like this. The gryphons from the Star Court come in every color you can imagine."

"Like Mercurial," Lyr said dryly.

"Like Mercurial," I said, more than aware of the anger in my voice. I was surprised that bastard hadn't shown up yet to gloat, or call in another fucking favor. But that was coming. Something to worry about later.

I turned my attention back to the gryphon. "I found him as a baby outside my window a few years back. Took care of him—well, Artem did. He had a broken leg. But he healed, and he was with me when I escaped. My only friend in exile." I looked at Sean. "At least, at first."

Sean smiled, and gripped my shoulder, his eyes full of emotion. "A good friend then."

"Well," Artem said. "You all better go. And win. Please. I have to be on my way—to the actual Alissedari. Rhyan," he pulled me back to him, and squeezed my hand, "You weren't supposed to come back. But you're here again, and this time, I have a good feeling, lad. But if I'm wrong, well—I've lived a good life." His eyes landed on Lyr's. "My lady, be safe." He went over to one of the smaller gryphons that had landed with him.

I turned to Sean and Lyr, my throat tightening, but it was time. And I stepped forward to address our soturi.

"This is it," I said. "I am so grateful to everyone who has come this far. Who has come here with us. Everyone who stands before me now is here for a reason. Because you all believe in a better world. In better leadership. In standing up to tyranny. We have seen horrors that no one should see, that no one deserves. It's time to stop those who enable such horrors, who help to bring them about. It's time to stop my father. To stop the man who has allowed far too many to suffer our fate. The man who has controlled the North, keeping too many oppressed and in danger for too long. You all know what to do. You all know where to go. And I know that in a few hours, we will claim victory as ours."

I looked at Lyr and nodded. She stepped forward.

"Rhyan and I," Lyr said, "will be right behind you. You go now with our full support, and full confidence. As well as our love. We all took an oath to stop the threat. And, today, that is exactly what we're going to do by ending the reign of Imperator Hart. Today, we free Glemaria."

Everyone cheered, and then Sean pulled them into formation while Dario and a Glemarian soturion named Rory began to round up the gryphons, feeding them some of the snacks we'd carried with us.

The soldiers began to climb onto their designated gryphons, some in groups as large as twelve on the biggest gryphon, while most had been placed into groups of six.

Lyr pulled out her sword, and at once, under the sunlight, it lit with flames, bright red light filling the meadow. Then she began to chant. "*Ani petrova* Rakashonim, *me ka el lyrotz, dhame ra shukroya, aniam anam. Chayate me el ra shukroya. Ani petrova* Rakashonim*!*"

Golden light exploded from inside her armor, lighting her up from head to toe, her hair a fiery red.

There was a thundering in my heart right then, my throat tightening. Because she looked just like … just like Asherah. Like my soulmate. And I had a flash of her. A flash of Asherah lifting her sword and riding into battle. In the same moment, I saw recognition in Meera's eyes—Cassarya. And Jules—Hava.

I wasn't sure, but Dario also had a strange look on his face as he watched her, like he'd seen this before.

I blinked and the vision faded, and she was Lyr again. She connected the sword to her stave—Asherah's stave—and then she took Aiden's hand, her stave connecting to his. A flash of blue light streamed between them. Then they went to work, glamouring each gryphon with an illusion spell. Slowly, each beast and the soturi they carried began to fade from view, their bodies blending into the surrounding field and trees.

It was a huge spell, and an even bigger undertaking. Glamour this advanced wasn't even studied, except by Aiden, and Ka Shavo in Bamaria. Lyr had practiced with him until the early hours. We'd decided that for a spell this large, and that had to last as long as it did, Lyr had to call on all her power. And if all went according to plan, this would be the only time she would have to use it today.

Dario stepped forward, his arms raised high. He signaled to the first gryphon. "*Volara!*" The gryphon, barely visible under the spell, began to run, roaring as its wings flapped, taking flight and soaring over the tops of the trees.

He signaled again, safely sending all but two gryphons out. Then he climbed up onto the one we'd designated for him, alongside Aiden, Jules, and Meera.

Aiden glamoured them all, and within seconds, my friends and Lyr's family faded from vision.

Then Lyr climbed up onto the red gryphon, and I followed, seating myself behind her, my hand wrapped around her waist.

"I'll see you on the other side," I called out.

"Keep them safe, Dario," Lyr yelled.

"On my life," he called back, and though I could barely see him, I knew his fist was at his heart. Then he cried out, "*Vra! Volara!*"

Wind gusted through our hair, pulling the hoods of our cloaks back. I couldn't see the moment my friends took off. But I could see the wind bristling through the leaves, and hear the flapping of wings.

And then it was just me and Lyr.

Her back heaved against my front as she breathed deeply. Then she turned around, pulling my chin to her, kissing me softly, and then pointing her stave between us.

"Ready?" she asked.

"I'm ready."

We disappeared.

CHAPTER FORTY-FOUR

LYRIANA

My heart pounded a heavy rhythm in my chest as I soared through the sky, flying over Glemaria. I nestled back against Rhyan, grateful I had him to hold onto.

On top of not loving flying on gryphons—though, the animals were starting to grow on me *slowly*—this flight was extra strange. The glamour magic meant I could hardly see the red gryphon beneath us. He was anything but red at the moment. I could barely see my body, or Rhyan's. We blurred into the sky, and the mountains, and sometimes the leaves of the trees as we passed them.

Rhyan remained mostly quiet as we flew, and I didn't want to say much to disturb his focus. I knew this was hard for him. There were so many moving pieces, and at the end, he'd face his father. Something I knew he still feared, still dreaded. So I mainly leaned back against him, stroking his hand which rested against my belly.

The flight was expected to take hours. We had to cross to the other side of the country, heading all the way north, and then east.

The arena known as the Pits was located to the west. But we weren't heading to the Alissedari.

Thanks to Kenna, we'd learned Devon had become aware of Sean's movements north. As had word of my presence in Korteria. Thanks to that Godsdamned innkeeper. But it was a blessing, in the end, because it allowed us to realize what he had been planning.

The entire tournament wasn't just a distraction for his people against a failing reign. It was a trap for all of us.

He wasn't going to be at the arena today. He was hiding in Seathorne, in his fortress.

By the time we would arrive, our soturi would have infiltrated Seathorne, making a path for me to easily reach Rhyan's father. Then I would bind him. Jules and Meera, guarded by Dario and Aiden, would locate the box that contained Rhyan's magic and bring it to us. Then, his magic restored, Rhyan would be able to reveal the extent of his crimes to the Council, and Glemaria would finally be free.

The hours passed more quickly than I would have thought. And I knew my time with Rhyan, just flying, alone, and momentarily safe, was about to come to an end. Rhyan's breathing quickened as the gray stone towers of Seathorne atop Gryphon's Mount finally came into view. Out on the cliff just beside it, lay the white seraphim. Asherah's tomb.

My tomb.

He released a shaky breath, then leaned forward, ordering the gryphon to land.

"*Dorscha*," he commanded, making sure to reach past me and touch the gryphon's head so our descent wasn't at the usual speed—the one that felt like a gryphon crashing out of the sky. I'd had enough of that for the next two lives.

I held onto Rhyan and the gryphon's claws touched down just outside the promenade.

It was eerily quiet. My stomach twisted.

Then Dario's voice sounded in my ear. "Lyriana." I touched the cool vadati stone with my fingers, feeling it warm as a blue light glowed in my peripheral vision. "Dario."

"Everyone's in place," he said calmly. "Showtime."

"I'm on my way inside." I turned in Rhyan's arms, reaching for his face, still blurred and difficult to see with my illusion spell. But I knew where his lips were, I had his face memorized, and pressed a light kiss to them.

"Partner," he said, his hand stroking over my waist, fingers running over the hilts of my weapons, and then down to my hip where he gripped me. "Remember, strike first, think later. Whatever happens in there, we survive this, and we leave together."

"Together," I said, my heart pounding.

He lowered his hand to my thigh for one more squeeze before I felt him frown against me. "Did Dario sound a little strange to you?" Rhyan asked, his voice formal and devoid of his accent.

"I don't know," I said, sweat beading at my brow.

"The blood contract," Rhyan hissed.

"If he's compromised," I said, "I have to get in there."

"Fuck." Rhyan stilled. The blue light hadn't gone away.

"Lyriana, everything's fine," Dario said, but he sounded even stranger than before. His accent softened. His lilt was usually the thickest of the three, devoid of any attempt to use the more formal accent of the nobility. The kind meant to mimic Devon's lack of a lilt.

Rhyan shook his head. "Something's wrong."

My pulse quickened. But Meera and Jules were inside. I had to get in there.

"I'm going." I pressed one more kiss to Rhyan's lips. And then I descended, my boots slamming down on the stone beneath us.

I pulled out my stave. One more spell.

And then I brandished my sword and I ran inside. I tore through the front hall, expecting it to be empty. That was the plan. Our soturi should have taken care of any guards, clearing the way. But then someone called out to me from behind.

"Stop!"

I heard two sets of boots. I didn't wait to see who it was. I ran, but only a moment later, two Glemarian soturi wearing black leather armor, silver gryphons stitched into the torso, seized me. My sword clattered to the floor as they grabbed my arms, and shoved them behind my back.

No!

It had been hours since I'd called on *Rakashonim*. My glamour must have faded as soon as I entered the fortress. And my strength, that had faded, too. Fuck! I gritted my teeth and struggled against them, but their grips were like iron.

"Lyriana Batavia, you're under arrest for trespassing in Seathorne, and conspiracy to assassinate His Highness, Imperator Hart. You're coming with us."

"NO!" I screamed. "NO!"

"Lord Dario and Lord Aiden have already turned you in. They confessed everything. Between that and your crimes against the Empire, it's time to accept, it's over for you."

Tears filled my eyes. "No. No!" Fuck! The fucking blood contract.

They gripped my arms tighter, pulling me down the stone corridors, past the giant gryphon statues that lined the walls. My feet dragged, and I tried to stop them by digging my boots into the floor, trying to break free of their hold. It was no use.

"Where are you taking me?" I asked.

"To the Seating Room. His Highness is very eager to see you," said the soturion on my left.

My throat dried and before I knew it, we were at the familiar double doors leading to the room where Imperator Hart ruled. Where he'd killed Rhyan's mother. A gryphon with his wings outstretched had been carved into the wood. I met the herald's eyes, and then he stepped back, the doors opening wide.

Imperator's Hart's aura blasted through the threshold. All at once, all the fear and trepidation I'd felt the first time I was there returned.

But unlike last time, the Seating Room was full. The entire Glemarian Council was in attendance, filling one of the plain wooden benches that Devon favored. The only opulence in the room was him, his golden Laurel of the Arkasva. The golden border on his black robes that marked him as Imperator. And the shining silver of the weapons slung through his belt.

He sat on his Seat now, on the raised dais, his face stern, his eyes blazing with triumph.

My stomach clenched as he stood, and the auras of his nobility blasted against me. Anger and hatred and disgust.

I searched desperately, looking for a familiar face. I landed first on Lady Amalthea, the fucking woman that had taken advantage of Rhyan when he was drunk. The one his father had tried to force him into an engagement with. I looked ahead at the dais. Kenna stood behind him, even more pregnant than before. Her stomach had been huge the last time I'd seen her, and I could have sworn based on its size that she'd have given birth by now. But her belly had only swollen more. And as I moved closer, my feet still dragging, my pulse racing, she looked down, refusing to meet my gaze. My heart sank.

"Lady Lyriana Batavia," Imperator Hart said in his deep and hateful voice. "It wasn't enough for you to kill His Majesty, Emperor Theotis."

"I didn't do that," I cried out.

"No? You still want to lie? Even with all the evidence stacked against you? Enough of this. Your men have been captured." Gone was any trace of the smirk I'd seen him wear when I'd dealt with him in the past. This wasn't Imperator Hart anymore. This was Rhyan's father. The vengeful, cruel man who had no shred of humanity left. I realized now that as dangerous as he had seemed before, it was nothing compared to the hatred burning in his eyes now. Nothing compared to the man he'd become to Rhyan. Sending him to his death.

I looked desperately around the room, my heart stopping when I didn't see any sign of Meera or Jules.

"Where's Dario?" I asked. "And Aiden?"

"Where they belong," he said and snapped his fingers. A door behind the dais opened, and Dario and Aiden both walked out, smiling viciously at me.

Dario laughed. "It was only too easy to bring you back here."

Aiden shrugged. "Sorry, Lyriana. But my loyalties will always lie with my Imperator. "He placed a hand over his heart. "With my country."

"Bind her," Imperator Hart ordered.

"No. No!" I screamed, but Aiden unleashed the rope from his stave. It shot at me, coiling around my body like a nahashim, burning against my clothing.

"I trusted you," I cried.

Aiden only shrugged, and looked away, his face stern, without any hint of warmth.

My chest heaved.

"Dario," he said. "Give this to her. Now."

Dario retrieved a scroll from his hand and walked it over to me, unraveling it before my eyes. It was another blood contract.

I'd broken free of mine when I'd last seen him in the arena. At Rhyan's stripping. My *Rakashonim* had burned through it.

There was another unspoken signal from His Highness and Dario held a knife to my throat.

"Now, Lyriana," the Imperator drawled. "You can sign this, and I may pardon you for your attempted crimes, speak on your behalf to the Emperor. Though, considering you have been named a traitor of the Empire, and wanted dead, I can have Dario execute you now, save you from further torment and torture. But you'll choose, and do it before all these witnesses."

I searched the depths of Dario's dark eyes, pleading. We'd become friends. I'd trusted him. Left him to protect my family. But he remained cold and unmoved, the way he'd been when I first met him, completely under the thrall of Imperator Hart.

A tear rolled down my cheek, and I looked up again, trying to catch Kenna's gaze. We'd been allies. Friends. But she continued to stare at the ground.

Where the hell were Meera and Jules? What had happened to them?

"Sign," the Imperator commanded.

"No," I yelled. Just another Godsdamned manipulation. If I signed, I signed my life away. My freedom. And in the end, he was likely to kill me anyway. "Fuck you! You lying, murderous, piece of shit."

"Dario," he commanded. "She had her chance. I sentence her to death."

My stomach clenched, sweat breaking out on my forehead.

And then the double doors slammed open with a thunderous bang, one powerful enough to shake the room. Someone cried out in fear. And a voice, angry and feral, filled with the vengeance of a God, roared out.

"You will die if you touch her!"

Everyone turned in their seats, and Imperator Hart's eyes widened in shock and fear, his face draining of color as Rhyan entered the room.

CHAPTER FORTY-FIVE

RHYAN

"But you're—you were ..." my father spluttered.

"Dead? Akadim? Apparently, that was just a phase for me. Something I was going through." I strolled into the Seating Room. Into the room I'd hated so much over the years. The room where my father had hurt Lyr, where he had forced her into an engagement with Kane, forced me to be with Amalthea. The room where I'd had to stand for hours in silence at his side, and it was the room where my mother had—where—where he'd murdered her.

He rose from his Seat, his face turning red with anger, his aura blasting. "Seize him," he screamed. "Now!"

Twenty-five soturi in the room all stepped forward, emerging from the shadows against the walls, their swords drawn and pointed at me.

I shrugged, unconcerned. "I am powerless now. You saw to that, Father. You took my magic. Ripped it from my body. The way you ripped everything else away from me. My title, my friends, my life!" My voice shook. "My mother."

His eyes narrowed, his brows coming together in a sharp, pointed V.

"So," I said, "it should be easy for your soturi to apprehend me."

But they didn't. They remained in place, not moving, not daring to take even a single step forward.

"I said seize him!" my father screamed.

I continued strolling forward, unconcerned.

"Dario," I said, my voice had gone cold. "Step away from Lyr. Now."

"No," my father yelled. "You keep that knife on her throat. And Rhyan," his eyes bore into mine, full of the same hatred they'd been filled with the day he tried to force me into a blood oath—the day he carved into the skin on my face. The day he took my mother's life. "One more step, and she dies."

"You wouldn't dare," I said. "You know the consequences. You know what I promised, what I swore."

If you hurt her, if you harm one hair on her head, there will be nowhere safe for you. Nowhere you can hide. Not in this lifetime. Not in the next. I will hunt you to the bowels of eternity.

"You have one chance," I told my father. "We don't want to hurt you. We want justice. Justice for all the akadim you allowed in, that you allowed to hurt your people. For all the blood contracts and blood oaths you've been wielding like weapons against your own Council. Your own Ka. And, for the murder of Garrett Aravain. On the day of the Alissedari you willingly allowed akadim into our country, akadim that attacked us on our way to the tournament. It took Garrett's soul, turned him forsaken. When I killed him in the arena that day, it was to let him die as himself. Because he asked me to. And when I confronted you about it, you admitted it. You knew all along what had happened, you knew the truth and covered it up."

"What?" There was a cry, and I knew at once it was Garrett's father, Kane's Second. I'd avoided looking at him the whole time we were back in Glemaria before. But now, now I looked, for the first time in over a year, trying to tell him how sorry I was for the role I'd played, and how sorry I was for hiding the truth. I wanted to apologize to Garrett's whole family. To make amends. But that would come later.

I glared at my father. "And you, you, are responsible for the murder of my mother, Lady Shakina Hart."

"You fucking liar!"

"It's true," Kenna said, looking up. "I was there. I watched it happen. And I was forced to lie."

"I will speak to you later, wife," my father spat out, his words like ice. "I've had enough. Dario. Slice Lyriana's throat. Now!"

"NO!" Lyr screamed, and so did I.

Dario's hand shook, as he tried to pull his hand back. He cried out clearly in pain.

"The blood … contract … fuck!" He gasped, tears in his eyes.

Lyr stumbled back. But my father barked an order at Aiden, and suddenly he was rushing toward Lyr, his face screwed in pain. He gripped her shoulders, shoving her towards Dario.

Fuck. Fuck. Every single part of the plan had gone off without a hitch. Had gone perfectly.

Until now.

Our soturi had infiltrated the fortress before Dario's team arrived. Every soturion still loyal to my father and on-duty inside Seathorne had been bound and moved to the dungeons.

It was Sean's men who stared back at me now, refusing to strike, refusing to harm me.

Lyr had removed her glamour, willingly getting captured by Harman and Sean when she entered Seathorne. Sean's hair had been glamoured to a white blond, and my father hadn't noticed. Hadn't recognized the green of his eyes.

But Meera and Jules were supposed to be back by now.

And there was no sign of them.

We knew as soon as Dario and Aiden got near my father, their blood contracts would reactivate. And we had counted on him using them to hurt Lyr. To be convinced he was still winning.

But I was supposed to have my strength now. I was supposed to have my magic back.

And now, the fear in Lyr's eyes wasn't feigned anymore. I knew the difference. It was real. Because Dario and Aiden had been given direct orders. Orders they couldn't refuse.

Dario was struggling, trying to hold back his knife as Aiden looked ready to vomit. They were trying, trying to refuse, to not hurt Lyr. But their strength was failing, and Lyr was bound, her body exhausted from calling on *Rakashonim*, using enough magic to glamour an entire army for the day.

"Dario," my father roared, and even I could feel the thrall of the blood contract. "Slit. Her. Throat."

"NO!" I screamed and watched in horror as Dario had no choice but to push his knife against Lyr's neck.

I ran, racing for them when suddenly something heated against my chest, illuminating my entire torso.

My armor. The shard. I had a sudden memory of being Auriel. Of him putting the armor on, trying to save Lyr from the Wall of the Prince. Of the armor starting to glow and heat, the shard activating. But it hadn't been him doing it.

It had been me. My soul returning to my body, coming back to life. Connecting to Auriel.

And now, this time ...

That's right. I'm back, Auriel thought in my mind. *But I can only hold on so long. So let's make it count, shall we?*

The room exploded with green light and suddenly Dario and Aiden yelled out, as did a dozen others. Aiden released Lyr. Dario turned away from her, his eyes like daggers, pointing his knife at my father, and drawing his sword.

"It's gone," gasped Aiden. "The blood contract. It's just ... gone."

I nodded at Aiden. "Unbind her." I turned to look back at the Council. "All of your blood contracts are gone now."

Lyr's ropes vanished, and she drew the red shard from her back.

"Surrender, Devon," Lyr ordered my father, her voice full of venom. "It's over for you now. You've lost."

His eyes were wild, searching the room in horror, looking for any of his soturi, anyone still loyal to him.

But no one would meet his gaze. Instead, they were focusing on me, like they were offering their support. Like they'd taken my side. My heart thumped, and I realized it was the first time they'd done so. Because it was the first time they were free.

"No!" my father screamed. He withdrew his sword and tore across the room, launching himself at me, tackling me to the ground.

As we fell together, the hilt of his sword landed on my face.

Stars and then darkness filled my vision. I groaned, a splitting pain running through my head. I hit the ground with an agonizing thud. My blade slid across the floor from me, and I strained to reach it, my vision blurry.

"If I die, you die with me," he seethed. "And this time, it will stick, because you are powerless. Like you always were. You were always weaker than me. Pathetic. Nothing." Spittle flew from his mouth and sprayed across my face.

"You. Are. Nothing," I gritted through my teeth. I was panting, and out of breath. His body weight shifted and for a moment I thought I would be able to reach my blade. But before I could move, his hands wrapped around my neck and squeezed.

I gasped, barely able to breathe, kicking helplessly. Lyr was screaming my name, telling me to get up, to fight back.

But I couldn't. Suddenly, I was younger. Back to a version of myself almost four years ago. Powerless, and bound by my father. Unable to touch my magic or my strength.

My father had beaten me brutally, like he always did. Because he was stronger. Had always been stronger. But that time, it was the first time I'd remembered what I knew about gryphons. That they never learned that they became stronger than the rope. That if they tried, they could tear the rope apart. And before that day, I'd never tried. I'd never fought back.

Until I did. And I'd won.

My power was gone. But I was more than that. I'd fought for my strength. I'd been fighting my entire life.

And I was done feeling weak, feeling lesser than him. I was ready to win. Finally. I threw my head forward, slamming into my father's. Blood spurted from his nose onto me, and his hands loosened. I landed a punch to his face, my body bucking and throwing him off. Suddenly, with an energy I didn't know I had flowing through me, I grabbed my sword and charged.

He swung, blocking my hit, and I turned, striking metal against metal. Our blades clashed, again and again.

I turned and spun, about to attack, when he struck a hit, slicing into my arm. I cried out, feeling blood gush from the wound.

And then suddenly, I stilled, the armor around me heating again.

I felt my eyes brighten, and my father, who'd lined up a killing blow, froze.

"Devon, you didn't think I'd miss this, did you?" Auriel spoke through me. "The big finale? No. I'm always one for a show. But I'm also here to remind you that when you die, our oath still stands. When your pathetic ruined soul leaves your body, I'll be here waiting on the other side, waiting to escort you to hell."

Then silently, in my mind, he said, *Now get him. And tell Lyriana, I said hello.*

I will. My chest heaved and he was gone. It was just me and my father.

He roared out, his sword lifted.

Our blades came together, clanging and reverberating, and then somehow, I lost mine. He did, too. They clattered to the floor and slid away.

We both scrambled for the nearest one.

Mine.

I reached it first, but my father's grip on it came a second later, and then we were in a tug of war for the weapon, both trying to turn it toward the other.

I hissed through my teeth and watched as I slowly bent his wrist back, turning the blade on him. I was winning. Finally.

I could see the fear in his eyes.

"Rhyan, he seethed, "I will kill you."

"No. You won't." My muscles burned, but I turned the blade on him and pointed its tip at his belly.

And suddenly there were two new voices in the room.

"We have it," Jules yelled out.

"Lyr," Meera cried. "Here."

A snake hissed, a nahashim, and I caught sight out of my peripheral vision, a black box being handed to Lyr.

There was a metallic clicking sound as it sprang open.

I pushed the blade into my father's stomach, ready to gut him the way he'd stabbed me before. I felt it, my muscles straining, every last ounce of my strength being tested.

And then bright, brilliant blue light filled the Seating Room. My magic.

Lyr began to chant, and as I pushed the blade through my father's belly, his eyes widening in pain, my body began to glow as the light seeped inside of me, sinking into my skin, knitting through my muscles, threading back into my bones.

I gasped, all at once, my strength renewed, any lingering hurt or pain gone. My sense of weakness and exhaustion vanished. My sight was clear, my head no longer hurt.

"I should have killed you that day," he said. "Instead of your mother."

"You should have. But you didn't. Now go to hell," I said calmly. "Auriel's waiting for you." I impaled him with my sword.

The light left his eyes, blood pouring out of his mouth and coating his black beard.

I kicked his stomach, pushing him off the blade, and watched as his body fell.

Right over the spot where my mother died. The exact same spot.

I dropped my weapon, tears in my eyes, and found Lyr, and all at once, her arms wrapped around me, holding me close.

It was done. It was over. My father would never hurt me or anyone else again.

The room erupted into cheers and applause. Fucking applause. Dario was clapping and Aiden was smiling and hugging him, and Sean was rushing toward me, his eyes watering, his arms open.

Everyone began to chant, their words coming at once in a cacophony of declarations.

"The tyrant is dead!"

"Arkasva Rhyan!"

"Arkasva Rhyan!"

"Lord Rhyan Hart, High Lord of Glemaria."

My chest tightened. The title I'd been given by a rebel army in the woods, it was now reality, now being shouted by members of the Glemarian Council. I looked up at the Seat of Power, at the dais I'd never wanted to stand on before, and my eyes met Kenna's.

CHAPTER FORTY-SIX

LYRIANA

Hours had passed since Devon Hart's demise, since Glemaria had been freed. Everyone in the Seating Room had immediately gone to the healing center to see to their injuries. It was mainly Rhyan who needed tending. But a few of our soturi had also needed attention from the fight to remove Devon's guard.

There'd been a huge meal after, served in the dining hall, all arranged by Kenna.

I sat with her, glad to be reunited, and glad to know she was okay. Not hurt. And no longer under Devon's threat. And never would be again.

She seemed lighter, happier, relieved. And finally told me then that she was having twins—that was why her belly had grown so big.

We both started laughing and crying, before she thanked me and Rhyan profusely. Because now, she and her babies weren't in danger from their father.

Following the meal, everyone had gone into meetings. So many meetings. There were so many decisions that had to be made by the Council. The first order of business had been questioning Kenna, to provide any proof she could to verify Rhyan's claims of his father's crimes. She had produced his journals, as well as a pile of scrolls he'd written, that detailed many of the decisions he'd made during his reign as Arkasva. He'd been so arrogant, he'd written it all down, believing himself untouchable. It was perhaps the first good thing he'd done. Made it easier to convict him by confessing—even if it was from the grave.

Then, there was what to do about Devon's funeral, how to announce his crimes, and who would rule in his place until the next Arkasva was crowned with the Laurel. Decisions had to be made about how they would proceed with the transfer of power.

I'd sat through most of the meetings, eager to help, and show my confidence in Rhyan, but I was also curious to see how all of the most powerful nobles would react to everything. To the change.

I'd never been so happy in my life just knowing that Rhyan had support. That he'd quietly had much of their support all along. The number of Council members and nobles who'd come forward admitting that they'd been forced into blood oaths, and then more recently, into Devon's sinister blood contracts, had been appalling. He'd had far less loyalty than he ever let on. The constant use of magic to force his will onto everyone around him, had in the end, weakened his power. He'd been losing control for a long time, scrambling to keep it.

Only Kane, who had left along with his legion, hadn't been compelled in any way. It was a true testament of how evil he was, how in line Kane's views were with Devon's.

And also... just how awful the promises were that Morgana and Aemon must have made to draw him away. I shuddered, and my heart ached. Morgana, who was my sister, who had felt like a part of my soul. Morgana, who I'd fought so hard to keep from losing because of her vorakh. Now I was losing her in a completely different way. The reunion of Moriel,

Ereshya, and Shiviel was going to have dire consequences. War was coming. Not just from them, but from the Empire. Glemaria was free, but Emperor Avery still ruled. Bamaria was still New Korteria. And we'd just thrown the first shot. When word reached him, he'd retaliate.

But I'd think about that tomorrow.

The consecration for Rhyan would be announced in every town. The ceremony would be in a week. There would be a visit to the temple, multiple parades throughout the country, and a habibellum in their Katurium—one with no killing allowed—to celebrate. Sean was sending out messages to every Glemarian in exile, everyone who wished to see Devon's demise, and would support the transfer of power.

In a week, Rhyan would become His Grace, Arkasva Rhyan Hart, High Lord of Glemaria in open defiance of the Empire.

Tears welled in my eyes. He deserved the title. He deserved all that went with it. The power, the prestige, the ability to decide to make things better for his country. Rhyan could pass progressive laws. Help so many people. As long as we could keep the wrath of the Empire back, he was going to be an amazing Arkasva. Glemaria had no idea just how fucking lucky they were to have him. And with the forces of Glemaria behind him, he would have the power to fully clear his name across Lumeria. And then, we would begin to separate the country from the Empire and the Emperor's cruel rules, policies, and exploitation. We also wanted to begin to abolish the laws forbidding those tied together by kashonim from falling in love. They were outdated, and a gross form of control. Plus, we'd seen time and time again how natural it was. How good it could be for kashonim partners to love each other. How powerful we'd become together.

And perhaps most importantly at the moment, far fewer innocent people would be killed and turned by akadim.

Because Rhyan would guard and protect his people against them. He was actually going to stop the threat, not encourage it, not use it as a crutch to keep his people afraid and docile. And of course, with what I could do now, with the red shard and my ability to heal, I was going to help. We were going to heal as many people as we could.

But despite how good everything sounded, the coming together of our plans, and the coming celebration of our victory, I was unsettled. My heart hurt just a little, my stomach twisting—and I felt so fucking guilty for it. Kenna had made arrangements for me and Rhyan to stay in his old room. So after hours of meetings and discussions, that's where I ran off to, needing a moment to myself.

I knew where we stood, Rhyan and I. I knew we loved each other more than anything in this world. We wanted to be together. We were *mekarim*. There was no doubt about that. There never would be. But duty sometimes made love impossible. Rhyan now had to remain in Glemaria for who knew how long. And now that Arianna had been named Imperator of the South and had willingly annexed Bamaria to Korteria along with Elyria, had allowed the creation of New Korteria, something had to be done. I couldn't stand back any longer and allow Bamaria to remain occupied, to allow my people to be abused by Ka Kormac. I had to go home. I had to get my country back.

But I didn't know where that left me and Rhyan.

Jules was the Heir of Ka Azria. Elyria was meant to be hers. And ... I'd spoken to Meera in depth. She'd changed since I'd last seen her. After discovering her identity as Cassarya, Goddess of the Blue Ray, and getting to work with the nahashim, away from the intrigue of court politics, she confessed to me that she had no desire to rule. No wish to become Arkasva.

It was up to me.

It had always been me. My dream. My desire. And now, my destiny. I was my mother's daughter. She'd named my father Arkasva because she knew Arianna couldn't be trusted, because she'd always planned for the line of power to come to me. The daughter she'd dreamed of, the daughter she knew was Asherah.

It was all I'd ever wanted to do, to fight for. But my heart sank. Gods. How was I going to rule Bamaria—if we got it back—in the South, while Rhyan, my love, was duty-bound to rule in the North? We'd be back on opposite ends of the Empire. Torn apart again. It was for the best for our people. We had to fulfill our duties to them, and we needed the support and backing our positions would offer. Would need them when we took on Morgana and Aemon. But I didn't know what that looked like. Or how long we might be apart.

I took a long, hot bath, and then discovered some of Rhyan's extra sleep clothes had been moved in. I changed into them, sitting down at the vanity to brush out my hair and add oil to the ends. Rhyan's red gryphon soared by the window, wings flapping, his eyes looking in, like he knew. He knew this was his place.

A tear rolled down my cheek.

"Partner," Rhyan said suddenly. He hadn't used the door. He'd traveled. His magic truly was back.

I smiled and watched his reflection behind mine in the mirror, my heart leaping. He'd changed into a fresh tunic and soturion uniform hours ago, all of his old weapons and effects restored to him. The only thing that was new—well, in a sense—was his armor. Auriel's golden armor, and the green shard. His shard.

My breath caught. He looked so handsome and strong and healed. He looked like a king.

And ... a God. Not Auriel. But like himself.

I turned in my seat, rising to greet him. He was already crossing the room to close the distance between us, his arms outstretched, ready to hug me. I sank into him, squeezing him tight, holding him as he buried his face against my neck. His eyes were wet with more tears. I ran my hand up his nape, into the soft brown curls that I adored.

He shuddered, and I led him to the bed, sitting down on the edge, my arms tight around him.

"You're okay," I whispered. "It's all right now." I let out a shaky laugh. "Everything's okay." Somehow. Miraculously.

"I just—I think, I'm grieving," he said. "I'm grieving. I feel like ... not exactly like I did when my mother died, when he—You know. But the pain, it feels similar. Heavy. It hurts."

"You did the right thing. You know it had to be done."

"I know," he said, his gaze distant. His throat bobbed. "He deserved it. He deserved fucking worse. If I could kill him again, I would." His voice broke. "So why am I crying for him?"

My heart hurt, wanting to take his pain, and I squeezed his hand. "Maybe ... maybe it's because you're a good person. With a big heart, and soul. Maybe," I bit my lip. "Maybe who you're really crying for is you. Because you deserved a father who was better, who loved you, who was kind." Tears rolled down my cheeks. "Maybe this isn't grief for him—it's okay if it is—even if he doesn't deserve it. Maybe it's grief for the father you should have had. The life that should have been yours, that I wish for you now. One that's safe and happy with joy. And love."

I wiped the tears from his eyes and he cupped my jaw, pressing his lips to mine.

"I love you," he said, his voice shaking still.

"I love you."

I held him then, letting him cry.

When he seemed to calm, he sat back, his emerald eyes blazing as they stared into mine.

"I don't want to do this anymore," he said. "I don't want to grieve for the life I didn't have. Or the life I wanted."

"You don't have to," I said softly. "Everything is getting better. Your father is gone. Glemaria is free. You're here, you're alive. Dario and Aiden love you. Sean is free to come back home. We found our shards. And … Gods. Rhyan, you're Arkasva. You're High Lord."

His jaw tightened and he looked away. His aura flaring.

"What is it?" I asked.

He turned back to me. "You. Your place is in Bamaria. It always was."

My stomach dropped. "I know." The backs of my eyes burned, my stomach roiled. Here it was. The thing that would separate us. I was going to be sick.

Rhyan slid off the bed, and got down on one knee. He took my hands in his, and stared up.

"Your place is in Bamaria," he said again. "And so is mine."

"What?" I nearly choked out the word.

He shook his head, his eyes alight as if the very shard of his Valalumir were behind them. I sank onto the floor with him, straddling his lap, our arms around each other.

"Lyr, Lyriana, my love, *Mekara*, all this time, since you saved me, I've been afraid. I was afraid of myself. Of what I had become. Of being akadim and how that was affecting me."

His throat worked, his hands squeezing mine.

"I burst into tears when the soturi named me Arkasva. Because I didn't think I deserved it. But also because … it was what my father was. Arkasva and Imperator. I told myself I didn't want the title because I was terrified that I might be like him. That in the way being akadim might change me, that he had, too. But that wasn't it at all." He smiled, pushing my hair off my shoulders.

"Lyr, I wasn't afraid of being Arkasva. Not at all. I just didn't want to be. Before I left here, before I was forsworn,

I asked Kenna to run away with me. I wanted to get out of here. I needed to be saved. I wanted to save her, too."

I nodded, remembering he'd told me about that.

"She refused. Her place was here. It was always here." He shook his head. "But that's not true for me." One brow furrowed. "I love Glemaria with all my heart. Gods, I love my country and its people. I love the land, the trees, the cold, the gryphons. I want nothing but the best for it, for everyone—even the assholes."

I laughed.

"So, I talked to Kenna, and the Council. She was the one leading the rebellion all these years, working to remove my father, communicating with the rebel groups, and sending messages to Sean. She's the one who was prepared to lead." His eyes blazed, his aura finally calming down. "And so she will. Kenna's going to be Arkasva, High Lady of Glemaria."

I gasped. "What? Rhyan, are you sure?"

He nodded. "I've never been so sure of anything in my life, except when it comes to how deeply I love you. The truth is, I like being Arkturion. I like protecting others, fighting against evil. I want to keep doing that. And I want to do it at your side. I have to be at your side. Because, my place, my soul, and my home," he placed his hand over my heart, "it all lies with you."

"You mean it?"

He placed his other hand over his heart. "*Me sha, me ka.*"

My lips found his, and his hands slid under my ass, lifting me against him, as he stood and laid me on the bed.

I stretched out beneath him, welcoming him between my legs. Welcoming him home.

"There's just two more things," he said, kissing my neck, his hands moving to pull up my shirt, as I started to unbuckle his belt, and shove his weapons aside. "Two humble requests on my part."

"Name them," I said, my top off. I reached for the clasps of his armor.

"When I died—" he stilled, "Sorry, it still gets me."

I caressed his cheek.

"It severed the kashonim between us."

I blinked. "It did?"

He took my hand in his and turned my wrist up, pulling it to his lips. He kissed it softly. "You didn't notice?" he asked, his voice hoarse. "Our scar from the oath ceremony is gone." He showed me his arm. And he was right—the scars had vanished. It was the first time since the night we'd sworn in the temple that we'd acknowledged them. It had been unspoken between us, a symbol of the fact that we couldn't be together. I was glad to be rid of it.

"I want to bind myself to you again. On my terms," Rhyan said.

"What do you mean?" I asked.

"Some nights when I couldn't sleep, I read Auriel's—*my*—Valya. Kashonim worked differently before the writings were lost. It wasn't forbidden. Or illegal to love. And it didn't drain the other's power. It was something that was shared and flowed freely back and forth between partners. It expanded strength, it didn't diminish. Of course, the Empire changed that. But, the Valya has the ceremony inside. A way to join us, freely, to make us stronger. Together. Will you do that with me? Will you be my kashonim?"

My heart was filled with love. "Of course, I will."

He grinned and his armor came off, along with his boots as I tore his shirt over his head, sliding my hands down the expanse of his chest and abs, feeling the way his muscles contracted and tightened.

"Good," he said, his hand sliding up my torso, cupping my breast.

"What was the other thing?" I asked.

He bent down to suck my nipple into his mouth, one hand lowering to the waistband of my pants. I reached down to his hips, and in seconds, we were both naked.

"This," he said, kissing his way down my breasts and stomach, until he pressed a kiss between my legs, then lowered his face, licking me from bottom to top. "Do you still want to marry me?"

His mouth closed on the bundle of nerves, his tongue flicking against it.

"Yes," I said, biting my lip before I cried out.

He hummed against me, the sensation making me buck.

"Was that a yes to *this*," he sucked on me again, his tongue lapping. "Or, yes to marrying me?"

"Both," I cried out. "Yes."

He laughed. "We can do both ceremonies together. Declare what we are to everyone."

"I want that," I said, breathless. Then he growled, unleashing himself on me, sucking and licking and kissing, until I was writhing under him, sweat breaking out across my body. I cried out, my orgasm rushing out through my fingers and toes.

"One last thing," he said, crawling back over me, his lips on mine, tongue diving in so I could taste myself.

"You know, since you abdicated the Seat of Power, you've become very demanding," I said.

He gripped his cock, rubbing the head between my folds. "You bring it out in me. Make me want things. Make me feel like I can have them."

"Well then, state your demand," I said, my hips moving against him. "And I shall take it under advisement."

"Marry me here," he said, his voice low. "In Glemaria. In the mountains. I want to—I want to start our new life together in the place where it ended for Auriel and Asherah."

"Start again," I said.

He bit his lip, too overcome with emotion, and nodded.

I reached down between us, and pulled him inside of me. "Yes. Yes. To all of it. To you."

He started to thrust, slow and gentle. "Once everything's settled here," he moaned, "when Glemaria is stable, we'll do whatever we have to do next." He placed his hand under my head. "Fight Aemon and Morgana," he hissed. "Fight the Emperor. And go back to Bamaria. We're going to take it back for you. Free it from Kormac."

I rolled my hips, my heels pushing into the mattress to get more friction. "And defeat Arianna."

"Yes," he said.

And when the time is right, you will strike and have your revenge. And then you will retake the throne of Bamaria.

Rhyan was panting, thrusting deeper inside me.

"Bamaria will be yours. I swear to you, I will lay it at your feet as your Arkturion, as your husband—"

I grinned, my heart thrumming and expanding, heat rising between my legs.

"I will personally melt down Arianna's Laurel of the Arkasva to make you your own."

I shook my head. "No. I have another request." And then I flipped us over, Rhyan landing on his back, as I sank down on his length.

"Name it." He reached one hand to stroke me where we joined, and the other took my hand, our fingers threaded together.

I lifted my hips, and sank back down, riding him faster and faster, my heart thundering. "I'm not going to wear a laurel. I'm not going to be Arkasva of Bamaria, or High Lady."

Rhyan frowned. "What do you mean?"

I leaned down, finding his lips, taking him deeper and deeper.

"When I go home and I retake Bamaria, you'll melt Arianna's laurel for me into a crown. Because I'm fucking done with the Empire of Lumeria. I'm not going home to be Arkasva. I will go home as queen."

CHAPTER FORTY-SEVEN

MORGANA

I emerged from the river, finished with my nightly bath and took my towel from Lissa. The water dripping off me felt cool in the night. Refreshing after a long day of meetings and plans on what to do next.

"My robe," I said. Lissa handed it over at once, and then I slid into my slippers, motioning for the two akadim who'd become my personal guards in the last few weeks to follow behind, watching me from the shadows.

Our court had turned in for the night, thank the Gods. My mind was exhausted. I'd had to restrengthen the onyx walls around my thoughts over and over as Aemon hounded me for details on everything I'd done while away from him. He'd been furious since he discovered that Lyr had managed to not just find Rhyan, my prized Arkturion, and cure him, but that she had acquired the red shard, and Rhyan the green. Not to mention, she had cured every akadim I'd left behind in the Wall of the Prince. Between him and Parthenay's gloating, as well as all the former chayatim we'd rescued constantly trying to pry, I was beyond ready to go to sleep.

I'd been penitent for the loss for days. And I knew he was harboring his suspicions. Blaming me. Ridiculous. I was going to explode if he asked me again. Why had I done it?

How could I have left Rhyan and his soturi so vulnerable? How could I have lost the green shard to the enemy?

As if I could see the future. As if that were my vorakh. It wasn't—not yet.

He had access to Andromeny and her visions and every other Godsdamned chayatim from the Palace. If he hadn't seen what was coming, how could I have? How could I have known?

I'd done nothing but serve him, helping our cause, betraying my own family, all so I could complete my goal. Bring down the Empire.

But after weeks of digging, Rhyan had been running the mines perfectly. They weren't raping, they weren't fighting, and they were hardly eating. Akadim could go months without a meal, and promising blood and flesh when the work was done had proved a mighty motivator.

So I'd felt safe leaving when I was called away. I'd performed the kashonim on Rhyan and his akadim to ensure the work was completed. To ensure we found the green shard, and that it was given over only to us. It would have been our third out of the seven. Between the shard and Rhyan, the amount of power we would have amassed, even I shuddered thinking about it. The Empire was going to crumble. And Rhyan was going to be the monster leading the force.

But that plan had died. Thanks to my Godsdamned sister, thanks to Lyr.

Still, we had another way. I had brought Arkturion Kane into our camp. Shiviel. Aemon didn't want to admit he was pleased, he preferred to blame me for the loss of Rhyan and the shard. But Kane was the real reason I'd had to leave my post. I had come to help *him*. A fact I wouldn't let him forget.

For years Aemon and Kane, the two most violent and powerful Arkturi in the Empire, had been at odds. Always fighting. Always antagonizing each other. It was no wonder he'd been unable to get Kane onto his side.

Me, however? Exploiting his mind was easy. He was weak. Not even in possession of a vorakh. Not since his soul was splintered. Not since Auriel and Asherah had created a secret eighth Guardian. It was the new incarnation that carried Shiviel's magic, Shiviel's power. And, Shiviel's soul-code to access the yellow shard.

Kane on our side was far better than not having him. But Kane on his own was proving to be somewhat useless. Little more than a vicious muscle.

I entered the cave where we were staying, torches lining the walls. My guards stepped into the shadows and Lissa, finally accustomed to their presence, stood just a few feet apart from them.

Aemon stood in the dark, a handful of his guards against the wall opposite me.

Still ruminating over what you've done, Aemon thought into my mind.

How can I not? But why do you worry? We're still stronger. We have two shards.

But so do they, kitten. Aemon walked toward me.

So? What will they do? I thought. *They don't even know how to use their power yet.*

Aemon's nostrils flared. *They will. You know that they will soon.*

I took his hand. *Soon. Not now. They are woefully behind us in strength, in planning, and in support. They are nowhere near our power. Or our purpose.*

His eyes darkened, flashing down my body. *Hmmm. They only have two shards. But now I hear Julianna and Meera have rejoined them. That's four Guardians.*

And? I scoffed. *My sister and cousin are weak. And we don't know yet if they will come to our side, if given the chance.*

Aemon laughed. *I can be persuasive. I think we can get them.*

I frowned, my stomach lurching. *What do you mean?*

You look worried, he thought. *Wouldn't you be happy? I thought you wanted them to be here with you.*

I swallowed roughly, trying to calm my nerves. *Of course, I do. I just don't want them to be hurt on their way to us. I'd rather they choose to come here willingly. Or at my request.*

I didn't say I'd kidnap them, I said persuade. His hand stroked my hair, twirling it in his hand, wrapping it around his wrist until he pulled my head back. His lips found mine. *But maybe you should convince them, if that's what you want.* His tongue pushed between my lips, one hand sliding my robe off my shoulders.

Maybe, I thought. *If you trust me to go to them, I will.*

Hmmm. He reached for my ass, grabbing it roughly.

Are you truly still mad at me? I asked. *I swear I did what I thought best.*

You lost us a shard, a powerful akadim, an entire fucking soturi. And—I brought a Guardian in!

I'd had to get into Kane's mind. Understand his twisted wants and desires. And then fuck him. It was always about fucking in the end.

But it worked. He was ours now. And so was Glemaria's first legion. The North was officially unstable. The Empire primed to fall. I just had to promise him more power than Devon Hart had ever allowed. Reveal the truth of his identity. That Kane was a God. And Devon Hart was not. Especially now. Now, he was dead. Everything was already working in our favor. The first hole in the Empire's strength had been made, a hole we would exploit.

"Well, I have good news," Aemon said. "We're going to be able to get to the yellow shard. Restore Kane's power. Very, very soon."

I frowned, willing my heart to beat normal. "How?"

"The eighth Guardian. Turiel has been found. Andromeny's got him and she's on her way here. They should be arriving ... right ... now." His lips widened into a grin.

A line of akadim marched into the cave, Andromeny walking behind. She was glowing, her black hair wild and unkempt. Right behind her, a giant akadim carried a mage in his arms, bound with magic and actual rope. His mouth had been gagged, his eyes blindfolded.

But I recognized the floppy brown hair of Tristan Grey.

Aemon laughed. "Sit him on the ground over there."

Tristan struggled as he was put down, moaning against his bindings, his body jerking as he tried to free himself from the ropes.

Andromeny leaned down, removing his blindfold. His brown eyes widened in fear. She ripped the tape from his mouth.

He let out a yell. "You. You! Murderer! You fucking bitch!"

Andromeny slapped him across the face. "Shut your mouth! I did what I had to for my king. If you had died, none of this would have happened. But here we are."

"Died? What—what wouldn't have happened?" His body trembled, and his brown eyes filled with tears. "Morgana?" he asked. "Morgana? Where are we, what is this?" Then he shook his head, like it didn't matter. "Help me."

"I'm sorry, Tristan," I said sweetly, my head starting to hurt. "I can't. Justice must be served, the way you served justice to my kind for so many years."

"No," he said. "No!"

"Welcome to our court, Lord Tristan," Aemon said.

"Arkturion Aemon? Please, I can pay, whatever you want," he begged.

Aemon shook his head. "It's King now. And I don't want your money. What we need from you, is something else." Tristan paled.

"Don't worry," I said. "You won't be here too long. We just need you for a little. Your life actually. Then Kane can activate his full power. Reunite with his full strength. And you'll be free." I shrugged. "Dead, but free."

His face fell, like his soul had just been crushed. "Morgana," he pleaded.

"Well done, Andromeny," I said, and snaked my hand down Aemon's back, reaching for his ass. The pain in my head was intensifying. "Now leave us. All of you. I need some time with my king." I looked away from Tristan, my head felt like it was going to split open.

"*Maraak*," Andromeny said and bowed. "*Maraaka*," she said to me. Then she turned to Tristan one last time. "Turiel," she crooned. "Welcome home."

Tristan's eyes widened, his skin paled, like he'd heard that name before. He knew. He'd seen it. Then she walked from the room, taking the akadim along with her.

It left me and Aemon with our guard, with Lissa, and a bound and terrified Tristan on the floor.

"I want you," I said to Aemon, my breath coming in short, painful bursts. "Now." *Fuck me.*

Aemon's eyes narrowed, looking back and forth between me and Tristan. *Are you sure*, he thought. *With our prisoner here?*

I grinned wickedly. *He's going to die. He's already had his last fuck and doesn't know it. We can at least entertain him.*

I let my robe fall. Tristan gasped, though he sounded like he was in pain, and averted his eyes.

Good. The prick had always deserved this.

Take me, I thought to Aemon. *Now, I can't wait. I need you.*

Aemon's pants were undone a second later. He lifted me up into his arms, my legs wrapped around his waist, my ankles locking behind his ass. He carried me to the wall, pushing me against it.

Watch him. Watch him suffer and writhe while I take you.

I did as I was told, making eye contact with Tristan.

I could hear his thoughts clearly. His fear of pain and dying. Dark thoughts about a Yellow Room and the Emperor. Galen flashed in his mind, sorrow, grief. But mostly he was missing ... Naria. Well, that was new. Though all the thoughts were tempered by the terror in his veins as he remembered who'd taken him. The vorakh who'd murdered his parents.

He was also busy trying to figure out a way to escape. Fool. He didn't know it yet. There wasn't one.

Aemon rubbed the head of his cock against my folds. *Kitten.* He frowned. *You're not wet.*

"I will be," I said, biting his lower lip. I lifted my pelvis, grinding into him, willing myself to become more aroused.

He sucked on my neck, one hand toying with my nipple.

I circled my hips, pushing against him from the wall.

"Distracted?" he asked.

"Maybe," I panted. "A lot has happened. And a lot lies before us. But I still want you. I need you." I pushed my hips forward, taking in the tip. *Please.*

He growled from the contact, no longer able to resist, and shoved inside.

I cried out, tightening around him. I hadn't been ready, but it didn't matter. The minute his hips began to thrust, I moaned in relief.

Fuck. Fuck. I gritted my teeth. That had been close. Too close.

I arched against him and cried out as I finally released the fucking onyx wall I'd wrapped around my mind. The secrets I'd been keeping, the depth of my thoughts, was exhausting, and draining me, even with access to the power of my shard.

Aemon grunted, thrusting deeper, and I closed my eyes, matching his pace, moaning every time he slammed back inside.

I had known what would happen to Rhyan. I had known before he died. I knew it would come to pass. I knew it had to. He would become akadim. Andromeny had seen it. And so I'd waited, and bided my time. Holding Aemon's shard captive, learning to control the akadim, to bind them to me. Because I had to be sure. I had to make sure he was mine. That I could protect him. Save him. For Lyr. For Lumeria. Bartering for Rhyan as my Arkturion, in exchange for the indigo had worked beautifully.

And I'd kept Rhyan from further losing his soul, from being unable to return to himself.

Aemon picked up the pace, his flesh slapping against mine.

Tristan was silently sobbing to himself.

I ran my fingers through Aemon's hair. "Not so fast," I purred. "Don't you want to give our company a good show?"

He bared his teeth, and pulled at my hair, baring my neck to him. "He'll get a fucking show."

He turned us around, laying me on the ground, pulling out just long enough to lift my legs over his shoulders, and then he slammed back into me with a grunt.

"Fuck," I cried out, turning my head in time to see Tristan look away in horror, his eyes tear-stained.

I continued to stare at him, just to keep Aemon happy. To keep him going. Because I needed him to keep fucking me, to give me just a few moments where my mind could be open, my thoughts my own. And Aemon unable to hear for once.

I had known, I had fucking known Rhyan would be cured, that they all would. Andromeny had seen him as a demon, seen him march on Glemaria. Seen fire spread from its highest peak and burn the Empire to the ground. She'd seen the sun come out. She'd believed that meant the daywalkers.

But I had known better. I had enough experience interpreting Meera's visions, seeing how the strange images always played out. Andromeny's visions were almost always straightforward. Accurate. Not this one.

I knew the sun meant he was healed. Meant he was cured. And so was his entire army.

There was never any need for me to perform the kashonim on Rhyan, linking the others to him. There never was. I had the akadim well under my control, and knew they'd continue to be long after I was gone. But I'd done it anyway.

So Parthenay would believe. So I could abandon them. So Lyr could save them. Rhyan was always meant to come to Glemaria, and from there fire would spread. Fire that would bring the Empire to its knees. But he was going to do it alive. And Lyr would be beside him. Already, it was starting.

I lifted my hips, urging Aemon on, making sure he didn't grow suspicious, or think for a second I wasn't enjoying myself. I was. Oh, I was.

Just not for the reasons he believed.

His movements grew faster, and I squeezed him inside of me, crying out his name.

He was not going to touch Jules, or Meera. Or Lyr. Or Rhyan. Not again. I'd see to that.

But first, I had to find a way to save Tristan. I had to get the reincarnation of Turiel away from here.

Because if Aemon killed him, if Kane's full Guardian power was restored, and he was reunited with the yellow shard, the power of the Yellow Ray, then Gods help us all. The world would end.

The story continues in Book Six:
Queen of the Drowned Empire

Appendix 1: The Empire of Lumeria

There are twelve countries united under the Lumerian Empire, Lumeria Nutavia. Each country is presided over by one of the Twelve Ruling Kavim. Each country is governed by an Arkasva, the High Lord or Lady of the ruling Ka.

All twelve countries submit to the rule and law of the Emperor. Each Arkasva also answers to an Imperator, one Arkasva with jurisdiction over each country in either the Northern or Southern hemispheres of the Empire. In addition to the Emperor's rule, twelve senators, one from each country, fill the twelve seats of the Senate. A senator must not belong to the ruling Ka of their country.

The roles of Imperator and Emperor are lifelong appointments. They are not passed onto family members, but must instead be elected by the ruling Kavim. Kavim may not submit a candidate for either role if the previous Imperator or Emperor belonged to their Ka.

Imperators may keep their ties to their Ka and continue to rule in their own country, but an Emperor will lose their Ka upon anointing and must be like a father or mother to all Lumerians.

Empiric Chain of Command

Emperor Avery, High Lord of Lumeria Nutavia
The Emperor rules over the entire Empire from its capitol, Numeria. The Emperor oversees the running of the Senate, and the twelve countries united under the Empire.

Devon Hart, Imperator of the North
The Imperator of the North is an Arkasva who not only rules their own country, but also oversees the rule of the remaining five countries belonging to the North. His rule includes the following countries, currently ruled by the following Kavim:

Glemaria, Ka Hart
Payunmar, Ka Valyan
Hartavia, Ka Taria
Ereztia, Ka Sephiron
Aravia, Ka Lumerin
Sindhuvine, Ka Kether

Arianna Batavia, Imperator of the South
The Imperator of the South is an Arkasva who not only rules their own country, but also oversees rule of the remaining five countries belonging to the South. The sitting Imperator is also the ruler of Bamaria. Her rule includes the following countries currently being ruled by the following Kavim:

Bamaria, Ka Batavia
Korteria, Ka Kormac
Elyria, Ka Elys (previously Ka Azria)
Damara, Ka Daquataine
Lethea, Ka Maras
Cretanya, Ka Zarine

The Immortal Afeyan Courts*
The Sun Court: El Zandria, ruled by King RaKanam
The Moon Court: Khemet, ruled by Queen Ma'Nia
The Star Court: Night Lands, ruled by Queen Ishtara

*Afeyan Courts are not considered part of the Lumerian Empire, nor do they submit to the Emperor. However, history, prior treaties, and trade agreements have kept the courts at peace, and working together. They are the only two groups to have shared life on the continent of Lumeria Matavia.

Appendix 2: The Bamarian Council

Each of the twelve countries in the Lumerian Empire includes a twelve-member council comprised of members of the nobility who assist the Arkasva in ruling and decision-making.

The Bamarian Council includes the following:

Arkasva: Arianna Batavia
Master of the Horse: Romula Grey
Arkturion: Waryn Kormac
Turion: Dairen Melvik
Arkmage: Kolaya Scholar
Master of Education: Shanna Kasmar
Master of Spies: Sila Shavo
Master of Finance: Trajan Grey
Master of Law: Kiera Ezara
Naturion: Dagana Scholar
Senator: Janvi Elys
Master of Peace: Brenna Corra

Appendix 3:
Titles and Forms of Address

Emperor: Ruler of all twelve countries in the Lumerian Empire. The Emperor is elected by the ruling Arkasvim. They are appointed for life. Once an Emperor or Empress dies, the Kavim must elect a new ruler. The Emperor must renounce their Ka when anointed, but no Ka may produce an Emperor/Empress twice in a row.

Imperator: The head of the hemisphere. The Empire always has two Imperators, one for the Northern hemisphere, one for the South. The Imperator will also be the Arkasva of their country. They have jurisdiction over their hemisphere, and act as a voice and direct messenger between each Arkasva and the Emperor.

Arkasva (Ark-kas-va): Ruler of the country, literally translates as the "will of the highest soul."

Arkasvim (Ark-kas-veem): Plural of Arkasva.

Heir Apparent: Title given to the eldest child or Heir of the Arkasva. The next in line to the Seat of Power or First from the Seat.

Arkturion (Ark-tor-ree-an): warlord for the country, general of their soturi/army.

Arkmage: The ruling mage of the country. Ethical disputes over the use of magic are brought to them. They lead the seven Watchers of the Light, and maintain the temple as well as the country's collection of Valya scrolls. They are granted a stave which allows them to exert the power of ten mages and preside over important holidays, rituals, and ceremonies.

Lady: Formal title for a female or female-identifying member of the nobility.

Lord: Formal title for a male or male-identifying member of the nobility.

Soturion: Soldier, magically enhanced warrior. A Lumerian who can transmute magic through their body. May be used as a form of address for a non-noble.

Turion: Commander, may lead legions of soturi. Must answer to their Arkturion.

Mage: A Lumerian who transmutes magic through spells. A stave is used to focus their magic.

Apprentice: A soturion or mage who has passed their first three years of training. As an apprentice, their time is divided between their own studies and teaching the novice to whom they are bound. This is done to strengthen the power of kashonim, and because of the Bamarian philosophy that teaching a subject is the best way to learn and master a subject.

Novice: A soturion or mage who is in the beginning of their learning to become an anointed mage or soturion.

Your Majesty: Formal address for the Emperor or Empress. Previously used for the Kings and Queens of Lumeria Matavia. It can also be used for the King and Queen of the Afeyan Sun and Moon Courts.

Your Highness: Formal address for Imperators. The term of address has also been adopted by the Afeyan Star Court.

Your Grace: Formal address for any member of the ruling Ka who is in line to the Seat of Power, including the Arkasva. A noble may only be addressed as "Your Grace" if they are in line to the Seat.

Appendix 4:
Glossary and Pronunciation Guide

Names

Lyriana Batavia (Leer-ree-ana Ba-tah-via): Previously third in line to the Seat of Power in Bamaria.

Morgana Batavia (Mor-ga-na Ba-tah-via): Previously second in line to the Seat of Power in Bamaria.

Meera Batavia (Mee-ra Ba-tah-via): Previously first in line to the Seat of Power in Bamaria (Heir Apparent).

Naria Batavia (Nar-ria Ba-tah-via): Heir Apparent, first in line to the Seat of Power in Bamaria.

Arianna Batavia (Ar-ree-ana Ba-tah-via): Current Arkasva and High Lady of Bamaria.

Aemon Melvik (Ae-mon Mel-vik): Warlord of Bamaria, Arkturion on the Council of Bamaria.

Rhyan Hart (Ry-an Hart): Forsworn and exiled from Glemaria. Previously was first in line to the Seat of Power (Heir Apparent).

Avery Kormac (Ae-very Core-mac): Current Emperor of Lumeria Nutavia. Theotis was previously from Korteria, and a noble of Ka Kormac. His nephew, Avery Kormac, is the current Imperator to the Southern Hemisphere of the Empire, and Arkasva to Korteria.

Devon Hart (Deh-vawn Hart): Imperator of the North, he rules over the six northern countries of the Empire, as well as ruling Glemaria as the Arkasva.

Names (Gods)

Asherah (A-sher-ah): Goddess, Guardian of the Red Ray. Original Guardian of the Valalumir in Heaven. She was banished to Earth as a mortal after her affair with Auriel was discovered.

Ereshya (Air-resh-she-ah): Goddess, Guardian of the Orange Ray. Original Guardian of the Valalumir in Heaven.

Shiviel (Shiv-ay-el): God, Guardian of the Yellow Ray. Original Guardian of the Valalumir in Heaven.

Auriel (Or-ree-el): God, Guardian of the Green Ray. Original Guardian of the Valalumir in Heaven. He stole the light to bring to Earth, where it turned into a crystal before shattering at the time of the Drowning.

Cassarya (Cah-sar-ree-ah): Goddess, Guardian of the Blue Ray. Original Guardian of the Valalumir in Heaven.

Moriel (Mor-ree-el): God, Guardian of the Indigo Ray. Original Guardian of the Valalumir in Heaven. He reported Auriel and Asherah's affair to the Council of Forty-Four, leading to Asherah's banishment, Auriel's theft of the light, and its subsequent destruction. He was banished to Earth, where he allied with the akadim in the war that led to the Drowning.

Hava (Ha-vah): Goddess, Guardian of the Violet Ray. Original Guardian of the Valalumir in Heaven.

Turiel (Ter-ree-al): The name of the entity created from part of Shiviel's soul. He holds the majority of Shiviel's magic and power as the unknown eighth Guardian.

Names (Afeya)

Afeya (Ah-fay-ah): Immortal Lumerians who survived the Drowning. Prior to this, Afeya were non-distinguishable from other Lumerians in Lumeria Matavia. They were descended from the Gods and Goddesses, trapped in the mortal coil, but they refused the request to join the war efforts. Some sources believe they allied with Moriel's forces and the akadim. When the Valalumir shattered, they were cursed to live forever, unable to return to their home, be relieved of life, or touch or perform magic—unless asked to do so by another.

Ma'Nia (Mah-nee-ah): The Moon Queen, head of the Afeyan Moon Court, and ruler of Khemet, one of three Afeyan countries that border the Lumerian Empire.

Mercurial (Mer-cure-ree-el): An immortal Afeya, First Messenger of her Highness Queen Ishtara, High Lady of the Night Lands.

Ramia (Rah-me-yah): Half-Afeyan librarian. Moon Court Princess, Daughter of Queen Ma'Nia.

Rakanan (Rah-kah-naan): The Sun King, head of the Afeyan Sun Court, and ruler of El Zandria, one of three Afeyan countries that border the Lumerian Empire.

Zenoya (Zen-oy-ya): Half-Afeyan librarian.

Places

Allurian Pass (All-or-ree-an Pass): Mountain cutting through the western border of Glemaria and the non-magical human lands. Marks the edge of the Lumerian Empire, and is the only way to enter the non-magic lands through Glemaria.

Aravia (Ar-ay-vee-ah): Country in the North on the southern border of Glemaria. Ruled by Ka Lumerin. It contains a vibrant system of caves.

Bamaria (Ba-mar-ria): Southernmost country of the Lumerian Empire, home of the South's most prestigious University and the Great Library. Ruled by Ka Batavia.

Cretanya (Creh-tawn-yuh): One of the northernmost countries in the South of the Lumerian Empire, ruled by

Ka Zarine. Known for its city of Thene and vibrant night life.

Elyria (El-leer-ria): Historically ruled by Ka Azria, rulership has now passed to Ka Elys, originally nobility from Bamaria.

Damara (Da-mar-ra): A Southern country known for its strong warriors, ruled by Ka Daquataine.

Glemaria (Gleh-mar-ria): Northernmost country of the Empire, ruled by Ka Hart. Imperator Devon Hart is the Arkasva and Imperator to the North. Rhyan Hart was previously first in line to the Seat.

Korteria (Kor-ter-ria): Westernmost country in the Empire. Magic is least effective in their mountains, but Korteria does have access to starfire for Lumerian weapons. Ruled by Ka Kormac.

Lethea (Lee-thee-a): The only part of the Empire located in the Lumerian Ocean. Ruled by Ka Maras, this is the country where criminals stripped of powers, or accused of vorakh are sent for imprisonment. The expression "Farther than Lethea" comes from the fact that there is nothing but ocean beyond the island. Due to the Drowning, the idea of going past the island is akin to losing one's mind.

Lumeria (Lu-mair-ria): The name of the continent where Gods and Goddesses first incarnated until it sank into the Lumerian Ocean in the Drowning.

Matavia (Ma-tah-via): Motherland. When used with Lumeria, it refers to the continent that sank.

Numeria (New-mair-ria): The Capital of the Lumerian Empire, home of the Emperor, and location of the Palace, and the Nutavian Katurium. Numeria is located in the center of Lumeria and not considered part of the North or South.

Nutavia (New-tah-via): New land. When used with Lumeria, it refers to the Empire forged after the Drowning by those who survived and made it to Bamaria—previously Dobra.

Prominent Creatures of the Old World Known to Have Survived the Drowning

Seraphim (Ser-a-feem): Birds with wings of gold, they resemble a cross between an eagle and a dove. Seraphim are peaceful creatures, sacred in Bamaria, and most often used for transport across the Lumerian Empire. Though delicate in appearance, they are extremely strong and can carry loads of up to ten people over short distances. Seraphim prefer warmer climates and are rarely found in the northernmost part of the Empire.

Ashvan (Ash-van): Flying horses. These are the only sky creatures that do not possess wings. Their flight comes from magic contained in their hooves. Once an ashvan picks up speed, their magic will create small temporary pathways to run upon. Technically, ashvan cannot fly, but are running on these magic pathways, which appear before them and vanish once stepped upon. Residue of the magic is left behind, creating streaks behind them, but these fade within seconds.

Nahashim (Naw-ha-sheem): Snakes with the ability to grow and shrink at will, able to fit into any space for the purposes of seeking. Anything lost or desired can almost always be found by a nahashim. Their scales are always almost burning hot, and they prefer to live near the water. Most nahashim are bred on Lethea, the country farthest out into the ocean, closest to the original location of Lumeria Matavia.

Gryphon (Grif-in): Sky creatures that are half-eagle, half-lion. Extremely large, these animals can be taken into battle, preferring mountains and colder climates. They replace seraphim and ashvan in the northernmost parts of the Lumerian Empire. They may carry far heavier loads than seraphim.

Akadim (A-ka-deem): The most feared of all creatures, akadim are literally bodies without souls. They kill by eating the souls of their victims. These demonic creatures were previously Lumerians, but grow to be twice the size of a Lumerian and gain five times the strength of a soturion. Immortal as long as they continue to feed on souls, these creatures are impervious to Lumerian magic. Akadim are weakened by the sun and tend to live in the Northern Hemisphere.

Jalamnavim (Jah-lahm-naw-veem) or **Water dragon:** Dragons with blue scales that live deep in the Lumerian Ocean. Previously spending their time equally between land and water, all water dragons have taken to the Lumerian Ocean and are usually spotted closer to Lethea. Their sightings have become so rare their High Lumerian name, *Jalamnavim* went out of use.

Agnavim (Ahg-naw-veem): Rarely sighted in Lumerian lands. These red birds with wings made of pure flame favor the lands occupied by the Afeyan Star Court. Lumerians have been unable to tame them since the Drowning.

Chimera (Kai-mer-ah): Ancient monsters from Lumeria Matavia whose existence were forgotten after the Drowning. Their history was only recorded in Auriel's Valya, but those scrolls were lost. The chimera favored the eastern shores of Lumeria, and migrated to unknown lands beyond Lethea prior to the sinking of the continent.

Terms/Items

Bind/Binding: A spell that ties a rope around a Lumerian to keep them from touching their power, or restricting their physical ability to move. A Binding is temporary, and can have more or less strength and heat depending on the mage casting the spell.

Birth Bind: Unlike a traditional Bind, a Birth Bind leaves no mark. It is given to all Lumerians in their first year of life, a spell that will keep them from accessing their magic power when it develops during puberty. The Birth Bind may only be removed after the Lumerian has turned nineteen, the age of adulthood.

Dagger: A ceremonial weapon given to soturi. The dagger has no special power on its own, as the magic of a soturion is transmuted through their body.

Ka (Kah): Soul. A Ka is a soul tribe or family.

Kashonim (Ka-show-neem): Ancestral lineage and link of power. Calling on kashonim allows you to absorb the power of your lineage, but depending on the situation, usage can be dangerous. One, it can be an overwhelming amount of power that leaves you unconscious if you come from a long or particularly powerful lineage. Two, it has the potential to weaken the mages or soturi from whom the caller is drawing strength. It is also illegal to use kashonim against fellow students.

Kavim (Ka-veem): Plural of Ka (see above). When marriages occur, either member of the union may take on the name of their significant other's Ka. Typically, the Ka with more prestige or nobility will be used thus ensuring the most powerful Kavim continues to grow.

Laurel of the Arkasva (Lor-el of the Ar-kas-va): A golden circlet worn by the Arkasva. The Arkasva replaced the titles of King and Queen that were used in Lumeria Matavia, and the Laurel replaced the crown, though they are held in the same high esteem.

Mekarim (Mee-kah-reem): Soulmates.

Mekara (Mee-kah-rah): Term of endearment, translates to "My soul is yours."

Rakame (Rah-kah-may): Term of endearment, translates to "Your soul is mine."

Rakashonim (rah-ka-show-neem): Link of power to one's soul, allows you to absorb the power of your own life lineage and past selves, but can be too volatile for the mortal body to sustain.

Seat of Power: Akin to a throne. Thrones were replaced by Seats in Lumeria Nutavia, as many members of royalty were blamed by the citizens of Lumeria for the Drowning. Much as a monarch may have a throne room, the Arkasvim have a Seating Room. The Arkasva typically has a Seat of Power in their Seating Room in their Ka's fortress, and another in their temple.

Stave: Made of twisted moon and sun wood, the stave transmutes magic created by mages. A stave is not needed to perform magic, but greatly focuses and strengthens it. More magic being transmuted may require a larger stave.

Vadati (Va-dah-tee): Stones that allow Lumerians to hear and speak to each other over vast distances. Most of these stones were lost in the Drowning. The Empire now keeps a strict registry of each known stone.

Valabellum (Val-la-bell-um): A traditional arena game in which soturi battle over the course of the day in honor of Asherah's Feast Day to reenact the story of the War of Light. In the final battle, soturi play the roles of the seven banished Guardians. The game ends when the fighter playing Moriel dies.

Valalumir (Val-la-loo-meer): The sacred light of Heaven that began the Celestial War, which began in Heaven and ended with the Drowning. The light was guarded by seven Gods and Goddesses until Asherah and Auriel's affair. Asherah was banished to become mortal, and Auriel fell to bring her the light. Part of the light went into Asherah before it crystallized. When the war ended, the Valalumir shattered into seven pieces—all lost in the Drowning.

Valya (Val-yah): The sacred text of recounting the history of the Lumerian people up until the Drowning. There are multiple Valyas recorded, each with slight variations, but the

Mar Valya is the standard. Another popular translation is the Tavia Valya, which is believed to have been better preserved than the Mar Valya after the Drowning, but was never made into the standard for copying. Slight changes or possible effects of water damage offer different insights into Auriel's initial meeting with Asherah.

Vorakh (Vor-rock): Taboo, forbidden powers. Three magical abilities that faded after the Drowning and are now considered illegal: visions, mind-reading, and traveling by mind. Vorakh can be translated as "gift from the Gods" in High Lumerian, but is now translated as "curse from the Gods."

Acknowledgments

Welcome to the acknowledgments of my longest book to date. Whew! If you're still here, thank you! Thank you for reading this far and for sticking with me, and for sticking with Lyriana and Rhyan on this journey we're all on. I've written a lot of words already. So let's get to it.

Sara DeSabato, my friend, my fellow pisces, and my developmental editor who literally kept me from crashing out. I could not have finished this without you.

Marcella Haddad, you have proven again and again what an amazing human you are, and I can't thank you enough for your support and for literally stealing and hiding my phone so I could finish writing.

Julia Paddison, thank you for always checking in on me and being willing to listen to me ramble about the plot and my worries and anxieties as I wrote. Also, you kept me fed, and that counts for everything.

Asha Venkataraman, I so appreciate your support and willingness to read the early and sometimes messy drafts.

Mom, you're always encouraging me and I can't thank you enough.

Dylan, Blake, Hannah, and Dani, the loves of my life. Thank you for being you.

Eva, Michael, Elissa, and Jules, you're probably the most amazing support team a sister could ask for.

Taryn Fagerness, thank you for all of your behind the scenes work.

Molly Powell, thank you for your continued support of the series.

Andy Ryan, I appreciate your copy edits so much!

Stefanie Saw and Saint Jupiter for the most gorgeous indie covers again!

Steve Kuzma, my guardian of the website!

And of course, my readers. I wouldn't be here without you! Thank you, thank you, thank you!

Love,
Frankie

About the Author

Frankie Diane Mallis is the bestselling author of the romantic fantasy Drowned Empire series. She lives outside Philadelphia, where she was previously an award-winning university professor, but now spends all of her time dreaming up and writing new worlds. Whenever she steps away from her laptop, she can be found practicing yoga and belly dance, drinking coffee, vintage shopping, or baking gluten-free desserts.

Visit www.frankiedianemallis.com to learn more, and sign up for the newsletter. Follow Frankie on Instagram (@frankiediane), and on TikTok (@frankiedianebooks).

HODDERSCAPE

WANT MORE HODDERSCAPE? JOIN US!

Sign up to our mailing list to get exclusive early sneak peeks and offers:

Follow us on our social channels:
 @hodderscape

Buy our books, find out more, and discover exclusive content:
www.hodderscape.co.uk

WANT MORE HODDERSCAPE?
JOIN US!

Sign up to our newsletter to stay up to date with our new books and more.

click here to sign up now

@hodderscape

www.hodderscape.co.uk